TOTAL SURRENDER

A Featured Alternate of the
Doubleday / Rhapsody Book Club

"What do I need to do?"

"I'll show you . . ."

He wanted Sarah Compton. Without limitation, withou constraint.

"For the remaining days that we are here," he explained, "we will have a sexual relationship . . . I will demonstrate the methods of loving, and you will practice on me until you grow proficient."

"Very well."

"You will do whatever I say."

"Within reason."

"No," he interrupted, quashing her bit of bravado. There would be no restrictions. "I will select the path. You will follow it. I will create the games; you will play. Enthusiastically and completely. Or not at all."

She stared him down, biting against her cheek, obviously deliberating refusal. His Sarah was tough and proud; she wasn't used to having a man tell her how to act . . . Half of his enjoyment would be attained from eroding her inhibitions, from her bowing to his stipulations, from her pleas for more . . .

St. Martin's Paperbacks Titles by
CHERYL HOLT

SECRET FANTASY

TOO WICKED TO WED

TOO TEMPTING TO TOUCH

TOO HOT TO HANDLE

FURTHER THAN PASSION

MORE THAN SEDUCTION

DEEPER THAN DESIRE

COMPLETE ABANDON

ABSOLUTE PLEASURE

TOTAL SURRENDER

LOVE LESSONS

Total
Surrender

Cheryl Holt

St. Martin's Paperbacks

This is a work of fiction. All of the characters, organizations and events portrayed in this novel are either products of the author's imagination or are used fictitiously.

TOTAL SURRENDER

Copyright © 2002 by Cheryl Holt.

ISBN: 0-312-94823-9
EAN: 978-0-312-94823-8

Printed in the United States of America

St. Martin's Paperbacks edition / July 2002

St. Martin's Paperbacks are published by St. Martin's Press, 175 Fifth Avenue, New York, NY 10010.

15 14 13 12 11 10 9 8 7 6

Chapter One

"My goodness!" Lady Sarah Compton murmured aloud as she sat up straight and peered out the window. "I didn't know things like that went on in the country!" Her voice resonated in the empty, elegantly appointed bedchamber to which she'd been assigned.

Down below, the grounds were immaculately tended, with walkways carved in symmetric lines through the shrubbery. Torches were flickering, and couples were strolling about, enjoying the summer evening. Far at the rear of the yard, one pair paused for a lingering kiss. Their lips melded, their arms wrapped tightly, the embrace continued on and on, and she watched, embarrassed about staring but unable to stop.

The man slipped his fingers inside the bodice of the woman's dress, tenderly caressing her voluptuous breast, and for some reason, Sarah's own breasts swelled in response. Her nipples tightened and elongated, rubbing irritatingly against her corset, making her aware of her body in a fashion she'd never been before. Uneasy with the odd sensations, she shifted about in the window seat where she'd reposed, but she couldn't get comfortable.

Eventually, the man lowered his hands to the woman's bottom, urging her closer by massaging her buttocks, and Sarah lurched forward, intrigued and amazed by the blatant spectacle, until gradually, the duo shifted away, heading into the shadows where she couldn't observe them.

Raising her fingertips to the glass, she held them against the pane, tracing in deliberate circles, her gaze lingering on the spot where they'd been. They looked so compatible, as if they unequivocally belonged together, and their display stirred in her an unbearable longing for a similar attachment with another.

Her room was cheerful and pleasant, decorated with light blue rugs, wallpapering and draperies. The furniture was serviceable, the bed large and soft, the chairs cushioned and snuggling in front of the small hearth. It was situated on the third floor in a secluded wing of the mansion, which meant that there were no guests' voices or servants' footsteps passing by in the hall.

Though it was early June, the night was cool, and one of the maids had lit a fire. The dry wood popped and sizzled, creating the only sound in the silent chamber, and she felt totally removed, as if she was the very last person on earth, so disconnected that she might have been sitting on the moon.

The twilight sky was a deep indigo fading to black, and a single star flickered on the horizon. As though she was a silly young girl, she nearly made a wish on it, but caught herself before engaging in the absurd flight of fancy.

Wishing was for fools.

Even if she still believed in such idiocy, what would she pray for anyway? A different fate? A fortune to fall upon her? A rich husband? How ludicrous! As if she'd marry on the spur of the moment just to rescue her brother, Hugh, from his current fiasco!

"What am I doing here?" she queried aloud, but no answer echoed in reply.

A sense of separation and disorientation manifested, which was out of character. Typically, she relished solitude and preferred her own company to the blathering of others. Yet, now, she found herself yearning for . . .

She wasn't quite certain what. A huge cloud of dissatisfaction hovered over and around her, and she couldn't shake it. Nothing interested her, and there appeared to be no appropriate remedy for what ailed her. Since she wasn't precisely sure of her affliction, she couldn't concoct a cure.

Until recently, she'd always been assured of her path.

Her reclusive life in the country, her management of the family's Yorkshire estate, those decisions had been easily made and the results gratifying. But no longer. Discontentment reigned supreme.

Perhaps her restlessness was due to her advancing age. At twenty-five, she was entitled to evaluate the turns in her road, to review the detours she'd selected because of her unwavering recognition of duty and responsibility. The men in her family had never shown a predilection for preserving the ancient Scarborough title or property, so she'd juggled a cumbersome burden.

In the process, she'd given up a chance for her own home and children. While in the past, she'd never thought she'd wanted them and had never obsessed over their absence, of late, the missed opportunities were weighing heavily.

Should she have wed all those years ago?

She'd actually had a Season in London, but when she'd gone at age sixteen, she'd been ungainly and socially inept. Teased and laughed at, she'd been tormented, and the butt of more than a few cruel jests. Girls had tittered behind their fans over her genuineness, her lack of sophistication. Boys had snickered over her inadequate breasts, her crimson hair, her unwillingness to hide her intellect.

She'd fled the city, vowing never to return. Despite their father's subsequent ultimatums and demands, his insistence that she marry to shore up the family's lagging finances, she'd rebuffed his attempts at wedding her to any of the cruel oafs of the aristocracy who had belittled her. A categorical spinster, she'd spent the intervening years flourishing in the country at the Yorkshire property she loved.

Since those early days, she'd blossomed and matured, and she could have selected another path for herself. If she had, her life would be so different. She'd be admired, cherished and respected, a nobleman's wife, a parent. Instead, she'd remained single, a sort of jaded nanny for her father and half brother—two adults who had no inclination to grow up, and who had thus required incessant mothering.

Somehow, someway, she'd succumbed to the insupportable existence, and she couldn't tolerate the untenable onus inflicted upon her by those she was supposed to love.

When her father had been alive, it hadn't seemed so difficult. He'd been a kindly man, with good intentions, but his judgment was perpetually routed by bad choices. His disasters had habitually left him perplexed over the size of the catastrophes he'd wrought, but with his death, Hugh had assumed the title of Earl of Scarborough, and he gambled and played as though decadent comportment was his preordained right.

In direct contrast to their departed father, Hugh never evinced any fondness for the estate or the people who depended upon its prosperity for their incomes, and he was even more apathetic now that his character had worsened. Drink and fast living had brought on strange mood swings, and he could be cruel, prone to violent outbursts and heedless conduct.

His latest gambling blunder was a perfect example of his slide to perdition, and she couldn't help but replay their horrid conversation, when they'd discussed the loss and the unknown man who'd prompted it. The words tumbled through her head like a bad refrain, flaying her with the evidence of the sorry state of her affairs.

"Was it the faro tables?" she'd asked him, as if the method of his downfall had mattered!

"No."

"But it was cards?"

"A few games of commerce is all."

"I see. How much?"

"All that's left."

"Define all."

"Whatever is not entailed to the title."

"The furniture?"

"Yes."

"The last of the farming equipment?"

"Yes."

"The clothes off my back?"

"Perhaps. I'm not sure how far he will dip into the personal possessions of the family."

"How about me?" she'd probed starkly. *"Have you wagered me away, too?"*

"He'd have no use for you," Hugh had retorted coldly. *"He typically likes his women a tad on the feminine side."*

The cut had been harsh, striking at her old insecurities, and it still hurt to think that he'd uttered it, but that was Hugh: rash, negligent, and caustic.

What she wouldn't give to throttle him! It was bad enough that he'd gambled away the last of their possessions, but the twenty thousand pounds he'd lost as well— money they didn't have and never would—was reckless beyond imagining.

When he'd visited at Yuletide, she'd given him the last three-hundred pounds from her dowry, and she'd warned him there was no more. Not that he'd listened. He'd forged ahead with his corrupt course and, while the villain holding his markers had allowed him three months to pay, there was no way they could come up with that amount of cash.

Of course, Hugh's solution was that she save him, once again, by marrying a wealthy husband as quickly as possible. The idea was absurd, yet she'd found herself agreeing to try, simply because she hated being at odds with him, but she was heartily weary of pandering to his needs, of adapting to his degeneracy, scrimping and saving, never having enough.

How she hated being poor!

Perhaps that was the real reason she'd decided to go visiting and had traveled to Bedford and Lady Carrington's house party—for it assuredly wasn't in order to snag a spouse as Hugh insisted she must.

Excessive, unrelenting poverty was so grim. Didn't she deserve a bit of fun? Hadn't she earned some frivolity and merriment?

There was so little joy in her days, no carefree, gay entertainments, no pleasurable meals or leisurely afternoons spent at capricious pursuits. There was just apprehension and despondency and gloom, and now—with Hugh's latest conundrum—there was desperation, too, but she'd been expecting the worst forever so the end was anticlimactic.

For once, she had no inclination to rescue Hugh. She'd delivered him from one debacle after the next until he'd begun to erroneously assume that she could rectify any exigency, and he obviously thought she was prepared, on this occasion, to work another miracle. Unfortunately, her patience had finally been exhausted, and her stamina for weathering another calamity had vanished.

She'd had months to brace herself for the sordid conclusion that was approaching; she'd felt it down to the marrow of her bones. All through the winter and spring, she'd kept peeking over her shoulder, as though Doom was lurking there, ready to overtake her when she least suspected it. Yet, her destiny had quietly arrived in the form of a nameless, faceless gambler.

Who was the man foolhardy enough to wager for Hugh's pitiful belongings? Down to the candle holders on the walls, it would all go. Such a meager pile! Who would want it? Who would be that greedy? Clearly, the blackguard was more addicted to gaming than Hugh. What a sorry individual he must be!

A knock sounded on the door, and she rose slowly and trudged to admit the serving maid and a quartet of burly men who carried large jugs of hot water for the bathing tub awaiting her in the adjoining dressing room. As they grappled with their task, she relaxed on a chair beside the fire, eyes closed, ears peeled, eagerly listening as the water splashed into and filled the basin.

A real bath! The maid had offered one, and Sarah had selfishly accepted the luxury. At home, she never had a full bath anymore. There were only a few elderly servants remaining, and she never had the heart to obligate any of them to lug the heavy load upstairs.

Her personal washing was done in the kitchens after supper, quick swipes with a cloth. How exotic it seemed to have the opportunity to immerse her body! The thrill she eceived just from thinking about it only underscored the miserably low level to which her fortunes had descended.

The men—buckets empty—departed, and Sarah had the maid unfasten her gown and corset, then she ushered the woman out. This extravagance was one she deigned to enjoy at length and privately.

With modest complications, she shed her dress and most of her undergarments. Clad only in a chemise that hung to mid-thigh, she went to the inner chamber. The room was small and cozy. A miniature brazier, the coals aflame and glowing, heated the air. A painted screen was set against one wall, and the tub hidden behind it.

Sarah approached. Steam drifted up, and she dangled her fingers, checking the temperature. On a nearby vanity lay a stack of towels, soaps, and other bathing accouterments. She opened bottles and sniffed at the contents, locating a rose-scented oil and adding it to the vaporous mixture.

Ready to begin, she almost stepped in, then paused. A sudden whim to be daring and bold ensnared her, so she reached for the hem of her chemise and pulled it over her head.

She'd bathe in the nude! She never had before, but who would know? The maid had been dismissed, she was far from home, on her own. Within reason, she could engage in any scandalous behavior without detection.

Feeling naughty and audacious, she spun about and saw her reflection in a mirror positioned next to the tub. Entranced, she realized that she couldn't remember when she'd ever inspected her nude torso.

As though taking inventory of a stranger, she tipped from side to side, searching for attributes and checking for flaws. Ultimately, she decided that she was beholding a fetching woman, slim, rounded, with stunning emerald eyes and glorious auburn hair. Her body curved appropriately—expansive at the shoulder, narrow at the waist, flared at the hips—and her slender legs made her appear taller than she was.

Shifting, she appraised her profile, but the stance high-

lighted her breasts in a manner that was as enticing as it
was disturbing. She couldn't quit looking, and she was
overcome by the disquieting notion that this was why one
didn't parade about naked. Too many unsettling and unusual sensations were provoked.

Under her visual inspection, her breasts felt fuller, heavier, and her pink nipples hardened into two taut little
buds—just as they had when she'd been spying on the two
lovers in the yard. Curious, she rested her palm against one
of the extended tips, and the action brought about a flurry
of physical agitation.

Her nipples started to ache and throb. With each beat of
her heart, the pulsation hammered through her chest. It progressed down her abdomen to lodge deep inside, at the core
of her womb, causing it to shift and awaken. The woman's
spot between her legs seemed to expand and moisten.

Unexpectedly, she was deluged by a wave of longing so
intense that she nearly crumpled under its strength, and she
grabbed for the rim of the tub to steady herself from the
onslaught. The impression was puzzling to describe. She
craved . . . though *what* she couldn't have explained.

Surprisingly, she envisioned the couple in the garden
again, and she scrutinized her smooth, bare flank, remembering how the man had stroked the woman's buttocks,
how he'd levered her closer. She recalled how the pair had
slipped into the dark, and she speculated about what had
occurred once they were in a more remote area. What sorts
of mysterious things had the man done to the woman?

The proceedings were beyond the ken of a virginal spinster, but she couldn't help wondering. Apparently, her
imagination was quite vivid, for the mental pictures increased her agonizing awareness of her breasts.

"Craziness," she muttered. Craziness to be alone and retired for the evening, and ruminating over lewd riddles.

Disgusted with herself, she plucked her roving hands
from her body and locked them around the edges of the tub
where they would stay out of trouble.

Carefully, she sank down, and she hissed out a breath

as she landed on her knees, and the blistering liquid slapped at her thighs. She proceeded with scrubbing her various parts, but much of the pleasure she'd hoped to delight in had disappeared. Every place she touched reacted. The rough nap of the washcloth aggravated her receptive flesh, so she gave up, sliding farther into the basin and reclining as much as she was able.

Struggling to relax, she balanced on her arms and tipped her head back, relishing the warmth. At some point, fatigue overwhelmed her, and she dozed. When she opened her eyes again, she'd slept for quite a while. The water had cooled, so she stood, letting it sluice off her skin, then she climbed out onto the rug and snatched one of the towels.

Commencing at her neck, she worked across her breasts, her stomach. Briefly, she rasped across the delicate cleft between her legs, but she didn't care for the stimulation it induced, so she bent over and rubbed down thigh and calf. As she straightened, movement captured her attention, and she glanced into the mirror.

A man was lounging behind her, perfectly at home, and casually viewing all! The sight was so startling that she was temporarily paralyzed, incapable of processing what she was witnessing. His appearance seemed like a dream, and she narrowed her focus at his reflection, grappling to make sense of the bizarre development.

Not an illusion, he was really and truly there.

Tall, with trimmed black hair and striking sapphire eyes, he was a ravishing man—perhaps the most handsome she'd ever encountered. He had high cheekbones, an aristocratic nose, a generous mouth. His wide shoulders tapered to a thin waist, lanky hips, long legs, and powerful, muscled thighs.

He wore only a pair of fitted trousers, no shirt or shoes, and she was tantalized by the absurd observation that she'd never before beheld a man's unclad chest. It was covered by an intriguing fur of dark hair, piled thick on top then dwindling across his flat stomach to a slim line that disappeared into the waistband of his pants. The top two buttons were undone, so she could see much farther than she ought, and the spectacle was perturbing and exhilarating in a manner she didn't comprehend.

"Lovely . . ." he murmured in an enticing baritone that skittered across her nerve endings and induced her abdomen to clench in response.

The peculiar salutation snapped her into action, and she whirled to face him. Nervously, she clutched at the towel, desperately striving to shield herself, but his probing examination slithered over her like a tangible caress, lingering on her lips, her breasts, the juncture between her thighs.

"How did you get in here?" she reproached, endeavoring to sound adamant and assertive, but the quaver in her voice communicated her uneasiness.

"Through the door." He gestured, and she noticed a second screen and a door behind it, adjoining her dressing room to the next bedchamber.

He took a step toward her, and she took a step back. "You're not welcome. Leave at once!"

"Are you sure you want me to go?"

"Absolutely!"

"But wouldn't it be more amusing if I stayed? You could climb in the tub again, and I could wash you. Or"—he glanced down at his pants that so graphically outlined his masculine form—"I could soak in the water, and you could bathe *me*. Either way, I promise the experience will be everything you desire. And more."

A man and a woman bathing? Together? Washing? Each other? A whirl of incredulous scenes flashed through her mind, and her heart raced.

His fingers went to the front of his trousers and touched the placard as though he was about to release the rest of the buttons and strip himself. Panicked, she kept her gaze bravely affixed to his. "What do you think you're doing?"

"Disrobing."

"Don't you dare!"

He chuckled, oozing charm. "I'd heard you were eager, but I don't mind prolonging things with a few games."

She had no idea what he meant and couldn't even ▪
a guess. Flustered, she resorted to the type of polite dis▪
she regularly employed with recalcitrant underlings. "I
politely requested that you leave, and now I insist."

"Before you've had your fun?"

The question was mildly raised, his tone one of intimate
promise about matters she didn't understand. There was a
confidence and subdued arrogance in his demeanor that
seemed to guarantee gratification.

He moved closer.

The mirror was directly behind her, the basin on one
side, the vanity on the other, and he was in front. She was
hemmed into the corner, unable to slip past, and it occurred
to her that—discounting Hugh—this was the only instance
she'd ever been closeted with an adult man. The doors were
closed, the room isolated, the servants abed, and if she'd
chosen to call out, no one was available to assist her.

She was totally at his mercy, and she was supposed to
be scared and alarmed, yet she found herself elated by the
scandalous interlude. Where the heady, ribald euphoria
sprang from she couldn't have explained, because she
hadn't realized she was craving a clandestine adventure.

Perhaps the man, himself, instilled the improper sentiment. He was overtly complacent about their situation, assured that he had every right to enter, confident that she
would appreciate the wrongful intrusion. When he stared at
her with those extraordinary eyes, she yearned to acquiesce
to whatever he suggested.

Still, she couldn't permit him to remain, and she pulled
herself up to her full height, which was distinctly lacking
considering how he towered over her. "I'll not ask again,
sir."

"I've been watching you."

He'd been watching her? From where? For how long?
Had he observed her whole bath? Mortified, she clasped
the towel more securely against her breasts. "How terribly
vile."

"You opened the peephole." He shrugged, his offensive

...ing of polite conduct apparently being of no import.
..y wouldn't I look through?"

"What peephole?" she inquired, aghast.

"The one between our rooms." He ignored her outrage.
"Your skin is so smooth. Like silk."

The simple statement disconcerted her. She'd never before received a flattering compliment from a man, especially not an attractive, virile, mostly naked one, and as she
stumbled for a response, he advanced like a large cat, a
graceful, predatory beast like those from the jungles of Africa that she'd seen at an exhibition in London. He was so
near that the fist she'd valiantly anchored to her bosom to
hold the towel was pressed against his ribs. His skin was
warm, and his matting of chest hair tickled the heel of her
hand.

She tilted away, but the mirror prevented evasion.
Though she fought to appear staunch and in control, her
dilemma had quickly spiraled beyond her ability to navigate. Anxiously, she licked her bottom lip, which instantly
had him studying her mouth as though intent on devouring
her.

"Sir, you're scaring me."

"How?"

"I'm not certain why you're here—"

"Aren't you?" His words were husky with a dangerous
lust that even she, in her sheltered, virginal state, couldn't
misconstrue.

"—or what you propose . . ."

"You know what I *propose*. I'll be very gentle if that's
how you like it." With a sure finger, he traced down her
cheek and across her neck, and his touch was so blistering
that she felt as if she'd been burned. She flinched, and he
soothed, "You don't need to be afraid."

She battled to comprehend what he was saying. It
seemed that he aimed to force himself upon her, but there
was no urgency in his demeanor. "If you were any kind of
gentleman . . ."

"I'm no gentleman, my dear lady. Never have ~ fessed to be."

Her pulse thudded at a higher rate. She had no noti~ how to interact with a man who uttered such a wild claim If he didn't deem himself to be a gentleman, then what code governed his behavior? "If you don't depart, I'll scream."

"I don't care if you scream. I'm happy to indulge any of your whims, just as you'll get to indulge mine, so you're free to do whatever makes our rendezvous more enjoyable for you."

What? She shook her head, perplexed and becoming frightened even though he'd done nothing that was outright menacing.

"Please . . . I'm here alone, and I'm . . ." She wanted to state the obvious—that she was undressed—but she couldn't speak the word *naked* to this unknown scoundrel, and she blushed bright red, the flush originating somewhere in the vicinity of her stomach and sweeping up her breasts to her cheeks. Unduly warm, she resisted the impulse to fan herself lest she drop the towel.

"I demand that you go."

"God, you're pretty." He reached behind her head and tugged at a comb that had helped to restrain her abundant locks, and the velvety mass cascaded down her back and hung to her waist. "I love your hair. It shimmers like fire."

For one, mad instant, she thought he planned to kiss her, but instead, he ducked under her chin and nuzzled against her shoulder at the site where her pulse pounded so furiously. A shiver of excitement tore through her, and she swallowed a baffled squeal that could have been either delight or indignation.

His lips were heated and soft, and he tenderly kissed against her nape then, to her astonishment, he licked across her skin. She jumped then twirled away, only to end up facing the mirror, with him behind her, and she assessed the two of them, evaluating the differences: his tall to her short, bronzed to fair, brawn to lean.

ıdly, he settled his hands on her hips and snuggled
ɔackside against him, and she was assailed by an array
unique anatomical impressions. As though she'd been
searching for this man all her life and had finally found
him, she ignited with sensation, every pore alert and animated, and her nipples tightened painfully, poking at the
towel.

The knave immediately noticed how they'd peaked. "I
can't wait to have my mouth on you."

The declaration kindled cryptic images, and restlessly,
she scrambled to flee—from the unusual fleshly perturbation and from him—but because of their positions, he
merely nestled her close and flexed against her. His groin
stroked across her bottom in a manner she'd never presumed a man might attempt with a woman. There was a
solid ridge along his abdomen that dug into her buttocks,
and her traitorous body reacted by squirming to get nearer
to it. He appreciated her participation and gripped her
firmly, flexing again.

"Your breasts are so beautiful," he murmured. "Just the
size I like on a woman. Not too big. Not too small." Before
she knew what he was about, he'd pushed the towel aside,
revealing one to his torrid gaze. He cupped it, weighing it
with his palm, then he pinched the nipple, twirling and
manipulating it back and forth.

The swirl of agony he instigated was like nothing she'd
ever previously experienced. The torment blazed a trail that
commenced at her bosom, then rushed out across her torso,
to the roots of her hair and the tips of her toes, and she
curled them into the rug.

"Please," she begged, but whether she was beseeching
him to continue or cease was impossible to surmise. On
some secret level, she surreptitiously craved what he was
vigorously inflicting.

"Look at us," was his rejoinder. There was a gleam in
his eye that made him appear wicked and beyond redemption. "Look at how exquisite we are with my hands on
you."

His gaze met hers in the mirror, and she could conclude that he was correct. Mesmerized, she was beguiled by the incongruous perception that she was magnificent in his arms: curvaceous, feminine, alluring. Their bodies were flawlessly reconciled, perfectly attuned, and the display titillated and disturbed. Much as she wanted to, she couldn't quit staring.

He could read her thoughts, and he smiled insolently. "You see it, too, don't you?"

"You're mistaken," she pointlessly asserted.

"Am I?"

Determined to prove her wrong, he unveiled her other breast, and she desperately grasped the towel around her waist, so it wouldn't fall to the floor and leave her uncovered. As she battled with her nude condition, he petted and fondled, squeezing the mounds and tweaking the nipples until they spasmed intolerably.

Her breathing hitched. Too much was happening too fast. The wanton episode was so inconceivable that it played out like a fantasy—except that he was really present, arousing and addictive. Her mind wailed for her to call a halt, but her body wouldn't obey.

"I'd planned to have you on your bed the first time"—his assertion brushed against her ear—"but maybe I should take you here, by the mirror, so you can see how splendid we are together."

An exotic fog may have temporarily immobilized her, but a fragment of sanity managed to seep in, and she was coherent enough to realize that her virtue was in peril, so she fought his restraint, but he scarcely noted her opposition. He lifted her and deposited her on the vanity, in a fluid move, scooting her back and positioning himself between her thighs.

They had rapidly vaulted to a different, more ominous, stage of involvement. There was an obstinate air about him; he wouldn't desist until he'd journeyed to a conclusion of which only he was cognizant.

He yanked the towel away, and she was completely ex-

..d, and he dipped to her nipple and sucked at it. The ..ried crest was raw and inflamed from how his fingers .ad handled it, and his mouth only increased her distress. With a yelp of surprise, she resisted his machinations, even as her body hastened forward toward an unfamiliar destination, and she had to combat the urge to spur him on.

So entranced was she by his concentration on her nipple that she didn't discern how he'd shockingly traced his hand down her stomach until he massaged across her womanly cleft. Without warning, he delved through the springy hair and parted the folds, then pushed a finger inside. She froze, wondering what he contemplated, but he caressed her gently, the maneuver at odds with the tension she could sense emanating from him. The foreign intrusion strengthened her conviction to escape, but retreat was blocked by his hips and thighs.

"Stop it!" she commanded, but he didn't appear to hear her; he kept on. "Stop it, now!"

Blindly, she groped about, latched onto a heavy decanter, and swung it at his head. The blow glanced off his crown, but it definitely got his attention. He wrenched away, patently confused.

"Jesus," he muttered, "what the bloody hell did you do that for?"

She swung again and caught him alongside the temple, tearing a gash. Blood welled into the cut, and he staggered, momentarily off balance, and she utilized his distraction to leap away, swathing the towel about her as she went. Dashing into the bedchamber, she considered sprinting into the hall, but she couldn't let anyone discover her predicament.

Commotion emanated from the dressing room, and she spun around. Her adversary, a cloth jammed to his head, had stumbled in behind her, and she cast about for a weapon but didn't see anything useful. She still held the bottle, so she smacked it against the marble of the fireplace, and it shattered effectively.

"Stay away from me," she ordered, brandishing the bro-

ken glass. "Depart at once—the same way you entered—
or I'll slice you to pieces like the swine you are."

The man paused for the slightest moment then, enraged
as a wounded bear, he stalked toward her.

Chapter Two

Michael Stevens stopped in the doorway to the bedchamber as the crazed woman before him smashed a decanter against the fireplace. Glass shards flew everywhere.

"I mean it!" she repeated in threat. "Go!"

He wasn't certain what had just occurred between them in her dressing room but, considering the aftermath he was now viewing, he had to sincerely wonder whether she was prone to lunacy.

What type of female invited a man to her boudoir, enticed him beyond reason, then panicked like a silly virgin? She was fortunate he still had control of his wits, that he wasn't the sort who would rush across the room and take what she'd initially offered but had obviously decided she didn't want to supply.

The woman was a menace, and he couldn't help but wonder what Pamela Blair, Lady Carrington, was thinking, welcoming such an unstable person to her fete. Pamela regularly opened her home to her decadent friends and acquaintances, providing them with a private and confidential environment where they could frolic at their leisure. They came in droves, to fornicate and debauch, both the men and women ready to wallow in every sick, ribald, immoral fantasy imaginable, and there were plenty of men currently visiting who wouldn't desist, despite these loud, fervent protests.

Pamela was risking disaster by bringing such a volatile guest onto the premises, and Michael couldn't wait to tell her so. In the meantime, he had to figure out a method of soothing this beautiful-but-deranged shrew before she shouted the house down.

To think that he'd let himself be lured away from a placid, civilized game of cards for this! If he'd utilized superior judgment, he could be downstairs—winning—while safely sequestered in the company of rational men or, better yet, he could have gone to cavort with any of the other female guests who'd asked, and he could at this very moment be copulating in peace, without being banged on the head for his troubles.

Considering the numbers of gorgeous, lustful women who were flowing in and out of the property, he'd had numerous other acceptable choices. As he was the most disreputable male in their midst, the wanton ladies of the *ton* were positively dying to couple with him, and for the past few weeks, he'd impulsively obliged their despicable caprices.

The party was every man's greatest dream come true. The level of decadence guaranteed that anything and everything was permitted, the women pleasing and amenable, and rules and inhibitions abolished. Raw interaction and meaningless sex, copious, insignificant, unrefined intercourse, was not only tolerated under Pamela's roof, but absolutely encouraged, with the prerequisite being that the people partaking of her hospitality were completely predisposed to misbehavior.

So what was this woman doing in Pamela's house? What did she hope to accomplish by this maidenly display of offense?

Belowstairs, he'd stepped from the card room in order to stroll outside in the fresh air, when he'd been accosted by a buxom blonde who'd pulled him aside and whispered insistently that the auburn-haired virago standing in front of him wanted him to visit, that she was too shy to come to him later on as others would, so she sought a covert rendezvous in the privacy and sanctity of her own bedchamber.

Supposedly, she'd never previously attended one of Pamela's parties, was nervous about her participation, and

therefore wished an inconspicuous orientation into the carnal routine.

When the request had been posed by her alleged friend,
he hadn't given much thought to who the blonde ambas-
sador was, or to why she was soliciting sexual congress on
behalf of another, but he was definitely curious now as to
her identity. Earlier, he'd presumed she was a lady's companion or perhaps her maid, so he hadn't ruminated over
the entreaty or why it had been oddly made.

Already, he'd grown bored with the proceedings that
Pamela had instituted and the situations she'd convinced
him to try. The available lovers were as jaded as himself,
and surprisingly, he missed the closeness and spark that
should have come with making love, so he'd readily consented to indoctrinate this novice but, in light of the manifest level of her upset, he had to admit that something was
seriously awry.

She hardly resembled a reticent, demure paramour. Instead of a lonely female awaiting a bit of subdued loveplay,
she appeared overwrought, shocked, outraged, and—if the
murderous gleam in her eye was any indication—ready to
kill.

Typically, he disdained the bored, unhappy aristocratic
noblewomen who had filled Pamela's country house to
overflowing. He detested their loose morals and their lewd,
lascivious lifestyles. They were pathetic in the lengths to
which they would go to find diversion from their tedium.

With no conscience and no integrity, they would commit
any contemptible act. They saw nothing wrong with cuckolding their husbands, with carrying on indiscreet liaisons,
or fornicating with little concern as to whether they bred
children not fathered by their spouses.

His aversion to them was only surpassed by his disgust
for their husbands, those lazy, impotent peers of the realm
who drank and wagered and debauched without regard to
the consequences. They assumed they had a God-given
right to inflict themselves on the rest of the world.

In London, he and his brother, James, owned a gaming

club where they pandered to and coddled the slothful lords.
Those earls and barons couldn't keep their blunt in their
wallets or their cocks in their trousers, and he and James
catered to their base whims, which was undeniably the reason their business was so popular.

If he'd been in town at the moment, he'd have been hard
at work, ensuring that there was adequate liquor and food
available, so that the exalted gentlemen would be comfortable while they complacently gambled away their estates
and their children's inheritances.

How he despised them all!

They were men of no principles or ethics, who would
spout their accursed code of honor until they choked on it,
but deep down, they were blackguards and cads with nary
a scruple, so he was more than happy to have sexual relations with their willing wives, which was why he'd traveled
to Bedford.

Whenever one of their spouses beckoned, he was entirely agreeable. In any manner, in any fashion, as often
and savagely as they could bear it, he'd dabble with them,
heedless as to the damage he might leave in his wake, because in his opinion, they deserved every bit of misery he
was able to mete out.

So he wasn't exactly sure what had gone wrong this
time. He'd been *invited* to the damned room. Asked to
watch. Asked to fondle. Asked to fuck. And all he'd gotten
for it was a cockstand so excruciating he could barely walk,
and a crack on the skull that had nearly put him out. As it
was, he'd probably end up with a stitch or two in his cheek
before the night was through.

Bloody, wretched woman! Didn't she know better than
to trifle with a precariously aroused man?

Though he'd never been the sort to raise a hand to a
female, he had half a mind to take her over his knee. In
his present mood, the chance to deliver a good thrashing—
especially to someone as reckless and idiotic as she appeared to be—sounded like a fabulous idea.

He stepped into the room. "Would you please lower your voice before someone hears you?"

"Stay back!" she commanded again, wielding her make-shift weapon, and she lifted one of her dainty feet as if she might actually wade into the sea of broken glass surrounding her.

Marvelous! Just what he needed, both of them cut and bleeding! Perhaps he should send down to the kitchens for a physician and the thread to sew them up!

"Are you mad?" he barked, but softly. Taking into account his dubious position with these illustrious personages, he never made a public scene, and he wasn't about to start, yet she didn't seem overly concerned about the opinion of others.

Not inclined to make matters worse, he threw aside the cloth he'd pressed to his wound, then he stormed toward her until they were toe to toe. A piece of glass pierced his heel, but he was so angry that the pain barely registered. "Give me that!"

He reached for the fractured decanter and yanked it away, hurling it into the nearby hearth where it clanked undramatically against the bricks. She squealed in protest and twirled to run, but he grabbed her from behind, slipping an arm around her waist and lifting her up. As he swung her out of the pool of shards and slivers, she struggled to escape, administering a swift kick to his shin that had him wincing, but, for the most part, her efforts were ineffectual.

The only true damage was to his abused, overinflated phallus, but it wasn't physical injury he was suffering. Their awkward position had deposited her shapely ass directly against his groin, and his cock swelled further and cried out for an excuse to finish what they'd started.

God, but he wanted her!

The woman possessed no secrets. From the beginning, when she'd entered the dressing room and tested the temperature of the bathwater, he'd been spying on her through the tiny hole affixed to the wall between their rooms.

The antiquated mansion was notorious in its design, a

veritable lecher's treasure trove of concealed rooms, secluded hallways, and peepholes so that when she'd pulled
off her chemise, he'd seen all: the graceful legs, the curved
hips, the crimson hair shielding her pussy, the pert breasts
with their beaded nipples.

She was a ravishing woman, with that spectacular hair,
those cheekbones, that cute nose with its upturned tip. And
that mouth! With its wicked tongue! How he longed to
learn how adept it could be when she wasn't busy using it
to spew sass and issue orders.

As she'd deliberately and languidly stripped herself bare
then knelt in the tub, seductively scrubbing her private
places, she'd seemed an intriguing mix of innocence and
experience, wholesome yet tantalizing. Knowing he was
watching—or so he'd believed—she'd presented a sensual,
galvanizing exhibition that could only have been designed
to titillate and inflame. The interlude had been the most
erotic he'd ever witnessed in a lifetime that had been filled
with naughty sexual activity.

Remarkably, the most intriguing segment had been when
she'd lain back in the water with her head tipped against
the rim and her eyelids had fluttered closed.

While she'd slept, she'd appeared young, ingenuous, and
removed from the worries that had marred her face when
she'd first arrived. She snored, and he couldn't help chuckling at the memory, or speculating as to how indiscreet
she'd deem him to be if he mentioned it.

Unwonted emotion had tugged at his heartstrings as
she'd slumbered so serenely. What had brought her to Bedford and Pamela's indecent party? What horrid episode had
transpired that would make her presume the gathering
would rectify her woes?

She doesn't belong here.

The conviction had spiraled through his mind over and
over again, and he'd been overwhelmed by the perception
that he understood more about her than he properly ought,
that he could sense things about her he had no reason to
distinguish. Absurdly, he was desperate to keep her safe

from harm, and he'd nearly persuaded himself that he'd be doing her an enormous favor if he spirited her away.

Eventually, he'd shaken off the ludicrous notion. Spurred by unfathomable motives, the woman had summoned him upstairs, which meant she was a pampered, amoral member of the *ton* who had come to Pamela's abode of sin and vice of her own accord, and who was downright eager to enjoy the licentious amusements the lady rendered to her guests.

Pamela habitually catered to the male libertines and roués of High Society, as well as to their degenerate women, so he was inordinately familiar with this termagant's type of debased disposition, and he'd relished the idea of having her.

There was a deceptive air about her that fascinated him; she was natural yet beguiling, and he'd calculated that copulation with her would be a refreshing development, that she would bring something to his sexual intercourse that had been lacking for a long while. By doing nothing at all, she fomented a diverse jumble of sentiment that had him craving more than a heedless carnal encounter.

Perhaps his heart had not turned to stone, after all.

With a great deal of excitement and anticipation, he'd approached her, enthusiastic to dispense the sensual attention she'd requested, while anxious to obtain a nebulous, but undeniable, benefit in return. He'd silently observed as she'd awakened and dried herself, scrupulously evaluating her saucy breasts, her rounded ass, and ultimately determining that she would be a perfect partner for the ribald sorts of libidinous recreation he enjoyed.

Initially, with her exclamations of shock and insult at his appearance, he'd thought she was playacting. So many of them did, feeling the need to blunt their depravity by feigning umbrage. As they'd studied their joint reflections in the mirror, she'd been so curious, so responsive and receptive, but as he'd moved to the next level, as he'd suckled at her supple breast, he'd received the distinct impression that she was unprepared for what she'd initiated, which left him totally bewildered.

Unceremoniously, he dumped her on the bed and tossed her towel after her.

"Cover yourself."

She hastily complied, but the towel wasn't wide enough to suit her purposes, and trembling, she cowered beneath it. He glanced about until he located a green robe draped over a chair; he retrieved it, and pitched it to her.

"Put this on," he dictated, then he showed her his back while searching the walls for peepholes. Behind him, he noted her hesitation, then she hurriedly moved about on the bed. When the mattress shifted and her feet hit the floor, he spun around.

Mercy, but she was an erotic sight, with that splendid hair curling across her shoulders. She'd cinched the robe's belt at her waist, and the fabric flawlessly outlined her magnificent body, her graceful hips, her pouty breasts with those tempting nipples. Their discord had elevated her pulse and flushed her cheeks to a flattering rose color.

Their gazes linked and held. Though she was shaking like a skittish colt, she meant to stand her ground.

"Who is your husband?" he quietly demanded.

"I'm not married."

"You're a widow?"

"No. I've never wed."

"You're single?"

"Yes."

Tersely, he bit out, "Then why did you ask me here?"

"Me? Ask you?"

"If you didn't plan an assignation, why invite me to your room? Are you so naive that you don't appreciate how dangerous it is to dabble with a man when you've no intention of following through?"

"You believe that I'm the kind of woman who would . . ." Aghast, she sputtered. "That I . . . that I . . ."

Apparently, she couldn't utter the words that would describe the type of person he suspected her of being. A niggling wave of doubt swamped him. "You fancied *me*. You specifically propositioned *me*."

"You wretched bounder!" Thoroughly insulted, her stunning emerald eyes glimmered heatedly. She clutched at the lapels of her robe. "How dare you concoct such a wild story!"

Taking her measure, he carefully scrutinized her affront. He was a good judge of character and always had been. In his line of employment, he had to regularly assess veracity and temperament, and he was convinced she was telling the truth. She had neither solicited him nor procured his services.

So, who was the blond emissary who had lured him to her? And why? Clearly, someone hoped to set a carnal trap. But for him? Or for her? And to what end?

Abruptly and gravely apprehensive, he raced to the door and locked it.

"What are you doing?" she queried, but he ignored her.

A painting hung on the wall, and he lifted it off its hook. Sure enough, there was a partially hidden peephole that would have allowed a voyeur to lurk in the hall and peek inside. He flipped the artwork upside down, and the opening was effectively shielded.

After a meticulous search of that wall and another, he discovered no more holes. The third wall faced the exterior of the house and the fourth, the inner dressing room, so they couldn't possibly contain any. The only other entrance—the door to his adjoining bedchamber—was barred from within. For now, they were relatively secure. No one could fortuitously stumble upon them in a compromising situation.

Wary and determined, he confronted her, once again. "Who are you?"

"I don't wish to say, and if we should ever have the misfortune to meet a second time, I insist that you pretend you don't know who I am."

"Not bloody likely."

He stomped over to her, and she straightened, distressed

yet striving to appear brave. Angrily, he stared her down until it gradually dawned on him that a strange energy was sparking between them, their bodies extending out to one another, and he grimaced with dismay. He didn't want to be attracted to her!

As a man vastly experienced with women, he readily recognized that they shared an acute physical affinity. Whether she emitted a covert signal or radiated a particular chemistry, he couldn't explain the phenomenon, but she aroused him as no other could, and he hastily squelched the bizarre erotic realization. At present, he had bigger problems to mull than an asinine, unwarranted amorous bond.

"Do you have any idea"—his hushed tone was scathing—"what would have happened if we'd been discovered just now?"

The question startled her. Evidently, she'd been so overwhelmed that she hadn't had the opportunity to reflect upon the momentous consequences. "What do you mean? Are you suggesting that someone aimed to catch us?"

"Your name, madam. If you please." Mutinously, she returned his glare but didn't reply. "Fine. Then tell me this: Who is a blond woman in attendance? She's about your age, petite but shapely, with big blue eyes." *And fabulous breasts,* he nearly appended, but he wouldn't describe her by such a crass method.

After a lengthy hesitation while she weighed all the angles, she retorted, "Probably my cousin. Why?"

So . . . she had a family member on the premises who proposed personal mischief. Interesting and terrifying! He was an expert at ferreting out suspicious facts and histories; he did it systematically at the club where he frequently unearthed the sordid details of their customers' lives. There were many ways to untangle this debacle.

"No reason," he responded enigmatically, which caused her to bristle.

"Why did you inquire?" she decreed authoritatively as

though she spent her days expounding proclamations that were instantly obeyed.

"I shan't confess, milady." Menacingly, he towered over her. He was purposely trying to intimidate with his size, but it wasn't working. "And might I recommend that you refrain from ordering me about? I'm not one of the lowly minions in your orbit who will leap to do your bidding."

"What is your name?"

"Michael Stevens."

He braced for the predictable sign of recognition . . . but none followed. Because of his gaming establishment, and the notoriety of his parentage, he was so infamous in her circles that he was inevitably identified and gossiped about wherever he went. The fact that she was clueless as to his renown was definitely a puzzle.

His mother was the celebrated actress Angela Ford, and his ass of a father, the wealthy and illustrious Earl of Spencer, Edward Stevens. Michael and his brother had to be the two most conspicuous bastard sons ever conceived. How could she not know? Had she been raised in a cave?

"Why are you here at Lady Carrington's party?" he snapped.

"I'm on holiday." Churlishly, she added, "Not that my schedule is any of your concern."

"Madam, I just mistakenly had my mouth on your breast, and my hand up your twat. I'd say that makes everything about you my business."

"How utterly crude of you to mention what transpired!"

Irritated, and tired of whatever plot someone was hatching, he harshly retorted, "I didn't hear you complaining."

"Are you implying that I instigated this fiasco? You despicable cad!" Steam was literally shooting out of her ears as she jabbed a finger in the center of his chest. "I didn't! I told you to leave! I advised you from the first, but you wouldn't listen! How dare you insinuate otherwise!"

Although he was loath to admit it, she was correct, and he burned with chagrin. He'd thought her introductory, tepid denials had been an eccentric version of lovemaking,

and despite how much he'd like to lash out, the debacle
was scarcely her fault.

"You're right, of course. My apologies."

"Thank you." At her acceptance of his olive branch, her
gaze united with his as she entreated, "What do we do
now?"

"*Now* . . . I get the hell out of here." But he instantly
atoned for his rough language. "Beggin' your pardon, milady."

"You won't discuss this with anyone, will you?"

"No."

"Swear it."

"I swear."

Her eyes were open wide, analyzing, delving far inside
to the spot where his black heart beat its steady rhythm.
"How can I trust you?"

"My word is my bond."

"But you said yourself that you're no gentleman."

"Nevertheless, I never make a vow unless I mean to
honor it."

Gad, but when she looked at him like that, she was so
exceptional. Fetching, impressionable, defenseless, she inspired a myriad of masculine instincts to protect and shelter,
and he yearned to wrap his arms around her, to hold her
close while whispering that everything would be all right.
The urge to safeguard her was so overpowering that he was
frightened by the strength of it.

He declined to feel any emotion toward her! He abhorred her kind! It was neither his affair nor his problem
if she had a corrupt relative who was endeavoring to drag
her into some sort of public calumny, of which he would
play no part.

Shifting restlessly, he merely wanted to exit the dreadful
scene. If he was extremely lucky, he'd never again have
occasion to cross paths with the hapless woman!

"I must be off," he lamely communicated, "and don't
worry. This incident will remain our secret. No one will
ever hear of it from me."

Her attention lowered to his bared stomach and, though he hated to acknowledge it, the sensation tickled all the way down to his toes. He instructed his feet to move away, but they wouldn't comply. Rooted to the floor, he let her look her fill. For a woman who'd purportedly been traumatized and assaulted by his male presence, she was distinctly inquisitive, and he was vain enough to admit that he liked how her absorbed regard roved over him.

Astounding him immensely, she spoke. "Would you explain something before you go?"

"If I am able."

"When we were in the dressing room"—she stopped, swallowed, fidgeted with her robe—"what were you striving to achieve?"

What! A damned virgin?

"Oh, Lord, spare me." He groaned and tilted his head back, pressing a finger and thumb against the bridge of his nose, praying for fortitude while fighting the fierce headache that was forming. "Say it's not true! You can't be a virgin!"

Silence was his answer, and he whipped his gaze to hers, requiring that she look him in the eye, but she wouldn't. She was excessively interested in a spot somewhere over his shoulder, her cheeks flushed with embarrassment. Forced to recognize how untried she actually was—she couldn't even verbalize what had occurred between them!— he calmed himself. "You don't have any idea what we were about?"

"I suppose you were . . . we were . . ."

White-hot anger set in. At her. At her family. At himself for the predicament in which he'd almost landed. How he'd like to march downstairs and have a chat with her scheming cousin! He never would, though, because he couldn't risk inciting a furor over their clandestine contact.

Michael was not his brother, James. James had few reservations about the upheavals he sporadically inflicted on the members of the Quality, and if the occasional innocent became ensnared in his wretched machinations, he didn't care and suffered no compunction to make amends.

Not so, Michael. He'd never furnish others with reasons to compare him with his father, the Earl of Spencer. The earl had seduced Michael's mother, sired two illegitimate boys on her, then left her alone to raise them while he went on his merry way.

Michael would never commit such a callous exploit, so while he had no qualms about copulating with the degraded wives and widows of the *ton* who sought his favors, those favors never extended to their chaste daughters, because he declined to end up shackled for all eternity to one of the selfish, spoiled snivelers.

And now that he thought about it, why the hell was she quizzing *him* about prurient behavior? She was hardly a girl fresh out of the schoolroom.

"How old are you anyway?" he peevishly posed. "Twenty-four? Twenty-five?"

"What's my age got to do with anything?"

"You're too old to let yourself get involved in a mess like this!"

"I am not old!"

"For pity's sake, you're a spinster—"

"I'm not a *spinster*!"

"—prancing about this dissolute mansion, where there are nothing but rakes and rogues lurking in the halls." He indicated her curvaceous torso. "You stroll about naked, with your doors unlocked. What did you expect might happen?"

"I never go visiting! I never guessed that a man would just . . . would just . . ."

To his dismay, tears welled into her lovely eyes. He couldn't abide female histrionics! If she commenced, he couldn't guarantee what he might do. "Don't you dare cry!"

"Then stop yelling at me!"

"I'm not yelling!" he hissed rabidly.

"Yes you are! This has been an horrendous event. You're not helping by being so grouchy!"

She was plainly not prone to sentimental outbursts; one

impeccable tear tracked a charming trail down her cheek,
and she glanced away. Flustered, she battled to stabilize her
breathing and regain control, and he heaved a resigned sigh.

The ice around his heart began to melt. Incapable of
sustaining his upset, he swiped his hand across her silky
skin, capturing the warm moisture on his thumb, then he
stuck it in his mouth and sucked at the salty drop. She was
out of her league in this residence and with these people;
a lamb led to the slaughter.

How could he leave her to her own devices?

"I was touching you," he patiently elucidated, "as a man
touches his wife. They do things to one another."

"What things?"

"They kiss and caress each other. It's arousing and pleasurable."

"But we're not married."

"We don't have to be. A man always relishes a woman's
passionate company, and the two participants need not be
wed to practice intimate indulgence."

"If we'd continued, you'd have taken my virginity?"

"Yes."

"In what manner is the deed accomplished?"

How on God's green earth had he fallen into the middle
of this conversation?

Gently, he admonished, "I hardly think I'm the one to
advise you."

"No, I don't suppose you are," she agreed, after a protracted contemplation.

"What is your name?"

"Sarah."

He nodded; it suited her.

"Sarah"—he determinedly rolled it off his tongue, and
it felt just right—"you can't stay here in Bedford."

"What do you mean?"

"This house, this party." He gestured around, including
all that was transpiring under the mansion's taciturn roof.
"I realize that you are desirous of a country holiday, but
this is not the simple rural assemblage you imagine it to

be. The people who have traveled from London . . ."
Briefly, he considered minimizing the gravity of her circumstances. After all, she was unsophisticated and would have no idea that men and women conducted themselves in such an egregious fashion. Yet he couldn't have her discounting the perils. "The guests are not here for socializing and entertainment."

"Then why have they come?"

"To have sexual relations."

"That's the only reason?"

"Aye."

She weighed this information then, skeptical, she grinned. "I don't believe you."

Capturing her arm, he ushered her toward the wall that faced the outer hall. "Look!" He lifted the painting he'd rearranged and pointed to the peephole. "Men can prowl in the corridor and spy on you."

On tiptoe, she flattened her eye to the hole. Faced with the bald confirmation, she was less assured when she shifted back, and she dubiously folded her arms over her alluring bosom. "Why would they want to?"

"Men like to watch. It's titillating for them—especially when the woman doesn't know. It makes a man wish to sneak inside and do things he oughtn't." She shivered, and he dropped the painting back into place. "This house is teeming with these blasted holes. Never permit this picture to be shoved aside or removed. Always check it."

Still doubtful, she moved to the bed and, like a sailor drawn by a mermaid's siren song, he followed. In a mere handful of minutes, he'd been captivated by her, powerless to separate himself. It was far past time he departed, but like a smitten lad, he kept prolonging their discourse so he could linger.

"This seems so far-fetched."

"Yet it's true, Sarah. The other guests have been in the city for months, and they're bored. They're seeking distraction. I won't go into the details because they're too delicate."

"I'm not a child!" she huffed, piqued. "What do they propose?"

He'd hoped that she'd be easily shocked, and thereby easily induced to return to her own home, but clearly, she was exceedingly stubborn, so he clarified starkly. "They will tarry in each other's bedchambers where they will engage in the sorts of physical sport I attempted with you. The difference is that the women are willing."

"But they're nearly all married."

"None of their husbands are here."

"So?"

"They plan to dally with other men."

This news gave her pause, and another, more disturbing possibility presented itself. "Will *you* philander with any of them?"

"However many ask," he candidly replied.

The fact troubled her, and her brow wrinkled in consternation. "Why would you?"

The answer to her interrogatory was so long, and so complicated, that he wasn't sure he could provide an accurate rejoinder if he'd had a week to contemplate one. He couldn't rationalize the sick recreation he pursued. She would never understand, and while he'd satisfied himself that he suffered no stabs of conscience over the state of his carnal dissolution, he found that he couldn't justify his conduct to her.

He settled for, "I'm bored, too." Declining to furnish an additional excuse for an inquisition, he parried with, "Promise me that you'll go home first thing in the morning."

"Why would I? These tales you're spinning are preposterous. My very own brother suggested that I attend this party. He wouldn't implicate me in such an abominable undertaking."

"Wouldn't he?" Her denial wasn't quite as vehement as he might have predicted. Had he heard equivocation? He sidled nearer, until the sparks were flowing between them once again. Unafraid, she glared up, challenging him.

"Sarah, listen . . . I've been acquainted with Lady Carrington for many years."

"So have I. Pamela is a friend of my family."

"But you don't know everything about her, or you wouldn't be here. She has a distinctive reputation."

"What sort of reputation?"

"For hosting lewd parties, the more wicked the better. I've attended many of them, and I'm not joking; it's risky for you to stay."

Unable to resist, he laid his hand on her nape, feeling the petite, fragile bones of her shoulder. She accepted the gentle caress, a major feat after what she'd endured from him earlier. He stroked up her neck and lifted her chin with his thumb. "I don't want you swept up in any disaster. Leave! Tomorrow!"

Just then, a soft knock sounded on the door, and the knob rotated unsuccessfully, but solely because he'd possessed the foresight to secure it when he'd had the chance.

Very softly, a female called, "Sarah . . . ?"

"My cousin Rebecca," Sarah whispered, and her eyes narrowed with trepidation and a hint of indignation.

Staring her down, he dared her to form the correlation, to deduce for herself that she was in the middle of something much deeper and larger than she could handle.

He leaned in, inhaling the smell of roses that clung about her. No gentleman by any stretch of the imagination, his lips grazed the curve of her ear. "I must be away," he mouthed. "Keep your doors locked—at all times. Both the one that opens out to the hall, and the one between our rooms. And *go home* in the morning."

She turned slightly as though she might argue, and the shift brought them so close that their lips were all but joined. Only a breath separated them. Their eyes connected, and expectation hovered in the moment.

Almost against his will, he was spurred toward her, but he was neither his impulsive brother nor his incorrigible father. He was a mature, twenty-eight-year-old man, who would control his unruly, libidinous cravings.

He bestowed the lightest kiss, just because he could and she couldn't refuse, but he didn't attempt more.

"Promise me," he mouthed, once more.

Belligerently, she simply smiled, and he ached to compel her acquiescence. Undeterred, her cousin tried the knob again, and he whirled away, not permitting himself a backward glance at her seductive form.

The lass was hazardous. To his equanimity. To his well-being. To his keen drive for self-preservation. So he'd make certain there'd be no further opportunity for stolen kisses.

On nimble feet, he vanished into his room, closed and barred the door behind.

Chapter Three

Sarah tossed and turned and finally gave up any attempt at sleep. She was uncertain of the time but figured it had to be after two. The fire was out, and a glimmer of moonlight glowed in the window. The mansion was unnaturally quiet, and she lay still, listening to the beat of her heart.

After the dashing Mr. Stevens had so fleetly fled her room, she hadn't closed her eyes a single second. How could a woman possibly rest when so much new stimulation had been thrown at her?

Everything was tangled in her mind: Michael Stevens, the house, the party, her brother, her cousin. The jumble of images played over and over, and she couldn't stop contemplating what had happened and what it all meant.

Mostly, she couldn't quit thinking about Michael Stevens. Now that she'd had opportunity to ponder their meeting with a clearer head, she wasn't angry or distressed. She was curious. Their corporeal adventure had been dramatic and thrilling and, though she was loath to admit it, he had left her hungry for more.

She felt as though she'd read the initial chapters of an exciting novel, but the book had been snatched away just when she was getting to the good part, the section that would have explained the secret intricacies of the plot. Yes, it had been inappropriate for him to come into her room, and yes, it had been wrong for him to have handled her as he'd done, but regretfully, she couldn't find the temerity to be sorry, and she wished she hadn't become overwhelmed and bonked him on the noggin. If she hadn't reacted so timidly, like the spinsterish virgin he'd accused her of being, she might now be cognizant of numerous libidinous particulars about which she'd ruminated for years.

Their encounter had been amazing, breathtaking. He'd touched her in ways she'd never imagined a man might touch a woman and . . . it had been wonderful. Shocking, too, but *wonderful* was the only accurate method of describing it.

All these hours later, her body was alive and thrumming with an unfamiliar, exotic energy, as though it had been in hibernation and had just been awakened. Her nipples were alert and aroused from how he'd pinched them. Whenever she shifted about on the bed, the fabric of her nightdress irritatingly rubbed against them and made her wish he was present to fondle them again.

He'd suckled against her! With his dark hair splayed across her chest, and his lips wrapped around her breast, he'd looked so beautiful. The episode had been brief and abrupt, but the agitation he'd inflicted with his atrocious teeth and tongue still tormented.

Her womanly cleft was overly aggravated, as well, and when he'd caressed her there, she'd been outraged by the intimate penetration of his conniving hand, but not now as she reflected upon it coolly and analytically. His shrewd finger had fit exactly right, had stroked across an itch she hadn't realized needed scratching.

Retrospection about him and his indecent gestures caused her to press her thighs together, but the movement inundated her with searing sensation, and she groaned in frustration. Her tender, feminine flesh was moist and swollen, and to her consternation, she wished he was available to continue his maneuvers. Without a doubt, he would be competent to ease her physical woes.

Michael Stevens, bounder that he was, had created this abject misery, and he would be aware of the route she needed to travel to assuage her unrelenting agony. The man was a walking, talking primer of information on the female torso. He knew more about a woman's anatomy than she knew herself.

Just before he'd departed, he'd kissed her. It had been

scarcely more than a peck, but considering that it was her first kiss, she lingered over the nuances. The transient embrace had been magnificent, and her mind wandered again to the couple in the garden who'd united so ardently, and she couldn't help speculating as to what it would have been like had Mr. Stevens kissed her like that. Long and deeply and passionately.

Her nipples began to throb, once more, and she rubbed her palm over one of them, presuming she'd allay the arduous distension, but the slight palpation initiated a fresh flurry of unusual perturbation. Alarmed and flustered, she rolled onto her stomach and stretched out, but the position made matters much worse. Each of the spots Mr. Stevens had rigorously provoked was in direct contact with the mattress, and she was inflamed anew.

Appalled by her state of affliction, she jumped out of the bed as though she'd discovered snakes in it. There was a bottle of wine on the dresser, and she poured a glass and paced slowly, sipping the red liquid and trying to calm her shattered nerves.

What had happened to her?

Her body had careened out of control, making her yearn for things she couldn't have, for things she'd never guessed she desired. She'd grown daring and reckless, and if Mr. Stevens had been with her at that very instant, she'd have let him do whatever he pleased as long as he promised to terminate her infernal suffering!

She was obsessed with him. Why was he at Lady Carrington's party? Who was he? Where did he live? How did he support himself?

He was certainly refined and self-possessed enough to be a member of an aristocratic family, but he was too bold and dangerous to have sprung from such a tepid background. With the cryptic comments he'd supplied about his participation in the festivities, he'd hinted that the female guests were zealously vying for his favors. Was he some sort of sexual servant? A man who made his way by pleasuring the women in residence?

The concept—that he shared his marvelous physique with anyone who asked—was so fantastic, and so far beyond her realm of experience, that she couldn't process it.

Who was he? *What* was he?

Any probable answers to her questions were too disturbing, so instead, she switched to pondering his warnings about the gathering, about her family. Critically, she strove to recall every tidbit of the conversation she'd had with Hugh that had led her to Bedford. The visit had been his idea, as had the choice of location, and other than his efforts to coerce her into rescuing him from his financial straits, she couldn't recall any untoward remarks with regard to the party or the people who would attend.

How about her cousin Rebecca? Rebecca's decision to accompany Sarah had also come about at Hugh's recommendation. Was she simply a congenial, innocuous traveling companion, or was she actually an instigator of trouble? Mr. Stevens seriously believed that Rebecca had steered him to Sarah's room, then stopped by—supposedly innocently—to check if Sarah was settled. Why? Was she anticipating that she'd catch Mr. Stevens on the premises? Could she have acted so despicably?

They were friends, relations. When Rebecca's parents had died four years earlier, Sarah had taken her in and provided food and shelter when Rebecca was out of options, when she'd had nowhere else to go. After prevailing on Sarah's generosity for so long, what could Rebecca hope to gain by sending an unknown man bent on ravishment? Had that been her aim?

Sarah refused to credit it.

And the party . . . Was it the lewd assembly Mr. Stevens insisted? How could she find out? She could hardly wander the halls and go sneaking into people's bedchambers.

Should she depart for home as he'd demanded? Did she wish to leave?

There was nothing for her in Yorkshire, no reason to rush back, and now that she'd met Michael Stevens, she was determined to stay. Distressing as it might be to chance upon him, she *had* to see him again.

Throughout her musing, her eyes had grown accustomed to the dark, and she noticed a sliver of light emanating from the dressing room. No lamps or candles were burning, so she couldn't fathom from where it emerged. She walked into the smaller room and was surprised and astonished to discover a peephole.

Intrigued, she marched over to it and stood on tiptoe, trying to peek, but the hole was too high, so she retrieved a footstool, climbed upon it, and peered inside.

A tiny room was visible. She couldn't see the entirety, just part of one wall, a chair, a table, and a narrow bed. Two candles flickered in a holder, illuminating the enclosed space.

Michael Stevens was there, alone, dressed as he had been earlier in a pair of tight-fitting trousers and naught else. He lounged negligently on the bed, his back against the wall, one ankle carelessly crossed over the other. From his rapt stare, Sarah assumed he was waiting for someone to join him. On the surface, he appeared relaxed and bored, but there was a restless energy hovering about him that piqued her interest.

Would he realize she was watching? Was she the only one? He was acquainted with the purportedly perverted workings of the manor and had intimated that there were copious peepholes, so there could be many people spying on him.

Did he know? Did he care?

Conspicuously unconcerned, he rubbed circles across the center of his chest, his fingers scratching through the mat of curly, tempting hair. Languidly, methodically, he arced lower, past the waist of his trousers, across the placard. He was swollen down below, the odd ridge of flesh prominently manifested, and he stroked the heel of his hand along it, a pained look on his face, as though he was extremely uncomfortable.

Despite the fact that she barely knew him, she sensed

many things about him—what he was thinking, what he was feeling—and she could tell he was eager, expectant, anticipating whatever was about to happen. She strained against the peephole, searching for clues.

Off to the side, a door opened, and a woman stepped into view. She was wearing a cloak, the hood pulled over her head and shielding her identity. Sarah rudely studied the goings-on, and when the pair began to talk, she pressed her ear against the hole so that she could eavesdrop on what was being said.

"What's your name?" Mr. Stevens asked, his voice husky.

The woman spoke softly, and Sarah couldn't discern her reply.

"Who is your husband?"

This response was also unintelligible, but Mr. Stevens chuckled over whatever he'd learned.

"What is it you would like to do for me?" He regarded the woman with a jaded, intense expression.

The woman gawked at her feet but didn't speak.

"You know the rules," Mr. Stevens advised sternly. "You have to say aloud what it is that you want." The woman hesitated, then leaned closer to Mr. Stevens and whispered something. "Ah . . ." he murmured, a brow rising, "one of my favorites. Are you undressed under your cloak?"

"Yes."

"Show me."

Her fingers went to the clasp at her neckline, then pushed the fabric off her shoulders but the hood remained in place. Sarah observed the woman's body in profile. She was naked, her breasts exposed. Her nipples were a brown color, elongated, and they jutted outward.

Mr. Stevens reached out and manipulated both of them with finger and thumb, inducing the woman to writhe uneasily, and Sarah's heart pounded. He was arousing the woman in the same fashion that he'd handled Sarah and, conscious of how it had felt, her own breasts reacted, tin-gling and hardening just from her watching. Though he was caressing someone else, it seemed as if he was touching her own bosom. Mesmerized, she was bothered and startled by how easily she was drawn in just from viewing the erotic interlude.

"Excellent . . ." he crooned seductively.

The sexy timbre of his compliment—bestowed on another lover—tickled down to her toes, and the realization confounded her terribly. The display was corrupt and deviant, and she understood that she should desist. Her behavior was improper, disquieting, and the outcome none of her affair. There was a shutter she could utilize to cover the hole, but embarrassingly, she couldn't force herself to use it.

Disgusting as it sounded, she was absolutely captivated by Michael Stevens. He was so handsome, so wholly virile, in a manner she'd never encountered before. Until they'd met, she'd had no idea there were men like him in the world, no inkling that people carried on in the shameless ways he welcomed, and a team of horses couldn't have dragged her away.

Like the worst sort of voyeur, she had to witness how the incident unfolded.

He moved behind the woman and turned her toward the opposite wall—one Sarah couldn't see—but it was clear that the couple was facing a mirror. Mr. Stevens was gazing over his lover's shoulder, just as he had with Sarah, and he cradled the weight of her breasts as he nuzzled against her throat. Whimpering with apparent ecstasy, the woman's eyes fluttered shut, her head tilted back, and he nipped against her nape.

"Do you like it when I do that?" he questioned, fiercely twirling at the woman's nipples.

"Yes." His lover was breathless, excited. "Don't stop."

"Your breasts are so beautiful," he declared, assessing the two mounds in the looking glass. "Just the size I like on a woman. Not too big. Not too small."

What!

"Maybe I should take you here in front of the mirror, so you can see how splendid we are together."

Sarah lurched away from the hole, the familiar words ringing in her ears.

"Look at us," he continued. "Look at how exquisite we are with my hands on you."

The cad! Only hours earlier, he'd uttered identical statements in her very own boudoir! How dare he lavish the same praise on another! It made their rendezvous seem so tawdry and ordinary when, on her end, she'd ultimately decided that it had been the most fascinating, enchanting event of her entire life. After reflecting at length, she'd persuaded herself that he'd been as charmed by her as she'd been by him, that he'd found her to be special as no other man ever had, that she was attractive and appealing.

Now, she simply felt like a fool.

In a temper, she whipped away from the peephole so rapidly that the stool wobbled and tipped, dispatching her to the floor with a loud thump. She landed crookedly on her rear and smacked her ankle against the vanity. Pain shot through the joint, and she moaned aloud, then clapped her hand over her mouth, wondering if the occupants in the adjoining room had heard the commotion.

If Mr. Stevens detected that she'd been snooping, she'd die of mortification!

Cautiously, she tugged herself up to a standing position. Though her ankle ached and her bottom smarted, nothing was injured but her pride. The beam of light from the hidden room was like a beacon, urging her to return to her perch on the stool, but she categorically refused to heed its beguiling call. However Michael Stevens might conclude his bizarre evening, she didn't care to know. She didn't *want* to know. Some mysteries were best left unexplored.

She hobbled out, shutting the door that separated her bedchamber from the dressing room. Confused, anxious, haunted by what she'd seen, she forced herself to bed and jerked the covers high. Eventually, after suffering through hours of wretchedness and chaos, she fell into a fitful sleep.

*   *   *

Michael heard a strange noise, as though someone had fallen, and it was followed by a restrained whimpering, but he didn't allow the sound to distract him. There were several peepholes into the Viewing Room so, no doubt, diverse people were watching, and anything could be happening just beyond the walls.

For a moment, he endeavored to conceive of who some of the spectators might be. Perhaps it was one of those eccentric men who enjoyed huddling alone and playing with himself during the proceedings, or one who became stimulated for later sexual congress by spying on others. Perchance it was one of the handful of aberrant men with baser appetites, those who were not attracted to women at all—but to himself as a potential partner. They would be impatiently waiting for a degenerate glimpse of his engorged member, an impressive sight by anyone's standards.

More likely, it was one of the women he hadn't had yet, a newcomer to the party who was wondering if she had the necessary lack of inhibition to take a turn with him. They were all so overtly titillated by the prospect.

After years of existing on the fringe of their society, he possessed a wicked reputation that was decidedly deserved, and they craved the chance to engage in carnal relations with him so that they could brag about their exploits later on. Come the morn, he would be the main topic of conversation over breakfast: who'd lain with him, how many times, in how many ways.

His own motives for participating in Pamela's lewd games weren't specifically comprehensible. It was as though he was driven to prove, over and over again, that nothing mattered. Yet his obscure purposes paled in comparison to those of the women who coupled with him. They were lonely, bored, degraded in their pursuit of entertainment, but he declined to feel sympathy toward them. Pamela had devised the rules for the tainted amusement, and they flocked to indulge, hoping that something especially

nasty would occur—the naughtier the better—so that they
would have more to bluster about to their friends.

He cared not. Not about their motives or their needs or
wants. They could all go hang.

Even as the contemptuous thought passed through his
mind, he suffered a pang of guilt, remembering the vixen
named Sarah into whose room he'd been stupidly drawn.
Her chamber was close by, and he was glad she had no
method of watching what he was about to do.

The notion that she might stumble upon him in the midst
of such corrupt conduct was unsettling and filled him with
shame, and he grimly pushed her memory away. He didn't
choose to consider her predicament, or what might befall
her. He didn't plan to worry over her, or have her interfering with his practice of pleasure.

Already, she was plaguing his battle-scarred conscience,
the one he'd carefully tucked away when he'd fled London
three months earlier. His heart had been bruised and battered by those he loved, and he'd had his fill of compassion
and empathy. Now, he was content to drift, indifferent to
his misdeeds, so he wasn't about to countenance some red-
haired witch burrowing under his skin.

If she finagled herself into his life, he'd start fussing
about her and chafing over her plight. He'd revert to the
type of sensitive fool he'd been before events had taken
their toll. The frivolous noblewoman had managed to insert
herself into the middle of treacherous intrigues that were
too abundant to mention, and if he wasn't circumspect, he'd
find himself checking on her, guarding her, keeping the
lechers at bay, unveiling the scheme of her brother and
cousin.

Dammit! The blasted woman wasn't any of his concern!
How she'd been lured to Pamela's house, why she'd agreed
to attend the party, what might transpire because of her
family—none of it was any of his business.

He was here to fornicate and to gamble, and for no other
reasons, and he wouldn't fret or fume over an imbecilic
spinster who didn't have the good sense to depart when she

should. The crazed woman needed a protector, but he wouldn't endeavor to assume the role.

He wouldn't care about her. He wouldn't!

Forcing his attention to the mirror, he scrutinized his current paramour. Her breasts were nicely formed, and he toyed with them overly long. He was hard, ready, willing to offer her however much she'd accept, but the woman herself did not matter.

No higher purpose lurked behind his actions. There was just the sex; vulgar and crude and risqué—just how he fancied it. The anonymous, blatant copulation fit his mood perfectly, and he intended to bury himself in this stranger until he couldn't continue, until his overeager phallus was limp, his raging sexual drive finally, but temporarily, slaked.

Gripping her hips, he deliberately flexed against her buttocks, letting her savor his enormous size, providing an indication of what was coming. Shoving the cloak off her abdomen, he eyed her pussy; it was bald and smooth as a babe's. "You've shaved yourself."

"Aye."

"Just for me?"

"Yes."

His male vanity was immensely stroked by the inane feat she'd performed for him. He cupped her, then roughly entered her with two fingers, conferring no ease, pilfering what he wanted, supplying what she craved, but as he worked against her in a fixed rhythm, another uncomfortable image of Sarah flashed, diverting his attention.

What was it about her? She'd bewitched him!

When he'd agreed to this evening of debauchery, he'd foreseen a leisurely, sating escapade with the woman in his arms, as well as with the various others who were scheduled to visit later, but intrusive thoughts of Sarah made this seem ridiculous; he was out of his element, unprepared to proceed. Suddenly, he felt unclean and profane—just when he'd resolved to feel nothing at all.

Desperate to chase Sarah away—quickly—he whispered into his lover's ear. "I'm ready now."

"Yes . . . all right." She consented haltingly, and stiffened, apprehensive about the hasty escalation.

"I'll lie down on the cot." He released her and moved to the bed, propping the pillows behind his head. She froze, either too disconcerted or too nervous to approach, but he was confident that she wouldn't leave without providing him a carnal release. Others might be watching, and she'd never embarrass herself by fleeing the scene. Her vanity wouldn't let her become a laughingstock.

"Come here," he ordered, and the terse command propelled her forward. She knelt down and fiddled with the buttons on his trousers. Her slender fingers slipped the top one through its hole. Soon, he'd be bared to her torrid gaze and able ministrations, and he braced for the rush of lust to flood over him, but it never arrived.

Dispassionately, he waited. He was incredibly hard, his cock never failing to rise for any dubious occasion and, in anticipation, his phallus swelled further. Ultimately, he was free and in her hand. She stroked him and licked him, until his hips responded of their own accord, then she leaned down and slipped her lips over the crown.

He was a big man, bigger than any of them ever supposed, and he didn't let his impressive proportions interfere with his gratification.

"Take more of me," he decreed. Reaching for the back of her neck, he eased her down, and she went without complaint, while he stared at the ceiling, focused on a crack that ran from one edge to the other.

The woman adeptly proceeded with her task, but true desire proved elusive until, without warning, Sarah once again rudely intruded into the center of the sensual exercise. He visualized her stepping out of her bath, wet and slippery and smelling like roses. He recalled the firm, taut nipples he'd suckled, the slick, tight pussy he'd fingered.

For some reason, she excessively excited him, so he closed his eyes and pretended that *she* was the woman stooped over him, that she was enticing him with her wicked mouth and tongue. Vividly, he imagined teaching her to suck at him, making her practice, encouraging her to master his favorite techniques. Adamant yet gentle, he'd be a relentless instructor, and she'd be an apt, enthusiastic pupil, set to learn what he deigned to impart.

Steadying his paramour, he held her in place, granting her as much as she could manage, urging her to take a bit more.

"Sarah . . ."

In his mind, he pictured her in all her nude, glorious splendor, and his level of desire soared to a previously unascertained height. He shuddered and let himself go.

Chapter Four

Sarah sat on the verandah, her face shielded by a bonnet, observing the other guests and enjoying the late afternoon sunshine. The fabulous summer day was quickly approaching evening, temperatures were balmy, the sky bright blue and filled with fluffy white clouds. Soon, everyone scattered about at the various tables and settees would venture inside to dress for supper, and she should have been content to relax, but disturbing ruminations kept creeping in, rendering it impossible to cherish the moment.

After her encounter with Mr. Stevens, then her subsequently stumbling upon him during his odd tryst, she was definitely in a state. He had cluttered her senses in indescribable ways, and though she screamed at her overly zealous mind to give it a rest, her active imagination wouldn't calm down. The only matter she could contemplate was him and what he'd been doing.

Surreptitiously, she scanned the long porch that wrapped around the mansion, wondering who his lover had been. She scrutinized the mannerisms of the women, evaluating how they moved, tipped their heads, and gestured, but to no avail. She couldn't tell.

During the night, she'd removed herself from the dressing room and the temptation it provided, but she'd spent interminable dark hours regretting her decision. To her ultimate dismay, she wished she'd continued on! She was frantic to learn how the rendezvous had developed and how it had ended.

Shocking as it seemed, she hoped she'd have the fortuity to watch him again before too much time had passed. There was something abominably erotic and alluring about spying. If she shut her eyes, she could pretend that *she* was the woman in the room with him, and that he was perpetrating those treacherous exploits against her own person.

What was the matter with her? Why did she find his comportment so titillating? Even as she recognized the impropriety of her conduct, and even as she exhaustively chastised herself for her wantonness, she was craving a repeat performance.

Her nocturnal reveries about him and his antics had grown cumbersome as he now commanded her entire daylight attention, as well. She couldn't stop conjecturing as to where he was and how he was spending his afternoon. Disgustingly, she was perpetually craning her neck, searching the crowd for a glimpse of him, but she'd not seen him anywhere.

While she'd never admit as much to another soul, she was fascinated by him and what she'd witnessed, and she was impatient for the chance to ask him: Why? Why did he act so decadently? Why did his physical peccadilloes hold such appeal? What was the attraction?

For some inexplicable reason, she felt as though she'd always known him and could interpret his thought processes, and she'd been left with the overwhelming impression that he hadn't actually wanted to be engaged in such depraved misdeeds. Deep down, he was a good man; she was certain of it, though why she believed so, or why she might presume to judge, was beyond her ability to explicate.

She perceived an affinity between them that she'd never had with another, and she couldn't shake the sensation that he didn't belong at the party any more than she did. Their strange assignation had so thoroughly disordered her world that she was convinced there was a larger purpose behind their meeting, and she refused to go home until she had occasion to explore what it might be.

As she fantasized about Mr. Stevens, her gaze wandered to the sloping green yard where several couples competed at an informal lawn game. They were hitting a ball across

the grass with a sort of mallet and aiming for a basket that
was located quite a distance away at the base of the hill.
She wasn't sure of the rules, but it seemed that whichever
couple landed their ball in the basket with the least amount
of strokes was the winner.

Rebecca was one of the participants and, when the contest had begun, she'd invited Sarah to play, but Sarah had
declined, and she was relieved that she had. On the surface,
the sport seemed harmless enough, with eager contestants
and innocuous jesting and wagering over the tough shots,
but there were undercurrents to the verbal banter that she
didn't grasp, and a great deal of unusual, intimate touching
that would have been disconcerting.

She couldn't pinpoint what was making her uncomfortable. Perhaps the laughter was a little too familiar, the subtle looks between the partners a tad too prolonged, but
whatever it was, there was a strain in their interacting that
bothered her.

As the women leaned down and positioned their sticks,
the men were constantly nearby, snuggling themselves
against the women in order to abet them with their swings.
After the episode with Michael Stevens, she recognized
how unsettling it was for a man to press himself against a
woman's buttocks. She readily recalled how he'd held her
hips and flexed his groin, and she shifted uneasily, relieved
that she hadn't allowed any of the men to act so familiarly.

However, she was striving to be fair about the entire
event. So far, she'd witnessed nothing that she would deem
downright inappropriate, and she was forced to speculate if
this wasn't how adults related when they were visiting. This
was unmistakably a fête for grown-ups. There were no children invited; only men and women who had plenty of leisure time and who required some means of occupying it.

Perhaps she simply didn't understand the social conven-
tions when a crowd of such people gathered together. Obviously, the standards were a trifle lower, but casting about,
she couldn't help but remember Mr. Steven's descriptions
about the assemblage. He'd contended that the women

wouldn't be accompanied by their husbands, and apparently, he was correct. While there were many gentlemen present, none were married to any of the ladies.

She endeavored to guess at the number of guests, but tabulation was difficult. Lady Carrington was adept at offering varied amusement, with concurrent merriment occurring, so visitors weren't convened in the same spot.

Card games were progressing in the house, gambling in some of the backrooms, where even the women were permitted to join in. Outside, there was horseback riding, meandering through the gardens, and one bunch had even commandeered several carriages for a picnic at the lake.

Just then, her hostess emerged through the French doors and blazed a trail through the guests. Sarah enviously studied her, trying not to be overly conspicuous. A beautiful woman, ten years Sarah's senior, Pamela Blair had been the fourth wife of an elderly earl, but also his favorite, and thus, upon his death, he'd graciously bequeathed several valuable properties and a significant income with which to enjoy them.

She regularly entertained huge groups, and her soirees were invariably the rage, with people begging invitations whenever she was having a particularly interesting masquerade or banquet.

Tall, blond, slender, and graceful, she murmured hellos and conversed with old friends. Eventually, she reached Sarah, and the two women chatted, while casually regarding the competitors in the yard.

As a girl of seventeen, Sarah had met Pamela during her failed debut outing, but they'd not crossed paths since that dreadful debacle. Pamela had been twenty-seven years old, already a widow, and Sarah much younger, so they'd not formed a confidential association. Nevertheless, Sarah had discovered her to be direct and forthright, which had been refreshing in view of how ghastly her brief excursion had been, and she retained fond memories of the woman who'd never been judgmental or cruel during a period when Sarah had been so terribly out of her element.

Pamela was amiable but detached, welcoming but not inordinately so, absorbed but not acutely. There was a coolness that kept others at a distance, especially someone like Sarah who had never made friends effortlessly, yet Sarah trusted the older woman and suspected that the fickle members of High Society preferred her fellowship for the same reason. She had a reputation for being loyal, reliable, and discreet, admirable qualities in a small, elite community where everyone attended to everyone else's business.

Pamela inquired after Sarah's family, her brother, their Yorkshire estate. As Sarah was uninformed as to Pamela's private life, she had difficulty making chitchat in return, so she stuck to flattering observations about the weather, the festivities, the company.

When Pamela quizzed her about the adequacy of her accommodations, Sarah finally found the opening for which she'd been waiting.

"Do you happen to know who's been assigned the suite next to mine?"

"Why?" Pamela laughed softly. "Were they keeping you awake?"

"No, nothing like that. I just noted a gentleman when he exited." She was dying to simply speak the name Michael Stevens aloud, but she was a horrid liar, and she couldn't fabricate an acceptable story as to how they might have met. "I recognized him from somewhere, but I wasn't positive of his identity."

"Hmmm . . ." Pamela brooded, pondering the arrangements of the sprawling mansion. "I didn't realize there was anyone in that room. Once Hugh advised me that you were coming, I intentionally gave you a quiet chamber away from the gaiety. Some of my companions can be . . . rambunctious . . . in the night, so I figured you'd relish the additional privacy."

"I do," Sarah agreed, while theorizing as to the woman's definition of *rambunctious*. "Thank you."

"What did this mystery man look like?"

"Handsome. Broad shouldered. Dark haired." More

wistfully than she intended, she added, "He has the most
spectacular blue eyes."

"Well . . . that would *have* to be Michael Stevens. He
definitely has eyes that prompt a woman to fantasize about
things she oughtn't." Pamela chuckled, then leaned over
and patted Sarah's hand. "I wasn't aware that I'd situated
him near you, but trust me, dear, you're not acquainted with
him. Nor should you be."

"Now I'm absolutely intrigued."

"To put it bluntly, Sarah"—Pamela stared out at the yard
for a lengthy interval, carefully choosing her words—"he
wouldn't be a fitting prospect for you, so there's no excuse
to amble down that road." At Sarah's raised brow, Pamela
hastily supplied, "Pardon me if I sound unduly harsh, and
please don't misconstrue. Michael is a great friend of mine,
but he's not at all what you're seeking."

Sarah blushed to the tips of her toes. Did Pamela suppose she was husband-hunting? Did everyone? What indiscreet statements had Hugh used to explain Sarah's
attendance? Flustered, she glanced around. Were the other
guests stealthily assessing her, eager to behold more of her
inept forays into the matrimonial quagmire performed by
the aristocracy?

"I'm not searching for a man," she felt obligated to clarify.

Pamela bent closer still, and Sarah was frightfully glad
that they were sequestered. If a single utterance of their
conversation was overheard, she'd expire from humiliation.
"Let me be frank, Sarah. I know why you're here—"

"No you don't," she interrupted. "Not if you think I'm
stalking after a husband."

"But Hugh said—"

"Hugh was wrong."

"Oh, my apologies." Confused, Pamela queried, "So,
why exactly *are* you here?"

"I'm not sure," Sarah replied with such candor that Pamela laughed aloud. "I was just so tired of being at home.
It's been . . ." She paused. Though she liked Pamela very

much, and the woman inspired confidences, Sarah wasn't ready to confess how dire were the circumstances, so she finished with, "It's been hard. I was anxious for a change of scene, and it's been terribly long since I've gone visiting."

"Too true," Pamela concurred. "This is so embarrassing. Hugh told me that you were set to wed, and he requested that I facilitate matters by introducing you to any gentlemen who might suit. I've been racking my brain and luring some of them out to the country. Hugh insisted you were disposed."

"That rat! I'll kill him."

"Don't waste your energy, dear," Pamela succinctly asserted. "Hugh can manage to *kill* himself without any assistance from you."

Because the proclamation was so agonizingly accurate, Sarah didn't respond. Hugh was in a descending spiral that couldn't have a satisfactory conclusion, but she'd deduced ages ago that there was nothing she could do but persevere while preparing for the worst. "Hugh presumes I'm in pursuit of a husband," she grumbled, "but really, I just came to get away from all the pressure."

"As you should have"—Pamela smiled conspiratorially—"and I'm honored that you selected my party for your holiday. How long will you stay?"

"How about three weeks?"

"Marvelous. We'll fill your time with engaging recreation, then send you home refreshed and primed to face whatever is approaching."

From Pamela's shrewd expression, Sarah suspected that the other woman had learned much more about Hugh's affairs than she was willing to divulge, but then, it was rumored that there were few secrets Pamela Blair hadn't uncovered.

Sarah affirmed, "The rest will be vastly appreciated."

"Then *rest* you shall. And who can say? Maybe my machinations won't be for naught. Perhaps some dashing beau will catch your attention."

"I doubt it," Sarah griped, which caused Pamela to laugh again.

"An innocent flirtation might be just the ticket." Ready to move on, she stood. "If I can do anything to make your visit more pleasant, please notify me." She turned to go, hesitated, then whispered, "And at all costs, avoid Michael Stevens. You don't need a complication like that in your life."

With a wink, she sauntered down the terrace, and Sarah jealously critiqued how she mingled with the crowd, how readily she belonged in any situation. The ability to fraternize was never a gift Sarah had possessed, and she suddenly felt all alone even though she was surrounded by dozens of people. She hated being so detached, and she yearned to fit in, so when Rebecca waylaid her a second time and urged her to attempt the game of balls, she grudgingly acquiesced.

As she walked down the steps and onto the grass, a man got up and followed her, and if Rebecca looked as though she'd beckoned him into action with an urgent tip of her head, Sarah chose not to heed her ruse.

What did she care if Rebecca was soliciting gentlemen to court attention on her? Their courtesy and civility didn't have to portend anything more than Sarah wanted it to. She was adept at the art of putting imprudent men in their places; she'd had a lifetime of practice with her father and Hugh, so she wasn't worried that one of them might take unfair advantage on Pamela's lawn.

Besides, she would be carrying a rather large mallet. If any of the men became exceedingly fresh, she wasn't averse to rendering a deserving smack!

Another contest was about to commence, and there were ten couples geared to shepherd their various balls down the grass. Sarah and two other ladies were new to the sport, so everyone chattered jovially about the necessary techniques. Bets and boasts were affably bandied about as the first pair took their turn. The woman always began, with her male cohort positioned behind and guiding her through the motions.

Sarah's partner had been introduced to her by Rebecca as George Wilson, a gangly, balding man with bad teeth and body odor. He'd bowed politely over her hand, but when he'd risen, she could smell alcohol on his breath, and there was a disquieting gleam in his eye. Evidently, he was sizing her up with dubious intent, and though he struggled valiantly to lock his gaze on hers, it kept dipping to her cleavage, so she faced the yard and the line of players, but the maneuver provided him with a profile of her breasts, and his stare was blatant and incessant.

The couple ahead of her hit their ball, then trailed after it, leaving her with George, and he gallantly offered her their stick, gesturing magnanimously. "After you, Lady Sarah."

As she stepped to the ball, he converged on her from behind. In a low whisper, revolting in its intimacy, he declared, "Allow me to show you how it's done."

Despondency had prompted her into the rash diversion, but reality had rapidly settled in, and she thought she might die if he laid a hand on her. She dithered, trying to conceive of a gracious retreat, just as a familiar voice spoke.

"Hello, Wilson." Michael Stevens casually strutted up as though his entrance was the most ordinary of occurrences, when it obviously wasn't. His interjection of himself into the proceedings had heads swinging from all directions. He called several people by name—he knew many of the male guests—and they grumbled their welcomes in return. No one was glad to see him but, almost as if they were fearful of insulting him, they couldn't show their displeasure too openly.

Surprised and thrilled, Sarah jerked around to face him, only to confront his resigned stare that seemed to say: *I knew I'd find you in the middle of a calamity.*

He was more dynamic than she recollected, his dark hair shimmering in the bright sunshine, and his piercing sapphire eyes silently scolding until he had her squirming under his meticulous assessment.

With his generous height and wide-shouldered physique, he towered over everyone, and the entire group appeared to be furtively analyzing him, while flagrantly pretending not to have taken excessive note of his arrival.

He exuded an energy and intensity that had the men discreetly checking him out, hoping to ascertain how he carried himself so effectively. The women were more impertinent in their evaluation, boldly examining him as one might a rare jewel or extraordinary painting.

Dressed as the finest gentleman, his light blue coat and tan trousers precisely outlined his muscled form. His black boots sparkled, the white of his shirt blinded, his cravat was expertly tied, and he was frowning at her with a severity that stole her breath.

When she'd fantasized about the subsequent appointments they might share, she assuredly hadn't dreamed of anything like this. Why had he put in an appearance? What did he contemplate?

"My apologies, Wilson," he was stating to her partner, "but her first game was promised to me long ago." He glowered at her, challenging her to contradict him. "Isn't that right?"

The onlookers were spellbound by the fascinating display. Not wanting to cause a scene, she lied affably. "I'd given up on you, Mr. Stevens, and decided you weren't coming. How kind of you to finally join me."

"I was detained." He ushered her away, efficiently dismissing George. "Perhaps you can have a subsequent match with her, Wilson, although I doubt she'll be inclined. Once she's had the best, it will be hard for her to lower her standards."

Sarah didn't exactly comprehend the implications of his remark, but she was astute enough to perceive that it had been uttered at her expense. Several men snickered, a woman briskly fanned herself, and Sarah's cheeks blushed bright red as dozens of meddlesome eyes fixed on her.

For a brief instant, George vacillated as if he might protest Mr. Stevens's usurpation, but Rebecca shot a quelling
glare that had him scurrying off.

Fuming, Sarah used the distraction caused by his departure to lean over and whisper, "What did you mean by
that?"

"Keep smiling," he whispered in reply. "Everyone's
looking."

"At you!" she hissed. "I was perfectly anonymous until
you abducted me!"

His lips grazed her earlobe—deliberately, she was sure—
his hand rested on the small of her back, and she was overwhelmed by having him so near. With all the attention lev-
eled their way, they were awkwardly conspicuous in a
fashion she hated, so she deigned to act as normally as
possible. She gripped the mallet, but just when she would
have attempted her initial swing, Mr. Stevens reached
around her, effectively trapping her in the circle of his arms.

"Permit me to instruct you," he said, and chills sped
down her spine. "The game goes like this."

Warm and magnetic, the entire front of his body was
flattened against the back of hers, and she could feel the
solid plane of his chest, the curve of his abdomen as he
arched over her, the strength of his legs as he balanced her
between them. His groin was directly against her posterior,
and the sensation produced an exhilarating swirl of butterflies that cascaded through her stomach.

Wrapping her small hands in his large ones, he controlled the arc of the stick as it landed with a firm thump,
and their ball careened down the hillside.

"Very nice," he murmured, though she was quite sure
he wasn't referring to the ball or the swing at all.

They straightened, and their gazes met and locked. Lord,
but it was sinful for a man to be so pleasing to behold. He
retrieved her arm, then gallantly steered her across the yard.
The nosy spectators still evaluated them, but at least they
were traveling away from all those perked ears.

As he'd advised, her smile was firmly in place, and when

they'd covered enough ground to initiate a candid conversation, she asked, "What were you implying about me?"

"Simply that you and I are acquainted."

"It was more than that!"

"Aye, it was."

"You intentionally made it sound as if we're . . . we're involved." Her stomach tickled at the delicious sentiment, but she easily feigned pique.

"Cross your fingers that everyone thought so."

"But it's a lie!"

"One that I trust will keep your sorry hide out of trouble."

"Of all the nerve . . ."

"Though why I should bother is beyond me." He sighed heavily, a man with the weight of the world on his shoulders. "You seem determined to plague me with your tribulations."

"The only *tribulations* I've sustained"—she attempted to pull to a halt, but he tugged on her arm, maintaining a slow and casual pace as they paraded down the lawn— "have been with you, Mr. Stevens. Now, I'm just trying to enjoy a peaceful game of ball."

"You're so oblivious"—he made a derisive sound low in his throat—"you don't even realize how badly you need my assistance."

She chuckled, treasuring this chance to engage in capricious repartee. "You're too rude and domineering to be of much help."

"That's what you think." He tucked her arm more tightly into his own and reassuringly caressed her hand; goose bumps shot up her arm. "Stick close, and perhaps the lechers and perverts will keep their distance."

Glancing around, she had to concede that those in viewing range were tediously normal, with nary a reprobate among them. "How will you contrive to restrain them?"

"I'll scare them off." He wiggled his brows. "I'm good at it."

"They *do* look afraid of you."

"They are."

"Are you a brute?"

"I can be."

"You certainly frighten me with little difficulty." From various positions across the grass, the other players continued to furtively spy on them, and she couldn't help but report, "They're watching you as though you might do something nefarious."

"They merely can't believe I've joined the game," he explained. "It's common knowledge how much I loathe your kind."

"My kind!" What was that supposed to mean? He was at a gathering full of the nobility! "There's an insult buried in there somewhere."

"Absolutely." He stopped their momentum while they waited for the couple ahead of them to swipe at their ball. "Ignore them like I do," he insisted, once the pair had moved off, shrugging them all away as inconsequential. "I've uncovered too many of their dirty little secrets, and they're simply embarrassed by what I've learned."

How interesting! What a mysterious man, and how wonderful that they'd met! Her musings were a jumble of possessive impulses and absurd longings that she couldn't set aside. She suffered from an insane urge to inquire as to where he'd been all day, but she hadn't a clue how to frame her question, because she'd never discerned how to engage in the coquettish flirtations at which other females excelled.

"If you abhor us all so much, why are you here?" Sarcastically, she batted her lashes. "What possessed you to grace us with your stupendous presence?"

"Would you rather I'd stayed upstairs and let Wilson fondle your pretty bottom?" He peered over her shoulder, baldly scanning her backside, and her knees weakened at the decidedly salacious gleam of approval he flashed once he'd finished. "While I admit it's quite lovely, I'd thought you'd applaud my intervention, but if you'd like me to go . . ."

"No, you bounder." Recalling how disgusted she'd been

by Mr. Wilson's advance, she gripped his hand more firmly than she should have, and he rewarded her by snuggling her a bit closer than was proper. "Don't you dare leave my side."

"What's the matter with your foot?"

The change of topic made her dizzy. "My foot?"

"You're limping."

Her ankle still throbbed from her ignominious fall off the stool, but she wasn't about to reveal any details regarding her mishap!

"I tripped."

"But you're all right?"

"Yes."

"You look very fetching"—her breath hitched at the unexpected compliment, and she peeked up at him from under the rim of her bonnet, when he appended—"with your clothes on."

"Oh, you horrid man!" she reproached as a dimple creased his cheek, making him appear wicked and irresistible. His words induced a swarm of recollection, both wonderful and horrid, and a blush started to rise again, somewhere above her ankles, and it swept up her body, heating her chest and face.

"Too fetching, in fact," he went on. He was distinctly flustered that he'd noted her comeliness, downright perplexed by their flourishing entanglement. "You can't go prancing about, looking so *fetching* at this party."

"My apologies for getting dressed," she retorted facetiously.

"Why are you still here, anyway?" he inquired cantankerously. "You swore to me that you would go home this morning."

"I made no such vow." She dug in her heels, ready to argue the point, but he serenely continued on as though they weren't having a bodily tug-of-war in the middle of the yard.

"I expected you to heed my advice, but perhaps I should

have stayed on the verandah, and let Wilson have his way with you."

"Ooh! You're an absolute cad to allude to such crude behavior."

"Of course, I've seen what you have to offer, so I can't blame him for trying."

She was amazed that two adults, who scarcely knew each other, could carry on such a shameless conversation. Still, she wouldn't have ended it for the world. Primly, she rebuked, "You, sir, are no gentleman."

"We've already established that fact."

They approached their ball, and she stepped next to it, then froze. He was staring at her so intently that she was completely mesmerized by the magnificence of his blue eyes. Up close, they were sharp and clear, cool as shards of ice, and she could have stood there all day, studying them, for they made her absurdly, recklessly glad that he *wasn't* a gentleman.

He pressed himself against her, and as they swung at the ball together, those idiotic butterflies swarmed anew, but she refused to chase them away. She was situated so that her backside was shielded from the prying eyes of their audience, and astonishingly, he indelicately stroked his palm across her flank.

"You have the most shapely ass."

"Desist!"

She whipped to a vertical position and nailed him with the penetrating glower that regularly turned Hugh in a bumbling, prevaricating idiot, but the practiced look was wasted on Michael Stevens. Belligerently, he met it, then his focus dropped to her lips and lingered, as tangible as the kiss he'd bestowed the previous night. He was much better at intimidation than she'd ever conceived of being, and she bravely strove to rival his hot stare, but could only persevere for a moment.

Irritated by her lack of fortitude where he was concerned, she whirled away, but he matched her stride for stride, moderating their progress so it seemed friendly and methodical.

Calmly, tenaciously, he propounded, "That's what they're all contemplating."

"What?"

"They're inspecting your bottom and your bust, and they're imagining how arousing it would be to catch you by yourself." They'd reached their ball, and she waved toward it so that he might strike at it alone.

"Be my guest," she said.

"Rules of the game, darling"—the endearment rolled off his tongue as though he'd spoken it to hundreds of women in his life—"we have to hit the ball together. It is specifically designed to provide the men with infinite opportunities to be naughty in public."

She peered about, cogitating as to whether he was telling the truth, because if he was, then the guests would infer that he'd come out onto the yard in order to touch her improperly, and with his disposition and posturing, he'd done nothing to squelch the notion. Plainly, they'd created a maelstrom of supposition, with the spectators patently curious as to why he'd sought her out.

The women regarded her jealously, wishing they'd secured similar prurient courtesy for themselves, but the men had a heightened awareness of her, as though—if Stevens was attracted—there must be something provocative they'd missed.

Were they all leering at her with indecent purpose? Or were Mr. Stevens's admonitions inciting paranoia?

"If what you say is factual, then your conduct has made matters worse. Not better!"

"Hardly. Don't forget that I'm the one who prevented Wilson from groping you."

More cautious now, she let him slip his arms around her, and she liked how she tingled when his body made contact with her own. The surroundings were more extreme, the grass greener, the sky clearer, the air fresher. When his hands encompassed hers, and they mutually bat-

ted with the stick, she relished the unadulterated power of
his torso. He moved with a fluid grace, inducing a myriad
of lurid images. Of his naked chest and brawny shoulders.
Of his adept fingers and seeking tongue.

Of the naked woman with whom he'd cavorted in the
small, dimly lit room.

Gad! She must never discount his natural proclivities!

The ball glided off, and she shifted away. "For some
reason, you want to alarm me, but it's not working."

"He'll try to sneak into your room."

"What?"

"In the night, Wilson will strive to gain entry. I succeeded with little difficulty, so he'll be able to prevail if
he's obstinate enough. Which he is."

"You're mad."

"He will," Mr. Stevens announced with such conviction
that she shuddered involuntarily. "How will you protect
yourself once he's there?"

Desirous of knocking the arrogant oaf down a peg or
two, but not sure how, she caustically stated, "I guess you'll
have to crash through our adjoining door and rush to my
rescue."

"What if I'm not about when it occurs?" He scowled at
her, patently puzzled by his burgeoning involvement in her
affairs. "I'm not joking," he reiterated. "You're not safe
here. Please go. First thing tomorrow." She glared at him
but said nothing, so he added irascibly, "Promise me you
will!"

"Mr. Stevens"—she was categorically exasperated by
his caution—"why does it matter to you whether I remain
or depart?"

For a single second—just one—she thought he would
answer honestly. Stark worry and bleak concern were evident, and she braced to hear a heartwarming comment that
would confound her common sense. Then, as though a
screen fell into place, his emotions were deliberately
masked.

"I can't tolerate insipid women, Sarah, and you don't

seem stupid. You must realize that dawdling here is foolish."

Idiot! she chided herself. As if this flinty scoundrel would have professed a kind sentiment!

The remark was issued just as they approached the end of the lawn, which precluded further discussion. All of the contestants' balls were in the basket but theirs, and Mr. Stevens administered a quick swipe that spun it into the middle of the pile. His overbearing demeanor precluded any gay jesting with the other couples. Not dallying to sociably tally with the rest of the group while they established the winner, he briskly escorted her toward the verandah.

Once they were out of earshot, she scolded, "You are the most discourteous person I've ever met."

"Yes, I am."

"You go out of your way to be uncivil."

"I thrive on it."

"I can't abide such churlish behavior."

"I don't care."

In two more strides, they were at the porch, and it dawned on her that she'd been given the perfect excuse to probe him for personal details, and she'd squandered it. He addled her wits as though she was still an awkward adolescent girl, dazzled by a dapper male.

She climbed onto the lowest stair, while he resided on the grass, and the extra height put them eye to eye. Regarding him painstakingly, she'd have been perfectly content to tarry, daydreaming and seeking to understand him, but others were tracking their every move.

"Thank you for the game, Mr. Stevens."

"My pleasure." He bowed appropriately over her hand. "Have a pleasant evening."

Brushing past her, he disappeared into the massive house without a backward glance, while she stood like a simpleton, reflecting on how terrible it would be if she never saw him again. For all his contemptuous manners and crude, imperious ways, she'd never hitherto encountered anyone like him, and she was undeniably enthralled.

At his departure, people gawked at her as if she'd
sprouted a second head, and she yearned for privacy, but
she couldn't retire so early. Casually, she strolled into the
residence, rambling about, until she deposited herself in the
music salon where two women were performing duets on
the pianoforte. She reclined on one of the couches and listened, the music washing over her and calming her racing
heart.

On the mantel, the clock ticked aggravatingly, and she
silently calculated how long it would be before she could
plead fatigue and escape for the night, and even as she
marked the slow passage of the minutes, she pondered
whether Mr. Stevens would later visit the secret room, if
he would cavort with another lover.

Sarah had no intention of forgoing the lewd distraction
Pamela had so obligingly furnished. She planned to watch
all; every riveting, disturbing, glorious aspect of Michael
Stevens's indiscreet exhibition.

Rebecca Monroe scrutinized her cousin from across the
lawn. She had always liked Sarah in the abstract, though
she was envious of her, too. Sarah was all that Rebecca
was not. Strong-willed, determined, and headstrong while
Rebecca imagined herself to be the opposite: inept, waver-
ing, and inefficient. Plus, Sarah had the unfair advantage
of being the daughter of an earl, while Rebecca had
emerged from the indigent side of the family, the only child
of a severe, incompetent merchant who'd died drunk and
penniless.

For many years, Rebecca had soothed herself with the
perception that she'd bested Sarah in looks and comportment, the only commodities that held any value for a
woman. Rebecca had been born pretty, and Sarah had been
gauche and plain. While growing up, Rebecca had seen
Sarah on a handful of occasions, and she could vividly recall how people used to privately despair over how she
would mature. Yet Sarah had blossomed, and her current

state of loveliness irritated Rebecca to no end.

Still, she struggled not to be petty or bitter over all the blessings that had been conferred on Sarah and that she perpetually took for granted. After all, Sarah had offered her shelter at a desperate time, and because of her generosity, Rebecca had managed to gain Hugh's regard. If Sarah hadn't asked her to live at the estate, Rebecca would never have had a chance at Hugh's affection.

Considering all that Sarah had done for her, she tried not to be resentful, yet she was irked that Sarah refused to utilize her assets to help Hugh. Through the simple step of marrying—which was unconditionally required for a woman of her class and station—she could fix so many problems.

That's why Rebecca had concocted her scheme to see Sarah expeditiously wed. Rebecca wanted Sarah gone from Scarborough, plus she wanted to make Hugh proud. He never was, always claiming she was useless and ineffectual.

Despite the three Seasons she'd joined him in town, acting as his hostess and more, he was never satisfied with how she carried out her tasks. But she'd show him!

For a long while, she'd been reflecting on how she could force Sarah into marriage. Sarah seemed in no hurry to accomplish the deed, so Rebecca merely intended to give her a little shove in the right direction.

When the invitation had come from Lady Carrington, Rebecca had instantly mulled the possibilities and decided it would be the ideal method of achieving her goal. Since he knew how ribald the party would be, it had been easy to convince Hugh that Sarah should attend. The opportunity to have her completely compromised was simply too good to pass up, and Rebecca wasn't about to be thwarted.

She'd invested too much energy, and endured too much of Hugh's distasteful conduct, to admit defeat. If Rebecca had anything to say about it, Sarah's reign at Scarborough was about to conclude, because Rebecca had other motives, more personal ones, for wanting Sarah gone from Yorkshire. She didn't dwell upon them, because she hated to

seem exceedingly covetous, but once Sarah wed and went
to live with her husband, Rebecca would finally get to
marry Hugh, just as he'd promised from the first time she'd
shared his bed.

She'd become the mistress of Scarborough.

And wasn't that a glorious notion? How she'd lord it
over all those slothful servants who perpetually treated her
like a dreaded poor relation! Once she was their countess,
they'd snap to when she passed! She'd dreamed about it at
length and often, and the fantasy was about to change into
eality.

So . . . though she liked Sarah well enough, she also believed that—sometimes—you had to lend fate a hand.
Sarah would marry eventually, and Rebecca pictured herself as simply hurrying matters along, and she wasn't unduly bothered about the identity of the prospective
bridegroom. As far as she was concerned, men were all
alike. Any of them would be acceptable so long as they
had money. Lots and lots of money to bail Hugh out of his
latest misfortune.

There were a half-dozen suitable prospects already on
the premises and, upon perusing Sarah, each had expressed
an interest in what they presumed would be a tiny taste of
her abundant delights, although with Rebecca's solicitous
facilitation, a *taste* would develop into the full meal. She'd
do anything to become Hugh's wife, and like it or no, one
of the blasted fellows would be betrothed to Sarah in the
impending fortnight.

She peeked over her shoulder, stealthily appraising Michael Stevens as he walked Sarah up the hill toward the
manor, and she couldn't help but notice how the two of
them were whispering as though they were fondly acquainted. Sarah was captivated by the notorious gambler
and ladies' man—just as Rebecca had suspected she would
be.

Now, all Rebecca need do was work on the timing. She
thought she'd had it arranged the prior evening but, for
some reason, Stevens hadn't followed through as Rebecca

had postulated he would. He hadn't been in Sarah's room when she'd *happened* to stop by, but clearly, something had occurred between them.

"Oh, well"—she reminded herself of the adage—"good things come to those who wait," and she was extremely patient.

How could Sarah resist the man's precarious charms? And if, at the conclusion, Sarah's husband turned out to be Michael Stevens, wouldn't that be the most apt resolution for all concerned?

Chapter Five

From somewhere distant, a clock chimed the midnight hour, and Sarah slipped from her bed and crept to the peephole in her dressing chamber. After retiring, she'd lounged and walked the floor, occasionally checking to see if anyone occupied the hidden room, but so far, it had been empty, and her apprehension and anticipation grew.

Michael Stevens completely absorbed her thoughts. Their nude encounter the previous evening, followed by their brief chat on the lawn that afternoon, had her head spinning. She'd kept tiptoeing to the door that separated their suites and pressing her ear to the wood, yearning to detect him moving about, but her attempts had been greeted by silence. No one appeared to be there.

Once, she'd even firmly and carefully turned the knob, though she wasn't certain of her intent should the loathsome thing have swung open. Almost with relief, she'd discovered it locked from his side, precluding any decision about how she'd progress, or there was no telling what heedless act she might have perpetrated.

Would she have brazenly entered? Searched his personal papers or read his diary? Hoping to find what?

Though she hated to admit it, she was desperate to breathe the air he inhaled, to inhabit the territory where he roamed, to handle his belongings, to rifle through his shirts, and examine his cuff links. Thank goodness he'd had the foresight to secure his door, thus preventing any such foolishness on her part!

Cursing her sorry, disordered mental state, she climbed onto the footstool and, silent as a mouse, adjusted her eye to the peephole. She froze; her heart pounded. The event for which she'd been waiting all day was about to commence.

Michael Stevens rested against the pillows and sipped red wine from a stemmed goblet. His steady gaze remained fixed on the entrance.

He was once again wearing only a pair of trousers, chest bared, and the sight was extremely arousing. All that naked male flesh, all that dark, swirled hair, was unsettling and thrilling. She longed to run her fingers through the matted pile, to rub her nose against it, while she traced over sinew and bone.

With a slow hand, he stroked the bottom of his chalice against his torso, arcing down in circles to his stomach, then lower, to the ridge in his trousers. The motion induced him to stir uncomfortably, and his groin flexed.

Just then, a woman joined him, another cloak shielding her identity, but she wasn't the same lover Sarah had spied upon the night before. She moved differently, and she was shorter and broader across the shoulders and buttocks.

Mr. Stevens rose up off the cot and stalked toward her like a predatory beast, all elegance and smooth, menacing purpose. His whole torso seemed to glimmer with an undefinable emotion that reached out to Sarah, billowing across her nerve endings, tickling her abdomen and breasts. A wall separated them, yet he beguiled her, and she couldn't prevent herself from wishing that his enticing regard was focused in her direction.

How she'd adore the chance to become the female enclosed with him! To stand next to him, to bask in his presence, to have those stunning blue eyes searching her own. If she was ever lucky enough to acquire a subsequent opportunity at being sequestered with him, she wouldn't be so quick to send him packing!

Mr. Stevens began with the same question he had the prior night. "What's your name?"

The woman spoke softly and, as before, Sarah couldn't detect her answer.

"Who is your husband?" There was a telling silence, a

muttered comment, then Michael's sarcastic grin, and Sarah
would have given all she possessed to behold the woman's
expression. Finally, he asked, "What is it you would like
to do for me?"

After a lengthy hesitation, the woman leaned forward
and whispered in his ear, hovering close. He'd cocked his
head, listening, and Sarah suffered a strange flash of envy
and jealousy at noting their nearness, but she impelled herself to remain calm. To watch. To study. No matter how
disturbing, she had to ascertain what they were contemplating.

"Ah . . . *I* get to choose . . ." he mused. "Have you been
informed about what I like best?"

The woman nodded and said something, but the only
word Sarah could decipher was *mouth*, and, upon hearing
whatever she was suggesting, Mr. Stevens's eyes glittered
with triumph. What was it that he liked *best*? There seemed
to be a cryptic code to these assignations that everyone
could interpret but herself, and not understanding the intricate meanings was the worst sort of torture.

"And you're still inclined to proceed?"

Another nod.

"I'm a big man. Bigger than most."

"Aye," the woman murmured, "so I've been told."

"Once you've started, you have to finish. You might find
it unpalatable."

"I'm sure you're wrong. I expect it will be *very* pleasant." The woman was obviously regarding him specula-
tively, appraising his marvelous physique. "I wouldn't have
scheduled an appointment if I wasn't disposed to continue
to the end."

For what precisely was he contracting? Sarah wondered.
How many ways could a man and woman delight in each
other's physical company? Plainly, there were many clandestine behaviors about which she was unaware, though
Mr. Stevens had hinted at some of them during his abridged
visit.

Eagerly, she eavesdropped, anxious to learn more.

"Are you undressed under your cloak?" Mr. Stevens inquired.

"Yes."

"Show me."

Coming up behind her, he trapped her in the corner, and she stiffened at the sudden contact. His hands fell to her waist, and the muscles across his back tensed and bulged as he pulled her against him. She unfastened the clasp, and he dictated, "Push it off your shoulders."

She complied, but the hood stayed on, so her face was still hidden, and Sarah's view included the woman's arm and back. Mr. Stevens's questing fingers lifted to cradle her breasts and, although Sarah couldn't see the maneuver, she sensed his ministrations.

He was trifling with the woman's nipples, twisting and twirling them as he had Sarah's own, and she observed, stimulated and agog. He rocked his front against his lover's backside, and he dallied, his searching hands never still, until he had her squirming. The woman groaned, as though in misery, but Mr. Stevens only gripped her tighter.

"Does your husband touch you like this?" he queried.

"No, never."

"How about like this?"

"No," the woman repeated, gasping and writhing, and Sarah received the distinct impression that he was smirking and preening.

Men! She'd never comprehend their thinking or their motives!

She strained against the peephole, but she couldn't discern exactly what he was affecting. He was caressing the woman, but how? How was he provoking her to dissemble so dramatically?

His paramour was definitely relishing his thoroughness. Guttural moans issued from her throat, a fist wrestled against the leg of his trouser, grappling for purchase against the taut fabric. In visible ecstasy, her head tipped back, and Mr. Stevens kissed and bit against her nape.

He rotated her, until they were facing the mirror, and

the moment became too personal for Sarah, because she recalled only too well how he'd positioned *her* when he'd been in her dressing room, how he'd cupped her breasts and toyed with her nipples. She could still vividly recall the heat and scent of his skin, the strength of his resolve.

Her nipples began to ache. With each beat of her heart, her pulse pounded through them. They cried out for a type of relief she couldn't describe and, hoping to ease their distress, she covered one of them with her palm. The contact set off a maelstrom of agitation that rolled through her chest and rushed down her stomach, centering between her legs.

Her womanly cleft dampened, the flesh swelled. In agony, she grazed down her abdomen to her wet core. Even through the fabric of her nightrail, she could feel the radiating warmth. Her total being pleaded for a release that was outside her realm of experience, and a frantic longing seemed about to sweep her away. Without a doubt, the novel, strange appetites were stirred by what she was perusing.

Stop watching! she ordered herself. *This isn't right or proper.* But she could no more quit than she could halt the sun from rising on the morrow. She was mesmerized by the sight of his bronzed fingers on the woman's pale breast. The display incited unnatural cravings and kindled formerly shrouded desires, desires that she had no means of quelling.

Although she should have felt ashamed or—at least—confused, she simply became more and more curious.

Unrepentant, she pressed against the peephole, braced for more.

Mr. Stevens's arm was draped across the woman's torso and spread low where Sarah couldn't investigate its performance. Presumably, he was fondling her cleft as he had Sarah's, and the woman zealously luxuriated in his intimate treatment. Their bodies rode together in an adapted rhythm, the woman making pitiful, begging noises.

"Look at us," Mr. Stevens commanded. "Look at what I'm doing to you, and say my name."

"Michael Stevens," she replied.

"Louder." She uttered it distinctly, and he appeared exultant. His hips ceased their perpetual movement. "I'll have you now," he declared. "On the bed."

Where the minute before, he'd been amorously attuned and greedy for her, he'd instantly changed, strutting away as though he hadn't a care, as though it didn't matter if the woman followed.

Sarah held her breath as he relaxed and arranged a pillow. What did he propose? What would he require?

She couldn't see enough of the room to know!

Frustrated, she attempted to alter her location on the stool, peering up and down, seeking a wider panorama, but to no avail. The peephole offered only limited access. Mr. Stevens's head and chest were discernible, but not his waist or anything lower.

His lover approached, and it appeared as if she knelt over him, but Sarah couldn't be sure, and evidently, she hesitated overly long, because he decreed, "The top button, madam!" A moment passed, then another, and he ordered, "The next one, if you please."

She was opening his trousers! To what end?

Sarah wanted to bang her forehead against the wall. How cruel to have been led down the carnal path only to have her journey obstructed at the last bend. For years, she'd ruminated and stewed about what men and women did when they were alone. Improbably, she'd stumbled upon a private, confidential method of determining the particulars, the mysteries of the world were about to unravel, but she couldn't observe the details!

How grossly unfair! Whoever had designed the spot had poorly planned the result. What was the point of contriving a peephole that didn't furnish a full vista? She hadn't wanted to witness some; she wanted to witness all!

"You're larger than I imagined," the woman remarked, uneasy.

"Yes, but you were advised at the outset," Mr. Stevens explained indifferently. "Take me at once. I'm ready."

Heeding his command, the woman did something that induced him to exhale in a slow hiss. His entire body tensed.

What? Sarah longed to shout. *What are you about?* But instead, she whirled away. Remembering her inglorious plunge the previous evening, she gingerly descended, then paced. A tangle of erotic images had her body throbbing and vibrating in places she'd never noticed before, and she strolled back and forth, scrambling to soothe her riotous breathing and thundering heart.

What were they striving so frenetically to accomplish? Unfortunately, her background and upbringing provided no mechanism for solving the riddle. She simply couldn't conceive of where their actions were leading, or why they would persist in the manner upon which they both seemed so intent.

At a loss, she sneaked back to the stool and quietly clambered to her perch. To her consternation, whatever adventure had kept the pair involved had been rapidly concluded. It was over. The woman's cloaked back was to Sarah, and Mr. Stevens faced her, looking apathetic. They were silent, unmoving.

Finally, the woman sputtered, "Did you enjoy yourself?"

"Yes." He was cold, devoid of emotion.

She wavered, then petitioned, "May I meet with you again?"

"As you wish."

The woman's shoulders sagged as though he'd just bestowed a great benediction, but Sarah could have sworn his tone was one of bored acquiescence. If he never saw the woman a second time, he wouldn't care.

The woman dawdled, clearly yearning to discuss what had just happened, but Mr. Stevens's lack of interest precluded her speaking further. Eventually, with a slight shrug, she departed.

Mr. Stevens paused for a lengthy interlude, apparently listening to ensure she'd actually gone. Then, mollified, he leaned against the wall and smoothed a weary hand over his brow. He looked more ominously handsome than she'd yet seen him. Rumpled and mussed and fatigued, he yawned and scratched across his stomach.

Unaware of her avid assessment, he turned so that he was directly situated for analysis, and his expression was one of despair and discouragement. His melancholia was so manifest that she wished there were no barriers separating them, that she could be by his side, resting her palm against his cheek, while she gently reassured him that everything would be all right.

Heaving a labored sigh, he blew out the candles and exited, shutting the door with a sharp click.

Stirred, stunned, distraught, and overwhelmed, Sarah peered into the darkened room long after his footsteps faded.

Michael stared at nothing.

The enclosed space was permeated with the odors of raucous sex, sweat, and candle smoke. The ambiance was stuffy and suffocating, and he had an urgent need for a cooling, invigorating breath of fresh air. From the strident sexual intercourse, perspiration had wetted and snarled his chest hair, and he swabbed across it, striving to wipe away the stench.

He could smell the woman on his skin and taste her on his tongue. She'd adequately tended to his ever-present lust, but he'd not been attracted to her in the slightest, and now that he was sated, her lingering essence was nauseating, and he forced down a wave of repugnance.

Disheveled and unkempt, he gazed at himself in the mirror that hung on the opposite wall. The man reflected back was in a sorry condition. His cock had been meticulously serviced, and it hung useless and limp against his leg, but he'd gained only temporary gratification. While most men would have reveled in the chance to engage in such an indecent, debauched oral ejaculation with an anonymous partner, he was not one of them. Try as he might to pretend otherwise, he was sickened by the corrupt level to which his conduct had fallen.

Pamela had concocted the offensive amusement, readily grasping how it would appeal to his sense of the absurd, how it would fan the fires of his enmity toward the aristocracy. When she'd urged him to participate, he'd agreed, thinking himself so detached that he could fornicate freely and without restraint. In past years, he'd sporadically and gladly acceded to her bizarre offers of carnal recreation, but to his surprise, at this current party his misdeeds only increased his despondency, further ravaging his anguished mind and troubled heart.

The women with whom he consorted were so willing to debase themselves, and he abhorred them for it, but he detested himself even more. As though a stranger had inhabited his body, he was lashing out at them, with his words and careless attitude, abusing them—and thus their husbands—with his cuckolding, but despite how often he copulated, he was never going to find genuine contentment, because the animosity he fostered wasn't for any of them specifically, or for the nobility in general.

He wasn't fooling himself: the actual object of his anger was his father, Edward Stevens, the Earl of Spencer.

Of late, memories of his father—and what he'd brought about all those years ago—were floating on the surface, and Michael could no longer push them down. Wherever he went, he seemed bent on wreaking paths of destruction in his efforts to run from the disturbing reminiscences that constantly cropped up.

His father, the king of all bounders, the epitome of all cads, was the catalyst behind his raging. The esteemed nobleman had been a thorn throughout Michael's life, jabbing and poking at his unstable existence at the most inopportune moments.

As a lad, Michael had loved Edward, had worshiped him with a godlike awe, but Edward was only a mortal man, comprised of human vice and bad behavior. When Michael was just three, his father had deserted their small family, had abandoned Michael's mother, Angela, and her two young boys in order to do his duty to his earldom by marrying a girl of the *ton*.

Angela had never recovered from his callous, contemptible act. James and Michael had suffered, as well, as they'd struggled to overcome the inexplicable loss of their father. They'd grown up to be undisciplined, impetuous boys, had matured into brutal, dispassionate men who did not trust or love, who never formed emotional connections, who never allowed anyone close.

Michael had neither forgotten nor forgiven those ancient sins that had been so casually and remorselessly committed. When his newly widowed father had dared to show himself in their peaceful, happy home—the one they'd created with no assistance from his illustrious self—and had lorded it over them by playing on Angela's interminable affections and seducing her anew, the resulting scene had been horrid.

Michael had felt betrayed. By his beloved mother. By his incorrigible, obstinate father. By his brother, James, who had placidly watched the debacle unfold but who hadn't done anything to stop what was occurring.

Edward had mistreated Angela for over three decades, yet she still loved the aging roué. There was no accounting for it, no understanding to be had for the affairs of the heart that propelled people to such insane attachment.

He'd fled London that day and, shortly after, Edward and Angela had eloped, tying the knot as they'd insisted they should have when they were young and foolish and less circumspect. Their marriage had completely numbed him, and he simply couldn't locate the fortitude he needed to carry on as though nothing had changed—when, in fact, everything familiar had been destroyed.

In response, he could only manage to wander, to gamble, to fuck and denigrate the immoral women who came to him, but deep down, he recognized that he could never vent the wrath he harbored for Edward. There were not enough hours in the day to totally unleash his malice, so why keep on? Why did he persevere?

Unbidden, an image of Sarah popped into his head, and he shuddered with disgust at himself. What he wouldn't give to laze in her virtue, to frolic in her untainted company. He felt unclean and impure, and his spirit begged for deliverance from the burdens that prodded him to comport himself so imprudently.

Earlier in the afternoon, when he'd glanced down into the yard from one of the upstairs windows, he'd been shocked to find her still in attendance. He'd been so positive that she would heed his frightening advice and go home. Then, when he'd seen that libertine George Wilson about to touch her inappropriately, outrage had compelled him to intervene. Against his will, she'd awakened his protective instincts and caused his forsaken chivalry to rear its ugly head. Like a magnet, she tugged at his resistant impulses to safeguard and cherish.

She was so original, so unsullied, and he couldn't abide the idea of her being tarnished in any fashion. In his current state, among these vile people, she seemed to represent the only good thing still thriving in his universe, and he shook away his thoughts of her. In such a foul atmosphere, it was wrong to contemplate her.

Scratching across his stomach, he could smell himself and the woman's cloying perfume. He reeked. The sticky residue from his seed had dried on his phallus. He was sickened by his degeneracy, and he desperately craved a bath to wash away the evidence of his degradation.

Initially, he'd told Pamela that he'd have carnal relations with two other women before the night was over. Usually, he accommodated her whims and caprices, but his desire to oblige her had waned, and he couldn't go through with it.

He blew out the candles and walked out to the secret stairwell, destined for his bedchamber. In the shadowed hall, a vision of Sarah flashed through his mind again, and he flinched.

What would she think if she ever discovered the depth of his depravity?

Chapter Six

Pamela Blair reclined on her sofa, her negligee loosely tied and widely parted to reveal bare cleavage and a smooth, waxed leg. Across her sitting room, Michael Stevens brooded and stewed and, as usual when he was near, he took up too much space. Such a virile, vital person, he was so different from the diverse gentlemen of her acquaintance who were watered-down versions of the male animal.

He exhibited none of the fluff or posturing, none of the pretension or swaggering, that the others practiced ad nauseum, but then, he didn't need to preen or pose. With that invincible combination of attitude, demeanor, and temperament, rivals could only jealously envy him. And he was so bloody good-looking. An amazing body, coupled with a comely face and those mesmerizing sapphire eyes, ensured that he cut a swath wherever he went. Heads turned, women coveted, men begrudged. It almost wasn't fair to the members of his sex that he possessed so much, while the rest of them had been graced with so little.

His dynamism came from his mother, she knew. Angela Ford, the flamboyant actress, had set society on its ear thirty years earlier through her notorious affair with the Earl of Spencer. She was now in her mid-fifties but remained a stunning, enchanting beauty, acclaimed for her keen wit, outlandish dress, and direct manner.

While his father, Edward Stevens, was a handsome, intelligent, and vibrant man, Angela's allure was responsible for Michael's constitution. He had inherited her fabulous traits, yet he incessantly carried himself as though he had no idea of his staggering impact.

She'd known him for over a decade, and had initially

become friends through his older brother, James, who was Michael's duplicate in sexy dispensation and bold demeanor. They had just returned to London after living in Paris for fifteen years. Angela had raised them there, out of the hurtful glare of the Quality's lofty snobbery. But once the boys were grown, she'd brought them to London, and Pamela chuckled whenever she recalled how introduction of the two Stevens sons had stirred the staid lives of so many.

What a commotion they had caused!

Wealthy, elegant, disreputable in their appetites, they had been rash, careless, out of control, eager to embrace any untoward behavior. Mothers had swooned at the very mention of their names. Fathers had wrung their hands over the potential disasters they might instigate. Girls had chased after them in a heedless rush.

Pamela, herself, had considered dabbling with one or both—how could a woman resist?—but as her dear husband had been alive at the time, she wouldn't have risked jeopardizing her cordial relationship with him, not even for a tumble with a luscious partner like Michael Stevens. Although that's not to say that she hadn't sampled his delectable charms on numerous occasions after her spouse had passed on.

He stood before her now, showing her his back. Restless, jaded, potent, he'd matured, and thus calmed some of his excessive conduct, but he wasn't averse to sporadically participating in periodic extravagant immoderation.

Sipping a glass of the strong Scots whisky he favored, he was ignoring her and gazing out into the yard, and as she studied him, she couldn't help wondering what had plagued him the past few months. Ordinarily, she had no problem ferreting out lurid details, but despite all her inquiries, she hadn't been able to uncover what had driven him from the city. And Michael assuredly wasn't providing any clues. He could be as tight-lipped as a jar of sealed preserves when the situation called for it.

Some disturbing circumstance had sent him into a bizarre downward spiral that was distinctly out of character. Instead of administering his duties at the famous gentlemen's club he owned with James, he'd been attending country parties, one after the next. He couldn't abide rubbing elbows with the exalted slackers and louts who also visited, frequently explaining that he was forced to put up with them at his establishment, but not in his private hours.

So ... what was he doing at her house?

Gambling impulsively, for incredibly high stakes, he no longer appeared to care how much he won or lost. Nor was he concerned over who was damaged in the process, even though he invariably harbored a reputation as deliberate in his games of chance. He'd witnessed too much of the havoc produced by wagering, so he seldom indulged more than the smallest bets, yet now, he was bent on destruction.

While she wouldn't have been surprised by such outrageous behavior from his brother, Michael had perpetually been the more reticent of the two, and more likely to refrain from excess.

His sport with the female guests was typical of the recent changes. While he wasn't averse to partaking in lewd entertainment, he wasn't usually the first in line to volunteer, either. Yet when she'd suggested her latest visual amusement, which allowed her to take full advantage of the manor's less savory attributes, he'd promptly agreed.

The lady party-goers were begging to couple with him, and the news that he was present and available had them scurrying from London. Though her fetes were constantly well attended, his appearance had made the gathering an absolute priority for many. She hadn't managed to generate such enthusiasm since the time his brother, James, had done much the same.

The silly ninnies of the *ton* were scared of Michael Stevens, and they weren't sure how to interpret his commanding personality. With his curt comments and fuck-me-or-don't attitude, the women were lining up in droves, greedy to experience his rough brand of illicit sexual intercourse and, though none of them would admit it, each slyly yearned to be the unique paramour who cracked through his hard shell.

Plus, he was just so damned pretty. There wasn't a woman in the kingdom who had the fortitude to deny herself such pleasure when it was freely offered.

"Let's engage in some loveplay," she stated baldly, wishing he'd acquiesce but figuring he wouldn't. She'd invited him upstairs for a tryst, but he'd yet to indicate any interest.

Further opening the lapels of her robe, she granted him an abundant view of her rounded breasts—if he'd ever deign to look in her direction—then she stroked with her hand and squeezed the nipple, effortlessly arousing herself as she thought about how agile he was with that wicked tongue of his.

"I don't think so."

"You cad!" she grumbled, though she was smiling. They'd not been lovers for an eternity, and she missed him, enough so that she'd lured him into her private salon in the middle of the day. He was a man with whom she could flagrantly trifle and not worry about an unwanted pregnancy. Michael was extremely careful and would never provoke a conclusion that might lead to disaster. "Don't you dare say you're not in the mood!"

"I won't," he concurred, and she was fairly confident he was smiling, too.

"I've undressed and everything!"

"Sorry."

"You can be positively lethal to a woman's pride!"

"I try my best."

"You bounder. Now that you've been so cruel, I don't think I'll share the dreadful news I've received from London." She playfully pouted, suspecting that her reference to the city would pique his curiosity, and she was correct. He glanced at her over his shoulder.

"I don't care to be apprised of anything that is occurring in town."

"Aren't you a fine friend! You won't fornicate with me, and you won't listen to my woes, either."

"I loathe your gossip."

"Men!" she chided. "Why do I keep any of you around?"

He sighed, trying to sound put-upon but failing. "What is it?"

"My stepson, Harold"—she exaggerated the appellation of her late husband's son, an ass who was ten years her junior, a boor whom she despised—"has resolved to marry. I'm about to become a dowager!"

The tidbit had the desired effect. He chuckled. "You? A dowager?"

"Yes, can you believe it!"

Mischievously, he regarded her scantily covered torso, inspecting the swell of her bosom. "Well," he mused casually, "you *are* starting to sag a tad here and there."

"Oh! You horrid wretch!" She laughed and grabbed a pillow, flinging it at him. "If the term *dowager* ever springs from your lips, I'll wring your neck!"

"Yes, ma'am," he avowed sternly, pretending to be thoroughly chastised. "Is he busy having the dower house cleaned and equipped so he can hide you away?"

"I'd kill the little worm if he tried."

"Yes," he asserted, "I suppose you would."

Her feud with the callow boy was protracted and had begun the day his elderly father had selected a youthful bride. "I'm fortunate my dear, departed Charles provided for me so well." If he hadn't, she'd have very likely found herself out on the streets about now, beseeching old friends for food and shelter. Early on, she'd learned how to survive; she was proficient at chasing after what she wanted—and retaining it once she had it.

"You'll be all right?" he prompted.

"Absolutely. My financial affairs are suitably arranged; he can't touch any of my properties or my money."

"You'll advise me if you need assistance? Because Harold owes me a fortune. I could fend him off quite easily."

His overture was typical. While he customarily displayed an inflexible front, the handful of people who knew him intimately recognized the soft heart that beat beneath the steel exterior. "I'd come to you and James, straight-away."

"I should hope so."

He poured himself another whisky, and the silence lingered as she indulged herself by assessing his marvelous anatomy. She couldn't wait to gauge his reaction to the next, so she delayed until he was completely comfortable once again. "I have other tidings from town—"

"And I told you that I've no desire to listen to—"

"James wrote to me." He seemed to cringe slightly as if hearing of James was rather like receiving a physical blow, but the impression passed so quickly that she was certain she must have imagined it.

He shrugged. "So?"

"He inquires as to whether you're here with me."

"You may inform him that I am."

"You don't mind?"

"Why would I?"

"You tell me." She raised a brow. "Are you two fighting?"

"Hardly. I don't *fight* with my brother."

That wasn't true, but she let it slide. "He writes that he hasn't received any correspondence from your parents, so he assumes that they're well and enjoying their honeymoon in Italy."

Michael was so unaffected by her pronouncement that she felt as if she'd mumbled in a foreign language. Two months after it had ensued, the hasty, unanticipated elopement of his parents was still the hottest topic of discussion in London. Michael hadn't uttered a word about it, but the incident had to be the reason he was raging and alone.

After a while, he remarked, "Bully for them."

"There's more."

"What?" He couldn't prevent the question from slipping out, for try as he might to pretend he didn't care, he did. Too much.

"James himself has married."

In light of the dramatic and shocking nature of her disclosure, she wasn't entirely positive what she'd expected, but not this overwhelming, imposing quiet. She rose and stepped to her desk, retrieving the letter and tendering it to him, but he didn't reach for it, so she dropped it to her side.

"To whom?" he ultimately inquired.

"Lady Abigail Weston."

"Of course . . ." he murmured.

"She's the Earl of Marbleton's sister.

"Yes, I'm aware of that fact."

Pamela was perplexed that the information invoked no rejoinder. James had already suffered through one horrid marriage to a *ton* princess, and taking into account Michael's entrenched dislike of the aristocracy, she had predicted a biting response. She—as well as everyone else in London—was dying to discover how James had involved himself with the beautiful, reclusive spinster.

"What the bloody hell is wrong with you?" she inevitably blurted out. "Aren't you curious about any of this?"

"Not really."

She rested a consoling hand on his shoulder. "What is it, Michael? You can confide in me. Your secrets will never leave this room. I swear it." He merely stared at her with those glacial, detached blue eyes that gave nothing away. More gently, she added, "I detest seeing you like this."

"I'm fine."

"Liar." He shrugged again, and she stifled the urge to shake him. "He wants you to come home."

"Not likely." *Especially now* resonated clearly, though he didn't speak the sentiment aloud.

"He's been searching everywhere for you; he was anxious to locate you before the wedding so you could be his best man."

"Well . . . that's one affair I'm glad I missed."

"He's worried about you, darling. What may I divulge to him?"

"Whatever tickles your fancy. It matters not to me."

Abruptly, he stood, momentarily towering over her, the masculine closeness of his body and the appealing scent of his skin making her light-headed. He slipped his fingers inside her robe, affording her breast a naughty caress, then he moved to the window, displaying his back once more.

"You're impossible." She sulked, retiring to the sofa and lounging as he gulped the last of his whisky and persisted in contemplating whatever was keeping him so fascinated down on the lawns. "I hate it when you don't pay attention to me. If you're not careful, you'll destroy my self-confidence."

"I doubt that," he muttered, laughing softly. Eventually, he queried, "Who is the fetching woman who's visiting? She has the most striking auburn hair. Her name is Sarah."

"Oh, no . . ." Groaning, she proceeded to pour herself a drink. First, Sarah was asking about him; now he was asking about Sarah. This was bad. Very, very bad. "I presume you're talking about *Lady* Sarah."

"Who is her family?"

"Compton."

He spun around, his fierce gaze on hers. "She's Scarborough's sister?"

"Aye."

"They look nothing alike."

"Different mothers."

"What's she doing in Bedford?"

"*He* maintains she's determined to marry and is hunting for a husband, but *she* insists she's just taking a holiday."

"But why here? For Christ's sake, she's a virgin!"

"How would you know that?" For once in her life, she actually had the opportunity to observe Michael blushing. Would miracles never cease? Two bright spots of color marred his cheeks.

"I can tell," he said lamely.

"What? Can you smell chastity or something?" Irritated, she approached, clutching the decanter, and refilling his libation while she peeked out the window. Below in the yard, Sarah was pointedly visible, sitting on a bench while sur-

veying the other guests and relaxing in the afternoon sun.
"Stay away from her, Michael."

"I have no idea what you mean."

"She's had difficult times lately, and there are even more
ahead. She scarcely needs you as a complication."

"I'd never involve myself with one such as she."

"She's a wonderful woman. I like her very much."

"Then send her home. Today. She doesn't belong with
this crowd; she's like a sheep among the wolves."

Pamela was regularly privy to confidential knowledge
about the clandestine intrigues of others, so she deemed
herself to be an expert at deduction. Obviously, these two
had done more than pass each other in the hall. Michael
seemed totally smitten, with Sarah in no better condition.

"She's delighted to be here," Pamela noted, "and I'm
glad she is. I won't demand that she depart."

"Do it because she's your friend. Protect her."

"She's safe enough." He shot her a penetrating glare that
said he didn't credit her denial, and she was affronted. Yes,
she hosted ribald parties, but her male guests had never
violated any of the females. There were too many convenient, willing women.

"You appreciate how Hugh acts," she admonished. "You
can't begin to understand the kinds of unpleasantness she's
had to endure by being related to him. She's entitled to this
break from her obligations."

"What she *needs* is a stern scolding. A swift kick in the
rear wouldn't hurt, either."

She bristled with dread. They were already dangerously
attached. How had this happened? "Michael, heed me: If
Hugh is spewing the truth, for once, and she *has* settled on
marriage, she deserves to find an appropriate mate."

"Absolutely."

"It can't be you."

"As if I'd ever want it to be me." He snorted crudely.
"I can't believe you feel you have to warn me off."

Disgusted with the sudden tenor of the conversation, he
set his drink on the table and prepared to stomp off in a

huff, and she took hold of his arm, halting him in mid-stride. "Don't be upset."

"I'm not," he finally remarked, and he acknowledged her expression of regret by wrapping a strand of her long hair around his finger and using it to draw her near.

"Will you play the game tonight?"

After pondering for a lengthy moment, he replied, "Oh, hell . . . why not?"

"Excellent. The ladies will be elated."

"I'll bet."

"And if you decide you'd like to dally"—on tiptoes, she brushed a kiss across his unresponsive mouth—"just knock. I'm still interested."

"I won't change my mind."

With that, he walked out, and she tied her robe and locked the door behind. Clucking in dismay over this newest turn of events, she went into her bathing chamber to wash. When she exited some minutes later, she peered outside again. There, bold as brass, was Michael Stevens sharing a garden settee with Sarah Compton.

"Bastard . . ." she grumbled, though not unkindly. Sarah was lovely, and Pamela couldn't blame Michael for being tempted. Yet, for all his impetuous disposition, and though he continually and zealously disputed her opinion, Michael was a gentleman. He was gravely cognizant of his status where a woman such as Sarah was concerned, and he wouldn't forget it.

Still, as she covertly watched the pair, their eyes sparking fire, their torsos sloped toward one another, a great wave of unease swept over her. They were attuned as only the most intimate of lovers could ever be. Their attraction was so blatant that she couldn't help speculating as to whether an innocent flirtation with Michael might be beneficial for Sarah. The adventure would definitely boost her lagging spirits before she traveled to Yorkshire to confront the future.

What's the worst that could transpire? she mused.

The dozens of frightening, sinister answers that rushed

to the fore were so distressing that she declined to reflect on any of them. She strolled from the window, refusing to prolong her spying.

Whatever Michael was about, she didn't want to know.

Chapter Seven

Michael was certain he'd lost his mind. Assuredly, he was deranged. Perhaps a wicked spell had been cast over him, or he'd been bewitched with a charm. Whatever the impetus, he was rashly and stupidly advancing toward Sarah Compton. Though she hadn't glanced in his direction, and didn't realize he was imminent, she was luring him in as firmly and methodically as if he was a fish impaled on a hook, and he couldn't arrest the progress of his feet. With each step, he marched to his doom.

When he'd answered the summons to Pamela's room, he'd gone with the unmitigated aim of coupling with her. They were highly compatible and, as he'd not partaken of her delights in many months, an assignation would have been an entertaining, amiable way to pass a boring afternoon. But when he'd gazed out her window and had seen Sarah sitting in the garden, on a cloistered bench where anything might happen, he'd lost his ability to concentrate. Suddenly, his plan for an uncomplicated sexual encounter with Pamela had vanished, only to be replaced with unwonted apprehension about Lady Sarah Compton.

Why was she still tarrying in Bedford? How could he persuade her to leave? What words could he utilize so that she'd go home where she'd be safe?

With all the dreadful news that continued to pour out of London, following him and unsettling him wherever he went, he was frantic to regain some semblance of control over his private affairs. As a man who cherished his independence, and his ability to direct his own course, he was frustrated and baffled by the swirl of events into which he'd been thrust. For once, he couldn't manipulate the conclusion according to his instructions.

He was desperate for one happy ending, and for reasons that were utterly unfathomable, he'd concentrated his attention on Lady Sarah, daftly assuming that hers could be the fitting resolution he so rigorously sought. If he could just get her to agree that departure was imperative!

Ludicrous and strange as his motives seemed, he craved the opportunity to have her reliably sheltered so that she would never be adversely affected by this harsh, unforgiving world in which they were both enmeshed. If he had to toss her over his shoulder and drag her off, that's exactly what he was prepared to do.

She must listen to him!

Quietly, he converged on the bench, and as he drew near, he was struck anew by how exquisite she was. Her spectacular auburn locks were pulled up, and a few ringlets dangled to tickle and glide across her nape. Distinctly, he recalled how soft her hair was, how thick and heavy, how silky.

Keenly and astutely, she surveyed the surroundings, her comely face puzzled, her pert brow quirked. Her lips pursed in an enticing pout. Moist, ripe, inviting, her mouth was the kind that had a man disposed to more than kissing. There were so many delicious diversions for which she could be trained that would put it to beneficial use.

The dark green gown she wore, with its scooped neckline, stretched tightly across her bosom and outlined her magnificent breasts. They were high and rounded, and he recalled how eager he'd been when he'd cupped them, when he'd sucked on those two taut nipples, and the graphic recollection set his male urges afire. Attracted to her as he'd been to no other before, he was incorrigibly titillated and aroused. Though his enchantment was unsuitable and could never be acted upon, he lusted after her with a foolhardiness that was frightening.

He wanted to have her and exploit her in every manner a man could possibly covet a woman. The sentiments she inspired were feral, animalistic, ungovernable, an irrepressible compulsion that was beyond his cognition or command. He couldn't fight the restless impulses she inspired nor was he inclined to; he simply desired her with a negligent impetuosity that was manic in its intensity.

The lowest of scoundrels, he'd invaded her boudoir, yet he wouldn't pretend to be repentant. Offered the least provocation, he'd intrude a second time, and very likely, he wouldn't depart when she ordered him out.

With a careless urgency, he yearned to hold her down, to fuck her until his passion was sated and his cock was limp. In the process, though it was lunacy to presume so, he imagined that by precipitously spilling his seed, he would finally find some peace!

Compelling himself onward, intent on shattering her serenity, he breathed her scent, and their exotic chemistry began to spark. Abruptly invigorated and enervated, he felt vibrant and exuberant; the colors brighter, the air purer, the sunshine more concentrated, just from lingering in her proximity.

The response she engendered in him was relentless and unyielding, beyond his ken. The only conceivable interpretation for his affliction was that they shared an incomprehensible affinity. However, his body needed no rationalization. His robust, unruly phallus sprang to attention and filled his trousers, causing him to ache intolerably. It was reacting as though he was, once again, a lad of fourteen and sneaking out to visit the French whores with James.

How could a woman incite such torment by doing nothing at all? Just by sitting there, looking so damned winsome, she ignited a flame that caused him to burn for her with an unremitting ardor.

Without requesting permission, he joined her on the bench. Obviously, she'd not discerned his approach, and his unforeseen move made her jump.

"Mr. Stevens!"

"Lady Sarah."

"You startled me." Distrustful, she scowled at him. "I suppose it would have been too much to expect that you could announce yourself like any other civilized man."

"There's nothing *civilized* about me."

"I enthusiastically concur!"

She shifted so that she was facing him and, because the bench was small, with an arm on each end, space was limited, so her torso was forced into closer contact with his. Suddenly, their shoulders were touching, her stomach curved against his side, her hip leaned into his thigh. Most delectably, a breast—the nipple pointed and easily apparent—brushed against him and, in shock at the suggestive impact, she reared back but encountered no means of escape.

He was behaving like an imbecile and a knave, yet he pressed his advantage. Employing only his greater size, by bending near and hovering, he worked her into the corner. A passer-by wouldn't have noted untoward conduct, but they were so confined that she couldn't flee. As it was, her hand instinctively rose, an ineffectual barrier, and she situated it in the middle of his chest where his pulse reverberated under her palm.

"Do you mind?" she queried.

A special musk wafted about her. If he'd been blindfolded and locked in a room with a hundred women, he could have picked her out by her distinct fragrance. The heady aroma called to his basest instincts, attracting and tempting him to experience her extraordinary charms.

"Not a bit."

"Oh, you are insufferable!" But she was laughing, her voice low and seductive and urging him on.

In the past, he'd never spent time with females of her station, because he hadn't the patience to weather their prattling, but oddly, he found Lady Sarah to be outrageously sexy and absorbing, and he hung on every word that popped out of her desirable mouth.

Her expressive green eyes flashed with what appeared to be delight at his nearness and, hoping to provoke her to chatter, he said, "I've provided you with sufficient admonitions about this party."

"Yes, you've been an unequivocal boor about it."

"Then why are you dawdling about out here?"

"It's really none of your business."

"You're incorrect. Since you're plainly bound to get into trouble, someone must watch out for you."

"And you've appointed yourself my guardian?" A contemptuous snort rumbled low in her throat. "Is that why you've stumbled along?"

"You're lucky it was I and not one of the other black-guards at this gathering."

"As if you're more honorable than another!" She sniffed contemptuously, turning up her saucy little nose. "You forget, Mr. Stevens, that I've previously witnessed the type of calamity that can arise when I'm in your company."

"I quit when you asked me to, milady," he reminded her quietly, even as he secretly wished he was the sort who could have proceeded despite her protests. Perhaps if he'd carried on, he wouldn't still be so intrigued. "Most men wouldn't have halted."

"Most men wouldn't have entered in the first place!"

Her glare could have melted lead, and it was so thoroughly mocking that he supposed she stood in front of a mirror and practiced to perfect it. With a brother like Hugh Compton, she probably had to bestow it often, but he rather enjoyed seeing her in a temper. The emotions that swept over her pretty features were interesting and pleasing to behold.

"You haven't answered my question," he reminded her. "Why are you here? I'd assumed you'd be traveling home by now."

"I am utterly fascinated as to why you conceive that you're in a position to order me about."

"Somebody should."

"I'll let you know when I'm ready for it to be you."

She kept pushing at his chest but with no success, because he didn't prefer to be shoved away. Crazily, he yearned to lean in, to capture her lips with his own. He focused on the hand that was touching him, and he even engaged in a transient flight of fancy where his avid imagination painted them secluded and alone. Those long, slender fingers would stroke across him, down his stomach and lower.

The very idea impelled him to grow hard as stone.

What marvelous sensations she invoked! She felt them, too. Her eyes widened in surprise, her nostrils flared, and she calmed, terminating her efforts to propel him away. He could almost see the wheels spinning as her mind struggled furiously, striving to process her body's devastating response.

There was no explanation. They enjoyed a physical bond. It was no more simple or complex than that.

The rendezvous became intimate, extremely so, and he was stunned by the compulsion he suffered to fully understand this woman, which induced him to suspect that he was losing his grip on reality. There was no other intelligent rationale for the sentiments she inspired.

"I saw you from the house," he absurdly mentioned.

"You were spying on me?" She smiled, enlivened by his disclosure.

"Yes, that's why I came down."

"You were worried about me. Again."

Though their conversation had evolved to a juncture where confidential remarks might be bandied about, he couldn't bring himself to acknowledge as much, so he chided, "Do you have any idea how isolated this spot is? Anyone might have blundered by."

"But no one did."

"Lady Sarah—"

"Sarah. And . . . may I call you Michael?"

"Certainly." He received a huge jolt of satisfaction from knowing that she wanted to call him by his name.

Slipping his hand under hers, he linked their fingers, then dropped them to his lap. Lazily, he caressed his thumb across the center, and he'd expected her to withdraw, but astonishingly, she seemed mesmerized by his bold gesture.

She studied their united hands, inquiringly noting the dissimilarities—of fragility and daintiness compared to his own broad proportions—and for an attenuated interval, they tarried under her silent, acute scrutiny. A gentle breeze rustled through the trees; a bee buzzed past in the flower beds.

When she lifted her gaze to his, once more, she was staring at him with such frank, visible veneration, that he determined he might be able to dissuade her from her incautious path. He had to persevere until he prevailed on her to depart!

He reiterated, "Tell me why you're out here by yourself."

"Since you demand a confession, I admit that I was searching for you."

The proclamation stopped him in his tracks. "For me?"

"Yes."

"Whatever for?"

"I've been waiting for you to wander by for the past two days, but you've been terribly uncooperative. You never join in any of Lady Carrington's entertainments, and you never appear at supper like a normal person."

The insult made him chuckle. "No, I don't."

"And I've been dying to talk with you."

"Why?"

The vexing noblewoman longed for a discussion? On what topic? She hardly seemed the type to simper over tea about her hair or clothes or any other tedious subject. They had no communal background, one mutual friend, and limited interaction, yet he couldn't tamp down the flair of excitement that had him mulling why she was considering him at all, or why she'd be dallying in the garden and anticipating that he might saunter by.

Out of the blue, she inquired, "Are you happy that you're here?"

"What?"

Shifting uncomfortably, he was disconcerted by her assessment. She peered far into the core of his black heart and made him wish he'd never been so idiotic as to seek her out.

"You keep imploring me to go home, but I must concede that I could say the same to you." She squeezed his fingers encouragingly. "You don't belong in Bedford any more than I. You're so discontent."

How had she noticed? How could she be so unerringly perceptive? "I'm not *discontent*," he was compelled to assert, "just bored."

"No. You're distressed—and dismayed because of it."

"For a woman who's scarcely acquainted with me, you're categorically convinced of your opinions."

"It is peculiar, but I comprehend much more about you than I ought. Why is that? Can you explain it to me?"

Nervously, he brooded over why she was able to glean so much. The enhanced awareness that drew them together defied all logic, and he hated that she felt confident enough to delve and pry. He'd never confirm her excessively accurate appraisal of his condition, so he didn't corroborate or deny her judgment, but still, she gazed at him with a genuine admiration that threw him off guard.

Wanting to lessen her impact, he grasped her arm. "Let's take a walk, shall we?" If they were strolling side by side, he'd not have to directly confront her during her annoying examination, and if he was clever in the route selected, he could maneuver her back to the house before she guessed what he was about.

"No, I'd rather not," she replied infuriatingly. "I'm quite cozy where I am."

Did she move just a tad bit closer? His hand was now unacceptably pressed to her side, and his naughty fingers—despite his strict command that they remain stationary—massaged against her tiny waist in a slow circle. However, his impropriety met with no complaint, so he didn't desist.

For an untried woman whom he'd nearly ravished two days prior, she'd become inordinately complacent! What had transpired to bring about this transformation?

"I don't think"—he fought to sound stern—"that it would be fitting for others to observe you loafing on this bench with me."

"Your reputation must be horrendous," she reflected, composed as you please, as though she'd been thoroughly apprised of his disgraceful notoriety and was wholly indifferent.

"It is." Amazingly, he was blushing. With the exception of his mother, he'd never cared what females thought of his character, yet he was ashamed that Sarah might have uncovered some of the less savory aspects of his constitution.

"I've never before been introduced to a despicable cad," she said lightly, "so I shall consider our meeting to be an adventure. It will be a learning experience; perhaps I'll finally ascertain why women are so regularly beguiled by a scandalous figure."

A definite twinkle glimmered in her eye. The impertinent woman was laughing at him! "You're evidently not bothered about appearances when you should be."

"Why don't you leave this place?" she queried softly, cutting off further dissection of his distinction or disrepute. "What is troubling you so?"

When had he become so bloody transparent? "There's nothing *troubling* me."

"You're upset. Has something happened?"

Before he could check himself, the words spewed forth as though bubbling from a fountain. "Well, I've always lived with my mother and my older brother, but my mother recently married a man I can't abide."

"That would be difficult."

"And a few minutes ago, I was informed that my brother has also wed someone whom I don't particularly like."

"Are you and your brother close?"

"We were."

"I'm sorry for you."

Bewildered by his folly, he endeavored to grasp why he'd divulge so much to this virtual stranger. He exhaustively shielded his privacy, yet he'd blurted out exceedingly personal details to her with barely any contemplation of the consequences.

Striving to mitigate the admission, he declared, "The matter is of no great import."

"You miss him."

He shook his head against her penetrating deduction. "No, I don't."

"Not true, Michael."

As she spoke his name for the first time, his heart hammered with an unaccustomed gladness, and with an unwavering conviction, he yearned to hear her murmuring it over and over again.

"So," she mused, "if you left this party, you'd have nowhere to go, would you? Is that why you stay?"

Instantly, she'd homed in on the very conundrum that had been driving him these many months. Life—as he described it—had ended when his mother had wed Edward. He had no home. No family. He was drifting because of it, and couldn't seem to find any good reasons to go back to London.

"I *stay* because this is precisely where I belong." He thought of the decadent women, the lewd couplings in which he engaged, the sick, ribald sport he instigated in his meager attempts to relieve his doldrums through sexual satiation.

Now, it seemed his entire existence was one, lengthy episode of debauchery and vice with nary a pleasant intervening interlude. He'd fallen so far into the abyss of corruption that he couldn't locate the road that would return him to a sane system of carrying on. There was no reality for him but these perpetual days—and nights—of dissolution and iniquity, and even if he determined to switch his course and tread a more virtuous path, he wasn't sure how to alter his direction.

"We've a lot in common, you and I," she contended.

He sniggered disdainfully. "Stuff and nonsense."

"Why would you say so? I don't really have a home,

either. Everything I've held dear is being taken from me. Perhaps that's why I feel this incredible association with you; we've both been cut off from all that's familiar."

A hideous stab of unbidden guilt slithered through him, but he quashed it ere it could flourish. "Kindred spirits?"

"Exactly."

"That's ridiculous."

Boldly, she set her hand on his chest a second time. Her steady gaze slid to his mouth and fixated on his lips, inducing him to crave and remember things that were best ignored.

She prompted, "Do you ever think about that night you came to my room?"

"No," he lied. "Never."

"I do. Constantly."

His thundering heart skipped several beats. She'd been reflecting upon their tryst? About their truncated foray into pleasure? About how they'd touched, kissed, connected? "Why would you?"

"I've just been speculating as to what might have occurred if I hadn't said no."

The earth seemed to stop spinning on its axis. On a thousand occasions since that despicable event, he'd pondered the same. If they'd forged ahead, if they'd coalesced in sexual ecstasy, would he now be languishing so wretchedly? Why was he so inanely positive that physical knowledge of her body would be a cure for so much of what ailed him?

"You've taken leave of your senses," he muttered, and he removed her hand. With it floating so near to his heart, it created the queerest sensation that she was massaging his woes. "It's this house that's making you contemplate such wicked subjects. All the better that you depart."

"But if I left, I'd never see you again."

"There isn't any reason you should want to," he stated, though the identical notion had crossed his mind. Somehow, she'd niggled into his consciousness, and he'd never be fully shed of her. With the information that Pamela had imparted—that Sarah's brother was Scarborough—any man who possessed a shred of integrity couldn't help but fret over her future.

"I can't account for why, but it just seems so . . . so *vital* that we spend time together."

"For what purpose?"

She deliberated, vexation wrinkling her smooth brow, her incessant attention captivated by his mouth. A weighty supposition clearly engrossed her, for she couldn't look away. The pink tip of her tongue flicked out, wetting her bottom lip, making it glisten, and the sight made him dream about the fabulous games she could be taught to play. That he could be her tutor!

A flush darkened her cheeks, her pulse elevated and pounded at the base of her neck. She probed far inside his being, examining his shallow depths, hunting for emotion that was long absent, and finally, she wrenched her torrid gaze to his own.

Humbly, fantastically, she requested, "Would you kiss me?"

He nearly fell over. "What did you say?"

"You heard me." She blushed a bright scarlet and stared at her lap. "It was difficult enough to ask. Don't be so crude as to insist that I repeat myself."

"I *heard* you, all right. I simply can't believe my ears."

A rush of images swamped him as he recalled his previous fleet effort at seduction: her slender body, impertinent nipples, and taut pussy. When her cascade of crimson hair was hanging loose, it shimmered and swirled about her hips.

Astoundingly, he could picture her in his bedchamber in London, a site where he'd welcomed no other paramour. He'd lay her back, sample and savor, have her until she was begging and pleading for him to cease, then he'd begin anew. He'd continue until he was drained, satisfied, replete.

Vividly, he recalled their one and only brief kiss. How delectable it had been! How undone he'd been afterward! And for so many hours! He'd craved so much more from her. More than she could ever give. More than he should ever receive.

"No, I will not."

"But why? You've come to dabble with the female guests. Why not with me?"

He'd been curious as to where her solicitation was leading, and now he had his answer: His innocent companion was intrigued, hankering for a few love lessons with an adept partner. He couldn't decide if he was angry or amused. "Because, milady, you are a virgin."

She flinched as if he'd slapped her. "What has that to do with anything?"

"I'm conversant with what you may have deduced about my character"—he fumed at the image of her eavesdropping while his indecent antics were dissected by some of the guests—"but I am not in the habit of debauching untried women."

"I didn't invite you to defile me. I merely requested a kiss!" A spark of temper flickered into full view, and he treasured the spectacle. "I may be unschooled, but I don't believe they're similar!"

The volume of their voices had risen, so he bent nearer and hissed, "Have you gone mad?"

"Perhaps!"

"It seems as if you're anxious to be ruined!"

"What if I am?" She haughtily threw out the potentiality, almost as if it was a dare. "It's no concern of yours!"

"That, my dear, is where you are wrong!"

"If you won't accommodate me, I'll just have to ask someone else. I'm sure I can locate another who won't deem the idea to be as unappealing as you obviously do."

The thought of some other man kissing her was so disturbing that he was forced to admit he was . . . was . . . jealous! How absolutely bizarre!

Perchance if he'd been born to different parents, if his childhood had been contrary to what it actually was, if his life wasn't occupied with immorality and vice, she might have been the sort of woman he'd have chosen as a bride.

She was good and kind and precious—the total antithesis of himself.

For her to wheedle and feign fondness, to tantalize and entice with a promise of unattainable possibilities, was beyond the limits of what he could tolerate. He was resolved to show her, once and for all, just how incredibly imbecilic she was acting. The insipid ninny was enmeshed in a perilous pursuit, but she was too foolish to realize it.

Glancing around, gaining his bearings, he saw a small gardener's shed at the fork in the walkway, discreetly hidden behind a row of hedges and sheltering oak limbs. He rose, seized her elbow and brought her to her feet, spurring her along as though she weighed no more than a feather.

"Come!" he ordered.

"Where to?"

"You're about to learn why we can't sneak about *kissing* each other."

With a hasty peek down the footpath, he could distinguish that no one was in sight, so he yanked at the shed door and crept inside, dragging her in behind. Turning the wooden latch, he secured them from detection. There was a window up high that allowed air to flow. Dust and sunlight danced through it.

He stared at her, then rudely and inappropriately advanced, so that her breasts brushed against him, and his abused phallus was cushioned by her abdomen. To her credit, she didn't shy away. She straightened, unafraid of whatever he proposed.

All beauty, temperament, and allure, she was splendid.

"You want a kiss? Fine! I'll give you a kiss." He grazed his thumb across her bottom lip, loitering, conscious of a gale of stimulation that extended to his extremities. "Close your eyes."

"Why?"

"Just do it," he scolded, exasperated.

Carefully, she studied him, then her eyelids fluttered shut, and without hesitating to debate the wisdom of his decision, he pressed his mouth to hers. Confounded, she stiffened but didn't pull away, not hindering him in the least, so he pretended that her placidity was acquiescence.

Holding only the back of her neck, he didn't deepen the embrace, nor did he caress her or flex against her. He simply merged with her and, as he'd suspected, he was immediately overwhelmed.

This is what heaven must be like. The transient concept drifted past, then evaporated.

Sweetly, almost chastely, he discovered her best-kept secrets, using scant pressure and bare coercion. With a feeling approximating joy, he teased and trifled.

Her reaction was just as instantaneous and staggering as his own. Her breasts swelled, her nipples beaded and buffeted against her corset, imploring their release from confinement. Her pulse escalated, her skin heated. Losing her balance, and needing to steady herself, she clasped his waist, her fingers kneading into the fabric of his coat.

A moan—one of bliss and awe—escaped, and he wasn't sure from whom it had emanated. Mayhap, it had been a mutual recognition of their collective exhilaration.

He couldn't have guessed how long he stood, deliberately luxuriating with her. Time had slowed, reality had no meaning. There was only her and the drab shed, and the divine impressions that swept over him.

When they finally separated, he was shaky, perplexed, and agitated—just as he'd known he'd be. His pulse was racing, his body ablaze, and his cockstand so painful that he wasn't sure how he'd walk inconspicuously to the house.

Gradually, he distanced himself, readjusting to being two distinct people when, for a transitory moment, they'd been a single entity unto themselves.

She breathed a soft sigh of regret, then her eyes opened, and she regarded him with artless candor and, if he wasn't mistaken, an extremely misplaced amount of tenderness.

He was a villain. A bounder. An undisciplined rogue with no morals or scruples, the fact that he'd now twice used her badly being the unequivocal proof.

"Oh, my . . ." Her confusion and wonderment were manifest. She held her fingertips to her lips, as though containing the blistering commotion.

"That, Lady Sarah," he stridently professed, "is precisely why I won't kiss you. Don't ask ever again."

Though he was desperate to continue, to keep on until he hadn't the power or inclination to halt, he went to the door, freed the hook, and peeked out. No one was about.

He peered over his shoulder. She was bathed in shadows, a lovely, sheltered, exquisite gem inexplicably dropped into his sordid world, and he wanted her with an unrelenting, reckless abandon.

"Good day, milady." He bowed stiffly. "Don't wait for me in the gardens or anywhere else. I shan't stop by."

With that, he departed, leaving her to her own devices, returning to the manor and the privacy of his rooms where he could contemplate the long, depressing hours till evening and the depraved night yet to come.

Chapter Eight

Sarah paced furiously from one end of her room to the other. She couldn't quit thinking about Michael Stevens, about their rendezvous in the yard, or their furtive trip to the gardener's shed. The kiss they'd shared had been the most thrilling, intriguing event in what she deemed to be her extremely eventless life.

He'd done nothing but lightly touch his mouth to hers, so how was it possible that such a simple gesture could be so riveting? All these hours later, long after he'd departed in a huff, and she'd returned to the house alone and more frustrated than ever, her body was completely disconcerted by the sensations the tender interlude had invoked.

She'd become uncomfortably conscious of her condition as a woman, a spinster, a virgin who was quite sure she didn't want to be one much longer. Yearning for his company, she was now eager to while away her time in wanton pursuits that she'd have previously considered patently ridiculous.

From the moment she'd first laid eyes upon him, she'd been drawn into his sordid realm, until she couldn't imagine an occurrence more lovely than the opportunity to revel in his sweet version of erotic excess.

How and why did he fascinate her so? What was it about him that overwhelmed her common sense, that had her mooning about the mansion, hoping to catch a glimpse of him? It was as though she'd reverted in age to a love-struck adolescent who was teeming with youthful, unrequited reveries which, given the state of their acquaintance, was absurd.

Three days prior, she'd met him in a shocking fashion,

but since then, she hadn't learned any detail of consequence about him. He was purportedly a cad and a bounder, a man of horrendous reputation. But what else?

He had a mother and brother about whom he cared deeply, he was marvelous at kissing, and he would commit any foul escapade with a woman. That was the extent of her knowledge.

Craving an in-depth interview, she'd spent her entire daylight hours wandering about in search of him. In the breakfast room. At the card tables. Out by the stables. She'd walked the grounds, peeking through hedges and selecting provident viewing locations where she might spy on the entrances to the manor. Yet she'd had no luck at chancing upon him, which had only induced her to stew about where he was, what he was doing, and with whom.

When he'd finally surfaced, it seemed as if she'd conjured him up, but once she'd had him within her purview, she hadn't discovered any useful tidbits. In his magnificent presence, she could concentrate on nothing but the physical: how he carried himself, the husky timbre of his voice, the dangerous glitter in his eye. The fact that he was fully clothed and looked superb.

Like a thunderstruck dolt, she'd pondered his corporeal attributes and conduct, while privately wishing that he might visit her clandestinely, once again, and reveal more of his sensual secrets. In too short an interval, she'd developed a strange and unexplainable attachment to him, and she didn't appreciate the notion of him bestowing his favors on his various paramours. If he was going to dabble in carnal indiscretion, she was prepared to insist that he seek out her and no other.

The impetuous decision had been so strong and pervasive that she'd even deigned to knock on the door that separated their suites, urging him to open, so that she could declare herself, but annoyingly, he'd not been there. Or, if he had been, he'd refused to answer her summons.

His absence had driven her crazy with anxiety as to his whereabouts. She'd impatiently prowled, hunting for him, so she could tell him not to visit the hidden room that evening, that he should allow her to be the one to bring him comfort and relief. He could teach her, then let her practice her new techniques on his fabulous anatomy.

Despite how he'd scoffed at her assertion that they were kindred spirits, she felt linked to him as she'd never been with another, and her impression of closeness caused her to worry and fret. About him. About his family situation. About his dissatisfaction with life and his place in it.

Her peculiar enlightenment as to his personal problems plagued her with an extraordinary level of concern for his welfare. She was convinced that he shouldn't be cavorting with the female guests. The lewd behavior was out of character for him, and she intended that he desist. At once. That he regroup and renounce his reckless conduct. Their kiss had been phenomenal, splendid, and she simply couldn't abide to learn that he didn't possess a similar sentiment about the whole affair. After their heated, bonding embrace, he absolutely couldn't go around making love with others!

The hour was late, the manor settled and quiet, and she contemplated whether she should endeavor to locate the stairway that led to the hidden room so she could stop him before he entered. For a good part of the day, she'd tried to ferret out the mode of access, but she'd been unsuccessful at deciphering its position, so she doubted if she could stumble upon it in the dark.

Baffled and apprehensive, she went to her dressing room, sneaked to the peephole, and stealthily climbed onto the footstool. To her dismay, Michael Stevens had magically appeared and was sequestered inside. He lounged, negligent as ever. Bored and delectable, he waited for another anonymous lover to join him.

Though she longed to pound on the wall and call his name, she restrained herself. She watched—as she always did. She couldn't tear herself away from his beautiful face, his furred chest, his tight trousers. As usual, the top buttons were unfastened, and her gaze was held captive by the male mysteries buried below.

How she craved to see him in the altogether! To run her hands across that marvelous torso! To massage and caress as he permitted his other paramours to indulge themselves on a regular basis!

From off to the side, the door opened. A woman stepped into sight, cloaked and concealed, and Michael straightened.

"Don't do this," Sarah implored, but silently. "Michael, please . . ."

Hating to observe, but unable to discontinue, she kept her eyes glued to the pair, bracing for what was coming, aware of the sick amusement in which they would engage, but she couldn't stop herself.

The titillation was extreme, the arousal disturbing and impossible to resist. Disgusted with herself and her motives, disgusted with Michael and his, she pressed her eye to the hole just as Michael rose to his feet.

"What's your name?" he inquired, and at the woman's casual response, he chuckled. Whoever was under the cape was a person Michael knew well, an associate whose company he relished. He stared at her with a bemused expression, and he chided her lightly, a hint of familiarity and admiration in his question. "Why are you here? You don't like showing off."

"You've been neglecting me, darling," the woman pouted. "You declined to oblige me this afternoon."

Sarah's mind swirled in panic. He'd been with this woman during the afternoon? When? Before or after her own assignation with him? Could he have kissed her so amorously, so passionately, then casually moved on to another? The concept didn't bear contemplating.

"I wasn't in the mood," Michael said somewhat petulantly, which caused his companion to laugh aloud.

"Well, you'd best be now," she scolded, though impishly. "Surely you wouldn't begrudge me a bit of a frolic."

Michael was clearly intrigued that the woman had visited, and he was ready to humor her whim with a friendliness and sincerity that Sarah had not noted in him before.

To her consternation, this novel attitude of his was more disconcerting than ever. It had been painful enough to scrutinize him as he'd manhandled his partners with a calculated, unshakable disregard, but it was so much worse to see him dallying with someone for whom he sustained an evident fondness.

A powerful, unaccustomed jealousy roared through her, and she cursed him and his lover. The affectionate tone and genuine regard were excruciating to endure. She abhorred witnessing the couples' amiable connection, but she'd already enmeshed herself so far in Michael's activities that she couldn't withdraw.

They were conversing, and Sarah struggled to hear.

Mockingly, Michael queried, "What's your pleasure, milady?"

"You shouldn't have to ask."

"And you know the rules," he advised. "You have to state your preference."

"Blast the rules!" she asserted, but she was laughing again.

Their bodies were melded, her hands massaging through the luscious matting of hair on his chest, then lower. Sarah couldn't distinguish the exact maneuver, but the woman seemed to be stroking his abdomen, rubbing across the protrusion in his pants. She huddled near and whispered her predilection in his ear.

"A pleasure to service you, milady," he intoned.

"You scoundrel! I'm perfectly willing to beg—if that's the only way I can garner your attention."

"Are you naked under your cloak?"

"Yes! How indelicate of you to mention it!"

"Let me see."

With a flourish, she whipped the cape off her shoulders and preened before him, nude and insolent. Her hair was wrapped in a white turban, supplying no clue as to its color, and her face was discreetly covered with an intricate purple mask, rimmed with feathers and golden sparkles, so her identity remained disguised.

"What do you think, darling?" She squared her shoulders and thrust her bust forward.

"Very nice . . . as always."

He reverently stroked a plump, rounded breast, and Sarah wanted to die! How could he worship at another woman's bosom when he'd so recently showered *her* with tenderness? She loathed the patent admiration that he showered on his lover, because she remembered all too well how it had felt when he'd gazed similarly at her.

Leaning down, he suckled at a nipple, gently and obligingly tasting the rosy nub. Enthralled, the woman smiled down on him, then shivered with delight as she ran her fingers through his glorious black hair.

Sarah's heart pounded, her womb stirred. As usual, it seemed as if he was manipulating her own breast. Her nipples throbbed and ached, and she squeezed one of them, hoping only to alleviate the furious pang of agitation, but pinching the distressed tip proved dangerously exciting.

She forced her hand away and focused her concentration on the duo, determined that she wouldn't miss a single second of their sortie, despite how difficult or stimulating it might become.

Michael fell to his knees and, whatever he was accomplishing, his companion's eyes glittered, her back stiffened. She bit against her lip, her breath coming in fast respirations, and her fingers gripping his shoulders.

"God, you are so good at that," she muttered.

"We aim to please."

"I'll be sure to recommend you to all my friends."

"I'm humbled."

Sarcasm dripped from his words, and Sarah strained against the peephole, desperate to discern precisely what had his visitor so preoccupied, but she couldn't identify the procedure.

The episode resumed, the woman increasingly distraught, her body exhibiting more tension. Then, for some inexplicable reason, she stepped away from him.

"Not just yet."

From his position on the floor, he glared up at her. "I'm not finished."

"Neither am I."

Winking playfully, she scooted to the bed and giggled when he grabbed for her. He climbed behind her, centering himself, and it looked as if he was unbuttoning his pants. The woman wiggled against his groin, and she was merrily preventing him from achieving whatever he intended.

"Behave!" the woman scolded as Michael bit against her neck, and she shrugged him off. "I advised you of my choice. And it's not this! You must honor my request."

They tumbled about, kissing and cuddling, until Michael was lying on his back, the woman on top. Down toward the bodily regions Sarah couldn't perceive, the woman's hands were busy stroking him in a fashion he greatly treasured, but Sarah couldn't begin to speculate as to their task.

"You are so hard for me," she asserted.

Apparently, she was proud of what her efforts had attained, and she brushed a chaste kiss across his lips. "Close your eyes, darling, and I can be anyone you want me to be." Mischievously, she added, "You can even pretend I have green eyes and auburn hair; I won't mind."

"Witch," he grumbled as the woman committed an exploit that caused them both to gasp with a sort of reciprocal anguish. Then . . . they were moving conjointly, much as one would when riding a horse. The motion went on and on, the lovers more involved, more intense in their enterprise. The woman adjusted herself so that her breasts dangled over Michael's zealous mouth. He pressured, milked, and suckled.

Sarah watched to the end, repelled, captivated, discomfited, wanting them to cease immediately, while at the same juncture, never wanting the torrid exhibition to conclude. They reached a mutual goal, a pinnacle, both crying out with a strangled elation, and she felt ashamed and sickened to have witnessed the intense emotion that flared between them, yet she was glad she had.

Their pace slackened, the tension abated, the pair relaxed, and Michael rubbed the woman's back.

Arrogant and satisfied with himself, he murmured, "Feeling better?"

"Oh, Lord . . . but you utterly kill me when you do that."

Balanced on her haunches, she studied him with a possessive smugness, and they shared a charged moment awash with cryptic meaning, and Sarah's heart twisted at having to acknowledge how closely acquainted they were.

Was she his mistress? His true love? She couldn't stand the thought that he might belong to another before she'd ever had the occasion to win him for herself.

Without speaking, they dressed and prepared to exit. The woman donned her cloak, then delayed to carefully inspect him.

"Will you be all right?" she gently interrogated.

"Of course."

"You have another appointment scheduled at two. Will you keep it?"

"I'm not sure. I'll need to think about it."

Evidently cognizant of his dark secrets, she assessed him scrupulously, then ultimately admitted, "I hate seeing you like this."

"I'm fine."

"You could come to me later."

"I won't."

"My door will be unlocked. Just in case." Sighing, she brushed another kiss across his lips, then swirled away and was gone.

Michael sat on the edge of the bed, his head down, arms on his thighs. Regret weighed heavily; Sarah could sense it as clearly as if he was articulating aloud.

Whatever foul incident had driven him to Bedford, with its hidden room, and the decadent females with whom he philandered, he found no solace. Not even the present encounter, and a lover he obviously cherished, brought contentment.

Sarah spied on him for as long as she could tolerate the scene, when it dawned on her that she had to find him. She

couldn't allow him to debase himself with another paramour. He had to abandon his plans for a subsequent tryst.

Without pausing to reflect, or to heed his warnings about
the nocturnal proceedings in the house, she grabbed a cloak
and a candle, then crept to the door and peeked out. The
corridor was dim and deserted, and she tiptoed away.

She was going to locate that accursed secret room if she
had to tear the mansion apart brick by brick!

At the end of her own hallway, she commenced her investigation by feeling along the walls, the floorboards. She
even tugged at a window and poked her head out, wondering if there was an exterior stairwell, but no entrance
was discovered. Retreating to the stairs, she descended to
the second floor.

As she started down, she thought she might have heard
a door shutting, and she glanced over her shoulder, but
there was no one behind her.

Hesitating, she was overcome by the strongest sensation
that someone had been lurking and awaiting the moment
she would leave her room. Which was nonsense. She'd only
been at the party for a limited time, had hardly met any of
the guests, and it was after midnight. Who would expect
that she might be up? That she might be roaming about?

Still, with those devious musings swirling, the shadows
seemed inordinately sinister. Hurrying to the next landing,
she was certain a footfall sounded behind her, and she tarried again, listening, but no one approached.

Chastising herself for being foolish, she went directly to
the rear of the passageway and persisted with her examination. As she passed bedchambers, no light emanated, yet
in one, a woman moaned. In another, a man was groaning
as if in repressed pain. The noises were unnatural, and made
her flinch nervously.

It's just the dark, playing tricks.

She'd always detested the dark. The fear had blossomed
after her mother's funeral, when she'd been a tiny girl.
Night terrors had originated and had never completely dis-

appeared but, as she was now an adult, she refused to have the old dread ruling her behavior.

Noticing no dubious signs that she had company, she returned to the landing, determined to proceed to the first floor, just as a man emerged out of the stairwell, impeding her progress. Fleetingly, she conjectured that it might be Michael but, as he neared, she could instantly ascertain that it wasn't he. The interloper was shorter, wider across the middle, and he smelled different.

Wary, she moved back, and her heart pounded as he moved with her. She narrowed her eyes, seeking evidence that might help her distinguish who he was, but nothing about him seemed familiar.

"Good evening, Lady Sarah," he crooned softly.

A chill ran down her spine. Her hood was in place. But for her candle, the area was black as pitch. How had he guessed her identity?

"You've mistaken me for another, sir." She ventured to elude him by shifting toward the steps, but he effectively blocked her escape either up or down.

"I've been waiting for you." His words seemed full of furtive significance and purpose. "Ever since you arrived, I've been waiting."

"I have no idea to what you refer. Now, if you'll excuse me . . ." Struggling to seem brave and in control of the situation, she shoved at him, but he was large and immovable.

"So . . . that's your game." He chuckled menacingly. "You act the innocent most credibly. Well, I enjoy it, too. We'll have some enormous fun, you and I."

Abruptly, he pinned her against the wall, circling her waist and binding her arms at her sides, and her candle dropped and flickered out. Their positions were angled so that her body was stretched out, her breasts mashed to his. Disgustingly, he'd insinuated his thigh between her own, and he pressed at her core, rocking toward her in a foul rhythm.

"Release me, or I'll scream."

He pushed her hood off her head and jerked his fingers

through her hair. "I don't mind a little commotion."

"I'll call for help," she threatened.

"But you shouldn't expect anyone to come to your aid. Should others happen by, I'm quite sure they'll delight in the spectacle. There are several here who'd love to watch while I give it to Scarborough's little sister."

His vulgar breath swept over her cheek, and he covered her mouth, muzzling her, as he reached under her wrap and fondled her breast. Wildly, she battled against his abominable groping, but he was too big, and she was obstructed by his excessive bulk.

"Such a pretty, pretty girl." His fingers fumbled with her skirts and began inching them up.

Sarah bit him as hard as she could, but she didn't have sufficient leverage to inflict significant damage. Still, he momentarily loosened his hold.

"Help!" she shouted just as he gagged her, again. He leaned nearer, his mouth at her ear, his hand laboring to insinuate itself between her legs.

"You like it rough, do you? Excellent."

Chapter Nine

Michael stepped through the secret door and into the pantry. A candle had been left in a holder for him, and he thought about lighting it but, after glancing out into the kitchens, he deemed it unnecessary. The moon was high, shining in the windows, and he could easily make his way.

He commenced down the lengthy corridor, leaving the serving facilities and proceeding toward the more social sections of the house. Passing the library, he paused and observed—unnoticed and unseen—the decadent revelry going on inside.

Pamela contributed the site for all of them to act out their lewd fantasies, but she never joined in, and he wondered if she realized the undignified level to which her parties sank in the dark of night. Early in the morning, her competent, efficient staff cleaned and tidied, affording no clue that anything indecorous had occurred. Perhaps she wasn't aware of how rashly events were wont to spiral.

Heavy, pungent smoke from a Chinese pipe swirled through the room, painting a grotesque, unreal scene. Two women were naked and embracing on one of the sofas while several gentlemen watched. The men were in a state of half-dress, and one of them walked over and began fondling, then fucking, the woman who was on top. Another man rose and mixed with the trio, taking the second woman in her mouth. Roughly, he proffered more of his cock than she could tolerate, but she was inebriated, lethargic, and thus compliant to his demands.

Michael stared, as did the others, as though it was the most common of sights. The four lovers were degenerately displayed, a ribald tableau of sex and sin that appealed to the onlookers' base desires.

How had his life sunk to such an appalling low? He'd exposed himself to degradation for so long that his moral compass was broken.

When had he become this callous and detached? He—who had formerly carried on with such fierce enthusiasm—could only scrutinize with an abstract, isolated disinterest.

The man came in the woman's mouth, holding her down until she swallowed, then he removed his wilting phallus and straightened his trousers while his companion continued to saw away between the thighs of the other woman. The male audience was laughing, spewing crude remarks, as a third man decided to sample of the orifice that had just been filled to overflowing, and Michael departed, unable to further bear the spectacle.

At the main foyer, he climbed the grand staircase, feeling unclean, sullied, and craving a bath. From past experience, he appreciated that the hot water would wash the taint on his body, but it would do little to cleanse the stains on his soul.

He was just about to reach the landing on the second floor, when he was jolted by a woman's soft cry of alarm. Her plea was cut off before the word *help* could be completely uttered.

Crude and harsh, a man's voice followed. "You like it rough, do you? Excellent."

A couple was struggling, their clothing in stark outline against the white of the wall. He could smell the odor of strong drink on the man's breath, and an earthy, familiar, unmistakable scent emanating from the woman. A sensation of inevitable destiny surged over him, and he sighed, then rushed to the pair, grabbed the man and, with hardly any effort, flung him aside.

"What the devil!" the scoundrel muttered as he stumbled to his knees.

Shielding Sarah from the man's furious regard, Michael inserted himself between them and glared at the cowering nobleman, recognizing him as one of the scores of debauched rakes of the *ton* who enjoyed the excuse to inflict himself on unsuspecting women.

"Good evening, Brigham," he menacingly articulated.

"Stevens!" Brigham griped. "I might have guessed." Wobbling, he rose to his feet, striving for bravado as he spat out, "Bastard!"

"Careful now," Michael cautioned. "Don't forget how much money you owe me. I might decide to call in your markers." He moved closer. "You've upset the lady. Apologize."

Brigham scoffed as if Sarah was a whore. "Bloody asshole, why don't you mind your own damned business?"

Brigham was a coward and a bully, so if he'd exhibit any sort of bluster, he was abundantly foxed. Michael clutched the front of his shirt and yanked him up, showering him with a close-up view of blazing temper.

"Last chance," he threatened.

Despite Brigham's level of intoxication, he possessed enough of his wits to recall Michael's pugilistic abilities, and he grasped that Michael was ready to tear him to pieces. Tentatively, he eased back, hastily shedding his confrontational mien.

"I apologize, milady."

The supplication was lukewarm, and he didn't so much as glance in Sarah's direction, but Michael let the slight pass. Later on, he'd deal with the contemptible swine. For now, he had to get Sarah back to the safety of her room.

"I'm positive you mistook her for another. Isn't that right?"

"Absolutely," Brigham concurred.

"You've got exactly five seconds to disappear." Michael hurled Brigham toward the stairs. "One . . . two . . ."

Michael's skills as a brawler were renowned, so Brigham needed no second warning. He scurried away like the rat he was. Michael waited until he'd vanished, then he turned, the voluminous force of his concentration falling on Sarah.

Brigham was notable in his reputation for violent and obscene fornications, and Michael shuddered at what might have happened. Why was the insane female wandering the halls? Did she think he was joking in his admonitions?

"Who was that loathsome individual?" she inquired, possessing a mere inkling of her usual vigor. She was trembling and distressed, but blessedly, appeared uninjured.

"Be silent!" he tersely counseled, as he tucked her hood over her auburn curls and clutched her arm. "Let's get the hell out of here."

Lest they encounter other guests, he spurred her along, scanning alcoves and doorways, but no one witnessed their passing. Briskly, he wound them through the maze of corridors until they arrived at their own secluded wing of the mansion, and he ushered her to her door, his lips pressed to her ear. "Go inside and secure the lock. I'll be with you momentarily."

Without affording her the opportunity for debate or dissent, he pushed her through the portal and shut it behind. Pausing until the lock clicked, he shook his head in dismay over the predicament in which she'd deposited them.

Didn't she comprehend that he'd have to call Brigham to account for his behavior?

He prowled around the corner and entered his own bedchamber, advancing to the door that separated their suites. Since his initial foray into her territory, he'd kept it barred, a signal to himself that he dare not submit to another rendezvous with the exotic meddler. Jerking it open, he sped through to her main sleeping chamber, first taking a quick inventory to assure himself that the peephole he'd previously blocked remained covered, then he marched over to her in the center of the room.

"What were you thinking, being unescorted like that?" He quizzed her softly, in case anyone was strolling by.

The hood of her cloak was down, and she quavered slightly. She looked young, confused, lost.

"He knew who I was." She was baffled and perplexed by the information. "He followed me."

"Of course he did!" He seized her by the shoulders, but handling her was a mistake. As if he'd burned his hands, he instantly dropped them. "Haven't you listened to a word I've said? About this gathering? About these people?"

"He wanted to have his way with me; because of my brother."

Michael could barely force the question past his clenched teeth. "Did he hurt you?"

"No. There wasn't time."

She shivered with distaste and, to his horror, tears welled into her pretty eyes. In his ragged state, he'd failed to reflect on how overwhelmed she'd be. He'd only contemplated his own frenzied reaction. Not hers. Very likely, she was stunned to the core, yet he was reproaching and scolding her as though she was a child. It seemed a madman had invaded his body, but he'd just been so upset at witnessing her abuse.

What if he hadn't chanced by? What then?

An alluring tear fell and slid down her cheek, and she swiped it away. "He scared me."

A low grumble—whether of disgust or resignation, he wasn't sure—erupted, and he snuggled her against his chest. The top of her head tucked neatly under his chin. Her rounded breasts, the two beaded nipples erect and alert, poked into his ribs. Her stomach gently cradled his phallus. Despite his recent exploits with Pamela, his body sizzled to attention, wild to dabble with a new partner.

He was a wretched excuse for a man! A detestable human being! She'd been tossed about, violated, and, even as he smelled of the sex he'd just had with another, he could only ponder what a precious carnal haven she would be.

At a previous time in his life, he could have promptly curbed his libidinous proclivities, but no longer. He was out of control, incapable of curbing his conduct, and he was afraid of what he might initiate. Not willing to risk alarming her further, or accomplishing something he oughtn't, he set her away, putting plenty of space between them.

Not comprehending why he'd declined to render consolation, she gazed up at him, making him yearn to comfort
and soothe, which was terrifying.

Never before had he been compelled to offer solace to
a distraught female. The women with whom he typically
consorted didn't generate concern for their predicaments or
woes. In contrast, he recognized Sarah as a dangerous adversary, for she instigated all manner of appalling sentiment, until he yearned to protect and revere, to treasure and
nurture.

He didn't want to be ensnared by her dilemma or problems, yet here he stood, rabid for the slightest excuse to
furnish assistance.

What a precarious path he'd trod!

"It is the middle of the night." He fought to remain calm.
"Why were you out in the hall?" Lord help her if she'd
been sneaking to an assignation with a lover. He really
wasn't certain what he might do if that was her response.

"I was looking for you."

"Me?" *Again? Why on earth* . . . He bit off a curse. "I
apprised you of the hazards of this house. Why didn't you
heed me?"

His temper flared, but he effectively reined himself in.
Not intending to be acrimonious. Not planning to lambaste
her with his furious comments. He'd just been so . . . so . . .
bloody *frightened* when he'd seen the mess into which
she'd stumbled, and he'd been deliriously and foolishly
anxious to charge to her rescue.

"I didn't mean to cause any bother," she quietly declared. "I simply had to find you."

"With all the blackguards residing under this roof!" He
repressed a quiver of abhorrence. "What was so idiotically
consequential?"

Glancing at her feet, she was suddenly shy and embarrassed. "I didn't want you to keep your appointment."

"What appointment?"

"The one scheduled for two o'clock in the hidden room
where you . . . where you . . . dally with those women while

others spy on you." Avoiding him, she went to the corner, untying her cloak and hanging it on a hook. Her back to him, her shoulders sagged. "I couldn't stand for you to meet with another lover tonight. It seems terribly wrong. When you behave so, I fear for you; I really do. I had to stop you."

He couldn't move. He couldn't speak. She knew about the Viewing Room? Frantically, he tried to recollect his current misdeeds. In the preceding days, he'd cavorted there on at least a dozen occasions. Had she beheld every episode?

"How . . ." he sputtered.

"There's a peephole. In my dressing room."

Feeling ill, treading like an automated machine he'd once viewed at a museum, he walked to the smaller chamber, casting about to get his bearings. Then he noticed the footstool, the visible dark hole with its shaft of light shining through.

As opposed to Sarah who was shorter, he didn't need the stool, and he toed it away, then flattened his eye against the opening. The room was empty, but a lamp still burned, the wick turned down. Barely breathing, he surveyed, letting the sordid surroundings register, remembering how he'd performed with the women who'd deigned to frolic.

The vista was tawdry, sleazy. What must Sarah have thought? He felt soiled, impure, unworthy to be in her company, yet in a daze, he blundered to her bedchamber. She was perched on the edge of the bed, patiently awaiting him, and though he'd resolved to keep his distance, declining to approach and sully her further, he couldn't stay apart. He loitered at the foot of the bed, using one of the frame's carved poles for balance.

What could he say to justify his actions? Why was an interpretation necessary? She was a stranger, an irritation, who'd been nothing but trouble from the minute he'd met her, so where did this overpowering desire spring from to mitigate and account?

He swallowed. Swallowed again. "How many times?"

"Three."

"Oh, God . . ." He leaned against the bedpost and stared at the floor. Flushing, he felt the wave of heat flash in his nether extremities and fling upward. His cheeks were tinged red with unaccustomed chagrin and something else. Shame, perhaps. Or guilt. "I'm sorry you saw."

"I'm sorry you were there!"

"You don't understand."

"No, I don't, and you could never rationalize it for me."

"I wouldn't even try."

He heard her arise, and he wished he could simply vaporize. Then she was directly confronting him, her skirts twirling about his legs, her body leaning into his. "Don't go again. Promise me!"

"Sarah . . ."

"Is it a manly wanting? Is that the reason?"

"No . . . no . . ."

"Then, why?"

"I couldn't begin to explain." His focus flitted to the wall, the ceiling. Anywhere but into those shrewd, verdant eyes.

"You're searching, and I'm not sure for what, but you won't discover it in that room."

"I'm not *searching* for anything." He was just fervid to achieve some peace!

"Come to me, instead. Let me be the one to love you."

Her unruffled entreaty obliged him to meet her gaze, and the intensity with which she regarded him was acute. "I've advised you before that there can never be a relationship between us. We've a strong physical attraction, you and I, and—"

"More than just physical."

"Perhaps," he ultimately allowed, the indications of their ardent connection too clear to deny. "But we dare not act on our impulses. We would be reckless to pursue such a passionate course."

Her hand was on his chest, and he couldn't locate the strength required to remove it. He was tempted to hug her tightly, once more, but Pamela's scent hovered over him, the evidence of his doomed moral character hanging about him like a damning cloud.

"You won't be intimate with me. Why? Is it that you think you're not respectable or reputable enough?"

"Yes, that's exactly what I think."

Detecting what he hoped was a safe harbor, he gripped her waist, and she responded warmly, wrapping her arms around his back and distending herself so that their bodies melded. He cherished having her so near, even as he ordered himself to ignore her marvelous presence. "You are so fine, so rare, and what am I? A man without honor or scruple. You observed my true nature."

"That's not who you really are. I'll never believe it."

Then, she did the very worst thing he could possibly imagine. She tenderly kissed the middle of his chest, over the spot where his heart ached so intolerably, and he lurched away, her affectionate position agonizing to endure. Accusingly, she stared up at him.

"The scent of a woman is on me," he mentioned baldly, constrained to display the extent of his failings. "I've just lain with another; I've just come from bedding her."

"I don't care."

"I do."

"Then wash yourself; return to me."

Oh, that he could obey her command! That he could have her in all the ways a man covets a woman! To his very marrow, he cried out to redeem himself in her arms, but how could he befoul her with his attentions when he thought her so extraordinary?

"I can't."

"Can't or won't?"

"Won't." His rejection of her overture pricked painfully, like a stab from a sharp knife.

"You'll dally with the others at the drop of a hat. Why not with me?"

"It is different with them."

"*Different* how?" A hint of ire flared.

"They don't matter. Not in the least."

Skeptical, she chuckled disdainfully. "And you're saying I'm important to you as they are not?"

"Aye."

His admission shocked them both. He was fascinated and surprised that he'd reveal so much. She was dubious, distrusting of his motives, and she released him and slipped away. Immediately bereft without her, he was impelled to hasten after her, to hold her close where she definitely seemed to belong, but he restrained himself.

She went to the window and studied the night sky, and he fought the urge to talk, to join her. He suffered the strangest compulsion to beg her forgiveness for being the man he was, for not being more suitable or more worthy, but he couldn't confess what was in his heart. Silenced by impossibilities and remorse, he was transfixed, powerless to make amends, incompetent to alter events. He could only impotently watch as she grappled with the quagmire in which his irresponsible conduct had landed them.

"I'm twenty-five years old," she finally said. "I've never had a beau. Never been kissed, or strolled in the moonlight with a handsome swain. My family's situation is a mess, so my future is very unsettled; I don't know what the impending months will bring."

At the veiled reference to her brother, he shifted uncomfortably but offered no comment. There was nothing to be gained by reviewing her wayward sibling.

"What are you implying?" he queried instead. "That your personal life is a muddle so you'd like to complicate it further by consorting with me?"

"No." She turned to face him. "I'm saying that I'll be here for two more weeks, and then I journey home to odious alternatives and extreme choices"—she stalwartly mastered a wave of emotion that made her eyes glitter with what he suspected were unshed tears—". . . and I am so desperately unhappy."

"Oh, Sarah . . ." He couldn't stand to hear her tragic disclosure, or to witness her anguish, but he had little remedy to contribute.

"But you're here, and I'm here, and something remarkable could ensue in the next fortnight. I feel it in my bones."

She was correct, yet he lied. "Nothing good could ever come from a liaison between the two of us."

"You're only fooling yourself, Michael," she unwaveringly asserted. "This affinity"—she gestured, indicating what couldn't be put into words—"you sense it, too."

"But I'm a grown man," he indicated, "and just because I lust after you doesn't mean I have to act upon it."

"It is more than mere lust, and you know it." She left the window and cautiously moved in his direction. "My entire blasted life, I've done precisely what was required of me, so this once, I'd like to reach out and seize some joy. I truly, truly would."

"You won't find any *joy* with me."

Scrupulously, she assessed him. "You're afraid to determine what it could be like."

"No, not at all."

"What is it, then?" She was growing angry, defensive.

"We're drawn to one another, so I grasp how it would be. There are physical ways in which I would use your body." Doggedly, he chided, "What I would take are gifts you should save for your husband."

"But I never intend to marry," she declared with a ringing finality. "So where does that leave me? Should I never learn of these secrets that transpire between a man and a woman? I admit that I'm selfish, and I crave some of your mysterious bodily titillation for myself. Should I deny myself this contentment?"

Michael was in agony. What man had ever been presented such an enticing feast? She was a mature virgin, primed and ready for sexual initiation. If he acceded, he could excite and stimulate her, teach and disclose to her the sexual methods he enjoyed. A devoted, zealous pupil, she would wield her distinct skills with lethal precision for his exclusive benefit and delectation.

His weary spirit wept in anticipation of how much succor he would obtain. His cock swelled from conjecturing how it would be. Still, he valued her too much, treasured her too much.

"The fact remains that you are a maid." He was reminding her—and himself.

"Your lovers"—she blushed, her chaste condition profusely apparent as she courageously forged ahead to discuss inappropriate carnal proceedings—"they do things to you with their hands and their mouths. You could instruct me."

Peeking down at her slender, adept fingers, then back up to those lush, moist lips, he could conceive of her kneeling before him, stroking and cupping him, while her tongue imparted dazzling pleasure.

"I touched you in a forbidden manner, once before," he pointed out. "You didn't like it."

"You're mistaken. I loved it; I was simply overwhelmed."

They'd gradually migrated across the floor until they were, once again, toe to toe. Her gown twisted around his legs, his boots dipped under the hem. Their frank conversation had elevated her pulse, her breathing was labored, her breasts toiled against her corset, the outline of her nipples conspicuous against the bodice.

Vividly, he remembered every detail of those two breasts, the shape, the size, the color of the solid tips. How firm they'd been! How sweet they'd tasted! With a flick of his wrist, he could have her bared to suckle and play, taunt and tease. He could introduce her to sensual gratification and, in the process, seek his own, but he simply couldn't behave so badly toward her.

He couldn't commit a despicable offense against her. As an untried woman, she didn't fathom the full implications of her proposition. If she was to bestow her virtue on some lucky fellow, he should hardly be the one. Practically any other gentleman of her acquaintance would be more deserving.

"You are curious. You've seen much that has your body eager and your mind intrigued." He slipped his hands into hers, and he felt as if he was holding her protected and safe. "But this is not the place, and I am not the man with whom you should indulge these whims."

"It is not a *whim*." She linked their fingers, the maneuver bringing them closer still. "Can't you feel it?" Her eyes were wide with delight, her smile brimming with wonder. "Can't you feel what happens when you're near?"

The sensation was genuine and profound, and perhaps that was the real reason he refused to dally. If he bought into her mad scheme and seduced her, where would she be at the affair's conclusion?

In a brief interval, their fates would illicitly entwine, and she couldn't possibly realize how thoroughly they would become embroiled. Nor could she comprehend that his level of involvement would be so much different from hers.

At an early age, from the period when his father had abandoned their family, he'd learned that it was perilous to love. So he didn't. Never forming sentimental bonds with his paramours, he sought out a woman's company for sexual alleviation and no other purpose.

Gad, but he wasn't confident he could ardently devote himself to a woman. The very idea seemed so asinine that he couldn't picture himself in such a negligent venture.

Briefly, he would share her life and her bed and—without a doubt—they would have fabulous sex, but that was all, and when she ascertained what she'd surrendered, she'd rail and hate, and he couldn't abide the notion of creating so much havoc, or of causing such wrenching tribulation.

He didn't want to discuss their association, or demonstrative shackles, or mutual dependence. Her feminine daydreams, her romantic hopes for ruination, only increased his longing for too many things that could never be.

Still, he was so terribly lonely. What did it signify if he looted just a bit more of her innocence? The kiss they'd relished earlier in the gardener's shack had been distracting him for hours. The lusciousness of the moment, the strength of the sentiments it generated, had him eager to repeat his folly until he was far beyond rational consideration or action.

"You are so lovely," he proclaimed. "Too lovely for the likes of me."

His statement puzzled her, and he took advantage of her consternation, catching her and seizing her mouth before he could change his mind—or she could change hers.

He nipped and reveled, toyed and tarried, thinking that her flavor was so infernally superb, like peppermint and spice. Needing more, he insinuated his tongue between her ruby lips. Beseeching. Persuading. As though she'd kissed him a thousand times before, she opened and welcomed him inside.

There was no hesitation, no inhibition; she joined in the vivacious kiss with a gladness and ebullience he'd never encountered with the scores of jaded lovers who littered his past. He worked against her, teaching her the tempo, and she met him stroke for stroke, sparring with him in a fervid dance.

His hands gripped her lush bottom, and he lifted her off the floor, until her feet were dangling, her perfect torso stretched out the length of his. Her breasts were crushed to his chest, her nipples jabbing like shards of glass. Stomachs, thighs, calves, they were forged fast.

Though he'd spilled his seed not an hour prior, his phallus was enlarged and alert, pleading for freedom from captivity. He felt like a robust, strapping lad of fourteen, ready to come at the snap of her fingers.

Not willing to deny himself a modest sample of the shattering excess, he spun her and propped her against the bedpost. Her thighs were spread wide and, though many layers of fabric separated them, his cock was wedged against her mound, her searing heat coaxing him, urging him on and in. Matching the thrust of his tongue, he flexed against her, slowly and meticulously, letting her savor his aroused condition, allowing her to distinguish his decadent invitation.

With a virulent obsession that confounded and amazed, he yearned to rip at her dress, to feast on her breasts, to wrench at her skirts and impale himself between her virginal thighs. She'd be tight, scalding, her maiden's blood charging him to erupt at will.

He never finished his orgasm in a woman's cleft, because the concept of planting a babe was preposterous, but with a glaring urgency, Sarah incited him to spurt his blistering emission across her womb, and he was so deliriously aroused that he deliberated whether to empty himself in his pants like an unseasoned boy.

Pulling away, he checked himself, quelling his appetite as much as he was able, even though he couldn't bring himself to completely disengage. Not just yet. Her feet touched the rug, and he rubbed her back as he trailed light kisses across her cheek, her brow.

"Why were you doing that?" She was short of breath, exhilarated. "You were pressing against me. Why?"

"It's the rhythm of mating. I want you . . . as a man wants a woman." He dipped below her chin and licked where her pulse throbbed at the base of her neck. Her skin was hot and salty. "My body is aflame, demanding that I make love with you."

"Then take me," she whispered against his mouth. "Touch me as you did when you were here that first night. Show me how it can be."

Poised on the brink of a drastic cliff, he was geared to jump off into a void from which he could never return. He desired her beyond wisdom or sense, but as with so much in his life, he simply couldn't have her.

Confused, reluctant, reeling, he removed himself from temptation by stepping back and permitting the chilly air of the room to swirl betwixt their heated torsos. Instantly, he felt deprived and forlorn, and he grieved the loss of her mollifying presence.

"Don't stop," she appealed, her gaze expectant and trusting. "I want you to be the one."

"I can't, Sarah."

"I feel as though I've been waiting for you all my life."

"You ask for too much," he insisted. "More than I am. More than I could ever be."

"No, I hardly ask for anything." Her hand rose and massaged his chest in a lazy circle, consoling him, recognizing how he craved her brand of comfort. "I request only these few days. This scant increment of time."

"The stakes are too high. If we were detected . . ."

"No one will ever know; I swear it." Her eyes probed his. "I'll never seek another boon from you; I'll never contact you again after I leave here. Please . . ."

Oh, that he could relent and appease them both in a fleeting erotic liaison. Her solicitation was outrageous, thrilling. Such ecstasy was meant to be acknowledged, but he simply, unconditionally, could not partake of what she was proposing.

"No," he said resolutely, while disgracefully pilfering a last kiss but, as he'd already stolen so much, what was one thing more? "Good night."

"Michael . . ."

He departed, not looking over his shoulder lest he see her lovely face and be dissuaded.

Into his own bedchamber he strode, shutting and securing the door. A servant had left water, though it had cooled. Stripping swiftly, he washed, lagging, the cold cloth soothing his torrid skin. Then, he crawled into his bed, naked and alone, determined not to think, not to recollect, not to care.

Chapter Ten

Sarah sat at a table on the verandah, admiring the grounds. The distinctive porch wrapped around the side and back of the house, and various guests surrounded her, sipping beverages and prattling amicably. The day had bloomed sunny and warm. The sky was blue, the lawns spectacularly green, and a few horses grazed in a far-off pasture.

A carriage wound through the idyllic scene, traveling up the lane leading to the manor. A quartet of gaily clad women chattered as they approached, their journey from London almost at an end. Numerous guests promenaded arm-in-arm along the meticulously groomed pathways of the gardens, serene and content to savor the lazy afternoon.

She watched all with a jaded detachment. The gathering appeared to be just another country party, attended by the bored members of the *ton,* but time, distance, and events had made her more wise.

A half-dozen couples competed at a licentious game of ball down on the grass, and she wasn't foolish enough to let loneliness or dissatisfaction lead her to join in. She pretended to be enthralled, but she really wasn't, not caring in the least who frolicked naughtily in plain sight.

Beside her, Rebecca gabbed convivially about the varied amusements in which she'd partaken. Two women wandered by, and they talked to her about London and a theatrical performance they'd all seen. Rebecca was in her element, fraternizing in a manner at which Sarah had never excelled.

For the past three years, Rebecca had accompanied Hugh to town for the Season, acting as his hostess, so she was familiar with many of Lady Carrington's visitors as

Sarah was not. Though Sarah had planned to be more friendly, to establish new relationships, she couldn't concentrate on the social intricacies of the situation.

The only topic she could mull was which of the women might have been with Michael in the hidden room. The pair before her laughed and joked, as Sarah methodically stripped them, searching for clues that would reveal if she'd viewed them unclothed.

Quietly, she inspected, politely expounding when necessary, but mostly appraising how they tipped their heads or squared their shoulders. Ultimately, she decided that neither had partnered with Michael, so she lost interest in the remainder of the discussion.

As she scanned the yard, her mind was in a whirl, her thoughts jumbled with images of Michael. He was so dashing, so handsome, so unlike anyone she'd ever known, and against her will and better judgment, she was drawn to him, to his life of debauchery and excess, to his powerful presence and dynamic allure.

Captivated, concerned, and worried about him, she was also physically infatuated as she'd never imagined herself being. They'd shared much that was inappropriate—kisses, caresses, words—yet she suffered no guilt over her lapses.

She simply craved some privacy!

What she wouldn't give to have the blasted man all to herself. To be away from prying scrutiny and nosy gawking! Oh, that they could be swept away to a deserted island, like lovers in the fanciful romantic novels she infrequently read!

Were they alone, and no one about to witness their misconduct, would he think differently? Would he act differently?

Just being in his company incited all sorts of magic, and she could only concentrate on the kiss he'd dispensed the previous night in her room. By picking her up and pressing himself against her, he'd ignited a searing fire of desire that hadn't waned in the least. If anything, it seemed to be spiraling hotter and brighter.

There was definitely an earthy, lusty facet to her personality that she'd never acknowledged before, because she wanted things from him that she couldn't even begin to describe, although why she'd allowed herself to become smitten by a scoundrel who had a veritable harem of women falling at his feet was a mystery.

After what she'd witnessed of his antics, she ought to have more sense than to be pining away after the cad, yet she couldn't desist. Like a moth to the flame, she was attracted to him with a tumultuous, unrelenting ardor that she couldn't explain or defend. When she closed her eyes, she didn't see any of his other paramours, but herself, cherished in the cradle of his arms. *She* developed into the lover he teased, seduced, aroused. *She* was the one fortuitous enough to enjoy his phenomenal attention.

With an almost oppressive longing, she recalled the turbaned woman who'd managed to break through his walls in order to garner his gentler style of affection. Sarah's goal was to reap some of the same tender courtesy, but she had absolutely no idea how to get him to agree to furnish it.

They could be so good together! She was convinced of it, and she couldn't fathom going home without sampling some of his enigmatic delights. With a yearning that was indescribable, she needed him to fill a void she hadn't recognized to exist before they'd crossed paths.

She was amenable and enthused to give herself to him in any fashion he might require, yet the prior night, without a backward glance, he'd left her lonesome and forlorn, in the middle of her room. The sound of him turning his lock had merely underscored the strength of his resolve that they not associate. His refusal to acquiesce in her mad scheme had irritated her so much that she'd very nearly stormed across the floor and pounded on his door to demand admittance.

Only the realization of how irrational she'd sound, of how completely she would debase herself, had kept her rooted to her spot. Numb with consternation, she'd prepared for her slumber by stripping to her chemise and stockings, then crawling under the cold, impersonal blankets. She'd attempted sleep, but instead, she'd tossed and turned as she'd pictured him lying in his own bed just a few feet away.

Foreign notions had kept her busy as she'd wondered what was beneath his sheets: how he looked, what he wore, how his body was formed. The unusual, outlandish ruminations made her own body tingle and burn.

Rebecca's voice intruded into her daydreams, engendering her to discover that the two women had departed. She and Rebecca were cloistered, once again, but Sarah had been so distracted by her carnal musings over Michael Stevens that she hadn't noticed.

"Honestly, Sarah," Rebecca reproached, "you can be so rude."

"I'm sorry. I was woolgathering." Sarah transferred her gaze from the horizon to her cousin. "You were saying . . . ?"

"You are impossible!" Clearly miffed, Rebecca leaned nearer as she tugged at the brim of her bonnet to protect her face from the sunshine. "There are many in the assembled company who would like to meet you—several of the gentlemen, especially—yet you set yourself apart. Just like always. I thought you were here for a holiday."

"I'm having a holiday. A very pleasant one."

"You could have fooled me." Rebecca harumphed, then stuck her dainty nose in the air.

Her pretty cousin effortlessly negotiated the daylight mingling and evening amusements. With her fair countenance, voluptuous figure, and polished comportment, she was a typical English lady. If their birth circumstances had been reversed, she could have readily been the daughter of an earl. Inordinately suited to the position, she adored the preening, the soirees and fetes, and she thrived on her months in the city with Hugh, always returning with exciting stories about the galas she'd attended, and the people she'd befriended.

"What have I done that's so appalling?" Though she

inquired politely, Sarah wasn't overly inquisitive as to Rebecca's opinion for she couldn't help recalling Michael's assertion that Rebecca was up to mischief. As he'd been correct about so many matters, she felt inclined to regard her relative with a jaundiced eye.

"You never participate in any of the entertainments that Lady Carrington has devised." Rebecca counted off Sarah's sins, one by one, on her fingers. "You rise early and have breakfast before anyone else. You spend your afternoons in the garden, preoccupied with your reflections. You dress for supper, come down at the last minute just as the meal is announced, then you eat in silence, rarely conversing with your companions. After, you retire to your rooms, and no one sees you again until morning."

"A perfect vacation."

"Everyone's whispering about you."

"Alleging what?"

"That you're a virtual stick-in-the-mud!"

"I always have been; that's hardly news."

"But how are you to make friends?"

"Maybe I won't." Glancing about warily, she grumbled, "Not with this crowd, at any rate."

"What about the gentlemen who are here? How are any of them to . . ."

There was a significant hesitation as Sarah stared her down, her shrewd gaze working as well on Rebecca as it always had on Hugh. Sharply, Sarah demanded, "To what?"

"Well, silly . . . to get to know you, of course. Hugh confided that you were hoping for a few introductions, and—"

Sarah cut her off. "I wouldn't put too much stock in what Hugh said if I were you."

"What do you mean?"

"I *mean* that I'm here to relax. Nothing more. Nothing less."

For the briefest instant, she was certain Rebecca scowled at her with an unobstructed amount of loathing, but as quickly as the sensation emerged, it vanished. She was her customary, affable self.

Sarah didn't intend to immediately worry about what the disturbing impression might portend, but she tucked it away for later. At the moment, she was too absorbed with Michael Stevens and her novel carnal quest. With her concentration so engrossed, Rebecca was like a bothersome fly, buzzing about on the edge of her consciousness, and she felt like swatting at her.

"Speaking of Hugh," Rebecca mentioned, smiling and nodding to a gentleman down on the lawn, "I received a note. He's bored in town and thinking about stopping by for a visit."

"How nice," Sarah murmured, though she was actually contemplating that his arrival would be utterly horrid. She had no desire to run into Hugh, or have him hovering about and trying to manipulate her. When she relocated to Scarborough, there'd be plenty of opportunity to worry about him and his recent fiasco. His irksome presence would ruin her blissful respite.

She pushed back her chair and rose. "I believe I'll take a walk."

"There! You've proven my point!" Rebecca complained. "A gentleman has been asking about you, and he has a friend whose companionship I enjoy. The four of us could play in the next game of ball."

"I don't think so." As she strolled away, she discreetly masked her disgust at the repugnant notion.

At loose ends, restless, she left the terrace and rambled out into the yard, roaming aimlessly until she found the bench where she and Michael had tarried. She soaked in the tranquillity, surveying, watching the house, peering at the gardener's shack where he'd lured her and kissed her so splendidly.

Where was he? What was he doing? Who was he with?

Behind her, a pair of gossiping women were gliding by. Sarah was separated from them by a thick, trimmed hedge so she could listen to them, but not distinguish who they were.

"Yes," one of them whispered, "it was Brigham and Stevens."

Suddenly frantic, her ears perked, Sarah bolted upright. Brigham was the knave who'd accosted her!

"No doubt about it?" the other prompted.

"George insists it's true," the first said. "Brigham was leaving for London, but Stevens caught him out behind the stables. Beat him to a pulp! Broke his nose, some ribs, perhaps an arm . . ."

"I'd like to have seen that." The woman giggled inappropriately. "How long ago?"

"An hour or two."

"Any idea as to the cause?"

"Well, George contends it was over an insult to a woman, but with Stevens, and his pride, who can tell? It might have been any slight."

"I can't imagine there's a female alive who could incite him to defend her honor."

"Not anyone here, certainly."

Their voices drifted off as they sauntered away.

"What's happening now?" The query drifted over the bushes.

"Brigham was destined for town, with a bloody cloth pressed to his face, and Stevens is . . ."

Sarah couldn't discern the remainder. The women had wandered too far down the footpath. She sat immobile, chaotically striving to come to grips with what she'd just learned.

Michael was fighting? With that libertine, Brigham? Was he insane? Wrestling in the barnyard like a ruffian! She couldn't decide if she was more alarmed or angry. Then, like a slow-wit, the truth dawned on her: She'd been the catalyst!

Where is he? This time, the question had a desperate edge to it. Was he injured? Did he need assistance?

She had to speak with him so as to ascertain his condition for herself. Jumping to her feet, she was eager to run for the mansion, but years of excellent breeding kicked in, and she slowed her step, lest others note her hurrying by. She was too intent on her destination to have anyone identifying her, interrupting her for a chat, or remarking on her haste.

Like the nonentity she was among the verbal, exuberant crowd, she flowed through the garden, up the verandah steps, and into the house without a single person nodding hello. Inside, she casually strode to the grand staircase that led to the upper floors. Luckily, no one was about as she ascended, and she climbed regally but determinedly.

Where else might he be but in his private quarters? She would check, and if he wasn't there, she wasn't positive of her next course of action. She couldn't plan that far in advance. He had to be in residence!

Seeming bored but firm, she slipped into her own apartment and barred the door. Shucking off her bonnet and gloves, she marched through the dressing room and knocked at his adjoining suite. If someone answered—someone other than Michael Stevens, that is—she hadn't thought about what excuse she'd render. She simply forged ahead, but no one responded, no footsteps trod toward her, so she rapped again, then reached for the knob and turned.

The two previous times, when she'd been impetuous and tested the knob, the entrance had been locked. Yet on this third attempt, to her immense astonishment, it opened. Almost disbelieving, she watched it swing back. In a matter of seconds, she stood facing his bedchamber, and she didn't have to hunt far to find him.

As though he'd been expecting her, he lurked on the other side of the room, frowning intently at her door, almost willing her appearance simply by peering at the wood. He didn't seem at all surprised to have conjured her up.

A bath had been delivered, and he was soaking—naked, she assumed—in a large tub brimming with steamy water. Leaned against the back, his knees were raised and spread. Though it was a pleasant day outside, a small fire had been laid in the hearth, and it cast his wet skin in shades of bronze. A table was next to the tub, and bathing accessories were stacked on it. A dark green robe had been casually thrown on the floor.

With his right hand, he held a glass of amber-colored liquor from which he vigilantly sipped, not taking his eyes off her as he did so. The hand was bandaged with a cloth. A second cloth had been folded over and was pressed against a bleeding cut on his brow.

Nervously, she stepped across the threshold, and she experienced the strangest sensation that she was traveling from one dimension to another, leaving her old life, her old disposition behind, as she moved forward to embrace his world and whatever she might eventually encounter within it.

"May I come in?"

He motioned with his libation. "Yes."

Compelling herself to be the assertive person she usually was, she crossed to him, refusing to be cowed by his nudity, by his maleness, or by their secluded environment. For once, she had him just where she wanted him: all to herself.

As she approached, he glowered up at her. There was a strange look about him, daring her to draw nigh, chafing to discover if she had the temerity, but she had no intention of disappointing him. She neared, bravely advancing until her thighs abutted the rim.

"I just heard," she mentioned, and she gestured toward the pad that was compressed above his eye. "Is it bad?"

He didn't answer but proceeded to stare and, when she might have vacillated or fled, she forced herself nearer still, bending and balancing her hip on the edge. She breathed in the scent of the sandalwood soap he'd used, and the pungent, healing bath salts that had been dumped into the water.

Without waiting for an invitation, she covered his hand with her own and removed the cloth from his head. The gash wasn't deep or long, but red and oozing, and it probably ached terribly. Tentatively, she traced along it. "How did you get this?"

He was silent for so long that she concluded he wasn't going to reply, then he conceded, "I'm not generally so clumsy, but I wasn't concentrating, and one of his coachmen blindsided me"—pausing, he shifted away from her questing finger—"or I might not have stopped."

His report painted distressing images of the altercation, of its brutality and violence. "And Brigham?"

"He'll live."

The admission disturbed her. He was so passionate and intense. How was a mere woman to deal with such potency? And if she tried, how could she emerge unscathed?

"Are you in pain?" A stupid interrogatory, since she knew he was, but she was struggling for something to say, which was odd. She was never tongue-tied around him; the man habitually induced her to jabber incessantly.

"A little." He shrugged. "I'll mend."

Ere she could deviate from her chosen route, she braced herself against the basin, bent over and placed a tender kiss on his forehead, just above the laceration. Lingering with her lips on his skin, his eyelids fluttered shut as he accepted the sweet ministration.

As she straightened, and his sapphire gaze captured hers once more, they were separated by only a few inches. He was incomparable, magnificently virile, and wonderfully masculine, and he smelled so fine. His hot, slippery body beckoned, and she couldn't resist touching him, so she massaged comfortingly against his shoulder.

"Why?" She had to understand. No one had ever defended her before, never rushed to her aid, or taken her side. Emotions warred; she was confused, furious, frightened, but in the same instant, enchanted that he would risk so much.

After a prolonged, charged moment, he retorted flippantly, "Why not?"

"But he didn't harm me or—"

"He *tried*. That was sufficient." Obviously, he considered the matter closed, his motives and behavior beyond debate or dissection.

She took the beverage from him, setting it on the table, then she loosened the bandage that bound his knuckles. They were bruised and swollen, flinty evidence of the thrashing he'd inflicted, and she suspected that they throbbed unmercifully. Blood was caked between his fingers, so she grabbed a clean cloth, dipped it in the bathwater, and sponged away the mess.

Observing, but offering no comment, he was silent and ponderous. When she'd finished, she kindly kissed across his fist, then cradled his hand in both of her own, hoping that by holding him in the simple fashion, she could provide ease for his afflictions.

"We need something cold for this swelling."

"There's special water in that pitcher."

He pointed to one of the dressers, and she rose and went to it, pouring some into a bowl. Indeed, its temperature was frigid—several ice chunks were floating—then she returned to him and applied the chilly covering. For a few minutes, she clamped it in place until his tension slackened, then she chanced another glance at him.

"Better?" she queried, but he didn't respond directly.

Instead, he narrowed his focus. "Why are you here?"

This was one of those occasions when she supposed she should simper and coo as a more accomplished female might, but babbling inanely had never been her style. Plus, she appreciated that he was watching her carefully, assessing her for a greater purpose, that she now had a chance to prove herself, to elevate their relationship to another level.

"I was worried about you, and I had to see for myself that you weren't seriously wounded." A tad scolding, she added, "I came upstairs the moment I learned of what had happened. It's a good thing I found you so easily, too, or I'd have torn the house apart, chasing you down."

"I've ended up in worse condition."

His casual dismissal made her wonder if sparring wasn't a typical diversion for him. What a wild, marvelous notion!

She'd never known another like him; certainly not the staid, stodgy gentlemen of the *ton*. None of them would act so impulsively, so outrageously. From birth, their sensibilities were quashed to where they hardly felt anything at all. He was an extreme individual, and she'd had some of his formidable personality aimed in her own direction, so she pitied the person who enraged him enough to provoke conflict. Michael didn't look as if he lost very often.

The frigid dressing on his battered knuckles had heated through, so she went over to douse the cloth, then gingerly swathe him again. He continued to study her, and there was a peculiar air about him, his stillness like that of a viper or other ferocious animal, and she wished she fathomed more about him so that she could properly deal with whatever was troubling him.

Struggling for levity, she smiled. "I didn't realize you were a brawler, Mr. Stevens."

"There are many things you don't *realize* about me, Sarah."

"Do you regularly engage in fisticuffs?"

"When the situation calls for it."

He shrugged again, so unforthcoming that she longed to box his ears. She was so curious about him. Yet their assignations had been so odd, and so accursedly condensed, that she never uncovered any relevant information.

What drove him? Why had he been so affronted on her account? What part of his character had urged him to act as her defender?

Needing more revelations, she probed, "When was the last time?"

"A few months ago. I had to drag James out of a dock-side tavern."

"James is your brother?"

"Aye."

"And he didn't wish to depart?"

"No."

With the modest revelation, a thousand questions popped up, but she seemed unable to voice any of them. His gaze had dropped to her mouth and stayed there. He was endeavoring to intimidate her, though she wasn't sure why, but whatever his incentive, he was in for a shock, because she wasn't about to shy away.

"I don't want to talk about my brother," he finally said. As before, the pronouncement made it indisputable that it would be fruitless to pursue the topic. "In fact," he proclaimed, "I don't want to talk at all."

Her heart sank. While she deemed that she belonged with him, and was ecstatic to offer comfort when he was suffering, perhaps he didn't feel the same. His dictum constrained her to suggest, "Would you like me to go?"

He shook his head, and she repressed a shiver of relief. A drowning woman thrown a rope!

"I'm glad you came," he admitted. "I'm glad you're here."

The disclosure severely astounded her, and apparently, him, as well. He scowled, pondering why he'd affirmed so much.

"So am I." Boldly, she reached out and rifled her fingers through his hair as she'd been itching to do. It was thick and silky and damp.

He seized her wrist, shifting her so he could kiss her lightly, almost chastely. When he pulled away, there was a suspicious sheen in his eyes that *couldn't* be tears. Yet she perceived that the frightful combat he'd waged on her behalf had gravely overwhelmed him, had loosened some compass that guided him. He was hovering on a cliff of despair and wretchedness over which he could leap. Or not.

She melted. For reasons she couldn't define, the man called to her, intrigued and amazed, daunted and exhilarated, and she couldn't bear his agony. Mothering instincts, to protect and hold dear, surged to the fore.

"Thank you." She cupped his cheek with her palm and bestowed a chaste kiss of her own. "For what you did today."

"You're welcome," he solemnly declared. Brooding and quiescent, he persevered in analyzing her when, more than anything, she yearned to be whisked into his arms and treasured in all the ways of which he was so capable.

But he did nothing. He said nothing.

There was so much she aspired to tell him. That she was in awe, thunderstruck, and very likely falling ridiculously and senselessly in love, yet she dared not share any silly ardent outbursts. With ominous certitude, she grasped that he wouldn't approve of a sentimental overture.

Still, she couldn't prevent herself from stating, "I hate that you're hurting. How can I help you?"

His focus sank to her mouth again, then lower, to her breasts. He caressed them meticulously with his eyes until the nipples peaked and rubbed against her corset, and she had to resist the impulse to squirm.

"If I requested that you disrobe"—his torrid examination slid up her torso—"and lie down with me on the bed, would you?"

There was a challenge in his solicitation. Evidently, he expected her to decline or feign offense. If he thought she'd retreat, he'd miscalculated, but then, he wasn't the first man who'd underestimated her, and he wouldn't be the last.

"Yes, I would," she rejoined, calm as you please. "I would undress, and after, I would happily do whatever you ask of me."

"That is what I want." His puzzling attitude intensified. "That is the one thing you can do that will make me feel better."

"Then, my precious champion"—she tipped her head, evaluating him, taking his measure, letting him see that she was unafraid of his shameless proposal—"that is what you shall have."

Chapter Eleven

Michael shifted against the edge of the tub, putting space between them, wanting Sarah to have plenty of time to come to terms with her brazen decision, but she didn't seem to have the good sense to be anxious or frightened. The look she was giving him had him utterly unnerved.

Across the room, his large bed beckoned, urging him to carry her to its pliant mattress, to lay her down, to obtain some comfort. Hovering below, shielded by the soapy water, was his fierce cockstand, his phallus painfully begging to be assuaged between her heavenly thighs.

Though she didn't grasp it as yet, once he stepped out of the bath, there would be no going back. His resolution was wrong, outrageous, idiotic, but he meant to indulge. Today and tomorrow and the next day and the next after that. For as long as Pamela deigned to impart her hospitality—though in view of her pique over his latest exploit, his stay might be cut short—he would contrive to debauch and defile Sarah in every despicable way.

Starting gradually, he would initiate and enlighten, tease and tutor, until her fabulous, compliant body was attuned and burning for his type of prurient excess. He would thrill, delight, enchant, supplying all the delectation she could possibly tolerate and, in the process, he would garner some satisfaction of his own. If it killed him, if it took every ounce of his resolve and strength, if he spilled himself a thousand times in order to achieve satiation, he was determined to eventually attain contentment.

Recent events had unleashed something inside him, something voracious and feral that scared him, because it was so powerful. He couldn't quit thinking about her. Her

. . . in the stairwell, accosted by Brigham. Her . . . in her bedchamber, admitting that she'd spied on him while he'd fornicated with other women. Her . . . begging him to seduce her, to ruin her.

Pacing and cursing, he'd passed the night, unable to rest, helpless to cease his ruminating, his yearning. With morning, he'd been like a wild animal, unruly, unpredictable. Perched at his window, waiting for Brigham to emerge, he'd known the coward would strive to slip away like the dog he was.

The fracas had been welcome, vicious, malevolent, and he'd thrived on each punch thrown, on each smack of bone on bone, each spatter of blood that flew across the ground. In every muscle and pore, he ached—his ribs, his head, his hands—but he wasn't repentant. Not over any of it, and he was so savagely delighted that he'd had the chance to vent his fury so meticulously. He felt as if he was coming back to life, reawakening after a lengthy slumber. But with the conclusion of the melee, a staggering emptiness had enveloped him and, as he'd soaked in his bath, he'd progressively deduced how to allay his troubled condition: He wanted Sarah Compton. Without limitation, without constraint.

When she'd appeared—as if his hulking thoughts had summoned her—he'd recognized, then and there, that the course he'd chosen was inevitable. He was ready to fuck and defile, to sate and purge himself; to finesse, beguile, and abuse her in every conceivable fashion, and he didn't intend to be penitent for whatever he might perpetuate.

"For the remaining days that we are here," he explained, "we will have a sexual relationship."

"I've been hoping," the insane woman freely assented.

"I will demonstrate the methods of loving, and you will practice on me until you grow proficient."

"Very well."

"You will do whatever I say."

"Within reason."

"No," he interrupted, quashing her bit of bravado. There

would be no restrictions. "I will select the path. You will follow it. I will create the games; you will play. Enthusiastically and completely. Or not at all."

She stared him down, biting against her cheek, obviously deliberating refusal. His Sarah was tough and proud; she wasn't used to having a man tell her how to act, but then, as she'd issued from a family of men like Hugh Compton, what could he expect?

Half of his enjoyment would be attained from eroding her inhibitions, from her bowing to his stipulations, from her pleas for more. She *would* become complacent to his demands.

"Well?"

"If I don't agree?"

"We won't begin."

Her dilemma was enormous. Just out of principle, she considered declining. She didn't like him mandating her behavior, yet she craved the opportunity to experience what he was offering. She sought an affair on her own terms but, by his very disposition, their *amour* could never develop in such a lame manner. He was the type of man who would set the tone and pace. Surely, she comprehended that about him?

"Fine," she ultimately said.

He had to prevent himself from shaking his fist in triumph. She would be his premium conquest. "I will require conduct of you that you've never dreamed possible."

"I realize that."

"You can't be timid or shy. You must be mentally prepared to attempt whatever I suggest, and you shouldn't be apprehensive or bothered by our conduct. Whatever transpires is allowed."

"I'm not afraid." She chuckled. "Or shy!"

"Your purpose will be to please me through the carnal acts that I teach you. In return, you will receive your own gratification. The sins of the flesh will overwhelm you; you'll wonder why you've never committed them until now." Shrewdly, he regarded her. "Do you still wish to proceed?"

"Aye."

"First, you must make one promise to me."

"If I'm able."

"You must promise me that you'll never be sorry. That you'll never harbor any remorse."

He didn't deem it feasible. In fact, he was quite convinced that the aftermath would be brimming with regrets, but perhaps if he instilled the concept at the outset, he might mitigate some of her later lamentation. "Swear it to me," he insisted.

"I swear it. I'll never regret what occurs between us." She smiled. "I never could."

He nodded, accepting her vow, pondering if she'd truly keep it. She was a woman of her word, but some transgressions—such as the ones he was about to perpetrate against her—were too serious to be forgiven.

"Have you ever seen a naked man?" he asked.

"When would I have?"

"Turn around."

Puzzled by his request, she didn't budge, so he clarified, "I'm going to climb out of the bath. I certainly don't mind if you watch, but I hardly suppose you're prepared for the sight."

Her eyes widened with comprehension. He'd managed to shock her, and she leapt to her feet, geared to bolt.

"Stop!" he commanded to her retreating back, and she slid to a halt as he suppressed a wave of male vanity at how promptly she'd complied. What an interesting seduction this would be!

He exited the tub, the water lapping against the rim, and she vigilantly listened to every sound. Her torso was ramrod straight, her fists clenched at her sides, her head cocked. Reaching for a towel, he approached until he was directly behind her.

"I'm drying myself," he declared. "I'll have my robe on momentarily."

"All . . . all right."

Commencing at his hair, he fluffed at the dampness, then he moved down, to his neck, chest, buttocks, and legs. But for their labored breathing, and the intermittent crackling of the log in the fire, the room was deathly quiet, and she tensed as the towel scratched across his bodily bumps and crevasses.

Leaning down, he intentionally let the towel brush along her hemline, and she jumped whenever he encroached. Eventually, he tired of his petty amusement, and he donned his robe, stuffing his arms in the sleeves and binding the cord at the waist.

"I am finished."

At the news, she endeavored to face him, but he prohibited the movement by wrapping himself around her and trapping her backside along his front. The sparse robe was the only garment covering him so, as he pressed his scantily clad form against her, it was as if he was wearing nothing at all.

In agony, he hardened to an obscene length.

Spreading his fingers wide across her pliable belly, he clutched at her and pulled her bottom against his groin. She had the most mesmerizing ass, perfectly forged for a man's appreciation. He flexed into her skirts, sensing her figure, her cleft. To his relief, she didn't shirk away from the intimacy, so he held her tighter and whispered in her ear.

"Do you have any idea what transpires when a man and a woman are alone?"

"No. I learned some from observing your behavior, but . . ."

He couldn't abide her talking about what she'd beheld of himself and the other female guests. His plans for her included nothing similar to those decadent diversions, and he didn't care to be reminded of how he'd debased himself and his partners. Impatient to brusquely silence her, he bit against her nape, and the sensation had the desired effect. With the unfamiliar impact, she sucked in a huge breath of air.

Their liaison would have nothing in common with the previous, lewd dalliances she'd witnessed. Her sensual fate was sealed. He wanted her; he would have her. But the journey would be languid and pleasant.

"A man and a woman," he continued, "like to kiss and embrace. To fondle one another. They undress, so that their bodies can connect"—he nuzzled along her shoulder, and goose bumps prickled down her arms—"bare skin to bare skin."

"Why?"

"A woman's nudity incites a man to physical passion. He's then eager to mate."

"Do you want to . . ."—she swallowed, swallowed again, her head tipped to the side, exposing more for him to sample—"to *mate* with me now?"

"Yes, very much."

"It's the middle of the day."

"You'll have no secrets from me."

"But we're not married."

"We don't need to be."

"I don't understand."

"All in good time, my little virgin." He laughed softly and swept his palms up her stomach to just below her breasts, not caressing them but drawing so near. She braced for the higher level of involvement, and was frustrated when it didn't arrive. "How many pieces of clothing are hidden under your gown?"

An adorable blush crept from deep inside and colored her cheeks. She seemed incapable of responding, so he asked, "Petticoats?" She nodded, and he queried, "Corset?" though he knew the reply.

The stiff contraption hemmed her in and, with her respiration elevated by the stirrings of desire, she struggled against confinement, and he couldn't wait to pull at the laces and whisk it away. Avidly, he recalled the size and shape of her breasts, and he couldn't wait to view them free and unencumbered.

"How about drawers?" he queried, referring to the new-fangled undergarment.

"Yes."

Infrequently, he discovered them on his lovers, but he never cared. The novel contraption was simply one more item meant to conceal and titillate, one more article to peel away and discard before he reached his destination.

"I'm going to remove your dress." He stroked her heated flesh, brushing her breasts in passing, bringing his hands to rest on her shoulders. "And your petticoats. I'll strip you—"

"Till I'm . . ."

She couldn't speak the word *naked* aloud, and he almost took pity on her, but he refrained. He wanted her fidgety, uneasy, off balance. "To your chemise. No further for now."

Frantically, her mind whirled. Her wishes were about to be granted, and she was terrified by the prospect, yet she didn't disappoint. "I believe"—she trembled slightly—"I would like it if you did."

With a few snaps of his wrist, her bodice was loose, and she reflexively grabbed to keep it clasped to her bosom.

"Put your arms at your sides," he ordered, and she obeyed as he pushed the gown past her waist and hips, and soon it was pooled about her feet. He lifted her out of the pile of silk and lace, setting her on the floor, once again then, quick as a wink, he undid her corset and flung it away, mollified when her lungs adequately expanded.

Her chemise was delicate, cream-colored, with a dainty floral pattern stitched on the borders. It fell to mid-thigh, and he glanced down, noting a hint of bare leg, garter, and stocking.

"Face me."

He allowed her to spin around. The fabric of the shift was thin and transparent, and he could see her breasts, navel, and woman's hair. His erection inflated further, and absently, he rubbed across it, bidding it to recede, but to no avail. The image of her, nearly nude and calmly anticipating his ensuing imprudence, was too enticing.

Already, he'd pushed her awfully far, but she courageously passed each test he meted out, though she wasn't
currently looking him in the eye, and she was careful not
to permit her attention to wander to his lower regions where
he continued to fondle himself.

Kneeling before her, he absorbed her essence, her sweat,
the musk of her sex. He tugged off her shoes, untied her
garters, and rolled down her stockings. More goose bumps
flourished, and he massaged up and down her calves, cuddling her, warming her.

He stole one, fleet kiss against her stomach, one deep
inhale of the tang on her abdomen, of the cushion of hair
surrounding her pussy, then he stood, regarding her exact-
ingly, curious as to how she'd survived the ordeal, but he
needn't have worried. She was unaffected, her shoulders
squared, and she didn't recoil in the slightest as his gaze
roamed across her, hot and potent as his hands might have
been.

"Take down your hair."

Obediently, she set about pulling at the combs and pins.
In seconds, the heavy mass swung downward, encasing her
in a stream of auburn and gold. It fell to her waist, a shimmering ribbon of crimson designed to inflame and corrupt.

"Run your fingers through it." She acceded, as he decreed, "Whenever you visit me, you'll have it unbound and
brushed out."

"As you wish." He advanced until his chest grazed her
nipples, his thighs encircled her own, but she didn't hesitate. "What now?"

"We'll lie on the bed. You'll learn to touch me." He
flicked his thumb across her bottom lip. Full, moist, red as
a ripe cherry, he stole a kiss then, twirling her in a circle,
they sank onto the mattress, with him on his back and her
stretched out on top.

She was a vision to behold. The strap of her chemise
had slid off her shoulder, a succulent breast was partly bare,
her hair cascading about. Beautiful, arousing, she was de-

sire incarnate, and for the moment, she was his—and his alone—to do with as he pleased. He could barely stand the suspense, the marvelous sense of expectation, yet he deigned to go forth deliberately, to savor and relish every delicious instant of her downfall.

Adjusting her legs, he opened her thighs so that she straddled him. Her pussy was directly over his cock, instinctively recognizing the appropriate sensual route, and she spread and slumped further, dramatically increasing the explicit contact.

Tugging at the belt at his waist, he loosened it, and pushed at the lapels of his robe, exposing only his chest.

"Touch me," he said and, when she vacillated, he gripped her hand and laid it over his heart, then rasped it in a slow circle. "Like this."

He should have seized control of the assignation and tormented her until she was writhing and pleading for more, but truth be told, he was exhausted after his vigorous combat.

As a bastard son, who had been shamelessly disavowed by his rich and noble father, he often engaged in altercations. Offensive comments—usually aimed at his mother—were regularly hurled, and he vented his wrath at any imbecile foolish enough to make an untoward remark, so his entering into a dispute was nothing new.

A skilled, seasoned opponent, he could hurl a punch as well as take one. However, the frantic display he'd delivered to Brigham had exploded with a ferocity he'd not exhibited before, and the intensity had left him thoroughly drained. He needed Sarah's sweet courtesy, was desperate to suffer through her virginal oohs and aahs, to bask in her fascination. The feel of her smooth hands, with those slender, questing fingers roving over him, was like a healing salve to his battered body and spirit.

She amused herself with his chest, rifling through the springy hair, exploring the ridges and valleys until her maneuvers felt as natural as breathing, as though she'd touched him just so a hundred times before.

Braver, she dipped lower, across the knobs of his rib cage, but he'd secured a grueling blow to his side and, before he could warn her to be cautious, she patted across the bruising, and he flinched and winced.

She froze. "You're hurt."

"Not badly."

"Let me see." She relocated, her lush pussy easing off his phallus as she shoved more of the robe apart. The spot on his ribs was inflamed, the abrasion ghastly, and she studied and inspected, then bent over and kissed it as she had the wounds to his temple and fist.

When she straightened, she flashed a stern look. "I don't like you fighting."

"It's occasionally necessary."

"But I can't bear it that you've been injured." Gently, she traced across the damage. "Promise you won't do it again," and she graced him with a tender kiss against his mouth. "Please?"

It had been a very long while since anyone had evidenced concern for his safety or welfare. In response, he could only offer a small concession. "I'll try."

"That's worth something, I guess."

The exchange concluded, the banter lagged, the quiet magnified. She focused on him with such penetrating, abiding affection that he couldn't stand to perceive it, so he said, "Touch me again."

Steadying her hips, he centered her so that she was, once more, lingering over his erection. How he longed to thrust against her! He was so hard, he ached. His balls wrenched and cried out, but he restrained himself. This was her first encounter with male nudity, and there would be abundant excuses in the impending days to rush toward total fulfillment, but not just yet.

More sure of herself, she now confidently nestled into his matting of chest hair, burrowing her nose, sniffing at his skin, and he caught her chin and steered her to his breast.

"Kiss me here," he dictated, and his brown nipple pebbled into a compact bud as her superb lips painstakingly submitted. "Suck me into your mouth."

An adept pupil, she instantly acquiesced, nibbling and toying until he could barely remain stationary. When her teeth nipped at the tiny nub, he couldn't block the groan that escaped.

She grinned up at him. "You like that, do you?"

"Very much."

"You did it to me . . . that night in my room."

"Yes. A woman's nipples are incredibly sensitive. When a man dabbles with them, he accentuates her titillation, and she is excited and relaxed. The stimulation prepares her for what is to come."

"And what is that?"

"Soon, milady, all your questions will be answered."

He ushered her hands to both his nipples, revealing the suitable pressure, the appropriate manipulation. She trifled and played, her eyes glued to his so that she could judge his reaction.

The minx! She was a natural! Too astute. Too disposed to attempt any risqué procedure.

Her unwavering concentration was extremely disconcerting, so he guided her mouth to his other breast, easing her to the nipple. His cock was throbbing, the crown oozing with his sexual juice. He stabilized her and partook of an unhurried flex against her cleft.

As though she'd been poked with a pin, she jerked upright. "Why do you keep doing that?"

"Doing what?" He pretended innocence, flattening her against his erection, and feasting with another leisurely flex.

"That thrusting motion. It just feels so . . . so . . ."

"Extraordinary?"

"Yes. But naughty, too. And forbidden." She wedged herself more fully along the crest of his phallus. "My body seems to fathom what you propose, when I've no notion myself."

"Absolutely." His wanton fingers slipped under the hem of her chemise and petted the smooth skin of her thighs.

"You are so ready for me to be your lover."

"How can you tell?"

"Even though you are a woman, you need sensual animation just like a man."

"I was told differently."

"You were told wrong."

The veracity of his statement sank in, and she acceded to the inevitable, initiating some flexing of her own, driving herself forward, using her knees and toes. Joyous, she smiled as though she was a child who'd just found a unique flavor of candy. "Do you feel it?"

"Aye, lass, I do." He gritted his teeth, speculating as to how he'd persevere at a sluggish pace, how he'd take minimal steps, when his entire being was spurring him to skip to the finale without delay.

Eliminating temptation, abandoning paradise, he levered her away. "You've never seen a naked man," he reminded her. "How about a boy?"

"I've bathed a few male children in my day."

"Then you're aware of how we vary."

Her brow furrowed, then realization dawned. "In our private parts." She peeked down, to what was concealed by his robe, but the solid vertex of flesh couldn't be missed. "I've always wondered why."

"It's for coupling. So that we fit together."

"How is it accomplished?"

"My cock swells, and by flexing, my seed is lured to the tip and rushes out the end."

"What does your *seed* look like?"

"White. Creamy."

"Where does it go?"

"Into the chasm between your legs. In the site from where your monthly blood flows." He rested his hand on her abdomen, his thumb pressing at her mound, but she wasn't equipped to handle more, so he didn't move downward.

At the mention of her menses, she flushed, but the delicate subject wasn't inordinately disturbing to her, which he took as an excellent sign. Before the afternoon was through, they would discuss many more distressing topics.

"And a babe is conceived in this fashion?"

"It could be. If the timing is right."

"Is this dangerous, then? I hadn't thought that we might create a child."

"We won't. I'll be circumspect."

She shook her head. "I say it again: I don't understand what we're about."

"There are techniques for dallying without proceeding to marital copulation. That is what I contemplate."

"But why would you simply want to . . ."—she searched for a term, but couldn't pick one of her own, so she employed his—"to *dally*?"

"For pleasure, Sarah." The mode in which *pleasure* rolled off his tongue caused her to stir, her loins descended, instinctively extending out to him. "A man derives great satisfaction from spilling himself. It is an activity he seeks above all others."

"So . . . *pleasure* will be our goal?"

"Yes. Our only one."

"What do I need to do?"

"You'll stroke me. With your hands and your mouth. I'll show you."

He placed her fingers on top of his bulging erection. Adding tension, he demonstrated the rhythm, but he abruptly realized that he could settle for nothing less than her bared flesh applied to his own.

He untied the knot at his waist. "Open my robe. All the way."

Chapter Twelve

Sarah didn't hesitate. She was trembling, not with fear or trepidation, but with anticipation, so she prudently masked her excitement, not wanting to give the impression that she'd become a coward at this late juncture.

By all accounts, he'd hardly done anything to her. He'd talked, he'd eliminated most of her clothing, he'd flexed against her through several layers of fabric. Yet her body was on fire, her nipples contracted so that they hurt, her skin stretched so tightly that it didn't seem to fit her bone structure.

He'd slackened the belt at his waist but, daring her to proceed, he hadn't untied it. As if she'd back down! Without being conscious of it, she'd craved this moment forever.

Carefully, she controlled her shaking fingers and unraveled the knot. Deliberately, prolonging her discovery, she drew the lapels of his robe aside, sequentially revealing his navel, then the arrow of hair that shot down his belly.

Her eyes dropped imperceptibly, and she encountered all. Like a supplicant before a shrine, she pushed at the remaining material, baring him inch by glorious inch, until he was totally naked, and the reality was like nothing she'd imagined.

At viewing the male accessory on small boys, she'd never postulated that it would enlarge, that it could mature to being so bold and manifest. Looking angry and alive, the attachment was red and distended, with a bulbous head and purple, ropy veins. It protruded from a nest of his dark hair, two sacs dangling beneath, and her visual assessment made it extend out toward her in entreaty.

She hazarded a glance at him, and he lay silent and still,

studying her with an impersonal, glacial intensity.

Had he planned to shock her? To have her tearful and swooning? To send her stumbling from the room in offense and alarm?

He was motivated by deep, unfathomable issues that she couldn't hope to understand. The chances were great that he'd merely instigated this as a bizarre diversion in order to gain a response from her, but if the man thought she was some prim, squeamish miss, he obviously didn't know her very well. She was fascinated, enthralled, and ardent to explore.

"It's larger than I supposed."

"I'm aroused."

"It changes size?" Her eyes widened with astonishment, and he chuckled at her naïveté.

"Usually, it's flaccid and harmless." Tensing his stomach muscles, the extraordinary appendage inflated even more. "But not when I'm here with you like this. I'm so hard for you. I ache with my desire."

There was a husky tone in his voice, a desperation that plucked at her common sense, leaving her reckless and rash, and just then, she'd have performed any impulsive feat he requested.

"What do you call it?"

"My cock."

She struggled for terminology, but her innocent background hindered descriptive dialogue, so she gestured over his erect body part. "Are all of these . . . these cocks so large?"

"Mine is bigger than most." He directed, "Touch me."

Tentatively, she reached out and traced a line from the base to the apex. The sheltering layer of skin was hot and smooth, pliant and malleable, but the timid contact didn't satisfy him, and he clasped her hand in his, and wrapped them together around his heated staff, so that she could adjust to handling him so privately. Then, he commenced moving them conjointly, showing her the most effective maneuvers.

"The tip is the most sensitive," he pointed out. "Try to run over it with each stroke."

"Like this?" she asked, drawing back the yielding skin, unveiling the crown.

"Yes," he muttered through clenched teeth. "I'll obtain the most gratification that way."

As she was an avid, enthusiastic pupil, he readily left her to her own devices. Fastidiously, she investigated, learning his shape, awed by the variations of velvet over steel. She pampered and played, altering the pressure, the speed, the length of her caress. Amazingly, with the slightest modification, he reacted accordingly.

What power she held over him! What marvelous authority! If she wielded this much dominance when she was unskilled, she'd be a holy terror after a few hours of practice, after a few days.

Her nerves galloped at the realization.

"What are these?" She cupped the sacs between his legs.

"My balls."

"What are they for?"

"They shelter my seed, and they're very tender." But she'd already surmised as much, and she'd decided to withdraw when, sounding afflicted, he interrupted her. "Don't stop. Just be gentle."

Cradling the precious pile, she scooted down his thighs so that she had more space to observe and manipulate. The new position brought her over his stomach, and her sudden comprehension startled her.

She remembered the lover she'd witnessed, the woman who had been bent over him, but Sarah hadn't been able to discern her activity, and she'd been so blasted curious.

Could it be?

A inexplicable tingle rushed through her fingers, up her arms, and she was jolted by her keen insight. She gazed up his broad expanse of abdomen and chest. The pillows were braced behind his head, and he regarded her dispassionately, his sapphire eyes glittering.

"They put their mouths on you, don't they?"

"Who?"

"Your . . . your women. That's what you require of them, isn't it?" She rose onto her haunches. "They take you into their mouths."

"Yes."

"Why?"

"*Why* do I prefer it? Or *why* do they go down on me?"

"Both."

"I fancy it because it's erotic and naughty, and they do it so that they can brag to their friends that they've sucked me off."

Her brow furled. "What does that mean?"

"It's a crude phrase." He shrugged, but didn't appear repentant for having recited it. "It refers to when a man thrusts his cock into a woman's mouth. He continues until the friction is unbearable, then he discharges his seed into his lover's throat."

"You really do this?"

"Yes."

"Often?"

"Well, I wouldn't say *often*." He seemed amused. "Whenever a woman volunteers."

"Your partners swallow it?"

"Aye."

"What is its taste?"

"It doesn't actually have one. It's heat and salt."

"Your very essence," she murmured.

He shrugged again.

"This deed . . . does it have a name?"

"A French kiss."

"It's enjoyable for you?"

"Beyond measure. I relish the opportunity to spill myself between a woman's legs, but I never do, because I might create a child. So I'm obliged to any female who renders such a stunning delectation."

"You always agree?"

"I'm not in the habit of denying myself. I have a strong

sexual drive, and I accept what is freely offered."

He could baldly analyze his scandalous conduct. Most likely, he'd reveled in so much lewdness in his life that discussion of his untoward behaviors was extremely easy. How could she break through that unruffled façade?

Her heart was racing, her body afire, her womanly places pleading for his intricate manual attention. She was anxious to bring him to the same drastic condition, to where he was out of control, his guise of ennui shattered.

"Open yourself to me." He nodded toward his groin. "Take me into your mouth."

"I'm not certain that I—"

"You are."

"You're demanding too much, too soon."

"No I'm not."

Once again, he arranged her hand on his pulsating member, leading her in a languid motion, and she stared into those mesmerizing eyes. They were sublime, reassuring, and they made her crazy to blindly effect his every command. As though enchanted, she found herself leaning forward, leaning down.

"Will you finish inside me?"

"Not today."

"Why not?"

"You're geared for some. Not all."

"When, then?"

"After you've had more indoctrination."

Still, she vacillated. What had she gotten herself into? She professed, "I guess I'm apprehensive."

"About what?"

"About what I don't know."

"I won't hurt you; I never could."

The strength of his avowal was encouraging. "I grasp that. I just . . ."

Just what?

Their rendezvous was so devoid of care or concern, and he was so indifferent. It seemed wrong to proceed in such a disjointed fashion. The somber, aloof stranger lying before her wasn't the man of passion to whom she was devoted. The *real* Michael was in hiding, but she wasn't positive how to draw him out. Perhaps if she complied with his proposition, she could melt the barriers he'd erected. She was eager to please him, yet she was skeptical of his motives and fretting over her own.

"I want you, Sarah. I need you now."

His declaration soothed her turmoil, urging her on, and she couldn't deny him. Starting at the bottom, she flicked with her tongue, by degrees working up his length until she was licking at the oozing crown. When she arrived at the blunt apex, she eased him betwixt her lips.

The sensation was indescribable, his nature and spirit embedded in the turgid, obstinate extremity. Inhaling slowly, she was surrounded by his masculinity, his virility, his potency.

His hand went to the back of her head, holding her, guiding her. He shifted to his side, rotating her, as well. With his leg, he steadied her, pinning her close, and she opened further, procuring more of him than she'd previously believed possible.

As he scrupulously thrust, the physicality was amazing. The indiscretion, the impropriety, titillated her, leaving her wild and hungry for more. She basked in the lengthy, ribald interlude while he overindulged and, as she adjusted to his movements, she became cognizant of his rising ardor. Then, with very little warning, he pulled away, and she instantly regretted the loss.

Her lips were sore, chapped and stretched as they'd never been, yet she wished he'd kept on. She sensed that the procedure could have grown particularly raucous, and that he was restraining himself on her account.

"Are we finished?"

"No, love, we're not."

The endearment rolled off his tongue to slither into her confused mind, raising innumerable questions: Did he appreciate what he'd said? Was it unintentional? Intentional?

If he was aware of what he'd uttered, what had been his true purpose?

Thrown off balance, she hardly regrouped before he was hauling her up into his arms. He was smiling at her, the blaze of it so stupendous that she was glad she was lying down when it fell upon her.

He covered her with his body, his weight pressing her into the mattress, and having him on top of her was a thoroughly primal experience. He was so welcome, and he fit so perfectly—flat where she was rounded, rough where she was soft—and she couldn't prevent herself from enveloping him, her limbs spreading so that she could lovingly cuddle him. Cautiously, almost gratefully, he settled himself between her thighs, his cock heavy and wedged against her leg.

He hovered over her, his fingers at the hem of her chemise, and with no hesitation, he tugged it up her hips, disposed to remove it.

At seeing her rapid panic, he explained, "I'm terribly aroused; I'm going to come against your stomach."

"Will it hurt?"

"Only me"—he chortled over matters she didn't comprehend—"and only in a good way."

"My breasts will be bared to you."

"Again."

"Yes, and I'm nervous that—"

"They're so magnificent."

Through the fabric, he caressed her erect nipple and, like a puppet on a string, she immediately acquiesced, hoisting her lower torso, then her shoulders, so he could yank her chemise up and over her head.

How was it that he so easily routed her ingrained propriety? He but complimented her, and she jumped to do his bidding. Was she so starved for affection? So greedy for flattery and adulation? Apparently, the answer was yes.

By spewing a few laudatory words, he could prevail upon her to commit any depraved act—even those that were completely foreign to her character. Yet, she yearned to make him happy, to prompt that rare smile.

She was an unmitigated fool!

Her body was now shielded only by a skimpy pair of bright-red pantalets.

The most recent whimsy from Paris, Rebecca had noted when she'd brought them home from London.

The gift—six pairs of silky, frivolous underdrawers— had enchanted Sarah. She had so few nice garments, and no money for new. The wardrobe her father had purchased years prior for her debut was either too small or threadbare, so she'd cheerfully embraced the scanty unmentionables. They made her feel pretty and feminine, and she liked how they brushed against her beneath her clothes.

But when she'd donned them that morning, it had never occurred to her that Michael Stevens would be evaluating them that afternoon. She blushed furiously.

"Why, Sarah"—he was amused and surprised, as though womanly attire was the last thing he'd expected from her— "you're wearing French underwear."

The knave was so familiar with women that he was well versed in the modern style of intimate apparel!

The assignation had become too oppressive. What was she striving to attain? Why was she allowing him to tease her? She never tolerated men's jesting, having learned the hard way how an uncouth comment could wound, and, needing to flee, she wrenched away, trying to scoot off the bed, but he held her down.

"Let me go," she decreed, focusing on the ceiling.

"No."

Odious cad!

His hand slithered under the crimson waistband and tangled in her secret hair, then traveled on to where she was wet and swollen, and she was embarrassed that he'd detected the unusual moisture—especially when he felt compelled to preen over his discovery.

"God . . . you are so ready for me," he asserted, as two questing fingers slipped inside her.

He'd touched her in the same manner once before but,

at the time, she'd been too astonished to pay attention. Now, she moaned, clutching and weeping into his palm as he stroked deliberately, entering then retreating. The abominable machination stirred an acute appetite for more than the simple massage. She wanted things she couldn't begin to enumerate.

"Michael . . . please . . ."

"Yes, beg me. I love it when you do."

With a tap of his thumb, he sent a wave of stimulation up her abdomen to her breasts, and she whimpered.

How mortifying! She wasn't a *whimperer*. Yet, how was she to comport herself rationally and routinely when she was splayed wide and being fondled by such an arrogant rogue?

He was in pure agony, as well, as if palpating her was painful and, as he hung his head over her chest, she couldn't get past the impression that he hadn't been so unmoved, after all. Throughout, he'd seemed to be a sort of unaffected bystander, and his calm detachment had been so frustrating. She'd longed for him to endure some of the same jubilation and upheaval she was suffering.

Evidently, he hadn't been so apathetic. He was seething with unreleased turmoil.

"I have to come," he said, and he bent down and licked at her nipple. "I can't wait."

"Tell me what to do."

"Just hold me tight. Don't let go."

She snuggled him against her bosom, and his cock dilated to an enormous proportion. Insistent and relentless, he impatiently thrust it against her.

"Fuck me with your hand." And he ushered her to his shaft, once again.

She took on the erogenous chore, and her firm grip was magic. In a half-dozen lunges, he tensed and emitted a haunting groan. Hot liquid spurted across her abdomen and fingertips, purging him, then he shuddered and sank onto her, collapsing fully.

His breathing was labored, heavy and erratic, his heartbeat thundering against his ribs, beating furiously with her own. He didn't speak—perhaps he couldn't—and for once, she was glad of the silence. Words failed her.

Nothing had prepared her for how personal the moment would be. She felt he'd bared his soul, that he'd exposed himself as he never could with another, and she held him close. Eventually, he mellowed, but he was motionless, his forehead pressed to her breasts.

Abruptly, he sat up and moved to the edge of the bed, showing her his back.

His legs were unsteady, and he fortified himself then proceeded to the tub, dipping a washing cloth in the water and returning to her side. He avoided her gaze as he conscientiously cleansed his seed away, then threw the cloth on the floor. When he faced her again, in an unguarded moment, she witnessed vulnerability and loneliness.

A wave of protectiveness flowed over her, and she needed to provide comfort, emotionally as well as physically. She opened her arms in welcome, and he joined her willingly, resting in the crook of her neck. Much as one might a young child who'd been scared or injured, she nurtured him and, as she rifled her fingers through his thick mane of hair, she couldn't help thinking that this was where she wanted to always be, where she belonged.

Gradually, she noticed that he was developing another erection, and shortly, his cock was stubborn and intractable against her belly. He started kissing against her nape, sending chills down her spine, then he abandoned his safe perch, trailing down her chest, to a breast, and her breath whooshed out when he closed over the extended crest. Like a babe, he suckled against her. Gently at first, then more fervently, he increased the tension, until he had her writhing and squirming.

"What are you trying to accomplish?" she managed to gasp.

"I'm pleasuring you."

"It doesn't feel *pleasurable*."

"It will. Trust me," he commented encouragingly. "The

sensations are new, so they seem foreign to you, but they're customary."

"I don't know what to do." She hated that he was in charge.

"You don't have to *do* anything," he contended, laughing softly. "Just relax while I dally."

Relax? Was he mad? How could she relax when a man the likes of Michael Stevens was on top of her and nursing at her breast?

He kissed across her cleavage to her other nipple, and he toyed ruthlessly until it was raw and irritated. His hand idly trailed down her stomach. In a pattern of agonizing circles, he descended lower and lower, never falling quite far enough.

Finally, he sneaked inside her drawers and honed in on the spot his thumb had located earlier. At the same time, two fingers glided into her cleft, and momentarily, he had her hips flexing in an infuriating rhythm. She strained toward an unknown goal—if the cad would just point her in the proper direction, the journey would be so much easier—and she teetered on a ledge of desire, needing to leap off but not confident of when or where.

"What's happening?" she spat out, scarcely able to find the air necessary for communication.

"Have you never touched yourself like this? In the night? When you're alone?"

"No . . . never . . ." The information delighted him, and she could sense that he was grinning. The presumptuous rogue!

"You're going toward a peak of pleasure. As I did." He delayed the tempo, just when she was burning for it to multiply, and, cognizant of the havoc he was wreaking, he chuckled again. "The first time can be scary. But I promise that it will also be wonderful."

"I don't know . . . how . . ." She couldn't elucidate, couldn't implore, couldn't talk.

Oh, when would this torment cease?

"Your body knows." As though supplying confirmation,

he rubbed where all sensation seemed to be centered, and she arched up and would have flown off the bed if he hadn't been hindering her escape. "Close your eyes, and I'll take you where you want to go."

"I'm afraid," she whispered.

"Don't be. I'm here with you."

"Michael . . ."

He paused. "Say my name again."

"Michael!" she wailed, on the brink, frightened.

The cliff beckoned and, when he latched onto her breast and suckled adamantly, she jumped, sending herself into freefall. She was shattered, undone, and careening through the universe. A voice called out, with an extraordinary kind of ecstasy, and she vaguely recognized that it was her own, then his lips were on hers, silencing her by capturing her wild cry of joy.

The frenzy persisted for an eternity until, sequentially, she commenced to reassemble. Sanity and reality returned, and she was in Michael's bed, in Michael's arms.

She dared a peek at him, and he lingered over her with a look that could only be tenderness. There was a hint of male pride there, as well, at having reduced her to such a wanton circumstance.

"Much better," he murmured, and he kissed her cheek.

"Yes." She endeavored to shift away but didn't get far. His weight still pressed her down. "What was that?"

"An orgasm. The French refer to it as the *petit mort*, the little death."

"Well . . . they've surely got the right of it." She lifted a hand and let it fall with a heavy thud. "My bones have melted. I can't move."

"You don't have to. Just rest for a bit."

"Then, what?"

"We'll do it again."

"You're joking!"

"I'm not."

"My heart would quit beating."

He kissed her once more. "It will get better."

"More intense?"

"Absolutely. And quicker to achieve the more you're with me."

"I'll never survive."

"Perhaps not."

He urged her over so that her back was spooned against his front. One arm lay under her head, a muscled, intriguing pillow. The other was over her torso, his fingers making lazy loops on her stomach and hip.

Her perception was heightened—the bristle of his bodily hair, the heat of his cock on her bottom, the smell of their mingled sweat and sex—and everything appeared more extreme and profound.

A yawn emerged; she was too tired to hide it, and he drew a blanket over them, sealing them in a snug cocoon.

What next? The vexing interrogatory flitted by, but she was elated, exhausted, and too fatigued to dwell on the future.

She slept.

When she awoke, she brooked only a minor instant of alarm while she sought to recall where she was, but the episode swiftly passed, and the scandalous memories flooded in.

Where he was concerned, she'd developed an elevated awareness, and she could sense him in the room, studying her. A light aroma of tobacco tickled her nose. He was smoking—a tidbit to tuck away in her limited collection of the Michael trivialities she'd gleaned. Her eyes fluttered open, even as she pondered how they would interact now that their sexual escapade was terminated.

He was in a chair by the window, but as distant as if he'd been all the way beyond the ocean in America. He was dressed only in a pair of trousers, his hair was swept off his forehead, accenting the cut over his eye, and he watched her impassively. A half-empty glass of brandy sat on the table, and he was holding a cheroot, the butt aglow, the smoke curling upward. Behind him, she could see outside. The shadows had lengthened and much of the day had passed away.

On seeing her stir, he snuffed out the cigar, but he didn't say anything.

She came up on one elbow, her cascade of auburn hair tumbling over her shoulder. The blanket drooped, baring a breast, and his brow rose in nonchalant disinterest. Their bedplay had been engaging and exotic when he'd been participating, but now, as he frigidly stared with no deference displayed on his beautiful face, she felt absurd.

Clutching at the quilt, she posed the only query that seemed to matter. "What time is it?"

"Almost five."

Unnerved, she speculated as to whether he'd napped at all, or if he'd enigmatically assessed her, wishing she'd rise and retire, but not quite rude enough to wake her and insist.

From her perspective, the romp had been the most resplendent, fabulous ever; from his, nothing out of the ordinary. In all likelihood, he regularly wasted his days in sexual frolic, and she'd merely been lumped in with the scores of loose women with whom he cavorted.

Troubled by her musings, she strove for levity. "I guess you wore me out."

"*Fucking* will do that to a person." He nodded toward the bed. "I fetched your robe."

"Thank you."

It was draped on the bedding, and she couldn't stifle a thrilling rush at the thought that he'd visited her bedchamber. For some reason, the notion of him invading her boudoir, searching through her armoire and examining her belongings, was fascinating.

"You're going to miss tea," he remarked casually, "so you need to bathe, then go down for supper. We've been here for quite a spell, so it's important that you put in an appearance."

So, he *was* eager for her to depart. How disappointing!

"I doubt if anyone will miss me," she was compelled to

report. "I'm not any more of a social butterfly than you are."

"Your cousin knocked a while ago."

His look was filled with inquisition and accusation, and she could picture him standing in the middle of her room, robe in hand, with Rebecca on the other side of the door. They'd been so close to detection! While she should have been frantic and appalled, she was exhilarated by the danger in which she'd deposited herself—and him.

What had come over her? The woman she'd been before she'd arrived, before she'd met Michael Stevens, had vanished.

"Did she try the knob?"

"Of course." He stared her down. "She's awfully determined to catch you in a compromising position. Why do you suppose that is?"

"I've no idea," she responded blandly, adopting his reticence. She had no desire to discuss Rebecca, to permit the outside world, her other life—her real life—to intrude on this flight of fancy.

Keeping the covers flattened against her bosom, she battled to don her robe, not granting him a view of her nakedness. While the state had seemed normal when they'd been making love, with him imperturbably glaring at her, she was embarrassed by her nudity, and she simply felt inappropriately undressed.

She scooted to the edge of the bed, but she couldn't take the necessary steps to leave. She was terrified that once she departed, they'd never cross paths again.

He was treating her just as he did his other lovers, as if the event hadn't had any effect on him, and she despised his composed, nonchalant disposition. His cool reserve and taciturnity were warning her off and away. Yet, she wasn't timid; she declined to surrender without a fight, because she craved a loving relationship with him.

"Would you like me to return after supper?"

His reply was the very worst. "As you wish."

The aggravating response, the one he habitually utilized

to chase off his paramours, set a spark to her temper. She wasn't some doxy! Not a woman of loose morals with whom he could randomly trifle! She was a chaste, upstanding female, who'd chosen him—scoundrel though he was—and favored him with a part of herself she never proposed to bestow on another, and she wouldn't have her boon discarded as if she was of no import.

Stomping across the floor, she halted at his chair, their knees tangled, their feet overlapping, and he was surprised by her audacious move. Let him be!

"Stop it!" she dictated.

"Stop what?" He was plainly uncomfortable with her directness.

"Quit pretending that this afternoon was of no consequence."

He fidgeted. "I never said that."

"But that's how you're acting." Didn't he realize how special this was to her? "Our meeting held little significance to you, but it meant a great deal to me." Quietly, she added, "Don't ruin it."

He scrutinized her, then tipped his head in acknowledgment. "I didn't intend to discount what happened. I just assumed you'd want to be about your business."

"That I've had my *fun,* and now I'm finished with you?"

"Aye."

"Hear me, Michael Stevens: It will take a bit more than your bad attitude and rude manners to make me conclude that we're through."

"I see that." One corner of his exquisite mouth hinted at a smile.

She figured that was as close as she'd ever get to an apology. There were many things about him she didn't understand, but many things that were clear, as well. When he let his guard down, he could be tender and unselfish, though he resisted her attempts at closeness, and it dawned on her that perhaps he never became amorously attached to any female, so he'd built protective walls.

While he hoped to diminish the magnitude of their affinity, she had other plans. He wanted her to visit him again; she just knew he did! And she would force him to say so if she had to literally drag the admission from his lips.

"Don't treat me with the disregard you exhibit to your other lovers."

"I wasn't," he lied.

"You could have fooled me." He had the grace to blush. Without a doubt, he'd been pushing her away, but she'd spoiled his scheme by refusing to go peacefully.

"I'm confused, Sarah," he ultimately confessed. "About you. About us."

"So am I," she agreed, "but I won't deny our connection, and I won't let you deny it, either. This is too vital to me." She laid her hand on his shoulder. "I ask you again: Would you like me to return later?"

"I believe I would."

Her relief was so immense that her knees sagged, and she yearned to confide so much more—to tell him how meaningful the interlude had been, how she'd been transformed—but words failed her.

She turned and walked to the door that connected their rooms, and she stepped through but, unable to resist, she stole a peek at him, grimly desperate for a final glimpse.

Bathed in the fading light, he was handsome, dynamic, dissolute. His solitude and isolation called out to her, swayed her, and beseeched her for recognition, for help, and a sustenance that she longed to confer.

The sensations he invoked—to love, to cherish, to esteem—were so poignant that she couldn't remain. He was so alone and apart, and she required seclusion and distance to mentally prepare for their next encounter.

Impelling herself away from the perilous, heartrending sight of him, she hastened into her dressing room and shut the door.

Chapter Thirteen

Michael tiptoed down the hall. The hour was late, and he was glad his room was at the rear of the house where he could come and go without meeting any guests. He passed Sarah's chamber, then proceeded to his own. When he reached it, he slipped the key into the lock, then paused.

Would she be waiting?

At the same juncture, he hoped she was and wasn't.

Deliberately, he'd absented himself from the premises, avoiding the lure of the Viewing Room and any of the wild schemes Pamela might have hatched for the evening. Most of all, he'd made an adamant decision to insulate himself from Sarah and the provocation she rendered.

The afternoon he'd passed with her had been a slice of heaven. When they'd finished, and she'd fallen asleep in his arms, he'd felt much as he might had an angel flown down for a frolic.

The fight with Brigham had unleashed an emotional torrent he'd not endured in ages. After, he'd been weary and battered, and feeling every one of his advanced twenty-eight years. He'd craved solace and comfort as he'd never craved anything before, which was saying a great deal.

Over the nearly three decades of his life, he'd hungered mightily, seeking respect and admiration from acquaintances, love and affection from his family. The worst times had been as a child, when his mother had moved them to France. Although he would never concede as much to another soul, he'd pined away seemingly forever, expecting that his father would travel to Paris and fetch them home.

Whenever a knock had sounded on the door of their small flat, his heart had skipped a beat, certain that it was the day Edward had finally arrived. But it had never happened and, as he'd grown, his father's abandonment had lain like a heavy yoke, a burden he'd never quite been able to cast off. On occasion, the pain of that early loss still wreaked damage as though the wound was recently inflicted. The old injury propelled him to indecent acts, as evidenced by how he'd thrashed Brigham to a pulp and left him in a gory heap in Pamela's stableyard.

Lest she hear the sordid tale from another, he'd immediately visited her to confess his transgression, and he'd stoically persevered through the tongue-lashing she'd meted out, knowing she was entitled to her fury. Her censure had chafed and nettled, but some of the sting from her harsh comments was deflected by the hot bath she'd instantly sent.

As he'd chased the servants away, then lowered himself into the steaming cauldron, he couldn't remember when he'd been so isolated or detached. His personality and upbringing being what they were, he'd always considered himself a solitary man, yet as he'd relaxed in the tub, eager for some bit of mortal contact, he'd gradually fixated on Sarah.

He'd wanted succor and consolation, and no anonymous stranger would have sufficed; he'd yearned for Sarah—with her soft hands and soothing words. Sarah cared for him as no one else did, and he'd needed her ambrosial regard as he'd needed food or water.

When she'd brazenly joined him, when she'd kissed away his hurts, he'd quit fighting his impulses, determined to have her in the only way that counted. He'd behaved crudely—more so than usual—and he shouldn't have forced her into their liaison, but he'd forged ahead anyway. For reasons that had nothing to do with his birth status, he'd regularly been called a bastard and, with his treatment of her, he'd once again proved how utterly ruthless he could be.

Despicably, he'd used her, coercing her to perform acts he wouldn't have required of a whore, and she'd amiably and favorably acquiesced to every sordid exploit he'd proposed. Yet, he wasn't sorry. Their tryst had been stupendous, blissful, amazing.

After all of his erotic play, beginning when he'd been no more than a child in a man's body, he'd never so much as dozed off with a woman. Even the two short occasions when he'd kept mistresses, he'd never succumbed. There was something about *sleeping* that disturbed him with its intimacy.

Sexual congress was his only objective for visiting a lover's bed, because any other goal would likely send a faulty message as to his intentions. He dallied, he fucked, he left. Any female silly enough to demand more never saw him again. While slumbering was an innocent occupation, habit hampered him from lessening his guard sufficiently to where he was comfortable in such an awkward position.

Yet, he'd snuggled next to Sarah with nary a thought to the consequences, and he'd been magnificently surprised at how it had refreshed him to cuddle with her. Just by having her near, he'd felt connected, less separate, so he'd actually rested, but once he'd calmed adequately, prudence had prevailed, and he'd slipped out of bed, putting distance between them.

For over two hours, he'd studied her, marveling at how deeply she reposed. Fool that she was, her level of trust was out of proportion to what it should have been, given their odd acquaintance. Her body and spirit were at peace with the notion that nothing vile would befall her while he was there to watch over her.

And watch he had. She'd looked pretty, young, innocent. He couldn't take his eyes off her, and the manner in which she'd bewitched him filled him with unease. What was his aim, trifling with a virginal woman of the Quality? Scarborough's sister, no less! He didn't like her kind, or what she represented, so his motives were definitely suspect. Perhaps he and his brother, James, had more in common than he cared to acknowledge!

James had been enthralled by the members of the *ton*,

inflicting himself into their domain and vying for their undivided attention—most of it never good—at every possible turn. Michael had never shared James's fascination,
convinced that he was the wiser for not being seduced by
their wretched world, but apparently he'd only been delud-
ing himself.

Sarah was a striking example of how he'd misjudged his
own disinterest. At a time when his defenses were depleted,
she'd developed into an obsession, and he couldn't prevent
himself from chasing after her. He shouldn't even speak
with her, let alone instigate a libidinous association. What
benefit could he attain? Why did he persist?

Their romance would last no longer than the handful of
days he'd offered her before he'd stepped out of his bath.
He had numerous personal flaws; he'd never fall in love
with her, never ask her to marry, never strive toward any
sort of continuing affiliation. While she was convenient and
available, he'd enjoy her company, then he'd leave Pamela's decadent house and travel to another country party,
then another, until he finally became so bored that he retired
to London.

Sarah Compton would never cross his mind again.

So why this fascination? Why this unrelenting urgency
to be with her?

As the minutes had ticked agonizingly by, a horrid concept had wormed itself into his musings: Was this how his
father had started out with his mother? Had Edward too
suffered these unyielding, unmerciful longings that didn't
abate or wane? Had he been powerless to resist Angela's
allure?

Rumors had constantly abounded that Edward Stevens's
relationship with Angela hadn't been a juvenile indiscretion, but an intense *affaire d'amour*. Considering how Edward had come panting after Angela and wed her shortly
after his lawful, aristocratic wife had died, Michael couldn't
discount the stories that had been bandied about town.

As a youth, Edward had been totally captivated by Angela, incapable of, or unwilling to, avoid the attraction she

generated—just as Michael, himself, was currently unable to avert the disaster he was courting by pursuing Sarah. Perhaps he was more like his father than he dared to admit!

The opinion was unpleasant and irksome, and had been disturbing him when she'd awakened from her nap, appearing lush and well loved. He'd tried to be brusque, to push her away, but she was eminently proficient at getting under his skin and poking at his vulnerabilities. She infuriated and intrigued; he wanted her gone, he wanted her to stay.

With his ruminations in this bizarre jumble, he entered his room. Their adjoining door was ajar, and a lamp burned on the dresser. The flame was nearly expired, composing eerie shadows on the wall.

Suffering a twinge of both relief and dismay, he promptly noted that she'd fallen asleep on his bed. His initial inclination was to rush over, to ease down and shower her with kisses, but his ingrained sense of self-preservation kicked in. He locked his own door, then went to her bedchamber and checked hers, as well, assuring himself that they'd have no uninvited callers. Then, he returned to her and approached the bed.

For their prurient encounter, she'd worn a lightweight summer nightgown of pristine white with shortened sleeves and embroidered flowers around the scooped neckline. A pink ribbon tied at the front, and the luxurious fabric fell in soft folds against her torso, delineating each delicious curve and valley. Her hair was down and brushed out, and it lay in scattered disarray, a crimson stain against the bedcoverings. Her cheeks were rosy-red, her lips pouted, and her eyes fluttering with the dream she was having.

Enticing and devastating, she caused his blood to boil through his veins. His fingers tingled, his cock throbbed viciously, nearly doubling him over as his vivid imagination kicked in, painting scenes of what he would procure from her, how he would allay her fears, how he would instruct and satisfy her, while lustily and improperly fulfilling his every deviant fantasy. Yet he hardly cared. She'd begged for the chance to attend him again, and she was a grown woman who knew her own proclivities. Whatever transpired was no more than she'd sought.

Silently observing her, his concentration never straying from her captivating anatomy, he disrobed. Briefly, he pondered prolonging the prelude by obliging her to undress him, but he hastily decided against it. There would be no delay. He was aroused and prepared for the impending hours of ecstasy. His cock jutted out, proud and defiant, and he wrapped a fist around the heavy flesh.

Oh, how he wished he could spill himself in her mouth! Or between her legs! How tight that virginal cleft would be! How welcome the alleviation!

But she wasn't ready for such an event, and neither was he. Though his moral constitution was at its lowest level, he wasn't cad enough to terminate her maidenhood. Despite his extensive, incautious prior sensual amusement, he'd never stooped to stealing a woman's virtue, so he wasn't about to start. Still, the idea was so bloody tempting. *She* was so bloody tempting. How could he decline such inducement? Especially when her copious charms were freely and graciously extended.

Not wanting to frighten her, he carefully slipped onto the mattress and stretched out. She was on her side, so he scooted over and rolled her to her back, pinning her by resting an arm over her chest and a leg over her thigh.

"Sarah . . ." he murmured softly, never tiring of the opportunity to speak her name. He bestowed a chaste kiss that confused her. The reverie in which she'd been ensnared abruptly ended, and she awoke.

"Michael . . . ?"

Momentarily disoriented, she gazed up at him, genuine delight spreading through her, and he resolved that no matter what occurred between them, no matter how inappropriate his conduct, or how indecorous his actions, his folly was worth it to see her smiling at him with such unfeigned devotion. The empty spot in the center of his chest, where

his heart used to beat, stirred and ached as though jolted
into operation after a lengthy respite.

"Hello." An imbecilic grin crept across his own face.

"I was sleeping so hard." Mussed but adorable, she appeared confounded and abashed to have been caught una-
wares.

"Yes, you were."

"I tried to wait up for you."

How wonderful that she had! "I'm glad."

"Is it very late?"

"Aye."

She sifted her fingers through his hair, then lovingly
placed her palm against his beard-stubbled cheek, and the
move was so familiar and dear that his breath hitched in
his lungs.

Why had he let his personal demons impel him out into
the night? Why had he spent so much time wandering and
carousing? He could have been sequestered with her and
basking in her tender disposition. Kicking himself, cursing
himself for his asinine tendencies, he would stop spurning
the relief he garnered in her presence. For as long as they
remained in Bedford, he would overindulge in her delectable refuge.

Suddenly, reality was seeping in, and her brow furrowed
with concern. "Where have you been?"

Without a doubt, his whereabouts were none of her business, and she had no right to question him as to his activities. In the past, any prying female would have received
an austere warning, but instead, he bit down on his sharp
retort.

Sarah Compton provoked him in new and different
ways, and he had to grow accustomed to their peculiar style
of association. He liked that she cared enough to inquire,
to needle, and he yearned to have her understand the issues
that were motivating him, and the devils that were nipping
at his heels.

Gad, but if she kept staring at him as she was, there'd
be no stifling his negligent tongue. He'd babble away,

spilling his sorrows and woes on the bed like a bottle of spilt ink.

"I was out walking," he professed honestly, "and I went clear to the village, thinking to have an ale, then I stayed for a game of cards."

"But you knew I'd be here."

From another, the statement might have sounded like an accusation, but from her, there was only bafflement.

How long had it been since a woman had missed him or prayed that he would hurry home?

"I was puzzled," he shocked himself by disclosing. "After this afternoon."

"So you concluded it was best to avoid me?" Even her censure was gently tossed.

"I wasn't going to return, at all."

"Why?" she reproached kindly.

"I like having you here." The revelation stunned him, even as he privately chastised himself for expressing the sentimental drivel.

"What a sweet comment."

Stupidity! Why encourage the woman's flights of fancy? The manner in which she was regarding him—as though he was smart, benevolent, and extraordinary—terrified him. He appreciated how women viewed carnal dealings, how they processed intercourse. They read *love* into it where naught but lust existed.

Lest he create a mire from which they couldn't extricate themselves, he had to exercise circumspection. Despite how attracted he was to her physically, he had no intention of allowing any sort of idiotic emotion for Sarah to flourish.

"What we're doing . . ." He started prudently, not anxious to hurt her with the truth. "It's not right."

She set a finger to his lips, quelling any further voicing of regret. "Whatever ensues between us could never be wrong. And I won't listen to your saying so. This is a special time we've grabbed for ourselves. Let's just be content with what *is*."

Nodding, he accepted the sagacity of her statement, for

wasn't that exactly what he'd deduced, as well? He planned to seize the moment.

"May I make love to you again?" He kissed the tips of her fingers.

"That depends." She moved her hand down his neck, to his chest, where she rubbed in slow circles. "Have you been with another woman since we separated this afternoon?"

"No," he was relieved to respond. He hadn't even *spoken* to a female since then.

"You haven't been to the secret room?"

"No," he repeated.

"Because I have to admit, I was frantic that you might have." She blushed a flattering shade of pink. "When you weren't here, I looked through the peephole, but someone had covered it so I can't see inside."

"I'm the culprit. I didn't like that you've been observing what goes on."

"I'm a grown woman," she felt compelled to indicate.

"Yes, you are," he acceded, "but that doesn't mean you should be exposed to the lewdness in this house."

"The only *lewdness* I witnessed was your shenanigans."

"And I'm exceedingly embarrassed by that fact."

"Really?"

"Aye."

Startling him, she chuckled. "So . . . you've—once again—appointed yourself as the guardian of my virtue?"

"I suppose," he grumbled.

His rigid phallus nudged against her thigh, his naked legs tangled with hers, and the ludicrousness of their situation shook them. They laughed together, then it died away to a companionable silence.

"When you didn't return," she stated, "I was so worried."

"You needn't have fretted." But oh, how splendid to discover that she had! He was inordinately pleased.

"I wasn't sure how to find you and, after last night, I was afraid to search."

"Good," he remarked. "Perhaps I've finally talked some sense into that thick head of yours."

"Perhaps," she agreed, and the quiet played out, once more. Almost shyly, she announced, "I was terrified that you were visiting a lover."

"Is it so important to you that I not?"

"Extremely so."

The implication flustered him. She was pleading with him for a pledge of fidelity! Her request was so far-fetched that he could scarcely grasp it. Monogamy connoted fealty, a promise he could never make because he could never begin to keep it.

He didn't believe in the ridiculous kinds of everlasting Grand Passion espoused by the poets. Even if he was stupid enough to become romantically entrapped, he'd never let it happen over such a fine, upstanding woman as Sarah, because he could never be the man she supposed him to be, and if they wound up together, she'd suffer eternal disappointment.

Reality was a bitter tonic to swallow, and he didn't intend that she ever detect how divergent her illusions were from the actualities of his circumstances.

Clearly, she'd developed erroneous assumptions about the type of person he was. Probably, she'd credited him with assorted asinine attributes that were merely fantasy, but he'd revel in her daydreams. Just this once, he would pretend to be whatever she wanted him to be.

She was hunting for a hero, and he didn't aim to disavow her of her perceptions. He had no desire to inform her that he thought faithfulness impossible, loyalty absurd, and long-term commitment nonsense. He couldn't fuck and love conjointly, and he never misconstrued the two. Sex was a method of assuaging his erect cock, and he fornicated in order to achieve mitigation for his masculine drives, but she didn't need to be apprised of his convictions.

Her thinking that he was a better man, a different man, was positively enchanting. What could it hurt to humor her? If it bothered her that he might carry on with his licentious distraction in the Viewing Room, it was simple to placate her. Appeasement justified the consolation it brought.

"I won't go again." Not while she was in residence anyway, but he figured he wouldn't advise her of all his awful truths. A few lies were permissible between lovers, weren't they?

"It would break my heart if you did."

When had anyone ever cared about him so much, admired him so much? They were barely acquainted, yet she was so assured that virtuous character lurked deep within him.

That he could be the man she visualized! Instead, to his shame and consternation, he was without scruple or restraint, beyond redemption, a ne'er-do-well who used women for his own despicable purposes. Didn't she see? Didn't she recognize him for who and what he was?

The agony of confronting his faults, of having them so distinctly displayed, was too excruciating. She dredged up his imperfections and failings without even mentioning them. Just by lingering in her presence, he found himself questioning his entire mode of living, focusing on his individual defects as though they could be corrected or transformed.

He didn't have the patience for perpetual self-assessment. His pride couldn't take the immutable recrimination and evaluation, yet since he'd met her, he'd been besieged by old memories, forgotten grief, foibles and fiascoes, and he wasn't going to waste any effort contemplating the varied paths he might have chosen. This quagmire of indecision and perplexity in which he was enmeshed was pointless, and he had to shift them back to a realm he comprehended.

Hoping to accomplish only one thing—that being carnal pleasure—he sought out women to grace his bed. A gifted, skilled lover, he could dally to maximum effect, and women flocked to copulate with him because of his seductive abilities. Sarah was the same as all the others. She'd chased after him, seeking an erotic relationship that she presumed—with misguided design—would turn emotional, but she was too inexperienced to realize the improbability.

By debauching her, once again, he could bring their rendezvous back to safer ground, to where he would be honed in on the only important goal: satiation. If he was lucky, perhaps he'd be so involved in his quest that he'd manage to slake his infernal preoccupation with her before it drove him mad.

Innocently, he brushed against her lips, not tarrying as he'd love to do, but refraining as was most wise. Kissing her was dangerous. Better, saner, to employ his mouth in more fruitful, innocuous endeavors.

He declared, "I thought about you all evening."

"And I, you."

"Did you enjoy our afternoon encounter?"

"Every second of it." She winked wickedly. "I came back for more, didn't I?"

"So you did."

Feeling grand, he laughed and flipped them so that she was on top. Spreading her thighs, he adjusted her till her tantalizing pussy was directly over his cock, then he braced his hands on her hips and painstakingly flexed along her cleft.

"I've been so hard for you ever since we parted." He nodded toward her body. "Remove your nightgown. Show me what you learned today."

Chapter Fourteen

Sarah glared at him, dismayed by his cool command. In her naïveté, she'd fantasized that they'd forged a new understanding and would now come together with kisses and professions of devotion.

One corner of her mouth twitched with a smile, and she bit it back. How imbecilic of her, assuming that a simple afternoon romp would have altered their relationship. He wasn't the sort prone to poetic prose or flowery welcome. He was who he was. A complex man, he'd never cuddle or coo, but then, his rough edges and belligerent attitude were what attracted her so desperately.

As usual, he was being crude and demanding, but surprisingly, she realized that she could easily tolerate his high-handed manner. While she might have bristled had they been elsewhere, in this secluded situation, poised on the brink of sexual ecstasy, she was thrilled by how he ordered her about.

Regularly, he sought out women who were predisposed to decadency. By his own admission, he had strong manly drives that demanded routine alleviation. Though he'd favored her for his partner, he hadn't ascribed any specific significance to the selection, but she wasn't about to consider his lack of deference an indication of defeat. He'd returned—after incessantly debating as to whether he should—which she would take as a sign of progress.

She harbored no illusions about why he hadn't been overly enthused about dallying with her, once again. No doubt, due to her inexperience, she'd failed to fully satisfy him. Yes, he'd spilled his seed, but as far as she could discern, she'd had very little to do with it. She'd simply been present and available. He'd toyed with her, and his ardor had spiked, but he might have engaged in the behavior with anyone, be it she or another. Given his wanton habits, any naked female would have sent him over that climactic precipice.

Yet despite his professed confusion, he'd come back to her. He'd kindly conceded that he'd enjoyed their interaction, but she was acutely aware that their tryst had been limited in quantity and quality—a circumstance she proposed to rectify as soon as she was able.

She was eager to please him in every fashion, for him to view their assignations as magical and enchanted, but perhaps she was expecting too much. For the time being, she needed to be glad that he'd arrived, when she'd been so worried that he wouldn't.

After leaving his room earlier, she'd scarcely made it through the interminable evening of socializing without dissembling. When she'd pleaded fatigue and sped up the stairs, she'd burst into his room, confident that he'd be waiting, as impatient as she for what lay ahead. Initially, the fact that he hadn't been pining away had been an incredible disappointment, but after she'd shrugged off her fit of pique, she'd stood in the middle of his bedchamber and chuckled aloud.

Of course, Michael Stevens would have better things to do! What had she been thinking! She'd calmed herself, then agonizingly paced. Each creak of the old house, every crack of the smoldering logs in the grate, the infrequent footstep in the hall, had set her heart to racing.

As the hour had grown late, and he still hadn't appeared, her self-assurance had flown out the window. She'd envisioned the places he might have gone and what he might be doing. When she'd braved a glance at the peephole, and discovered it shuttered, she'd sagged with defeat, certain he was on the other side of the wall with an anonymous lover. All her scheming and planning had been for naught!

Disheartened, but incapable of remaining in her lonely, solitary bed, she'd proceeded to his chamber and lain on his pillow, instantly pacified by his smell. Drifting between despair and sleep, she'd stayed, resolved to hash it out. He could protest and complain and deny, but they shared a destiny, and he belonged with her—at least for the next few days.

After that, what might transpire was anybody's guess, but she'd always been an optimist. Any marvelous occurrence was conceivable.

Physical intimacy would bring them closer than words ever could, so she reached for her nightrail, yanked it up and over, and pitched it on the mattress. She straddled his lap, naked but for a pair of the exotic French underdrawers that amused him. His eyes locked on her bare chest, and her nipples responded, the tips constricting.

"Your body is so fabulous."

Irreverently, he pinched one of the elongated nubs between thumb and finger. The move had her squirming as did the comment, and her cheeks flushed She wasn't accustomed to compliments, especially such indiscreet ones. Spurring her hips, he tipped her forward, and her hands steadied on either side of his head, her nipples dangling over his enthusiastic mouth.

"I'm going to make love to your breasts."

"Yes . . ." she gasped on a rush of air as he sucked at the enlarged crest. "Whatever you want."

"I'll keep at it until you can't stand any more. Until you're begging me to stop."

"No, never. I'll never ask you to stop."

"Until you're crying out my name."

Now that was a definite possibility!

Pinning her to him, he worked atrociously, and he suckled till she was raw and distended, then he detached and shifted to the other, rummaging across her bosom like a nursing babe. He located the delectable morsel, taking it with his searching, zealous lips.

Below, his cock was rudely insinuated between her legs, and his hands descended to her bottom, squeezing and manipulating the rounded globes, and utilizing them as leverage to stroke his aroused member. His hot flesh tantalized her silky undergarment, pushing it into the heated cleft, causing her body to weep.

His hands were at her thighs, spreading her so that her swollen mound was titillated by his slightest movement. Exhaustively, his cock massaged her, every delicious inch, so that when he fumbled with the tie on her drawers, when he glided inside with those resourceful fingers, her entire being was adjusted for the pleasure she now fathomed to be winging in her direction.

With a few flicks of his devious thumb, he led her to the yawning crevasse and shoved her over. Cognizant of the pending tumult, she freely leapt into the void, the jubilant anguish staggering. He swallowed her cry of delight, kissing her thoroughly to consume some of her rapture as she soared to the heavens then floated back to earth.

As he'd invariably seemed reluctant to kiss her, she'd thought he would end it abruptly, but for once, he didn't. He treasured and sampled, and she relished the attention he'd suddenly decided to lavish on her. This was *kissing* as she'd always visualized it, at its most magnificent and exciting. Their breath mingled, their hearts beat in unison, his very essence flowed through her. The embrace went on and on, and she savored the display, letting him feast for as long as he was inclined.

Gradually, the interlude spiraled to a conclusion, and their lips separated. He gazed at her with such an intense, dangerous expression that she was completely unnerved.

Struggling for levity, she smiled and queried, "How do you do that to me so easily?"

"I take it milady was . . . *satisfied*?"

"Yes, you bounder," she grumbled. "Don't look so damned pleased."

Unrepentant and overconfident, he was positively lethal to someone of her limited ability, and she heartily wished she'd steeled herself against his onslaught. A mere woman could never successfully contend with such potency.

He chuckled, then stole another stormy kiss. "I adore

how I make you come," he said impudently. "You call out
for me . . . right at the end."

"I can't abide such arrogance in a man!"

"Get used to it, love."

Once again, he'd tossed out the endearment as if it was
of no import. Handsome as the devil himself, his sapphire
eyes blazed with desire, an abominably alluring dimple
creased his cheek, and she pondered how she'd let her poor
heart get into this fix. After she left for home, she would
never be the same.

"You are horrid. I don't know why I permit you to abuse
me."

"Because I'm irresistible?"

"Too true," she retorted. "More's the pity."

"Oh, Sarah . . ."—he chuckled again—"you are so good
for me."

"Am I?"

"Absolutely."

The air was charged as before a lightning storm, full of
promise and foreboding. Powerful emotions roiled through
her, and she was unable to ferret out a suitable rejoinder.

"I am so hard for you," he ultimately said.

He pressed his phallus against her, and it dawned on her
that whenever their verbal repartee became too intimate, he
reverted to talk of the sexual. She didn't mind, though,
because she wielded the most authority over him when they
were naked. The more he lusted, the greater her chances to
lure him toward the bond she hoped would eventually develop.

She partook of a slow flex of her own. "I like feeling
you close, but it's not enough."

"No."

"Why?"

"The normal conclusion for your orgasm would be for
me to penetrate you." He cupped her, fondling the silk
crotch of her pantalets, then a finger slid underneath the
hem, easing into her animated cleft. Sounding pained, he
huskily noted, "You're so tight."

"Will you . . . ?" She didn't possess the necessary vocabulary to interrogate him as to whether he would make love to her there. Now that he'd explained her emptiness, she recognized that her body was anxious to be relieved of its virginal condition.

"Not today. Maybe not ever," he asserted. "I don't know . . ." Appearing baffled and bewildered by his reticence, he let his voice trail off as he rolled her onto her back. "I'm going to put my mouth on you."

"What?" He caressed her moist pantalets, leaving no doubt as to his purpose, and her eyes widened in shock.

"When I come, I want to have the taste of your sex on my tongue."

"You're not serious."

"Oh, but I am."

Before she could prevent it, he was tugging her drawers down her thighs, and he had them over her toes and on the floor. He dropped down and centered himself, geared to advance, and she squirmed, flustered by his bizarre request.

"Michael!"

"When you say my name like that, you sound like an expensive whore."

The odd compliment grated; she didn't care for the coarse comparison, at all. "Whatever you're up to . . . I'm not ready for . . . for . . ."

The tip of his tongue dipped into her navel, and she writhed with trepidation, and he halted. He wrenched his torrid gaze up her torso, his blatant assessment calculated to remind her of her previous acquiescence, of how promptly she'd succumbed, of how overwhelmed she'd been.

"You trust me, don't you?" he asked.

"No, I don't!" She didn't trust him any further than she could throw him.

He had the audacity to laugh at her candor, then he continued with his ministrations. Lower, past her navel, to her feminine hair. He nuzzled his cheek in it, rubbed his nose in it, rooting and sniffing as though implanting her scent in his consciousness.

"Michael . . ." she tried again, "this is too personal."

"I told you"—he lifted up from his precarious perch—"that nothing is forbidden. *Nothing,* Sarah."

"But I had no idea you'd contrive something so . . . so . . ."

"Depraved? Outlandish? Improper?"

"Precisely."

He merely shrugged. "Having you in this manner will make me happy. Isn't that why you're here?"

As he was unerringly correct, protest seemed futile.

Somehow, despite her objection, he'd managed to inflict himself betwixt her legs, and he settled her thighs over his shoulders. When he spread the mysterious folds, she arched up, seeking escape, but he was holding her down, and she couldn't get free.

"Relax," he murmured soothingly. "Close your eyes and just feel."

"I don't like it."

"You will," he insisted, cheeky knave that he was.

Baldly, he scrutinized every aspect of her feminine opening. Then . . . his tongue. There and meddling and invasive, and she flung an arm over her face, hiding, longing to disappear. She felt humiliated, ravished, yet strangely intrigued by his thrust and parry.

He kissed her leisurely as he had her mouth, piercing her in an unremitting rhythm, and the unyielding seduction began to take its toll. Her thighs parted further, offering him more space in which to perform his devious, tricky assault. Try as she might not to enjoy the maneuver, she couldn't resist being drawn in. Her traitorous body reacted until she was straining against him—not in an attempt to get away, but in another skirmish toward carnal release.

"No, I can't," she wailed, when she detected where he was leading her. "It's too soon."

"It's never too soon. Do it again. Just for me."

The invidious rogue! He acted as if she was doing *him* a courtesy by finding sensual gratification.

His fingers were at her breasts, furiously kneading her ravaged nipples, as his tongue focused on the sensitive protuberance that he finessed with such devastating effect. With minimal effort, he—once again—hurled her over the ledge of desire.

As the stimulation abated, he was towering above her, imperious cock in hand, and he guided the ample crown across her cleft. "Can you imagine how it would be if I entered you now? I would ride you so hard."

For the longest time, he didn't move, poised on the brink of a terrible impasse, and she bit against her lip, incited, prepared for the next, but it never ensued.

Sweat pooled on his brow, and he meticulously fondled her, her bodily moisture wetting the tip, then ever so slightly, he inserted himself. Vividly foreseeing what could transpire, he stared at the spot where they were barely connected. She looked down, too, agitated and aching, contemplating that his presence seemed so appropriate.

Her hips clenched, and he jumped back as though burned, but he'd been forced beyond his limits of restraint, and he demanded immediate satiation. He clutched her to his chest and stroked his cock against her, twice, thrice, then he spewed himself on her stomach and leg, the fiery liquid blanketing her, its pungent aroma filling the air.

"Oh, Sarah . . ."

Moaning, he collapsed on her, and he held himself motionless as his breathing and pulse slowed to tractable levels. Finished, he strove to slip away, but she wouldn't let him, snuggling him to her bosom, his beautiful face nestled between her breasts.

The act of mating created such a unique serenity, and she wanted to sustain the moment, but unfortunately, the lull provided plenty of opportunity for reflection about subjects best forgotten—like a home and family of her own. She'd perpetually insisted she didn't require either, but now, with the smell of his sex in the air, and the sweet sound of her name reverberating off the walls, it was perplexing to remember why she'd shunned her chances for such contentment.

How had it resulted that she was twenty-five and so alone? Why had she settled for a pittance? She always believed her existence was eventful and consequential, and it had never occurred to her that she was lonely, or that she would like to live happily ever after with the man of her dreams—that man having a suspicious resemblance to Michael Stevens.

Shutting out reality, she wished for all the things that could never be, but concluded that she wanted them anyway. What was the harm?

Then, she kissed the top of his head, and he stretched and groaned languidly.

"Are you married, Michael?" The interrogatory popped out before she could snatch it back.

"No, why?" He peeked up at her. "Are you worried about my character?"

"I'm unequivocally *worried* about your character, you cad," she remarked, "but not because you might be cheating on your wife. You have many more severe flaws."

"You're right about that."

"I'm just relieved that marital infidelity is not among them." She said it lightly and, from the way he grinned, he'd taken it as a jest, but she sincerely meant it.

"I was just curious; I know nothing about you." And in the pause that followed, the rat didn't supply any information, though she'd presented the perfect excuse. She sighed. "Do you ever think about getting married?"

Her heart skipped several frantic beats. Where had that come from? If only the mattress would swallow her up so she could vanish! What a ninny he must deem her to be! A few tumbles in his bed, a few lessons in carnality, and she was babbling about matrimony! After she'd waxed on for days prior, feigning sophistication in affairs beyond her ken and supplicating for a meaningless fling!

"No, I never do," he answered more gently than she

deserved. He kissed the underside of her breast, then he balanced himself on an elbow. His seed was drying, and he toweled it away with her nightgown. "Is that what you're hoping might happen between us?"

There was no censure or rebuke in his tone, so perhaps if she was prudent, she could worm herself out of this debacle before she made an even bigger fool of herself. "I'm just beginning to grasp that I missed much by not marrying."

"It's only natural. Sex stirs many new and strange emotions. Particularly in a woman."

"But not in a man?"

"No. Women confuse sex with love, when they really have nothing to do with one another. For a man, fornication is simply a physical discharge."

"Is that how you see it?"

"Yes." The truth hurt her, and he added, "I'm sorry to be so blunt."

"That explains why a man can have different lovers."

"Yes."

"Why a man can purportedly love his wife, but keep a mistress."

"Exactly."

"Why you can go to the hidden room and cavort with women you don't know."

He stirred uncomfortably. "Aye."

She'd totally positioned herself to weather the frank statements, staring into his blue eyes and showing as little interest as he in the laborious topic. "Was this just *physical discharge* for you?"

"It was a good deal more," he puzzled her by acceding, "but that doesn't mean we'll wed when we're through." He ran a finger across her cheekbone, her chin, her lips. "Be careful where you allow your heart to wander," he declared tenderly but firmly. "Guard it well, for I will assuredly break it if you lose it to me."

"As if I would!" she commented dryly, nudging him in the ribs. "I'd like to think I have better sense."

"I would be a very bad mistake."

"You don't have to remind me."

She was lying horridly, but he had the decency to pretend that he didn't know it, and when she held out her arms, she was immensely gratified that he burrowed himself into them without hesitation. They lay together, his leg draped over her thigh, his wrist on her waist, and he scrutinized her as if committing her to memory.

"Why have you never married?" he queried, and his examination was as startling and as peculiar as when she'd posed hers.

How wonderful that he would inquire! Schooling her features, she affected a bored demeanor, even though she was dying to confess so much.

"I always supposed I would. I even had a Season in London."

"Really?"

"When I was seventeen, but it was quite terrible."

"Why?"

"Let's just be kind and say that, back then, I wasn't a beauty."

"I find that very difficult to believe."

The compliment was as welcome as it was astonishing. As he was not given to flattery, especially over something as nebulous as a woman's comeliness, she grabbed onto his words as though they were a merciful benediction. He kissed the tip of her nose, but the soft touch dipped down to her very core where so much of her past heartbreak lingered. The sentiment sank far inside, comforting her, and she yearned for his sympathy and approval for the woman into which she'd matured. The old torments were pieces of the whole.

"Back then," she offered, "I was all gangly limbs and red hair, and I was so unprepared for what London would be like. They ate me alive."

"Your peers can be a vicious lot," he concurred wholeheartedly.

"Yes, they can." God, but she loved him for agreeing!

"And my father was pressuring me to choose one of the boys, but they were all so unacceptable. I couldn't decide."

"You wouldn't let him pick for you?"

"No!"

"So you refused them all?" The twinkle in his eye was genuine. "You defied your father?"

"I can be extremely stubborn."

"I've noticed that about you."

She could have lain there forever, hugging, and laughing and trading jibes, and she was struck anew by how much she'd lost out on by denying herself this closeness with a man, just as she appreciated that this was the sole occasion she'd ever have to endure such bliss.

Michael Stevens was a unique individual, and after this interval was terminated, she'd never experience anything similar. This singular, rare encounter would have to take her through her intermediate years and further, the constant memories of their abbreviated liaison stark and distinct.

Sadness engulfed her at the conviction that she'd never again sustain this quiet joy, and she shoved it away. She refused to be unhappy! Not while she was here with him like this. There would be many, many days down the road when she could bemoan her fate and lament over what might have been. For now, she would be content with what *was*.

"And what about you?" She was desperate to learn more and, as she'd formerly deduced, gleaning tidbits from him was like pulling teeth. "Divulge something embarrassingly scandalous that will leave me aghast."

"You've uncovered all my worst secrets."

"Then, what about something personal?" She wouldn't let him avoid a few meaningful disclosures. "How do you earn your income?"

"I own a gentlemen's club with my brother, James."

A straight answer! Encouraged, she fired off a second round. "Where?"

"In London."

"You live in the city?"

"Yes. In the theater district."

"With your mother and brother?"

"I'm not sure."

"How can you not be *sure*?"

"With their recent marriages, I don't know the arrangements now."

"You haven't been back since their weddings?"

"No."

For once, his cool detachment was markedly absent, and she trod cautiously, aware that these were sore spots. "Who is your family?"

"My mother is Angela Ford. She's quite a renowned actress."

"Really?" Amazed, she sat up.

If she'd been advised to guess his antecedents, she'd have said he was a third or fourth son of a wealthy nobleman, the bane of his family's existence, the black sheep. But the son of an actress! She'd never been acquainted with anyone quite so disreputable. "How fascinating. I saw her once on the stage when I was in town. She's legendary."

"She is at that."

Sarah recalled the dynamic woman. She'd exuded a charisma that even Sarah, with her rural underpinnings, couldn't fail to note. That the notorious celebrity had birthed Michael didn't surprise her in the least.

"Who is your father?"

He gaped. Then . . . he laughed. Loudly. At her, and what he plainly considered a ridiculous question. "Sarah, I could swear you were raised by wolves in the forest."

He was teasing her, and she was thrilled that he liked her enough to expend the energy. "Why do you say that?"

"I just never meet anyone who isn't exhaustively versed as to all my gory details."

"Well, I'm not."

"Obviously."

He chortled merrily, enjoying himself at her expense, but she didn't mind. As long as he resumed his accounting! "Are there many? *Gory details,* I mean."

"Enough to fill a book."

"Oh . . ." Just how did one reply to such a statement? No advantageous retort cropped up, and silence reigned, once again, as he regarded her with an honest affection, evidently cherishing the verbal banter as much as she.

Finally, he stated, "My father is Edward Stevens."

She had to ponder for a moment before she placed the appellation. "The Earl of Spencer?"

"Yes, but I don't claim him, and he doesn't claim me."

His admission was so quietly pronounced that she almost didn't hear it, and she studied him thoughtfully. This was a seeping wound, one that had never entirely healed. "You're not joking."

"No, I'm not."

He rotated to his back, hugging her so that she was stretched out along his side, relieved that they'd shifted positions, because she could look somewhere besides into those astute blue eyes while she weighed his background.

His paternal parentage explained a great deal: his regal bearing, his haughty attitude, his imperious demeanor. She'd convinced herself that he was an aristocrat's offspring, someone of her social standing, yet he was an illegitimate bastard. Even if by some quirk of the wildest fate he determined he loved her, they could never marry.

How was it that she could so acutely grieve the loss of something that had never been feasible to begin with?

Striving to appear blasé, she countered with, "Now that you've confessed the identity of your father, I understand why you are so incurably arrogant."

"I can't believe you didn't know."

"I probably did"—fragments of an ancient gossip rumbled but not enough for her to recall any fine points—"but I would never have connected him to you."

"Does it make a difference?"

She was now more attuned to his style, so she recognized that his was not an innocent query. It was a test, an analysis of the type of person she was, and he braced, anticipating repudiation, and she couldn't help speculating as to why he sought her affirmation.

Unless he cares more than he's willing to admit.

The idea came unbidden, loudly and clearly refusing to be muted, so she acknowledged it for the superb concept it was, even as she wished that everything could be contrary to the reality with which she was now confronted.

"No," she lied deliberately, "it doesn't signify. Not in the slightest."

The evident pleasure he received from her fabrication was impossible to calculate or describe, and she was delighted that she'd provided the petty deception. For what did her opinion matter anyway?

He'd warned her not to become attached and with valid reason! No outcome was probable save heartbreak, so there was no use indulging fantasies.

Still, as his lips found hers, as he moved over her and commenced to suckle at her breast, as his cock extended against her thigh, she couldn't recollect why this was so improper. She'd never felt so alive, so gay or fulfilled.

"I want you," he avowed.

"Again?" And she was overjoyed that he did.

"Yes." He was confounded by his burgeoning need for her. "Already. Always."

"I'm glad."

And as he escorted her on that extraordinary journey, down the path that he so expertly traveled, she didn't regret any of her choices. The *future,* such as it was, would arrive soon enough, and for now, she didn't intend to fret about what it would hold.

Chapter Fifteen

Sarah rushed into her bedchamber, hastily stripping off her gloves, ready to make a mad dash to Michael and the ecstasy that awaited. First though, cognizant of his extreme caution, she checked the lock on the door—twice—but her fingers trembled with such apprehension for the impending libidinous event that she could scarcely manipulate the mechanism.

He wouldn't appreciate any overzealousness on her part, so she struggled for calm. Walking to the mirror, taking several deep breaths, she evaluated herself, distractedly straightening her coiffure. Not that her hair needed rearranging, but the fussing gave her a few extra minutes to compose herself after flying up the stairs in such a dither.

Despite what was actually transpiring, Michael sternly contended that theirs was simply a meaningless fling, so she had to appear cool and serene, which was what he expected of her. Through his subtle demeanor and fatiguing persistence, he'd clearly indicated that they would interact in an indifferent fashion. They would fully vent their shared lust and rising ardor, but any recognition of emotional connection, or profound affinity, was forbidden and had to be discounted and ignored.

With scant difficulty, he evinced equanimity. Except in the depths of excessive passion, Michael exuded a reticence that was distinctly upsetting. When he was naked and lying in her arms, they were as close as two people could ever hope to be, but once he donned his clothes, he reverted to being reserved and aloof. Assuredly, he was a polite and interesting associate, but he'd erected a wall between them that he would not let her scale, despite how fervently she tried.

Unlike him, she had her problems with the enforced apathy, and she had to compel herself to remain remote and uninvolved, when all she really wanted was to confess how much she cherished their furtive, stolen interludes. She endured solely for those glorious moments when she strolled in and his admiring gaze fell upon her. There was nothing quite so marvelous as having his undivided attention, seeing him smile, or knowing he'd been impatient for her arrival.

With each passing hour, it was growing more arduous to feign distance. He'd filled her life to overflowing, had given it meaning and purpose: that being to wallow in his splendid presence.

Why, oh, why had she denied herself such pleasure for so long? And now that she'd experienced his special brand of revelry, how could she return to Yorkshire and persevere as though nothing had happened?

The woman who'd efficiently and exhaustively tended the estate for so many tiresome years had disappeared, replaced by a woman for whom only sex—with Michael Stevens—mattered. Where once she'd treasured her placid, unchanging rural existence, she now couldn't imagine herself in that monotonous, boring world. She'd expire in such a tedious environment!

As a plant needed air and water, so she needed Michael in order to flourish. The idea of suffering through a day—or a night—without touching him, talking to him, kissing or holding him, was a torture beyond contemplation, yet when they were together, she was supposed to act nonchalant, and she wasn't having much luck at maintaining the ruse.

Her anticipation of imminent bliss was all-consuming and meant that she couldn't socialize at the gathering. While she'd never been much for fraternization, when Michael was waiting for her, she couldn't tolerate the inane prattle, the innocuous topics, or the frivolous substance of the other guests.

Braving a meal or an entertainment was so distasteful

that she could hardly descend the stairs, yet she forced herself to go, bowing to the necessity of putting in an appearance. She'd much rather stay sequestered and allow Michael to continue his proficient, thorough instruction in the carnal arts.

Just as Michael had predicted, she'd become enmeshed in the sordid dissipations he preferred, and she couldn't figure out how she'd avoided seduction until the ripe old age of twenty-five. Of course, she hadn't previously met Michael, either. Without a doubt, her attraction to him had melted some internal bastion of propriety, for she was now enthusiastic and willing to commit any lewd, indecent exploit he suggested—the more ribald the better. Total surrender—to him and the games he instigated—was her singular aim and goal.

In fact, she was wild for the debauchery to commence so that she could discover just how naughty he would ask her to be. How could she have guessed that underneath her proper, demure shell resided the soul of a complete wanton? All these years, her true proclivities had been so carefully hidden! What a joy—and a relief—to set them free!

With a final glance in the mirror, she adjudged that she was composed enough to head for his room. Fixing a pleasant smile on her face, she stubbornly endeavored to shield any untoward longing. There was no reason whatsoever to let him surmise that she was pining away, that she was already floundering as she fretted over how she'd carry on after they parted.

Since she was the one who'd insisted on an affair, and she'd quite verbally contended that she could participate with no strings attached, she wasn't about to admit a grave mistake in her reckoning: Detachment was impossible. He was too handsome, too thrilling, too dynamic, and there wasn't a woman in the kingdom who could avert a burgeoning infatuation after spending so much uninterrupted time with him.

She was no exception. If anything, she was more susceptible to his charm and wicked ways than another, and she incessantly pondered how she'd bear up once she left in two weeks, but she could never tell him so. They seemed to have adopted a secret pact not to mention the future; they dallied but neither spoke of, nor alluded to, that nebulous by-and-by when they would separate.

Their circumspection lent a recklessness to the assignations. The *dénouement* was drawing nigh much too quickly, so every encounter held a special semblance of finality. As though they were destined for the gallows come the morn, each rendezvous was more intense than the last, with both of them desperate to wring every speck of passion out of their communal experience.

This one, she was positive, would exceed the prior ones in excess, excitement, and satisfaction, and she would do everything in her power to ensure that the evening was merry and gay. When it ended, she wanted Michael to be ever so glad he'd passed his leisure hours with her rather than another.

Knocking softly, she opened the door without pausing for a response. They were so comfortable—like an old, married couple—that polite comportment was superfluous. She came and went, never hesitating to intrude on his individual quarters. Even if he wasn't about, she'd make herself at home, and those were the occasions she liked best. With his absence, she could snoop and pry among his belongings. Rifling through the wardrobe where he hung his shirts, or sifting through his tray of cuff links on the dresser, was enervatingly erotic.

And, of course, the dearest moments of all occurred when she fell asleep on his bed—a dreadful invasion of his privacy—and he arrived later, awakening her with kisses and more. The memory of those luscious appointments was too potent, so she steeled herself against their onslaught and walked in.

As usual, he was reclined in his chair by the window, a glowing cheroot dangling from his fingers. He lounged negligently, like a carefree prince or an Arabian sheik whose harem was about to fawn all over him. But as she'd learned early on, with Michael Stevens, appearances were deceiving.

From the manner in which he immediately examined her, from how he rose to greet her, she suspected that he wasn't nearly as unruffled as he strove to pretend. Magnetic, preposterously virile, he crossed to her. He was all grace and smooth motion, and there was a tension emanating from him that dispelled the affectation of ennui he labored so valiantly to sustain.

She buried a smile; he'd been missing her, at least a little, and she hugged the phenomenal notion close to her heart for subsequent dissection and contemplation.

He'd dressed for supper, even though he never went down, and she admired the superb sight. Rarely did she behold him primped and preened. By the time they had a few solitary minutes for themselves, he was ordinarily naked or, if he deigned to cover himself, he sported a robe.

She acutely appreciated this side of him, this civilized coating over the rough core. In the middle of a London ballroom, surrounded by the *beau monde,* he'd be spectacular. With his refinement and arrogance, he'd fit right in, his aristocratic Stevens bloodlines keenly apparent.

The fabulous dark blue of his velvet coat set off the vividness of his spectacular eyes, eyes that were focused on her with a dazzling potency. Without a polite word of welcome, he turned her and nibbled at her nape—a spot he particularly relished—and goose bumps slithered down her arms.

"Where've you been?" He was chafing, restless, lusting for her. His cock firm and obstinate against her bottom, he gripped her waist, pulling her closer. "I thought you'd be here an hour ago."

"I couldn't leave until that blasted soprano finished her aria." And what a hideous delay it had been! When the concert had begun, she hadn't been paying much attention to her surroundings, distracted as she was by her musings of Michael, and she'd permitted herself to be seated near the front, making it impossible to slip away undetected.

"You're here now."

"So I am." She tipped her head, granting him more space to sample.

"Are you hungry?"

"Famished." And hoping he was geared to indulge in a prurient feast.

"Good."

Gradually, her vision sharpened to encompass more of the room, and she saw that he'd had an intimate supper for two delivered. A square table, covered with a pristine white cloth and immaculate china and silver, had been placed by the fire. Candles glimmered romantically in the center, and the crystal stemware gleamed, reflecting the flames in the hearth.

"What's this?"

"Supper, milady."

"What a sweet idea."

He kissed up her neck, toying with her ear. "Will you join me?"

"Absolutely."

As though parading her into a grand dining room, he slipped her hand into the crook of his arm and escorted her across the floor, gallantly holding out a chair.

Scarcely capable of breathing in her elated state, she glided into it, clinging to every second of the unexpected, impulsive surprise. Up until now, she'd persuaded herself that—from his perspective—their trysts were purely sexual, that he'd prevailed with his objective of downplaying their significance, but evidently, she'd been mistaken. For him to have initiated this nonlibidinous activity was the most precious, most dangerous, eventuality he could have concocted.

Sharing a repast was a wholesome diversion, the sort of enterprise friends might undertake, and made it seem that they were companions and confidants, rather than two strangers who'd more or less bumped into each other and who were illicitly dallying after a succinct acquaintance.

"What brought this on?" she couldn't help inquiring, peeking up at him over her shoulder.

As if they regularly met for supper, he kissed her, then casually rounded the table, seating himself across from her and pouring the wine. "I decided that I wanted to have one memory of you with your clothes on."

"Beast," she chuckled. "If you wished to see me dressed, you only had to request it."

"Plus, it's so fun to remove everything"—he stared at her over the rim of his stemmed goblet—"piece by piece."

"Would you like to start straightaway?" Deliberately, she leaned forward, and the low-cut neckline of her evening gown provided him with an arresting exhibition of creamy flesh.

"Momentarily," he murmured, transfixed by her bosom. "Let me enjoy the view for a bit."

"Certainly." She adjusted herself so that he had an unobstructed display of cleavage.

His brow rose. "Are you flirting with me, madam?"

"Naturally."

"A hazardous business, considering my state of enamoredness with your copious charms."

"I'll risk it."

Vigilantly, he studied her. While he'd always been an intense man, suddenly he seemed vastly altered, as though he'd reached an intricate resolution, as though he had confessions to make, tales to tell, feelings to recount.

But instead of relating the introspections that plagued him, he shifted back. "Are you really hungry?"

"Ravenous. I left the party before the buffet was presented."

"Let's eat, then." He stood and went to the dresser where an array of covered dishes had been arranged. After filling several plates, he carried them back, situating them before her with a grand gesture. *"Voilà!"*

"Thank you."

Fleetingly, he looked abashed. "Sorry about the lack of servants, but we're fending for ourselves."

"We'll manage."

"I'd thought about engaging one of the footmen, but they're such tattlers that I couldn't have offered a bribe large enough to keep them from spilling all to Lady Carrington." Braced for her to object to the isolation, to the informality, he gazed at her across the table.

Was he mad?

She was euphoric that they were alone, and categorically enchanted that he'd gone to so much trouble. There was fish and fowl, vegetables and fruits, cheeses and breads. Everything was perfectly prepared, eye-catching, and when he stabbed a miniature carrot with his fork and held it out for her to taste, she was spellbound by how effortlessly he wended his magic.

"This is the main course," he declared. "Later, I'll provide dessert."

From the salacious gleam in his eye, she understood that he wasn't referring to food. "Do I get to pick my favorite?"

"With my avid assistance."

She nibbled, taking the tiniest possible morsels, drawing out the delectation. In the process, she learned—with no small amount of surprise—that it was abominably romantic to have a man feed her. He rendered various delicacies, and she eagerly participated, feeding him, as well. Lingering, delaying, savoring, they puttered with the cuisine, and it was fascinating to watch him perform such elementary feats as chewing and swallowing.

Inevitably, she was full to bursting, and she pushed her plate away, laughing when he coerced her into one bite, then another. She had difficulty refusing him, even over so trivial a subject as how much he wanted her to eat.

While he cleared the table, she loafed like a pampered princess. He tidied until there were only the wineglasses and the candles he'd shoved off to the side. When he sat across from her, once again, she was balanced on her forearms, and he assumed the same pose, the position bringing him so near that she could make out the gold flecks intermingled in the blue of his pupils, the mark where his razor had nicked under his chin.

His left eye was slightly blackened underneath, from a blow he'd sustained in his fight with Brigham, and she reached out and traced a finger across the wound, never tiring of the excuse to touch him.

"Where will you go when you leave here?" he queried, taking her hand, linking their fingers. "Back to Scarborough?"

"Yes." She was relieved that he'd thrown the prohibited topic of *the future* out into the open, but as delighted as she was that he'd raised it, she also regretted that he had. His interrogatory reminded her that the time for separating was very close indeed, and she had to prod her next comment past the lump in her throat.

"How about you?"

"I'm not sure. Another party, I suppose."

The thought of him persisting with his licentious habits was disturbing, and she couldn't bear to conceive of him whiling away at cards, women, drink, and other senseless pursuits.

"Why don't *you* go home? I wish you would."

"I will eventually. I can't just now."

"Why did you leave in the first place?"

"I was angry at my mother. I walked in on her and my father when they were . . ." His cheeks flamed with color; apparently, he couldn't describe what he'd caught them doing.

"They're married?"

"They weren't then, which made me angry; they tied the knot a month or two ago."

"You're not close to your father, are you?"

"No, not at all. He was horrid to my mother over the years, and I've never forgiven him for his bad behavior."

"It must have been quite shocking for you to stumble on them together."

"It was, and I behaved like an ass." He chuckled, but

without mirth. "At the time, it seemed appropriate to be furious . . ."

His voice trailed off, and he couldn't explain why he'd fled or why he couldn't go back. Gently, she nudged, "You can't deduce how to return?"

"After making such a monumental fool of myself in front of my entire family, I find it's easier to wander." Shrugging, he gulped at his wine and deftly changed the subject. "I'll try to picture you in Yorkshire."

"Then get a 'picture' of something very dull, very mundane, very sedate." He laughed, which warmed her. With her eyes, she added, *And 'picture' me missing you. Every second. Every minute. Every day.*

The silence stretched, jarred, and she boldly suggested, "You could visit me. If you were in the north."

Meticulously, he scrutinized her and, after a good deal of painful deliberation, he ultimately pronounced, "I never would."

Nodding, she stoically accepted his rejection. Probably, she should have been hurt but, as he'd rebuffed her proposition, he looked so forlorn that she couldn't be aggrieved.

A stronger woman might have argued or begged for a different response, but she couldn't elicit a single lure she could utilize to induce him to travel so far. Besides, if she believed he might actually come, she'd very likely spend the rest of her life gazing down the road, moping and hoping that it would be the day he'd show his sorry face. She repeated, "You should go home."

"I know."

"I hate to imagine the calamities you'll create if you trot off to another party. You've been an utter terror at this one."

"I didn't mean to be. Pamela proposed various diversions, and I agreed, and then—"

She interrupted. "You're blaming Pamela?"

"No, I just . . ." He languished again, the color on his cheeks heightening, his chagrin conspicuous. "Come here," he interjected, and he tugged on her hand, guiding her around the table till she was sitting on his lap.

Dipping under her chin, he nipped against her neck, causing her to giggle and writhe. "I don't want to talk about me," he asserted. "I want to talk about *you,* and how rapidly I can have you out of these clothes."

Whenever she probed into his affairs, he adroitly steered her away from further review of his dubious character by reverting to sexual banter but, for once, she wasn't irritated by his evasive action. She was as anxious as he to move the assignation to the physical realm where they connected so naturally.

"I'll ring for the maid."

"We don't need the maid."

"You'll aid me?"

"I'm renowned for my ability with corset strings."

"And you are a cad to mention such a disreputable skill," she teased, but she abhorred having him refer to his other women, those scores who'd come before her and who'd come after, but she cast off her dolor. He was determined to warn her that she must never get too close, must never crave too much, or desire too badly. It was but a component of the odd game they played. Their meetings were vital to her subsistence and peace of mind, but he was bent on acting as if they were trivial and inconsequential.

He squired her to the dressing room. She carried the candelabra and held it while he lit the lamp, and she perched herself on the stool in front of the vanity. Silently and expertly, he took down her hair, combed it out, then worked at the tiny buttons on her dress. With great interest, she observed, loving how he tarried to brush his lips in just the correct spot, how his hands loitered, or his fingertips explored and searched while he seemed to be innocently proceeding with his tasks.

The haphazard touching wasn't any such thing, and by the time she was stripped down to drawers and chemise, her body was thrumming, her feminine parts on fire, so that when he was done and urged her to her feet, she zealously spun into his arms, ready for a blistering kiss, but she was graced with a tender one, instead.

"Thank you," he said, his breath warm on her cheek as he pulled away.

"For what?"

"For humoring me." He fluffed her hair about her shoulders and back. "This was another memory I fancied."

"Of you undressing me?"

His manifest sentimentality had him overtly perplexed, and he could only mumble, "Well . . ."

"I'm delighted. It was wonderful."

"Yes, it was," he managed to express. "I'm *delighted* that I had the opportunity."

Stark emotion, on which he'd never expound, was visible in his beautiful eyes, and she dared to take a chance, pointing out what was so onerous to discuss. "We don't have many days left."

"No."

The heat in his gaze seared her, and she was convinced that he would finally profess how much he'd valued their time together, or how much he'd miss her after, but he merely stared, then stared some more, committing the interval to his budding store of reminiscence.

"I'm glad we did this—" she started.

But he cut her off before she could wend the conversation in a direction he was bound and determined it wouldn't go. "I want to love you all night."

"I'd like that."

"In your bed, for a change."

"I'd like that, too."

He blew out the lamp, then clasped her hand in order to lead her out into the other room. In the abrupt darkness, a glow penetrated the shadows, and she glanced up, amazed to discover the peephole shining like a flare.

She stopped.

"What is it?" Michael inquired, and she pressed a finger to her lips, signaling for quiet.

"Someone's in the hidden room." Turning, she went

back, grabbing the footstool and positioning it below the hole, then climbing up on it.

"What are you doing?"

She peered at him over her shoulder. In the past hour, he'd shed his coat, but nothing else, and he surveyed her with his arms folded across his chest, a bemused expression on his face.

"I want to see who's in there."

"You have become an unmitigated voyeur."

"Without a doubt."

"A wench. A wanton. A hussy."

"Yes."

"Get down at once," he soundly ordered, but he was chuckling.

"Ssh . . ." she cautioned dramatically. "Not till I find out what's happening."

He approached from behind and playfully whacked her on the rear. "I've been told that you can be struck blind from witnessing so much vice."

She chortled jovially. "I'll try to pace myself."

"Trollop," he muttered, and she swatted at him while he ducked.

Jamming her eye to the hole, she peeked in. The sordid scene was exactly the same, although it wasn't quite as thrilling since Michael wasn't the main attraction. Still, the unknown man within was handsome and appealing, so she was intrigued to examine his antics. A fetching brunette, with long, straight hair and big brown eyes, frolicked with him, but Sarah had never previously seen the woman, either.

During the occasions she'd spied on Michael, she'd thought she was drawn to the decadent viewing because *he* was involved in the debasing exposition. However, she was compelled to realize that lovers could furnish a stirring display, whether she was acquainted with them or not. The carnal scene before her was disgustingly titillating. The nudity, the malfeasance, the inappropriateness—both of the couple's conduct and of her watching them—made it difficult to desist.

The man was good-looking—not as comely as Michael, of course—but he was blond, so comparison wasn't exactly fair. He had a fabulous male body, which she could readily deduce since he was naked, though all she could behold was his backside. With a cherubic countenance that promised innocence, he appeared to be an angel who'd fallen into the wrong room, but he was definitely a devil.

"I wish he'd turn around," she grumbled. She had an atrocious inclination to inspect his cock. She'd only perused one in her life and, while she was sure it was a magnificent specimen, she wasn't averse to covertly analyzing another.

"Why?"

"Because all I can see is his buttocks."

"Would you get down?" he hissed.

"Oh, my goodness!"

Clucking her tongue, she couldn't believe the spectacle into which she'd blundered. This was certainly more lewdness than she'd counted upon. Such a thing had never occurred to her! Was there no end to the eccentric, depraved behavior in which these guests would engage?

"What?" he grouched. When she didn't reply, he recited an aggravated, "What!"

At first, there'd only been the one woman, but a second female was in the room, and they were statuesque, buxom twins. The man had been facing one and kissing her, his tongue in her mouth and his fingers pressuring her nipple, when the other loomed in from behind. Rubbing her breasts over his back, she wrapped her arms around his waist and commenced fondling him.

He was wedged between the pair, and obviously in a state of bliss. The women were happy, too. They were kissing and cooing, never stationary, their lips and hands busy and adept.

Sarah couldn't look away. Shamefully, her nipples stiffened, her pulse accelerated. Perhaps Michael was correct, and her moral constitution had sunk beyond redemption—just like his own.

"Twins?" Incredulous, she shook her head and scowled down at him. "Really, Michael, how do they—"

Before she could complete her query, he lifted her off the stool and deposited her on the floor. Flattening his eye to the hole, he glared into the room.

"Oh, for pity's sake!" he growled when he recognized the erotic trio. "I might have known. John Clayton . . ."

"The viscount . . . ?" In a whisper, she started to inquire as to the man's title, but Michael slapped the covering over the peephole.

"Don't close it," she admonished somewhat petulantly. "I'm not finished."

"Yes you are."

Prepared to scramble back up, she headed toward the stool, but he swooped her up and tossed her over his shoulder like an unwieldy sack of flour.

"Brute!" She pounded him on his back, but she was laughing too hard to have any effect. "Put me down!"

"No."

"Were those women twins?"

"Yes."

"Who are they?"

"His mistresses."

"Plural?"

"Aye."

"How do the three of them fornicate together? You didn't answer my question."

"And I'm not about to, so quit asking." He smacked her on the rear. "I swear, tomorrow I'll have that bloody thing nailed shut. Now, be quiet!"

Marching out to her bedchamber, he ungraciously dumped her on her bed. Then, he followed her down and, within moments, her curiosity about the threesome had vanished. She didn't need to ponder how others were trysting in the next room, for she was thoroughly overwhelmed by how *she* was accomplishing it in her own.

Chapter Sixteen

Pamela stared across the small table in her breakfast salon, and she wished that she'd had the formal dining room set. By its very nature, a country party meant that guests would arise at varying hours, so it was more convenient for them to grab a quick bite in the intimate room. However, with Hugh Compton occupying the space with her, she'd relish the excuse to observe him down a long expanse of oak— the longer the better.

She hadn't seen him in months, so she was surprised by how his dissolute lifestyle had recently ravaged his appearance. A blond-haired, blue-eyed, thirty-two-year-old dandy, he'd always been handsome, but intemperance and immoderation had wreaked havoc. His skin was now lined and sallow, his torso inordinately thin and sagging, his face aged and wrinkled.

The prior night of drink and revelry was taking its toll. His eyes were bloodshot, his fingers shook, and she couldn't help but suspect that his worsened condition was due to his current addiction to an exotic pipe an acquaintance had brought back from India and presented to him as a gift.

On a frequent basis, he experimented with forbidden Chinese opiates. Liquid courage, in the form of stiff whisky, was also habitually ingested. He constantly overimbibed on an abundant mixture of foreign herbs and alcohol.

A slight odor of smoke, spirits, and sex hovered about him and, in the mirror on the far wall, disapproval and dismay were reflected in her penetrating gaze, so she shielded her disgust.

She couldn't tolerate Hugh, with his weaknesses and complaints, and she couldn't stand having him visit, yet she could hardly ask him to leave. An open invitation had been issued in London to those who might be interested and, as Hugh was one of the most perverted, lewd members of the *ton,* she couldn't gripe when he showed up, expecting hospitality.

As an earl, he was highly esteemed, and she couldn't fathom why, but then, she'd married into the aristocracy and, as an outsider, it was frequently puzzling to grasp the reasoning of those with whom he shared his blue blood. His peers, despite his particular flaws, liked and accepted him, so she had no option but to keep a smile pasted on her face and pretend she was glad he'd come.

It irked that he'd had so many advantages, that he'd been coddled and cosseted, and what did he have to show for it? A gambling habit that had bankrupted him, and a control problem that induced him to gluttony, be it with women, intoxicating drink, or any other vice.

Though she could sanction much in the way of decadence, she wasn't excited about the type of iniquity he would bring to the assemblage, which was definitely saying a lot. The evenings were already spent in behavior that even she—in her jaded condition—deemed disgusting, and Hugh would lower the offered amusements to new and despicable levels.

Then, there was Michael with which to contend. What if Hugh and Michael ran into one another? Michael rarely inflicted himself into the gathering, but he was wont to roam at night, watching and randomly participating, and she could imagine the uproar that would develop if their two paths happened to collide. It would be an unqualified disaster.

While Michael was a great friend, and she delighted in his presence, his personal problems were growing intolerable. She was happy to extend a refuge when he obviously needed one, however he'd become too unpredictable. His temper was at flash point. Evidence his thrashing of Brigham.

She didn't much care for Brigham, either, but regardless of what he'd done, she couldn't have Michael lurking in her stables, trouncing her various male guests when they displeased him. He'd never been the sort to suffer fools silently, and Hugh Compton was the biggest *fool* Michael had encountered in a long while. She was sitting on a powder keg that could blow at any moment.

With a regretful sigh, she determined that she'd have to ask Michael to depart. Given his prevalent volatile state, he would view her decision in the worst possible light, so the odds were high that she'd damage their eccentric camaraderie.

What a detestable turn of events, that she could only allow one of them to stay, and the choice had to be Hugh!

"So"—Hugh dug into a pile of eggs—"how's my sister?"

"She's well; she's enjoying herself."

"Good, good." Imperiously, he held out his cup, not deigning to glance toward the servant who poured for him. The retainer was well trained and, if he had any opinion about the fact that he was serving brandy-laced coffee as Hugh's morning beverage, he gave no sign. "Any progress on the introductions we discussed?"

"Actually, no." She was disturbed by the conspicuous ingenuousness infused into his inquiry, and thus, absolutely on guard.

Looking at her plate, she stirred her breakfast around and around but didn't eat anything. Her mind whirred, striving to make sense of Hugh and his schemes. Without a doubt, he'd concocted some mischief concerning his sister, but Pamela didn't aim to augment the plot.

After her discourse with Sarah, she'd left Sarah in peace to treasure her holiday, and Pamela couldn't help wondering if Hugh hoped that she, Pamela, would spur things along by urging Sarah into a compromising position from which she couldn't extricate herself. Then, whatever transpired, the end result would be Pamela's fault. Hugh, as was his tendency, would remain innocent of any malfeasance.

He drained his refreshment then tendered the cup for refilling. "I allowed her to call upon you for the exclusive purpose of meeting with different gentlemen."

"Yes, but she hasn't seemed inclined to socialize." Pamela carefully sipped her chocolate, locking onto Hugh's glare with a guileless one of her own.

The pompous ass really believed that he had a say in Sarah's comings and goings! As if he could have *allowed* her to visit or not! Sarah was an adult woman and, at her advanced age, no longer under Hugh's thumb. She could do as she pleased. Hugh, with his customary dearth of acuity, hadn't realized that fact, but Pamela wasn't about to disillusion him. She liked Sarah very much, and she wasn't about to further Hugh's conspiracy—whatever it was.

As though their dialogue had conjured her up, Sarah entered, and Pamela peeked at the clock on the mantel. The hour was fast approaching noon, and she could barely prevent herself from clucking in dismay. From the first, Sarah had been the earliest of risers, yet in the past few days, something had caused a drastic alteration in her rigid schedule.

Pamela endeavored to detect as much as she could about her guests, so her proficient staff—spies all—meticulously tracked Sarah's movements. Luckily, there'd been very little to report.

For the most part, she ate her meals at off times, strolled the gardens for sun and relaxation, read in the library, and rested in her room. She appeared to be having the tranquil, restorative respite on which she'd planned, and Pamela would have been positively ecstatic had she not also been apprised that the adjoining door between Sarah's and Michael's chambers had been discovered ajar on two separate occasions. That the maid who serviced Sarah had thrice been rebuffed, with Sarah insisting through a barred door that she didn't require morning assistance. That a footman who'd been sent to fetch Michael's bathing tub, when Michael was purportedly absent from the premises, swore he heard Michael talking in Sarah's room.

Then, of course, there was the mysterious supper *à deux* Michael had had delivered to his room, yet despite her dogged persistence, she'd been unable to surmise even a clue as to the identity of the woman he'd invited when, considering the sorts of females on the premises, his special *guest* ought to have been crowing about her conquest.

Not damning by any means, but enough to have Pamela kicking herself for placing the pair in such proximity. The instant Sarah had inquired about him that day on the verandah, Pamela should have removed him to another section of the house, but forcing Michael to other quarters would have been so awkward. With the mood he was in, he would have bristled at the mandate, and she couldn't bear the idea of upsetting him more than he already had been by others.

Besides, it truly hadn't occurred to her to worry, because she couldn't picture Michael permitting himself to be drawn into a jeopardizing predicament with the stunning beauty. His brother James, yes, but *not* solid, dependable Michael. He had more scruples and conscience than James, and he'd always exercised more restraint, but apparently in this case, lust had won out.

Sarah was mature enough to have known better, but Pamela wasn't about to chastise her. Michael was the kind of man who women couldn't resist, and Pamela—with her own unwarranted physical attraction to the rogue—comprehended his allure more readily than anyone. When he deigned to focus his attention, there wasn't a female alive who could refuse him. Worldly women regularly scrambled to be the object of his dubious affection, so a person of Sarah's limited experience would have no defense against his substantial charms or expert lovemaking.

Plainly, she'd succumbed, though just how far down the road of passion she'd ventured was still in dispute. Taking into account Michael's sexual proclivities, Sarah was very

likely beyond redemption, and Pamela laid the blame, such
as it was, squarely at Michael's feet.

In light of his relationship with Hugh, his actions were
reprehensible. Hugh notwithstanding, Michael was aware
that, because of her stature and rank, he couldn't dally with
Sarah, but Sarah—with her rural, unpretentious background—didn't recognize the dangers.

Pamela frowned, speculating as to how this would end,
even as she was chastising herself for handling their budding romance so badly. The merest hint of intervention
would have averted the entire, probable debacle.

She beheld Sarah before Hugh did, and she concluded
that she ought to warn her or at least run interference. With
a burst of feminine intuition, she was consumed by the
notion that Sarah wouldn't be pleased to see him.

As Sarah stepped over the threshold, Pamela sneaked a
hasty assessment: hair neatly combed, gown appropriate,
demeanor perfectly poised. Yet, the sparkle in her eye and
the glow in her cheeks removed all supposition. Sarah had
unquestionably spent the night basking in multitudinous episodes of carnal bliss.

She's in love with the bounder, Pamela swiftly deduced,
shaking her head at their folly.

"Surprise, Sarah," she welcomed a tad too heartily,
"look who's joined us."

Sarah halted in her tracks, deep in thought, or perhaps,
lost in her memories. Almost in a trance, she seemed confused by the brisk greeting and, with Pamela's indicatory
gesture, she honed in on her incorrigible brother.

"What are you doing here?" she asked irascibly.

"Always a pleasure, *dear* sister," Hugh snarled, then
smiled—for Pamela's benefit, she was sure—although she
received the distinct impression that he'd throttle Sarah as
soon as he had the chance.

Upon his oration, Hugh's company fully registered, and
Sarah's countenance transformed. She'd been daydreaming,
and the sight of her sibling had rudely awakened her to

reality. Her spine straightened, and the glow that had pre-
ceded her disappeared.

"My apologies, Hugh. I've just risen. I guess I'm not
quite myself." The corners of her lips turned up in a smile,
but the salutation didn't reach her eyes, and she sounded
deferential, but not very. "Rebecca had mentioned that you
might be coming. How delightful that you've finally decided to attend."

Pamela studied the two of them. When they'd both been
younger, and in London for Sarah's debut, their father had
been alive to act as a buffer, so Pamela hadn't been able
to gauge their feelings for one another, but she had no trouble now.

From the taciturn manner in which Sarah watched him,
there was no love lost, but from what Sarah had endured
due to his recklessness, her disregard was completely understandable. On his best day, Hugh was difficult, and
whatever deference Sarah might previously have possessed
had vanished. As was typical of his type of highborn male,
Hugh didn't notice his sister's disdain. He would simply
never assume that he wasn't liked or, at the least, greatly
respected.

The siblings clearly had no knack for idle prattle, which
meant that tarrying with them would be unpleasant. She
desired no knowledge of, or participation in, whatever conversation might follow.

Momentarily, she pondered if she should abandon Sarah,
but one glance assured her that the other woman was
equipped to manage Hugh. Sarah was filling a plate, seating
herself, and nibbling on a scone, very much behaving as if
Hugh was no more than a pet in the corner, admitted but
ignored.

"Well"—Pamela chose the coward's avenue of retreat—
"I'm sure you two have lots to catch up on. I'll leave you
to your chat." She rose and went to the door, but not before
pausing to peek over her shoulder at Sarah, and she was
certain she spotted a love bite on her neck, though it was
mostly shielded by a scarf. "I have a guest who must depart.

Today," she emphasized, but neither Sarah nor Hugh was listening. "I'm off to tell him good-bye."

Without delay, she headed for Michael's room

Hugh lay on his bed and fluffed the pillows, the quarrel he'd just had with Sarah replaying in his mind.

The blasted woman! Arguing with him. Laughing at him. Why . . . she had the audacity to treat him as if he was still a lad in short pants! With whom did she think she was dealing?

Though he was technically her legal guardian, the arrangement wasn't taken seriously by either of them, because Sarah wasn't the type of female a man could rule. She was too quick-witted, too self-assured, and too stubborn to be ordered about; she could make a man cower and vacillate, induce him to distrust his purpose and objective. Even their dear, departed father hadn't known how to control her. To the dismay of both of them, she'd always behaved exactly as she pleased but, for once, he wouldn't permit her to call the shots.

"Not this time, little sister," he muttered.

His father's heir in every respect, his life was in London where pleasant diversions were available. He hated the country and always had, and he declined to waste his energy on any of the boring tasks that kept Sarah so enthralled. In his mind, it was sensible that they both aspire to occupations they enjoyed—his being gambling, debauchery, and vice.

Sarah refused to understand his position, but he was a man, an earl, a peer of the realm, so he need not justify himself to her. Theirs were separate worlds but, as she was about to brutally discover, her personal happiness and well-being were uniquely dependent on his, and her tranquil rural odyssey was about to come to a smashing conclusion. He was her brother, her master—her lord, by God!—and she would not trifle with him when there was so much at stake.

Against his better judgment, he'd left Scarborough and returned to town, graciously granting her the first opportunity to select a suitable match. Sarah was at her best when she was helping others and untangling their problems, and he'd wrongly presumed that she'd rectify this mess, too, as she typically had in the past.

With a confused rationality, he'd planned it all out: He'd facilitate an advantageous marriage for her, to a rich husband. As part of the settlement, her spouse would pay off Hugh's debt. If he was extremely shrewd, perhaps he'd even negotiate a quarterly allowance into the deal. Sarah's precious home would be preserved and restored, Hugh could go about his business in London, and they'd all carry on as before.

He'd been so desperately assured of the result! She was skilled at taking command and being in charge, and her efforts precluded him having to expend any of his own.

But he'd erred in acquiescing. She'd never intended to search for a husband, and he'd been played for a fool. All along, she'd simply thought her trip to Bedford was for recreation and relaxation. For weeks now, he'd gadded about town, stupidly believing that she was toiling toward a resolution, only to discover that she'd never meant to faithfully do her part!

How dare she circumvent his wishes!

Based on his expectations of her success, he'd ordered several new sets of clothes, checked out a team of horses for the coach he planned to purchase as soon as the marital contracts were drawn up, bid on a painting at an auction, and directed the housekeeper at the town house to have the furniture recovered—furniture that would be confiscated shortly, along with the property itself, if a financial rescue wasn't finalized.

The commoners who flitted around on the fringes of his life wouldn't confess as much to his face, but they were nervous about accepting his credit. Word of his arrearage had circulated, and everyone was convinced that he would loose all, so he was having a devil of a time making purchases or hiring workers. He'd flat out promised numerous people that he was about to have an infusion of cash, but they had the gall not to believe him, a low blow that perpetually chafed.

Indigence was the worst sort of torture!

Now, with Sarah's clever thwarting of his manipulations, he had to acknowledge that he shouldn't have deposited such an important outcome in her hands. The accursed female hadn't a clue as to how a woman attracted a man, and she was thoroughly incompetent at any situation that involved amorous matters, her failed *entrée* into society being the most striking evidence of her deficiencies in that arena. He should have recollected as much from the commencement, but he'd been so eager to have Sarah supervise the details of her betrothal.

Well, there were methods for obtaining what he wanted. In this, he would not be denied or dissuaded. He'd given her her chance, he'd trusted her, but she'd wasted it, and she was going to be shocked when she learned just how determined he was for a beneficial ending.

The door opened, and Rebecca rushed in. At age twenty-four, Rebecca was a year younger than Sarah, but different as night from day. A blond, voluptuous beauty, with features as perfect as a porcelain doll, she'd resided with them for the prior three years, after having survived a lifetime of excessive poverty inflicted on her by her profligate father. Never badgering, never complaining, never wailing over their pitiful lot, she appreciated—as Sarah never had—that affairs could be much worse.

While Sarah was likely in her room lamenting over the latest debacle, Rebecca was looking ahead to an auspicious conclusion. Sarah's appearance at Lady Carrington's gala had been her idea. Hugh could never have arrived at such a marvelous solution all on his own.

He studied her, his disapproval unequivocal. When she'd broached the asinine concept of luring Sarah to Pamela's party, she'd contended that she could execute the required eventuality in a handful of days, that she could rapidly have

Sarah totally ruined, but Sarah was proving too elusive for even the generally effective Rebecca's machinations.

Hugh was furious with her for her blunders. He'd sent Rebecca to Bedford with Sarah, thinking that their cousin would lend legitimacy to the finale. There was the additional benefit that Sarah considered Rebecca a friend, and Sarah would never suppose the other woman to be involved in any nefarious plot.

Sarah's fiasco would seem utterly forthright, and she would never have guessed his role or his maneuvering. Even if she had a subsequent inkling, there would be nothing she could do to change the outcome, but regardless of whether Sarah ultimately ascertained who had precipitated her downfall, he should have journeyed directly to Bedford to set the proceedings in motion. Matters had become too grave, and she would wed if he had to tie her down and force the seduction, himself.

He was tired of being poor, tired of having others thumbing their noses at him, tired of being spurned at his favorite clubs, gambling houses, and brothels.

He would have his way!

"Did you find a key?"

"Yes," Rebecca answered, approaching the bed, "although it was difficult without any help from the staff. Lady Carrington's people are so dreadfully loyal."

"Imagine that," he muttered sarcastically.

"When I suggested their assistance, they gawked at me as if I was speaking in tongues."

"But you acquired one?"

"I've tested it in six different doors." She held it out for his inspection. "It catches, but with some jiggling, it's fine. I filched it from a rack in the kitchens."

"Honestly, Becky, how common."

"It's not as if any of the employees would abet me. I felt like a wretched pickpocket." As she imparted a withering glare, she tossed the key, and it bounced on his lap. "I stole it for you. You might at least try to be a bit gracious."

"You'll see my gratitude when we've accomplished our goal."

"You'd better mean it, Hugh. If you're lying . . ."

He couldn't abide her flip attitude, and he'd had his fill of her whining and evasions. Since she'd been in Bedford, she'd penned three separate letters, defending her mistakes, and justifying her lack of success. He'd had to endure her continual bungling, so he didn't need to suffer through a feminine mood, as well.

"Are you threatening me?" he queried quietly. "*Me*, Rebecca?" His stern tone caused her to blanch, and she backed down immediately, once again the meek, solicitous female he demanded she be.

"No, Hugh," she said. "I apologize."

"As you should. You prevail upon our relationship too much. It makes you forget yourself." He patted the bed, urging her closer, and she obeyed. She might pout and brood, but she never stayed angry. "Did you locate any of the Chinese herbs I like?"

"Yes. In the library. Lady Carrington keeps a box for the guests. I took what was left. Here."

She rendered a neatly wrapped parcel and, as though it was the rarest of jewels, he wildly clutched at it. In London, his supplier had been out, as had his various friends, so he'd been frantic, and he was horridly relieved that Rebecca had stumbled upon a stash.

Apprehensive and irritable, he struggled to curb his obdurate craving. Realizing that the anticipation would be worth it when he finally imbibed, he laid the packet on the table, compelling himself back to his task, to his strategy for Sarah, and how it was likely to unfold.

He dictated, "Tell me again why you infer it is Stevens with whom she's dallying."

"From how they were acting when I witnessed them together. They have a much deeper acquaintance than anyone suspects. It's the manner in which she looks at him."

"How is that?"

"She's in love. It's the only explanation."

"Sarah? In love? Bah . . ." He waved away her deduction. "You're mad."

"No, a woman knows these things."

God, how he wanted her to be correct! And if it was Michael Stevens! The revenge would be so sweet!

"Did you ever ask him about that first night? When you sent him up to her room?"

"No, a second overture would have sounded suspicious. When I made the initial proposition, I'm sure he thought I was a servant, and I didn't want to disavow him of the impression."

"You needn't have fretted," he mused, recalling Stevens's history with beautiful women. "If he saw you again, he'd never remember you." He was too self-absorbed to notice the hurt that came over her, and he perked up. "Well, then, we'll pay a call on her this evening. Not too late. How about an hour or two after she retires?"

"She won't be hurt, will she, Hugh?"

How ludicrous for Rebecca to be experiencing a belated stab of conscience! "Where's the injury in her marrying a wealthy, successful businessman? By having the chance for a home and children of her own? That's what all women crave, isn't it? Now . . . be a dear and fetch me another brandy."

Without argument or condemnation of his bad habits, she proceeded to the sideboard, retrieved the decanter, and filled his glass.

"There's a good lass." He tossed it down in a single swallow as she hovered over him, seeing to his comfort, and he was struck again by how pretty she was. With that lavish blond hair, and those magnificent breasts squeezed into that fiercely laced corset, she was an arousing spectacle. In her glorious sapphire eyes, he could read the bald— but idiotic—affection she harbored for him and, after the arduous interview with Sarah, her fondness was soothing.

While Sarah was content to wallow away in the country, Rebecca periodically accompanied him to London where she acted as his hostess—and more when the occasion presented itself. He'd never admit to another soul that he lusted after his cousin, but she was so bloody accommodating. So bloody convenient. How could a man spurn what was so graciously offered?

"What if she's alone when we barge in?" Rebecca inquired. "What will we say?"

"We'll simply invite her down to the party—as though that was our sole purpose."

He'd worked it out in his head, in his disordered state, satisfied that he was making flawless decisions. Rebecca cheerfully assented as he'd predicted she would. She wouldn't question him, not after she'd created such a mess when left to her own devices.

"And if we don't catch her with Stevens," he pointed out, "we'll opt for another fellow. We'll unlock the damned door and shove someone inside—if that's what it takes."

"Too bad about Brigham," Rebecca noted.

"Too bad, indeed."

Rebecca had discreetly orchestrated Brigham's interest in Sarah and, with his fortune and title, he'd have been an excellent choice as her husband. Yet, nothing had progressed properly. Not only had the man *not* crept into Sarah's room, he'd been forcibly removed from possible consideration by his run-in with Michael Stevens.

No one had unveiled the basis for their violent disagreement, and Hugh shuddered over the pummeling Brigham had received. The nerve of Stevens, handling a peer as he'd done! The talk was all over town, though nothing would come of it. The man was a raving lunatic who ought to be hanged, or at the very least, transported at the earliest juncture.

Only Stevens's father, the Earl of Spencer, stood in the way of the contemptible scoundrel getting what he truly deserved. With his connection to Spencer, Stevens was untouchable.

Factor in the number of markers he owned, and the damning, confidential secrets he'd unearthed, and who was safe from the bastard's wrath? He was a menace, one that Hugh would be delighted to destroy.

All in good time, he counseled. Stevens would get his due, but for the moment, Hugh wasn't going to fuss about him. He was exhausted from traveling, and the constant trepidation induced by his fiscal dilemma, and he was geared up for some entertainment.

While he was anxious to retrieve his pipe from his bag, he pushed his impatience aside. Once he partook of the herbs, he wouldn't be able to adequately savor Rebecca's ample charms. After he'd debauched her a time or two, he'd indulge in his favorite pastime.

Obscurely, it occurred to him that sex had previously been his *favorite* diversion. When had that changed? And why? But the sentiment was fleeting as were so many. Recurrently, concentration proved elusive.

As he contemplated Rebecca, a welcomed stirring tickled betwixt his legs, and he almost wept with relief. Sporadically, with all the liquor and herbs he consumed, he was unable to perform his manly duties, and the incidents were beginning to frighten him. His inability to generate a cockstand had advanced into a recurring problem, and he was increasingly concerned that his aptness might vanish forever.

"Come here," he ordered.

More and more, women failed to spur his male urges. Even the most disgusting, unconstrained whores had no rousing effect on his limp manhood, so when he felt another prickle of desire in his nether regions, he was deluged with optimism and abruptly ablaze.

"Really, Hugh," she huffed, affronted. "Since you arrived, you've done naught but chastise me, and now you presume that I'll just blindly do whatever you require." Her pert nose went up. "Well, you've just pushed me too far."

"Come here," he repeated more forcefully.

"I won't, I tell you!"

"You will," he crooned softly, "or I'll be extremely angry."

"For once, I don't care."

The bitch spun away, as though she'd march out in a snit! Who did she think she was, putting on airs? For the first time in months, he could fornicate without any disconcerting obstacles, and by the heavens, she would oblige. Just the notion that she had the temerity to reject him inspired him to a fierce cockstand.

Embarrassingly, there were many available women at the party besides his cousin, but he couldn't seek out any of them for fear of being incapable of maintaining an erection. So far, Rebecca was the only person who'd been with him when the worst had ensued, so Hugh never had to brook any discomfiting rationalizations or humiliating elucidations. She was in no position to discuss their sexual relationship with others, and she hadn't sufficient carnal enlightenment to grasp what was amiss.

She couldn't depart; he wouldn't allow her to.

Exhibiting uncommon agility, he leapt to the floor, grabbed her, and whipped her around. "Get back in bed."

"Hugh, stop it," she sniveled as he urged her toward the mattress. She attempted to stare him down, but her defiance waned—as always—when confronted by his firm insistence. "You're hurting my arm."

"I won't be denied, Rebecca."

In a visible rage, she lay down, and he fell on top of her. He bared her breasts and suckled, but she was unmoving as a corpse, declining to participate as he'd repeatedly instructed. He thought about slapping a response out of her, but didn't. At the moment, he was unconcerned by her deficient cooperation.

Stimulated by the fierceness of her insubordination, he spread her legs and feasted. Elated that he was able, he climaxed in haste, then pulled out and collapsed on his side. She scooted away, scurrying to right herself.

"Don't leave," he decreed. "I'll have another go at you in a few minutes. As soon as I've rested." But the haze from his orgasm was clouding his deluded brain, and he faded into a disturbed slumber.

Chapter Seventeen

Michael was resting impatiently on his bed when he heard Sarah's arrival in her room. Though the hour wasn't overly late, he'd been waiting an eternity for her to return from supper. She'd begged him to join her, but he'd rebuffed her invitation—not out of his customary disdain for fraternizing with the other guests, but because of their diverse positions.

They wouldn't have been able to converse in the parlor before the meal was announced and, due to their disparate statuses, they'd have been seated at opposite ends of the table. He couldn't conceive of watching from afar, pretending they weren't intimate, as she chatted and mingled. If she was in proximity, he couldn't feign disinterest.

How he wished he could have accompanied her downstairs! That he could have proudly stood with her, her arm slipped through his. That he could have escorted her into the dining room, held out her chair, whispered in her ear throughout the banquet.

Astoundingly, he was chomping at the bit, hating the elite restrictions that kept them from acknowledging one another in public. While usually he could have cared less about the constraints upon him, for once, he was keenly feeling the divisions that his dubious parentage had engendered.

Over the years, he'd ridiculed James for his fascination with the members of the *ton*. Michael had always assumed that he had more sense, but since meeting Sarah and becoming involved with her, he recognized that he wasn't immune to the enticement of her world.

In Paris, with his mother a lauded, sought-after celebrity, his paternity hadn't seemed important. He'd been wel-

comed into the looser French society, befriended by the
noble sons of the wealthy families, eyed for future marriage
by the daughters of the prosperous merchants. His ancestry
hadn't had any effect on his behavior, so he hadn't worried
about fitting in.

But in London, where lineage was everything, he'd been
slapped in the face with reality. A trespasser, he'd fluttered
on the fringes of their exclusive domain, an interloper simply because his father and mother—two dynamic, charis-
matic, selfish individuals—had never wed.

Edward Stevens had four adult children—three daughters and a son—who were legitimately born to him during
his lengthy marriage, and it had been painful to discover
how differently they were viewed. Michael and James were
Edward's shameful indiscretion, and despite how much
they looked like Edward, or acted like him, how much they
postured and strutted, they could never be anything but his
bastards.

The inequity had been harrowing, and he'd eventually
accepted their situation, but not James. Though to be fair,
James had suffered more due to the fact that he'd been
older when they'd moved away. His recollections of their
father were precise and ingrained, so his loss had been
greater. He was the firstborn son of the prominent aristocrat, but he could never hold his rightful place, and he had
yearned for approval, while Michael had perpetually conjectured that he was beyond those youthful daydreams of
assimilation.

Then, Sarah had bewitched him. From the start, he'd
been infatuated with her, even though attraction was pointless. When he should have run fast and furiously in the
opposite direction, he'd acceded to her bold petition for an
affair, and as a result, they'd instituted some of the most
lusty, ribald sex he'd ever encountered.

Interspersed with the erotic sessions were tender words,
quiet interludes, and gentle sharing that had left him enchanted, enraptured, and utterly immersed in the liaison until he couldn't eat or sleep. His entire life now revolved

around the handful of stolen moments when he could tarry in her arms. The past had disappeared; the future had no meaning. He existed solely for their episodes of carnal bliss.

Thoroughly besotted, he never tired of watching her, never wearied of her company, of her pretty face or lush body. Considering his enchantment, he couldn't have gone to supper with her, because he would have spent the repast gazing longingly down the large table like a lovesick boy.

He listened to the muffled noises she made, and he could picture her perched on the stool at her vanity. As the maid unbuttoned her gown and unlaced her corset. As she washed, then slipped into her nightrail and robe.

Amazingly, he visualized himself—instead of the serving girl—assisting her, once again, with her private ablutions, and the notion was unsettling. The desire to aid her was irresistible, and he'd previously given in to it on that one occasion when they'd dined together, but he'd carefully prevented himself from doing something so idiotic a second time.

Never before had he been prone to dawdle in a woman's boudoir. With all the lovers he'd had, nary a one had inspired him to loiter. He'd never cared how they undressed, how they bathed, or readied themselves for slumber, but with Sarah, his beguilement had flared, early on, and he couldn't seem to get enough of her mundane details.

How unfortunate that this remarkable relationship would terminate before it had begun. There would be insufficient opportunity to explore these strange and wondrous sensations, and he sighed regretfully. What would Sarah think when she learned that he was packing his bags? Would she be upset or, more likely, would she be relieved that their *amour* had been so easily concluded?

Though he hated to admit it, Pamela had done them both a favor by forcing him to depart, and the request hadn't been a surprise. After the incident with Brigham, he'd been expecting it. She'd been courteous and compassionate; he'd appreciated her tact and, bearing in mind that Hugh Compton had arrived, she could hardly have acted in any other fashion.

But how to disengage from Sarah?

When he'd rashly initiated their romance, it had never occurred to him that it would be difficult to end it. He'd always been a competent, shrewd fellow, who examined every angle and option before proceeding, yet he'd permitted this slip of a woman—whom he barely knew and with whom he had so little in common—to totally inflict herself into his life and heart. He couldn't predict where he'd travel next, because he couldn't envision being separated from her.

What a foolish, foolish man he was!

The adjoining door opened, and she peeked in, smiling when she saw him. As he ached over the dreams that would never come true, he was confronted with the ample depth of his folly.

How could he endure losing her?

"I asked to have a bath delivered," she said. "Would you wash me?"

"I'd like that."

His cock hardened at the idea of touching her when she was wet and slippery, and she immediately noticed. Her delighted appraisal lagged on the bulge she'd produced in his trousers.

"Then, when you're finished, we'll switch, and *I* will bathe *you*."

The gleam in her eye was lecherous, and he chuckled. "I've created a monster."

"Yes, you have. Are you sorry?"

"Not a whit."

"I didn't think so."

A servant rapped on her door, and she motioned him to silence, then vanished in order to direct the hauling in of the jugs of water. Many minutes later, she entered again, clad only in one of her functional chemises. She approached the bed, her thighs pressed against the frame.

"Did you lock the door after they left?" he inquired.

"Yes."

"Did you double-check?"

"Yes!" She was riled by his caution.

"Are you certain?"

"Michael!" She was regularly exasperated by his overt vigilance. Even after everything that had happened, she was too trusting. With Brigham routed, she declined to suppose that there were others who might have designs on her.

"Are you ready for your bath, milady?" he teased.

"The water is too hot, so it needs to cool." She batted her lashes. "How will we pass the time?"

"You minx! You'll be the death of me yet."

"I hope not. I have too many licentious plans for you." She chortled merrily, then abruptly halted as she discerned a hint of his underlying distress that should have been prudently hidden. "You're upset."

"Not really."

"Don't lie to me." She possessed an innate insight where he was concerned. "I can tell when you are."

"Maybe a tad," he averred.

"Is your mother all right?"

"As far as I know."

She shuddered with relief, as though his mother was an old friend about whom she habitually fretted as the older woman flaunted herself across the Continent on her honeymoon.

During the cloistered supper they'd enjoyed in his bedchamber, he'd opened these doors to his personal history, and she'd gladly stepped through, then wheedled him to divulge some of his reflections about Angela and Edward, about James and his new bride, too, though why he'd discussed such delicate, private topics was a mystery. She'd just been so determined to drag his family's misery into the open, convinced that airing their dirty laundry was the best method for coming to grips with what had transpired.

Between bouts of frantic loving, they'd chatted incessantly until she was well versed in his foibles and squabbles. He had always been a detached, solitary man, and he couldn't believe how extraordinary it had been to confide in someone for a change, and he was disturbed by how much he'd miss their verbal intimacy once he moved on.

"Sit." He patted the mattress, and she stretched out as if she'd done just that on a thousand prior occasions. Her body perfectly conformed to his, and he situated her so that he could peer into her green eyes. He intended to always recall how brightly they shimmered, how scrupulously they assessed.

"What is it?" she queried.

"I'm leaving in the morning."

He wasn't sure what he'd anticipated from her. Weeping? Pleading? Assorted female histrionics? Assuredly not this dreadful calm.

"I see," she finally stated. "Why?"

"Lady Carrington asked me to."

"Why?" she repeated.

Many answers would satisfy, but so far, he'd deftly skirted the issue of his association with her brother, and he didn't contrive to address it at this late date. Apparently, she'd never guessed that he and Hugh might be acquainted, and he'd like her to remain ignorant of their sordid alliance.

He grinned, trying to make light of the circumstances. "She claims I've abused her hospitality."

"I thought you two were friends."

"We are"—he shifted uncomfortably—"but even Pamela has her limits."

"Brigham?"

"Yes."

"Where will you go?"

"I haven't decided. I've a dozen invitations to other parties, but I might journey to my brother's country house. It's remote and secluded, and I could benefit from the solitude."

"Will you continue on to town?"

"Eventually." His job at the club was the only decent method he'd ever detected for keeping himself out of trouble.

"You should head for home," she scolded. "The sooner the better."

They'd rigorously debated his plight, and he knew she was correct, but he couldn't seem to turn toward London. Not yet, anyway.

"If you went to your brother's rural residence . . ." She paused, contemplating. "Would you like me to join you there? I could probably find a way."

His heart pounded, then generated an odd rumble, and he was quite certain it might be breaking. More than anything, he wished she could follow him to James's house. The discreet staff would provide an exclusive haven in which to romp and build permanent memories, but it simply couldn't be.

"No," he ultimately declared, even as he marveled as to how he'd located the fortitude to refuse her. "We must say *adieu* tonight."

Unblinking, not breathing, she casually absorbed the news. "Are you positive?"

"Aye." She didn't argue or disagree, but still, he felt inclined to add, "It's for the best."

"I'm sure that's true."

He sustained a vicious impulse to shake her out of her acquiescence. Why didn't she react? Why didn't she quibble? Would it be so easy, then, for her to walk away?

When he'd instigated this insane business, he'd never projected ahead to the wretched finale. If he had, he'd definitely have fantasized that *she* would be the one dissembling, not himself. He was too confident, too in control. He could fuck a woman forever without growing attached to her.

Couldn't he?

"I want to make love till dawn," he said.

"So do I."

Yet, he couldn't seem to begin. Instead, he exhaustively regarded her, chronicling every particular. Dozens of words were poised on the tip of his tongue, and oh, how anxious he was to expound! If he'd been brave enough, he'd have confessed how much he'd treasured meeting her, how he'd valued their brief interlude, and how he hoped she would find happiness and serenity in the future, but he said nothing.

What good would it do to babble a pile of fatuous sentimentality? If he professed how much he cared, she'd likely do the same, and there they'd be, ensnared in an impossible circle of yearning and affection from which there could be no retreat.

Better to keep silent.

"It will be hard to say farewell," was all he could manage.

"I know."

"I'll miss you." *Always,* he was avid to append.

"And I, you."

They stared, neither willing to volunteer more, and he was so relieved. He couldn't bear to hear her actual ruminations, so he pretended that her internal musings adequately matched his own, though he didn't fathom how they could. His fondness for her had completely consumed him, and the concept of carrying on without this chance for sharing at the close of the day was beyond imagining.

The stirring, pensive moment ended when their lips touched in a quiet embrace filled with all that couldn't be uttered aloud. She riffled her fingers through his hair, stroked his neck and shoulder, until her hand settled on the center of his chest, resting over his heart, massaging and affording solace. Her tongue united with his in a peaceful dance that was familiar and delectable.

He'd never been much of a one for kissing, but with her, he couldn't withstand the slow provocation. Their breath mingled, their pulses beat in a constant rhythm. The sheer rapture of having her so simply and sweetly overwhelmed him, and he could have lain there in perpetuity, doing nothing more than pressing his mouth to hers.

The languid exchange couldn't help but grow more heated. Before long, her robe was off, and he was tugging her nightgown up her legs. He cupped and caressed her, relishing how her hips set the tempo.

His unskilled virgin had blossomed! She knew how to tantalize and arouse, how to originate and seduce, but also how to receive what she craved.

He toyed until she was wet with desire, her nether lips swollen and stimulated, and he succumbed to the lure of implanting her scent on his tongue. Her sexual essence was a potent aphrodisiac; it inflamed him and chased away his common sense.

Licking and tasting, he drove her toward her peak, but the wench was so proficient at restraint, so attuned to her body and his, that she was a veritable master at prolonging her pleasure. Tracing a path up her body, he lingered at her navel, at the valley between her breasts. He pushed her nightgown higher, revealing the undersides of those two spectacular globes, then higher still so that the nipples were bared and screaming for attention. Like a hungry babe, he nursed, indulging his carnal whims while her smell and warmth furnished unremitting succor.

Unable to delay, he yanked the sleepwear over her head so that she was naked, and his greedy eyes feasted on her comeliness, on her trim waist and flared hips. The sight caused his manly blood to flow until his cock was demanding surcease.

He jerked at his shirt, then tore at the buttons of his trousers, barely sliding them off his hips. Needing to be free of confines, in her hand, in her mouth, he was so hard for her, and he manipulated his turgid length as she watched then enthusiastically took over the task. She scooted down, bringing him to those chaste, pristine lips, that he loved to defile.

As adept as any courtesan, her tongue flicked out, again and again at the sensitive tip, then she sucked him in. He gave her all she could handle and more, probing deep, his titillation increasing because she couldn't seem to get enough.

Quickly, he'd arrived at an irrepressible zenith, and he

extricated himself, his heartbeat ragged, sweat pooling on his brow, his cock beseeching.

"Come in my mouth," she implored.

During all their rough antics, he hadn't yet, for despite how often she entreated, he didn't think she was prepared for the extreme experience.

"No."

"Michael . . ."

She protested as he skimmed down her body, removing his querulous phallus from temptation. He stroked the crown along the soft skin of her abdomen.

Powerless to avoid torment, he delved into her pussy, just the slightest inch, letting her erotic juices dampen the flaring tip. That he could plunge inside! Just this once! That he could have her in the only way that truly counted!

When he balanced on his haunches, she raised her legs and draped them over his thighs, offering herself. He could see her pink center, see the hairs that were slick and glossy. Her core was a slippery, menacing refuge, and he couldn't understand why he perpetually denied himself such unrelenting gratification.

As though reading his mind—a tactic at which she excelled—she chided, "It's our last time. Take me."

"Oh, Sarah . . ." He moaned in misery, poised at the apex, wondering where his willpower to desist would come from. "I'm not a saint. Don't give me permission."

"How can it matter?" She was panting, strained, eager.

"We've been over this and over this." He rubbed along her cleft. "If I destroy your maidenhead, you can't ever erase the damage."

"I won't ever want to. I'll never marry." She clenched her leg muscles. "Do it!"

Glaring at the ceiling, he was vacillating, ambivalent, unable to tolerate how she was pleading with her eyes. His buttocks tensed, and he flexed. He was playing with fire, at the point where he couldn't stop.

"I want to be your first," he inevitably affirmed, dropping his gaze to hers. "I want it to be me, so that you'll always remember."

"As if I could ever forget!"

She widened further, the move bringing him nearer, and he abandoned the fight. No going back. He steadied her, establishing himself to take her in a single, smooth thrust.

"This will hurt."

"Badly?"

"Just a little."

Tremulously, she smiled and arched up, lifting her breasts. He fondled a nipple, then trailed a hand down her front, to her waist and lower. Guiding himself, he rubbed across her, extensively moistening the blunt crest until he was sufficiently lubricated.

"No regrets," he reminded her.

"Never."

With a deft lunge, he was sheathed to her womb. As he sensed the tear, she cried out, and he leaned forward, looming over her, craving the chance to shelter and protect.

"The pain will pass," he whispered.

"It already is."

"Hold me tight."

She made a sound, and it could have been a laugh or a sob. "I never believed you'd actually fit."

"Told you," he murmured, kissing her again, struggling for composure while she acclimated to his abnormal invasion. Her pussy convulsed, permeated as it was with her virgin's blood, and his cock floated in a scalding, writhing sea of ecstasy.

At the first sign of her body's capitulation, he fervidly commenced. He'd desired her too badly for too long—all his life it seemed now, though he hadn't known it—and they simply couldn't have a tame copulation. Her tight cleft milked him, spurred him on, and he was able to allow himself free rein to vent his building lust.

Her admiration was visibly manifest, her veneration shining, and for once, he didn't shield his own feelings. He let the masks fall away, and he showered her with his ad-

oration, mutely imparting that this interval with her had
been a boon he had never foreseen, a gift he would infi-
nitely cherish.

She responded to his every ministration, her desire trans-
porting her beyond the initial discomfort. At the edge, he
tossed her over with a well-aimed swipe of his thumb, then
he accompanied her, though his trajectory was a bit altered
from its natural course.

At the very last, he withdrew, the blistering spew of his
semen shooting across her belly, and he snuggled into the
crook of her neck, resting there while the tremors shook
him, then waned. Gradually, he relaxed, but he didn't raise
up because, in reality, he was a coward, afraid to look her
in the eye and see what truths were lurking.

With the light kiss on his forehead, he couldn't thwart
the inevitable. He peeked at her, only to discover that she
was engulfed by such a profound sadness that he couldn't
figure out what to say or how to react. Of all the emotions
he might have named as to how she'd survive her deflow-
ering, he'd have never picked despondency. His heart
lurched and missed several beats.

"What is it, love?"

"I didn't realize you would pull out."

"I had to," he explained. "We daren't make a babe."

"Could we have from just one time?"

"It's possible."

She stared at him a long while, then proclaimed, "I wish
we had."

He was shocked and awestruck, his senses reeled. A
babe! With her! How he yearned to plant his seed so deep
that it took root and flourished.

Biting back a groan, he clamped his eyes shut, but unwelcome, beguiling images of young children waltzed
across his field of vision: little auburn-haired cherubs with
their mother's alluring ways and soothing countenance;
rowdy blue-eyed boys, with his sass and attitude.

Desperately, he craved the excuse to sire a babe on
Sarah; he wanted it more than he'd ever wanted anything.

Frantic to inject reality into his fantasizing, he struggled to speak but what emerged was, "Would a babe make you happy, Sarah?"

"I'd love to give you a son." She brushed the hair off his face. "I'd be so proud."

"I'm so sorry that we can't." Even as he said it, his body leapt to readiness. Though he'd just emptied himself, his cock swelled to a rude, vehement length, arranged to commit an almost predestined, irrevocable mistake.

The bathtub!

The phrase screamed out as a mode of rescue from the deviant course his anatomy was imploring him to trek. He required involvement in a less ardent endeavor, although why he would view washing her flawless torso as *safe* was a question he didn't stoop to meditate upon. His lurid reveries had to be instantly curbed before he did something reckless, something irreversible.

Hoping that space would allay his wanton urges, he stepped to the floor. He was covered with her blood, his phallus and crotch a red smear, evidence of the sin he'd committed against her, his semen a drying pile on her stomach and leg.

Grabbing a towel, he wiped her clean, then himself, and stuffed his irritated privates into his pants. Through it all, she observed his every move, and he liked how he felt revered and precious under her blatant scrutiny.

"Are you sore?"

Undecided, she shifted against the mattress, and her body emitted a wail of protest. "Ooh . . . yes."

"Then let's sit you in your bath for a soak." He helped her up. "The water will ease the tenderness, and wash away the blood."

"Am I injured?" She glanced down and scowled, not understanding the physical consequence.

"No, but you're no longer a maid." Insolently, he preened that he'd been the one to relieve her of her virtue.

"Will I bleed every time?"

"Just this once and"—he steered her toward the dressing

room—"when your lovely bottom is healed from tonight's adventure, it won't hurt ever again, either."

"I feel as if you split me in half."

She glared at him over her shoulder, and she was a charming vision, all shapely ass, long legs, and smooth, naked skin.

"I'm a very big man." He shrugged, conspicuously over-bearing, but like the cad he was, he couldn't resist gloating over what he'd just purloined from her. He stole a kiss before she could whirl around. "You make me wild with passion. I couldn't be gentle."

"You are such an arrogant rogue. Maybe I won't tell you how glad I am that it was you."

Her comment delved far into the spot where he was so lonely and alone. They were at the edge of the tub, so he bent down and tested the temperature of the water, finding it to be warm and inviting.

Pretending a detachment he hardly felt, he casually mentioned, "Are you . . . glad . . . that it was me?"

"Very."

He met her gaze then, and she was smiling at him with such an affectionate expression that he had to swallow three times before he could communicate further.

"In you go." He stabilized her as she climbed in and slid down.

"Aah . . . I'm a tad tender." Lowering herself, she winced as her beleaguered pussy coped with the heat, but then she rapidly acclimated, and she reposed, braced against the back, her knees spread wide.

For a few minutes, her body mended in the mild broth, and he knelt by her side, entranced by her loveliness and disposition. She turned toward him, her forearms on the rim, so that they were nose to nose, skin to skin, eye to eye.

"Will you let me wash you?" she appealed.

"Absolutely."

"And will you make love to me again afterward?"

"All night long"—he took a cloth and swabbed her

breasts—"if you're not too sore." At the wicked wink she flashed, he ducked under her chin and nibbled at her neck, inducing her to squirm and giggle.

"I get to be on top."

"Lord have mercy," he grumbled.

Presently, a noise vaguely registered—a throat being cleared—but it was so out of place that many moments passed before he honed in on what it was. He hesitated, then his focus went to the door that connected the dressing room to her outer bedchamber.

"Well . . . well . . ." oozed a familiar, much-loathed voice, "look what we have here."

"Bloody hell!" Michael cursed.

Sarah whipped around, gasped in dismay, and sank into the water, striving to shield herself.

Hugh Compton and Rebecca Monroe studied them, every decadent detail of their nude caper, and Rebecca's mouth gaped open like a fish pitched onto a riverbank. The four of them were a frozen quartet, then her brother had the decency to shove Rebecca away, so that she couldn't witness more of their lewd escapade.

Stationed by himself in the doorway, Hugh was framed by the threshold.

"Hello, sister," Scarborough intoned with a mocking bow. "And Stevens! How damned *interesting* to encounter you with Sarah." He tsked. "And in such a disgraceful condition!"

Michael had never felt so vulnerable, had never been caught so off guard. Warily, he vaulted to his feet. "What the hell are you up to, Scarborough?"

"I might ask you the same."

Scarborough was leering, straining on tiptoe for a glimpse of Sarah's breasts. The coarse attempt brought Michael's temper to a fast boil, and he sprang to action.

"Get out"—he jumped in front of the tub, so that Scarborough's glimpse was cut off—"or I'll kill you where you stand."

"Bastard . . ." Scarborough ground out. "Of course, you realize what this means."

"Go!" Michael shouted with such authority that both Sarah and Scarborough flinched. "Now!"

Not cowed in the least, Hugh straightened to his full height, which didn't match Michael's own, but nonetheless, he appeared threatening. And gleeful. The churl was ecstatic, and Michael longed to clutch him by the throat and squeeze until there was no air left in his lungs.

How had he, Michael Stevens—the most cautious and circumspect of men—fallen into an ambush set by such a despicable swine?

His heart plummeted as a horrid supposition cropped up, one he could scarcely give credence to, but he couldn't silence it. He wrenched his angry glower from Scarborough to Sarah who was huddled down in the basin. As he speculated, and evaluated, old doubts and misgivings crept in, and he couldn't help suspecting the worst.

Had she orchestrated this debacle with her brother? Had her seemingly gracious esteem been feigned? Scarborough wasn't clever enough to initiate such a scheme, or to pull it off successfully. Neither was his cousin. But Sarah?

It must have been her.

There was no other explanation as to how shrewdly and effectively the trap had been baited and snapped shut, snaring him in a coil of his own creation.

Earlier, when she'd arrived in his bedchamber, he'd interrogated her as to whether she'd locked her door, and she'd adamantly said yes. He'd been so befuddled by her that he'd simply taken her word for it; he hadn't gone to verify as was his custom. The depth of his enamoration had provoked him to act out of character, to trust and assume.

Such foolishness! Such stupidity!

He jerked his gaze to Scarborough, once again, and the earl laughed and nodded, confirming his excruciating deduction.

"My compliments," Michael coldly declared. "Well done."

"Yes, it rather was, wasn't it? We've all worked so hard on this," Scarborough observed smugly. "I'll meet you down in the library. In fifteen minutes." He spun around to depart, then cast a scathing glance over his shoulder at Sarah. "Leave our little whore to her bath. I'll deal with her later."

Chapter Eighteen

Hugh waltzed out, his egress marked by a resounding slam of the door as he exited into the corridor. For a brief moment, Michael glared down at her, his countenance a medley of fury, regret, and disbelief that was swiftly masked. Without speaking, he marched to the outer room where she heard the lock turning, and a heavy piece of furniture being dragged as a barricade so that no one else could surprise them.

Did he suppose that she'd contrived this fiasco? That she was in league with Hugh? She cringed. Of course he would! The blackguard!

Abruptly feeling not just naked, but exposed, she was desperate to cover herself, and she scurried from the tub. Not bothering with the towel, she was just tying the belt of her robe when he stormed back in. His sapphire eyes blazed with fire, his body trembled with controlled rage. Then, he checked himself, exhibiting the icy composure he displayed to the world. He'd reerected the protective walls that kept him safe from those who would maltreat him, and evidently, he now included her in that number.

"You assured me that you'd locked your door," he reproached.

"I did!"

"Then, madam, how did your brother get in?"

"I have no idea."

"So you say—"

"Yes, I say!" she interrupted. "Don't you dare charge otherwise!"

They angrily stared at one another across a hopeless expanse, and she couldn't have him suspecting that she'd betrayed their relationship. Tendering her hand, begging him to take it, she reached out, but he didn't so much as glance at it.

"Michael," she beseeched, "don't let's fight. We must figure out what to do."

"What to *do*?" He lurched away as if she'd admitted she had the pox.

"Yes, we're intelligent people. We can devise a practical solution. I'll talk to Hugh."

"You're very good at this"—he narrowed his eyes, scathingly assessing her—"and you play the innocent excellently, but there's no reason to maintain the ruse. You've snared me most effectively."

"You think I . . . that I . . ." She'd already deduced that he suspected her of duplicity, but his indictment stirred a surge of wrath. How could he distrust her! After they'd just lain together! "You bastard!"

The approbation spurted out before she could chomp down on it, and a dangerous, probing malice enveloped him. "I've never claimed to be anything but—"

"I apologize. I didn't mean that," she injected, yet he kept on, his voice brittle.

"—so why you would wish to tie your life to mine is a mystery." He spun toward his room. "But I guess we'll both have copious opportunity over the years to decide why you would agree to such a reckless path."

He was nearly at the portal, and she was terrified that he'd step through and disappear, that these pernicious, vehement declarations would be the last they ever uttered. She hustled to his side and put her hand on his arm, stopping him.

"Michael . . . wait. Let me explain." But as she'd had no part in what had befallen them, she wasn't sure what her *explanation* could be.

"You needn't justify your conduct"—his chilly façade was frightening—"and I won't suffer through an accounting of your rationalization. Or your brother's."

"But that's just it. None of this was my doing."

"Lady Sarah," he frigidly intoned, and his use of her title cut her to the quick, "the time that I would believe you is long past. Now, if you will excuse me, I've an appointment belowstairs."

"Give me a minute to prepare myself. I'll accompany you."

"Milady, your presence is neither necessary nor required."

He bowed slightly, then shut the door in her face, and she was so dazed that, before she could react, he'd bolted it with a determined click. She pounded on the unyielding barrier, roaring, "Michael Stevens! Open up this instant!"

Her command was greeted with silence.

She beat on it again and again till her fists ached, but her attempt went unacknowledged, and she inevitably ceased, holding very still, putting her palm to the wood. On the other side, she could sense his movements as he dressed in his fastidious manner, readying to descend for the momentous showdown with Hugh.

How would they respond to one another? What would they say? Would Hugh call him out? She blocked the ghastly notion, unable to abide reflecting upon her brother and her great love dueling, perhaps to the death.

"Damn you, Michael," she muttered, certain that he was listening. "I won't let you walk away." No rejoinder. "Do you hear me?" She kicked the bottom of the door so solidly that her foot throbbed from the impact.

Limping to the bedchamber, she cast about for some clothes, but she couldn't don the dastardly garments on her own, and she declined to confront the two men unless she was completely contained and self-possessed.

Fuming, sucked into an inferno beyond her ken, she hurled her corset on the bed and rang for a maid, then paced by the clock, counting each agonizing second until the woman appeared. With a relief that bordered on madness, she seized the retainer and drew her inside, and the servant—prudently cognizant of acute distress—made no comment, but efficiently went about her task.

The final comb in her chignon was scarcely in place when Sarah grumbled an insincere platitude and hastened out. Though she vividly remembered Brigham and the perils of wandering the halls, she wasn't worried. In her current mood, just let some brigand try to accost her! She was fixated on getting downstairs, and Lord help the gentleman who sought to detain her!

She was irritated at Michael for his proceeding without her. So much time had elapsed! Would he and Hugh still be conferring? What would be the topics? How could Michael mitigate what Hugh had witnessed?

Better than anyone, she understood Hugh, his mind, his disposition, his short-fused temper. *She* was the one who should be dealing with him. Not rash, imperious, benumbed Michael. What a disaster, to have two such intractable men at odds over a situation that was exclusively her fault! She had to intervene with Hugh before they exchanged so many insults that neither could back down.

Maneuvering her way to the bottom floor, she didn't encounter anyone, and she looked a sight, but she didn't care. As she raced toward the library, activity was audible in the various salons, the guests immersed in evening merriment, but who occupied them, or what they were doing, was a blur.

The door was just ahead, and she hurried to it, geared to knock once, then fling it open, but her desire for a grand entrance was spoiled as Michael emerged. Larger than life, he bristled on espying her, and she slid to a halt lest she plow into him. Behind them, Hugh's grating laughter rang out.

"Come with me." His dictatorial tone irked her, and he squired her away from the library and the battle she'd planned with her brother. She dug in her heels.

"No"—she grappled against his tight grip—"I must confer with Hugh."

"That's not going to happen."

He continued hauling her toward the foyer as though she was a naughty youngster about to be disciplined. She con-

templated loudly bellowing her displeasure, but there were
people about so she couldn't cause a scene, though she was
relieved to note that no one paid any attention to her passing. While she wasn't overly acquainted with any of them,
she wasn't about to have others watching as she was towed
along like an unruly child.

Crude jocularity drifted over a threshold, and she peeked
back, afforded a fleeting glimpse before Michael whisked
her on. A naked woman posed on a table while a half-naked
man tarried before her, kissing her breasts. A thick, hazy
smoke provided a grotesque, hallucinatory ambiance, ob-
scuring the many spectators who were hovering in the corners.

As she flinched, Michael yanked her away so quickly
that she wasn't positive she'd seen it at all. Could it have
been real?

She shuddered with distaste.

Before she could gather her wits, they were through the
main door of the manor and out into the quiet, fresh night
air. She breathed deeply to shed the pall that had hung over
the residence, but Michael ceded her no enjoyment of the
brief serenity. He ushered her to a carriage, and questions
flew—why were they leaving? what did this portend?—but
mostly, she inanely concentrated on how the infuriating
man had arranged for a carriage to be brought around so
promptly.

In the past hour, too many outrageous catastrophes had
arisen. Her thoughts were in chaos, her emotions in turmoil,
and she was convinced that she shouldn't absent herself
from the property, but Michael was even now hoisting her
in, and she struggled to arrest his progress, managing to
pitch back onto his chest.

"Get in, madam."

"I won't."

She whirled around, stomping her foot, and she imagined she resembled a petulant toddler, throwing a temper
tantrum. Throughout her life, men had endeavored to manipulate her and force her to do their bidding, but she'd

never acquiesced, and she wasn't about to start now. If Michael wanted something from her, all he had to do was ask. Manhandling her was not the way to go about it!

"You will. Now, or I shall lift you in bodily."

Indignant, she bit at her bottom lip, crossed her arms, and affected the mien that regularly set adult males to trembling. "I insist that you apprise me of your intentions, or I will raise such a ruckus that the entire household will come out to see what's transpiring."

He was unfazed by her threat, his eyes glittering menacingly, and if she hadn't been persuaded as to the type of man he was, she might have feared for her physical safety.

"As you obviously do not comprehend this about me"— he leaned close, articulating softly so that no one lingering nearby could perceive their quarrel—"I must advise you that I *never* prance about in public, engaging in discord where others might observe my personal squabbles. That said"—the presumptuous knave clasped her waist and tossed her in—"I will not loiter in the drive, arguing with you."

"Fine!" As incensed as he, she'd like nothing more than to whack that insolent smirk off his pretty face.

She moved to the far corner and huddled against the squab, as Michael delivered a few abbreviated commands to the coachmen. Then he climbed in behind her, his huge form blocking the small hatch so that she couldn't have vaulted out even if she'd considered it, which she hadn't. Crazy as it sounded, she was excited about the prospect of traipsing off with him. Whatever ensued, she intended to make the most of it.

He settled himself and rapped on the roof. The carriage clattered away at a brisk speed, and she clutched at the strap to keep from sliding off the seat. They cruised down the long lane toward the village, and then the road to London that lay beyond. He stared out the window, pretending he was the sole passenger, so she pulled back the curtain and peered outside, as well.

The moon was full, the countryside brilliantly illuminated, and she surveyed all for a quiescent, passion-charged interlude.

She'd meant to ignore him, but he simply pervaded the enclosed area, and she wasn't about to demurely submit to his carting her across England without having some idea of where they were bound or why.

"Where are we headed?"

The lengthy pause made her conclude that he wouldn't reply. Then ultimately, he focused his rabid gaze on her. "*You* are to stay at an inn."

"At this hour? How will we locate one?"

"We are near enough to town that there are several suitable choices."

"We couldn't have left in the morning? Like two normal, decent people?"

The word *decent* had him snorting derisively. "For over two weeks, I have been suggesting that you vacate the premises, and you would not heed me. Previously, I hadn't the authority to enforce your departure." His eyes constricted with an ominous venom. "Now, I do."

"Who made that decision?"

"Your brother"—he hesitated, striving for maximum effect—". . . and I."

The two cads! She wasn't some incapable young maiden. How dare they initiate a resolution without seeking her opinion!

"You might have permitted me to communicate my thank-you and good-bye to Lady Carrington."

"I'll offer your apologies."

"What about my belongings?"

"I'll have them packed and sent to you."

Ooh . . . and wouldn't she just like to shake him! This was how he'd acted when they'd first met, before they'd become lovers, and she abhorred this calculated indifference. She was wiser now as to his comportment, and she recognized that the hostile, flinty demeanor indicated he was hurting.

He presumed that she had schemed with Hugh, but after

all they'd shared, how could he be so willing to assume her complicity?

"What did Hugh say to you?"

He chortled. "As if you didn't know."

"Tell me!" she decreed.

"Be silent, woman! I don't propose to bicker with you all the way to the inn."

"We haven't begun to argue!"

"Don't push me!"

"You're behaving like a lunatic."

Seeming to deflate, he sank back and gaped out the window, once again. "Give it a rest, Lady Sarah."

"And quit addressing me by my title. It wounds me when you do."

Weary, he tipped his head toward the leather, and she longed to close the distance between them, to sit on his lap and guide them back to that special spot where they talked and loved so easily.

"I want to help," she murmured, but he had no retort. At a loss, she perused the outside landscape. Eventually, they slowed, and the driver urged the horses into the circular courtyard of an inn. Lamps were burning on the lower floor. Their conveyance rattled to a stop, and a postboy ran out from the stable to drop the step.

"Wait here," Michael exclaimed, springing out and banging the door behind.

She was half-tempted to pursue him just to have the satisfaction of disobeying his spurious mandate, but she wasn't about to meander into an unfamiliar establishment in the middle of the night without an escort. Reposing in the shadows, she scrutinized the surroundings, the only noises coming from the horses as they calmed themselves, the driver as he shifted about.

Many minutes later, Michael returned and assisted her to the ground. A serving girl held a lantern and, without debate, they followed her inside. Voices and revelry emanated from one of the common rooms, but Michael directed her past and up the stairs and, without incident, they ascended to a clean, tidy chamber at the end of the hall on the second floor.

She balanced on the edge of the bed while the girl lit a fire in the brazier. Michael guarded the door, a fierce, tempestuous sentinel who hovered over all while the girl finished her chores, then withdrew.

The stillness left in her wake was instantly oppressive, and Sarah stirred nervously, afraid to learn what was coming, just as afraid not to.

"Well . . . ?" When it seemed he'd never commence, she rose and listed his recent transgressions on the tips of her fingers. "You kidnapped me from Lady Carrington's estate. You won't divulge the contents of your conversation with my brother. You brought me to this strange inn. Explain yourself—immediately—or I guarantee that I shall hie myself downstairs, and find my way to Pamela's—if I have to hike every bloody mile through the dark to get there."

Without her being aware of it, she was essentially shouting, and someone in one of the adjoining apartments pounded on the thin wall and bellowed for her to "be quiet." Mortified, she lowered her volume to a harsh whisper. "I've had enough! This brooding, rude attitude may stand you in good stead with others, but I will not tolerate it. Now, speak to me like a sensible, civil grown man, or leave me be!"

"As you wish, milady." Apparently, he wasn't used to anyone remarking upon his ill humor, and he was jolted. Whispering as well, he informed, "Please break your fast and be dressed so that you are ready by eleven."

"What's occurring at eleven?"

"Why . . . we're off to the church." He gestured as though she was a simpleton. "To marry."

"We're to wed?" Naturally, that's what Hugh would demand. How stupid of her not to realize it! With how rapidly circumstances had escalated, she hadn't had two seconds to reach the inescapable conclusion. She'd simply been scared that they might grab for their pistols.

Her heart was suddenly thudding so fast that she felt it

might burst from under her ribs, and she eased down on the mattress, her legs unable to sustain her weight. Emotions warred: unconditional joy, fury, desolation.

To marry Michael Stevens! If the chance had been presented earlier in the evening, she'd have soared to the heavens, but not now. Not with him in such a snit. And most especially not when he and her brother had come to some sort of agreement without consulting her. She would not be bullied. Not by either of them.

She couldn't stop her flippant query: "Are you proposing?"

"No, because your answer is of absolutely no consequence."

Sighing heavily, she battled tears. How had her great fondness for him brought them to this hideous juncture? She blinked, then blinked again, recalling that she never cried—about anything—yet since he'd crashed into her staid, boring existence, she was constantly prone to weeping.

"What a coil . . ." Reduced to sniffling, she studied her lap, longing for solitude so that she could compose herself. As it was, a tear dribbled out and slipped down her cheek.

"There's no call for theatrics," Michael mentioned upon noticing. "Your display will produce no response from me."

Legs braced, hands secured behind his back, he was handsome, refined, aloof, and so very alone. This cold, hard stranger was no one she knew, no one she had ever known. The affection he'd harbored for her was totally lacking, and she couldn't bear its absence.

Their situation had revolved to where marriage was an option. While he brooded and stewed, her heart sang with the possibilities. She wouldn't view this calamity in negative terms.

He didn't love her; she appreciated that. In view of the type of man he was, and the world from which he'd evolved, perhaps he never would. But she loved him, and if he would just allow her to, she would spend the remainder of her days making him happy and, in the process, obtaining no meager amount of contentment for herself.

There had to be a method of chopping through his bul-
wark of animosity and suspicion. She simply wouldn't let
him spurn her. Whatever it took to restore their unique relationship, she would gladly do—if it meant she had to
grovel at his feet. This was no time to be timid, and she
carefully tucked away her pride where it couldn't interfere.

"Don't growl at me," she entreated. "I hate that you're
so upset, and I don't accept that this is a horrid turn of
events. I'd be proud to be your wife. I love you."

"How extremely convenient."

His curt rejoinder was like a slap. She'd never uttered
love to another soul, and it was painful and humiliating to
have her attestation callously hurled back in her face. Resolved to prevail, she forged on.

"It's true, Michael. You know it is." She went to him
and rested her fingers on the center of his chest, but touching him was like caressing a cool slab of marble. "I understand that you don't love me in return, but you hold me
in some esteem."

"Don't flatter yourself." He removed her hand, then
stepped away, creating space as he coarsely evaluated her
breasts. "What I've felt for you is lust. Naught else."

Making him see the bright side would be much more
difficult than she'd anticipated, but she wasn't about to capitulate. He could be stubborn, rigid, and headstrong, but
she wasn't exactly a shrinking violet.

Refusing to be brushed off, she persevered. "You can
bark and protest, but you'll never convince me that your
feelings aren't genuine. As far as I'm concerned this is a
marvelous predicament, and I can't fathom why you're so
annoyed."

"Perchance, milady, it has something to do with the fact
that your brother arrived with a fully prepared Special License."

"What?"

She couldn't have discerned his pronouncement correctly. A Special License would authorize an immediate

wedding. It negated the necessity of calling the banns; any waiting period was void. Why would Hugh have one in his pocket?

An unwelcome pot of disturbing ruminations bubbled over, hinting at deception and betrayal, but the implications were so stunning that, after everything that had already unfolded, she couldn't begin to process them. Only through sheer force of will did she prevent herself from falling on the bed in a state of shock.

"You're not joking, are you?"

"It was signed by the archbishop, no less." He whipped out the paper and waved it under her nose.

"We were so discreet. How could Hugh have discovered what we were about?"

"How indeed?"

The lull that resulted was damning. What could Michael surmise but that she'd had a stake in this? Hugh had as much as said so. She was furious at Michael for accusing her of such deviousness, but she was more enraged at her idiotic, deceitful brother. What did Hugh hope to gain?

Just to scurry the absurd cabal Hugh had hatched, she had half a mind to reject the marriage, yet even as she mulled the sentiment, she knew she wouldn't. Hugh had positioned her on a collision course with Michael, and she wasn't sorry.

They would marry, and Michael would calm down. Time would pass, he would adapt, and they would build a solid life. They would have children, a family. She would support him in his business ventures, and he could recommend how she should restore the Scarborough estate after it was pillaged by Hugh's latest gambling nemesis.

Michael owned a gentleman's club. He might know the scoundrel who had bested Hugh. Once they were wed, he could approach the villain on her behalf, or he might have contacts who could plead her case.

She whirled with excitement. They belonged together. Down to the very marrow of her bones, she sensed that this was the proper route for both of them, and she wouldn't be dissuaded, no matter how he grouched and snapped.

"I'll be a good wife to you, Michael. I swear it."

"Well, bully for you, Lady Sarah, but I've never wanted a *wife*. And"—he stalked to the door—"if I had ever thought to select a bride, it would hardly be a conniving, duplicitous aristocrat such as yourself."

"Will marriage to me really be so terrible?"

"Milady, I can't conceive of anything worse." He departed without a backward glance.

Horribly afflicted, she sank onto the bed, wondering how she'd ever make this right.

Chapter Nineteen

Rebecca tiptoed down the hall toward Hugh's room. Her pulse tripping with excitement, she couldn't wait to hear the joyous news of what had occurred during his meeting with Michael Stevens.

A smile tugged at her lips as she recollected every delicious moment of Sarah's fall from grace. She was glad she'd accompanied Hugh so that she'd been able to witness it for herself. Though she'd only snatched a fleeting glimpse before Hugh had shoved her away, she'd seen enough to understand Sarah's impossible situation. The bathing tub, the nudity, their scandalous seclusion, the imbroglio couldn't have transpired more perfectly if Rebecca had staged it.

The fact that Sarah had humiliated herself so thoroughly was amazing. In her wildest fantasizing, Rebecca hadn't anticipated anything so decadently marvelous. When they'd decided to enter, she'd thought they might catch Mr. Stevens in Sarah's bedchamber, that the pair might be talking or even kissing. But to stumble upon them naked and washing each other!

The reality was simply too sweet.

Her ruse to ensnare Sarah in a matrimonial web had been risky, and she hadn't really been convinced that she'd prevail, but she'd been desperate to prove herself to Hugh. So often, he treated her as though she was of no value, that she was stupid or ineffectual, and his disregard stung.

For the past three years, she'd toiled to situate herself so he'd conclude that she'd be a wonderful countess. She'd minded his town house, administered his calendar, hosted his parties, warmed his bed. In every fashion, she'd ingratiated herself so that he'd see her as viable to his enduring happiness. While her duties—especially the intimate ones— hadn't always been pleasant, she'd performed them competently, confident that he'd note her proficiency, yet he was never satisfied. He reproached and ridiculed, and she wasn't sure why she persevered.

The sole incentive that made it worth the effort was envisioning herself as the future mistress at Scarborough. She would revel in the position as Sarah never had. The house and property amply restored, a skilled staff at her beck and call, dressed in luxurious gowns and exquisite jewels, she would be society's most notable, embraced hostess. With her exalted husband by her side, she would dine on the finest foods, drink the rarest vintage wines, throw lavish balls and parties, and be envied by all.

Thanks to Sarah and her lustful conduct, Rebecca's reveries were about to come true. Who would have imagined that levelheaded, proper Sarah would be so freely led down the carnal path? Of course, from the looks of Mr. Stevens, it was easy to see why even a saint might be tempted.

Nearly skipping with delight over how circumstances had unfolded, and deliriously exhilarated as to her involvement, she hurried the last few steps. Hugh would be so proud of her! So gratified! He would finally behold her as a driving force, as the woman he wanted forevermore. They could be married, as he'd been guaranteeing for so long. With Sarah provided for, there was no reason to delay.

"Rebecca Monroe Compton, the Countess of Scarborough," she practiced, liking how regal the title sounded.

Close to giggling, she reached the door to Hugh's suite and stealthily slid inside.

Hugh was in a plush chair in front of the fire, clearly foxed, a half-empty decanter of brandy in his hand. There was no glass in sight, but she wasn't about to castigate him. This was a night for celebrating. If he chose to crudely swill from the bottle, who was she to say nay?

"Is Sarah with you?" he testily inquired.

"Sorry, Hugh, but she's still not in her room."

"Damn! Where could she be?"

"I searched everywhere." One of the servants had left a supper tray, and she grabbed some cheese off it before going to sit on his lap. "Her belongings are still in the wardrobe."

"Indubitably. Why would they be gone?" He downed a swig of his libation. "How about Stevens? Was he lurking about?"

"No, he wasn't there, either."

"Do you suppose they went off together?" Disturbed by the possibility, he stared into the fire, then slammed his fist on the arm of the chair. "Blast! I need to discuss this with her before Stevens does."

"What's to discuss?" She snuggled her bottom in the manner he enjoyed, but he was too distracted to notice. Though imbibing heavily, he certainly didn't seem to be jubilant. Suddenly worried, she prudently queried, "Everything proceeded as planned, didn't it?"

"The blackguard refused to sign the contract I'd drafted."

"How could he?"

"He laughed in my face!"

Instantaneously, her euphoria evaporated. Would her scheming be for naught? "He'll marry her, though, won't he?"

"He said he'll need to *contemplate* whether his sense of *duty and honor* would require it."

"But what about the marriage settlement you demanded?"

"He wouldn't agree!"

Not recalling that she was perched on his thighs, he jumped to his feet and sent her sprawling, and she scrambled to latch onto a bedpost so she wouldn't land on the floor. "So . . . we're to get . . . nothing?"

"He swore he'd see me dead and buried before I received one farthing of his blessed fortune."

How dare Mr. Stevens spoil her hard-earned victory! Utterly flabbergasted by this unseen turn of events, she sank down onto the mattress, thinking she might be ill.

Pacing back and forth, clutching his accursed bottle of spirits as if it was a magic talisman, Hugh ranted and raved about Michael Stevens and his tyrannical procedures.

"What about Sarah?" she injected into his diatribe. "Could she convince him?"

"That's what I'm hoping. She absolutely must consent to speak with him."

"And if she won't?"

Hugh didn't reply or perhaps, in his overwrought condition, he simply wasn't paying attention. He resumed his march across the rug, while she pondered how quickly her dreams had dwindled to ashes.

She'd plotted down to the smallest detail: Whichever fellow eventually ended up compromising Sarah, he would be a gentleman who recognized Hugh's status and rank, and he'd feel obligated to rectify the slight he'd committed against Hugh's family. The unlucky bridegroom would apologize in the only mode that mattered—by tendering money. Lots and lots of money.

Who would have thought that her strategy would be subverted by the likes of Michael Stevens? The man didn't comprehend the rules of civilized behavior! He was so far below Sarah's exalted station; it was a privilege for him to have been granted the opportunity to wed her! Didn't he grasp that his actions constrained him to make amends?

Rebecca brooded, heartsick and distressed, listening to Hugh rail against fate, watching him stagger and fume.

She remembered Sarah, and the expression of joy she'd exhibited that odd afternoon on the lawn when she'd been in Michael Stevens's presence, and one truth became abundantly clear: Sarah would never solicit Mr. Stevens on Hugh's behalf. Never in a thousand years.

Their conspiracy had been to no avail, though Hugh didn't know it yet. He never could face the consequences of his acts, but then, for much of his life, he'd had his father to hide behind, then Sarah, then herself. Despite their divergent interests, she and Sarah had shielded him from himself, but this decisive fiasco had proved too great a folly. She wanted to weep for what was forfeit.

The town house, with its pretty furnishings and lovely view of the park, was gone. As was the jaunty carriage, with its high-stepping chestnuts, that Hugh drove when he was squiring her about town. So too her closets of fancy clothes and baubles.

Most painful to consider was her loss of Scarborough. What a charming vision she'd painted, and what a fool she'd been to assume that it might come to pass. For just a moment, she closed her eyes and pictured herself floating down the grand corridor on the main floor of the mansion, her skirts brushing the tiles, as she waltzed to the parlor and greeted a new group of guests who had stopped for a visit.

The illusion faded, and she focused on Hugh, once more. Much like a petulant child who'd been denied a treat, his tantrum was terminated, and he was reclined again by the hearth.

"We won't be able to marry, will we?" She knew the answer, but she had to hear it from his lips.

"What?" He glared at her as if she was mad.

"You promised that we'd marry once Sarah was established, but we can't now. Not without any blunt coming in."

"Honestly, Rebecca." As he stared her down, he didn't seem quite so handsome; just inebriated and obnoxious. "You actually expected that we would marry?"

"But you said . . ."

"Bah . . ." He gestured obscenely, dismissing her—and her hopes—with a single motion. "I could never marry *you*. The notion is ludicrous."

Frightened, she swallowed down a panicked breath. "The very first occasion when you coaxed me to your bed, you vowed that we would."

"How could I?" Heedlessly, he trembled with mirth. "God, you're my cousin! And you're a commoner. Are you *that* naïve? I'm a man; I was just trying to lift your skirts. Surely you realized that?"

"No, I didn't," she mouthed.

"It worked, too!" Guffawing, he slapped his leg as though he'd just pronounced a hilarious joke at her expense, and she sincerely felt her heart might quit beating.

"I believed everything you said."

She thought of his disgusting habits and temper, of his grumbling and fussing, his lewd bedroom antics. Because she so fiercely craved the future he could have rendered, she'd braved all.

"Gads, just last week, I offered for Tilsbury's daughter"—he was babbling, having forgotten she was there— "but he insisted that I reverse some of my debt predicament before he'd reflect upon it." He shook his head and studied the flames. "That deal's shot to hell."

The embers glowed, and his morose meditation continued while she meticulously evaluated him, an unvoiced rage at his betrayals brewing dramatically. Gradually, his eyelids fluttered shut, and he began to snore. The decanter fell and clanked on the floor, but the noise failed to stir him.

Quiet as a mouse, she rose and sneaked away, even as she was deliberating on how she would retaliate for everything he'd done.

"I now pronounce you man and wife," the vicar intoned. "You may kiss the bride."

A lengthy, uncomfortable silence ensued, and Michael gawked at him as though the man had snakes in his hair.

Taken aback by the virulent appraisal, the minister gulped then muttered something that sounded like ". . . or not . . ." and snapped his prayer book closed.

At the intentional slight of his new bride, Sarah stiffened and shifted away, unable to tolerate his boorish company.

Good, Michael mused. *Let her be wary.*

When he'd arrived at the inn to retrieve her shortly before eleven, she'd been eagerly awaiting him in one of the private parlors. Perplexingly, she'd primped and preened in preparation, as if the farce was a real ceremony. Wearing a simple gown, but with her hair curled and swept up on her head, she'd appeared cheerful and beautiful.

Any man in the kingdom would have deemed himself fortunate to wed her. Not Michael, for he knew that looks could be deceiving. Underneath that pale elegance and allure beat a black heart.

He was a cautious individual who'd been whisked up in a disaster. This was the type of wretched debacle more suited to James than himself, and if anyone had suggested that he might one day find himself repeating his vows as reparation for a moronic carnal misstep, he'd have laughed aloud. He'd always presumed that he was too astute, too smart, too calculating, to end up on the wrong side of a marital calamity.

Once he'd learned that she was Hugh Compton's sister, he should have resisted his attraction instead of being beguiled by a virtuous flare and a pair of emerald eyes. How they'd sparkled when she'd beseeched him to engage in an abbreviated tryst! How they'd glistened when she'd shed enchanting tears! How they'd intensified when she'd called his name and cried out in sexual ecstasy!

What had possessed him to be so reckless, so negligent? He took pride in his self-control and discipline, and he couldn't accept the depth of his idiocy where she was concerned.

Well, he had no one to blame but himself for this catastrophe. While he wanted to chastise Lady Sarah and her brother, they couldn't have succeeded if Michael hadn't been so atrociously gullible.

On principle, he should have declined to marry her, but he wasn't that kind of person. Even before he'd gone down to the library the previous night, he'd been aware that Scarborough would insist on matrimony, just as he'd acknowledged that he would acquiesce.

After all, he could hardly argue that he wasn't culpable.

Yes, Lady Sarah had begged for the affair, and yes, she'd placed herself in his way at every turn, but he was a mature, experienced man, who should have withstood her campaign.

He was *not* his father, and he wouldn't shirk his responsibilities, but that didn't mean he would play Scarborough's game, either. Scarborough had hit him up for money—big money—as Michael had predicted he would. Yet, as Lady Sarah and her conniving brother were about to discover, Michael's sense of accountableness only extended so far.

For his crime of ruining Lady Sarah, he was constrained to wed her. Regretfully, he would impart to her the respectability that came with being a married woman, but that was all. He would never offer them a single penny in reparation.

Hugh and Sarah Compton could choke on their poverty.

The country chapel, with its pews, dark walls, and stained glass, smelled of wax and polish, of travail and prayers, and it occurred to him that he hadn't set foot in a church in years. He was surprised that he hadn't been struck by lightning when he'd stepped through the doors. Bearing in mind the plight of his immortal soul, a fiery, celestial thunderbolt wouldn't have been unexpected.

"Are we finished?" he irritably inquired. The sooner this travesty was concluded, the better off they'd all be.

"Ah . . . yes . . ." The vicar was still flustered by Michael's unwillingness to kiss the bride, but he pulled himself together, adjusting his spectacles on his nose and leading them to a table at the rear. "We just need your endorsement on the registry. And the license."

The vicar's wife, an older, crafty-looking sort, was the only witness to the sorry business. She kept sizing him up, readily distinguishing him as a sinner. Michael signed his life away while she held a lamp, and she regarded him with such disdain that he was positive she would comment on his insufferable deportment. He stared her down, daring her to utter a word, and she ultimately glanced away as Sarah too inscribed her name on the appropriate lines.

She's left-handed, Michael absurdly noted, as she shakily gripped the pen, and the cheap gold band that he'd slipped on her finger was highly visible in the dim light, a jarring reminder of how she'd abused his trust and shattered his illusions.

The ring wasn't even authentic. There was no jeweler in the area, and he hadn't had time to have a genuine one delivered. Not that he would have. He'd purchased it from a serving girl in the taproom at the inn, and he almost wished he'd be around to observe when the Comptons tried to pawn it and found out it was worthless.

Sarah stood, the signatures completed. She clasped a meager bridal bouquet, a bundle plucked from a vase near the altar after the vicar's wife had ascertained that Sarah had no flowers. Slightly wilted, petals drooping, she clutched them to her chest as though they were the finest hothouse roses.

"You've been very kind," she murmured to the older woman, brimming with transparent bliss as she hugged her tightly, mangling the blossoms in between their bodies.

"You're welcome," the woman asserted, and she added a phrase that he couldn't decipher, but it sounded like "Be strong, dear."

They parted, and the vicar's wife cast him a scathing look, and he blanched under her irascible examination. Obviously, she'd bonded with Sarah in some incomprehensible, feminine show of support, and she erroneously conjectured that Sarah was a put-upon, downtrodden bride who needed a champion. If he'd cared in the least—which he didn't—he might have taken a second to set the woman straight.

No doubt, she and her husband were dying of curiosity. After all, it wasn't every day that a country vicar was presented with a Special License and asked to immediately marry two strangers who were so aggravated with each other that they weren't conversing. It was extremely apparent that they were involved in a serious, odious dilemma, yet Sarah managed to seem innocent and vulnerable.

What would the other woman think if he apprised her of Sarah's capacity for deceit and artifice?

Michael furnished the vicar with a heavy bag of coins, an amount sufficient to quell speculation or gossip. Without contributing any further remarks, he exited the chapel, the noonday sun temporarily blinding. By the time he'd regained his equilibrium, Sarah had joined him and, as he advanced down the narrow path, she matched his strides.

His carriage awaited, as well as a horse he'd borrowed from Pamela that was tethered to the boot. Beyond, a trio of people gathered under a shade tree. His driver and a coachman, who were also bodyguards, were huddled with a widow he'd employed as Sarah's companion for the next week. As he and Sarah approached, the group leapt to attention, but he waved them off so that he and the lady could have a private good-bye. The servants could ruminate forever about what was transpiring, but they'd get no confirmation from Michael.

He reached for the door, while she hovered, pressing her tiresome bouquet to her nose.

"That wasn't so bad, was it?" She smiled gaily, her evident rapture setting him on edge.

"Get in." He lowered the step, but she didn't move.

"Don't be such a grouch," she chided. "You look as if you've just been to the blacksmith and had a tooth pulled." Embarrassingly, she captured his hands and whirled herself around in a circle, swaying with gladness over what they'd just accomplished. "What a gorgeous day! The sun is bright, the sky is blue, and I am so happy! Thank you!"

He hadn't the faintest inkling why she would be grateful, but then, he'd secreted her away before she could talk with her brother, so she wasn't cognizant that their contrivance had been foiled. She was laboring under the mistaken impression that there were grounds to rejoice.

"You sourpuss!" she was saying merrily when he displayed no reaction. "I won't allow your bad temper to spoil my celebration."

Ere he could stop her, she rose up on tiptoe and stole a kiss. As he inhaled her familiar, beloved scent, his hands inched to her waist, and he just desisted before he perpetrated a reprehensible gaffe.

He *did* take hold of her, but only long enough to set her away.

"Come on, Michael. Cheer up!" She laughed and danced a little jig. "This is our wedding day; not the end of the world. How long do you intend to be angry?"

As long as it takes. He eyed her dispassionately, wondering how she could be so bloody ecstatic, how she could prance about, reveling in her purported good fortune while throwing her cunning in his face.

Had she no shame? No remorse? No conscience? Did she care—even the tiniest bit—that she had devastated him?

"Get in," he repeated and, with his sharp tone, she finally heeded his irate condition. She ceased her bobbling and prattling.

"Oh, all right, you sorehead." Stabilizing herself, she placed her foot on the step. "Where are we off to? Have you selected some totally decadent spot in which to spend our wedding night? I'll have you know that I prefer chocolates and champagne!"

What was causing her to suffer these outrageous flights of fancy? Why pretend this was anything other than a sham? "*We* aren't going anywhere. *You* are going home."

The abrupt news stunned her. Her eyes widened with astonishment and hurt, and he steeled himself against all the ways in which she was still capable of provoking a response in him.

"To Yorkshire?"

"Yes."

"But I thought . . ."

"Thought what, Lady Sarah?"

"Well . . . that we would . . . travel to London." She

scrutinized him fervently, carefully choosing her words, beginning to appreciate that no matter the comment, it would be inappropriate. "I'd hoped we'd visit your family."

"I have no desire for you to meet my family. Not now. Not ever."

"You don't mean that."

"Oh, but I do."

She paused, searching his eyes, dissecting his demeanor. Something tripped and cracked—perhaps it was the final piece of his heart fracturing—and he forced himself to remain unmoved as perception dawned on her.

"You don't consider this a real marriage, do you?"

"Hardly."

He might as well have slapped her. As though her bones had transformed to mush, she sank down, the carriage stair impeding her progress, and she balanced against it.

"But . . . but why? You care for me. We could make this work. We could turn it into something wonderful."

"Why would I want to?"

With each harsh utterance, she deflated a tad more, and he felt he'd evolved into someone else entirely, that he'd been inhabited by an alien being who was bent on tormenting her until she crumpled into a heap.

What a *fine* man he'd grown to be, the son Angela Ford had raised to be such a chivalrous fellow. Michael Stevens—the eminent despoiler and defiler of women! If his mother could witness him now, in all his wretched, miserable, scurrilous glory, she'd never forgive him.

How had he fallen to such a contemptible state that he would behave so despicably? The only plausible explanation was that his feelings for her had been so pure and sincere—as close to love as he might ever come—and he simply couldn't countenance how grievously she'd wounded him. He could only react by striking out. By keeping on and on—until she went away, as agonized as he.

"When will I see you again?"

"I have no idea."

With the admission, sadness engulfed him, and he

shoved it away. If she had any concept of the profundity of his regret over their acrimonious split, she'd have incredible power over him, so he couldn't let her deduce how much he'd miss her, or how long it would take him to inure himself to their horrid farewell.

"Where will you be?"

"I'm not sure."

"What if I need to reach you?"

"I can't fathom why you would."

God, but he felt he was kicking a puppy. With each retort, she shrank back as if he was physically striking her. He couldn't endure much more, nor could she, so he helped her to her feet and guided her into the coach. Thankfully, she didn't resist or argue.

The driver and others neared, ready to discharge their duties, and she peered out the opening, her brilliant green eyes silently begging.

"It doesn't have to be this way."

"Doesn't it?" he interrogated caustically. "Next time you talk with your brother, give him a message from me."

"What?"

"Our marriage makes no difference. His debt stands. The inventory of the Scarborough property was effectuated while you were here in Bedford. My men will be around to collect my chattels on the appointed date. Unless, of course, he can locate the cash he owes me before then."

For a lengthy interlude, she assessed him. Mute, confused, she seemed to have no clue as to what he referred. Was she daft? The purpose of her seduction had been a misguided attempt to coerce him into returning Hugh's markers, so why was she so baffled? Scarborough's gambling debt was the reason she'd started it all.

Wasn't it?

Her revolting brother had contended as much during their contentious meeting in the library.

Unease swamped him. Doubts—vexatious, persistent, unavoidable—crept in, inducing him to hesitate and falter.

"You!" she howled, and she was horrified. "You're the one!"

"Don't act dumb, Sarah. It doesn't become you."

"You're a gambler?" She articulated the term with such loathing that it sounded like the worst epithet.

"When the spirit moves me."

"But you claimed you own a gentlemen's club."

"I do." He frowned at her affront. "Wagering is our main source of income. It's how *gentlemen* entertain themselves."

"A gambler," she wailed. "I've married a gambler! After everything I've been through!" She was teeming with righteous indignation. "Why Hugh?"

"Why not?"

"Why not! That's all you have to say for yourself?" Her fury was growing with each exchange. "Tell me why!"

"Because he's an ass. He deserved it."

"Give it all back! The markers, the property! Whatever you won, I order you to refund it to him."

"No."

"I demand it of you!"

"No," he reiterated. "Your brother wrought exactly what he deserved."

"That may be true, but he gambled away *my* home and the clothes on *my* back. *My* retainers will have no food in their bellies or coal for their stoves this winter."

"It's Hugh's doing," he callously barked, "and none of my concern."

"Why am I not surprised by your impervious attitude?" Scornfully, she shook her head. "While you were making love to me here in Bedford, you had men in my house, counting the silverware! What kind of pitiless monster are you?"

The damning question hung in the air, but there was no adequate answer he could supply. How had it happened that it suddenly seemed *he* was in the wrong?

Her traveling companion had been prowling on the fringes of their quarrel, pretending to ignore the heated exchange, and Sarah beckoned her on and in, then pulled the door shut in his face. At the last, she leaned out the window, her shrewd gaze running up and down his broad frame, taking his measure and plainly finding him lacking.

"Don't ever contact me again," she declared.

The curtain fell back, and she impatiently rapped for the driver, signaling him to carry on. The man looked to Michael, seeking permission, and Michael untied his horse, then consented with a nod of his head.

He yearned to plead his case, to explain or justify the belligerent contest with Hugh, but he was caught off guard by how the tables of outrage had been so promptly turned, and he couldn't defend himself.

As the carriage jingled to life and rolled off, her arm shot out the window, and for a brief instant, he sustained a foolish, thrilling rush as he presumed she was waving good-bye. Then, he saw that she was only flinging out her bridal bouquet, unable to bear having it in the coach with her. The pitiful arrangement rippled to the dirt, a morose, poignant statement of her abhorrence. The *faux* wedding band followed.

Walking down the dusty lane, he scooped them up, crushing the petals in his fist as he watched her disappear in the distance. He should have been savoring some moment of satisfaction; he should have been shouting good riddance and *adieu,* but all he felt was alone again and very much like the young boy in that Paris flat, waiting . . . waiting . . . for the father who never arrived to fetch him home.

Chapter Twenty

Michael paused on the stoop of the London home where he had passed the prior decade of his life. The three-story row house was situated on a narrow, busy street, a few blocks from their gambling club, and a few more from the Chelsea Theater where his mother spent so much of her time.

They'd moved into it shortly after leaving Paris. He'd been seventeen, and for all intents and purposes, a Frenchman, having been whisked away to the exotic country at the age of three so that he had few memories of England or the world they'd left behind. He'd loved their Continental lifestyle and friends, the foods, the wines, and the pretty, generous French girls, and he'd greatly begrudged his mother her decision to return.

What a shock the change of cultures had been! In Paris, he had been the son of a renowned celebrity. In London, he was merely a scorned oddity, one of the dozens of bastard boys of the aristocracy, trying to find their place in a community that shunned them.

Luckily, he'd fared better than most, due in no small part to his father, Edward Stevens. Though he hated to admit it, he had to give the man credit. Edward had purchased their gaming establishment for them, presenting it to James as a gift after his first marriage when he was but a lad of twenty in the hopes that the guarantee of regular employment would curb some of his more wicked tendencies.

The ploy had worked. Overly proud, they'd refused to flounder in front of Edward's peers—especially when those exalted nobles were positive that he and James would never amount to anything. In a big way, they'd proved everyone wrong.

They had a knack for earning money, possessing an innate aptitude for gambling, and for commerce with the types of fools who were drawn to it. They knew how to amuse and divert even the most surly guest, and they'd lined their purses in the process.

Their effective management had gained them powerful prominence on the fringes of High Society where they were admired and despised in equal measure. Customers detested their success, but still they came to play, unable to avoid the lure of the club that was the best spot for a fashionable gentleman to be seen while in town.

From the wagering and their dubious side ventures, they had grown obscenely wealthy, and they'd used the profits wisely, investing for the future and caring for their mother. They'd bought her this residence, and she'd constantly adored it. The sturdy abode of brick and mortar had shielded them from the harsh glare of London's snobbery and contempt. Theirs was a high-profile existence that provided scant privacy, and they'd been safe and carefree behind the closed front door.

He'd loved its spacious salons, comfortable furnishings, and efficient staff. A peaceful haven from his hectic hours at the club, the rooms were warm and cozy and, whenever he'd arrived home after a long night, he'd been soothed by shedding his cloak in the foyer as the aroma of James's American-style coffee wafted down the stairs, as his mother's laughter rang through the halls.

Tarrying for a moment, he relished the memories before he stuck his key in the lock.

Would it still fit?

With James's wife shaping her own domestic arrangements, he had very likely forfeited his freedom to come and go and, though he wasn't personally acquainted with the new Mrs. Stevens, he was quite sure that the ambiance created by his flamboyant mother would be a tad too extravagant for the composed noblewoman. He couldn't help

pondering how much reorganization he'd confront and how
he would deal with it. While he desperately needed the
solace of hearth and family, the traditional might have vanished.

Surprisingly, the door opened, but as he stepped through,
he vividly recalled the last time he'd entered. He'd just
rescued James from a pub where he'd been drinking and
carousing and suffering from the aftermath of his burgeoning love affair with the woman—Abigail Weston—who
would become his wife.

Distraught, afraid for his brother, Michael had wearily
trudged home, only to walk in on his parents and the tidings
that they were lovers, that they were finally destined to
marry. The scene that followed had been dreadful, and
every word Angela had uttered in Edward's defense had
stabbed like the sharpest blade.

After all the ways Edward had dishonored her, she'd
fallen for him like an infatuated girl. Her decision had
seemed abhorrent and crazy, disgraceful, and he still
couldn't comprehend why his proud, strong mother had
been so willing to debase herself over an aging reprobate
who'd never given her anything but heartache.

Affronted and dazed, he'd left London that day, filled
with exasperation and rage, and he truly hadn't known if
he'd ever return. He'd simply had it—with his mother, his
brother, his father—but his pique had ultimately faded, so
there was no reason to have stayed away so long, yet he
hadn't been able to make his way back.

His mother had wed, and Michael wished her happy. He
really, really did, for he loved her very much, and he could
never send her a bad thought. But if Edward hurt her
again . . .

Michael repressed a shudder. If Edward hurt her, Michael couldn't imagine what his response might be.

He stood in the silent anteroom, feeling a bit lost. Recollection swamped him: the marvelous years with James
and Angela, the terrible conclusion wrought by Edward.
His father was a bane, like a cloud of poisonous gas hov-

ering over Michael so oppressively that he couldn't shed the onerous cargo.

Edward's treachery when Michael was but a child had made him permanently wary, unequivocally cautious, and he had never let his guard down until Sarah Compton had ripped through the fabric of his staid environment, inducing him to yearn for things he couldn't have, encouraging him to dream, to speculate over what *could* be instead of settling for what *was*.

The burden of relinquishing Sarah—before he'd ever had her—was more than he could bear. When he'd lingered in that rural churchyard, and his carriage had lumbered away with her inside, he hadn't known where else to go but to London. *Home* had been the only option.

After their sham of a marriage ceremony, and the brutal comments they'd exchanged, he'd been perplexed and rankled. He was an excellent judge of people and their veracity, and on learning that he was a gambler, Sarah had been aghast and outraged that he was the individual who'd destroyed Hugh Compton.

Had Sarah been innocent? Had she been a pawn to Hugh's manipulations—just as Michael had been? Hugh insisted that she was culpable, but her categorical pleasure over their marriage had been authentic. If she'd acquiesced solely to placate Hugh, why feign such joy and affection?

If she was guiltless, he'd treated her abominably, and he couldn't face the notion that he'd erred, that he'd jumped to a faulty verdict. He'd just been so bewildered and angry that he couldn't think straight, and he'd craved a stable destination, a refuge where he could rest and regroup. So London had beckoned.

But now . . .

This was a mistake. I don't belong here anymore.

The concept spiraled through his head, and he couldn't remain. He turned to depart, but before he could escape, Abigail Weston strolled into the corridor. Completely absorbed, she was reading a letter, so she didn't notice him, and he furtively studied her. She was slender and petite, with pale creamy skin and eyes as green as Sarah's. Her hair was long and blond, and though it was the middle of the afternoon, she wore it down and tied with a ribbon as a young girl might.

He'd always been aware of who she was, because he made it a habit to investigate the family members of their clientele, but he'd never been this near to her before, had never judged her comeliness.

No wonder James couldn't resist, he petulantly conceded. She was a raving beauty, but then, his brother would have settled for nothing less.

Sensing his presence, she glanced up, and her brow furrowed, as she searched to deduce his identity.

"Michael . . . ?" she asked haltingly. The letter dropped and fluttered to the floor.

He tipped his head and acknowledged her in French, though he had no idea why he would. *"Bonjour."*

"I'm Abigail Ste—"

"Yes, I know." He cut her off. "I stopped by to pick up my belongings, but I'll try later when I won't be a bother."

"No, no, it's not a problem." She acted as if he were a frightened dog that might scurry off if he moved too rapidly.

An accurate description, he mused, for that was exactly how he felt, as if he'd been stranded on a desert island and no longer understood the rudiments of speech or civilized behavior.

"Please, won't you come in?" She gestured toward the receiving parlor, but he couldn't compel himself to meander in the direction she'd indicated. "We've been distressed by your absence," she said quietly, "and James will be so relieved that you're here."

He'd meant to speak his good-byes, but her overt concern had him dawdling like a mute imbecile.

More footsteps reverberated down the hall, and a new maid approached. Lady Abigail shifted toward the girl, but her focus was fixed on Michael, apparently afraid he'd evaporate into thin air.

"Would you fetch my husband?" she advised the servant. "Fast as you can?"

The maid hustled up the stairs, and momentarily, James hastened toward them. He skidded to a halt at the top step, his trousers scarcely on, his feet and chest bare.

His wife beamed up at him as if he controlled the moon and the stars. "Look who's here."

"Michael . . ." The appellation spewed out in a rush.

"Hello, James." He replied casually, pretending that his arrival was perfectly normal, and he was pleased at how unemotional he seemed. There was no tremor in his voice, and none of his anguish poked through.

James froze, anxious, then he took the stairs two at a time, racing down until they were face-to-face. "You bastard!" he crudely exclaimed, totally forgetting himself in front of his wife. "It's been three months! You had me frantic with worry!"

"You shouldn't have fretted," Michael asserted. "I told you I'd be all right."

"Liar! You look like death warmed over. What's happened to you?"

He grabbed Michael and crushed him in a fierce hug that continued on and on. Michael didn't reciprocate, but endured the reception like a statue, though he did close his eyes and inhale James's pacifying scent. James ended the embrace, but he kept touching, running his hands up and down Michael's torso and limbs, checking for injuries, or perhaps, verifying that Michael was real and not an apparition.

Locking an arm around Michael's neck, James pressed their foreheads together, whispering, "Don't ever scare me like that again!"

"I'm sorry."

"I'm just so glad you're here." He pulled away, once more, but not before bestowing another tight squeeze, and Michael garnered the distinct impression that James was cushioning him for a blow.

James said, "Many events have occurred while you were away. Mother married."

"I know."

"So did I."

"I heard."

"Abby, come."

James motioned to his bride who was across the foyer. Nervous, she didn't step toward them, so James went to her, and the manner in which he smiled at her caused Michael's heart to reel in his chest.

Clearly, this was not a marriage of convenience, not a misdeed James had righted by offering his name. There was steadfast devotion between them, stalwart emotion. James appeared exhilarated and smitten, and Michael was stunned to discern that his brother was terribly in love.

From the genuine regard mirrored by Lady Abigail, it was obvious that she loved him, too. Their open, irrefutable affinity afforded glaring evidence of how reality had been transformed while he'd been away. His worst suspicions were confirmed: The house was no longer his home. James now shared it with another, and though James would never say as much, he would need abundant private opportunity to establish himself in his new life with his wife.

While Michael wanted to castigate his sister-in-law for instigating the modifications, he couldn't. Yes, she'd thrust herself at James, and her tenacity had been the catalyst that had brought the disasters crashing down, so Michael longed to condemn her, or at least dislike her but, on discovering how fond she was of James, it was difficult to maintain any aggravation.

James had encountered little tenderness in his thirty years; few people had truly cared for him, and Michael was heartened to see Lady Abigail displaying such warm, visible sentiment.

"Abby," James proclaimed, "this is my wayward brother, Michael."

"Hello, Michael." She gifted him with a dazzling smile. "It's splendid to meet you."

"How do you do, Lady Abigail."

"Please call me Abigail."

"I will."

"We were just about to eat so that James can be off to work. Won't you join us?"

"You must!" James asserted. "We'll catch up on your travels, and then we'll go to the club. The staff will be so excited to have you back."

Bright, expectant, they stared at him, a paired unit of like disposition and purpose, eagerly anticipating the dissection of his adventures over a leisurely meal.

On innumerable occasions, he and James had come home at dawn, intending to sleep the day away, but before they took to their beds, they'd relaxed in the dining room, replaying the hours of vice and sin they'd experienced. Their mother was usually with them, adding her pithy observations and insights.

He missed those times and, while he ached to participate in the modest ritual, he recognized that he dare not. They would quiz him as to where he'd been, what he'd been doing. How could he possibly explain? He didn't understand it, himself, so he could hardly render an accounting to others.

James wouldn't bat an eye over his antics, but there was very little he could speak about to Lady Abigail, and any explication would lead to the end and Pamela's party. How could he describe what had transpired? He would have to relate the details about Sarah. About loving her and hating her.

He couldn't think about her; he couldn't talk about her. He simply could *not*. Not now. Perhaps not ever. He could only carry on.

"No, but I thank you." At his rejection of their hospitality, they deflated. Doubtless, James hoped he'd befriend Lady Abigail, and he would eventually. But at present, he couldn't stand viewing James's palpable bliss, not when his own life was such a mess. "I have a thousand errands to run."

"Will you at least visit the club?" James inquired hesitantly.

"Yes." He nodded, deciding as he went along. "In fact, for the time being, I'll take a room there."

"No!" Abigail announced. "We insist that you stay with us. Don't we, James?"

"Absolutely." James laid a hand on Michael's shoulder. "This is still your home, Michael. Nothing's different."

Did James really believe as much? Probably. His older sibling could be horribly oblivious.

"It's best if I go." He forced cordiality into his tone as he politely bowed over Lady Abigail's hand. "It was a pleasure, Abigail." But the informal mode of address seemed foreign on his tongue. Then, before James could detain him, he spun and walked outside.

Needing to be away, but not sure of his destination, he hurried off. Though he felt he was wandering aimlessly, he gradually perceived that his feet were reflexively leading him to their gambling hall.

He'd perpetually enjoyed his position there; the crowds, the pace, the action, the money. Employment had kept him out of mischief and off the streets and, in his prevailing disordered state, he definitely required the steady diversion and stabilizing influence. Increasing his stride, he realized that he'd forgotten how attached he was to their business, and now more than ever, his job would keep him occupied so that he'd have no chance for reflection or deliberation.

Work . . . that's what he craved. He would immerse himself so thoroughly that there wouldn't be a single, idle moment when Sarah might cross his mind.

Rebecca scowled down at Hugh Compton, unable to conceal her contempt. He was unconscious on his bed, his breathing ragged, his odor foul. Liquor bottles were scattered about, his pipe tipped over. Like a helpless infant, he'd wet himself but, in his intoxicated condition, he wasn't cognizant of anything.

"Some fancy *lord* you are now, my Hugh." She glanced around at the disgusting chamber, part of the three-room flat she'd located after Michael Stevens had foreclosed on the town house. She'd convinced Hugh to vacate before the embarrassing date, declining to grant Stevens the satisfaction of tossing them into the street like a couple of beggars so, as his men had carted away the last of the furniture, she hadn't had to watch.

What a low level she'd reached by allying herself with Hugh!

When her parents had died four years earlier, and she'd accepted Sarah's invitation to live at Scarborough, she hadn't expected much. A roof over her head, food, companionship. But after she'd ingratiated herself, the possibilities for more had seemed so distinct and so easy to achieve. Especially after her initial excursion to London with Hugh.

Rebecca had been captivated by the gay parties, the jovial people, and she'd quickly determined that she belonged in the city, at the center of the merriment. She'd analyzed and plotted, then she'd promptly set her cap for Hugh.

In the beginning, she'd liked him well enough and had been content hosting his entertainments, supervising his household and social calendar. If he wasn't drinking and carousing, he could be pleasant, but his addiction to his precious Chinese herbs had weakened him until he'd grown surly, impetuous, and, at times, downright dangerous.

Rubbing her side, she felt the bruising from where he'd punched her the prior evening. How had her circumstances been reduced to this? To surviving in a hovel, with a cruel, vicious man who'd double-crossed her at every juncture?

She deserved so much more.

Of course, Hugh charged her with the entire debacle. He never thought anything was his own fault. Having failed in their attempt to bring down Michael Stevens, Hugh had incessantly railed over how she'd misread the outcome.

Sarah had scurried back to Yorkshire—how she'd accomplished the feat was still a mystery—before they could

parlay with her. Michael Stevens had returned to town, bold
as brass, and proceeded about his business as though he'd
done nothing improper.

Rebecca and Hugh had been left standing with their hats
in their hands, like witless fools, and Rebecca was compelled to confirm a lone mistake in her careful planning:
Only she and Hugh had witnessed Sarah's disgrace; they
hadn't brought along any spectators. With Hugh's word
against Stevens's, and considering their history, who would
believe Hugh?

Stevens had deftly rebuffed Hugh's financial stipulations, leaving Hugh with a duel as his sole means of re-
dress, but Hugh would never have challenged Michael
Stevens. Stevens was a master at pistols and swords. Fists,
too. Cowardly Hugh, with his shaky, meager physique,
couldn't have acquired an agreeable result through threat
of violence.

They'd been so assured that Stevens would capitulate,
but they hadn't comprehended that he had no sense of
honor, so he had successfully outmaneuvered them both.
Nary a whiff of scandal had affixed to himself or to Sarah
who was, once again, ensconced as the mistress of Scarborough, persevering as if naught untoward had occurred.

At Rebecca's insistence, Hugh had made a single trip to
the estate, demanding information and assistance, and the
scene between brother and sister had been appalling. Sarah
was furious over Hugh's machinations, and she'd rejected
every proposal and ultimatum, firmly declaring that she
never intended to set eyes upon Michael Stevens again.

The actual particulars as to what had happened between
the two lovers was unclear. Sarah wouldn't say, so Rebecca
didn't know how her cousin had readily moved from a romantic, naked bath frolic to a heightened case of loathing.
Sarah wasn't about to confess that Michael Stevens had
compromised her, and she'd vociferously avowed that if
Hugh so much as hinted of the scandal to others, she would
deny it to her dying breath.

Hugh blamed Sarah for all—when he wasn't blaming

Rebecca. In the wake of the fiasco, he'd selected his usual route for tackling a catastrophe: over-imbibing, smoking herbs, and decrying his fate. When she'd wearied of his diatribe, and had pointed out his specific liability, she'd procured a few hard punches to her rib cage.

"Well, dear Hugh," she murmured, "nobody hits Rebecca and gets away with it."

And nobody breaks a promise, either.

She frowned at the message that had just been delivered. It was from the father of a rich girl he'd been secretly courting. The wealthy merchant had politely and wisely spurned Hugh's offer of marriage, and if Rebecca hadn't been so enraged over Hugh's duplicity, she might have laughed aloud.

The precious heiresses wouldn't have him! Not even to buy the title of countess!

Walking over to him, she held her fingers over his face. The special concoction she'd mixed in his brandy was rapidly taking its toll. He was barely respiring, and it would likely be just a matter of minutes before he ceased altogether, so time was of the essence.

He didn't eat much anymore, so he'd lost weight, and his last ring slid off smoothly. She pocketed it, along with the gold buttons from his coat.

While she'd pinned many hopes on Hugh, and the largess he might eventually supply, she was no fool, either. Her mother's daughter, she'd covertly squirreled away a nest egg, so she'd get by. Not in the lavish mode to which Hugh was accustomed, or in any manner he would have deemed acceptable. But she had enough to buy a small house, and she'd have an income, though insignificant, that would keep her from the poorhouse.

Her only other option was to hie herself off to Scarborough, to dawdle about in the empty mansion with Sarah while her cousin tried to salvage the remnants, which Rebecca wouldn't do. She abhorred the country and thrived in the city, and without Hugh to ruin her prospects, she imagined she'd find ample serenity.

Through her contacts with Hugh, she'd met many gentlemen who delighted in her company. If she calculated correctly, she might still make an advantageous marriage. In the meantime, she'd become friends with a widow who needed lodging. They were compatible and sharing a domicile would decrease expenses. Rebecca would have her own home, where she would look after herself, and she wouldn't have to rely on a lush like Hugh Compton for her daily security.

In the wardrobe, she rifled through in a final search, ferreting out several pound notes, an ivory cigar case, his silver flask. She critically surveyed the rest of the apartment, stumbling on other incidentals that, in her initial haste, she'd omitted. Stuffing all in a drawer, she retired to her cot and snuggled down under the single blanket.

The night passed with agonizing slowness, and she steeled her emotions so that she could manage to appear shocked and overwrought when the serving woman arrived in the morning and found Hugh dead in his bed.

Chapter Twenty-one

Sarah stood in the silent mansion, peeking out the window as a small, black carriage plodded up the drive. The instant it had turned off the main road, she'd noticed it, and the sight filled her with unease, because she couldn't fathom who it might be.

No one visited Scarborough anymore. Between Michael Stevens's despicable avarice, and Hugh's untimely death after a squalid episode in town, she'd become a pariah. Neighbors had been rabid to gossip, chewing over her wretched plight like dogs over a bone, and they'd abandoned her to her fate. She was the talk of the countryside, so she never ventured out, because she couldn't abide the pitying looks, subtle remarks, or false sympathies of those acrimonious people whose welfare she'd valiantly fought to sustain.

In the village, they blamed her for what had transpired at the estate, for the foiled commerce and trade that had unmercifully affected their connected livelihoods, so she stayed at home with the elderly retainers who'd kept working for her merely because they had nowhere else to go.

With Hugh's demise, merchants now made no pretense of denying assistance. Without monetary resources to back up her petitions for coal or edibles, she'd had to survive on what she could scrounge from the gardens, or the pittance of animals that had escaped Michael's notice.

"Wait until we hear from the new earl. We'll decide then," was the standard response to her entreaties.

The sentiment had been expressed on copious occasions, until she'd ultimately realized that it was fruitless to reason with any of them. They were aware that she was at the end of her financial rope. No money would be forthcoming in payment, and if they offered her items on account, they'd never collect.

They were irrationally optimistic, presuming that the unknown earl would fix what she'd broken, and she shook her head at the ludicrousness of their misguided expectations of rescue.

Hugh had died without an heir, and his successor was a distant cousin whom she'd never met and who supposedly resided in Virginia. She'd sent a letter, but with the impeded speed of ocean crossings, it wouldn't reach its destination for weeks, and then several months would pass before she received a reply. And that was *if* she had the correct address and *if* the man was still alive.

She knew nothing of his fiscal assets. If he was a gentleman of modest capital, and he took over the reins of Scarborough, how could he succeed? Very little land came with the inheritance—the unentailed acreage had been sold off long ago—so he couldn't revive the estate through farming, yet the villagers absurdly hoped for an impossible miracle.

Clearly, however, they were no more foolish than she, sitting as she was in the cold, bleak mansion, cursing her fate, and waiting for something—anything—to happen.

What was she going to do? The American earl might not wish to support her, or if a wife accompanied him, the other woman might not care to have Sarah hovering about and interfering. Sarah would have to make her own way, but how and where?

She'd never resided anywhere but Scarborough, had never imagined any other life. With no skills, or the funds with which to alter her fortunes, she had no choices. She was too independent and proud to hire herself out as a maid or governess to an affluent family. The only other option that presented itself was to head for London, to demand her rightful place by her husband's side, but she couldn't debase herself so completely.

Whenever she recalled how he'd exploited her, how he'd

lured her into the mess with Hugh, how he'd swindled Hugh then refused to back down, she saw red.

A gambler! After all she'd endured, she'd cast her lot with a capricious bounder, and she passed her days—when she wasn't fretting about where she'd find food for supper—worrying that he'd publicize their marriage, that he'd forfeit his last farthing in a card game, and then *his* creditors would start pounding on her door.

If that moment ever arrived, she'd journey to town and shoot him right in the middle of his black heart. She didn't own a gun anymore—his henchmen had snared her remaining pistol—but she'd obtain another somehow, and she derived incredible satisfaction from reflecting upon how loud the bang would be, how shocked he'd appear when he fell dead at her feet.

Ooh, she could conceive of it so vividly!

The dark conveyance approached, stark against the white snow that littered the yard and sparkled like brilliant diamonds in the winter sunshine. Eventually, it halted out front. The coachman was bundled in a greatcoat, a cap pulled low. His skin was ruddy, and his breath swirled about his head in a cloud.

"Who could it be?" she pondered aloud, her voice jarring in the empty salon. But for a writing desk and two dilapidated chairs, the furniture was gone, her husband having carried out his threat to call in his markers.

Three weeks after she'd returned from her disastrous visit to Pamela Blair's party, several dozen men had shown up with large freight wagons and pages of lists that enumerated the household items. They'd seized the lot, down to the inkwells and stirring spoons, all those insignificant belongings that her father and Hugh hadn't previously squandered simply because they were so trifling that their value was negligible to any gambler of means.

Apparently, her absent spouse wasn't included in that group. No trinket was too minor to escape Michael Stevens's penurious revenge.

They'd loaded their carts, then departed, weighted down
/ith the scraps of what had been her world.

How could Michael have done this to her? How could
he shame her so terribly? She couldn't begin to theorize as
to what he wanted with the last of her things, or why he
would care about them so vehemently and, when she was
extremely vexed, she'd wonder where he had taken them.

Infrequently, she'd foresee packed boxes, covered with
cloths in a sterile warehouse, drawing dust and mice. Other
times, she'd envision him selling everything at a fair, and
some other faceless, impoverished woman buying all, then
relaxing on what had been her sofa, or seating herself at
the table that had once filled the breakfast parlor.

Given the rundown condition of most of it, perhaps he'd
just dumped it in a pile and burned it. Those ancient beds
and chests of drawers would have burst into a ball of
flames, quickly devouring the evidence of how hard she'd
tried to preserve a heritage that the men of her family had
never respected.

"Bastard . . ." she muttered crudely, though she wasn't
sure to which man she referred.

Unquestionably, her spouse—with his irascible will and
irrational disposition—fit the bill, but the epithet could also
apply to her irresponsible brother who'd had the audacity
to die prematurely at age thirty-two without a cent to his
name.

Sarah's only link to the event had been her receipt of a
disconcerting message from Rebecca, informing her of the
sordid details. Another had come from Hugh's solicitor,
with a polite request as to when Hugh's account might be
squared. The third was from the undertaker, outlining mis-
cellaneous burial costs, but she hadn't had the money for
his London funeral, let alone the quantity required to trans-
port his body to the estate for interment.

Between the two of them, Michael Stevens and Hugh
Compton, and the despicable level to which they'd reduced
her state of affairs, her mind was so disordered, so disjointed and rambling, that she couldn't adequately grasp

what had occurred, nor could she forge a plan for the future. She was bogged down, powerless to advance out of her current doldrums, because she couldn't move beyond her ruminations over their mutual duplicity.

Michael had known Hugh long before she'd ever crossed his path. Their tainted history had crashed into her, running her over like a runaway coach. She'd had the misfortune to be swept up in the catastrophe the pair had instituted, and she wasn't even sure why she'd been at the center.

What had they both been trying to accomplish? Michael, especially. Why had he corrupted her?

On her end, she'd desired him with an uncontrollable, stubborn passion and, because of it, she'd been determined to instigate a liaison and damn the consequences.

But what was his excuse? How did he justify his misdeeds? Was her seduction simply a cruel attempt to further *take* something from Hugh? Was she just one more chattel of Hugh's that Michael wanted to confiscate in order to prove whatever point he'd been so adamant about making?

If she was naught but a pawn in his machinations, then he'd not been fond of her in the slightest. The idea hurt unbearably, for though she was loath to admit it, she'd tossed and turned many a long night, reliving those glorious assignations where they'd learned to love fully, thoroughly, and without reservation.

The loss of that closeness, of the joy and passion they'd shared, was too painful to acknowledge, so she didn't. She declined to ponder why he'd married her, why he'd sent her away immediately after, why she hadn't heard from him since. She wouldn't torture herself with what-ifs and what-might-have-beens, or chastise herself over how she might have handled that final, dreadful day any differently.

Despite the awful factors that had brought them together, she'd been deliriously ecstatic at their wedding, elated over her destiny, only to discover that he considered marriage to her an embarrassment or worse.

Shuddering, she recoiled from the opportunity to wander farther down the road of personal recrimination. She absolutely would not mourn Michael Stevens another second!

The driver hopped down and lowered the step for her visitor, and Sarah was stunned to see Rebecca descending. She was snug in a plush, black cloak, with a matching fur muff and hat. Her china-blue eyes were bright, her cheeks rosy. She looked pretty and flourishing and, by comparison, Sarah felt dowdy in her brown wool gown and heavy boots, her knitted mittens with the fingertips cut out so that she could work on her correspondence, her thick shawl wrapped tight against the chilly temperature.

She hadn't seen Rebecca since that hideous encounter when Hugh had traveled to Yorkshire for the sole purpose of convincing Sarah to seek reparation from Michael. Rebecca had joined with Hugh in spewing outrage over Michael's behavior, but their concern for her welfare had rung false, and she'd ignored their interrogation as to Michael and what had transpired in Bedford. Something—arrogance? stupidity?—had prevented her from confessing that she'd married the blighter, though she couldn't have explained why.

Perhaps it was Hugh's firm resolve to compel Michael to pay for sins that Sarah believed were her own. Or perhaps it was the way Rebecca had gleamed as she'd cajoled over what they could *get* from Michael Stevens.

Sarah wasn't about to help them wheedle their way into Michael Stevens's pocketbook, because she wouldn't humiliate herself by confronting him again when he so obviously despised her. His disregard would have killed her, so she'd denied all and, as far as she knew, no one had a clue that she was wed to the notorious London gambler, the man who'd broken her heart by spurning her on her wedding day. And if she had anything to say about it, no one would, either. She'd cut out her tongue before she'd ever confirm their union.

Rebecca entered on a rush of frigid air, definitely fine, in spite of her ordeals in the large metropolis. She was plump and healthy, plainly not worried about where her next meal was coming from. Her black mourning outfit was beautifully tailored and sewn in a quality fabric.

Sarah had no black attire to wear in order to grieve for her unlamented brother. She'd outgrown the garments she'd donned at her father's passing, and she couldn't employ a seamstress for any excessive alterations. As her cousin walked into the foyer, cocky as a rooster on a summer morning, the very image of perfectly coifed English gentility, Sarah caught herself jealously staring, speculating as to how Rebecca had managed so well.

This isn't fair! she thought irritably, and she didn't even try to quash the petty opinion. Too much had happened in the past six months for her to be feeling charitable.

Since Hugh's death, she and Rebecca had exchanged intermittent letters. Rebecca had purchased a modest residence, had a roommate, and sufficient funds to engage a cook. While she didn't move among the highest echelons of society, she wasn't lacking for entertainment. She attended the theater, various musicales and poetry readings, balls and soirees. Where she'd gotten the money for her new lifestyle was a mystery Sarah didn't prefer to explore.

In her missives, she always urged Sarah to forsake Scarborough and come to town. Sarah regularly declined, and she had the sneaking suspicion that Rebecca tendered the recurrent invitation simply because she was so positive that Sarah would never accept.

Rebecca huddled in her fancy cloak as she scrutinized the vacant space, the bare walls and floors. Sarah had been explicit in her written descriptions, but still, she supposed the changes were difficult to visualize. Rebecca evinced such pity for Sarah's diminished circumstances that Sarah was overcome by a strong desire to slap her.

She didn't want or need this woman's sympathy. She needed cash and time and alternatives, but—heaven forbid—not empathy and certainly not compassion.

"Hello, Rebecca."

They embraced halfheartedly, and her cousin brushed at a few flakes of snow, and Sarah could only peevishly note that the hat, by itself, had probably cost more than she had spent on food in a year.

"My, my, Sarah"—Rebecca disdainfully assessed her surroundings—"you endeavored to elucidate, but I didn't appreciate your desperate predicament until now."

"It could have been worse."

"I don't see how."

"Well, Stevens's men could have set a torch to the house on their way out."

Sarah led her to the parlor, the only room that had a fire going and two chairs to drag next to it. Luckily, the adjoining salon was closed off so Rebecca wouldn't detect that Sarah had made a bedchamber out of it. There wasn't fuel for the elevated floors, so she slept downstairs, heating just the two rooms. Not that the discontinued use of the upper chambers mattered; they contained no furnishings.

"What are you doing such a distance from London?" Her pitiful situation precluded chitchat, and she was glad. She couldn't comprehend why Rebecca had come to call, and she wanted her gone.

"I'm off to a Christmas house party near Middlesbrough, but I couldn't pass so close without stopping."

She then regaled Sarah with boring anecdotes about her fashionable friends, and about her roommate who was awaiting her at the coaching inn in the village, and Sarah was relieved that Rebecca hadn't brought her associate along to witness how far Sarah had fallen.

Sarah was polite and commented where it seemed appropriate, but she couldn't quite enjoy their odd conversation. Rebecca appeared so happy and contented, while Sarah viewed herself as doomed and devastated. The contrasts in their personalities had never been more glaring, and Sarah resentfully discerned that she envied her cousin for her freedom and adaptability.

"I've been thinking about Hugh's body," Rebecca said.

Her bizarre pronouncement terminated Sarah's shallow reverie. "What about it?"

"He needs a proper burial."

"Wouldn't that be nice," Sarah responded sarcastically. "How could I afford it?"

"Well, I understand that you don't like to talk about Mr. Stevens"—her mention of Michael had Sarah fuming—"but he was overly fond of you once, and I was simply curious as to whether you might prevail upon him to have Hugh shipped home. Hugh would have liked to be entombed with some fuss and pomp in the crypt here at Scarborough, and it's a tragedy about his grave in London. Why . . . there isn't even a stone."

"I couldn't pay for one," Sarah testily replied.

"That's just my point, dear." Rebecca leaned over and condescendingly patted Sarah's arm. "My roommate slipped on some ice and injured herself, so we've had unanticipated expenses. I went to Mr. Stevens, myself, just two weeks ago, and appealed for a few pounds to tide us over."

Sarah was murderously calm; her ears must be deceiving her. Battling to maintain an unaffected smile, she blandly declared, "You asked Michael Stevens for money?"

"Yes."

"What did he say?"

"He was exceptionally generous, and he donated much more than I'd solicited."

"How did you dare?"

"I felt he owed us some recompense. After all"—she shifted, her plush skirt swishing at her legs—"you and I weren't involved in his quarrel with Hugh, but look where it left us."

Where it left us, indeed, Sarah thought acridly, gazing around the barren chamber and adjusting her bulky clothes against the cold.

Rebecca preened as though her contacting Michael Stevens was eminently suitable, and Sarah resisted the impulse to scream with frustration.

How could Rebecca communicate with Michael! How could she degrade herself like a common beggar! Didn't she have any pride? Didn't she recognize Michael Stevens for the scoundrel he was?

"I'm surprised he had any blunt to bestow," Sarah stated with more bitterness than she'd intended to show.

"Whatever do you mean?"

"Well, with his being a gambler, I can't believe he has two pennies to rub together."

"Michael Stevens?" Rebecca laughed gaily. "Oh, Sarah, the man is richer than Croesus."

"From gambling?"

"No, silly, from the club he owns with his brother. It's the most popular spot in the city for a gentleman to pass his leisure time."

"But I thought he survived from game to game."

"That he gambled to earn his income? No," Rebecca clarified. "And when he plays for any kind of stakes, it's only with fools."

Like Hugh, was the unuttered reproach.

"But if he's so wealthy . . ." Sarah couldn't say the rest: Why did he do this to me? Why did he leave me like this?

"Why did he take everything?" Rebecca finished for her. "Sarah, his and Hugh's dispute was protracted and bitter. You don't know what Hugh was like in town."

"No, I don't." But she had a fairly good notion. She'd observed Hugh at his worst many, many times. He'd been insufferable.

"While I'm not definite on the particulars of his game with Mr. Stevens, there have been stories. I hate to tell you this, but Hugh probably deserved what he got; he was a total ass, and you must remember that Mr. Stevens's animosity was provoked over a lengthy period of numerous insults."

"Possibly," Sarah mused.

Her mind was reeling, but she could only focus on one, novel fragment of what Rebecca had imparted: Her husband was wealthy. He was economically settled, so much so that he would graciously lavish several pounds on a woman with whom he wasn't acquainted simply because she had the gall to inquire.

Slowly, her temper ignited. For months, she'd been struggling to recover from being captured in the whirlwind that had enveloped Michael. She'd been languishing from terrible bouts of melancholia, incapable of dealing with how Michael had burst into her life, then vanished like a magician in a puff of smoke.

She was enraged. About how he'd failed to trust her. About how he'd manipulated and abused her. About how he'd abandoned her to flounder and wallow in the poverty he'd inflicted.

While Rebecca was smartly dressed and on her way to Christmas festivities, Sarah was scrounging for the barest necessities, grappling with debt collectors, searching for pen and foolscap so that she could draft her daily rationales as to why they must continue to wait for compensation.

Fury burst upon her in a wave of unrelenting ire. How could he treat her so shabbily? And why had she allowed it?

He'd sent her to Yorkshire like a naughty child, and she'd scurried home, with nary a complaint or thought as to whether his decision was correct.

His conflict had been with Hugh, not her, and she was tired of being painted the villain. Hugh was dead, interred in a pauper's grave, and Sarah was Michael's wife. The man had responsibilities to her. No one had forced him into marriage; he'd done so freely, albeit reluctantly, and it was past time he honored his vows.

Suddenly sensing that she'd overstayed her welcome, Rebecca rose and prepared to depart, prattling on as to how her companion would be getting anxious.

"Don't let me keep you," Sarah advised, sounding horridly uncivil.

"I wish you'd come to London." Rebecca repeated her overture. "I hate to see your dire straits, so please say yes. We've an extra room that could be yours. Would you like me to stop by on the return trip? You could ride with us. We'd have space for a bag or two."

"No, Rebecca, but thank you."

Then and there, she decided she'd make her way to town, but not for any of the reasons Rebecca might conjure up. She had words—a few nasty, indelicate, rude words— that she planned to speak to her *husband.* And by God, he was going to listen to every one of them, if she had to tie him down while she said her piece!

"At least, let me give you this." Rebecca held out a bag of coins, and Sarah didn't hesitate to grab it. "It's some of what Mr. Stevens dispensed."

"How wonderful!" She derived perverse pleasure from knowing that she would pay for her excursion with the cad's very own money.

Rebecca strolled out, and the carriage whisked her away. Sarah watched until it was just a dot on the horizon, then she marched to her lonely, desolate parlor, delighted that Rebecca had visited, relieved that the woman's disclosures had spurred her to action.

"Well, Mr. Stevens," she announced to the dying fire, "I'm off to London. What do you think of that?"

Pitching the bag from hand to hand, she relished the coins clinking together as she pictured how astonished he'd be when he opened his door to discover her on his stoop.

Was he in for it! Very likely, his ears were already ringing.

Chapter Twenty-two

Abigail Weston Stevens was walking down the stairs when she heard a knock on the front door. Previously, she might have ignored it, anticipating that the butler would take on the mundane chore that she would have deemed beneath her station but, in the past year, her life had been transformed. For the better.

She wasn't in her brother's grand mansion, filled with dozens of servants, but in James's small house that was truly a home. Fondly, she tended to, and oversaw, the cheery abode in her recurrent efforts to instill the sense of serenity and closeness that James had missed out on while growing up.

Marriage had definitely generated changes! By allying herself with the nefarious rake, she'd been altered in more ways than she could count. Lovingly, she traced a hand along the swelling in her abdomen, the babe he'd so lustily planted just beginning to show.

As always happened when she thought of her robust, vital husband, butterflies swarmed through her stomach. She was so appallingly happy! Each day was superior to the last, just as she'd surmised they would be when she'd begged him to make her his bride.

Since they'd been together, James had calmed and matured, delighting in the simple pleasures. They were a family, and with the approach of summer, their number would increase by one more when she gifted him with a beautiful son or daughter. A wave of tender sentiment brought tears that moistened her eyes. With her pregnancy in full bloom, she cried about everything and nothing, and she tried to quell the surge of emotion but, as she sauntered over to greet her visitor, she could barely contain her joy.

She turned the knob, and she wasn't really thinking about who she might encounter—perhaps one of James's business associates or one of his employees—but the pretty woman lingering on the stoop had her snapping to attention. Her comely face and unique auburn hair were mostly shielded from view by her dark cloak, and Abigail suffered a moment of uncanny compassion as she recalled her own furtive trip the prior spring to see James's mother, Angela Ford, and her beseeching Angela to aid in convincing James to wed.

"May I help you?" Her curiosity was thoroughly piqued.

"I hope so. I realize this is terribly forward of me." The woman blushed becomingly, and nervously glanced about, checking that she had the correct address, then she braced herself. "I was advised that this is the residence of Michael Stevens, and I must speak with him."

"And you are . . . ?"

"Sarah . . ." Nodding authoritatively, she added, "Sarah Compton . . . Stevens." She pronounced *Stevens* as though it didn't fit on her tongue.

"I'm Abigail Stevens. I'm married to James. Are we related?"

"Yes." The woman studied her carefully. "Michael is my husband."

"Your what?"

"My husband," she repeated, daring Abigail to dispute her allegation.

"Oh, my . . ." Abigail was totally flustered. Could it be true? With Michael and his bizarre mode of carrying on, she supposed anything was conceivable. Even an unknown wife! "When . . . ?" she managed.

"In June."

"But that was six months ago!"

Just about the time his excursion to the country had ended, and he'd stumbled into London, so lost and forlorn. Little had varied since then. He was reclusive, morose, incomprehensible in his conduct and methods. Abigail had struggled to befriend him, but he was an elusive thorn in her side, rebuffing her and James's attempts at reconciliation—when she wasn't positive what they needed to *reconcile*.

"Forgive me," she said, as she recalled her manners and gestured. "Come in, come in."

"Thank you."

Abigail ushered Sarah into the foyer and, as the butler retrieved her cloak, Abigail quietly counseled a footman to dismiss Sarah's rented hack. Their pending discussion would last more than a few minutes, so the driver needn't tarry.

They entered the parlor, and Abigail noticed that Sarah was chilled to the bone and, as Abigail ordered snacks and tea, she wondered how far the woman had traveled—and how dreadful had been her journey!

She was brave to show up unannounced, but Abigail was tickled that she had. Whatever hideous misery was gnawing at Michael, perhaps the basis was about to be revealed, which was an immense relief. There was a mystery here, and she was determined to get to the bottom of it.

Michael had undergone numerous modifications in his personality that had reshaped his relationship with James, and James was bewildered by the loss of their friendship. He couldn't mend the rift that had developed, and it was tormenting him.

Introspective, pensive, covert, Michael had always been somewhat reserved, but now, he was taciturn to the point of absurdity. James swore that something was terribly wrong, that an egregious incident had occurred while he'd been away. Michael wouldn't—or couldn't—talk about it, and James couldn't break through Michael's melancholy.

His younger brother lived by himself, in a house James owned a few blocks down the street. Michael worked, he ate, he slept, but he was like a person who was dead inside. There was no enjoyment or satisfaction as he went about his responsibilities. The contentment James assured her had once been there was gone.

Had this woman been the root of his affliction? If so, would she be the cure?

Optimistic, she sat forward. "We're sisters-in-law."

"You believe me, then?"

Sarah was so clearly relieved that Abigail could only smile. "Of course I believe you." Who would lie about being married to Michael? While the man was as good-looking and intriguing as her husband, he was so enigmatic that he frightened her. "Why wouldn't I?"

"Well, my impromptu visit is rather odd."

No more *odd* than when Abigail had confronted Angela Ford, but she didn't mention it. "What shall I call you? Since we're both *Mrs.* Stevens, the formality is a bit ridiculous."

"Sarah."

"And I'm Abigail."

From Sarah's comportment and demeanor, Abigail discerned her to be of the Quality. "Who is your family, Sarah? Did you say Compton?"

"Yes."

"Are you, by chance, related to the recently deceased Hugh Compton, Earl of Scarborough?"

"He was my brother."

An earl's daughter! An earl's sister! Abigail was stunned. Michael had privately and clandestinely married into the aristocracy, and he'd kept it a grand secret. Why?

The shocking gossip about Hugh Compton rushed back. While he'd been alive and provoking mischief, it had been impossible to avoid the sordid stories. James, who was a constant fount of discourse on the rich and infamous, had imparted his portion of them, but no one had ever hinted at this information.

Michael had surreptitiously married Scarborough's sister, and neither Hugh nor Michael had ever whispered a word about it. Had Hugh Compton even known? What did it all mean?

Abigail relaxed on the sofa, the preposterous revelation sinking in. She almost couldn't credit the woman's statement, yet she did. A deep wound had been haunting Michael, plaguing him heart and soul, but in their ruminating over the probable cause of his injury, they'd never conjured up an explanation like this!

"Sarah, I imagine you have a very fascinating tale to relate. Would you mind waiting for my husband? He'll be interested in your comments." At the reference to James, Sarah appeared ready to bolt, and Abigail laid a consoling hand on her arm. "Whatever it is, he'll be an incredible help to you."

"Are you sure?"

"He has an extraordinary knack for sorting out problems and devising solutions."

Abigail walked to the hall and conferred with their majordomo Arthur, who efficiently hovered nearby. His brows flew up in amazement as he learned of their guest's identity and, with no further urging, he hurried off to roust James out of bed.

A maid brought refreshments, and Abigail was offered a reprieve from conversation while Sarah wrapped her fingers around a hot cup of tea and absorbed its warmth. From how she gobbled down the slices of meat, cheese, and bread, it was obvious that she was famished.

When did you last have a decent meal?

Abigail was saved from posing the indelicate question aloud because, just then, James hustled in.

Considering how rapidly he'd been awakened, he was flawlessly dressed, and intent on beholding Sarah Compton Stevens with his own two eyes.

"James"—Abigail rose placidly and went to him, silently begging for calm—"I'm so glad you're here. The most marvelous guest has stopped by."

"Yes, Arthur informed me." He stomped across the floor until he was directly in front of Sarah. "Excuse my abruptness. I'm James, Michael's brother."

"No apology is necessary," Sarah graciously indicated. "My arrival was unforeseen, but I was so eager to meet with Michael. I came here straightaway."

Abigail conceded, "And we're delighted that you did."
James made no signal of agreement, so Abigail poked him
in the ribs. "Aren't we?"

"Yes," he then replied emphatically, "we certainly are."

Sarah stood, and they scrutinized one another like pred-
ators circling before combat. Seeming astonished that two
such attractive, potent men could exist simultaneously, she
eventually noted, "You look just like him."

"No"—James's smile heated the room—"you're mistaken. I'm *much* more handsome."

"Oh, James," Abigail chastised, but his stab at humor
was successful. Sarah's tension eased as she finally comprehended that she was safe and wouldn't be sent packing.
"Let's sit, shall we? I gather we're in for a lengthy and
engaging narration."

"And I for one," James retorted, "can't wait to hear the
details."

They adjusted themselves on the furniture, facing one
another, and Abigail discreetly pressed food on Sarah while
the woman regaled them about her adversity with Michael.
Although she omitted the juiciest parts, they concluded that
Michael had compromised her and married her because of
it.

But as her recital continued, as she depicted how he'd
sent her home to fend for herself, as she described the autumn and the seizure Michael had accomplished of all
Hugh's belongings, as she itemized the poverty and hardship she'd been constrained to endure, they stiffened with
outrage. James, especially, was disturbed by how badly Michael had behaved.

As she reached her summation, explicating how she'd
decided to head for London, Sarah's ire equaled their own,
her temper rekindled by her accounting.

James was irate, unable to be still, pacing behind the
couch, and Abigail received the distinct impression that Michael was lucky he was absent. Her husband and sister-in-
law had allied against him, and they were dangerously bent
on getting answers from the unsuspecting man. Abigail

would have felt sorry for him had he not acted the categorical bounder toward Sarah.

"What now?" she asked into the deafening silence that ensued once Sarah finished her chronicle.

James summoned Arthur to fetch his coat. "It's high time my brother and I had a chat."

"Do you know where he is?" Sarah queried.

"I might." His response was intentionally ambiguous.

"I'll go with you." Sarah crossed the room, prepared to join in the search.

"Perhaps it would be best if you stayed here with Abigail." He stared at Abigail, seeking her intervention. "I'll be back shortly."

"I've planned this moment for six months," Sarah asserted, "and I won't delay another second. I'm going!"

She proclaimed it with such finality that Abigail couldn't see how James would dissuade her. Nevertheless, he visually spurred Abigail to intercede as he implored, "I really don't think that's wise."

James was outright pleading now, and suddenly, Abigail got his message. "Oh, dear . . ." she grumbled, not meaning to grouse audibly.

"What is it?" Sarah asked.

Abigail sighed. Poor Sarah had been through so much; she didn't need any grave tidings. "James is right," Abigail gently cautioned, "perhaps you should remain behind."

"I'm not a child." Sarah glared testily at both of them. "I demand the truth."

James flashed Abigail a tortured look, in typically male fashion, incompetent to elucidate, forcing her to do the dirty deed. "Michael probably isn't alone."

"With whom would he be?"

Abigail yearned to soften the blow but couldn't decipher how to make it sound less damaging than it was. "Presumably, he's with Pamela."

"Pamela . . . Pamela Blair?"

"Yes." Abigail drew near to her. "He's been cavorting quite shamelessly with her since last summer."

"There've been rampant rumors they might marry," James felt obliged to append.

"James!" Abigail scolded, and he reddened at how his disclosure affected Sarah.

Her legs had ceased to support her, and she sank onto the sofa. "But she's my friend."

"I'd bet my last pound that she doesn't know about the two of you," James inappropriately interjected. "Michael hasn't confided in anyone."

Abigail was exasperated with James. His remarks were cutting like a knife. Obtuse creature! In light of his employment and the uproars in which he typically became embroiled, he was usually adept at handling the most difficult situations. The fact that he was stumbling only underscored how rattled he was by Michael's deportment, so she couldn't be too aggravated.

She sat with Sarah and held her hand. "What James is clumsily saying"—she optically threatened him with dismemberment—"is that we don't understand Michael anymore or what's troubling him. He's been so contrary that we hardly know him."

"Exactly," James put in. "He's so strange, and he's been so uncommunicative, that he and I scarcely converse. I've always assumed that he endured a trauma while he was away, but I've never ascertained what it was."

"He seems heartbroken to me. Very sad," Abigail volunteered. "He's grieving." Encouragingly, she suggested, "Perchance, he's hurting over what transpired, and he can't figure out how to mend your differences."

"Carrying on with Pamela . . ." Sarah muttered to herself. "I will *absolutely* wring his pitiful neck!" Blatantly furious, she marched over to James, fists clenched, eyes sparking with rage. "Take me to him immediately!"

James appealed to Abigail for guidance, but she merely shrugged. "Maybe you should." She brightened. "We'll all go."

"*We* will not!" James declared, then cleared his throat. "I mean . . . I want to keep you out of it."

"Why? Sarah may need me."

"Abby . . ."

She bristled over his reticence. He was, once again, treating her like some wilting noblewoman, and she hated it. "You're embarrassed to introduce me to Michael's"—she almost said *mistress* but couldn't utter the despicable term in front of Sarah, so she switched to—"companion. Honestly, James, I won't expire."

"This might not be pretty, and I won't have you involved." Disconcerted, he reminded her, "The babe's been making you ill all morning."

"But I'm fine now."

Not wishing to induce dissension, Sarah interposed, "James is prudent to fret over you, Abigail. Michael and I both have tempers, so what I have to say to the cad won't be pleasant."

"Please?" James sweetly requested. "For me?"

"All right," she griped, powerless to refuse him anything. "But you must promise that you'll relay all the gory particulars; you can't leave anything out! And Sarah . . ."—she went to her newfound sister-in-law and enveloped her in a tight hug—"if your meeting with him is overly wretched, return here at once. You're family; we'll help you."

"You're very kind, Abigail."

They departed together; James guided Sarah into his carriage, then he scrambled in behind, and Abigail watched, feeling left out.

"Come for supper," she called at the last, "and bring Michael with you—if you can!"

Sarah waved her confirmation, as James pulled the door closed and motioned to the driver. Abigail lingered until they disappeared around the corner.

Sarah loitered in Michael's bedchamber and critically surveyed her surroundings. There had been a few signs of Pamela's occupancy, but after James had acquainted her

with the staff, they had readily complied in assisting her to
erase any evidence of the other woman. The handful of
combs, the red silk petticoat, and the slinky peignoir she'd
located were currently being delivered to Pamela's own
domicile.

Satisfied with her afternoon's endeavors, she descended
the stairs to sit with James in the parlor where he was patiently sipping on a brandy while awaiting his brother.

Michael's house was a charming place that James had
purchased years earlier for his first wife and, from the moment they'd arrived, James had acutely enjoyed himself as
Sarah had stormed about. Her fury had escalated as she'd
proceeded from room to room, witnessing how comfortable
Michael had been while she'd been scrimping and freezing
in the country.

The three-story row house was nearly identical to the
one where James and Abigail lived. On a busy, affable lane,
it was cozy and plushly decorated with a welcoming ambiance. There was a feminine flavor to the decor that she
liked, and she couldn't move beyond the despicable, petty
notion that this warm, snug abode could have been hers—
had she not been a coward and let Michael contend that
their marriage was a fraud.

When they'd shown up at his door, Michael had been
out, but the servants had insisted he'd be back soon, so
they'd bided their time rather than track him all over London. Yet, once they'd settled in, Sarah couldn't abide the
dawdling. She'd begun exploring, and though Michael's
personal mark was scarcely apparent, his clothes were in
an upstairs bedchamber—along with some of Pamela's. If
Sarah hadn't been so angry, she might have been shattered.

While they'd been separated, she'd convinced herself
that she had no feelings for her husband. During those long,
lonely months at Scarborough, she'd persuaded herself that
their brief affair had been an aberration, that she hadn't
loved him madly and passionately but, as she'd fingered his
apparel and shaving equipment, as she'd rifled through his
dresser—just as she'd loved to do when they were together

in Bedford—the sorry truth had crashed down on her. His presence had been so strong that she'd been impelled to admit how much she still cared.

How could he have set her aside so easily?

From what James had imparted, she was aware that Michael had come back to the city, then started up with Pamela shortly after. He'd hardly blinked between taking a wife and taking a mistress.

What was she to make of such disrespect?

She appreciated that he was overly virile and had an unrelenting sexual drive, that he regularly assuaged it with any woman who acted the least bit interested, so she harbored no illusions about his carnal attributes. Yet, she was stunned that he'd so hastily turned to another lover.

Oh, how it distressed her to acknowledge that she hadn't mattered to him! That she very likely hadn't crossed his mind after he'd walked away from the small church where they'd wed.

Well, Michael Stevens was in for a surprise. Sarah had had plenty of opportunity to reflect during the laborious, frigid trek to London. She craved a valid marriage, and she wanted a house full of boisterous children, with Michael as their father.

With the exception of the unfathomable Rebecca, her own family was nonexistent. Her father and mother were dead, and Hugh—pitiful Hugh, whom she didn't mourn or miss—the last of their line. The Scarborough estate she'd fought so valiantly to protect wasn't hers. She belonged nowhere and felt as if she had no past or future, and the single component that connected her to the rest of the world was that she had a spouse; a husband who didn't fancy her, but that was about to change.

If the trying killed her, they would come to terms with what had transpired. Michael Stevens hadn't discovered what her father and Hugh had always known: She was stubborn and determined. She didn't quit, she didn't surrender, and she never capitulated until she'd achieved her goal.

From her perspective, conditions looked desperate; she

was out of options, and she wouldn't desist until she had, once again, broken through Michael's wall of reserve. She hadn't forgotten what it was like to have his undivided attention, to bask in his admiration, to win his regard. There was nothing quite so fine as holding him close while knowing that she was the sole person who had ever loved him. He was no match for her in resolve or persistence.

She stepped into the parlor just as a key clicked in the lock. Her heart skipped several beats, her step faltered, but she regrouped, ready for battle.

"Are you up to this?" James asked.

"Yes."

"Abigail and I are here for you."

She smiled at the man who was already a good friend. "I'm grateful."

"If he tosses us out on our ear . . ."

"I won't permit it," she scoffed. "Your brother's days of bossing me around have ended."

"I can see that." James chuckled at her pluck and tucked her arm in his. "But in case you've miscalculated, you can stay with us for as long as you like."

What amenable news! To be granted shelter! Somewhere clean and safe, where people cared about her! Until that precise moment, she hadn't truly believed that she could escape her seriously dire straits.

"Your hospitality won't be necessary. Michael will be thrilled to see me." They walked out to the foyer. "It just might take him a while to realize it."

They halted in front of the door, and Michael strolled in—with Pamela by his side. She was lovely as ever, fashionable in a dark fur cloak and hat, with red feathers dangling over her shoulder. Her nose and cheeks rosy-red, she was laughing over something Michael had just said.

It had commenced snowing, and a flurry of huge, white flakes cascaded in behind them. Michael stamped his feet against the cold, then spun around and espied them huddled, critical and condemning, but as was his habit, he displayed no outward sign of consternation or recognition.

Sarah might have been crushed by his seeming lack of reaction, but she wouldn't allow herself to grapple with pity or regret. She simply stared, then stared some more.

He was more handsome than she remembered, and her heart ached at observing his masculine beauty up close. She had never been able to gaze upon him without being moved. He was too dynamic, too commanding, and her pulse wasn't steady.

With the snow dusting his hair and shoulders, his blue eyes aloof and withdrawn, he appeared distant, unapproachable, unattainable, and she steeled herself to the daunting task that lay before her. She would not fail in claiming him for her own!

"James . . ." Michael nodded. "Sarah . . ." he adjoined cautiously.

"Why, Sarah Compton," Pamela gushed merrily. "How wonderful that you're in London! You're the very last individual I expected to see in town today!"

"I'll bet," Sarah responded miserably, reining in her resentment. Pamela wasn't cognizant of the circumstances; the blackguard had never told her!

Pamela clutched Sarah's hands and gave her an affectionate kiss on the cheek. "How have you been?"

"Fine," Sarah lied.

"In June, you abandoned my party so fast that we never even said good-bye!"

"I'm sorry." Sarah threw Michael a quelling glare that he coolly mirrored. "Michael promised he'd make my apologies."

"Oh, he did, but you know men!" Pamela gestured gaily, flinging them all off as unreliable. "He wouldn't say why you'd gone. I hope you weren't upset about anything . . . ?"

There was a question posed in her remark, and Sarah's wrath intensified. How dare Michael do this to Pamela! How dare he put Sarah in such an awkward position!

Tired of the ruse, wishing the acrimony over, she barked at Michael. "Tell her."

"Tell me what?" Pamela innocently grinned up at Michael who was wholly unaffected.

"Tell her!" Sarah repeated sharply.

"Sarah and I married," Michael acclaimed, calm as all get out.

"When?" Pamela choked, instantly looking sick.

"That last day in Bedford."

Pamela's mouth fell open. "All this time . . . you were . . ." She couldn't complete her sentence, and her expression was so full of indignation that Sarah was somewhat appeased. "Oh, you unmitigated rogue! How could you!"

"That's what I've been dying to know," James accused, tensing with virulent menace. "I'd love to have your answer, brother—if you think you could possibly provide one that I would tolerate."

Michael was firmly, doggedly silent, though his eyes glittered with a peculiar fire. A thousand words were poised on the tip of his tongue, but Sarah knew him well. He'd never speak up in the middle of this vile scene.

"Sarah," Pamela interrupted, "forgive me! I had no idea!"

"I believe you."

"You're my friend. I would never . . ." She cast Michael another scathing look. "I am so mortified! I should go . . ."

But she didn't depart, and an awkward interlude developed, so Sarah said, "I'm going upstairs to dress for supper. You have five minutes to make your farewells. Then, I don't want you over here again."

"No, I won't come by," Pamela vowed, shaking her head in dismay, "but would you . . . would you visit me later? After everything is more settled?"

"We'll see," Sarah blandly acquiesced.

Sarah turned to James. "I won't be having supper with Abigail this evening. I'm dining in—with my husband. I'll send a note to her on the morrow."

"No need." James expressed. He leaned near and whispered, "If it turns out that you can't bear to stay, send one of the servants to my club. They'll know where. I'll come and get you. Despite the hour."

"I won't require any assistance." Climbing the first two steps, she spun around, then glared down at Michael and Pamela. Michael still exhibited no emotion, while Pamela looked as though she yearned to shrivel into a ball and die. "Pamela, I'm sure you didn't mean any harm, but I intend to keep my husband. If I catch you sniffing around him again, I'll break both your legs. I swear it!"

"Oh, God . . ." Pamela blushed furiously.

"Even if he begs, don't meet with him ever again. Don't make this any worse than it already is."

"No, I won't, Sarah. I promise you!"

"And do me a favor?"

"Anything."

"Spread the word to his other paramours: I won't have him philandering. He's mine. And I'm not sharing!"

As she hurled the challenge, she met Michael's gaze, and something dangerous and unreadable flickered in his eyes, then vanished. She stormed up the stairs, not glancing back.

Chapter Twenty-three

Michael frowned at Sarah's pretty backside as she marched up the stairs. She was a sight, with all that wifely affront directed at himself and Pamela. With her proprietary disposition, and that affectation of umbrage and offense, it almost seemed as though she was truly perturbed, but then, she was a terrific actress. She could have made a name for herself on the stage alongside his mother.

Once the sound of her wrathful retreat had faded, he stirred uncomfortably, sequestered as he was with Pamela and James. Their joint censure was tangible, their anger explicit, their dismay substantial.

"I could wring your bloody neck." Pamela seethed with righteous indignation, and he couldn't blame her.

He'd longed to confide in her, but he couldn't discuss the anguish and disappointment he'd suffered at Sarah's hands. Pamela would have listened and advised, but Michael couldn't bring himself to confess.

Straining, he tried to decipher where Sarah's footsteps had led her, and he surmised that she was in his bedchamber. Sighing, he pondered why she'd feel free to rummage around in his personal apartment. She couldn't be moving in and making herself at home! They weren't destined to cohabitate, and he was curious as to why she'd finally come slinking to town.

What was she doing here? Why now? What sort of disaster did her presence portend?

On dozens of occasions, he'd picked up a pen, aspiring to write and inquire after her circumstances—especially after Hugh had died—but he hadn't been able to put ink to parchment.

When her cousin had solicited money, which he'd supplied with nary a thought, he'd been hard-pressed to keep
from plying her for details as to how Sarah was faring.
After Miss Monroe's departure, he'd stewed for hours,
searching for some method of mending their predicament,
but he'd generated no ideas, and he'd ultimately determined
that any communication would have been pointless. If he'd
contacted her, what would he have said?

That he was sorry? He wasn't.

That he missed her? He didn't.

That he apologized? He wouldn't.

That he wished things had ended differently? Now, that
was a question worth considering.

Whenever he closed his eyes, he envisioned her dancing
out of the church after their wedding ceremony, clutching
her pathetic bouquet and smiling joyfully. Her emotion had
seemed so real, as though she'd developed a genuine *tendre*
for him that had nothing to do with Hugh or his scheming.

How she'd feigned such valid sentiment was a mystery.
Why she would pretend such extreme affection had kept
him up many nights since they'd separated. On that fateful,
hideous wedding day, he'd been so angry, and she'd been
so happy, and there hadn't been a way for those two human
conditions to meld.

Since then, there'd been no suitable opportunity for reconciliation, though he couldn't fathom what needed to be
resolved. She and her dubious brother had endeavored to
blackmail him into a financial rescue that he would never
undertake. He and Sarah were strangers, from opposite
worlds, and she was Scarborough's sister, by Hugh's own
admission, as fully capable of deceit as Hugh had ever
been. They had no common ground, or mutual foundation
of trust, so why had he married her?

He'd asked himself as much a thousand times and still
hadn't marshaled a viable answer. During the fiasco, he'd
just been so shocked and overwhelmed. Her chicanery and
betrayal had wounded him, and he'd needed to ruthlessly
react, so marrying her had seemed a sufficient punishment.

Since meeting her, he'd become a fool. Where Sarah Compton—*Stevens* a tiny voice added—was concerned, he couldn't locate solid ground. The earth kept shifting under his feet, inducing him to sway and vacillate from one bad decision to the next. He'd wed her in a fit of pique, he'd sowed the oats of his wretched future, and she was his now, whether he wanted her or not.

She'd arrived, demanding respect, recognition, most likely money, and he couldn't begin to guess what else.

What a tangle!

Pamela stepped in front of him. "You'd better hie yourself up those stairs and do some fast talking. Tell her the truth, or I'll never forgive you." Snapping the clasp on her cloak, she huffed to the door. "I may not forgive you anyway!"

"If you can wait just a bit, Pam," James injected, "I'll see you home."

"My carriage is parked out front," she said, and she paused, not quite geared for farewell. Squeezing Michael's fingers, she entreated, "Don't call on me, darling. I'm not interested in your justifications, and I'd die if she learned that you'd stopped by!" In parting, she stole a quick kiss. "I don't understand any of this, but you need to work it out with her. You won't regret it."

As she walked out into the cold afternoon, he made no *au revoir*. In a smattering of minutes, he'd gained a wife he didn't want and lost a friend he'd truly miss. The day had gone to hell, and it wasn't even four o'clock. He leaned against the door, physically bracing himself for whatever James was about to say.

Through the awkward silence that followed, he couldn't look at his brother, so he stared at his feet instead, remembering all the prior occasions when they'd had a good row, when they'd argued and fought, counseled and coerced, consoled and constrained. How he had always loved James! But just now, he couldn't bear to hear the questionable words of wisdom his older brother might choose to impart.

"What happened?" James queried with much more calm than Michael had predicted.

"You're aware of the card game Scarborough and I played last spring."

"Yes."

"So, you know how he was acting. His derogatory remarks. I couldn't back down."

"I'm surprised you didn't call him out. I would have."

"I judged it more gratifying to have him alive and paying through the nose." His blasted pride never ceased to get him into trouble. Why had he let Hugh goad him to such absurdity?

"What about *her*?" James referred to Sarah.

"She was at Pamela's party."

"Did you debauch her to retaliate against Hugh?"

"No . . . yes . . ." He dug the heels of his hands into his eyes. "Maybe. I'm not sure. She was staying in the room next to mine. I couldn't resist." Brimming with memories recollecting all, he reminisced over how sweet it had been, and his heart constricted and ached. "I wanted her," he inevitably affirmed, "and it didn't have anything to do with her brother."

"I never suspected it had. She's quite stunning."

"Aye."

"So . . . you seduced her?"

"Yes, but she was simply plotting with Hugh, working us into a compromising situation so they could extort money—and compel the cancellation of his markers."

James bristled. "Who told you that?"

"Scarborough, himself."

"You believed him?"

"Why wouldn't I?" Michael's sizzling gaze locked on James's, and he encountered conspicuous skepticism. "She left the door unlocked."

"Are you positive?"

No, he yearned to shout, but he was no longer certain. "Hugh insisted that they'd concocted it together. That she'd been involved every step of the way."

"If you buy that nonsense"—James advanced until they were toe to toe—"why did you marry her?"

He gulped, struggling to breathe. "Because I didn't want anyone to think I'm like our father."

James laid a hand on his shoulder, and for once, Michael didn't shake it off. "Hugh was lying to you. About her. About her participation."

"How can you be so confident?"

"I quizzed her extensively. She was caught up—just as you were."

"What if you're mistaken?"

"I'm not," he said evenly. "Promise me you'll let her explain her side of it. And get a few things off her chest. She's fairly vexed with you."

"As I am with her."

"She's had a difficult few months."

"So have I," Michael irascibly contended.

"And with Scarborough dead"—James wouldn't argue when Michael would have loved nothing more than an enthusiastic spat—"she has nowhere to go, and no visible means of support. She needs your protection."

The information made him hesitate. Many a night he'd tossed and turned in his lonely bed, wondering what would befall her, but he'd refused to fret. His cup overflowed with recrimination, but immature as it sounded, his vanity wouldn't allow him to grovel before her, offering unwanted aid that he was convinced she'd throw in his face.

"What would you have me do? Beg her to take advantage of me? To rifle through my pockets so she can pilfer the last of my coins?"

"The solution is up to you," James stated, "but you're going to have to *do* something. She's here, she's your wife, and, from what she told Abigail and me, she won't be leaving anytime soon." His grin was full of mischief. "I hauled her trunk upstairs. She's already unpacked."

"Why, thank you, brother," he remarked sarcastically, gnashing his teeth.

"Glad to help." James chuckled and bowed mockingly,

and strangely, the silly display made Michael feel better than he had in a long while, and he realized that they hadn't joked in ages.

"God, what a mess," he mused.

"Look . . . she came to you," James indicated. "She took the first step. Can't you meet her somewhere in the middle?"

"Count on you to say something thoroughly idiotic."

"Now . . . now . . ."—James lectured like a seasoned old man—"being married is *not* the end of the world. If you give it a try, you might even grow to like it."

Michael looked at his brother, *really* looked for a change. He was contented as he never had been before. The rough edges of dissatisfaction and disappointment that had shadowed his character, and driven his reckless behavior, had vanished, replaced by a disgusting veneer of blissfulness that only the newly married could ever manifest.

"Go home, James." He was eager to be spared this novel glimpse of his brother. Besides, it was time to confront his wife, so he opened the door and pushed James out.

"For once in your life," James admonished, "do the right thing, will you?"

"I don't know what the *right* thing is," he rejoined truthfully.

"Yes you do," James asserted with smug confidence. "If you need me, send a message. I'll come back immediately."

"As if I could stomach more of your bloody assistance," he grumbled as he shut the door, his final view of James, his complacent, irritating grin.

The silence of the house enveloped him. His handful of well-trained servants were politely absent, leaving him to his bitter introspection. Then, the inevitable couldn't be avoided, and he mounted the stairs, his tread heavy, like a condemned man to the gallows.

Where she was concerned, he'd developed a second sense, so his intuition easily guided him to her. From the threshold to his bedchamber, he could distinguish her movements in the adjacent room where she was boldly preparing to take a bath. As was her habit, she'd added rose oil to the water. The smell permeated the air and tickled his nostrils.

The sleeping arrangements were very much as they had been in the country: two bedchambers divided by a communal dressing room. For a brief instant, he presumed that she'd moved into the adjoining salon, but then he saw her combs on his dresser, her corset draped over a chair. He stalked to the wardrobe and peeked in. Three of her dresses were hanging next to his shirts.

Did she propose that they would share a bed as man and wife? They wouldn't spend any time sleeping! Surely, the insane woman realized that fact! His physical fascination with her hadn't waned in the slightest. Just the thought of her readying to bathe sent the blood surging to his loins.

His temper flared. Six months had passed, and without notice or warning, she had the audacity to show up and insinuate herself into his house and his bed. How was a man to cope rationally with such a contingency? Did she hope for a platonic accord? Or did she fancy they would carry on as lovers?

At the notion, his cock distended brutally, and he resolved not to give her a choice. She'd foolishly inserted herself into his life, so she would suffer the consequences— although *suffer* was probably not the correct term. After he'd initiated her into the sexual arts, she'd developed into an adept, proficient lover so the *suffering*, such as it was, would be magnificent, and he would wallow in every erotic, disturbing minute of it.

He approached the dressing room and, through the crack in the door, he could see her. She was undressing, and he stealthily and inappropriately spied. Had she decided to use a flash of bare skin in order to entice him to commit acts he didn't intend?

Well, whatever her game, she'd miscalculated. If she was careless enough to imprudently disrobe before his very eyes, she would pay whatever price he extracted.

Poised on the brink, cognizant that he should announce

his presence, he couldn't impel himself to stop her. Like a practiced courtesan, she'd undone the buttons and ties on her gown and was slowly tugging it to her waist, past her hips, until it pooled on the floor.

She lifted her foot onto a stool, furnishing him with a wide expanse of naked thigh as she removed one shoe and the other, pitching them with an unceremonious clump. In a smooth motion, her chemise was off, and momentarily, she wore only a pair of her sheer French drawers, stockings, and garters.

A gentleman with even the smallest measure of civility would have departed, but like a perverted voyeur, he wrongly watched her stripping. Irreverent as always, he didn't care as to her opinion of his conduct. She appreciated the sort of scoundrel he was, yet she'd come to him anyway, and he wasn't about to deny himself such outlandish carnal pleasure. Morals and manners be damned!

She faced him then, and she did nothing to conceal herself. Her flawless breasts, nipples peaked, invited his crude investigation. The two mounds were ungodly in their perfection. No mortal man could gaze upon them and behave himself, and he wasn't about to. She'd disrobed in his bedchamber, so whatever transpired was no more than she deserved.

Once again, she placed her dainty foot on the stool, bending over to untie her garters and roll down her stockings, then she stood, her hand pulling at the bow that laced her drawers, and she conducted them over her hips, her legs, until she was exquisitely, sinfully naked. At ease now, with her body, with her nudity, she stretched her arms high, flexing her muscles and arching her back.

Her hair was piled on her head, so none of her charms was hidden. Observing all—the wide shoulders, the nipped waist, the flared hips—his brow creased with anxiety as he noted that she'd lost weight. He was intimately familiar with every inch of her torso, his tongue having traced over curve and valley. She was slimmer, but from what?

Shaking off the disturbing insight, he focused instead on

the crimson hair shielding her pussy. Its dangerous lure impelled him to the door just as she moved to the tub.

She perceived his presence and halted in mid-stride, her foot balanced on the rim, the pink of her cleft winking at him from between her legs. He fought down the impulse to rush to her, to touch her there, to kiss her there.

"You can't expect to watch," she complained.

"Absolutely."

"I don't want you in here."

"Milady, we are far past the time when what you *want* matters to me at all."

Her emerald eyes sparked with ire, and she held his gaze, set to engage in verbal fisticuffs, but the warm water beckoned, and she turned away.

"Why am I never surprised when you act like an ass?" Then, she proceeded to ignore him, testing the temperature with her toe. Deeming it adequate, she slipped in, a moan of delight bubbling from her ruby lips. "Aah . . . I haven't had a hot bath in an eternity."

He declined to examine the statement too closely, wouldn't ask: how come? Instead, he concentrated solely on the sensual illustration, rejecting the chance to discern more than he dared.

There was a mirror behind the tub, so he could rudely analyze her antics. He'd always relished seeing her at her bath; she lowered her guard, cherishing the occurrence like a sailor; maidenly modesty forsaken.

Relaxing, she widened her legs. Her thighs were spread, and he could conceive of her pussy below the water, wet and swollen from the heat. He neared to obtain a better view, and her breasts floated on the surface.

"Is your mistress gone?" She stared at their posed reflections in the glass.

"I have no mistress."

She scoffed. "I meant what I said."

"What was that?"

"If I catch her panting after you again, I'll kill her"— her rabid regard dropped to his crotch where his overblown phallus prodded blatantly against the placard of his trousers—"then I'll castrate you."

He marveled at the threat. She was so bloody enticing when she was exhibiting her true character, and he grappled with the significance of her caveat. Did she consider him worth having? Worth keeping? Worth fighting for? She seemed to be jealous of his alleged indiscretions with Pamela, which could only arise from her harboring valid emotion.

His confusion increased.

"You have a wicked tongue, madam."

"Mrs. Stevens to you," she proclaimed caustically. "Have the decency to acknowledge who I am."

At the reminder, he flushed, two bright marks of red staining his cheeks. "Dear *wife*," he emphasized, "you've only just arrived. Don't command me about."

"You'll seek me out"—she raised a defiant brow— "whenever you have need of a woman's services. You'll not embarrass me by cavorting with every whore in London."

"Pamela is not a whore," he felt obliged to relate.

"I never said she was," Sarah conceded, "but you won't dally with her again. I'm afraid my mind's made up, and the subject is not debatable."

So . . . she thought to employ her corporeal wiles to keep him on a tether. An excellent ploy. In light of how attracted he was to her, how captivated he'd always been, the concept of having her regularly was acutely tempting.

Did she assume that she was imposing an untenable burden? He had no qualms about slaking his lust with her. If she was heedlessly volunteering, he'd promptly assent.

Weeks—nay months—of lewd excess stretched ahead, and he tried to calculate why he'd denied himself. She was his wife, he'd seen to that by speaking the vows, but he'd only perceived the onus brought on by allying himself with her. Not the incomparable satisfaction.

His body had never known such outrageous luxury and, at that very moment, it was pleading to be assuaged. Why not submit? What reason could possibly justify restraint?

He toed off one boot, then the other. Only when he drew off his jacket and dislodged his cravat did he garner any undue scrutiny from her. She came up on her knees, glaring at him over her shoulder.

"What are you doing?"

"What does it look like?"

"You're removing your clothing!"

"An accurate assessment."

"To what purpose?"

"I'm joining you."

"After all your misdeeds! You're mad if you suppose you can saunter in here, snap your fingers, and require me to fornicate!" In a snit, she shook an accusing finger at him. "You thought I contrived against you with Hugh. You didn't trust me. You didn't believe in me." She paused, swallowed hard. "I'll do whatever you ask," she said, "but first, you must admit that you were wrong about me. Tell me you're sorry."

"I'm not."

Gad, those eyes! They tortured him! They delved to his core, exposing how much he'd missed her without his even knowing he had.

"Well, *I'm* sorry," she quietly professed, "for everything. For doubting you, and maligning you. For letting you chase me home to Scarborough. I should have stayed with you. There's a fine connection between us, and I'm willing to put our differences aside. To start over."

Her gracious expression of remorse felt like a noose around his neck, strangling him and, consummate villain that he was, he couldn't reply. While she was disposed to mend and heal, he was hurting too much to make concessions, not even something as simple as the apology she craved. He had to protect himself—at all costs!

She waited in vain, until she understood that he wouldn't beg her pardon, and she sagged in defeat as he plucked at the front of his pants, the top button popping free.

"Didn't you hear anything I just said?"

"I'm aroused." Another button flipped from its enclosure. "I've tolerated a lengthy period of sexual abstinence."

"I'm to infer that you and Pamela have merely been attending the opera?"

"Exactly."

"I discovered some of her clothes. In this very room."

"She frequently overimbibes"—he shrugged away the untoward rumors—"and has spent the night."

"You must conclude that I'm appallingly gullible."

She tried to exit the tub, but he rested a restrictive hand on her shoulder, adding tension, impeding escape. He was being cruel, but he simply couldn't let her wheedle herself under his skin again. If he opened his heart even a minute amount, she'd barge in, and he was terrified by the prospect.

"Have you had any lovers?" he boorishly inquired, and it dawned on him that her answer had better be *no*. An alien torrent of jealousy coursed through him; he'd very likely have to slay any man who'd had the audacity.

"No." She was emphatic, insulted. "How about yourself, my dear and *faithful* husband? Can you make the same vow?"

"Yes." He was just as definite. "Now that the issue is settled, I plan to indulge."

"Not until we hash this out."

"I've no intention of talking this to death. You're here, and you're naked in my bath. You'll do what I say, and you'll do it gladly."

"And *you* are a dreamer." But she continued to avidly peruse him as he shed his trousers.

Languidly, prolonging the ecstasy, he dragged them down his legs and kicked them away, then he rose beside her. Naked and hard, his cock an offensive size, he gripped it in his fist, easing some of the urgency. His phallus was mere inches from her plush, alluring mouth. He stroked himself, revealing the tip, knowing how fabulous it would feel to be inside that moist haven, to have her kneeling before him and sucking at him until he was imploring her to stop.

"Touch me," he commanded.

"No." But he wasn't about to be denied.

Before she could react, he slid into the tub and sank down behind her. They were wedged in the narrow space, her backside pressed to his front, his thighs mashed to hers, their calves and feet overlapping. Slippery and smooth, she smelled like sex, and woman, and roses, and he centered his cock on the cleft of her ass, his hands gripping her waist.

Her bounteous hair pricked his nose, and he yanked at the combs. It swung down in a cascade, the ends dangling on the water, and he shoved the heavy mass aside, then leaned forward and bit against her nape, causing her to writhe and squirm.

Insolently taunting, he held her firmly against him. "Have you been pining away for me?"

"Not for a second."

His fingers slipped down her stomach, kneading through the springy red curls, dipping into her, and she tensed at his unexpected invasion. Her pussy had only previously endured his unrefined style of penetration, and at the vain realization, his cock inflated further.

"I hate you," she charged but without conviction.

"Then why have you come?" He kissed up her neck, nuzzled her hair, and was pleased to detect goose bumps.

"So that I could tell you—to your face—what a wretch I think you are." Jostling him with her elbow, her blow glanced off, the only tangible result being that she inadvertently rubbed her shapely ass across his erection.

"Ooh . . . do that again." He bit at the lobe of her ear, and raucously grasped her nipples, as he studied their joint reflection in the mirror. Her abundant breasts and lush pussy were discernible. He lurked behind her, a dark, looming menace who boded ill.

"Look at us, Mrs. Stevens."

His cajoling dragged her attention to the mirror. With a

TOTAL SURRENDER   337

strained intensity, she evaluated the placement of their bodies, of his lips at her cheek, of his fingers at her nipples.
As lovers, they were impeccable together; they always had
been.

"Do you remember the first time I visited your bedchamber at Pamela's country house? I fondled you like this,
and you watched in the mirror. You were so hot, so beautiful. Just for me."

"Your conceit knows no bounds," she mutinously maintained. "I was bored and lonely; I might have welcomed
any man stupid enough to enter."

"I was the one. The *only* one."

"You flatter yourself."

With one hand, he manipulated her breast, while the
other fell to her pussy. Palpating her vigilantly, he probed
and explored, and eventually, he secured what he'd been
seeking: a scant response from her hips. He pressed against
her mound, eliciting a groan she didn't want him to discern.

"You are so ready for me."

"Arrogant beast!"

Like a scientist with a new invention, he found her clit
and began to play, working, toying, and teasing her. Her
hips succumbed, more brazenly adopting his rhythm.

He'd forgotten how much he treasured her sexual predilection, how he was attuned to her every need, how his
spirit soared at her prurient nature. Bending down, he
doused his cock, wetting the erect member. "Take me inside you."

"I won't," she argued. "I haven't forgiven you."

"I don't care."

He inserted the blunt tip, gave her a tad more. Her eyes
widened, as if she didn't recall how big he was, and he
could barely stifle a moan of pleasure at having her, once
again. "I love fucking you," he indelicately mentioned. "I
always have."

As he intruded slowly, meticulously, their gazes linked
in the mirror. Cautiously, she reached behind her head, tracing along his neck, his face, his lips, and he kissed her

palm, awed by the emotion that blazed from the simple gesture.

He couldn't stand this effect she so easily managed!

The only thing he wanted from her was spicy, tempestuous sex. Nothing more. Clutching her hips, he attempted to ardently thrust, but the tub was too cramped, and he couldn't exert the pressure he longed to wield, but apparently, excessive endeavor wasn't necessary. After minimal effort, he was at the sharp edge of release.

Almost without warning, he started to come, and he frantically grabbed for her, striving to withdraw so that he could disgorge his seed across her back and keep it away from her womb, but she'd been anticipating the maneuver. She ground her buttocks into him, their awkward poses propelling him against the rim of the tub and blocking his egress. Her cleft milked him with its severe stimulation, and his body arced, his cock throbbed, his seed shooting into her body in a sizzling river.

He couldn't recollect when he'd last spilled himself inside a woman. The wrongness of it, the folly, the impropriety, produced a bizarre thrill that billowed through his loins as he primally delighted in his ultimate possession.

She was *his*.

With a decisive, possessive plunge, he buried his forehead in her hair, treasuring the sensation of having her so completely, a feeling of rightness flooding over him, then gradually, sanity was restored, and he pulled away as much as he could, alarmed by what he'd just accomplished.

How did she so freely overwhelm him? He'd come like an untried lad of thirteen, ejaculating inside her as though it was a normal course of events. How could he defend his negligent incursion?

Wary of what he would discover, he met her gaze in the mirror, once again. A strong emotion flickered in her green eyes, but he couldn't decipher it.

"I'm sorry for my lack of control—" he commenced falteringly, but she cut him off.

"If you've decided to apologize for something," she replied scathingly, "don't you dare let it be for coming inside me. I do believe I might strangle you before I'd listen."

She huffed out, water splashing onto the floor with her departure. In a temper, she snatched her robe and stomped away, silence left in her wake. Pondering the perplexity of females, how incomprehensible they were, how mysterious, how irksome, he sank down in the tub.

His knees weak from the potency of his orgasm, he rested his arms on the edge of the basin as he took a cloth and scrubbed himself, recovering from the vigor of their copulation. Incrementally, he calmed enough to dry himself, then don his trousers.

When she'd stormed out, he hadn't nettled over where she'd gone, postulating that she'd run downstairs, or fled to one of the other bedrooms to fume and seethe.

To his dismay, she was lying on his bed, her head on his pillow, her body curled into a ball and covered with a knitted throw. Facing away from him, she appeared petite and vulnerable, and he knew with a glaring certitude that his bed would never be his own again. From that moment on, no matter when or how he looked at it, he'd always picture her there, seeming to have staked out her spot with no intent of relinquishing it.

Baffled, abashed, he huddled in the doorway, not sure what to say or how to say it. He could never find his balance with her.

"Where are my things?" Her question was so quietly voiced that he wasn't sure she'd spoken.

"What things?" he inquired.

"The furniture and possessions that belong at Scarborough."

"They're stored in a warehouse. Why?"

"I want everything sent back."

"All of it is mine," he couldn't stop himself from peevishly pointing out. "Your brother—"

"Hugh is dead," she tersely interjected. "Whatever happened between the two of you, it's not important anymore. The new earl is on his way. From America. He's a distant

cousin whom I've never met, and I won't permit you to
shame me by having the manor in a shambles when he
arrives."

It was easier to relent than he'd imagined. He'd never
wanted the blasted chattels in the first place. The entire
cargo had been nothing but a daily, constant reminder of
his mistakes. "I'll see to it."

"I have some elderly retainers who need to be pensioned
off, but I've never had any money to help them."

"Done."

Trembling, she breathed deep, then exhaled, and he
watched the rise and fall of her rib cage. "And I want
Hugh's body shipped home so that he can have a proper
burial." She gave a soft laugh that sounded very close to a
sob. "His grave is here in London, and I don't even know
where."

His initial inclination was to deny the modest request,
but he couldn't. What did he care where Hugh Compton
was buried? He acceded again, even as he marveled that he
was being so accursedly cooperative. Next, she'd demand
the shirt off his back, and he'd be jerking it over his head
and presenting it to her on a silver platter.

"I have a secretary who works for me at the club," he
said. "He'll visit you tomorrow. Tell him what you need;
he'll handle it."

"Thank you." There was a protracted pause, then she
forged on. "I'm prevailing on you horridly, but there's one
thing more."

She was still staring at the wall, and it annoyed him that
she wouldn't roll over. Usually, she was stubborn enough
to confront any obstacle, to slave through any disagreement, and he recognized that he'd succeeded in pushing her
past her limits.

"You're my wife." As he acknowledged her, he experienced an extraordinary rush of pride at claiming her. "I'll
render to you whatever I have the means to provide."

"Then . . . I ask that you put some money in a trust for
me. Not very much," she hastened on, lest he rebuff her.

"Just enough so that if you gamble away what we have, I will have some funds to tide me over. That way, I won't be cold, or hungry, or scared ever again."

His heart flipped over in his chest. What had he done? While he'd inflicted a terrible price on Hugh Compton, he'd avoided estimating the probable repercussions to her.

"Oh, Sarah . . ." Like a blind man, he stumbled toward the bed and glided down onto the mattress, resting a hand on her back, massaging in soothing circles. "I'm not a gambler," he declared. "I wager on occasion, but rarely, and only for meager amounts. I'm not obsessed like your father was. Or your brother."

"Swear it."

"I swear it to you," he reassured her. "You'll never go without."

Her body shuddered, then she nodded, accepting his pledge, and he caressed across her hair as though she was a young child in need of comfort. Her tension dissolved, and he turned her onto her back. Tears streaked her cheeks, and his heart lurched once more. He couldn't bear to have her unhappy.

"Don't cry, love." He swiped at the residue with his thumb.

"I didn't plot with Hugh," she fervently attested.

He examined her, scanning for deceit or cunning, but there was no sign of duplicity and likely never had been. Hugh's treachery had instigated an anger that had burned furiously, but it was rapidly waning. She was wiser than he, pursuing a new beginning, and his initial step toward her had to commence with a speck of trust. Of her, and her motives.

"I believe you."

Chastely, he kissed her, with the simple embrace, tendering apology and receiving pardon. When he tried to move away, she held him just there against her mouth. She opened for him, and the tranquil kiss became something more, something profound and poignant that brushed his very soul.

As their lips parted, she was beholding him with a clear, abiding affection, and he earnestly stated, "I haven't been with Pamela. After you . . . after we . . ." How to divulge this? His chagrin was excruciating. "I went to her bed once, and I couldn't go through with it."

"I believe you," she said, as well.

"I kept thinking about you"—he hated to disclose that she was his greatest—his only—weakness—"and about how much it would hurt you if you knew."

"I'm glad."

"So am I."

There was so much more he yearned to say, but powerful sentiment rocked him, and he was frightened by its strength. Suddenly out of his element, he extended himself next to her, burrowing himself in the crook of her neck, tasting the salt of her skin, inhaling the musk that was her very essence.

He snuggled down to her chest, where her pert nipple poked at his cheek, and he sucked at it, nursing at her breast, easing his woes and consternation. But when she was near, his need for succor transformed, and he grew hard with wanting her, the force of it never ceasing to amaze. He positioned himself, bracing his weight on his arms, and he gazed down at her with what could only be unbridled joy.

Flexing his hips, he dallied until he was fully sheathed, snug in her succulent haven, and his cock expanded as her muscles clenched around him.

"Let's make a babe, Michael." She smiled up at him, welcoming him home. "Give me someone to love besides you, you miserable oaf."

She loved him! Pulse racing with excitement, he was desperate to repeat the sentiment, but the words—never uttered to another—were lodged in his throat, and he couldn't push them out.

His dread of abandonment reared up. It had ruled his life, ever since the day when he was three and his father had forsaken him, and he was overcome by his dormant, destructive fears.

"I can't get you with child!" He was almost wailing. "I'll grant you anything but that!"

"Why?"

"I couldn't bear it."

"Michael . . ."—her exasperation with him was evident— "we're going to have beautiful children. Many, many of them."

"But if you left me, or if something happened . . ."

"I promise you"—she laid her palm on his cheek—"that I will never leave. No matter what." She grinned wickedly. "Despite how obnoxious you are, or how horridly you try my patience, I'll always remain by your side."

He felt driven to explain his anguish, but he wasn't sure he could. After the upheavals of his childhood, he'd survived by becoming a creature of habit, needing regularity and normal routine. He loathed change; it was too painful.

Candidly, he admitted, "I don't know where I belong anymore."

"That's easy. You belong with me. You always have."

He filled her then, entering and retreating, slowly, mindfully, basking in the delectation, but he couldn't restrain himself for long. His hunger ran fierce as ever, and he was frantic and precise, taking them both beyond space and time to where they could soar as one.

When she called his name, he captured her rapturous cry on his lips, cherishing the exquisite and total wantonness with which she let herself go. United with her, his body quivered and, at the last, when he would have pulled away, something mighty—his love for her—prevented him from disengaging.

He longed to gift her with her heart's desire. In a fiery torrent, he emptied himself against her womb, flooding her, and he whispered a prayer that his seed would take root, that he could give her the child she craved.

They floated back to reality, and he was safely cradled in her arms. He kissed her hair, her cheek, her mouth, and his fondness for her wrenched the avowal from his very core.

"I love you," he choked out on a hitched breath.

"Yes, you do," she said, "and I love you, too."

"Will you marry me?" She was confused, so he clarified, "Again? So everyone will know that you are mine?"

She assessed him, checking for cowardice or indecision, but saw neither. "I'd like that very much."

In accord, he nodded, and she nodded, too. Then, he kissed the middle of her hand and laid it on his chest, directly over his heart so that she could feel it beating in a tempo with her own.

He was sated, assuaged, reposed, and as sleep took him, he rested peacefully, aware that when he awoke, she would still be there. That she would be there forever.

Chapter Twenty-four

Sarah dallied in her bedchamber, admiring the beautiful emerald band that Michael had placed on her ring finger, and listening to how quiet the house had grown. With the exception of James and Abigail, the wedding guests had departed, and she was relieved by the pending solitude. Although the occasion had been happy and jubilant, she was impatient to have her husband all to herself.

Day was rapidly turning to evening, and Michael's efficient staff—with a few female members added for her comfort—had the fire burning, candles lit, and a bath laid out in the dressing room.

Iced bottles of French champagne, and an assortment of delectable chocolates, were arranged on a table in the corner, and she couldn't help but be warmed by the sight. On her *first* wedding day, that horrid event at the chapel in Bedford, when she'd erroneously presumed they would have a wedding night in which to partake of them, she'd impishly demanded the treats of Michael.

To her delight, he'd remembered her request, and the humble gesture seemed to be another quiet apology for the things he'd done. In every feasible manner, he continually let her know he was sorry, and she was consistently touched and moved.

Michael had even offered to suffer through the grandest nuptials London had ever seen—if that's what she'd fancied—but he'd have been miserable with an elaborate fete, and opulence had never been her style, either, so she'd opted for an unpretentious affair, one that could be effortlessly planned and hastily thrown together.

With Rebecca still visiting in the country, Sarah hadn't

had any guests to invite, so they'd filled the list with Michael's handful of friends, the senior staff from the club, and a few of his and James's more prominent business associates. They were an engaging, entertaining group of people, their wives amicable and accepting, and the celebration had been extremely merry.

The group was cordial, and they'd appeared sincerely pleased to have Michael married and settled. Any fears she'd harbored about fitting in had vanished. With ease, she could envision herself established in his world. What a blessing that she'd finally escaped her doldrums and traveled to town!

At the window, she stared down into Michael's backyard. *Her* yard, too, she reminded herself, amazed at how she'd barged into his life, at how quickly she'd begun to think of the property as her own. With no trouble at all, she'd made herself at home.

The modest, neatly groomed garden appeared forlorn and dilapidated in the cold of the late December afternoon, and she could just picture how pretty it would be in the spring, when the trees started to bud and the flowers to bloom.

James and Michael were huddled in the center, their heads pressed close, their breath mingling and swirling in a white cloud. The grays and blacks of their formal wedding attire blended with the decaying foliage, but clothing couldn't dull their appeal. They shone brightly, too intrepid, too bold, like exotic birds who'd been dropped from the sky into an alien habitat.

She raised her hand to the pane, feeling the cool glass against her fingertips, as she furtively watched them and wondered what they were discussing. Their relationship had realigned to the steady, firm condition they'd previously enjoyed, their bond devoted and true as it had been before Michael had fled to the country.

Although she wasn't cognizant of what had transpired to resolve their tensions, she supposed that they were simply too attached to be at odds for long. They were different, yet so alike—two peas in a pod, as the saying went—and it was fascinating to be in their company. Their minds worked in similar patterns, their thoughts so attuned that they frequently finished one another's sentences.

James uttered a remark that made Michael laugh aloud and vigorously shake his head, and she couldn't stop smiling. She loved the sound of his joy.

Though she'd only been in residence for two weeks, he'd been transformed, and she liked to secretly postulate that her presence had brought about the striking, welcome changes.

Now, if she could just figure out how to convince him to emit even a fraction of the same openness and solicitude for his parents when they returned from their honeymoon on the Continent, she'd consider herself to have accomplished a major feat.

Sensing her presence, he focused on the upper floors, searching the windows. His blue eyes locked on her, glittering with approval, roving over her form in a languid, sensual perusal. Her nipples were instantaneously alert, her corset laced too tightly, and she was boorishly anxious for James to leave, for her wedding night to commence.

Behind her, footsteps resonated in the hall, and she glanced over her shoulder as Abigail entered the room. With her own family gone, Sarah had every intention of replacing it with Michael's, so she called upon Abigail at every opportunity. In a smattering of days, their relationship had evolved to where it seemed they'd been companions since childhood, that Abigail was the sister she'd never had.

"May I come in?" Abigail asked, her demeanor disheveled and a bit bewildered.

"Please do."

With her pregnancy playing tricks, Abigail had dozed off on a couch during the noisy, boisterous reveling that ensued after the ceremony and, without the woman stirring, James had affectionately carried her upstairs and tucked her in bed for a nap.

"I fell asleep."

"Yes."

"For how long?"

"Only about two hours."

"Aren't I interesting company! How embarrassing."

"Don't worry. No one noticed."

Actually, everyone had, but they'd discreetly watched how sweetly and tenderly James had seen to her welfare. Apparently, James's circle of acquaintances was amazed by the modifications that matrimony had contributed to his character, and the variations were a perpetual topic of gossip by all.

"I was never informed that a woman underwent so many bodily alterations when she was increasing." Abigail moved to Sarah's side. "Just wait till it happens to you."

Sarah absently ran a hand across her abdomen, speculating as to whether it might have already occurred. As though he'd stored up months of lust, Michael couldn't get enough of her. Evidently, he'd merely been biding his time until he could show her how much he needed and wanted her, and now that he could unleash his desire, there was no reining him in.

Since the afternoon of her arrival, they'd rarely left their bed. They couldn't make it down to the parlor, or sit through an entire meal, without rushing back to the bedchamber for another experiment with passion. When they'd been in Bedford, Michael had taught her much, but the brief stint had provided her with only an inkling of the vast array of rapture that was available under his tutelage.

Abigail sidled nearer in order to see what had Sarah so preoccupied. On perceiving the two men, she murmured, "What a dashing pair of rogues they are."

"It ought to be a sin to look so splendid."

"I've always thought so."

Abigail sounded almost petulant about it, and Sarah laughed as they surreptitiously spied on their husbands. Eventually, the duo concluded whatever conversation had them so engrossed. James wrapped an arm across Michael's shoulder—very much the elder, wiser sibling—and they vanished into the house.

For several lengthy moments after they'd disappeared, the two women peered at the spot where they'd been, then the observation burst from Sarah: "Lord, but we're fortunate, aren't we?"

"For a couple of girls from the country," Abigail concurred, "we didn't do too badly for ourselves."

"We certainly didn't."

Downstairs, the men were moving about, the soft hum of their voices drifting up, and Sarah concluded that they were in the parlor, having a last whisky.

She and Abigail shifted away from the window, causing Abigail to heed the candlelight, the covers that had been turned down on the bed, the rose petals strewn about, and Sarah hoped her zeal to be secluded with her husband wasn't too manifest. While she liked Abigail very much, she was ready for some privacy.

"I should be going," Abigail judiciously pronounced, but then she didn't budge. A tad flustered, she ultimately said, "Ah . . . I have something for you."

"Really?" Abigail had planned and hosted the reception, so Sarah had insisted on no other wedding gift from her. They'd agreed, so she couldn't conceive of what it might be, and her curiosity flared when she noted that Abigail was clutching a small leather satchel.

"A few weeks ago," Abigail explained, "I found these pictures of Michael in an old trunk in the attic, and I . . . I . . . didn't imagine they should just be lying about. I thought you might like to have them."

Unable—for some reason—to meet Sarah's gaze, Abigail proffered the portfolio. Sarah opened the flap and pulled out a dozen pen-and-ink drawings. Of her husband. Outrageously handsome. A decade younger. And naked. Very, very naked and disturbingly sexy in each one.

"What the devil . . ." Sarah briskly skimmed through the stack.

"You're aware that they grew up in Paris, aren't you?"

"Yes."

"Well, in their teen years, they had a friend," Abigail clarified. "An artist, who painted this sort of thing for money."

"You have some of James?"

"Three sets," she admitted, blushing a bright scarlet. "It's a long story," was all she added by way of elucidation. "Until I stumbled upon these, I hadn't realized that Michael posed, too."

As she persevered with her chatter, Sarah was energetically thumbing through the pile. From every angle and perspective, Michael was graphically, diligently depicted. He was etched with great care; front, back, side, no position remained unportrayed, and the artist was clearly a master at detailing the human form.

Michael was sumptuous, smug, vainglorious and, while much of his torso was narrower—his muscles and bones not thoroughly matured into the manly physique he would ultimately acquire—other parts of his anatomy were painstakingly delineated, and she couldn't quit gawking.

Even at such a tender age, his *best* attribute had been fully developed.

"Oh, my . . ." She used one of the drawings to fan her face against the sudden temperature of the room. "Did you peek at these?"

"I told James I hadn't, but"—a wicked and naughty disposition glimmered in Abigail's eye—"I especially like number six."

"You brazen hussy!" Sarah giggled like a schoolgirl as she swiftly hastened to the sixth picture. Michael was a negligent model, with an arm leaned against a window frame as he insolently pouted over his shoulder at the artist. The posture was provocative, arousing, his hind legs tight and defined. And his bare posterior was so damned cute.

"Number *six* is definitely entertaining," she promptly assented.

"Anyway"—Abigail was almost stammering—"you might have fun with them. Tonight and whenever . . ." Her cheeks colored to a blazing shade of crimson, and she clasped her hands over them, trying to ward off the flash of heat. "Oh, mercy me! I'd better be off."

They made their good-byes, with Abigail contending that Sarah needn't accompany her downstairs, and Sarah was glad. With only James and Abigail still in attendance, there wouldn't be much time before Michael joined her, and she needed every second to prepare. Now that she was in possession of Abigail's marvelous gift, she required a few moments to deduce how to utilize it to premium advantage.

Abigail started out, then halted in the doorway. "Don't you dare tell James I snooped at those pictures!"

"I won't," Sarah vowed, chuckling as Abigail scuttled away.

Immediately after Abigail's exit, one of the maids conveniently popped in. Sarah flung her pouch of illustrations on the bed, then mellowed as she was stripped of her clothes, her hair brushed out, but she declined the other woman's offer to apply lotions or perfumes.

Dismissing her, Sarah instructed that they not be disturbed till the morn, then she proceeded to her bath, sinking into the hot water and attempting to relax while she waited for her husband.

Her husband! The luscious concept tickled her stomach and ignited her anxiety. He would arrive anon, animated, domineering, urgent for her and what she could give him, and she couldn't stand the anticipation, so she strove to contemplate some other topic, but diversion was impossible.

Her ears perked, detecting the faint noises of James's and Abigail's farewells, which meant Michael would enter directly. She slumped down in the tub, immersing her breasts, her shoulders, aiming for every inch of her body to be wet and slippery.

Presently, he was ascending the stairs, then advancing down the hall. She paused until he was in the outer bedchamber, then she clambered to her knees, lazily stretching her arms, showing him her backside. Knowing he was at the door, she pretended she hadn't noticed, but she could sense him behind her, prowling like a caged animal.

Coming up on her feet, she stepped onto the rug, whirling about just as he moved into the room.

"Good evening, Mrs. Stevens." He formally greeted her, tipping his head in acknowledgment, and her heart did a colossal flip-flop at his mode of address.

"Mr. Stevens," she answered just as precisely.

His sapphire eyes shimmered with desire and something more, something she wouldn't even try to name. The cooler air had hoisted goose bumps on her skin, her nipples constricted, and he reached out and stroked an erect nub. "Always a pleasure to find you at your bath."

"Would you like to take one, too?"

"Momentarily. First, let's share a glass of champagne."

Remarkably, he wasn't his customary poised, confident self, and it was odd that, after their lewd frolicking of the past days, he could be nervous. Then, she recognized that she was tense, too. Assuredly, speaking those binding vows could unsettle a person; it hadn't been any less austere the second time around.

"I'd like that." The delay would be appreciated; the libation would calm them both. "It's a tad chilly in here. Would you dry me?"

Retrieving a towel off the vanity, he rubbed it up and down her back, front, bottom, legs, then he enfolded her in the large cloth, tucking the flap at her cleavage to secure it in place. His arms went around her, and he pulled her close.

"How was your wedding, madam?"

The query was lightly hurled, but his wasn't an idle question. With him, they never were. There was a lost little boy lurking at his core who desperately sought approval, though she'd never disclose that she pictured him as being so vulnerable.

"Everything I'd hoped for and more," she responded honestly. She lifted up on her tiptoes and kissed him on the mouth. "Thank you."

"You're welcome."

"I like your friends."

"I don't have many," he broached as though it was a crime.

"You're just choosy."

"No. I admit it's the beast in me. I scare people off."

"Without a doubt," she chuckled, "but not me."

"Aren't I the lucky one?" The opinion was voiced with much more sentiment than he'd meant to show.

"Yes, you are," she admonished, and she intended to regularly remind him just how fortunate he was. "Is everyone gone?" she inquired, though she knew they were.

"Yes, praise be." Breathtaking and magnificent, he smiled down at her. "I thought I'd never get you alone."

"Poor baby," she crooned. "Were you pining away?"

"All day."

The gentle admission incited profound emotion. How she loved this man and always would! Since he could be rude, overbearing, and pushy, there was no accounting for it, but who could ever rationalize why two people belonged together?

Occasionally, they discussed their novel connection in the dark of night, when shadows made it comfortable for Michael to confess what was in his heart. Why had they met? From where did this impression of abiding affinity emanate? Early on, she'd sensed it, and since her arrival in London, it had flourished anew.

How would it burgeon as time progressed? What would they feel in a month? In six?

She looked down the road, through their middle years and beyond, and she could behold him by her side, the radiant center of her life. The notion brought such exultation and contentment that a few blasted tears sprang to her eyes, and she tamped them down, refusing to exhibit an uncontrollable, maudlin rush that would likely leave her foolishly blubbering.

"I'm ready to drink that champagne now." She clasped his hand and led him into the bedchamber.

"Will you be naked while we are?"

"Is that how you'd like me to be?"

"Eternally."

"You're insatiable."

"Only since you stumbled into my life."

"Liar." She laughed, proceeding to the table laden with food and drink. "I saw how you misbehaved before I came along."

"And you'll never let me forget, will you?"

"Maybe in forty or fifty years."

While she tracked his every move, he opened the champagne and filled one glass, then toasted her. "Here's hoping it'll be that long. Or even longer."

"Here's hoping," she echoed.

"I love you."

Not a man to bandy about the word *love,* it was only the second instance he'd proclaimed himself, and her heart skidded with felicity and bliss. "I love you, too. I always will."

He tendered the glass so she could take a sip, and he twisted it so he could drink from the same spot on the rim. Then, startling her, he gripped an arm around her waist, and hauled her next to him. Using the stem of the goblet, he pushed down her towel, baring a breast, and she hitched a breath as he dribbled cold champagne across the extended tip, inducing it to pucker even further.

Leaning down, he laved it clean with his tongue, soaked it again, then dropped to his knees and indulged, slowly and exhaustively sucking at her. She adored how his lips toiled, how he dabbled and played. Her womb stirred, her thighs flexed; between her legs, she was moist and inclined to dally.

Sifting her fingers through his hair, she let it fall across her chest. Huddled there over her bosom, he looked sublime, and she rested her hand on his neck, imploring him, urging him on.

Inevitably, he pulled away, and he peered up at her, more wicked and dangerous than usual. He grabbed her buttocks and spurred her nearer, burying his face in her stomach, inhaling her essence. "You make me so hard."

"Good."

"I better have that bath. Or I'll never get it done."

"Would you like me to wash you?"

"Wench!" he chided, grinning, but he abruptly sobered. "Actually, I don't think so. I need a few minutes to myself." Mystified, confused, he asked, "Am I crazy?"

"No. It's been quite a day."

"Yes, it has." Briefly, it appeared that he might expound, but as she'd discovered, his revelations were saved for the wee hours. "You don't mind?" he probed.

"Go on." She assisted him to his feet and waved him toward the door, snatching a kiss as he passed by.

As he went about his business, she tended to her own, slipping into black stockings and mules, a sheer black robe. Checking her reflection in the mirror, she liked what she saw and decided to don nothing more. A hint of her nipples was defined through the thin fabric, and the middle of her torso was visible, showing her cushion of woman's hair, and a flash of smooth thigh, that added highlight and intrigue to the seductiveness.

On their bed, she fluffed the pillows, then reclined. The door to the dressing room was ajar, and she caught sporadic glimpses of Michael leaned back, his arms balanced on the edges of the tub. The familiarity of his motions should have been soothing—the water lapping, the washcloth rubbing over his skin—and she shut her eyes but couldn't calm herself.

Craving distraction, she picked up the portfolio of illustrations Abigail had given her. Avidly, she perused each picture, lingering over his various nude positions, assessing the width of his shoulders, the tuck of his waist, the curve of his rear. The representations were so lifelike; she felt she could jump into the drawings and tarry with him at will.

One, in particular, was mesmerizing. Spread out on a daybed, an arm casually bent behind his head, he was aroused, his phallus elongated and potent, and his fist was loosely clutched around it. Arrogant, imperious, intent on gratification, he focused resolutely, his body strained, as though he was expecting a lover who would eagerly service him in any fashion he demanded.

Had a woman been present when the picture was sketched? The notion had her recalling the other instances when she'd seen him engaged in ribald behavior, and she couldn't refrain from recollecting how riveting they had been. How improper. How utterly thrilling and wanton. Perfect musings, for the perfect wedding night.

Michael was climbing out of the tub, drying himself. "You're awfully quiet in there," he mentioned. "Are you all right?"

She couldn't help smiling. "I'm just doing a little light reading."

"I've got plans for you, so don't become too engrossed."

"Too late." She ran the tip of her finger across the shape of his cock. It was an odd tactile sensation, as if she was really touching him, and it made her completely wild to experience the genuine article.

What was it about nudity, about indecency and vice, that had such a stunning effect on her character? There was something so marvelously inappropriate about studying displays that she oughtn't to witness, or espying scenes she was never meant to view. Once she encountered a licentious spectacle, she couldn't prevent herself from wanting to see more.

"My goodness . . ." Just as he set foot in the room, she flipped to the next portrait—a bodily profile that flawlessly outlined his jutting cock. "I'd always heard that things like this went on in Paris, but I never believed any of the stories."

"What about Paris?" He filled another glass of champagne, then approached the bed, savoring the sparkling liquid. "I grew up there, remember?"

"Oh, yes. I remember."

"I'd like to take you visiting sometime, when the national upset is ended."

Garbed only in a towel, swathed at the waist, his eyes were tinted to a more absorbing shade. Smelling clean and manly, like soap and heat, his skin was damp, the tips of his hair curly from the steamy water. His crotch bulging deliciously, he was sin and iniquity swaddled in a dark blue package.

"What do you have there?" he inquired.

"A belated wedding gift from Abigail." She examined him carefully. "Turn sideways, would you?"

Unsuspecting, he complied without pondering her request.

"Drop your towel."

He started to, then stopped, the peculiarity sinking in. "Why?"

Endeavoring to keep a straight face, she glanced at the drawing, then dragged her torrid attention to those private parts that never ceased to intrigue and captivate her. "You've matured well over the past decade, but I want to compare."

"What are you talking about?"

Just then, he detected her treasure, and she prankishly shoved the stack under her hip, striving to hide it but not succeeding. Giggling, she scooted across the bed, but he leapt onto the mattress and pinned her down before she could escape. His hips pressed into her, his cock swelling ample and solid against her leg.

"Let me see!"

"No."

Playfully, he wrestled her prize into the open and, when he yanked it from her, there was no doubt that he recognized it for what it was. For once, he was rendered speechless. Mortified, too. A red flush initiated down low and swept up his chest and onto his cheeks.

He was aghast. "Where did you get these?"

"From Abigail."

Issuing a strangled groan, he rolled off her and onto his back, throwing an arm over his face. Chagrined, he stared toward the ceiling for a lengthy interval, then his elbow rose, and he peeked out at her. "Did she look at them?"

"Only number six." Snuggling over his chest, she hauled his arm away, and kissed him. "She thinks you have a cute bottom."

That strangled wail recurred. "James will murder me if he finds out. You'll be a widow."

"So I gather." She winked. "Your unique male beauty will remain Abigail's and my special secret."

"I'll never be able to go to supper at their house again. She'll constantly be assessing my rear."

"Probably." Considering his recurrent, dubious antics with women, it was charming that he could be so easily embarrassed. "You're very sexy in these. Young, too. You realize that we *older* women are extremely fascinated by younger men, don't you?"

"I've created a monster." As this was not the initial circumstance in which he'd made the point, he sighed. Resigned, he spun on top of her, trapping her to the mattress once more. "What will you do with them?"

"I guess I'll have them framed and hung in my boudoir, so I can gaze at them whenever I'm in the mood."

"Jezebel." He dipped under her chin and nipped at her nape. "Strumpet."

"You know how much I like to watch." She batted her lashes. "I learned from the master."

"And I suppose that's another topic of which I'll never hear the end."

"Maybe in forty or fifty years," she repeated.

"How wonderful"—he smiled at her, the power of it dazzling to behold—"to have you whispering in my ear all that time."

He took the collection and laid it on the stand next to the bed. Then, he rotated across the mattress, bringing her with him until she was on top. Her sex hovering eagerly over his, she braced herself on one arm, staring down at him as he sprawled against the white bedcoverings.

His mat of alluring chest hair begged to be stroked, causing her nerves to quiver and tingle. His tempting mouth—

that had simply been made for kissing—enticed h   sample. During their wrestling, his towel had come free, and his nether regions were exposed, cajoling her to look, to taste, to touch.

"Who needs to watch," he indicated, "when you can enjoy the real thing for yourself?" Taking her hand, he stroked it across the pebbled bump of his nipple.

"My thoughts exactly."

Stretching and purring like a contented cat, she splayed her fingers and rubbed in slow circles, feeling his heart thundering beneath her palm.

Suddenly ablaze, expectant, and wild with her desire for him, she tugged off her robe and tossed it on the floor.

To the law enforcement community. We deeply appreciate your service and dedication.

Chapter One

Eden Sinclair positioned the cursor over the send button, then paused. Hopefully, this email would be the one that brought the heirs of the Beaumont estate together regarding the future of the historic home. Then again, it might just make matters worse.

Biting her bottom lip, she winced as she clicked and sent the email on its way. As the assistant director of the South Mississippi Preservation Society, she'd been put in charge of dealing with the current owners of the antebellum home. The six heirs had been bickering over the future of the house for nearly two years. Eden had tried everything she could think of to bring them together. Still, each had a vision for the home, and none were willing to compromise, which complicated the society's desire to purchase the home and

restore it. Beaumont was historically significant to the small town of Blessing, Mississippi, and Eden was determined to save the unique structure.

Leaning back on the sofa, she exhaled a heavy sigh. If only there were more hours in the day or fewer obligations. Closing her laptop, she let her gaze drift to the view outside the large windows that ran the length of the cozy sitting area and kitchen in Oakley Hall. It, too, was a historic home and had been the Sinclair family residence since the late 1800s. She and her five-year-old daughter, Lucy, had moved in here after her husband, Mark, had passed away two years ago. A bitter swirl of anger and sympathy spurred her emotions. Would she ever come to terms with his duplicity?

Shaking off the sour mood, she allowed herself a moment to enjoy the winter camellias blooming in the backyard, their red-and-white flowers adding a welcome burst of color to the late January landscape. She would like to enjoy the quiet a little longer but knew there was no time to dillydally. Eden was due at work in half an hour. Rising, she moved to the kitchen just as friend and caregiver Jackie Gibbs entered with a plate in her hand and a scowl on her face.

"Old fool! I don't know why I put up with him. We should have him committed."

Eden smiled. She knew why they put up with Owen Sinclair. Because they loved him. Or rather, the man he *used* to be. The losses in her father-in-law's life had taken a toll and since the death of his oldest son, her husband, Mark, he'd lost all reason to live. A heart attack shortly after Mark's death had left Owen with a restricted lifestyle, which he'd fought tooth and nail. Depression had also set in, stealing much of his usual enthusiasm.

Thankfully, his latest project kept him occupied and reasonably stable. He'd purchased the historic Saint Joseph's Church and was creating a private museum dedicated to the history of Blessing, and he'd put her in charge of it. A mixed blessing.

"Then I guess we should be grateful for the museum. At least it keeps his mind occupied."

Jackie grunted. "Silly notion if you ask me."

Eden chuckled. She'd be lost without the woman. As an old friend of the family and a professional caregiver, Jackie had come to Oakley to nurse Owen after his illness. She'd quickly become like family, eventually moving in to help Eden as well. Eden had floundered since Mark died, trying to raise her daughter amid learning that her upright, re-

sponsible husband had left them financially destitute. It was only due to Owen's kindness that she and Lucy had a place to live with him in this old house.

Jackie dumped the toast into the trash and rinsed the plate. "I did manage to get one of his meds down him. He wants to see Lucy when she gets home from school. He adores that child. She's the sunshine in all our lives."

Eden couldn't agree more. Her daughter was always smiling, happy and eager to help. But also a constant source of worry, always looking around corners and climbing fences to see what lay beyond.

Jackie took a glass from the cupboard. "I've been meaning to ask, how are things at the museum?"

Eden eased into a chair at the breakfast table. "Not good. I can't be there full-time and things at work are so busy I can't get away like I did a few months ago. Owen has promised to find me some help, but he doesn't want to pay anyone, which leaves volunteers, and you know how that goes."

Jackie nodded in understanding. "The town is not too happy with Owen opening a private museum. He should have given that building to the historical society and let them manage things."

Eden didn't disagree. "I know, but it's the only thing he's interested in now and I don't want to let him down. But I don't know how much longer I can do it alone..."

Jackie poured a glass of water and held it up. "I'm going to see if I can get a few more pills down our bullheaded grouch. And I'll slip in a comment about the museum, too." She winked.

Eden smiled. "Good luck with that." She was beside herself with worry over Owen's health, mainly because he refused to take his medications. She and Jackie had tried all kinds of persuasions, but Owen had only dug in his heels. With his heart condition, he was supposed to avoid excitement of any kind. However, his volatile personality could explode at any moment, which made the danger of another heart attack an ongoing concern.

A shadow passed over the kitchen window and a firm knock sounded on the back door. Eden opened it to a tall, dark-haired man with deep-set brown eyes. He held a large duffel bag and gripped a cane in his right hand. A kernel of concern formed in her chest. "Can I help you?"

The man cleared his throat and shifted his weight. "Is this the Sinclair home?"

Eden debated whether to answer his question, but finally replied, "Yes."

The man's brown eyes narrowed. "Is Owen Sinclair here?"

Her defenses rose. No one came to visit anymore. Owen had few friends. "May I ask what your business is?" The man's eyebrows rose as if he was offended.

"Who are you?"

Eden stiffened at the authoritative tone of his voice. "Please state your business or I'll have to ask you to leave." The man's jaw worked side to side.

"I'm Blake Sinclair. Owen is my father."

Eden blanched. A chill shot up her spine followed quickly by a jolt of anger. This couldn't be happening. The last thing they needed now was for her coldhearted brother-in-law to suddenly reappear. "What are you doing here?"

He shrugged. "I've come home."

The half grin he gave her lit the fuse on her irritation. "This hasn't been your home for twelve years. You're not welcome here."

He nodded slightly. "I expected that, but I'd like to see my father."

"He's not well. He can't have visitors." The man's demeanor shifted from pleasant to challenging and he squared his shoulders.

"And who are you and why are you in my father's house?"

Eden stood her ground. "I live here. I'm Eden Sinclair. Mark's...wife."

The man's attitude shifted again, his shoulders lowering and his gaze softening. "Mark. *Married.* I should have expected that. Where is he? I'll talk to him."

Eden fought the sting of tears that always formed when she thought of her husband. Whatever his faults, she'd loved him. "Mark died two years ago." The shock on the man's face gave her a twinge of satisfaction, which she promptly smothered. She needed to remember this was her brother-in-law. He was family.

"I... I didn't know. I'm sorry."

"Blake? Oh my word, is it you?" Jackie slid past Eden and wrapped the man in a hug, speaking softly and rocking him back and forth. When the hug ended, she took his face in her palms. "It's so good to see you. So good."

Eden crossed her arms over her chest and waited. Jackie might be happy to see this prodigal son, but she had no use for the black sheep. She'd heard all about the younger brother's reckless, self-centered behavior and knew firsthand about the shattered lives he'd left behind when he turned his back on his family.

"Come in, kiddo. I want to hear what you've been doing. It's so good to have you home." She turned toward Eden. "Please pour a glass of sweet tea for our lost sheep."

Eden did as she was asked but every fiber of her being protested. Jackie and her brother-in-law sat down at the breakfast room table. After handing him the tea, she leaned against the counter. Blake glanced her way several times and she returned the look with a glare.

"It's good to be home and come across a familiar face. I haven't seen you since before Mom died. What are you doing here?"

"I live here now. I take care of the family." Jackie placed her hands over his. "Are you okay? You look pale and tired."

"It was a long trip here from California."

"Oh my, I should say so. And what about this?" She pointed to the wooden cane, and his leg, which was held stiff in front of him. "What happened?"

Eden didn't want to be curious, but she was. Blake was in his early thirties, five years younger than Mark. He should be in his prime. No doubt his years of wild living were to blame. She wiped that thought aside. It wasn't in her nature to be harsh or judg-mental, but when it came to her brother-in-law, the stories she'd heard did little to endear

him to her. The way he'd cut his family out of his life made her blood boil. Family was the only thing that mattered in life.

Blake shrugged. "An old football injury."

Jackie grunted. "You didn't play football. You were the star pitcher of the baseball team." Jackie studied him a moment, then glanced at his leg. "What really happened to put you in such a state?"

He glanced at her again, then looked away quickly. His hands worked the handle of his cane, which was positioned between his legs. Eden waited for the big confession. Like maybe he'd jumped out of a plane or fallen off a mountain. She kept her arms crossed over her chest defensively. Whatever the reason, this should be good.

"I've been in rehab for the last year and a half."

Jackie reached over and laid her hand on his. "Rehab? You didn't get addicted, did you?"

He smiled and shook his head. "No. I took a bullet in my leg. Nearly lost it a couple times but the doctors pulled me through."

"A *bullet*! Oh, Blake, what were you involved in?"

He chuckled softly. "My job. I was a police detective. I was shot in the line of duty."

Jackie stared at him. "You were a policeman? All this time?"

"Pretty much. I was working for the Stockton, California, PD. But that's all over now. I got a medical discharge from the force. No more chasing bad guys for me. They tried to assign me a desk job but I turned it down. Not my style."

Jackie smiled. "A policeman. Your mama would be so proud."

He made a dismissive gesture. "She'd be the only one." He shifted his cane to his other hand. "I'd better go."

"Are you here to stay, BJ?"

Blake smiled. "I haven't heard that name since Mom passed. I don't know how long I'll be in town. That depends on Dad."

Jackie nodded. "I need to tell him you're here."

Eden couldn't remain silent. "No! I mean, what about his heart? This could be a terrible shock."

"What's wrong with his heart?" Narrowing his eyes, Blake looked to Jackie for an answer.

"He suffered a serious heart attack shortly after Mark died. We almost lost him." She paused and clasped her hands. "Since then, he's had to be careful and avoid any excite-

ment. The whole thing has left him depressed and difficult to deal with."

Eden spoke up. "Having you suddenly pop up might be too much for him to handle."

Jackie sighed. "She has a point. I'll see if I can smooth things over before you see each other." She stood. "You wait here, and I'll go talk to him."

"I don't want to cause trouble. I just wanted to try and set things straight between us."

Jackie smiled. "I know."

As soon as the older woman left, Eden turned her gaze on Blake. "Don't you think it's a little late to try and fix things?"

"It's never too late to seek forgiveness."

The calm, smooth tone of his voice fueled her irritation. "You won't find any of that here."

Blake held her gaze, his dark eyes shadowed. "I know."

The man was insufferable. "Then why come back? Why now?"

"I had no place else to go and it was time."

Before she could respond, loud voices from the front of the house could be heard. As she'd expected, Owen wasn't pleased that his second son had returned. The voices grew louder, then suddenly stopped. Eden knew that meant Jackie had left the room. When

Owen became unreasonable, she turned her back on him. It was the only thing that would get his attention.

When she returned to the kitchen, Eden knew they had reached an impasse.

"Your father is a bullheaded, hard-hearted old coot."

Blake nodded. "I didn't expect a warm hug and a fatted calf."

"Where are you staying?" Jackie asked.

"No place yet."

"I thought not. I'd offer you a room in the house but that might not be smart right now. You can stay in the studio for the time being. I'm sure I can get him to come around."

Eden stepped forward. "No, Jackie. He can't stay there, either." Eden glanced at Blake, who had stood and was leaning heavily on his cane. "I mean... It's too risky. If Owen should see him and not be prepared, his heart might not be able to take the shock."

"I realize that, but this is his *son*. His only living child. I'll not turn him out in the cold. They both deserve to face each other. And I'll not let Owen hide and pout for a week nursing his resentment, either. We're going to have supper together tonight. After that we'll let the Lord work it out."

"Jackie!"

She rolled her eyes at the sound of her name. "Oh dear. Round three is about to get underway. Eden, you help Blake to the studio. And I'll see if I can calm our grumpy old man down."

Eden started to protest but she knew Jackie was the only one who could deal with Owen when he was in this state. Lucy could lift his mood but she was at preschool this morning.

Eden walked past Blake and pushed open the back door. She was aware of him behind her, walking slowly and awkwardly across the long back porch with his stiff leg. She ignored the twinge of sympathy. Where was *his* sympathy when the family was grieving, and Mark struggled to keep the family business afloat?

"I know my way to the studio. My grandma lived there for years."

Eden ignored him. She strode down the long covered porch that jutted out from the east side of the historic home, stopping at the last door. The space had served as storage after she'd sold her home. The boxes were mainly filled with Mark's belongings that she hadn't known what to do with and hadn't been ready to give away. One day, she'd have to sort through it all, but not yet. It was easier to ignore it.

She unlocked the door and stepped back, allowing Blake to enter.

He glanced around, emitting a low whistle. "This doesn't look like I remember it. Grandma had a lot less stuff." He smiled over his shoulder at her. "She liked things clean, neat and free of clutter."

Eden pressed her lips together. He was already finding fault. She put the key on the table next to the door. "Most of these things belonged to Mark. You can put them in the old car barn if you want." She walked back along the porch, entered the kitchen, then stopped at the sink, emitting a loud groan of aggravation. "Unbelievable. Ungrateful. Arrogant."

"Are you talking about Owen or Blake?" Jackie came to her side. "What's the problem?"

Eden pushed away from the counter and gestured toward the back of the house. "Him. He's already complaining that the studio doesn't look like it did when his grandmother lived there."

Jackie shrugged. "That's understandable. Grandma Fuller was an artist. She was very persnickety about her home. Seeing the place filled with boxes would be a shock. He's come home to find everything changed."

Eden set her jaw and crossed her arms over

her chest. "Why did he come home in the first place?"

"I think he felt it was time." Jackie gently stroked her arm. "What is it you're afraid of?"

"That he'll make things harder for Owen. He's not strong. He can't handle this kind of stress."

"Don't sell the old goat short. He's stronger than he lets on, and this might just yank him out of his depression. I'd rather have him feisty than lifeless."

"It's not just that. I've heard the stories about Blake's behavior—his reckless streak, the self-centered approach to everything. He's too disruptive."

Jackie held up a hand. "I know what you've heard and some of it *is* true, but don't you think we should give Blake the benefit of the doubt until we see otherwise? He's different. Calmer. Not the fidgety hothead he was as a young man."

"All I know is that Mark never had a good thing to say about him, and Owen would get enraged whenever his name was mentioned."

"I'm not denying there was bad blood between the three of them, but there are two sides to every story, and I think we need to hear Blake's side before we kick him to the curb."

Eden's anger eased and her conscience pricked. Tales of bad-boy Blake's escapades had been drilled into her from the moment she met Mark and had been underscored by her father-in-law. She didn't want to be unfair, but she wasn't about to risk Owen's health, either.

"I don't want Owen to be hurt. He and Lucy are the only family I have."

Jackie smiled and squeezed her hand. "And me."

Eden smiled. "Yes, of course."

Jackie patted her shoulder. "Just give the boy a chance."

"I'll try."

"Good girl. Now, I'm going back into the black bear's cave and see if I can convince him to see his long-lost son."

His son…the policeman. Eden couldn't ignore that fact. A wounded cop. Not the image she'd carried all these years. She had a tough time reconciling his job with his reputation. Was he telling the truth or was it a story meant to elicit sympathy so he could worm his way back into the family? What did he really want here?

Eden ran her palms over her face. The man had only been here a few minutes and she was already suspicious of his every move. Jackie

was right—she needed to give him the benefit of the doubt.

But how was she supposed to do that?

Detective Blake Sinclair watched Eden walk toward the house, stiff-backed and disapproving. Her resentment was obvious. He wasn't sure what his surprise sister-in-law had against him, but he expected he'd find out soon enough. She sure hadn't hesitated to express her opinions. However, he suspected her attitude was based on more than concern for his ailing father.

He turned to survey his new lodgings. The rooms had been added for his grandmother in her later years and consisted of a living room and kitchen at the front of the studio and two bedrooms with a bath in the back. The best feature was the front porch. When she wasn't painting or working on a craft project, Grandma would sit in her rocker and watch the seasons change.

He ran a hand down the back of his neck. So much had changed in his family since he'd left. Foolishly, he'd assumed everything would be the same. Instead, he'd learned his brother had died, his father was ill and he'd acquired a sister-in-law and a niece.

They may have gotten off on the wrong

foot, but there was no denying that Eden was a very attractive woman. Her blond hair flattered her delicate features and highlighted the bluest eyes he'd ever seen. Mark always had an eye for the prettiest girl in the room. Though he'd usually been attracted to the cool, sophisticated types. Eden was more of the sweet, girl-next-door variety.

A sharp sting of grief jolted his mind. His brother was gone. The loss augured deep inside. So many years lost, years that might have given them a chance to grow close again like when they were kids.

But he had a sister-in-law and a niece to get to know. Mark's family. Though he had a feeling forming a relationship with his brother's wife would be difficult. She'd been cautious when she'd greeted him, but after he told her his name, her expression had darkened with the suddenness of a summer storm. She had gone pale and swayed as if her knees were going to buckle. Mostly, she looked like she wanted to skin him alive.

He was definitely *not* welcome at Oakley Hall.

Blake scanned the studio again. The living room was serving as storage for random items and stacks of boxes. Eden had said they were Mark's things. He touched a box labeled

Books. His brother had always been an avid reader, unlike him. Reading was a sedentary activity. He wanted action.

He trailed his hand across the box. What had taken his older brother's life so young? Perhaps Jackie would explain if his dad let him hang around long enough to find out.

Blake stopped at the bedroom window that looked out along the winding driveway. He'd had a bad feeling when he'd approached the house. The old home looked the same but tired and worn down. Like him. The house needed painting, the yard was overgrown and the roof was missing some shingles. He'd sensed then that something was very wrong. Owen Sinclair took as much pride in his home as he did his company. And Mark. His *perfect*, oldest son.

He shoved aside the old resentment. Maybe he should leave and not cause any trouble. No. He'd come too far and learned too much to back out now. He'd walked out of Blessing twelve years ago with no intention of ever returning. Yet here he was, the prodigal returned. He slipped his hands into his pockets and closed his eyes. Only there would be no rejoicing parent to run to greet him with open arms.

A dull ache began along his thigh, and

he rubbed it vigorously to ease the spasm. He was feeling the effects of his two-mile walk from town to Oakley Hall. Blessing had grown in his absence, and the woodlands surrounding his home now boasted retail space and new homes. He suspected the big bicentennial this spring had caused the growth in the small town.

A zinger of pain lanced through his thigh. He groaned. He needed to sit. After carrying his grandma's old rocker from the living room to the porch, he eased into it. The gentle motion quickly drew away some of his fatigue and unearthed old memories of Grandma Fuller watching him and Mark playing ball in the yard. Blake had been a bit lost when she passed. She and his mom had understood his desire to break free from this town. Whereas Dad expected a stricter code of conduct and assimilation into the family business. Sinclair Properties was the only acceptable career for Owen's sons.

His stomach growled and the fatigue settled upon his shoulders again. He needed more than a rocker; he needed sleep. Back inside, he made his way to the bedroom and retrieved his meds from his duffel, downing two pills. His leg was throbbing. He'd overdone it today and his thigh was letting him

know it. Wincing, he kicked off his boots, then sprawled across the bed and closed his eyes. An image of his surprise sister-in-law filled his mind. Why did she resent him so much? She'd behaved like a fierce protector of his father. She might be an obstacle to their reconciliation.

At least she was an attractive obstacle. He groaned and draped his arm over his eyes. It was not something he should be noticing about his brother's wife. No matter how lovely she was.

He rolled onto his side, buried his face in his pillow and drifted off.

A loud knock on his front door drew him from a restless sleep. It was still daylight. He couldn't have slept long. A quick glance at the clock showed it was late afternoon. He rose and started toward the living room only to have his leg start to buckle. He grabbed his cane.

Jackie stood on the front porch. "I came to deliver news. Not sure if it's good or bad."

He motioned her inside, but she shook her head. "I just wanted to let you know that your dad has agreed to have supper with the family this evening."

Blake frowned. "The whole family?"

"Yep. He's promised to mind his manners."

He huffed out a breath. "Right."

"Anyway, I thought you could use a heads-up." Her eyes narrowed. "You look tired. Everything okay?"

He nodded. "Fine. I overdid it today, that's all." Jackie looked skeptical but didn't challenge his comment.

Supper with the family. It should have made him happy. So why was his stomach tied in a huge knot? Probably because he doubted Owen could mind his manners for longer than a sip of sweet tea, but he knew he had to face his father eventually. The sooner that happened, the sooner he could move on with his life.

Blake stepped out onto the porch and eased into the rocker, his fingers worrying the carved handle of his cane. The big question was, where was his life headed now? Law enforcement was off the table. His bum leg ruled out many of the things he liked to do, but he could sort that out later. Right now, he had to figure out how he'd get through supper with his father.

A car pulled up and he watched as a little girl got out. Eden hurried across the patio and wrapped her in a hug, waving goodbye to the driver. This must be his niece. Lainey. No... *Lucy*. The thought took a moment to regis-

ter. Mark, a husband and a dad. His heart ached for their loss. They must have been very happy. At least he hoped so.

From what he could see from the porch, the little girl was a carbon copy of her mother. They held hands as they walked to the house, Lucy's ponytail swaying playfully. The charming picture left him with an odd, hollow feeling in his chest. It also reminded him that the leg was still aching. He'd have to take it easy as much as possible today because tomorrow he had to get his life reinstated. A year and a half in a rehab facility had caused important parts of his life to lapse. His driver's license had expired, he had bank accounts to be activated and he needed to find a local physician to oversee his ongoing recovery. Now, however, he needed rest. If he was going to face his father shortly, he needed to be clearheaded.

Back in the bedroom, he stretched out, but sleep didn't come. His mind was clogged with a hundred ways the evening meal could unfold. None of them good.

How would his father respond to his unexpected homecoming?

Chapter Two

Eden shut the kitchen door behind her, then looked toward the studio. Blake had been on the porch in the rocker watching when Shirley Kirby brought Lucy home. Eden had been aware of his presence but had chosen to ignore him. What did he expect to find here? And why had he come home after all this time?

She'd only heard about the bad-boy brother, had never even seen a picture of him, which was odd, come to think of it. But from the time she'd known Mark, she'd heard nothing good about Blake. So now that he was here it was only natural she'd be on her guard against this threat.

"Mommy, can Cuddles have a treat?" Lucy was stooped down petting her little Shih Tzu puppy. It had been a birthday present last month from Owen.

Eden turned from the window and smiled at her daughter. "I know what you really want is a treat for yourself."

Lucy grinned. "Ice cream."

"Well, you can have one of the little ones but nothing else until supper." She reached into the jar on the counter decorated with puppy paws and handed the small bone-shaped dog biscuit to Lucy. "That goes for Cuddles, too."

Lucy carried her ice cream to the table. "Who was that man on the porch?"

Eden's heart skipped a beat. She'd hoped the child hadn't noticed. She searched for an answer that would satisfy her little girl. She had no idea what Blake's position in the family would be, and she didn't want Lucy caught up in all the family drama. "He's visiting Miss Jackie."

"Oh."

Thankfully, Lucy was more interested in her treat than the stranger. It was times like this Eden wished Mark was here so they could discuss the best way to handle things. Though, he'd rarely been around most days. He'd been too busy at the office.

"There's my little Lucy Belle. Did you have fun at preschool?"

Lucy nodded. "Then I went to Addie's house to play."

"Wow, you had a big day." Jackie gave Lucy a kiss on the top of her head, then sat down. "That looks like good ice cream."

"It is. I ate it all. See…?" She held up the empty Dixie cup. "Mommy, can I go see Grandpa?"

"Sure. I think he's in his office." Lucy hurried off, Cuddles on her heels. Eden sank down into a chair and looked at Jackie. "What are we going to do about Blake?"

"I was going to ask you the same thing. What do you think of our long-lost son?"

"He's nothing like Mark."

Jackie chuckled and shook her head. "No, he is not. If you didn't know they were brothers you'd never suspect. That was part of the problem. Blake was like his mother and that was hard for his dad and brother to understand."

Eden considered her friend's words. "They don't even look alike. Mark was so slender and elegant. Blake is more muscular, more the outdoors type."

"And more handsome."

Eden almost agreed but hot shame clogged her throat. "No one was as handsome as Mark."

Still, she couldn't deny that Blake possessed a kind of blatant masculinity that

was hard to ignore. But somehow she would. *Not her type.* She pushed thoughts of Blake aside. She had bigger concerns. "I'm worried about what his sudden reappearance will do to Owen. His heart can't withstand this kind of emotional stress. Won't this be like adding fuel to a fire?"

"Maybe, but it's time that fire was put out." Jackie patted Eden's hand. "Don't worry, I won't put Owen at risk, but neither am I going to play along with this family feud or the pity party in which he's been indulging. I know what your father-in-law is going through. I've lost a spouse and I grieved, but eventually you have to accept it and start living again." She stood. "Which is why I'm starting a new campaign today. I'm calling it the B&O Railroad. Connecting the tracks between Blake and Owen."

Eden grinned. She loved Jackie's unquenchable spirit. "How do you plan on making that happen?"

"Hopefully tonight at supper. I'm fixing their favorite meal."

Eden didn't like Jackie's plan, but she also knew that the woman was the only one who could handle her father-in-law. All she could do was pray the meeting between father and son went peacefully.

Her anxiety was in high gear later as she filled the glasses with sweet tea and arranged one at each place setting. Everything was ready for the family meal. Secretly, she hoped that something would happen to change the plan. Anything would do. Owen changing his mind, a power outage, even a hurricane would be welcome, though in January that was impossible.

The timer on the oven beeped. Within minutes the food was on the table. With one last look to make sure everything was in its place, Eden walked to the family room. "Supper is ready." Not wanting to see Owen's reaction, she quickly turned and went back to the kitchen.

Lucy and Cuddles hurried behind her. "I'm hungry."

Eden smiled and helped her daughter onto her booster. "I like to hear that." She glanced at the door. Blake hadn't shown up. Maybe her prayers had been answered and he'd decided it was too difficult to meet his dad this way.

Before she could turn around, Blake tapped lightly on the door, then let himself in. Lucy greeted him.

"Hi. My name is Lucy. Who are you?"

Normally, Eden was proud of her daugh-

ter's friendly demeanor, but this was not one of those times.

Blake smiled. "I'm your uncle Blake."

She thought about that a moment. "What's an uncle?"

Blake leaned forward. "I'm your dad's brother."

She frowned as if the concept was too complicated, then glanced at her mother.

Eden set her jaw. "It just means we're family."

Blake held her gaze a moment before reaching out to pet Lucy's puppy. "Who's your friend?"

"He's Cuddles. He's a boy."

Blake nodded thoughtfully. "Good to know."

Behind her, Eden heard Jackie and Owen enter the kitchen together. She tensed. She did not want to be present when father and son saw each other for the first time in over a decade, but here she was literally standing between the two.

She watched as Blake looked at his father. His mouth was in a tight line, his dark eyes shadowed. Was that a hint of pain in the brown depths?

"Hello, Dad."

Owen grunted, yanked a chair out and sat down. Eden moved to take a seat, only to re-

alize that she'd be next to Blake. Owen and Jackie were on the opposite side and Lucy was tucked between her and Owen. Wonderful. Not only did she have a front-row seat for this encounter, but she was also in the line of fire.

Owen kept his gaze lowered to his plate, his jaw working back and forth as if trying to control his emotions.

Jackie smiled. "I hope the chicken pie is good. It's been a while since I've made it. It's from your mother's recipe, Blake."

"Then it's bound to be delicious."

Owen started to reach for the bowl of green beans, but Lucy interrupted him. "Grandpa, we have to say the blessing, remember?"

Eden tensed. Owen's expression looked like it was the last thing he wanted to do, but he could never deny a request from his granddaughter. Lucy held out her hands. Owen took one and Eden took the other, only then realizing that she'd have to take Blake's hand as well. It took a full second for her to decide to accept the moment. Get the blessing over with and let go.

His hand wrapped around her fingers, warm and gentle, the contact creating a ripple in her pulse. Apprehension no doubt. Still, she couldn't ignore the surprising strength

she found in his large hand. She'd expected his grasp to be weak.

Lucy said her favorite blessing. "God is great, God is good, let us thank Him for our food. Amen!"

Everyone chuckled at her enthusiastic amen. Before Eden could reclaim her hand, Blake released it like it was on fire. Apparently, he didn't want to be any more connected to her than she did to him. Fine with her. So why did she feel slightly offended?

Jackie started a conversation about Lucy's latest art project while passing around the food. Eden tried not to look between father and son, but as the minutes ticked by, she grew increasingly apprehensive. Surely this peace couldn't last for the entire meal.

Jackie finished her story, but no one took up the conversation. After a long silence, she tried again. "It's so nice to have the family together around the table."

Owen aimed his gaze at Blake. "It's the wrong son. It should be Mark. Not him."

Eden froze, shocked at Owen's harsh words, and felt a rush of sympathy for Blake. How awful to be reviled by your father. She looked at Blake, but his expression was unreadable. She braced herself. *Here it comes.*

The fireworks are about to begin. If they got too heated, she'd have to take Lucy away.

Blake was silent a moment, then looked at Owen. "You're right. He should be here. But he's not."

The older man shook his head. "You're not welcome here. You're dead to me."

"I know that, too, but I'm not dead. I'm here and I want to try and make amends somehow."

"Impossible. You can't take his place."

Eden nearly choked on her bite of pie. She never expected to hear these things coming from her father-in-law.

Jackie patted Owen's arm and whispered softly, "Calm down. Take a deep breath."

"Jackie, this chicken pie is even better than I remembered."

Blake's comment drew a grunt from his father.

"It must be the only thing you remember. Did you forget where you lived? Who you were? Who you were supposed to be? Your obligations?"

Owen's tone grew angrier with each word.

Eden sensed Blake stiffen beside her and braced herself. His calm response surprised her. "Jackie, would you pass the corn?"

Owen set his glass down with a loud bang. "I'm talking to you."

"No, sir. You were interrogating me."

"Have you no answer?"

Blake set his fork down. "Yes. I never forgot where I lived. I found who I was and where I was supposed to be. And I met all my obligations."

"Not to your family."

"To *myself*."

"Ha. You were always a self-centered brat." Owen fisted his hands on either side of his plate. "Why did you come back here?"

Blake didn't flinch at the cruel question. "It was time. I don't want to be at odds with you any longer."

"Too late for that. What did you hope to accomplish?"

"I thought we could be a family again," Blake answered. "And that I could help around here or lend a hand at the office."

Owen slammed a fist on the table, rattling the dishes. "Stay away from my business. You didn't want it when I needed you and I don't need you now. If you really want to help, then help her."

Eden blinked when her father-in-law pointed directly at her.

"She needs help at the museum if it's going to be ready for the bicentennial this spring. Make yourself useful."

Blake's shocked expression mirrored her own. "What? I mean… I'm not sure that I—"

"Just as I expected. You only want to help when it suits you. You want to mend fences, then prove it. Get yourself over to my museum and help Eden. You can start tomorrow."

"I can't be there tomorrow."

Owen waved off Eden's comment. "Then he can show up when you need him." Her father-in-law pushed back from the table and walked out.

Eden watched him leave, unable to speak for the tightness in her throat. Owen couldn't be serious. This was *disastrous*. She couldn't work with Blake. He'd be underfoot, complicating things and slowing her progress. Not to mention she didn't like the way he made her feel. Being near him left her confused and angry…and edgy. All the things she'd heard about him kept swirling in her mind. Only now she didn't know what to believe.

She looked at Blake, who had leaned forward with his elbows on the table, his hands clasped and resting against his forehead as if in prayer. Obviously, he wasn't eager to work with her, either.

Then he looked up, a sad smile flickering on his lips. "Sorry you had to see that. I

should have been prepared, but I guess I expected too much."

"He shouldn't have said those things. I think he was just caught off guard by your sudden appearance after all this time."

Blake gave her a tolerant smile. "No. He's genuinely angry that I'm alive and his real son isn't. Nothing I can do about that." He raked his fingers over his scalp. "Well, looks like we're going to be working together."

She shook her head. "No, really, it's not necessary. I'm fine." Eden searched for a way to avoid this plan. "Owen didn't mean what he said."

Blake made a skeptical grunt. "I've known him longer than you and I recognize an order when I hear one."

She knew it, too, but was unwilling to agree so quickly. "The museum is on track. I'm behind at work so I can't spend as much time there as I'd like. I only have weekends to devote to it, and the evenings I like to spend with Lucy."

He frowned. "The museum isn't your regular job?"

"No. I work for the local Preservation Society. The museum is a part-time job." He studied her a moment as if wanting reassurance. "The museum will be done in plenty of time."

Blake pushed up from the chair using the tabletop for support. "I know it will. You and I will make sure of it." He grasped his cane. "Just let me know when to report to work. I'll be there." Then he turned and walked out.

Eden stared at the door, wishing she'd turned the man away this morning. Owen's command had turned her life upside down and she had no idea how she'd set things right again.

Lord, why did You send this man into my life? I can't handle this now. Please send him away.

She released the tense breath she'd been holding and shifted awkwardly in her seat, wondering how to proceed. The blowup was over. It hadn't been as physical as she'd expected but crueler than she'd imagined.

She ran through the scene again in her mind, puzzled by what hadn't happened. For years she'd heard about the epic battles between Blake and his father. Stories of the door slamming, fists pounding, nose-to-nose arguments. Even coming to blows at one time, but that hadn't happened. Instead, Blake had responded by calmly deflecting Owen's ugly words. Why hadn't he exploded?

On the other hand, her father-in-law had been angrier and viler than she'd ever seen

him. The hateful things he'd said sparked a surprise sympathy in her for Blake. In all the years Eden had known Owen, she'd never heard him like this. Since his heart attack, he'd become easily irritated or frustrated when things didn't go well, but never so hateful and cruel.

Sighing, she watched through the large windows as Blake made his way along the porch to the studio. He looked defeated. His shoulders were slumped and he leaned heavily on his cane as he walked. Despite herself, she felt for him. Was Jackie right? Was he a different man from the one described to her over the years? She'd always chalked Mark's resentment up to sibling rivalry. But now she wondered if there was more to it.

Mark had always said his brother was a charmer, able to sway people to his side with a smile and skillful manipulation. Apparently, that was true because here she was after barely twelve hours in his presence, and she was feeling sorry for him. That said, she reminded herself he'd been a detective, wounded in the line of duty, which meant there must be more to him than the cold-hearted man she'd heard about.

She stood and started to clear the dishes away. Setting the plates on the counter, she

stared at her palm. She could still feel the touch of his hand and the way his fingers had curled around hers at the dinner table, not tight, just firm. Secure. It had been a very odd reaction.

She shook off the memory. Maybe this confrontation would convince Blake he wasn't wanted, and he'd move on. He'd made his attempt at reconciliation, and it had failed. End of story.

Blake stood in the doorway of the studio, his shoulder pressing against the frame. His first meeting with his father had been worse than he'd expected. Though why he should have anticipated anything else was ridiculous. He'd pinned his hopes on the passage of time softening the old man's heart.

He stared at the kitchen window, where he could see Eden clearing off the table. His one bite of chicken pie had been delicious. He hadn't been able to eat after his father's outburst. His chest had tightened like a vise as old memories choked off his air. The yelling, the ugly words that would escalate until his mother would physically come between them and defuse the situation. Most of the time it worked, but toward the end, she was too weak to keep the peace. He blamed that

on Owen. His father always put his own concerns ahead of everyone else's.

Coming here might have been a mistake, but his desire to set things right with Owen was still his driving force. He wasn't ready to give up so soon. Not until it was completely hopeless. He'd known hopelessness in his life, and he wasn't there yet.

He had to keep trying, but he needed to keep the fights away from Eden and Lucy. He glanced at his hand. The memory of holding her hand during the blessing lingered. He could still feel the silky softness of her skin. Strange. He'd never known that sensation before. Not even with his ex-fiancée, Monica. Eden's touch was like a brand on his palm. It had given him a moment of connection, of being part of the family again.

He looked at the kitchen once more and saw that Jackie had joined Eden as they worked together. He hoped they saved some of that pie. He might be able to have it for lunch. Or he'd try to sneak back into the house later after everyone had gone to bed. His stomach rumbled. He was really hungry. Blake hated that the meal had been ruined for the others, but then Owen was good at creating drama.

He went inside, noticing the boxes he'd shoved to one side. Tomorrow he'd carry

some to the old car barn. He needed more room if he was going to stay here. Despite the disagreement this evening, he wasn't ready to leave Blessing. He wasn't ready to say good-bye to the rest of the family, either. He'd been alone a long time. It had been four years since Monica had called off their engagement. He hadn't seen it coming. He should have, but the shock had wounded him deeply and had pushed him toward taking more risks in his job, which had led him to his current situation.

Being back home, even with his dad's rejection, was what he needed right now. He needed the comfort of familiar surroundings. Ideally, he'd like to have been in his old room, but the studio was almost as good. He'd spent a lot of time here visiting his grandma. Jackie was like a second mother to him. She'd been his mother's close friend and her son Tony had been Blake's best buddy all through school. And finding Eden and Lucy was a happy surprise.

As he walked past the box marked Books, he noticed it also said Personal. Intrigued, he pried it open and pulled out a file folder stuffed with paper. Below it was a small stack of books, mainly software tutorials. Underneath them was a laptop. He pulled it out just

as a knock came on his door. He laid it back in the box and went to answer. "Eden."

She looked uncomfortable, her hands fidgeting nervously. "I just wanted to say that I'm sorry for the way Owen behaved at supper. It was… I've never seen him like that before. The things he said to you were cruel."

He smiled, caught off guard by her words. Earlier her blue eyes had shot daggers at him, yet now she was expressing sympathy. She must be a woman of deep compassion. "That's kind of you to say, but he wasn't as angry as I'd expected."

She bit her lip. "He's always been so sweet and kind to me and Lucy, and he and Mark always got along so well. I don't understand this side of him."

Blake nodded. No need to ruin her opinion of Owen. "That's because Dad and Mark were cast from the same mold. My father and I never could find common ground."

She studied him a moment, as if trying to understand. "And you and Mark?"

How much should he share? There was no reason to tarnish his brother's memory. "We got along great until he was about twelve. That's when he decided to follow in Dad's footsteps, and we drifted apart. We saw the world differently. That's all." She nodded but

something in her eyes made him take a closer look. Worry? "Don't worry about Dad and me. I'm going to give reconciliation a good try, but if I can't make that happen, then I'll move on. I won't disrupt the family forever. I don't want to burden you or Lucy with this mess."

She nodded. "Thank you for not making the situation worse tonight. I was prepared for —" She stopped, her cheeks turning pink, and she looked down.

Blake smiled. "You've heard about the old donnybrooks, huh? Well, I've learned a few things over the years. Patience being one of them."

She held his gaze a long moment as if she was trying to look inside him. He told himself to turn away, but he got caught up in the warmth of those blue eyes and it was hard to break eye contact.

"Well, it's getting late..." she murmured.

"Wait." He spoke without thinking. "Before you go, I suppose we should talk about my helping you at the museum."

"Not now. Maybe tomorrow."

"All right," he replied, trying to mask his disappointment.

"Good night, Blake."

He watched her walk back to the house, unable to take his eyes off her. She was an

interesting woman. He grunted and shut the door. Her concern for his feelings had left a warm sensation inside his chest. Mark had married an amazing woman. Beautiful, smart and caring. Not the type he would have expected him to choose. But then, his brother had undoubtedly changed over the years the way he had, and the way Owen hadn't.

Eden had given him a small kernel of hope that he could be reconciled with at least one member of his family. He'd like to be friends with his sister-in-law. Especially since they'd be working together at the museum. The last thing he wanted was to stir up more division in the family.

Perhaps her unexpected display of understanding was a good sign that she didn't want him drawn and quartered after all.

Chapter Three

Blake eased open the back door of the main house the next morning, scanning the room. No one here. He'd found a coffee maker in the studio kitchen but no coffee so he decided to risk running into the family in search of a cup and maybe a biscuit or roll.

The smell of fresh brew drew him to the end of the kitchen counter. Everything he needed, cups, spoons, sugar and cream, was right there. The first sip was pure nectar. He closed his eyes and savored the taste, letting the warmth chase away the chill in his bones. Yesterday the weather had been balmy and sunny. A front had moved through overnight, bringing colder temperatures for the day, but tomorrow would be warm again. He'd forgotten how erratic winter in the South could be.

"Hi, Uncle Blake."

He glanced down and smiled at his niece. She looked adorable with her ponytail all askew and a big smile on her face. He might enjoy this uncle thing. "Good morning, Lucy."

"Are you going to fix me breakfast? Miss Jackie always makes me pancakes."

"Really? Well. I suppose I could do her job this morning. If you help me."

Lucy nodded, smiling. "I like to help."

"Perfect. Can you show me where everything is?" After a few misdirections, Blake located a skillet and the ingredients for basic pancakes.

Lucy dragged a stool over to the counter and climbed up. "I'm a good stirrer."

He chuckled and handed her the spoon. "Then you should do the honors."

Within a few minutes, the pancakes were being piled on a plate and carried to the table.

He'd made them silver dollar–size to amuse Lucy. They were halfway through the first batch when Eden showed up. The look of shock and surprise on her face would have been entertaining if he hadn't been so aware of her attitude toward him. He stopped mid-bite and waited for the scolding to begin. He didn't have long to wait. "What are you doing?"

He smiled, hoping to dilute her irritation.

"I was hungry, so I made pancakes. Lucy was hungry, too."

"Uncle Blake makes baby pancakes. See. Aren't they cute?"

Eden's jaw slid side to side. "So, you just made yourself at home?"

Blake met her gaze. So much for the friendly approach. "It's still my home."

"Mommy, I helped, too. I stirred."

Eden placed a possessive hand on Lucy's head. "That was nice of you to help, sweet pea."

She may have been speaking to her daughter, but her eyes were on him. "You can't make amends by fixing breakfast."

"I wasn't trying to. I was hungry. That's all."

"You want some baby pancakes, Mommy? They're yummy."

"No, thank you."

"Can Cuddles have one?"

"No. It's not good for him."

Jackie strode in, a big smile on her face. "Good morning. It's good to see you sitting here, BJ. Oh, and you made pancakes." She looked at Eden. "Blake and his mom would have them every weekend. They were the only ones in the family who liked them."

"Mark hated pancakes."

Blake saw Eden's cheeks redden, as if she hadn't meant to say that out loud.

Jackie nodded. "He and Owen preferred French toast."

Jackie kissed Lucy on the top of her head and touched Eden's shoulder as she came toward Blake and bent and kissed his cheek. "I'm glad you're making yourself at home, BJ." She moved to the coffee maker and poured a cup. "Did you sleep all right? The studio hasn't been lived in for a long time."

He glanced at Eden, but she'd turned her back and was staring at the orange in her hand. He forced his gaze to Jackie. "I rearranged a few things. It was fine and the bed was comfortable. I slept like the proverbial log."

"Good. I'll bring you fresh linens today and if you'll make a list, I'll pick up a few groceries." Jackie pursed her lips. "You certainly need to eat better. You look like a scarecrow. We need to fatten you up."

Blake smiled. "I remember what a good cook you were. I used to find any excuse to eat at your house."

"You and all of Tony's friends, as I recall."

He took another bite of pancake. "How did you end up living here, Miss Jackie?"

"I'm a caregiver now and when Owen be-

came ill, I came in to help. Eden was working full-time and caring for Lucy. We all sort of clicked and I ended up moving in. It's been a blessing for all of us." She patted his shoulder. "Maybe it will be for you, too."

Blake doubted that. Between his father's unforgiving attitude and Eden's resentment, he feared his time at Oakley would be short. He changed the subject. "Is Paul Grayson still the manager at the Blessing bank?"

"He is."

"Good. I need to get some things taken care of." He rose and carried his plate to the sink. Eden drew away as he came near. Her bitterness toward him ran deep, and he wanted to understand why. He walked to the door, then turned back. "Eden, let me know when to report for work." She shot him an angry glare. He grinned and opened the door.

Lucy waved at him. "Bye, Uncle Blake."

"Bye, Lucy. Bye, Cuddles." He glanced at Eden, but her expression was much the same as it had been. *Disapproving.* It was going to take more than pancakes and a smile to forge their relationship.

Eden wiped the sticky syrup from Lucy's hands and carried her empty plate to the sink.

"Is Uncle Blake going to be here every morning? I like his pancakes."

She wanted to reply with a firm no, but she had no idea how long he'd hang around. A wave of unwelcome sympathy surfaced once again. He'd suffered a serious gunshot wound. Maybe coming home was something he needed.

Jackie refilled her cup. "I should have guessed BJ would end up in law enforcement."

Eden hated that she was curious. "Why is that?"

"Blake was a lot like his mom. Angela loved helping others. She was always volunteering for one thing or another. That's how we became so close. We both volunteered at the food bank and at Madeline's Clothes Store. She had a huge heart."

"I thought Blake was a wild child."

"He was rambunctious, always looking to try something new, wanting to see what was over the next hill. But he was never in trouble."

That information didn't mesh with what she'd always heard. "I don't understand."

Jackie plucked a muffin from the stand in the middle of the table. "Owen expected his sons to follow in his footsteps. The plan was

that they would get a business degree and join the company. But Blake never wanted that. He was taking criminal justice classes and Angela made sure Owen didn't know. When she died, it all came out and the relationship between BJ and Owen fell apart. Owen felt Blake had betrayed the family. He delivered an ultimatum. Come to work for the company or get out. Blake left and that was that."

Eden shook her head, trying to understand. "Mark always said Blake was the one who had walked out without even a goodbye. He said it broke Owen's heart."

"I'm sure it did, but not in the way you think. He was heartbroken because his big dream of having both his sons in the company was shattered." She stood and went to the sink. "You know how much I care for your father-in-law, but he's always had a selfish streak. Angela was the only one who could temper it, especially when it came to BJ. But after she was gone, there was nothing to keep the pair from locking horns."

Eden couldn't deny that Owen had a one-track mind about certain things. He and Mark had both been workaholics when it came to Sinclair Properties, but she hadn't thought of it as selfish. However, maybe she hadn't been seeing him clearly. Her perceptions

about Blake were taking a hit. "Why do you call him BJ?"

"It's what Angela always called him. Blake Jonathan. BJ."

"Oh." She brushed hair from her forehead and shoved aside her curiosity about her brother-in-law. "All I know is that whenever Blake's name came up, neither Mark nor Owen had anything good to say. They only talked about his contempt for family and his irresponsible lifestyle."

Jackie grimaced. "Deep down I think Owen felt guilty for the way he ordered Blake away, but he's a proud man and it is difficult for him to admit when he's been wrong."

Eden chafed at the observation. "You make him sound so self-centered."

"Right now he is." Jackie touched her hand. "He's stuck in his grief. Losing Mark was the end of his big dreams."

Eden teared up. She understood. The loss had been unbearable at times. If she could have shut down and hid in the house the way Owen had done, she would have, but she had a job and a child to take care of. "Can you blame him?"

"Yes, I can blame him, and no, he hasn't lost a dream. Blake is here. He's a Sinclair, too. And you and Lucy are Owen's legacy, but

all he can see is that one big dream is gone. Sometimes I want to shake his head off his shoulders. The stubborn old man needs to see into the future. I'm hoping Blake will force him to do that."

Eden was hoping Blake would see how unwelcome he was and leave. She bit her lip, immediately regretting the unkind thought.

Jackie stood. "It's my day to get Lucy to preschool. I've got errands to run so I'll see you later."

A glance at the clock told Eden she had nearly an hour before she had to be at work at the Preservation Society. That gave her plenty of time to work on cataloging some of the museum pieces Owen wanted on display.

Opening her laptop, she got to work, grateful that she had plenty to keep her mind off her brother-in-law. Movement out the window drew her attention. Blake was sitting on the porch steps outside the studio, his hands clasped on top of his cane, gazing thoughtfully out across the lawn. It was hard to find any family resemblance between the brothers.

Mark had been supremely confident, self-assured and controlled. Everything he did was neat, precise and planned. He'd been handsome, with sharp features and hawk-like eyes. Even his wardrobe was crisp and

sophisticated. Mark always made her think of the men in suit advertisements. Lean, neat and classically handsome.

Blake, on the other hand, was a different kind of attractive. With his strong features and deep-set, probing dark eyes, he was the very picture of the rugged, outdoors male. His hair was dark brown, and he had a lazy smile that captured your attention and highlighted his chiseled jawline. It was easy to see how he earned his reputation as a charmer.

The differences between the two brothers extended far beyond their looks. Mark had been a driven man, always focused on the next thing. He had a way of commanding the world to bend to his will. Much like Owen. However, Blake had a more easygoing way about him, as if he took life as it came. No doubt it was a quality that came in handy in his career in law enforcement.

Eden jerked her attention back to the computer screen. Why was she making comparisons? There was nothing about her brother-in-law that was admirable. Certainly not his ability to cut his family out of his life, then pop up suddenly and think he could fix years of neglect and estrangement with a pancake breakfast.

Yet, her mental image of Blake was find-

ing it hard to align the man with the things she'd always heard about him. She pressed her hands against her warm cheeks, trying to chase away the guilt over her thoughts. She'd truly believed what Mark had told her about his brother. While he may not be the villain she'd expected, she couldn't forget what he'd done. Any man who would turn his back on his family to chase a reckless existence didn't deserve her sympathy. Then her conscience mocked her. Blake *hadn't* been living a frivolous life. He'd been a policeman. He'd served the public and taken a bullet in the process.

Was she judging him too harshly?

"Time will tell, girl." The man was still a stranger to her, and she wasn't going to change her opinion on twenty-four hours of exposure. Sooner or later, he'd show his true colors.

Curious, she stood and moved closer to the window for a better view. As she watched, Blake rose and started walking toward the old barn. Why would he be going there? It was filled with junk, as far as she knew. What was he up to? Impulse took hold and she headed out the back door to question him. He'd disappeared inside before she caught up with him. Filled with suspicion, she stepped inside. "What are you doing?"

He turned and smiled. "Hello, Eden. I'm looking for something."

"Obviously. What? And who said you could snoop around the property?"

His smile widened. "I did."

She'd expected him to stop and explain, but he kept moving farther into the gloomy space. The man had no shame. "What are you looking for?"

"A treasure."

Eden mentally rolled her eyes. "There are no hidden treasures here."

He grinned and waved a finger. "Ah, you might be surprised. Though, it's only a treasure to me."

Blake moved behind an old wagon and a stack of plywood kept on hand for hurricane season. "Bingo."

She wound through the odds and ends and found him in the far back corner. She watched as he pulled a large tarp away, revealing a dusty old motorcycle. "What's that?"

He grinned widely as if he had truly found a treasure. "That is Roxy. Roxy, meet Eden."

She frowned and shoved her hands into her sweater pockets. "I'd hardly call an old rusty motorcycle a treasure."

"She may not look like much now, but she's

a rare beauty. All she needs is a little spit and polish, new tires and she'll be good to go."

"I might have known you'd have a bike."

"Why is that?"

There was a challenging look in his eyes. She raised her chin. "Mark always said you were a daredevil."

"He did, huh? Well, he's wrong in this case. Roxy belonged to my Grandpa Fuller. My mother's dad. He got this bike from a friend and he and I spent the summer I was fourteen fixing it up. He left it to me when he passed." He brushed his hand slowly over the seat. "Best time of my life. Special memories."

Eden's protective feelings for Owen swelled. "No memories from your father?"

He shook his head. "Sinclair men were only interested in work. Not family or hobbies."

Eden bristled, insulted at his implication. "They had a strong work ethic. They were building something important."

"True, but what good is it if it blinds you to the needs of your family?"

Eden didn't want to pursue that topic. "So, what are you going to do with it now that you've found it?"

Blake set his hands on his hips. "Clean her up and make her hum again."

"And ride off into the sunset." She hadn't meant to sound so hopeful. Her cheeks warmed.

He held her gaze a moment, then tapped his bad leg. "Don't think that would be a good idea. You need two good legs to make her run."

Eden swallowed the lump in her throat. She should have thought of that.

Blake replaced the tarp over the bike and came toward her. "I wouldn't believe everything Mark told you. He and Dad have a certain way of looking at things. Especially the past."

She raised her chin and looked him in the eyes. "He was my husband. I think I'll take his word over yours."

He came toward her. "One thing I learned as a detective was that five people can observe the same incident and yet each give a different account. The truth lies somewhere in the mix. You have to take the time to dig it out." Blake cleared his throat. "Well, I'm off to town. Have a good day."

He walked past, leaving her in the dim barn with thoughts swirling like dust mites in her mind. He was a very confusing man.

She stepped outside to see him pick up a small backpack and his cane and start walking down the driveway. She glanced around.

She'd assumed he had driven here, but she realized she didn't remember hearing a car yesterday. Had he walked here from town? Is that what he planned to do now?

She hurried after him. "Blake!" He stopped and looked back. She gestured for him to wait, then went inside the house, grabbed a set of keys, then hurried toward him. He looked puzzled. She couldn't blame him. Eden hadn't intended to be kind, but after learning of his injury, she couldn't allow him to walk the two miles to town on that leg. She handed him the keys. "Mark's pickup is parked in the new garage. I'm sure he'd want you to use it. It's just sitting there. I haven't taken the time to sell it."

Blake studied her a moment, then smiled, causing a blip in her pulse. She pressed her lips together.

"Thank you. I appreciate this. I'm not sure my brother would be in agreement with this loan, but I'm not one to pass up a blessing."

He tossed the keys into the air, grabbed them, then turned and walked to the garage. Eden turned and made her way quickly to the house, not wanting to see Blake behind the wheel of her husband's beloved vehicle. She was already regretting loaning him the truck. Because, no matter what he'd been through, she was *not* going to get chummy

with the man. It would break Mark's heart. The thought quickly followed that he hadn't thought about her heart when he'd left her penniless and devastated at his betrayal.

Still, her first loyalty was to her husband. Blake would be gone soon enough, then she could get back to her job of saving the Beaumont house. She tried not to think about the time wasted on Owen's private museum that could have been spent on negotiating the purchase of the historic home. That's where her heart was. Saving old homes had always been her goal. But she loved Owen dearly; he was family, and she was determined to see his dream through no matter what.

Even if it meant working with Blake.

Eden's unexpected consideration swirled in Blake's thoughts during the drive into town. It had been nice seeing kindness in her eyes instead of the resentment that was usually there. He suspected much of her low opinion of him was due to his brother. What had Mark told her about his younger sibling? He knew they hadn't been close for a long time, but he'd never suspected his brother held such strong feelings against him. It must have started after he left the family and no doubt his dad had added to the rift over the years.

There had to be more to Eden's animosity, he just needed to find out what. He didn't like seeing the look of anger in her eyes. He wanted to see her smile like she did whenever she looked at Lucy. His adorable niece was a miniature version of her mother. Seeing them together always made him smile. Lord knows he'd had little to smile about in the last few years.

Maybe he could find a way to win her over by helping at the museum. Though he wasn't sure how he felt about working with her so closely, he couldn't deny he found her to be an intriguing woman. Strong, kindhearted and loyal to a fault. Not to mention beautiful.

His brother had picked a special lady. A sting of realization hit him. Eden was his brother's wife. His widow. He needed to keep his thoughts about her purely platonic. Turning on his blinker, he pulled into the bank parking lot. Nothing like cold financial matters to keep a man's thoughts in line.

Hours later, Blake turned the truck toward Oakley Hall. He'd accomplished a lot today. His finances were in order, his driver's license renewed, and he'd met with a physician about his leg. His last stop had been at the church to renew his friendship with Pastor Miller. He'd need a spiritual specialist as much as he needed a medical one.

He turned on the radio and tapped his fingers on the steering wheel in time with the music. He almost had a real life again. As he drove past the old Saint Joseph's Church, he saw the new sign declaring it the Blessing History Museum. He wasn't looking forward to working there. He'd never enjoyed history. Especially with a woman who despised him. But when Owen Sinclair gave a command, it wasn't disobeyed.

Back home, Blake stopped the truck near the new garage and leaned forward to peer out the windshield. Eden and Lucy were holding hands and walking Cuddles across the lawn. He smiled. The chill of early morning had evolved into one of those sweet Mississippi winter days that felt more like early spring. He would like to join them and stroll between the trees. Had Mark realized how blessed he'd been? A beautiful, loving wife and sweet little girl to call his own.

His chest tightened. Those were things he would probably never experience for himself. He'd have to be content to witness them from a distance. He grunted softly as he got out of the truck. Coveting someone else's life wasn't something he'd ever indulged in. His life had been too full to long for more. But he was starting to envy his brother and the life

he'd had with Eden and Lucy. A hot rush of blood scorched his veins. He had to stop these feelings from getting out of hand.

Slamming the door closed with more force than necessary, Blake retreated to the studio, glad that Eden and Lucy had already gone inside. He'd found himself wanting to watch them together. Not a good habit to develop. He had to watch his p's and q's while he was here. Because he didn't want to create any new awkward situations. Especially with Eden.

He winced. His leg was complaining. He'd walked a lot today and it was time to rest.

Blake headed toward the bedroom, noticing that there were bags from a local grocer on the kitchen counter. Jackie had come through. He could eat in his room and avoid the main house, he thought with relief as he stretched out on the bed. Though isolating himself wouldn't accomplish what he'd come here to do, which was to settle things with his dad.

Blake draped his arm over his eyes in an attempt to sort out the tangled mess he'd uncovered at Oakley Hall. He wasn't sure how to approach the various conflicts. All he knew was that he couldn't sort it out on his own. He needed someone with greater wisdom

than he possessed. He might need a visit to the Blessing Bridge to untangle his confusing thoughts. The complications he'd found here were overwhelming.

Unable to still his troubled thoughts, Blake rose and went into the living room and fixed a glass of tea, then glanced at the stack of boxes near the door. Mark's things. Driven by a need to understand, he placed one box on the coffee table and opened it. He had so many questions. Why was Eden living with Owen? What had caused his brother's death? There was always an impression of secrecy when Mark was mentioned.

He sorted through one of the file folders, but it only held the usual company papers. After lifting out the laptop, he opened it and booted it up. While he waited, he examined a small datebook. Why his computer-savvy brother would have such an old-fashioned item intrigued him. He leafed through the pages, skimming the odd notations. Dates, numbers and appointments were all scribbled on the pages, but none of them made any sense.

When the laptop was up and running, he scanned the various files. Some were familiar names of properties Sinclair managed. Others were names he didn't know, but then his dad

was always taking on new clients who wanted him to manage their buildings or condos. It was one of the reasons Blake had left. Keeping track of payments and tenants was the most boring thing he could think of. Numbers in neat rows and balance sheets with every penny accounted for were more to Mark's liking.

Give him a good criminal collar any day.

Digging through the boxes only created more questions. There was still plenty of daylight. Maybe this was a good time to see to his spiritual dilemmas, and the best place to start was a visit to the Blessing Bridge.

A short while later he pulled to a stop in the parking lot. A large sign marked the location now officially called the Blessing Bridge Prayer Garden. The bridge had become a destination for the residents in the midfifties after a mother prayed for healing from polio for her son. When he recovered, people started coming to the site to lift up their prayers.

Blake started down the path, which was covered in fine gravel and neatly trimmed. The area had been landscaped with perfectly placed flowers and benches, creating a picturesque park. Years ago, when he used to come, the grounds had been natural and un-

touched. He'd practically forged the path himself with his frequent visits. It was the only
place he could come to fully escape the dark
shadows of home.

He stopped at the top of the arched bridge
and leaned on the rail, taking in the changes.
The park was lovely and peaceful, but he preferred the primitive state it used to be in. It
suited his mood back then. His mind was wild
and unruly. Pieces of his spirit were broken
like the limbs and branches that cluttered the
ground. He always left feeling hopeful, but
also more determined to escape Blessing and
the Sinclair name as soon as possible.

Today, he let the quiet of the site seep into
his spirit. He knew the Lord would hear his
concerns and it didn't matter if the land was
pristine or natural. Yet something was to be
said for the orderly arrangement of the park.
It allowed him to focus on the immediate concerns and not the tangled mess of emotions
that used to bring him here.

The focus of his emotions now was almost
as jumbled.

He was developing a growing interest in
his brother's wife. He found himself looking
at her, watching her, and each time he did he
had to smile. He was not on her glad-to-meet-

you list, and he hated that, but he admired her devotion to his dad. Misplaced as it was.

He rubbed his forehead. So much to adjust to. His brother dead before his time and leaving behind a wife and child. Mark was always that rock-steady type, a family man who prided himself on constantly doing the right thing, staying on the path laid out in front of him.

Unlike his younger brother, who was never satisfied, always restless and looking for what lay beyond the trees, over the next hill and down the road ahead. Well, he'd seen it all, done it all and now he was paying the piper. He sucked in a sharp breath as a zinger of pain shot through his thigh. Time for meds and rest, and those exercises he was supposed to do every day.

He needed to remember why he was here. To make peace with Owen. Nothing else mattered.

Chapter Four

Eden set her purse and laptop on the bench inside the back door and headed to the fridge for a drink. It had been a long workday with little accomplished and she was glad to be home. Lucy scurried into the room and wrapped her arms around Eden's waist.

"Hi, Mommy. I missed you today."

Eden scooped her daughter up in her arms. "I always miss you when I'm at work. Did you have fun at school today?"

"Yes. I made you something." She slid to the floor and darted to the sitting area, bringing back a piece of green construction paper. "I made you a macaroni flower. You can hang it on the wall."

Eden's heart melted. The pasta artwork vaguely resembled a flower, but Eden knew Lucy had poured her whole little heart into

the project. "It's beautiful, sweetie. I love it. Where should we hang it?"

"On the 'fridgerator so Miss Jackie and Grandpa can see it."

"Good idea."

"I made one for Uncle Blake, too."

Eden froze. "You did? Why?"

"'Cause he needs one on his fridge, don't you think?"

Eden sincerely doubted the man would appreciate the artwork. "I'm sure he does. Well, you can give it to him next time he's here."

"I made him a cane like the one he uses. It's purple."

Eden examined the creation. It looked more realistic than the flower did. She smiled. All that mattered was that Lucy had fun. Eden placed the flower art on the fridge and added a magnet to secure it in place.

Jackie entered the kitchen and beamed at the artwork on the front of the appliance. "I see you got your present."

"Yes, I did. It's beautiful."

She stepped closer and spoke softly. "Did you see the one she made for Blake?"

"Yes." Eden paused. "I saw him pulling out when I got home. Where do you suppose he's going this late?"

"I have no idea. By the way, that was nice of you to loan Blake the truck."

Eden turned away. "Kindness had nothing to do with it. I thought if he had transportation maybe he'd finish his business and be on his way sooner."

"Wow. That doesn't sound like the Eden I know."

Warmth crawled up her neck before her defenses kicked in. "He called Mark a liar."

"What are you talking about?"

"He said I shouldn't believe anything that Mark told me about him."

Jackie inhaled a slow breath. "He's not wrong, you know. Everyone has a bias to something or someone. And the truth is, we all experience things differently. Mark was always jealous of Blake. He felt he got away with things because he was the youngest."

"I'm sure he did." She could easily see Blake flashing his smile and getting his way.

"And Blake felt Mark was the favorite because he always spent more time with Owen."

Eden hadn't considered his point of view. Maybe she should have. The problem was, which one was true?

Blake slid behind the wheel of the truck Saturday morning and cranked the engine.

He was not ready for today. He'd rather stay in bed, or work on Roxy, take another round of physical therapy—anything besides going to the museum and helping Eden.

She wasn't thrilled by the prospect, either. He'd seen the dread in her eyes. Blake honestly had no idea what his father had been thinking when he'd ordered him to assist. No, that wasn't entirely true. Owen wanted his museum and that was that. Though why the old man wanted to start a museum in the first place was beyond him.

Eden's car was in the parking lot when he pulled up at the old church. A small sign pointed the way to the entrance. He turned the knob and stepped inside. "Eden? It's Blake reporting for duty."

He moved farther into the large room, the old fellowship hall, which was now filled with display cases and wall hangings. He frowned. It looked like a sad collection of high school projects.

Eden appeared from the far end of the room along with a welcome aroma.

"Good morning. Is that coffee I smell?"

She nodded and gestured him forward. He followed her past a room cluttered with boxes and a kitchen before stepping into a small

office. Eden waited while he poured his cup and sat down.

"Where do we start? I'm not sure how much help I'll be, though. Not been in many museums. I don't like history."

"I suspected as much."

Her attitude irked him. "But I'm a willing worker and I always finish what I start. So what do we do first?" He smiled but Eden turned away.

"This isn't going to work."

Blake moved to her side. "Of course it will, but I think we need to declare a truce first."

"What do you mean?"

"We need to reach an understanding that while neither of us chose to be here, we'll do our best to finish the project on time for Owen's sake."

She favored him with a skeptical expression. "You think you can do that?"

"Absolutely." He held out his hand. "We have a deal?"

Eden hesitated, but finally slipped her palm against his. The contact created a sensation he'd never experienced before. Not unlike the moment they'd held hands during the blessing. This time, however, he was acutely aware of her delicate fingers, the warmth of her small hand in his and the way it felt as

if their hands were meant to be joined. He looked into her eyes and saw them widen. Was she feeling it, too?

Suddenly, she pulled her hand away and touched her neck. "Then you can start by assembling a display." She showed him to the storage room and pointed to a carton. "I assume you know your way around a toolbox." She met his gaze, her blue eyes icy. "I hope you aren't the type that has to have your hand held every minute."

The image she'd presented bloomed, then quickly wilted in his mind. He focused on her arctic tone. "No, ma'am. No hand-holding necessary."

"Good. You can start with that." The box she indicated was large but narrow.

"What is it?"

"A wall display for large documents and pictures. It has panels that swing back and forth like for posters and such."

Blake looked around the storage room. No space here to work. "Okay if I take it out to the other room?"

"Suit yourself." She went back into her office, leaving him on his own.

So much for working together. He wasn't sure they'd come to an agreement or not.

Maybe completing his first task would gain him points.

Leaning the box against the wall, he slit the tape and opened the top. "Whoa." There were at least two million pieces to put together. This might take the rest of the day. If it weren't for his leg, he'd spread it out on the floor, but that wasn't an option. He looked around for a table to use but something familiar caught his attention. The large photo on one wall was of his great-great-grandfather Randolph Sinclair. He'd been a prominent businessman in Blessing and a local congressman. He moved to the next display and the next, then placed his hands on his hips and scanned the room again. "Eden."

She quickly came to his side. "Something wrong?"

He looked at her. "This is all my family stuff. I thought this was supposed to be a museum for Blessing, not the Sinclairs." Some of the color drained from Eden's cheeks.

"Is this all of it?" he continued. "Where's the history of the first way station on the river? The railroad coming through and the timber industry? This looks like the history of Owen Sinclair." When Eden still didn't respond, he turned and faced her. She was staring off into space. "What's going on?"

She met his gaze, her blue eyes clouded. "It's a private museum."

"What does *that* mean? Doesn't this belong to the city?"

She shook her head. "It belongs to Owen alone."

It took only a second for Blake to grasp her true meaning. "Let me guess. This is Owen's private museum so he can show everyone how important the Sinclairs are to the town. He wants to make sure no one forgets their contributions. Right?"

Eden took a long moment to reply. "He feels the family played a big part in the founding and growth of the town."

"They did but so did many other families."

She stiffened. "That's true, but this is Owen's project. He wants to leave a legacy behind for his family."

Blake shook his head. "No, for himself."

"You're wrong. You don't understand."

"Then explain it to me because all I see is re-creation of all the junk in our attic."

"Your dad is passionate about this museum. It's the most important thing in his world at the moment. It gives him a purpose and I'm going to support that in any way possible. I just wish I could have been here more often." She faced him, her eyes shooting daggers.

"And I'm not interested in your opinion. If you don't want to help, then you can leave."

Blake realized he'd let his feelings about his dad cross a line. "No. I'll stay. I shouldn't have said what I did but, I've got to ask, how does the town feel about this?"

"They have strong opinions but it's not up to them. This is a private display. Owen can put anything in here he wants."

"You don't expect anyone to pay to look at this stuff, do you? No one cares about someone else's personal history."

"That's not my concern. I promised to have the museum open for the bicentennial and that's what I'm going to do."

It hit him then that she really loved his father. He didn't understand why, but she did. He smiled and picked up a screwdriver. "Then we'd better get to work."

"Thank you."

The look of relief on her face gave him a twinge of regret. He'd have to watch his words around her. Her loyalty was impressive. He suspected she knew the folly of this project, but she was willing to ignore any negative comments to see Owen's plan fulfilled.

Eden leaned back from her computer and stretched. She'd been writing information

cards for the displays, something she'd been putting off. It had given her a reason to stay away from Blake as he worked in the main area. She'd peeked at him a few times, just to make sure he hadn't walked out, but he'd been working diligently each time.

Apparently, he'd inherited the family work ethic because he hadn't even taken a break. In fact, he'd set up a nice work area for himself. She hadn't considered how his leg might affect his capabilities. Unable to stoop down to do the job, he'd set up a folding table to use as a workbench.

Despite her doubts, Blake might be an asset to the museum after all. As if reading her mind, he suddenly appeared in the office doorway.

"I've got that display thing finished. Where do you want it hung? I may need your help. It's a two-man job."

"Of course." Blake held the frame up to the wall as she gauged the perfect spot. They worked together, her holding, him drilling, until the piece was secure. Then she handed him each frame and he slipped them into the slots.

She hadn't expected him to be so confident about the job. Mark had not been handy around tools or any kind of repair work.

Blake, on the other hand, had picked up a variety of useful skills.

"There you go." He swung one of the frames back and forth. "Smooth as butter. Want me to put the pictures inside them?"

She caught herself staring at him. There was a light in his dark eyes that surprised her, as if he really had enjoyed putting the complicated display together. "Uh, no. It's past lunchtime. Are you hungry? The Dixie Deli is just down the way... I could get us some sandwiches." She blanched. Where had that come from? She didn't want to bond with this man. Working together was one thing, but becoming friends was something else.

"I'm starved. You place the order and I'll pick it up."

"No, I'll take care of it. You've worked hard and I'm sure your leg must need rest."

He shrugged. "I won't argue."

Within fifteen minutes, Eden had placed the order and arranged for it to be delivered, and before they knew it, they were seated at the kitchen table unwrapping their sandwiches. They ate in silence for a while.

Blake took a bite of his sandwich and groaned softly. "I'd forgotten how good these were. It's good to know some things stayed the same."

Eden smiled. "The best in town. A new place opened up on Peace Street, but it can't compete." She took a sip of her drink, watching Blake. He'd surprised her today in several ways. "Thank you for your help. That display would have taken me days to put together."

He smiled and nodded. "I figured it would take me that long. But then, I read the instructions." He laughed out loud. "Go figure. No man ever wants to read the instructions. That's the first thing we throw away."

Eden couldn't help but smile. His delight was infectious. "Why is that?"

"Pride, ma'am. Pure pride." He held her gaze, and she thought about the handshake that had started the day. Touching him had been a jolt to her system. As if he'd transferred some of his abundant energy to her through his fingers. His hand had been warm, strong and secure. Like a safe place to stand.

"What's on tap for this afternoon?"

She jerked her thoughts back into line. "Uh, I have a few large documents that can be put into the frames and there's a couple of boxes I need moved around, if you're able."

"I'm ready when you are." He reached for his cane, which he'd hooked over the back of his chair, but it crashed to the floor. Eden

quickly retrieved it, intrigued by the cross carved into the curved handle.

"This is beautiful. I've never seen anything like it."

"Thank you. It's hand carved. One of a kind. A buddy at the rehab center made it for me. He'd give them to anyone who needed one."

She held his gaze, her mind swirling with curiosity. "How long was your recovery?"

"Start to finish, nineteen months. That was between surgeries, and complications and more surgery. The good news is I got to keep my leg."

"It must be hard for you. I mean you were so active and now you're..." Her cheeks heated. She was always blurting out things without thinking.

Blake smiled. "Crippled? Nah. I'm just slowed down a bit, that's all. I can't chase after the bad guys anymore, but I can walk, and in time, I might be able to play golf or hike again."

"So, you'll get better?"

"That's the plan. I'm still doing physical therapy, and I see a chiropractor regularly. Which I need to locate if I'm here long enough." He winked. "Not sure how long my reservation will last."

"I'm sure Jackie will let you stay as long as you need."

He shrugged. "But it's not her house. I'm afraid I may wear out my welcome quickly if my dad has anything to say about it."

Eden turned away. Her warm feelings toward her brother-in-law faded. She couldn't forget what he'd done. "You broke his heart."

"That's a nice explanation. The truth is that Mark followed his plan. I didn't. That's unforgivable in his eyes."

"Can you blame him? The family business was important to him, and you and Mark were the third generation. It makes sense he'd want to hand his heritage over to his sons. I don't see what's so awful about that."

"Nothing, provided the sons are in agreement. Mark always wanted to work for the company. I didn't."

Eden's defenses rose along with her anger. "Why couldn't you have just done what your father wanted? Why couldn't you set aside your own selfish desire for his sake?"

Blake held her gaze, his eyes hard and angry. She hadn't meant to upset him, but she refused to feel guilty about her position.

His jaw flexed. "Why couldn't he set aside his selfish desire and allow his son to live his own life?"

Eden placed her fingertips on her temple. He'd countered her assault with the truth. "I'm sorry. I just thought if you'd been here to help, then none of this would have happened."

Blake met her gaze. "None of what would have happened. The museum?"

"Yes. No. I mean, Mark's stress trying to save the company, Dad's heart attack. All of it."

"What do you mean *save the company*?" he demanded.

"It was in trouble. Something happened, I never knew what, but Mark was desperate, almost frantic to turn things around. But he couldn't. We had no idea at the time he was sick."

"Sick. What do you mean?" Blake leaned forward, his dark eyes probing. "How did my brother die?"

"Mark had a brain tumor."

"He didn't tell you about the cancer?"

She shook her head. "He complained of headaches, then he started becoming short-tempered, easily aggravated and angry over the smallest things. I thought it was the stress of the job. Then he started to withdraw, keeping to himself and spending more time at the office. Some days I wouldn't see him at all, and when he did come home, he'd sleep in the

spare room. I tried to get him to see a doctor, but he'd only get angrier." She tugged at her collar. "I thought he was having an affair. I didn't recognize my husband any longer. Things had gotten so bad, so volatile, I couldn't allow Lucy to live in that environment, so I contacted an attorney to begin divorce proceedings."

"Was the tumor to blame?"

She nodded. "We only found out after his death. The doctor said it wasn't uncommon for the tumor to cause significant changes in personality. Some patients can even experience delusions." What would Blake say if she told him the whole truth, about the gambling habit, losing all their savings and investments, the house and life insurance?

"Where was Owen during this?"

"He'd retired several years earlier. He had supreme confidence in Mark. He used to brag about how well his son was doing, and how he was taking the company in a new direction."

"What about now? Is the company still struggling?"

She shrugged. "I think so."

"Then why isn't Dad back at work?"

Eden took a long moment to reply. "He did at first. Then two months later, he had his heart attack. After that he stopped caring

about anything. Until he got the idea to start his museum. That gave him a focus, and he threw himself into the project. And he enlisted me to spearhead it."

"Despite your full-time job?"

Eden nodded. "I couldn't refuse him. He was struggling and this was the only thing that gave him hope, that he got up for each morning."

"Who's running the company?"

"Norman Young."

"I know him. Good man." Blake leaned forward and laid his hand on her forearm. "Well, I'm here now. You don't have to do all this alone. We're a team. Okay?"

Eden told herself to remove her arm but she didn't. There was comfort in his touch, and his words. She realized how much she'd needed help and encouragement. She'd been battling alone for a long time. But she hadn't expected help to come from her bad-boy brother-in-law. *He's a charmer.* Her husband's words flashed in her mind, and she pulled her arm from his touch. Time to turn the tables. "Now can I ask you a question?"

"Shoot."

"All this time, you didn't call or let anyone know where you were. The family needed you. The company took every ounce of en-

ergy Mark and Owen had. They could have used your help." She heard the accusation in her tone and took a deep breath to calm down. She looked at Blake. "I suppose you never thought about the family, did you?"

He toyed with his drink, avoiding her gaze. "At first, I thought about calling, but the truth was, I didn't want to know what was going on. Then after a while it was easier to not think about life back here."

She pressed her lips together. "Mark told me how you were always disrupting things, wanting the attention, getting him into one mess after another."

Blake studied her a long moment. "Is that how he remembered it?"

Her defenses kicked in. Was he calling her husband a liar again? "Why couldn't you have just done what your father asked and joined the company? Would that have been so difficult?"

Blake held her gaze. "Yes. I had no choice. After Mom died, I couldn't stay here. I had a life of my own to live. Not the one Dad had mapped out."

She squared her shoulders to regain her composure. They would never see things the same way so it was futile to keep rehashing everything. "Well, I appreciate your help…"

"You're welcome." He stood, gripping his cane. "Point me to the next project, Madam Curator."

Eden kept her expression neutral but inside she smiled at his levity. Maybe working with Blake wouldn't be so bad after all.

Or was she slowly succumbing to his charm?

Chapter Five

Blake eased open the back door to the kitchen early Sunday morning and glanced around. No one here yet. He made his way to the coffeepot and poured a cup. For some reason, the coffee here in the main house tasted better than what he could make in the studio. Today he felt like taking a chance on seeing family. So far so good. He turned and stopped in his tracks as Lucy, Cuddles and Eden entered the room. His niece and her dog stopped at his feet. However, Eden halted and turned away.

"Good morning, Lucy. How are you and Cuddles today?"

"Good. It's Sunday school day."

"Do you like Sunday school?"

Lucy nodded vigorously. "We sing songs and color and do finger plays. Watch." She entwined her little fingers into a fist. "It's the

church and the people are inside." He chuckled as she tried to duplicate the old finger play. She stole his heart every time he saw her.

Eden placed a bowl on the table. "Lucy, eat your cereal, please."

Owen came into the kitchen and Blake sensed a sudden drop in the temperature. His dad always could bring a chill with his presence. Owen stopped at the coffee maker, his back to them as he spoke.

"You're still here." He turned and glared at Blake.

Blake fought back his emotions. "I am." Not a good start to the day. He debated whether to stay and irritate his dad or go and leave the rest of the family in peace.

"Morning, everyone." Jackie breezed into the room. "Y'all need to shake a leg or we'll be late for church."

Blake spoke without thinking. "Would you mind if I came along?"

Jackie gave him a broad smile. "We'd be delighted."

"Thanks. It's been a few weeks. I could use some spiritual fortification." He set his cup on the counter and took his cane. "I'll go change and meet you there."

Jackie gave him a hug and whispered in his ear, "I think your dad is coming around."

Blake highly doubted that, judging from the scowl on his parent's face. He nodded but his stomach was doing flip-flops. He'd greatly underestimated the depth of his father's response to his return.

Attendance at church was exactly what he needed, and he hoped Pastor Miller gave one of those sermons that felt like it was directed at him personally.

Blake waited until the family had driven off before sliding behind the wheel of the truck. Attending the same church service as his family was one thing, sitting with them was a different story. There was no way he could share a pew with his dad. That would only create tension for everyone and that was the last thing they needed. There was enough of that swirling around at home.

Blake managed to enter the church without having to speak to anyone and took a seat in the back row of the sanctuary. He searched for Eden and found her sitting toward the front next to Jackie. Owen was on Jackie's other side. Lucy must be at children's church.

A touch of envy settled in his chest. It would have been nice to sit with his family, but he had a feeling that was a wish that would never come true. Owen Sinclair was a hard, stubborn man who never admitted to being wrong.

Blake paid only scant attention to the first part of the service. The music swirled around him, but his thoughts were settled on the conversation he'd had with Eden yesterday at the museum.

As if the family dynamic wasn't complicated enough, he'd learned that his brother had endured cancer alone. His tumor had put his marriage at risk, and something had happened at the Sinclair Properties office that had put the business at risk.

Hearing Eden talk about Mark's change in personality, isolating himself from everyone, and his frantic behavior at the office, left Blake more conflicted than ever. Mark had been more like their father than he'd understood. The workaholic nature and the pride that refused to ask for help were all traits that Owen had displayed daily.

His gaze sought out Eden again, a knot of resentment forming in his chest at the way she'd been treated over the last few years. Mark's selfish approach to his illness honestly made his blood boil. A husband and wife were to stand alongside one another and share the burdens for better or worse. And the way Owen had further burdened Eden by putting her in charge of his pet project when she was already spread thin with her regular job and

raising Lucy was outrageous. Not to mention helping Jackie with his self-centered father. He wanted to rescue her from it all and take her someplace safe, where she could find a little peace. She deserved that. And more.

But it wasn't his place to provide her with any of that. Blake pinched the bridge of his nose, then trained his gaze on the pulpit. Eden was starting to get under his skin. He thought about her constantly. It was a dangerous habit to start. She was his brother's widow. Off-limits. Out of bounds.

He'd come home to make amends. Falling for his sister-in-law would be the ultimate sin.

Pastor Miller stepped to the pulpit and Blake set aside everything but the words he was about to hear. It was time to worship, not worry. As he hoped, Pastor Miller's sermon hit home.

The benediction was spoken, and the pastor made his way to the door to greet people as they left. Blake intended to slip out unnoticed, but the reverend stepped forward and caught his attention.

"Good to see you here, Blake. Not sitting with your family?"

He grinned wryly. "Things haven't come to that yet."

"I understand. Come see me this week.

We'll pick up our conversation where we left off the other day." He glanced at the cane. "You still have to tell me about your adventures."

"I'll be there."

Blake returned to the house ahead of the family and changed into jeans and a T-shirt. The weather was as close to perfect as you could ask for on a Sunday. Sunshine, warm gentle breezes and azaleas budding out gave a man's spirits a lift. He had no plans today but to sit here on the porch and soak it all in.

"Uncle Blake! What ya doing?"

He smiled as Lucy came toward him at full gallop, ponytail bobbing. She looked cute in little jeans and a shirt with a glittery flower on the front. "I'm just enjoying the nice day. What are you doing?"

"Visiting you. I brought you a present. I made it at school. You can put it in your house."

Blake took the construction paper and chuckled as he recognized the image of his cane executed in macaroni.

"Wow. This is beautiful. Did you do this all by yourself?"

Lucy grinned and nodded. "Yep. I'm good at art. Where you gonna put it?"

Blake stifled a laugh and rubbed his chin. "Well, how about on the fridge? No, that's too ordinary. It needs to be someplace special.

How about in the living room where I can see it all the time? And I'll take a picture of it for my phone, then whenever I think about you I can look at my cane picture."

Lucy nodded. "Yes. I like it."

She reached for the handrail on the steps leading to the porch but instead of taking them she swung around to the opposite side and inched up along the narrow border. "Be careful there. Don't fall."

"I won't." She gave him a big smile. "I do this all the time." At the top of the steps, she transferred her feet to the outside of the porch rail and continued along the edge. "This is my trick. No one else can do this."

Blake watched her closely, hoping she wouldn't fall because with his leg, there was no way he could get to her quickly. Thankfully, the porch was only a foot and a half off the ground. "How long did it take you to learn this amazing trick?"

Lucy shrugged, then let go and jumped down to the ground. She turned, smiled and threw her arms in the air. "Ta-da."

Blake laughed and clapped his hands. "Very good."

She hurried up the steps and came to his side. "I like climbing. You want to play with me?"

How could he refuse this adorable child?

"Sure. What are we going to play? Tea party, dolls, dress-up?"

Lucy scrunched up her face. "No. I want to play ball. I'll go get it."

She scurried off, disappearing around the side of the house, then reappearing with a small soccer ball. "See. It's pink and purple. 'Cause it's a girl's ball."

"Of course it is. Well, Lucy, I can kick the ball with one foot but not the other, if that's okay."

He joined her on the lawn. He kept his cane with him. The ground could be uneven. "Are you ready?"

She stared at him. "Do you have a boo-boo?"

"Yep. A big one."

"Is that why you walk funny?"

Blake nodded and held his leg out. "It won't bend."

"Oh." Curiosity satisfied, the little girl set the ball down and kicked it. He sent it right back to her and she giggled. "You kick better than Jeffery."

"Who's Jeffery?"

Lucy made a sour face. "A boy at school. He kicks like a girl."

"I'll take that as a compliment of the utmost significance."

Blake could easily lose his heart to this

child. An ache had begun inside him, wrapped in envy and pierced with hopelessness. His brother had been a fortunate man. Had Mark fully appreciated his family? Having a lovely wife and sweet little girl like Lucy would be all that he'd ask for. It wasn't in the cards for him, though.

He doubted it ever would be.

Eden looked up from her laptop when Owen entered the kitchen and went to stand at the window. He was unusually quiet since they'd come home from church, almost thoughtful, which was out of character for him. "Can I get you a drink or something to snack on?"

"No." He clasped his hands behind his back and continued to stare outside. Curious, she rose and went to his side. Lucy and Blake were kicking the soccer ball in the yard. Lucy was bubbling with energy and from the big smile on her brother-in-law's face, he was having fun, too.

He had a great smile. She winced at that thought. Not that it mattered.

"She's like him."

Eden looked at Owen. "Yes, she resembles Mark in many ways."

"He was always moving. Always active. Never could sit still."

She realized he was talking about Blake. She looked at the pair in the yard. They were thoroughly enjoying each other. Despite his bad leg, Blake was moving well. Was her daughter really like her uncle? The thought was both disturbing and oddly comforting.

"He was a climber, too."

Eden's throat tightened. She'd tried to curb Lucy's desire to climb anything in sight but with no success. She studied Owen more closely. What was he saying? That Lucy would turn out to be a rebel like her uncle? Her heart skipped a beat. Though Blake actually turned out to be an honorable man. Perhaps Owen didn't know. "He was a detective wounded in the line of duty."

Owen worked his jaw. "Reckless fool." He turned and abruptly left the kitchen. What had he seen that had prompted those observations? There'd been no bitterness in his voice, just a statement of fact.

Her text alert sounded, and she hurried to pick up her phone and quickly scanned the message from her boss, Virginia Thomas, director of the South Mississippi Preservation Society.

Mrs. Langley has given us permission to photograph Beaumont. She'll meet you there tomorrow with the key.

Eden started to type a reply but dialed her boss's number instead. "Hi, Virginia. This is great news. What do you suppose changed their minds?"

"I have no idea. Honestly. It shouldn't be this difficult to decide whether to sell us the house or not."

"True, but when you're dealing with six heirs, living in five different states, the first thing to go is communication." The bickering had been going on ever since the owner, Mrs. Vincent Harper, had passed and left the home to her distant nieces and nephews.

"If you ask me, it's all about greed. The heirs know that property is worth more if they doze the house and sell it to a developer for retail space. They could make millions."

Eden chewed her lower lip. "Maybe granting us permission to take pictures is a step in a positive direction. At least we'll have documentation, if nothing else. If we could just find the key to getting that Ohio heir to change his mind… Everyone else is on board. At least they were at the last teleconference."

"Their lawyer is pushing for a settlement. Everyone wants a payday."

Eden couldn't disagree. The society had tried everything to convince them of the importance of the nearly three-hundred-year-old

structure. However, the nephew in Sandusky, Ohio, wasn't budging. As a real estate broker, he knew the land on which Beaumont sat was worth a small fortune today, and he was determined to get as much money as possible.

"Thank you for letting me know. I'll be at Beaumont first thing tomorrow."

"Oh, I meant to ask, did you ever find someone to help you at the museum?"

Eden took a moment to measure her words. "Yes. Owen ordered Blake to help me."

"Blake? The prodigal brother-in-law? How are you going to work with that man every day?"

A twinge of regret skittered through Eden's mind. She'd unfairly talked Blake down to her boss. "He actually started yesterday, and he was very helpful. He's not what I expected. He likes dogs." She wasn't sure where that thought came from, except he'd made friends with Cuddles, who now treated him like a long-lost friend.

"Well, will wonders never cease."

After the call ended, Eden opened her home page and looked at the image of Beaumont that served as her wallpaper. She wasn't sure why, but the old home had become special to her. She'd worked on several other historic homes in Blessing, but Beaumont had

touched her soul. It would break her heart if the society lost the home, though she was beginning to think that was inevitable. She knew the heirs would likely sell it and the new owners would bring in an excavator and demolish it, destroying centuries of history in the process.

Why couldn't people see the value in pre-serving the past?

Eden and Lucy entered the kitchen the next morning to find Blake sitting at the breakfast table. She hadn't seen her brother-in-law since yesterday. He'd come to church alone and ap-parently sat in the back. She'd caught sight of him speaking with Pastor Miller at the end of the service. Why hadn't he sat with the fam-ily? Probably because of Owen. It would have been uncomfortable for them all.

"Uncle Blake. I'm happy to see you."

Blake lifted Lucy onto his lap and smiled as his niece gave his neck a big hug. "I'm happy to see you, too."

"Are you going to make baby pancakes for us?"

Blake chuckled and glanced at Eden with his eyebrows raised. "I don't know. Are we?"

"Sorry, Lucy. Not this morning. Mommy has an appointment and you need to get to

school early today for the field trip to the library. I'll fix you a muffin and a glass of milk."

Blake joined her at the sink, rinsing his cup and setting it aside. "Do you want me to go to the museum and start on those boxes in the storage room?"

"No. I'll need to be there as we go through them. You have the day off. I'm meeting someone this morning, so we'll have to postpone that for now."

She glanced at her watch a few minutes later. "Lucy, are you almost finished? I have to be at Beaumont on time, so we need to get moving."

"Yes, Mommy. I'm done."

Blake moved to the table and picked up after Lucy. "Beaumont. Is that the old rickety hodgepodge place out on Thompson Road?"

Eden bristled at his assessment of the historic home. "It's not a hodgepodge. It's a perfect compilation of the history of Blessing."

He grimaced. "If you say so. When we were kids it was always the place you toilet-papered because it was so ugly."

"Stop! It's not ugly… It's unique. And it's rich with history."

"Why are you going out there?"

"I'm meeting one of the heirs. A Mrs. Bar-

bara Langley. She's given us access to the home to take pictures." She quickly explained the situation to him. "We may not acquire the house, but at least I'll have archival evidence of every nook and cranny for future reference."

Blake held her gaze a long moment. "That old place is important to you, isn't it?"

"It's important to *Blessing*. Lucy, get your backpack."

"Mind if I tag along?"

Eden spun around and stared. "To the house? Why?"

Blake grinned and shrugged. "Why not? I'm free and it's a big place. You might need some company."

She didn't have time to discuss the issue. "Suit yourself. Just don't get in my way."

"No, ma'am. I'll try not to."

She picked up her purse. "I have to drop Lucy off at school on the way."

A short while later, Eden pulled into the end of the long winding drive leading to the Beaumont Plantation. She would never say it out loud, but Blake wasn't entirely wrong about the place. While historically a treasure trove of Blessing history, aesthetically it was a hodgepodge of periods and styles.

Perched on the edge of a deep ravine above

the river below, the original rustic building had been a way station and inn during the 1780s and was one of the earliest structures in the area. Its low-pitched roof shielded a wide porch with hand-hewn rails and posts. Attached to the east end of the small building was a two-story brick Federal addition complete with portico and Doric columns.

The addition on the west end, added in 1858, was a three-story Greek Revival. The formal structure had become the front of the home, complete with Corinthian columns and double galleries. Each section had been designed according to current trends and requirements of the time.

Eden couldn't explain her affection for the old home. But it was the embodiment of three centuries of history and she wanted to see it preserved and not bulldozed for another apartment or retail complex.

Blake leaned forward and peered out of the windshield as Eden pulled to a stop near the middle of the sprawling home. "It hasn't changed. Maybe a bit shabbier than I remember."

She shot him a scowl. "It's been empty for two years. What did you expect?"

Another car pulled up and a woman got out. Eden greeted her warmly. "Thank you

so much for allowing me access. The society really appreciates this."

"I'm glad to help. I'm on your side. I would love to sell the home to the society and see it preserved the way it deserves. But I'm afraid most of my cousins have no heart for anything old and only see dollar signs."

"I know. It'll break my heart to see the home destroyed." Eden sensed Blake slowly approaching. She turned and saw him waiting patiently with his hands in his pockets. He looked relaxed and at ease. It occurred to her that Mark had never looked that way. "Uh, Mrs. Langley, this is Blake Sinclair, my... brother-in-law."

They chatted a few moments, then the woman left, and Eden held up the keys. "Finally, I get to examine this place inch by inch."

"How 'bout I leave you here and come back when you're done?"

One look at his expression and she realized he was joking. "Oh no. You asked to come along. You have to stick it out."

She smiled as she hurried up to the door in the oldest section of the home. Her heart beat quickly with anticipation. Today was better than a birthday. Inserting the large key into the lock, she turned it. Nothing happened.

She tried several more times with no success. Blake reached over and took the keys from her hand, brushing against her fingers and sending an electric jolt through her system. She kept her eyes averted for fear of him seeing her reaction. Eden thought she heard him clear his throat.

"Maybe it just needs a firmer hand." He inserted the large key and was rewarded with a sound snap. The knob turned and the wide, thick door swung open. Blake smiled and gestured her to enter.

She did so quickly, moving ahead of him to find space to breathe. That proved harder to do than expected. The air inside was stale and musty. She coughed. Blake did likewise.

"I don't suppose we can open a window?"

"No, but we can leave the doors open." She pointed to the door on the opposite end of the long entry room. "We can get a little cross-ventilation."

Blake saw to the door while Eden retrieved her camera.

"So where do we start?" He gestured with his hands. "The old section, the older section or the *really* old section." He smiled but Eden only scowled and turned her back, focusing on the long dark room.

"Why don't you see if you can find lights? I

know the house has electricity. Mrs. Langley arranged for it to be turned on today."

By the time Blake returned, Eden had completed her inventory of the center room, and its side rooms, snapping photos as she went.

Blake approached her, brushing dust and cobwebs from his head and shoulders. "Sorry. It took a while to locate the fuse box. It was in the cellar underneath the back portion of the house."

She smiled. "I should have told you to wear old clothes." She opened the door to the brick Federal structure at the rear. Blake followed, bumping into her when she stopped to snap an overall shot of the first room. She turned and frowned. "You don't have to stick to me like glue. Go wander around or something. This is going to take a while."

Blake looked at her in disbelief. "Are you kidding? This place is huge and we're all alone. This whole house is a disaster waiting to happen. Rotten floors, crumbling ceilings— even the furniture looks like it would collapse if you sat on it. No. I'm not leaving your side."

A slow rising heat moved through Eden's body. He was being protective. Willing to be bored for several hours just to make sure she was safe. She looked away. No one had ever cared enough about her interests to stand by

her. Not even Mark. He never understood her love of history and her passion for saving old buildings.

"I'll try not to take too long."

Blake shrugged and flashed her a smile. "No rush. Indulge yourself."

Eden studied him a moment. Blake was a completely different man from what she'd expected. He continually surprised her with his thoughtful gestures. It was getting harder to maintain her old image of him. An image she'd pasted together from bits and pieces she'd heard from Mark and Owen. It was unsettling to think that they were wrong, and the prodigal might have been the victim all along.

Free to concentrate on her work, Eden captured photos of every detail of the Federal section of the house, shocked to discover that it had been over an hour since she'd checked in with Blake. He'd followed her upstairs earlier, then took a seat on a sturdy-looking ottoman in the upper hall.

She hurried back. He was still there, staring at his cell phone. He grinned and slipped it into the back pocket of his faded jeans. The pale blue V-neck sweater he wore drew attention to his dark brown eyes. She swallowed. "Sorry. I forgot about you."

Blake chuckled. "That means you're having a good time. Where to now?"

"The Greek Revival addition. It's in the best shape."

They made their way downstairs and headed toward the front of the house. "Mrs. Harper lived in this part. She used the front parlor and kitchen and main bedroom upstairs." She looked around. "I can't imagine living here all alone. It's sad. All these beautiful old antiques and paintings but no one to share them with."

Blake looked skeptical. "This whole house is sad, if you ask me."

"I disagree. It's filled with stories, family dramas and happy times, from the 1700s to today. It may not have the beauty of some of the old Natchez homes like Dunleith or Longwood, but it has more stories to tell." She reached out and touched an old hall table. "And it's been owned by succeeding generations of the same family. A family with deep roots."

They walked into the front foyer of the house and Blake uttered a grunt of approval. "This at least looks like an antebellum mansion. What will happen to all this furniture and the crystal chandeliers?"

"The heirs will probably hold an auction.

There's a lot of history sitting in these rooms. These furnishings are fine examples of Empire and Rococo Revival styles." She set her bag and camera on a petticoat table. And brushed a stray strand of hair from her cheek.

Blake smiled at her. "Are you thirsty? What say we run to the store and get a drink and bite to eat, then come back."

She shook her head. "No need. I have water in the car. And if you like applesauce and yogurt in a pouch, we can use some of the stash I keep on hand for Lucy." Blake's skeptical expression made her chuckle.

"A pouch? That's a new one."

She returned his grin. He was making this task more enjoyable than she'd ever imagined. "Stick around long enough and you'll learn all kinds of new things."

His smile shifted and his eyes narrowed slightly. "I'm looking forward to that."

Oddly enough, so was she.

Chapter Six

Blake carried the remnants of their snack back to the car, then turned to look at the sprawling ancient house. For whatever reason, Eden loved this shabby old place. He didn't understand it, but he liked watching her enjoy it. She was dressed in a bright blue sweater and faded jeans, looking like a spring flower in the middle of winter. He swallowed and coughed. He shouldn't be noticing his brother's wife. Widow.

Back inside, he found her in the formal parlor, looking at her phone. She turned to him and his heart jumped sideways in his chest. Her cheeks were rosy, her blue eyes sparkled with joy and her smile stole his breath. She was the most beautiful woman he'd ever met. It took him a long moment to regain his composure.

"So, what do you think now about my house?"

His eyebrows rose. "*Your* house?"

"Wishful thinking, I suppose." She shrugged. "But I really love it. If only I could afford to buy it and bring it back to its former glory."

Blake emitted a long whistle. "That would take a huge amount of capital."

Eden sighed. "Go ahead and be practical. But a girl can dream, right? I'd love to own an old home someday."

He came and sat beside her on the small settee. The wistful tone in her voice made him curious. "What is it about this place, other than the history, that intrigues you so much?"

"I don't know. Maybe because it's neglected, unappreciated. It's a little cottage that managed to hang on through three centuries and grew into a mansion. Changing and adapting. The three disjointed sections stuck together over time, making a home for several generations."

"Do you feel disjointed or neglected?"

She met his gaze, then quickly picked up her camera and stood. "I need to finish up."

Blake followed, gently taking her arm. "Eden, did Mark neglect you and Lucy?"

She jerked from his grasp. "You have no right to ask such a thing. You don't know

anything about my husband, or our relationship, just like you don't know anything about Owen and his life."

She marched off across the wide hall and into the room on the other side of the house. He decided it was best to keep his distance for the time being. He'd obviously hit a nerve. His own nerves were vibrating, too. Had his brother neglected his family? Had things between Mark and Eden been worse than she'd let on? He made a mental note to seek out Jackie and ask some questions.

Blake waited for Eden to finish downstairs, but it was obvious she was taking extra time and keeping her distance. He took the broad curving staircase to the second floor and the wide upper hallway. The double doors leading to the second-story gallery beckoned him. He turned the knobs and stepped through the double doors and walked to the railing. "Wow. I could get used to this view. These live oaks are unreal," he mused out loud, drinking in the sight. "This must be one of the highest points in Blessing."

Footsteps alerted him to Eden's presence. He heard her moving about in the bedrooms. When the click of the camera sounded from the upper hall, he turned and looked at her.

She was taking pictures from the doorway. "You'll get some great shots out here."

"I can get all I need from here."

"But you can't appreciate the view from there." He motioned her to join him but she stood still as if frozen. She'd gone pale, her eyes wide with fear. Realization hit him like a blow. "Eden, are you afraid of heights?"

"No. Yes. Maybe."

Slowly he walked toward her and stretched out his hand for the camera. "I'll do it." He could see she was shaking. "Tell me what you want."

It took her a moment to speak. "The moldings, railing..." She made a sweeping gesture. "All of it."

Blake took snapshots of everything he could imagine she would want, then started back to the open door. Eden had moved back four or five feet from the opening. He returned the camera, studying her closely. "Are you all right?"

"I'm fine." She turned and started for the stairs, hurrying down them and disappearing down the center hallway.

He found her standing beside the car and he decided to let his curiosity linger awhile and not press her for an explanation.

"Ready to go?"

She stared at the camera a moment. "I need a few more shots if you don't mind."

He couldn't imagine what they'd missed. They'd captured the entire house and the outbuildings. "Okay. Where to now?"

She handed him the camera. "Would you go around to the back side of the house and take pictures?"

Odd request. "Sure, but why don't you— Oh." The back of Beaumont ran along the deep ravine. The last place she'd want to go if she was afraid of heights. He smiled. "I'll be back in a flash."

A short time later, he returned. "Mission accomplished." Back in the car, they drove home in silence. Blake fought hard not to press for answers. She was so strong and capable. Where had the fear come from? She sighed heavily and glanced at him.

"My parents were killed when I was six. I was ten when my foster mother took several of us to a carnival, and we rode the Ferris wheel. We were at the very top when it got stuck. We were there for over an hour while they fixed the problem. But it was windy that day and the car kept swinging. After that, I didn't want to be anywhere too far from the ground."

"I don't blame you."

She gave him a skeptical glance. "Go ahead. Say it."

"Say what?"

"What everyone says when they learn about my phobia. It's all in my head. There's nothing to be afraid of. Don't be such a scaredy-cat. The teasing and scolding would go on forever."

"Nah. I wouldn't do that. We can't help what we're afraid of." The look of gratitude in her blue eyes brought warmth to his veins.

"I suppose you're not afraid of anything. Being a big, brave policeman and all."

Blake chuckled. "Oh, I'm afraid of plenty of things. Snakes, quicksand, monsters from outer space. My dad…"

Eden giggled. "Which one is the scariest?"

Blake considered his reply. He wanted to tell her the truth. "I'm afraid of being alone the rest of my life."

Eden froze, her hands tight on the steering wheel. "We're all afraid of that."

He stole quick little glances at her on the way home. She'd always given him the impression she was content, that Mark had been the perfect husband. Now he was beginning to wonder if Eden was keeping part of herself hidden and putting on a confident mask to face the world.

Or was he just a man who was attracted to a lovely woman and wanted to know all about her? Either way, he needed to take a step back. Because he could quite literally be stepping into emotional quicksand with no way out.

Eden parked the car near the garage and waited as Blake climbed out. "Thank you for going with me."

"Anytime. You going to look at all your pictures now?"

"No. I have to go to the office for the rest of the day. Virginia will want to know how it went today."

She watched him walk slowly toward the studio leaning on his cane. The time at Beaumont must have taxed his bad leg. She regretted that but she was very grateful for his help this morning. Turning the car around, Eden started for work.

"Did Mark neglect you?"

Her throat closed up. The question had thrown her for a loop. Why had he asked that question? What had she said or done that might have tipped him off? Mark hadn't meant to neglect his family. He hadn't intentionally destroyed their life. He'd been sick... It was out of his control. Tears stung her eyes.

Even so, the truth of his question hit home. Mark had neglected them in a way, working long hours, missing events and time with Lucy. She'd never said anything, never allowed herself to acknowledge that she felt obligated to maintain the image of perfection Owen always placed around her husband.

Mark wasn't perfect. She'd loved him dearly, but it had always felt one-sided. Suddenly, a spark of anger coursed through her. She was his wife. Mother of his child. How dare Blake expose these feelings!

Her hands gripped the steering wheel. Why didn't Mark tell anyone he was ill? Why didn't he ask for help? She could have made his remaining time special, meaningful. But he'd chosen to go it alone, turn his back on everyone and everything.

The same way Blake had done. A sobering thought.

Guilt boiled in her chest. What was wrong with her? Mark had *cancer*. He couldn't help what happened. It's not like he deliberately ignored her or planned to lose everything they'd worked for.

Oh, but how she craved the support and understanding Blake had given her today. But it was wrong. So wrong. She could never have

feelings for her renegade brother-in-law. What did that say about her own flawed nature?

Was she so lonely that she'd accept attention from a man who walked away from his family? She wished, at this moment, that Blake would choose to walk away again.

Blake fixed a sandwich and a drink and sat down at the small table in the studio. His mind wasn't on his lunch but on the morning at Beaumont with Eden. He'd asked to go along on a whim, having nothing lined up for the rest of the day. But he'd discovered a new side to his brother's widow. So far, he'd experienced her compassion, her devotion and her love of family. Today he'd been introduced to her tender heart.

Eden possessed a deep affection for the old, run-down plantation house. He wasn't surprised since she did work for the Preservation Society, but he was curious about the significance of the old house in her life. Her comments about neglect and being disjointed held a deeper meaning. She'd denied she'd felt those things personally, but he was beginning to think there was more to the story. He wondered if it might have something to do with being orphaned at a young age. She'd con-

nected with the place for some psychological reason, and he wanted to know what it was.

In the meantime, he'd try to help out by continuing to work at the museum. There were still a couple of furniture pieces to assemble. Provided he could get his dad to give him a key.

He headed to the house, praying his old man was in a cooperative mood. Owen was seated in his favorite chair in the family room watching golf on TV. He looked at Blake briefly, then looked away. "What do you want?"

"A key to the museum. Eden isn't there today, so I thought I'd keep working. There are a lot of boxes to unpack still."

Owen didn't look at him but gestured toward the back of the house. "There's a spare on the key rack in the kitchen. Take care with those items. They're valuable."

Blake set his jaw. "Important *Sinclair* things, you mean."

"Watch your tone. The Sinclair name is respected here in Blessing."

Blake tried to rein in his anger. "So are the names of Tierney, Kovak, Jackson and Summerville. They have all contributed to the town."

Owen snorted. "Hardly the same thing."

He took a moment to calm himself. There was no use trying to open his father's eyes. They were blind to everything but his own point of view, but Blake could at least try to help his sister-in-law. "You do realize that Eden has a full-time job, and a child to care for. Do you think it's fair to put the burden of the museum all on her shoulders?"

"Eden is more than capable. And willing. She does as she's asked, unlike other members of the family."

The selfishness of the man had no end. "You mean she follows your orders? You have no right to stress her out this way."

"And you have no right to question my decisions."

Clenching his jaw, Blake turned and walked out. Some things never changed. He needed time to regain his equilibrium. Something to keep his hands busy. It was the only thing that helped.

Time to work on Roxy.

Chapter Seven

Eden scrolled through the photos she'd taken at Beaumont. As she did so, her emotions were pulled between delight and gratitude for having a detailed catalog of the historic home, and sadness that, in all likelihood, the house would be demolished, and all this architectural evidence would be lost.

Her gaze drifted to the sitting room window and the studio at the far end of the east wing of Oakley Hall. If someone had told her a week ago that she would enjoy time with her brother-in-law, she would have scoffed. But she had. Blake had been the perfect companion. He hadn't talked too much, hadn't made her feel rushed and, most importantly, hadn't made any snide comments about her love of the old place. As a result, she'd come away with more photos than she'd ever expected.

It had been several days since she'd toured Beaumont with Blake. She hadn't seen much of him since then. He'd kept to himself, presumably working in the barn on his beloved motorcycle. Just as well. She had left that day with a mound of confusing emotions and thoughts. Blake Sinclair wasn't what she'd expected.

She tapped a key on her laptop and scanned the next set of pictures. Blake's image appeared. She hadn't intentionally taken his picture, but somehow, he'd managed to insert himself into several. She leaned forward and looked closer at the one with him in the yard when they'd gone to the car for a snack.

Blake was standing with one foot on the lower step of the original house. He was looking over his shoulder and his expression was one of amusement. She was struck once again by the difference between her husband and his brother. Blake wore jeans and a V-neck sweater with the sleeves pushed up, exposing his strong forearms.

He looked comfortable, relaxed, the way he always did when he played soccer with Lucy.

In all their years of marriage, she couldn't recall Mark even owning a pair of jeans. His casual dress consisted of khaki slacks and a polo shirt. He was always conscious of his

position in the town. Looking anything less than presentable was not his way.

Eden couldn't help but wonder, if her husband had been more willing to shed his work persona, if they might have had more family fun together. But Mark was never willing to let his hair down. Not even with Lucy.

A wave of guilt shot through her like lightning. What was she thinking? She had no business comparing Mark with his brother. The two men bore no resemblance to one another in any way. Blake might not be the man she'd expected him to be, but that didn't elevate him to the level of her husband.

Eden chewed her lip. So why was she having nightmares again after all these years? They all had the same theme and involved a shadowy figure approaching her in the dark. She'd turn to run away but her feet were made of lead. She'd come awake, breathing hard and sweating, and filled with a sense of impending doom.

The dreams had started up again when Blake had come home. Closing her laptop, she reached for her purse and her keys. She needed time away from Oakley Hall and the museum. She needed to find a quiet, peaceful place to think and find some answers.

She needed to visit the bridge.

There was only one car in the parking lot when she arrived at the Blessing Bridge Prayer Garden. She hoped the person was secluded away in a quiet spot. She needed alone time to work through her emotions. It had been several months since she'd come here and laid her fears and worries at the foot of the cross. During Mark's last year, she felt as if she'd worn a trench from the parking lot to the bridge, she'd been here so often.

At the apex of the arched bridge, Eden stopped and let her gaze drift around the lovely landscaped grounds. Spring flowers were emerging, azaleas budding out, making the area bright with color.

Color was the thing she was missing in her life. With the exception of Lucy, who was like a ray of sweet sunshine. Her daughter was her whole life now. But the joy and exuberance had been missing for a long time, replaced by worry, obligations and responsibility. The last time she'd had fun was…

The morning at Beaumont with Blake.

Guilt washed through her once again, and she bowed her head. Her prayer rose in a flurry of appeals, confessions and supplications. Her emotions were a mishmash of feelings and she blamed Blake's return for her disjointed state. His presence here was dis-

turbing her predictable routine and ramping up her worry for her father-in-law. The four of them, Owen, Jackie, Lucy and her, had a comfortable life. Blake threatened it all.

She'd found a measure of peace over Mark's death and his decision to keep his cancer from his family. Only afterward she'd learned that the tumor in his brain had been the cause of his personality change and erratic behavior. She was still working through the anger over his destroying their future, but her anger was always followed by the reminder that Mark had been ill. He hadn't deliberately lost their money. He wasn't himself. At least that's what the doctors said. Small comfort. She would likely never know the whole story around his illness and death.

Eden closed her eyes and sent up one more prayer. *Lord, help me find my way out of this maze of confusing emotions. Show me the path forward.*

Blake bent over the old motorcycle and checked the oil. It was a congealed mess. The engine wasn't in any better shape. It was frozen solid. He'd have to rebuild it from the bottom up. No surprise since it had been sitting untouched for years. He should have prepared the bike for storage, but he'd left in a hurry.

His only thought then was getting away. Now he had a mountain of work to do to get Roxy back in tip-top shape, but reclaiming the old bike would be a joy. This must be the same way Eden felt about Beaumont. Maybe he should have been a little more understanding about her love of the old place. He vowed to make a point to speak more kindly about it in the future.

"I thought I'd find you here. How's Roxy doing?"

Blake wiped his hands on a rag and turned to smile at Jackie. "She'll be good as new with a little work. Nothing too drastic."

Jackie nodded. "Then what? You going to sell her?"

"Bite your tongue, woman. Roxy is family. She's the only memory I want to hang on to from here. I'll never let her go."

Jackie took a step closer. "I heard you toured Beaumont with Eden the other day. She's been working a long time to save that place."

"She certainly has a strong affection for it." Blake stepped to the workbench, gathering his thoughts. "Can I ask you a question about Mark?"

"Sure. I might not know the answer, though."

"Was he a good husband to Eden? A

good father to Lucy?" The shadowed look in the woman's eyes sent a twinge of concern through him. He had a feeling he wasn't going to like what he was about to hear.

Jackie took a seat on an old metal stool and crossed her legs. "I wasn't with the family then, but from what I gather, he was a loving husband who adored Eden. Lucy was his pride and joy."

He sensed a *but* coming. "Did he neglect them at all?"

Jackie glanced down at her hands a long moment before answering. "Probably not intentionally. However, Mark was a Sinclair. His first thought was always for the company. From what Eden has told me, there were a lot of missed dinners and events, and trips that got canceled at the last minute. But Eden said she always understood. She loved Mark dearly. She thought he could do no wrong."

"But he did?"

The older woman sighed, then leaned forward. "You have to remember that neither Eden nor Owen knew he was ill. He'd started to complain of headaches, but he always blamed it on the stress of the job. Eden said Mark grew more and more volatile and short-tempered, then he started to withdraw

and spent long hours at the Sinclair offices and rarely came home."

"Why didn't Owen do something?"

"I don't think he wanted to face the fact that his son was behaving oddly." She released a breath. "I've tried to talk to Owen, but I think he turned a blind eye to what was happening. To this day he claims things at work were fine and that Mark had kept the company on track."

"And Eden?" Blake asked quietly.

"I think she was lost and confused. She confided in me once that she thought Mark was having an affair and she was crushed."

Blake couldn't imagine his straight-as-an-arrow brother cheating on his wife. Especially someone as amazing as Eden. He cleared his throat to chase away his wayward thought. "That doesn't seem like Mark's style."

"I agree. We were all shocked when we learned he'd been battling cancer."

Blake tried to speak but his voice cracked. "Why didn't he tell anyone? Why suffer alone?"

"I can only guess, but I'd say that he had his father's bullheaded streak and then the tumor changed his personality further, confusing his thinking."

Blake mulled over Jackie's observations the

rest of the day. He didn't like what he'd heard, but he had gained a better understanding of Eden and her situation.

What he wanted to know now was, what was his brother going through at the end of his life? Had the tumor been responsible for his drastic change in behavior, or was it something else? A surge of guilt rushed through him. If he'd been here, maybe he could have helped. At least he could try and understand what his brother had endured.

He had an appointment with his new physician tomorrow. Maybe he could get some insight from him.

Something wasn't right about the whole situation, and he wanted answers. And as soon as he could, he would go talk to the man who might have them.

Blake fastened his seat belt a few days later and started the truck. He was still pestered by Eden's comment about Sinclair Properties having difficulties. What had she meant? He'd like to ask his father but that would only create another angry scene.

Turning on his blinker, he headed toward his father's office at the west end of town. Hopefully he'd get answers from his old buddy Norman. They had gone through

school together. He, Norman and Tony, Jackie's son, had been inseparable. It would be good to see him again and catch up. A twist of anxiety formed in his chest. He had a feeling that things at the company were more serious than he wanted to believe.

Blake made his way through the entry of Sinclair Properties and up to the second floor, stopping at the first door on the right. It was open and he could see Norman seated at the old walnut desk. His father was overly proud of that desk because his great-great-uncle had commissioned it to be made from timber on the Sinclair property.

Blake tapped lightly on the doorframe. Norman looked up and smiled, motioning him in. His old friend had changed little. He still had the same big smile and red hair. He stood as Blake came near, offering a hand and a pat on the shoulder. "Good to see you, buddy."

Blake held the handshake a moment longer. "It's been a long time." Norman and he had played high school ball together and dated the same girl at one time.

"It's good to see a Sinclair in the building. I'd heard you were back in town. Sit down, fill me in. What brings you back home?" He glanced at the stiff leg and the cane. "And what happened?"

Blake filled him in quickly, skipping the details. "And what about you?"

Norman smiled. "Married Gina Kohl. We have two daughters and a baby boy on the way."

A ping of envy touched Blake's mind. A wife and family. Things he hoped for someday. "That's great to hear."

"What brings you to the office?"

"I'm really here to ask you about the company. Eden hinted that there were problems."

Norman sighed and clasped his hands on the desktop. Blake braced himself for bad news when his friend's expression grew somber. "That's a long story."

"How bad is it?"

"Bad enough that if something isn't done Sinclair Properties might cease to exist. I've tried to get Owen to come back and take the reins, but he won't even consider it."

Blake leaned forward, meeting his old friend's gaze. "Dad's not himself anymore. He's not happy I'm back, but if the company is in trouble maybe there's something I can do to help."

His friend nodded. "Honestly, I had no idea what kind of chaos I was taking on. I've managed some tough businesses, but Sinclair Properties was the worst I'd seen. It's been

two years and I'm still trying to keep the ship from sinking."

"How did it get so bad? Dad was always obsessive about keeping things on track."

Norman dragged his finger over his lower lip. "I don't like to speak ill of the dead, but Mark made a string of poor decisions and over time they led to the cliff we're on right now."

Blake frowned. "That doesn't sound like my brother. What did he do?"

"When I took over, I discovered Mark had purchased a property management company out of Meridian."

"Meridian. Why would he take on something so far away?"

"From what I've learned, Mark was eager to expand the company, only he went about it all wrong. We're a small business with a handful of employees and we weren't equipped on any level to assume the debt of another company. He also made every wrong move possible trying to get things back on track."

"Did you tell Dad about this?"

"Yes. He would nod, then tell me I was doing a good job, and leave. It was like he didn't care what happened to the company at all." Norm took a deep breath. "I managed to unload the Meridian company shortly after

I got here, but the damage had already been done. Now it's just a game of dodgeball trying to keep things going."

"What about the properties Dad owns outright? This building and the Grove Hill Mall?"

"Things aren't going well there, either. The mall is old and needs upgrades, but there's no money to do that. The tenants are making noises that they will move to another location if the repairs aren't done." Norman sighed and leaned back in his chair. "If that happens, it's all over."

Blake stood and paced. "This doesn't make sense. Dad was always so fanatical about being responsible to our clients and keeping his properties in order. How could this happen?"

"It only takes one bad decision for things to fall apart. I don't suppose you'd consider coming on board for a while? Our clients might feel more amenable with a Sinclair at the helm."

Blake shook his head. "No. Out of the question. I never wanted to work at this place."

"Then maybe you could talk to your dad, make him see how precarious the situation is. If something doesn't change in the next few months, there won't be a Sinclair Properties.

Frankly, I don't know what losing the company would do to his health and I don't want to be responsible for that."

Norman had a point. Sinclair Properties was Owen's driving force. Losing it would be like a knife to his heart—a heart that was fragile. It might literally be the death of him.

"All right. I'll see what I can do."

Blake knew he needed to get to the bottom of this. Fast. Approaching his dad about his company issues would be like lighting a fuse to a box of dynamite, but he had a feeling if he didn't, things would explode.

He stood and held out his hand to his old friend. "Thanks for filling me in. I'll do everything I can to help."

"Don't take too long. I've already started looking for another job."

"Understood. Let me look into things before we talk again."

"I hope you have more success than I did."

Blake left the office with a headache pounding in his skull and a knot in his chest the size of a melon. The decisions his brother had made with the company were mind-boggling. Mark was a levelheaded, conservative man. What had suddenly made him want to take such a risk by expanding the business?

Norman had told him the facts of the situ-

ation, but he still wanted to know why. What had been going on with Mark that had up-ended so many people's lives? Was his tumor to blame or was there something else motivating his decision?

Maybe it was time to look through Mark's files. His family needed answers.

Eden parked her car next to Blake's truck at the museum the next morning and huffed out a sigh. She wasn't looking forward to working with him today. She'd spent a restless night trying to sort out all the conflicting thoughts she'd been having toward her brother-in-law, finally concluding that caution and wisdom should be her guide. Yes, he was different from what she'd expected, and he'd shown her kindness along the way, but he also had a reputation as a charmer. And she would not fall under that spell. She was too smart to get caught in that trap.

Inside the museum, she found the main room empty. Blake wasn't in the office or the kitchen or the storage room. A quick glance out to the yard found no sign of him, either. Where could he be?

"Blake?" Only silence replied.

A faint sound pulled her back into the main room. "Blake?"

"In here."

The reply was so soft she wasn't sure she'd heard it at all. She moved to the door leading to the sanctuary. He was sitting in the second row, staring at the altar. There was a peaceful look on his face she'd never seen before. "Are you okay?"

He grinned and nodded. "I've never been in Saint Joseph's before. This is a peaceful place."

"It's one of the oldest churches in Blessing."

He gestured toward the brass pipes of the old organ that took up the back wall. "Does it work?"

"No. It could but it needs a good bit of restoration."

He fell silent again, and Eden took the opportunity to appreciate the old church. She'd rarely been in the sanctuary since it wasn't slated to be part of the first stage of the museum.

Blake was right. There was an unusual kind of quiet peace here. The shiny pipes of the organ behind the pulpit contrasted with the dark-stained wooden pews waiting silently for the sermon to begin. And the magnificent stained glass windows depicting scenes from the Bible lining both walls shone in the

sunlight. Her eyes drifted upward. The hand-carved hanging lights in the ceiling spoke to a slower, more reverent time.

Blake reached for his cane, fingering the handle a moment. "It's a shame it's not a church any longer."

"Saint Joseph's built a new campus. They outgrew this one."

He took one more glance around the room. "My mom would have loved this place. Was Mark a believer?"

It was a question she'd asked herself many times. "He claimed to be."

Blake looked at her, his dark eyes troubled. Her husband's religious beliefs weren't something she wanted to discuss. She squared her shoulders. "There's not much to do today. There's a handful of boxes to go through, and I have labels ready to be placed. Oh, and a bookcase for you to assemble."

"I'm getting pretty good at that." He stood and followed her back to the museum. "By the way, I brought some boxes from the house. Dad said they were important."

Eden frowned. "Okay. We'll go through them later today."

Blake headed to the storage room and she took the opportunity to print out a copy of an old document and slipped it into the small

clear case she'd prepared. It was the official record of Blessing becoming the county seat signed by Arthur Avery Sinclair, mayor of Blessing at the time. After carrying the frame to the display cabinet, she stood it up on the middle shelf next to an old photograph of the courthouse during construction under the guidance of engineer William Winslow Sinclair.

She stood back and glanced around. Sometimes she felt as if she were being held captive by Sinclairs. She squelched the unkind thought and went back to work. This was her father-in-law's passion. He had lost so much. It was the least she could do by helping him achieve his dream.

Sounds of hammering filled the air as Blake worked on the bookcase. Eden's heart skipped a beat. *Blake.* She hadn't spoken to him since the tour of Beaumont. He'd taken his meals in the studio, and the few times she'd seen him, he was either playing ball with Lucy or heading toward the car barn, presumably to work on his beloved motorcycle.

At first, she'd been glad he'd stayed away. She needed time to sort through her tangled emotions. The kindness and understanding he'd given her had been difficult to process.

She wished he'd been the way she'd expected. It would be easier to deal with him if he was rude and selfish, but he wasn't and that worried her. But she was glad he was here today. She'd started to like him. A lot. Bad idea.

Blake strolled into the display room a few hours later carrying a large box, his cane hooked over his forearm. He set them on a worktable, then coughed as dust flew up around him. She had to smile.

Eden opened the top and peered inside, then blew out a quick breath. "Great, more books and papers. This is going to be more of a library than a museum."

"Maybe we should change the name outside."

She didn't comment. "Every time I think Owen has exhausted his collection of memorabilia, he finds more." Glancing around the main room, she fought off discouragement. She should never have agreed to this job. No matter how much she loved her father-in-law.

Blake looked at her. "I could get started if it would help. I've got a pretty good idea now what you're looking for."

Eden studied him a moment. That was a mixed blessing. The extra pair of hands and broad shoulders would be more than welcome, but they were attached to a man she

needed to avoid. There was an aura about him that made her nervous. Like a stone tossed into a still pond, the ripples just kept expanding.

She forced a smile. "Thanks." On the other hand, many hands make short work. Blake retrieved the second box and placed it on the table. She opened the lid and lifted out an old, faded, moth-eaten uniform jacket. "Ugh."

Blake waved a hand in front of his face. "Is that supposed to be on display?"

"Eventually." She laid the garment aside and reached back into the box, pulling out breeches, a kepi hat and a deteriorated leather shoulder bag.

He winced. "Who do you suppose these belonged to?"

Eden sighed. "Thaddeus Franklin Sinclair. Civil war hero. Died at age nineteen."

"You know way too much about my family history. I've never heard of him." He glanced into the bottom of the cardboard carton and lifted out a wooden box and opened it, emitting a low whistle. The case contained two matching pistols. "These might be worth showing off."

Eden nodded. "At least they're ready to display. The clothing is another matter. What else have we been gifted with?" The third

carton contained a small jewelry box resting on top of a set of old dishes and several figurines. She doubted they were worth anything.

Blake had opened up the jewelry box. "Huh. Suppose any of this is real?"

Eden moved to his side and glanced at the sparkling trinkets, lifting one from the box. "It's costume. We might be able to do something with it." She picked up a pocket watch. "I'll research this and see what Owen can tell me. It looks like an old train timepiece. The kind a conductor would carry."

Suddenly tired, she sank down onto the stool. "I thought I was almost done with all the items."

"You can't just lay them on a shelf and call it a day?"

Eden brushed hair from her face. "Yes and no. I can put them in a case quickly, but first I have to label and catalog them so everyone will know what they're looking at."

"How do you do that?"

She gave him a resigned smile. "Sit down with Owen and ask him to tell me about each piece."

Blake groaned. "Glad it's you and not me."

His plaintive attitude made her smile.

Eden closed the box and shoved it aside. The amount of work in those boxes was going

to be far more than she could manage. Out of nowhere, a sob rose up in her chest. She pressed her lips together and turned away, hoping Blake hadn't noticed. But he had.

"Hey, you all right?"

He was at her side, scrutinizing her with his dark eyes, stirring up a mixture of emotions in her. It was nice to have someone sensitive to her mood, but she wasn't comfortable with it being Blake. She forced a smile and nodded. "I'm fine. Just tired. I thought we'd been through all the boxes from the attic." She wrapped her arms around her waist. "Sorry."

Blake touched her arm lightly, sending little tingles along her nerves. She told herself to pull away but it felt good to have someone understand and listen.

"Tell me the truth. Is this museum really worth all the trouble?"

"Of course. It'll be a big asset to the town." She hoped her tone was convincing.

He looked skeptical. "Really? A display of all the things the Sinclairs have done over the last two centuries is going to have people lined up to view? It's my family and I wouldn't come to see it."

Eden opened her mouth to protest, then changed her mind. Blake knew the truth. No

sense in denying it. "I know it's not a real museum, but I promised Owen I would do this for him and I'm not going to let him down."

"Why are you so loyal to the man? I don't understand."

"Because I love him and I keep my promises." Blake's expression tightened and his jaw flexed. Maybe she should share a little more. "I didn't have a family growing up. Meeting Mark was like a dream come true. He gave me a family, a name and a history, things I never thought I'd have. Owen was kind and welcomed me with open arms."

Blake stood abruptly. "Are you thirsty? How about a glass of tea to chase away that dust."

She nodded. "Thank you." She watched him duck into the kitchen and return with two glasses.

He handed her a glass, his gaze pinning her to the spot. "With all this new stuff, will you be able to have the museum open on time?"

Eden stared at her glass a moment before replying. "I don't know."

"So Dad was right. You do need help."

"Yes, but not just any help. It needs someone in charge who knows what to do. I'm no museum curator. I'm a librarian. Owen thinks that because I work for the Preservation So-

ciety I know about museums. I need someone who can do the research and knows the proper way to display things." She blew out a breath. "There arc all kinds of requirements for starting a museum."

"Did you try to explain this to him?"

She gave him a smile of resignation. "Several times. He just pats me on the back and tells me how much he believes in me. The way he did Mark."

Blake nodded. "Manipulation tcchnique number one. I've been on the receiving end of that many times."

Her defenses swelled. "He's not trying to be mean… He just wants this so much."

He reached over and laid his hand on hers. "Tell me the truth, Eden. Shouldn't this be in the hands of the local historical society? What do the townspeople think of this?"

Eden bit her lip. She should be supporting her father-in-law, but it felt good to be able to tell the truth to someone. "They aren't happy about it."

"Then why didn't he just donate the building and the items to the city? Shouldn't it be the Blessing History Museum and not the Sinclair Shrine exhibit?"

Eden nodded. "Yes, but Owen wants it private. A public museum was too restrictive

and far too complicated. A personal museum has fewer requirements."

Blake made a skeptical grunt. "What he really wants is total control. The same way he tried to control his sons."

"Try and understand. He lost his dream of Sinclair and Sons. There's no one to leave the company to now. The museum will cement the Sinclair name in the town's memory forever so the contributions of his family over the last hundred and fifty years won't be forgotten."

Blake shook his head. "This is about pride. Nothing else."

"Stop! Don't say that. Can't you understand he's hurting. He's lost his only son and his dream. I won't deny him this small request." She saw Blake stiffen. His expression darkened and his eyes bored into hers.

"His *only* son?"

The sharp edge to his tone sliced through her. Her heart burned, setting every nerve on fire. "Oh, no, I mean… I'm sorry, but you've been gone so long I don't think of you as—" Eden rubbed her temple. She never meant to say anything so cruel to him, but she still couldn't reconcile the Blake that was here with the one she'd heard about for so many years. Her shame gave way to anger, and she

faced him. He had no right to be upset. It was all his fault for coming back!

She stood and turned away. "Everything was working fine here until you returned to town. You've upset everything and everyone. Why don't you leave? You're making everything worse."

Blake stood, his eyes dark and stormy, his jaw rigid. Pivoting on his heel, he turned and walked out, shutting the door quietly behind him.

Eden put her hands on her face and cried. How could she have been so unfeeling? She'd hurt Blake to the core because she hadn't been thinking.

And because her feelings toward him were growing murky.

Chapter Eight

Blake drove home struggling to decide if he was hurt or just angry. Eden's comment had pierced his spirit like a scalding-hot sword. He was still bleeding from the words. He was also furious at Owen for taking advantage of Eden, and at Eden for being so blindly loyal to his father. And deep down he resented being shoved back into the bad-boy role again. But Eden was right in one regard. He had been gone a long time. She had never met him so all she had to go on were the things Mark and his dad had told her, which apparently were all damning.

He parked the car and sought refuge in the studio. His leg was throbbing. He'd carried those boxes and now he was paying the price. Swallowing two pills, he eased onto the sofa, his heart still stinging. *"His only son."* He'd hoped Eden's opinion of him had softened.

He wanted to be her friend. Family. He'd felt a bond starting between him and his sister-in-law. He thought they were reaching common ground, and a comfortable working relationship. But it had all been shattered with three words.

While he admired Eden's loyalty to his dad, he felt it was misplaced. Owen was a master manipulator, skilled at getting his own way. Blake just didn't want her to be taken advantage of. She was too honest and kind. She was everything a man could want. Everything he admired in a woman.

He rested his head on the back of the sofa. Time to be honest. He was strongly attracted to his sister-in-law. Eden was starting to seep into his system. Bad idea. He'd caused enough animosity in his family. Having feelings for his brother's wife would be the ultimate sin.

Blake rubbed his eyes. But the more he was around her, the more he was drawn. He had to get his mind off Eden. He caught sight of Mark's computer. He hadn't looked at it since he talked to Norman. Maybe now would be a good time. He needed to figure out why his brother made such a mistake and he needed a distraction from thinking about Eden.

Did she really want him to leave or was she upset by his comments about Owen? Maybe

they both needed time apart. He certainly did. His attraction to Eden was growing stronger every day. He'd even started dreaming about her. She'd flitted in and out of his dreams, flashing a smile or a wave. He'd see her walking across the lawn with Lucy, the sunlight kissing her hair. He'd tried to ignore his feelings, but it was getting harder each day.

Somehow, he had to find a way to shut down his infatuation before it got out of hand.

If he didn't, he could say goodbye to any connection to his family forever.

Eden went in search of Jackie and found her curled up with a book in the living room. She glanced up and smiled. As Eden approached, her smile faded.

"Oh dear. I know that look. What's on your mind, Edie?" She patted the cushion beside her. "Come sit down."

Eden eased down, welcoming the touch of Jackie's hand on her knee. "I did something horrible today and I don't know what to do about it."

"I doubt you could do anything horrible, but go ahead. What was it?"

"Blake and I were at the museum talking and he said some things about Owen that upset me, and I tried to explain why the museum is

so important to him and me." She covered her mouth with one hand. "I told him that Owen was still hurting for losing his only son."

Jackie inhaled a slow breath. "I see. Well, that sure comes close to being horrible."

Eden's eyes teared up. "It is, isn't it? I don't know what I was thinking. I tried to explain but then I got mad and told him he was ruining everything here and he should just leave."

"What did Blake do?"

"He just turned to stone and he didn't say a word." She wiped at her tears. "He just walked out. I don't know how to fix this."

"An apology would be a good start."

She nodded. "I know and I will but I'm so ashamed I don't think I can face him. I never meant to hurt him like that."

"Which bothers you more, that you hurt him or that you asked him to leave?"

Eden slumped back on the sofa. "Both."

"Do you think he's ruining everything? More importantly, do you really want him to leave?"

The questions brought her up short. Did she? "No. But everything is changing since he returned. Owen is hateful to him, and I don't understand why. Lucy loves him and I don't understand that, either. It's like he's uncovering all these hidden parts of the family."

"Maybe it was time," Jackie murmured.

Eden released a quavering breath. "He's not like I expected."

"In what way?"

"*Every* way. He's calm, steady. He was a policeman, not a daredevil, and he's kind and patient and understanding and thoughtful." She sat up and clasped her hands in her lap. "He's easy to talk to. He understands where I'm coming from. With Mark, sometimes it was as if we spoke two different languages."

"And you're developing feelings for him."

"No, of course not! I mean I like him, but he's Mark's brother."

"What does that have to do with anything?"

Eden recoiled inwardly, horrified at the suggestion. "Jackie, that would be wrong. Shameful. It would be like betraying my husband."

"Why? He's not here any longer."

"I couldn't stand the guilt," Eden admitted.

"Guilt over what? Loving again?"

"Yes, I'm not ready."

"Widows remarry all the time. We're allowed to fall in love, to live again. Would you be surprised to know that I'm falling in love again and I've been a widow for eight years?" Jackie sighed softly. "Yes, I feel bad sometimes and worry what my husband would

think. Especially since the man is so very different from William."

"Really? Who is it?"

Jackie waved off the question. "Not important. Would it help you to know that Blake is falling in love with you?"

Eden had never considered such a thing. "No. You're wrong."

"I see the signs. I've known him longer than you. I knew him before he went away, and I know how much he's changed. The man that returned home is not the same one who walked out all those years ago."

Eden stood and paced. "I don't know what to do. Everything is so messed up."

"Perhaps you need someone wiser than me to discuss this with?"

She realized exactly what Jackie was suggesting and she was ashamed she hadn't thought of it herself. Time to visit the Blessing Bridge again.

But what if she didn't find her answers there, either?

Eden toyed with the glass in her hand and stared out the sitting room window at the winter gloom hovering over the area today. She should be getting ready for work but she lacked the motivation. Winter in Mississippi

was always a roller-coaster ride. She was glad the winters were short, barely two months. But just when you got used to the temperate days, the chill factor would return and plunge everything into the cold. It made for a constant change of wardrobe from day to day.

"Eden." Jackie walked toward her. "I forgot to tell you Owen's doctor's appointment was changed, and we have to be there at four this afternoon. So you'll have to take Lucy to dance class."

"All right. I'm sure I can get away a little early."

The older woman placed a hand on her shoulder. "You feeling any better about Blake?"

She nodded. "I still have to apologize. I'm just waiting for the right moment."

"Uh-huh. Take it from me, right moments rarely materialize. Just walk up to him and say you're sorry."

Eden wished it was that simple. Her visit to the bridge the other day hadn't been easy, but it had given her the courage and conviction to tell Blake how sorry she was and that she didn't really want him to leave. That had been a hard realization. She liked her brother-in-law. A lot. *Too much.* He was taking up space in her thoughts more and more.

Her cell phone rang, drawing her from her

confused thoughts. Her boss was calling. Probably wondering why she was late for work. She should have been at the office twenty minutes ago. "Hi, Virginia. I'll be there soon."

"I have good news. The heirs to Beaumont have reached a consensus. They want to sell the house to us. All we need to do is agree on a price."

Eden yelped. "Really? That's wonderful! I can't believe it. I'd given up hope."

"Me, too. We have a conference call here today at four o'clock to discuss it. Don't be late."

"I won't." She ended the call and spun around with happiness. She had to tell Blake.

Grabbing a sweater, she hurried to the studio and knocked. No answer. His vehicle was parked in the drive so that meant he was working on Roxy. She hurried across the lawn and through the door of the car barn and to the back corner. He was there, bent over the motorcycle. She was always intrigued by the joy he found in the old machine.

She was suddenly tense. They hadn't spoken since her hurtful comment. He looked up and saw her.

"Hey." He smiled and her heart skipped a beat. It shouldn't. Apparently, Blake didn't hold a grudge. "How's Roxy?"

"Coming along. You look happy. Did you get good news?"

She could barely contain her excitement. "My boss just called. We might get Beaumont after all."

He set aside the tool he'd been holding. "That's great news. You must be overjoyed."

"I am." A part of her wished there wasn't a bike between them because she would like to have given Blake a hug. "We have a video-conference this afternoon to go over things." She stopped. "Oh, I forgot. Lucy has dance class this afternoon and Jackie is taking Owen to an appointment."

"I could take her."

She blinked. Had he just offered to take a five-year-old to a dance class? "Oh no. I couldn't ask you to do that. I'll call one of the other mothers and see if they can pick her up."

"I don't mind. Really."

His kindness reminded her of something she'd been putting off. "Blake. I want to apologize for what I said at the museum the other day. It was thoughtless and cruel, and I didn't think. I never meant to say something so unkind. Please, can you forgive me?"

"I already have. You know, it was never my intention to disrupt things here. I underestimated my father's capacity for holding

a grudge. I never wanted to make everyone miserable."

"You haven't, and I don't want you to leave. Lucy would miss you." Heat shot up into her neck. She'd almost said she'd miss him, too. Big mistake.

"I'd miss her, too. Well, I'd better get cleaned up. I have a date with a sweet little lady."

Blake stepped into the kitchen of the main house later that day and was grabbed at the knees by a ponytailed princess. He chuckled. He'd never felt such a warm, happy sensation. This must be what being a dad felt like. He bent and patted Lucy's back. "I'm happy to see you, too."

"I'm glad you're taking me to dance. You can see my purple tutu. It's gonna be so much fun!"

He wasn't sure about that, but he smiled. How could he not with those big blue eyes looking up at him. "Awesome."

Eden came toward him from the sitting room. "I can't thank you enough for this. I hope you don't regret it."

Blake laid a hand on Lucy's shoulder. "No way. I love being with my niece. All I need is directions."

Eden smirked. "You might need more than that. You do realize you'll be surrounded by

little girls, laughing and screaming the whole hour." She leaned toward him and lowered her voice. "Just FYI, little girls scream over everything." She shrugged as if to say there was nothing he could do about it. "But you'll have the other mothers to help you out."

Lucy looked up at him with sparkling eyes. "You can meet my friend Addie. She's my bestest friend ever."

Blake glanced at Eden. "Everyone should have a best friend." Were he and Eden becoming friends? He hoped so. He looked at the little girl, who had taken his hand in hers. "Are you ready to go?" She nodded. "Are you driving?" Lucy giggled and his heart did that warm melty thing again.

"No, silly. I'm too little."

"Then I guess it's up to me."

Eden ran her hand over her daughter's blond hair and smiled at him. "You'll have to take my car. It has the child seat."

They exchanged keys. "Where are we going?"

"Tina Corday's School of Dance. Duncan Street just off the square."

A jolt of alarm shot through him. What did he know about tutus, or five-year-old little girls for that matter? He looked at Eden, who gave him an encouraging pat on the shoulder.

"Don't worry. All you have to do is watch."

Feeling somewhat relieved, he smiled at Lucy. "Then let's head out."

He found the studio with no trouble, but when they got inside, he had no idea where to go. His niece tugged him along to the dressing room now filled with a half dozen little girls in various stages of costumes.

Blake felt like a bull in a china shop. His six-foot-two frame wasn't designed to fit in this little room. Lucy sat on the floor and unzipped her small satchel. She pulled out a length of purple nylon and held it up to him. "I need help with my tights."

Blake looked at the stretchy purple fabric. It had a waistband, but he had no earthly idea how to get the thing on the little girl.

A hand lightly touched his shoulder. "I can do that."

He looked up at a slender woman with kind eyes. "Thanks. I'm out of my comfort zone here."

She started to gather up one leg of the garment, then proceeded to slip it over Lucy's foot before quickly repeating the process. Once the child was on her feet, the purple nylon fit her little legs perfectly. Next came a purple body suit with a ring of fluff around Lucy's hips. Suddenly she looked like a min-

iature ballerina and Blake's heart melted like warm butter.

Lucy hurried out with the other girls and the woman introduced herself. "I'm Shirley Kirby, a close friend of Eden's. You must be Blake Sinclair."

"Guilty."

"Let's go find a seat."

Blake was intrigued by the little girls fluttering around the large dance floor.

"I've heard a lot about you."

Blake grimaced. "Ouch. I'm afraid I'm not Eden's favorite person." Though he hoped that was changing. Maybe his trip to dance class would earn him some brownie points.

"I wouldn't be too sure of that. She told me how you helped her at Beaumont the other day and what a help you've been at the museum."

"I'm glad I was able to help. She's a very..." He chose his words carefully. "Capable woman."

Virginia gave him a skeptical glance. "Um. She's more than that. But I'm sure you've discovered her other sterling qualities."

Blake was grateful when the teacher called the class to attention. He was well aware of Eden's many attractive assets, but he wasn't about to voice them to anyone right now.

Dance class had started, and Blake kept his

gaze trained on his niece. She wasn't the best dancer in the group, but what she lacked in coordination she made up for with enthusiasm. He found himself chuckling at her happy movements. She smiled at him and waved, and his heart started the quick melt again.

For the first time in years, he allowed himself to think about a family of his own.

When the instructor dismissed the class, Lucy raced toward him all smiles. "Did you see me dance?"

"I did. You were the best one of all."

She giggled and gave him a hug. Blake looked at her precious face and realized he wasn't ready for their time to end. "I think we need to celebrate. How about we go for ice cream?"

"Yay! I'll hurry and change."

Blake looked at her tiny purple ballerina outfit. "I think you should leave it on. Then everyone will know you're a dancer."

She thought about that a second, then nodded.

The ice-cream shop was still in the same spot he remembered. After selecting their flavors, they sat by the window to eat.

A woman walked by and stopped. "Oh, how adorable. You are the cutest ballerina I've ever seen."

Lucy smiled. "Thank you."

"And so polite. You and your wife have done a good job with this little one."

Blake returned the lady's smile but his throat was so tight he couldn't speak. Lucy, his child. What a blessing that would be. He'd be proud to call her his own. He'd be proud to claim Eden as his also.

He shook off the notion. That would never, ever happen.

But it was nice to think about.

Eden heard Blake breaking down boxes in the storage room Saturday morning and sighed in relief. After her cruel comment last week about Mark being the only son, she feared he wouldn't come to work today. Though he'd been more than willing to take Lucy to dance class. Her daughter was still talking about how much fun they'd had and begging for him to take her again next week.

After placing her belongings in the office, she went in search of her helper, hoping her father-in-law had exhausted his collection and hadn't sent more boxes. She found Blake in the kitchen holding a cup of coffee. The sense of relief that he was here washed through her with more force than she expected. "Good morning." The smile he gave her sent a warm tingle down

her spine. There should be laws against a smile like that. "Did you bring any more boxes?"

He chuckled. "Nope. I guess that means we're all out of important Sinclair memorabilia."

"Let's hope so."

It was late morning when Eden took a moment to step back and examine their work. They'd made good progress. Blake had assembled the last few shelves and cabinets, and she'd made as many information labels as she could. Though some were simply described as *old watch*, or *antique jewelry*. Owen had been reluctant to share his stories with the last boxes he'd donated. Strange since he was always up to bragging about his family and their treasures.

Eden tapped her lower lip with her thumb. She'd been discouraged this morning when she came to the museum. Blake was right. No one would come to see this collection of Sinclair belongings. They were a part of Blessing history but not the whole history.

Blake stepped into the room, brushing dust from his shirt. As much as she'd resented him helping, he'd proved to be a blessing. And she'd come to enjoy his company.

"I'm starved. How about I run and get us something from the deli?"

It sounded good and her stomach was rumbling. "Okay." She gave him her order. He smiled, then gave her a little salute and left. She noticed he wasn't using his cane today. He must be feeling stronger. She'd worried the other day when she'd noticed him leaning on it heavily.

Walking to the side window, she looked out to the grassy side yard of the old church. There, under the sprawling branches of a giant magnolia tree, was a picnic table. After inhaling all that stale dusty air from the boxes, fresh air sounded like a wonderful idea. Eden gathered up utensils and paper plates and carried them out to the picnic table. She added a red, yellow and green plaid tablecloth for a splash of color to the drab landscape. As a final touch, she picked a few camellia blooms and placed them in a paper cup on the table.

She loved decorating and preparing a meal for her family. It was something she and Mark rarely did because he was always tied up at work. Quickly, she shoved that negative memory aside.

"Eden?"

"Out here." Blake emerged from the side door and winked as he approached the picnic table. "This is a great idea. I haven't been on a picnic in years."

"I thought we needed a little fresh air after all that dust."

"Agreed." He stepped over the seat and sat down. "It's a perfect day, too. Temperatures in the seventies, a clear sky overhead and a gentle breeze." He leaned forward and grinned. "The forecast calls for this to continue through Mardi Gras next week."

"That would be nice. It's been too cold the last few years to enjoy the parades." Eden handed him a paper plate and fished out the sandwiches from the bag.

Blake took a bite of his sandwich. "Did we accomplish much this morning?"

Eden took a moment to reply. "We did. I'm afraid there's not much more that can be done. The bicentennial is only five weeks away and there's no way I can get this place the way Owen wants it in time."

"I'm sure he'll understand. Though I still think a soup kitchen or homeless shelter would have been a better idea."

"Certainly easier. I wouldn't have to face your father at the end of the day and report that I didn't get much done."

"Yeah, that has to be tough," Blake murmured. "Did you and Mark always live at Oakley Hall?"

She toyed with her drink container for a

long moment. "No. We had a home in Bridge Way Estates. Lucy and I moved here after Mark died." Might as well tell him the whole story. "I had to sell the house after he passed away. Owen offered to let us live with him."

His eyes widened. "You had to sell your home?"

She nodded and folded the edge of her napkin back and forth. "The house, the contents, the cars, the boat. All of it. Mark developed a gambling habit and he lost everything we had. He left me with a mountain of debt to pay. I'm grateful for Owen taking us in."

Blake set his jaw. "I can't believe my brother would be so careless. And *gambling*? That doesn't make sense. You must have been furious."

She studied her hand. How could she ever explain the pendulum of emotions during that time? "I was in shock. I was horrified, hurt and angry. Mark died in a car accident, so there was an autopsy. That's when we learned about the tumor. How could I blame him for something that wasn't his fault?"

"That's very generous of you. But I don't think I could be so forgiving. Especially after learning he kept his illness to himself."

"I wasn't. I still have moments when I'm so angry that I… But I had Lucy to think of.

Being angry all the time wouldn't be good for her."

"No, of course not."

A squirrel hopped onto the end of the table, chirped and rose on its hind legs. "Oh, look. Isn't he cute?"

"And hungry." Blake tossed a piece of his roll out onto the ground. The squirrel glanced at each of them as if saying thank you, then hopped down, grabbed the treat and scampered off under the tree. "That's the closest I've been to a squirrel."

Blake was staring at her. His dark eyes held a light of affection she'd never seen before. Was Jackie right…? Was he attracted to her? Did she want him to be? What if he was? What then?

She searched for a more comfortable topic of conversation, but Owen marched out into the yard.

"What are you doing playing outside when there is work to do?"

Blake met her gaze, his jaw flexing. "We're eating lunch, Dad."

Eden spoke up. "It was such a nice day and I thought we needed a break."

"I saw the boxes inside strewn all over the place. Why aren't the items I sent over on display?"

"They will be, but I have to catalog them first, then—"

Owen waved off her explanation. "Nonsense. Hang it up, put a sign on it and move on. Time is short."

Owen pinned Blake with a cold stare. "This is all your fault. Always looking for a way to shirk your responsibilities. Get it together. This is important."

Eden opened her mouth to respond but the man pivoted on his heel and walked away.

Blake exhaled an angry breath. "I'm sorry. He has no right to talk to you like that. He's always been oblivious to others' feelings."

Eden folded her napkin. Blake was proving to be right. "I don't think the museum will ever satisfy Owen, no matter how hard I work."

"No, it won't. He's asking the impossible."

"I don't like to fail. I keep my promises."

"Some promises can't be kept. No matter how much we'd like them to."

Eden nodded. "You're right but how do you keep from feeling like a failure?"

Blake reached over and squeezed her hand. "You could never be a failure at anything you put your heart into."

His encouraging words lingered in her heart for a long time.

Chapter Nine

Blake closed his brother's journal and leaned back in the recliner. Reading Mark's private thoughts was awkward and disheartening. He battled guilt each time he opened the cover. But he was also beginning to understand what was going on in Mark's mind and the pressure he'd been under.

He rubbed the cover with his thumb. His older sibling had kept his cancer and the problems at work from Eden because he didn't want to upset her. Unfortunately, the progression of his tumor had started to distort his thought process. The last entry Blake had read revealed Mark's sense of panic that he might lose the company. His fear of letting Owen down had brought Blake near tears. He delved into how much their dad trusted him to take the company from a small firm

to something bigger. And how terrified he was of never bringing that dream to fruition.

But the comment that had torn Blake's heart to shreds was when Mark wrote that Owen had told him to grow the business or resign. He knew that feeling of receiving an ultimatum from their father, but he never expected it to be directed to Mark.

Blake stood and went to the window. It was clear that Owen had been pushing Mark to expand the company, and his brother never considered standing up to their father.

The question now was, what did he do with this information? If he told Eden, it might destroy her memories of her husband. And if he confronted his dad over what he'd learned, it might kill him. How would he handle the truth? Was it worth the risk that it could bring on another attack? But did he have a right to keep this discovery to himself?

He shoved a hand through his hair, his mind whirling. And then there was the matter of Sinclair Properties. If it was going to survive, then things had to change. His dad had to come out of his fog of denial and step up.

As far as he could see, there was only one way to tackle this, and that was head-on. He had to talk to his father. If the company was going to be saved, something had to change.

There was no one else who had a chance of getting through to Owen. It was up to him.

And, as it turned out, there was no time like the present. Eden was at work, Lucy was at school and Jackie was running errands. Inhaling a fortifying breath, he made his way to the main house. Owen was in the living room reading. Blake watched him a moment. For the first time since coming home, he took a good look at his father and realized with a jolt how old he looked. He was in his midsixties, but he looked older, as if life had worn him down. A heart attack and the aftermath could explain it but maybe it was something more.

"Dad. We need to talk."

Owen didn't budge. "No. We don't."

"We do if you want Sinclair Properties to survive."

Owen looked up, his eyes narrowed. "I'm not discussing my company with you."

Blake took a seat on the coffee table, close enough to his father to see his eyes. "You'd better or it'll be gone forever." Owen grunted and looked at his book. "I've talked to Norman, Dad. He told me about the trouble the company is facing."

"He had no right to tell you anything."

He leaned forward. "The company is fail-

ing, and he puts the blame on you and Mark. I want to know what happened."

"Not your concern. Norman is in charge, and he'll work it out."

Blake kept a tight rein on his temper. "Why are you turning a blind eye to this? Sinclair Properties has been your passion for as long as I can remember. Why did you step away from it?"

"Mark has everything under control," Owen bit out.

Blake reared back. "Mark is gone, Dad. Norman is in charge."

The look on his father's face sent a chill down Blake's spine. Shock. Fear. Horror. All emotions he'd never seen his father display.

"I said *Norman*. Don't put words in my mouth."

Blake set his jaw. Time to pull off the Band-Aid. "Why did Mark buy that Meridian company? We're a small business. We couldn't afford to take on another business."

Owen's eyes widened. "I wouldn't know. Maybe he wanted to grow the company." Owen stood and walked to the fireplace, keeping his back to his son.

Blake's heart sank. His suspicions were verified. "Did you push him to expand? Is that why he rushed into the deal?"

"Mark was his own man. I didn't question his decisions."

He chewed his lip. "Maybe you should have. That one mistake put the company in jeopardy. It may not recover if someone doesn't take charge. It's time to go back to work, Dad. If you don't you could lose it all."

"Mark knew what he was doing."

"No, he didn't. He was sick and he wasn't thinking clearly. The more he tried to fix things, the worse they got. Why didn't you stop him? Why didn't you take matters into your own hands?" Owen remained silent and closed off. "Dad, you have to open your eyes. Norman says you'll have to file bankruptcy soon if something doesn't change."

"That's not true. It'll be fine. Once the museum is done…"

Blake could maintain his composure no longer. "Stop it! Stop thinking about that museum and focus on the business. And stop expecting Eden to fulfill your dream. It's unfair." He jumped to his feet and glared down at his father. "She'd do anything for you and you're taking advantage of her. She has enough on her plate with a job and Lucy. She doesn't need your pet project on top of that. She's working overtime, worried she'll

let you down, and for what? A place no one will come to see."

Jackie hurried into the room. "What's all the shouting about? Owen, you need to calm down. Take a few deep breaths." The man waved off her concern with a growl. "Blake, what's going on?"

Blake crossed his arms over his chest. "I just found out that the company is falling apart because of something Mark did, but Dad won't do anything about it."

Jackie took his arm and steered him to the kitchen. "Sit down. I'll be right back."

Blake leaned back in the chair and tried to calm himself. What was wrong with his dad that he wouldn't fight for his business? It was alarming.

Jackie returned and took a seat at the table. "He's calmed down for the moment. Now tell me what's going on."

"What's going on is that he acts like he doesn't care if the company folds or not. Worse, he talked as if Mark was still here."

She sighed and nodded. "He's in denial. Has been since shortly after Mark passed. When we learned about the tumor, it upset everyone. Eden had been furious about losing her home and being left broke. But she changed when she learned Mark had been ill."

"And Dad?"

Jackie shook her head. "He grieved hard. He tried to go back to the office but after a few months he came home and shut down. I had a feeling something happened, but I never found out what. I think he's trapped in his grief. He's channeled it into that museum." She leaned toward him. "For some reason he can't fully accept that Mark is gone."

"Does he know about the mistakes Mark made at work? The mess he created?"

"I don't know. He doesn't talk about the company anymore."

"Something has to happen to wake him up. He needs to know what Mark did."

"It might be too much for him to handle."

A wash of concern replaced Blake's irritation. "Is his heart condition that precarious?"

"It's bad, but no, Owen likes to play it up for the attention."

"Yeah. No surprise there. Still, his whole life was in the company. What changed?"

Jackie shrugged. "Mark died and his big dream along with him. I can't get through to him."

"Well, someone better or Sinclair Properties will be gone."

Jackie held his gaze. "I'm not sure he would care."

* * *

Blake was still simmering with frustration over his father's lack of concern for the business well into the evening. He'd eaten alone, unwilling to face Owen again. From his front window, he'd watched the family around the table. They weren't smiling or even talking, from what he could tell. Even when he wasn't in the house, he had the ability to upset everyone.

He rubbed his jaw. Maybe Eden was right. Coming home had only stirred up a hornet's nest of problems and old resentments. Feeling restless and trapped, he went out onto the porch and sat in the rocker. The cold evening air calmed his tension and chased the fog from his brain.

He closed his eyes and concentrated on the soothing motion of the old chair.

"Blake!"

He opened his eyes and saw Eden running toward him, putting his heart rate into overdrive. Something was wrong. He hurried to greet her. "What's happened?"

"Beaumont is on fire!"

"What?" He took her shoulders in his hands. She was shaking and the pain in her blue eyes tore at his heart.

She clutched at his arm. "Virginia just

called. It's on fire. I've got to go. Will you take me?"

His first inclination was to agree, but then his practical mind kicked in. "I'm not sure that's a good idea. You won't be able to get close. The fire department will be there, and the police will have it blocked off."

"I know but I have to be there." She grabbed his shirtfront. "Please, Blake."

He nodded. He would take her, but he'd make sure she stayed far away from the chaos. "Come on."

He kept one hand in hers as he drove, second-guessing his choice. He should have convinced her to stay at home where she'd be safe, but he knew how much the old house meant to her, and how hard she'd worked to save it.

Eden didn't speak on the ride. She held his hand and stared out the window, crying silent tears that clawed at his heart.

The driveway to Beaumont was blocked off, but other gawkers were standing up on the lawn. Eden was out of the car before he could stop her. "Eden, wait!"

She pushed through the spectators, only stopping when the policeman stepped in front of her. Blake stood behind her, taking her shoulders in his hands. She was shaking,

tears were streaming down her cheeks and she muttered softly.

The roof of the rear addition collapsed with a loud noise and sparks shot into the sky. One wall broke loose, sending bricks tumbling to the ground with sickening thuds and stirring up ashes as they hit the ground.

"Oh no."

Eden's soft cry raked over his nerves. "Maybe we should go." Watching this had to be torture for her.

She shook her head. "No. I have to be here."

Firefighters turned their hoses on the central portion, keeping the roof wet in an attempt to save it.

They watched as the flames relentlessly consumed the original wooden structure and advanced to the Greek Revival addition at the front. Eden shuddered each time a portion fell prey to the flames. He wished he could do something to help, but all he could do was stand with her and offer what little comfort there was.

The firemen were working to contain the fire but even she could see it was hopeless. A house this old would succumb quickly to the blaze. She yelped when the west side of the home collapsed, crumbling into a pile on

the ground, leaving only the chimney chase standing.

She turned her face into his shoulder. And he cradled her head with his hand. A loud popping pulled her attention back around. The fire had leaped onto the roof of the Greek Revival home in the front and was devouring it like tissue paper. Even the firefighters had turned their attention to keeping the flames contained.

There was no hope of saving the historic home. A piece of Blessing was now a pile of smoldering ashes. As they watched, the upper gallery, where he'd stood a short while ago, tilted, then tumbled to the ground amid plumes of ash and debris. The lower gallery was quickly devoured. The death throes of the old house were the hiss and pop of the remnants of its life slowly ceasing.

Eden had turned and buried her face against his chest. Her trembling had eased but he could sense she was drained and weak. "Are you all right?"

She nodded. With nothing more to see, Blake gently turned her away, keeping his arm around her shoulders. She walked with unsteady steps as they made their way to the car. The smell of smoke hung in the air, leaving an acrid taste in their mouths. He could only

imagine the emotional pain Eden must be in. He needed to get her someplace quiet and safe.

He reached to open the car door when she looked up at him, her eyes brimming with tears.

"It's gone, Blake. It's all gone." A sob caught in her throat.

He pulled her into his arms and made soothing noises. He felt so helpless.

She looked up at him again and his heart rate tripled. She was so beautiful, such a strong, kind, amazing woman, and he was falling in love with her.

She said his name, softly, holding his gaze. The air around them stilled, grew warm, and he was aware of her breath, the little pulse in her neck. He tilted his head, drawn toward her with a power he didn't understand.

Mark.

She was his brother's wife. He braced and stepped away. Eden blinked, held his gaze a moment longer, then turned and got into the car.

Blake limped to the driver's side, his emotions surging like a tsunami. He fumbled with the keys, fighting to regain control of himself. They rode in silence toward home. Eden's sorrow was like a third person in the vehicle. "How are you doing?"

She wiped tears from her cheeks. "I'm fine."

"I'm sorry. I know how much that place meant to you."

She nodded. "We've been working so hard to save it and the heirs were finally coming together. Now, it's gone."

Blake glanced at her. "I wonder what started the fire."

She shrugged. "It could have been anything. A house this old can have any number of threats. It doesn't matter. That part of our town history is lost."

Blake heard the agony in her voice and longed to comfort her somehow. He searched for an appropriate way.

"Would you like to stop for a drink to gather yourself? The coffee shop should still be open." He braced for her to refuse. He was sure she wanted to go home and grieve for a while.

"I'd like that. Thank you."

Seated near the window of the small café, Eden savored the richness of the special roast brew. There were few people in the café, but those who were there were all abuzz about the fire. The house had been important to all of Blessing. Its loss would be keenly felt, especially during this bicentennial year.

She turned her gaze to the window, enjoying the lights of the downtown. Blessing had donned a sparkling facade this year in celebration of its anniversary.

Her nerves calmed and her emotions began to settle into place. She found Blake's quiet demeanor comforting. He'd brought her coffee to the table and sat silently, not attempting any conversation. She was grateful. Mark always felt he had to be talking, solving a problem. He'd never understood that sometimes she just needed to soak up the silence.

Blake was a more comfortable companion. He'd been so kind to bring her to the old house despite his objections, and he'd stood by protectively as the house was destroyed. It was something Mark wouldn't have even thought of doing. He never understood her love of old homes.

The thought shocked her, and she took a quick sip of her brew to regain her composure. And to avoid looking at her brother-in-law. She had to stop comparing the brothers. Not only was it pointless but it was an affront to Mark. Yet, she found herself doing it more than she should.

To her dismay, each day she saw a different side of Blake. She'd seen his gentle way with Lucy and Cuddles, his patience with Owen

and his dedication to helping at the museum. Now his tender compassion and consideration were starting to endear him to her even more.

"If you're done with your coffee, I thought you might like to take a walk along the river."

The sound of his voice jolted her back to reality. Being outside sounded like a good idea. They were too close here in the small coffee shop.

They walked in silence down the block and onto the sloping sidewalk that curled along the edge of the river. The city had turned the once-overgrown bank into a charming garden of lights and flowers and cozy seating.

"I love it down here. I wish I could come here more often."

"It's quite a change from what I remember."

As they walked, her grief began to surface again, her mind filled with the horrific image of flames and the house crumbling into the ground. "I loved that house. It was special."

"But it meant something more to you."

"Yes. I felt an attachment to it from the moment I came to Blessing," she admitted. "Then when I went to work with the preservation group and learned about its history and the families that lived there, I wanted to save it. I think in the back of my mind I adopted it. Silly, huh? But it felt like home.

I even mentioned to Mark that one day we might be able to buy it."

"Did he like the idea?" he asked.

"No. He had a different kind of home in mind. We built it the next spring."

Blake reached over and squeezed her hand, and she squeezed back, unwilling to break the contact. She stole a quick glance at him. He'd almost kissed her back at the house. She wouldn't have resisted if he had. But she'd seen the light dawn in his eyes, the realization that she was his brother's wife. She appreciated his strength of character. He was far stronger than her.

The problem was, now she would be tormented by the thought of what his kiss would have been like. Her cheeks flamed. She slipped her hand from his. "I think I need to go home now."

Blake gave her an encouraging smile and they turned their steps back toward the car.

Eden watched with a smile as Lucy and Cuddles played on the rug in the kitchen sitting room. The picture warmed her heart. It was moments like this that helped her keep the loss of Beaumont in perspective. She grieved the demise of the old home, but she was so blessed in her personal life she had

little cause to be sad for long. Blake's sincere compassion had helped, too.

"Mommy, I want Uncle Blake to come to my daddy-daughter lunch tomorrow."

Her contented mood vanished. "Wouldn't it be nicer if Grandpa came instead?"

"No. Uncle Blake looks more like a daddy."

She had a point, but the idea didn't sit well. "I'm not sure Uncle Blake could come. He might be busy tomorrow."

"No, he's not. I already asked him."

Wonderful. How did she navigate this one? Blake enjoyed time with Lucy, she had no doubt about that. But standing in for his brother, taking the role of father, might be asking too much. "We'll see. I'll talk to Uncle Blake, okay?"

Eden was still mulling over how to broach the topic of stand-in dad when Blake entered the kitchen a short while later. "I ran across a box of my grandfather's belongings in the car barn. You might want to take a look and see if they would add to the museum displays."

"Oh goody. More stuff." She smirked. "We can always use more Sinclair artifacts." She heard Blake chuckle. "Sorry."

He waved off her concern. "Hey, I'm on your side, remember?"

She did and she was more grateful than she

should be. "While you're here, I understand Lucy asked you to go to the school lunch tomorrow."

He smiled. "You mean the daddy-daughter thing. Yeah, I was flattered. But I didn't commit. I wasn't sure how you felt about it."

How *did* she feel? On one hand, she wanted her daughter to have a parent with her for the special event, but having Blake take the place of her father left her feeling guilty. "I suppose it would be all right. But don't feel obligated."

"Are you kidding? I'm looking forward to it. We're buddies. And I kinda like the idea of being a parent. I hope to try it myself someday."

The thought popped into her mind that he would be a wonderful father. She squelched that thought and opened her laptop and got to work.

Eden rubbed her eyes an hour later and looked up and smiled. Lucy was draped over the back of the easy chair by the sitting room window, staring outside. Cuddles was up on his hind legs beside her. She was glad her daughter was so close to her uncle. He was a noble role model.

Owen strolled into the kitchen and stopped beside Lucy looking out the window.

"What are you staring at?"

Lucy smiled at her grandpa. "That place." She pointed to the car barn.

"Why?"

Eden smiled at the gruff tone in Owen's voice.

"I'm waiting for Uncle Blake to come out so he can play with me."

Her father-in-law turned to her for an explanation. Eden stood and came to his side. "They play soccer every day."

"There he is." Lucy scrabbled out of the chair and dashed to the back door, Cuddles on her heels.

Eden watched with Owen as the pair nearly knocked Blake over with their excitement. He lifted Lucy with one arm and swung her around, then bent down to tussle with the dog. She noticed he was using his cane today. Was he hurting? He had a habit of not acknowledging when he was in pain. Like father like son. But at least Blake knew enough to use the cane when he needed to.

Owen shoved his hands into his pockets. "What was he doing in the car barn?"

"He works on his motorcycle."

Owen frowned. "That piece of junk his grandpa left him? I forgot it was in there."

Eden studied him a moment. "It's his prize possession. He said working on it with his

grandpa was his fondest memory as a young man."

Owen was silent as they watched Lucy and Blake kick the purple-and-pink ball around the yard. Cuddles joined in as well. Eden chuckled at the cute picture they made. Even with his stiff leg, Blake made a valiant attempt to return the ball in Lucy's direction.

"Does Lucy have any memory of my son?"

Caught off guard by the question, Eden took a moment to measure her words. "No. Not really. I show her his picture and tell her about him, but she was only three when he died."

"Did my son play with her?"

She knew what he was really asking. He wanted to know if Lucy would have cherished memories the way Blake did. Her heart broke for him. "Mark would read her a book each night before bed when he was home. They enjoyed eating ice cream together." It was a pitifully short list. "Mark adored her." She touched his shoulder, compelled to speak her mind. "Owen, Blake is your son, too. He's a good man. He was a police detective. He helped people. He's kind and thoughtful and he has a big heart."

Owen nodded, then turned and left the room, leaving her wondering what was nagging at his mind.

* * *

Blake's heart was a tangled mess of emotions when he walked into Lucy's classroom the next day. He was filled with pride over his adorable niece, but tense about filling his brother's shoes. How did a dad act at one of these things? Hopefully, watching the other fathers would give him a clue.

"Uncle Blake!"

Lucy scurried from her chair and raced toward him. He scooped her up and gave her a hug.

"Come see my desk."

Lucy proudly showed off her chair and her crayons and all her other school supplies until the teacher announced that it was time to go to the lunchroom. The cafeteria smelled like hot dogs and cake, just as he remembered. Some things never changed. After filing through the food line, they took a seat at tables and chairs that were not designed for a grown man. He was listening to Lucy's chatter when a hand touched his shoulder.

"Never expected to find you here."

Blake smiled as he recognized Norman's voice. "Same here."

Norman took a seat beside him. "This is Sadie, my middle one."

Lucy smiled. "Sadie is my best friend."

Blake chuckled. Lucy had introduced him to a dozen little girls she claimed were her "bestest friends."

"I was going to call you this afternoon. We have a problem at the office. Can you swing by when we're done here?"

"Sure. It sounds serious. What's up?"

"I'm afraid the end is in sight."

Blake's enjoyment of the lunch dimmed. Thankfully, once the meal was eaten and the principal thanked all the grown-ups, he was free to leave. But not before getting a hug around his neck and a kiss from Lucy.

He and Norman arrived at Sinclair Properties at the same time and entered the office together.

Norman quickly filled him in. "The bottom line is, if we don't replace all the AC units in the Grove Hill Mall, the tenants are threatening to withhold payment until repairs are made."

"How much will it cost?"

"You have six figures lying around you don't need?"

"Ouch. Sorry. I'm on a police pension." Blake envisioned the twenty-unit complex Sinclair Properties had owned and managed for as long as he could remember. "Can we make repairs?"

"We have been but it's to a point that won't work. One of the things Mark did when he was trying to fix his mistake was change contractors. The one he hired is useless, and as a result, we've been delivering shoddy repair work to our clients. And it's finally caught up with us. I've tried getting a bank loan but we're a bad risk right now. I don't even have a rich grandpa to call on."

Blake's mind did a quick spin as an idea formed. "How much do you need exactly?"

Norman quoted the cost of replacing all the units. Blake smiled and pushed up from his chair. "I might have a solution. Give me a couple of days."

"What are you going to do?"

"Break up with an old girlfriend."

Eden turned out the lights in the museum and glanced around. It had been a long day with little accomplished. Blake wasn't here today. She hadn't expected to miss him. He'd left her a text yesterday that he'd be unable to help this weekend. She been irked that he hadn't said what he'd be doing, but then, he had a right to lead his own life and not report to her.

She was glad to see Jackie in the kitchen when she arrived home that afternoon. "Do

you know where Blake is?" She tried to keep her tone even and not show too much interest in his whereabouts.

"Oh, he's out of town for a few days. He told me he had personal business to take care of. He's hoping to be back Sunday night."

"What kind of personal business?" And why did she feel left out?

"He didn't say. He looked really happy when he told me. Maybe he's met a girl."

Eden set her jaw. "I wouldn't put it past him."

Jackie turned and looked at her, a frown on her brow. "Would it bother you if he'd found someone?"

Eden turned away and started rinsing the head of lettuce. "Don't be silly."

"Funny, but I had a feeling you were starting to have tender feelings toward our prodigal."

"You're wrong. Besides. Even if I did, which I *don't*, he's my brother-in-law. That would be out of line."

"Why?"

"I'd feel like I was betraying Mark. Falling for his brother seems so sordid."

"Maybe it would if Mark were still here, and you were cheating on him behind his back."

"Are you saying I shouldn't honor my husband's memory?"

"No. But you're still young and you have a child to raise. Turning your back on love because they were related is a bit drastic. What if you started to care for someone who was a total stranger? Someone you didn't know anything about. Would you admit your feelings then?"

"Of course not. But Blake is family."

"Not your family. He was a stranger when he showed up here. You'd never met him and the only thing you knew about him was a load of bad things that his family fed you."

Jackie came to her side and slipped an arm around her waist. "I know what I see on your face when you look at him. I hear what's in your voice when you talk about him. It's time you started to pay attention to yourself."

Eden shook her head but she couldn't get the woman's comments out of her mind.

Lucy came into the sitting area dragging her teddy bear and looking lost. "Mommy, where's Uncle Blake? I miss him."

Eden pulled her daughter onto her lap. "I know, sweetheart. He'll be back soon but you couldn't play outside. Look, it's raining. Why don't we make cookies?"

Lucy pouted but nodded. "Okay. Then can we play Barbies?"

Eden chuckled. "Yes, of course. Now, what kind of cookies should we make…?"

Her thoughts were all in a different direction as she mixed up the batter for cookies. She missed Blake, too. She enjoyed seeing him and Lucy play soccer in the yard. He was much more athletic than Mark had been. There were so many differences between the brothers it was puzzling at times.

Maybe, that was because they *were* two different men. When she looked at things logically, the only thing Mark and Blake had in common was blood and a name. If that were true, then how would that affect her growing feelings for her brother-in-law? She was attracted to him. It was hard not to be. He had a way of making her laugh and smile, he showed an interest in her and listened to her concerns. She'd been telling herself she was lonely and simply drawn to a man who showed her some attention. She knew now that she'd been lying to herself. But each time she enjoyed his company, she always came away feeling guilty.

What did she do about that?

Chapter Ten

Blake folded up the tarp Monday morning and shoved it into one of the cubbies on the wall. Working on Roxy had left a mess in the barn, and he needed to clean it up. He could hear his mother fussing about leaving his things all over creation.

He smiled. He'd used those words at Lucy the other day when she'd scattered all her yard toys around the grass. His niece had taken to following him around, but he'd told her to not go into the car barn without an adult. There were too many things that could hurt her. She'd crossed her little heart and promised, but he still kept a watchful eye on her. She was a speedy little critter.

He scanned the work area, satisfied he'd put it all in order. He had a twinge of regret letting Roxy go, but it was for a worthy cause,

and it might be years before his leg was able to straddle a bike.

"Uncle Blake."

He stopped and listened. Was that Lucy? The call came again, louder and with a twinge of fear.

"Uncle Blake."

It sounded like Lucy, but she shouldn't be in the barn. Curious, he walked to the front of the building that used to be the storage space for the old cars. Before that it had been a true barn with a hayloft in the rafters.

"Uncle Blake. I'm scared."

He looked up and saw Lucy in the loft peering over the top of the ladder fourteen feet off the ground. She looked terrified. Her blue eyes were wide, and her lower lip poked out. Blake's heart stopped beating. If she fell from that height, it could be disastrous. He tried to stay calm. "How did you get all the way up there, Princess?"

"I climbed. But I can't get down. Come and get me."

Blake's blood turned to ice. He cursed his bum leg. There was no way he could maneuver the ladder with one leg and still bring the child down safely. He needed help, but he couldn't leave her and his phone was still in

the workshop room. "Lucy, just sit still, okay? Stay away from the edge."

"I want my mommy."

Blake searched frantically for a solution. "Okay, I'm going to call her. Don't move." The main door was only a few yards away. He could still see Lucy and maybe shout for help. Uttering a silent prayer, he inched toward it, keeping his eyes on the child. Then, to his relief, he heard Eden calling for his niece.

"Eden. Come here, please."

She came toward him smiling but he stopped her at the door. "We have a problem."

"Mommy! I'm scared." Tears were streaking Lucy's face and sobs shook her little body.

Eden looked up and breathed out a cry of alarm. "Oh no. I'm here, Lucy."

The little girl had leaned forward, reaching out for her mother. Eden held up her hands. "No, Lucy, don't move, sweetheart. Scoot back from the edge for Mommy, okay?"

"I want to come down."

Eden hurried to the ladder, then looked at him expectantly. Blake knew she assumed he'd climb up and bring her down. His stomach lurched. He was failing her and Lucy. The two women he cared most about. He met her gaze, then tapped his leg. "I can't climb a ladder, Eden."

He saw her turn pale, then her expression filled with horror. "How can we get her down? No one's here but you and me."

Blake hated what he was about to say but there wasn't another solution. "You'll have to go up and bring her down."

"No!" She backed away. "I can't. You know I can't."

Blake took her shoulders in his hands. "You *can*. I'll talk you through it… I promise."

Trembling, she shook her head.

"Mommy." Lucy reached out her arm, stretching over the edge.

Eden tensed. "Don't move, Lucy. Sit still. Please." She looked at him, her eyes pleading. "Isn't there another way down?"

"Unfortunately, no."

"Mommy!"

Blake's heart was racing and his spirit was being shredded. Lucy was growing more panicked. They needed to get her down quickly.

"Eden, you can do this. I'll be here. I'm afraid she might get too close to the edge."

She placed her hands on her cheeks. "But I—"

He gave her shoulders a gentle shake. "There's no other choice." He was relieved to see realization form in her blue eyes. "I believe in you."

Eden looked up at her daughter, who was sobbing. "I'm coming, Lucy."

Blake turned toward the ladder, staying close. "I'll walk you through each step and I'll be here to catch you if you fall. I may have a bum leg but my arms aren't broken."

She swayed and for a moment he feared she'd pass out. "Eden?"

She cringed, then bowed her head in defeat and turned away. "I...*can't*."

Dread swept through him. If he couldn't get her to try, he'd call the fire department, but even the few minutes they took getting here might be too long.

Eden looked up at her daughter and her vision blurred. Her baby was in danger, and she had to save her. She looked at the old wooden ladder attached to the post. It went straight up with narrow and very old slats for rungs.

She closed her eyes and groaned. *Lord, help me. I'm so scared.*

Blake took her hand and led her the few steps to the ladder. "You can do this. I'll be right here."

"Mommy." Lucy's cries suppressed some of her terror. She took hold of the sides of the ladder, fighting nausea. Eden tried to swallow but her throat was closed up. She shook

her head, then felt Blake close behind her. His hand on the small of her back gave her comfort and a measure of courage.

He whispered in her ear, "Lucy needs you."

She looked up the length of the ladder. It was a long way up. Her body tensed.

"It's just a hayloft, Eden, not a Ferris wheel."

She closed her eyes, then placed her foot on the first rung, aware of Blake close at her back. "I'm coming, sweetheart."

"Keep your eyes on each rung as you go, Edie. One hand, then the other. One foot, then the other."

She took one more step, then glanced down and froze. But Blake's calm, steady voice pierced her paralysis.

"Don't look down. Keep going. You're halfway there."

Eden forced her gaze to Lucy, who was watching her anxiously, tears on her cheeks and two fingers in her mouth. She always did that when she was scared.

One more step. Reach and step. Reach and step. She realized with a jolt that she was at the top. But now what did she do? "Blake?"

"I'm right here. Take one more step, then crawl onto the loft and catch your breath. You did great."

Eden did as she was told, and the instant she settled on the rough floor, Lucy crashed into her arms. "It's okay, baby. I'm here. You're okay..."

But she knew they *weren't* okay. They still had to get down. How were they going to manage that? She looked down at Blake, who was looking up at her and smiling. As if reading her mind, he started giving her directions on how to get down.

"Eden, you need to help Lucy get onto the ladder and start down."

She didn't want to do what he said, but they couldn't stay up here. She pried her daughter's arms from her neck. "It's okay, sweetheart. You can climb down that old ladder. You're part monkey, remember? And Uncle Blake is there to catch you if you fall. See how strong he is?"

Blake flexed his arms to demonstrate.

Lucy slowly turned around and put her foot on the first rung.

Eden watched with her heart in her throat. It was up to Lucy now. There was nothing Eden could do from up here. She prayed Blake could catch her baby if she fell. Lucy moved slow and steady with Blake speaking to her all the way. He plucked her off the ladder as soon as he could reach her. The little

girl clung to him, hugging his neck. Eden wished she was in that position.

Blake set Lucy down and turned his attention toward her. "Your turn, Madam Curator."

Knowing Lucy was safe had allowed her old fear to flood back into her mind, along with the nausea in her stomach. She stared at Blake. He was so far down.

"Eden, please. I can't help you climb down, but I'm here to catch you if you fall." He patted his shoulder. "Muscles, remember. But you're not going to fall. Show Lucy how brave you are."

It was the perfect encouragement. She didn't want her child to think she was afraid. She turned and reached out her foot for the first rung but couldn't find it. She yelped and froze.

"Try it again, Edie. Just an inch more and you'll touch it."

Eden glanced down and saw Lucy. She was smiling. If a five-year-old could do it… She trained her gaze on the loft and reached for the rung again. One by one, with each step conquered, Blake muttered encouragement. When she saw a horse stall between the rungs, she knew she was close.

Two more. One. Her foot touched solid ground and her knees started to buckle. Blake

caught her around her waist and gathered her into his arms.

"I knew you could do it! You've conquered your fear of heights."

She shook her head. "No...not really."

He held her tighter. "I'm proud of you."

Her heart thudded, but it was a different beat from the drumming of fear. Lucy grabbed her around her knees. Eden picked her up and hugged her fiercely. "You and I are going to have a long talk about climbing things."

"Okay, Mommy."

She set her down and took her hand.

Blake took Lucy's other hand and they started toward the house. "Well, all I can say is I've never seen such brave ladies. I'm feeling pretty useless right now."

Eden looked at him, holding his gaze. "Don't. You were more help than you know."

"I think this calls for a celebration. How about some ice cream?"

"Blake, we'll be eating supper shortly," she protested.

"All the more reason to celebrate. Dessert before supper."

She wasn't going to press the point. All that mattered was Lucy was safe and Blake had made it happen. She'd be forever grateful.

* * *

Blake entered the studio and clasped his hands behind his neck. He'd escaped Eden's and Lucy's company as soon as possible. His adrenaline had faded quickly, leaving him tense and drained. The ice cream had tasted like sand in his mouth.

He sank into the recliner, massaging his forehead in an attempt to ease the pounding headache in his skull. Never had he ever felt so useless, or so worthless, than when he realized that Lucy needed him and he couldn't rescue her. He'd hated forcing Eden to go up the ladder, but he was incapable. Not even during the worst of his rehab had he ever felt so powerless. He was a cop, but he was incapable of saving the two people he loved most. The thought of losing them had shredded his heart.

He'd have to keep a closer eye on Lucy. He hadn't realized how quickly little ones could get into trouble.

Blake closed his eyes. The bigger issue was what the incident had revealed. He could no longer deny his feelings for Eden. All he wanted to do was keep her safe, make her happy and spend the rest of his life at her side.

Lord, why did You place this amazing woman in my path when I can't have her?

He jerked when his cell phone rang. He was surprised to see Eden's name on the screen. His heart jumped. Had something happened to Lucy?

"Blake, I'm sorry to bother you but Lucy won't go to sleep until you tuck her in. Would you come over and tell her good-night?"

Relief coursed through his veins. "I'll be right there."

He started across the yard, not sure if he was feeling flattered because Lucy wanted to tell him good-night, or nervous because once again, he was assuming the role of parent, the job that belonged to his brother.

Eden greeted him at the door. "I'm sorry. She just won't lie down unless you're here. I hope you don't mind."

"Of course not. She's my little buddy." He looked into her blue eyes and added silently that she was the woman he loved.

He followed Eden upstairs to Lucy's room, drinking in a feast of girlie, ruffled curtains, pink-and-purple bedcovers, frilly dolls and a few pieces of sports equipment for good measure. He smiled. It was exactly what he would have expected from the little princess.

"Uncle Blake. I wanted to tell you good-night." She held out her arms and he sat on the edge of the bed and accepted her hug.

"Good night, Lucy." He held up his fist and she popped her small one against it. "You were very brave today, coming down that ladder."

His niece glanced at her mother. "I'm not going to climb it again."

"Good to hear. You scared us a big bunch."

Lucy smiled at him. "But you and Mommy helped me down."

Blake looked at Eden. "Mommy did most of the helping. She's very brave."

Eden broke eye contact and gently pressed Lucy back down on the bed and tugged up the covers. "Now, please go to sleep."

"Okay. I love you, Uncle Blake."

Blake's heart twisted and throbbed and melted into a lump in his chest. "I love you, too, Princess."

Back downstairs, Blake made a beeline for the door. The faux-family scenario was closing in on him, stealing his breath and clouding his mind. He reached for the doorknob as Eden called his name.

"Thank you for coming. And thank you again for helping me and Lucy." She took a step toward him and gently touched his arm. "I don't think I'm over my fear of heights, but I know I can if I have to."

Blake lost himself in her blue eyes. "You're

braver than you think. Brave and beautiful, and the most amazing woman I've ever known." She looked up at him, tilting her chin just so. All he had to do was kiss her. There was no way he could resist.

He took possession slowly, surprised and encouraged by her response. She melted against him and somehow his arms were around her, her hands gripping his shoulders.

Realization slammed into his mind at where he was heading. "Eden, I shouldn't have. I didn't mean... Good night."

He turned and walked out, taking refuge in the studio. He might be able to put walls and locked doors between him and Eden, but he couldn't find any barrier that would keep her out of his mind and heart.

What kind of man did that make him? A weak one who had fallen for his brother's wife.

Eden pulled up at the museum a few days later and found Owen's car parked near the door. A rush of dread touched her heart. "Oh no. More stuff." She regretted her words as she went to the door. She loved her father-in-law, but his constant criticism of her efforts was wearing thin.

She expected to find Owen in the main

room, but it was empty. He wasn't in the storage room or the office or in the yard out back. As she walked back through the church, she noticed the door to the sanctuary was open. She peeked in and saw him seated in the front pew, staring at the pulpit and the large cross mounted on the back wall. A jolt of alarm chased along her nerves. "Owen. Are you all right?" He didn't respond. "Do you need something?"

"Jackie quit."

Eden wasn't sure she'd heard him correctly. "What do you mean? Quit what?"

"Us. Me. She's walked out."

Eden struggled to understand. "No. She can't quit. She's family. Why would she leave us?"

"Me. She left *me*."

The dejection in Owen's voice broke her heart. She sat down beside him and put her hand on his arm. "What happened?"

"She said she was tired of trying to climb over my wall of pride." He raised his chin. "She's like my wife."

Eden was more confused than ever. Only one thing was clear. "Call her, apologize, do whatever you have to do, but convince her to come back. She's family, she belongs here

with us." Owen continued to stare at the altar without responding.

A thought suddenly intruded into her confusion. Lucy. If Jackie was gone, then someone had to pick her little girl up from school in…she checked her watch…ten minutes. Hurrying to the office for some privacy, she punched in Blake's number to her phone. "Blake, we have a problem. Owen is here at the museum—"

"Let me guess, he has more important things for you to add to the shelves."

"No. Blake, I found him just sitting in the sanctuary staring. He told me Jackie has quit."

"*What?* Are you joking?"

"No. I tried to find out what happened but he's not making sense."

"I'll be right over."

"No, wait. I need you to pick up Lucy from school. It was Jackie's day to do that. Take her home and I'll be there as soon as I can. I want to sit with Owen for a while."

When she rejoined her father-in-law, he was standing at one of the stained glass windows. She debated whether to speak to him. "Owen?"

Slowly, he turned and faced her. His eyes were filled with sorrow, his shoulders slumped.

Her heart ached. He looked older, tired and defeated. She'd never seen him like this. She started toward him, but he met her gaze.

"You go on. I want to stay here awhile. I need to think."

"Are you sure?"

He nodded and looked away. Reluctantly, Eden went to her car and slid behind the wheel. She wanted to cry. She needed Blake. They had to sort this thing out.

Her thoughts had been rotating over and over like a taffy pull machine reliving his kiss, which had felt so right, and the guilt over letting it happen. He'd become a friend and she valued his advice but she'd allowed that to overcome her judgment.

Lucy and Blake were in the yard kicking the ball around when she arrived at Oakley Hall. The sight gave her a welcome sense of security. He was a man who would always take care of those he loved. He came toward her, his expression filled with concern. "What's going on?"

"I don't know but I'm scared. I've never seen him like this. Blake, we have to get Jackie back. We need her."

He took her hand. "I know. She's family."

Eden had half expected him to say they needed her around the house for all the things

she took care of, but he'd only thought about
how much they needed her as a family member.

Her eyes filled with grateful tears. He had a
kind heart. "I tried calling Jackie, but it goes
to voice mail."

"Where would she go?"

"I don't know. This has been her home
since she came here." Tears rolled down her
cheeks. "Why would she suddenly walk out?"

Blake squeezed her hand. "I'll check with
Tony. He might know what's going on. Don't
worry. I'll talk to Owen, too."

He started to stand but she grabbed his
arm. "Thank you. I don't know what I'd do
without you here."

"I'm glad I came home so I could help."

Eden watched him walk away, struck by
how much things had changed. She'd wished
Blake away but now she couldn't imagine
Oakley Hall without him.

When had her opinion changed?

Keeping his promise to Eden to bring
Jackie back was proving to be more difficult
than he'd hoped. For the last four days, his
calls had gone to voice mail, and Tony had
been as shocked as anyone to hear his mother
had quit. He promised to look into things.

And Owen... Well, he was a closed book. The stubborn old man refused to talk about Jackie and had taken to sitting in his office.

Blake sought solace in the car barn, wishing he still had Roxy to tinker with and keep his mind off everything else. The empty spot in the workshop mocked him. He doubted his sacrifice had made any difference. Footsteps on the wood floor drew his attention. Eden was coming toward him. He couldn't help but smile. The bright yellow sweater she was wearing made her look like a ray of sunshine walking through the dim interior. "Hi."

She smiled. "Hi. I was wondering if you'd gotten in touch with Jackie yet. I keep trying her number but no luck."

He looked at her and his heart pounded in his chest. Since the kiss, he'd been consumed with thoughts of her along with a hefty dose of guilt. She'd kissed him back, but he couldn't put too much stock in that. Eden was vulnerable after that scare with Lucy. "Uh, yeah, I talked to Tony this morning. She's in Gulfport with her daughter for a while. He said he'd call her and see if he could convince her to talk to one of us."

Eden sighed. "I miss her so much. Owen is like a statue. He just sits and stares. I found him in his office the other day staring out the

window. He wouldn't even answer me when I spoke. I—"

She stopped and looked past him, her forehead creased. He braced for what was coming. "Where's Roxy?"

Blake took a nonchalant tone. "Oh, she has a new boyfriend now."

"You *sold* her? Why? I thought she was your prized possession. Your fondest memory."

He shrugged. "I have new memories now. There's a time to every purpose under heaven." He held his smile as she studied him. "I'm thinking of getting another one to restore. Something to keep me busy."

She nodded but her blue eyes were filled with doubt. "Okay. Well, if you hear from Jackie, let me know."

"Sure thing."

Eden turned and started out, then spun around. "Blake, thank you again for saving Lucy."

He shook his head. "You saved her. I just stood watch."

"You did more than that. You literally encouraged me every step of the way. I'm eternally grateful."

"It's what family members do."

"No. Not all members."

She walked out and Blake exhaled a heavy sigh. Gratitude. That's not what he wanted from Eden. But that's what he'd settle for. Nothing else was possible.

Eden had barely left the barn when his phone rang. He answered without looking at the name on the screen, expecting it to be Jackie. When he ended the phone call, he smiled. He would never stop marveling at the way the Lord worked things out. It was never the way he expected or planned, but it was always the best situation and usually from out of left field.

A swirl of excitement surged through his system, making him grin again. He had a job offer. A job with the police. There was an opening for an academy instructor at the Mobile Law Enforcement Training Center. It wasn't a desk job, either. There would be paperwork, of course, but mostly he'd be working with the cadets, teaching them the things he'd learned.

Blake glanced out at the main house. He wanted to tell Eden the good news. He'd tried not to dwell too much on his future. Working at the museum, spending time with Lucy and digging through Mark's files had kept him too busy to think.

This was truly an answer to his prayers,

but now it meant leaving Eden and Lucy behind and he wasn't sure how he could do that.

Eden glanced out the kitchen window later that day and saw Blake step off his porch and out onto the lawn. His limp was obvious today. That usually meant he'd overdone things. Probably playing with Lucy again. Their ball games were always fun to watch and her little girl looked forward to them, but she suspected they took a physical toll on Blake. Each time she saw him with Lucy she hoped his leg would improve over time so he could actually run and play and not have to always use his cane for support.

On impulse, she went outside and intercepted him on his way to the car barn. "Hello, Blake."

He turned and smiled. The look on Blake's face should have been her first clue. She'd never seen him so happy. "You're in a good mood."

"Yes I am. I just got offered my dream job. I never imagined something like this would come along."

Eden couldn't help but revel in his exuberance. There had been little joy in his life since coming home, and he deserved to be

happy, but an uneasy feeling settled in her chest. "Where will you be working?"

He set his hands on his hips and expanded his chest. "I'm going to be an instructor of academy cadets at the Mobile, Alabama, training center." He came toward her. "It's perfect. Not too much desk work and lots of time working with the trainees. I didn't think I'd ever get to work in law enforcement again, other than being chained to a desk."

Eden's heart burned and her throat began to close. Her worst fears had been realized. She set her jaw and crossed her arms over her chest. "So, you're leaving?"

"I guess so. They want me as soon as I can report."

Her initial excitement was quickly turning to anger. "What about the museum? And the bicentennial?"

"Well, I suppose…"

"And your father, and the company?" She choked back tears. She would not let him see her cry. "And what about Lucy? She'll be heartbroken."

"It's not like I'm moving to Dubai. I'll come and visit."

"I should have known you'd revert to your old ways."

A muscle ticked in his jaw. "Meaning?"

"Turning your back on your family when they need you most."

"No. It's not like that. The bicentennial will happen if I'm here or not. The museum is all but ready to open, such as it is." He swallowed. "As for my dad, he's made it clear from the get-go that I wasn't to get involved with his business. He won't be sad to see me go."

"That's not true. He's mentioned you several times. I think he is starting to change his mind about things."

"Not likely," he muttered.

Eden backed away, her emotions threatening to explode at any moment. "I knew you showing up here was a bad idea." She spun around and hurried back inside the house, her vision a watery blur. Seeking refuge in her room, she curled up in the window seat, her heart in shreds. Blake was leaving. She wasn't surprised. She'd been balancing her emotions for a long time, wondering when he'd display his true colors. She should have realized when he sold Roxy that he was preparing to cut ties to the Sinclair family. Walking away from her and Lucy.

A sob caught in her throat. Foolishly, her heart had begun to believe that the real Blake was the one she'd come to know and love

these last weeks. Love? How had she allowed this to happen? When had Blake burrowed into her heart and past all her defenses?

A wave of guilt washed through her. But she wanted him to be happy and this job was perfect for him. If only it were here and not in another state.

Wiping tears from her cheeks, she looked out the window, her gaze finding the studio. She'd come to depend on him being there and seeing him every day. Maybe with him gone, her feelings would change. Perhaps it wasn't love but only infatuation.

Hugging her knees, she bit her lip. No. What she felt was more than attraction, but along with that came the guilt over him being Mark's brother.

She had no idea how to sort out her tangled emotions.

Eden had found no answers to her conflicting feelings as she left the grocery store later.

"Eden."

She turned at the sound of her name and saw Norman Young coming toward her across the parking lot. She smiled. "Hello. Good to see you. I hear you had a fun time at the school lunch."

Norman smiled. "We did. Blake seemed to enjoy playing parent."

She sighed. Apparently not enough to hang around.

"I have to tell you, Blake has been a real blessing since he returned. It's a shame Owen can't see what he's done. Don't know what makes the man so bullheaded."

"What do you mean?" she murmured.

"Thanks to him Sinclair Properties can survive awhile longer. If he hadn't sold that motorcycle of his, we'd be in bankruptcy right now."

"I don't know what you're talking about."

"That old bike of his. Who knew it was worth six figures. He got top dollar for it at the auction in Nashville last weekend."

Eden's mind was churning with questions. "He sold Roxy to save the company?"

"Yeah, didn't he tell you?"

"No."

She mulled over the things Norman had told her as she drove home, trying to sort through the information. Had Blake really sold his beloved bike to save his family business? Did Owen know? The one time Blake had suggested helping at the office, his father had exploded. Had Blake ignored the warning?

The way she was ignoring her feelings? How did she reconcile her guilt with her affection? How and when had it happened? She thought back and saw a trail of little things

that had led her to this point. Blake's attention to Lucy and his willingness to always help. He hated history but he'd been at the museum every time she'd needed help. He'd even taken over on several occasions.

Then there was his kindness and understanding when they first visited Beaumont, and his comfort when it had been destroyed. And his strength in helping her and Lucy from the loft couldn't be discounted. But all of that didn't change the fact that he was her husband's brother, and her first loyalty was to Mark.

Wasn't it?

Chapter Eleven

Blake closed the small journal, his emotions a familiar mix of anger and sorrow. His father had always been a manipulator, skilled at getting others to do what he wanted, but he never expected Owen to be so selfish that he'd press his own son to take any risk necessary to grow his business.

He stared at the thin gray journal on the table. That one small book had answered all his questions about Mark, his dad and the crisis at the family business. Now, what did he do with that information? If he was leaving Blessing for Mobile, then he couldn't, in good conscience, keep what he'd discovered from Eden and his dad.

He'd imagined every scenario of his revealing the truth about his brother. The fallout could be huge, or it could finally answer so

many questions both Eden and his dad had about why Mark had made some of the decisions he had.

Eden was expecting him to leave. He doubted that telling her the truth would make him any worse in her eyes. Eden was obsessively loyal to her husband, so this news wouldn't dent her image of him for long. She was the type that would hold fast to the good memories and excuse the bad.

Owen was another matter. Exposing his role in this situation could go many different ways. Most likely Blake would be banned from Oakley Hall again, this time for life. The shock of what Mark had done and why could set off the granddaddy of all tirades. Or it could bring about another heart attack.

By the time dawn had made an appearance, Blake had reached his decision. First thing was to tell Eden and judge her reaction. Then worry about telling his father later. Blake had no idea how Eden would react. Anger, disappointment, shock, maybe even relief. Most assuredly she'd hate him for digging up the facts.

Maybe the bright spot in all of this was that it would place a wide barrier between them. Neither of them could come to terms with their feelings with Mark's memory looming

over their shoulders. It was an impossible situation.

Blake stepped into the kitchen of the main house and found Eden in her favorite spot on the small sofa in the sitting area. "Morning." For a moment he feared she'd ignore him. News of his job hadn't been received well. He breathed a sigh when she finally met his gaze.

"Come for more coffee?"

He slipped his hands into his jeans pockets. "No. I thought you might like to take a walk around the grounds. It's a really nice morning." The suspicion in her eyes nearly sabotaged his plan.

"Okay. But what's wrong?"

"I need to talk to you privately. It's about Mark." Her expression closed up and he feared she'd refuse to come with him. "It's important. And for your ears only."

"All right." She slipped on a light sweater as she came toward him. "You're scaring me."

"I don't mean to, but I have information you might want to hear."

They strolled toward the back of the three-acre lot in silence. Finding the courage to tell her was harder than he'd expected. "I've been puzzled by many of the decisions Mark made the last years of his life. It didn't make sense.

My brother was a solid, controlled, detail-oriented man."

"I know."

He took a deep breath. "I started looking into his papers and the files left in the studio."

Eden glared at him. "You went through his personal things?"

"Not at first. I just looked at the business documents and I found the purchase agreement for the Meridian company. That was the start of everything falling apart. Then I examined his date book, and his journals."

"What journals?"

"He started keeping one shortly before he bought the Meridian company."

"You read his diary?" she spat. "All his deepest private entries? You're despicable. That's low even for you."

He winced at her accusations. "Probably but I had to understand what happened."

"And what did you find?"

"Mark was pressured into buying that business," he told her. "Owen practically ordered him to grow the company or he'd be replaced."

"That's ridiculous. Owen would never fire Mark."

"No, I don't believe he would. But he wasn't above threatening and coercing to get what

he wanted, and Owen wanted Sinclair Properties to be a bigger fish in a bigger pond." He released a harsh breath. "And he put all his manipulative skills to work on Mark to make it happen."

"No. Owen wouldn't do that."

His tone softened. "I don't think he meant to, Eden, but it's his way. He sees his criticism and pushing as a way to get people to achieve their full potential, and Mark fell into the trap."

"No," she said thickly. "Mark had a tumor. He was sick and he wasn't thinking clearly..."

"All that's true, but it all started with Owen's pressure to grow the company. I think the pressure became so fierce that he did what Owen wanted only to realize that he'd sealed the company's fate. I think that's when he started gambling."

Eden had her arms wrapped around her waist, clearly distressed at what he was telling her.

"Mark wrote how he went to a conference in a Biloxi casino," Blake continued. "And he decided to try his hand at the games, and he won. Big. He thought, if he could win enough money, he'd be able to save the company and grow it at the same time and make Dad happy."

"Are you saying my husband was to blame for the company's troubles?"

He stopped and faced her. "Mark was desperate to save it in any way he could. He wrote about his frustration and his sense of failure for letting Owen down. He deeply regretted his separation from you and Lucy. He planned to make it up to you once he got things back on track."

"But he didn't."

"No. He found out about the tumor around that time, and it made him more determined to get things right. I think from then on, the tumor was distorting his thought process and there was nothing he could do."

"Why didn't he tell me he was sick?" she cried. "I could have helped."

"He said he wanted to spare you the pain and sorrow."

Eden turned away. "What kind of man doesn't tell his wife he's dying? And Owen, why would he drive his son to make such a reckless decision?"

Blake had no answers.

"Why didn't he tell me? I could have helped somehow. I would have understood his isolation, helped shoulder his burden. Isn't that what wives are for?" She covered her face with her hands. "How could he be so selfish?"

"He was trying to protect you."

She spun around and faced him, eyes shooting daggers. "That's the Sinclair way, isn't it? To go it alone, keep it all inside. Pursue your way no matter what." She lifted her chin. "That's what you did, too, isn't it? Your way was to be a cop instead of standing by your family."

"Eden—"

"Now you get to do it again. Ride off to Mobile and leave the rest of us to clean up the mess."

He clenched his jaw. "I thought you had a right to know the truth about what Mark was going through."

"Thank you for opening my eyes. Now I can sleep easy knowing my husband shut me out of his pain and sickness because he didn't want me to worry. And my father-in-law drove his son to the brink of disaster for his big dream." She turned away again, but muttered under her breath, "I deeply appreciate your shattering my image of my family."

The sarcasm and hurt in her tone sliced through him. "Eden, that wasn't my intention."

She was striding toward the house and didn't look back.

Now she could add his name once again to her hate list. Instead of seeking her input about

delving into his brother's past, he'd taken matters into his own hands, assuming that she'd be relieved when she learned the truth.

Eden was right. He should never have come home.

Eden's blood was still boiling later that day. Blake's "helpful" revelations had unleashed all her old anger at Mark and piled on resentment toward Owen. No. He hadn't stirred it… He'd dug it up. She'd buried all those old feelings deep and staunchly refused to examine them.

Now she had no choice.

She glanced at the clock. Time to start supper but she had no idea what to prepare. She'd seriously considered ordering pizza, but Owen was not a fan. Maybe he'd agree to takeout from his favorite restaurant. She was in no mood to cook.

Without Jackie to oversee meals, this last week they hadn't been eating as well. Owen hardly touched his food. She couldn't decide if it was her cooking or just that he missed Jackie.

"Mommy. I'm hungry. Can I have macaroni and cheese for supper?"

"I have a better idea. Why don't we eat out tonight. I was going to ask grandpa where he'd like to go. Want to come with me?"

"Okay."

She started down the hallway as Owen stepped from his office. He was holding his chest.

"I need...help."

"Owen!"

She quickly helped him to a chair and pulled out her phone. "Lucy, run and get Uncle Blake. Tell him Grandpa is very sick."

The next several minutes were a blur of fear and worry and confusion waiting for the ambulance, and watching Owen being carried off to the hospital. Blake had been her rock and helped her sort out what she should do next. He sent her on to the hospital and took Lucy to Addie's.

Now she sat in the ER waiting room, terrified of losing her father-in-law. He was the father she never had. Her tension eased greatly when she saw Blake coming toward her. For the first time she fully understood that Blake wasn't the man she expected, but after what she'd learned about Mark, neither was he. She'd begun to wonder if deep down Owen wasn't who he tried to be, either.

"Any news? How is he?"

"The good news is that it wasn't a heart attack. They think it was anxiety. He's stabi-

lized but they're going to run tests and keep him here a few days for observation."

Blake exhaled a tense breath and bowed his head. "I was afraid I'd be too late. I was afraid he'd be…"

Eden touched his shoulder and he slipped his arm around hers, then she rested her head against him a moment.

Blake looked down at her. "I called Jackie. She's on her way."

Eden breathed an audible sigh of relief. "Good. He'll be glad to see her. I think he missed her more than he let on."

The doctor came out and spoke to them, assuring them that Owen was being moved to a room and would be resting the rest of the night. He encouraged them to go home.

Eden shook her head. "No. I'm not leaving. Someone should be here with him."

"All right. I'll stay, too."

Eden took Blake's hand. "Thank you." He smiled and her heart skipped a beat. "We might be in for a long night."

"I know. I kind of like the idea."

She smiled and settled in beside him. In fact, she'd like to be at his side forever.

Blake yanked his phone from his pocket the next morning when it rang, expecting to

see the name of the hospital, not Norman's name. "Hey, what's up?"

"I thought I should tell you right away about some changes that have occurred."

Blake braced himself. "Okay."

"I've been offered a job in New Orleans. It's a great opportunity and I can't turn it down. Sorry to leave you in the lurch right now but I have to let them know tomorrow."

Blake rubbed his forehead. Just once he'd like to get good news. "I understand. I appreciate you letting me know. How soon will you leave?"

"Two weeks. The thing is, who's going to take the reins here? I was hoping you could convince Owen to come back."

"Owen's in the hospital. He suffered some kind of attack yesterday. He's not in any shape to run the business." Norman was quiet a moment.

"I'm sorry to hear that. But, maybe another Sinclair could step up to the plate. Having you associated with the business would go a long way to restoring clients' confidence. The only other option is to sell Oakley Hall."

"No. That's out of the question."

Blake's insides were being squeezed like a vise. He never wanted the company, never wanted to work there. Now he was faced with

running the whole show. It was the last thing he wanted to do, especially with his dream job within his grasp. But he couldn't let his family home be sold to save a dying company. Not now that his dad was ill. In all the years he'd been gone he'd never considered that his father wouldn't be there, giving orders, being in charge. But seeing him in the hospital bed frail and weak had forced him to face the truth.

Time was running out. It was up to him now. Eden's words rang in his ears. *Running away. Turning his back. Rejecting his family.* Maybe she was right. Maybe, in his own way, he was as selfish and bullheaded as his father. Maybe he'd been running all his life from the thing he was destined to do. He'd come home to repair his relationship with Owen and to make amends. What better way than to step in and save the business that meant so very much to him?

"Blake? You still there?"

"Yeah. I'm here." He blew out a long breath. "Looks like I'm going to be here for a long time."

"Does that mean you'll come and run the business?" Norman asked.

"Yeah."

"Friend, I know this isn't something you're

thrilled with. But, in all honesty, I think you'll do a wonderful job."

Blake hung up the phone, his heart like lead in his chest. The only small ray of hope was that Eden might be happy that he was staying to help the family.

But first he had a call to make and a job to turn down.

Blake stepped into his father's hospital room the next day to find Jackie at Owen's side and Eden seated in a bedside chair. She'd arrived last night and sent him and Eden home to rest.

"Good morning, Jackie. It's good to see you with the family again. You know you belong here."

Jackie scowled in Owen's direction. "It seems so. When I'm not here everything falls apart and people end up riding in ambulances."

Owen harrumphed but he had a faint smile on his face, which Blake found odd.

He approached his father. "How are you doing today?"

Owen held his gaze a moment. "Ready to go home tomorrow."

"Good." Thunder rattled the windows. "Better than trying to get home in this rain.

It's supposed to get worse. They're predicting heavy downpours and high winds this afternoon."

The nurse brought Owen lunch and Eden and Blake took the time to grab a bite to eat in the cafeteria. On their way, Eden took his hand. "He's doing so much better. The doctors confirm it was an anxiety attack. It's very strange but I'm just glad he's feeling better."

"Me, too." Blake studied her a moment. Should he tell her about his decision to stay and run the company?

He paid scant attention as Eden filled him in on the tests the doctors had run and the recommendations they'd laid out. But he knew that no matter what the doctors said, Owen would do as he pleased. The man always had and always would. But he was just grateful that his dad wasn't seriously ill. He might need his help going forward.

Blake really could use Eden's support with his new decision, but he wasn't sure how she would react. He finished his drink. No. Now wasn't the time to stir up the waters. Later, when Owen was home and settled, he'd tell Eden about Norman leaving and his taking charge.

"What do you think?"

Blake jerked back to the moment and realized Eden was staring at him. "What?"

"About Owen's anxiety. What do you think could have caused it? I doubt if Jackie's leaving would have upset him that much."

He had trouble organizing his thoughts. "I don't know. Mark was the only one who understood him. I could never figure him out."

Eden held his gaze a moment. Then she huffed out a breath of irritation and shook her head.

Obviously, he'd not responded the way she'd hoped. He watched her walk across the cafeteria and disappear into the hall before he stood and started walking back to Owen's room.

Eden wasn't in his future whether he stayed in Blessing or moved to Mobile. Not with Mark's memory between them.

How was he supposed to live with that?

Blake made his way slowly back to Owen's room, his thoughts in a jumble. The family were all staring at the television, which was tuned to the local weather report.

Jackie shook her head. "Looks like the storm is getting worse. They're predicting hurricane-force winds. Maybe you and Blake should head home." Thunder and lightning flashed and boomed overhead as rain pounded against the window. "Or maybe it's too late."

Eden whirled away from the window. "Lucy. She doesn't like to be away from home when it storms."

Blake grabbed his jacket and umbrella. "I'll get her. I'll swing by the museum first and make sure everything is secure. Eden, you stay here until the storm passes. I don't want to have to worry about you driving in this."

The rain was coming down hard when he pulled up to the museum. He picked up the potted plants near the entrance that Eden had placed there and set them inside the door. The wind was picking up and slammed the door back against the outside wall. It resisted when he pulled it shut. He turned on the lights but before he could walk to the middle of the room, the power went out. Using his phone, he made a quick survey of the windows and doors and checked the back entrance, where a few discarded items had been left.

As he made his way back through the building, his phone wailed with a weather warning. A quick check told him he might not be able to make it out to the edge of town to pick up Lucy from her friend's house. His best plan would be to hunker down and wait it out. He selected Eden's number to let her know about the change in plans, but his phone lacked service.

The wind screamed overhead, and he headed to the innermost room of the old church. As he ducked inside, a loud crashing noise assaulted his ears. The building shook and glass shattered.

Blake covered his head and crouched in the corner of the room.

Eden stood staring out the hospital room window, her thoughts a downpour of confusion. Her father-in-law was going to be all right but what about Blake? Had this health scare changed his mind about leaving Blessing? She hoped so because she wanted him to stay. But she wanted him to be happy, too.

If only there was a way to make this right for everyone. Try as she might she couldn't find a way to make that happen.

"Eden, come away from that window. What if it breaks in this wind?" Jackie tugged on her arm and steered her toward the chair near the bed.

But she couldn't sit down. She was too worried about Blake. Addie's mother had called and told her to tell him not to come. The weather was too bad. She assured Eden that Lucy was fine. Addie's older sisters had built a blanket fort in the living room, and they were having popcorn and ice cream

while they waited out the storm. If need be, Lucy could spend the night again and come home in the morning.

Eden held her phone to her ear, waiting for Blake to answer, her gaze riveted on the darkness outside. The storm was worse than they predicted, and she needed reassurance that he was safe at the church. This was her third call with no response. The worst of the storm had passed through a short while ago, but she kept getting an unavailable notice.

She heard a soft gasp from Jackie and turned to look at the older woman. Her gaze was glued to the television screen. Eden saw a video of the museum and a reporter in rain gear talking about the storm.

"Straight-line winds of over ninety miles per hour ripped through downtown Blessing, leaving destruction in their wake."

The video showed the roof being torn off the local motel and the metal canopy over one of the gas stations blowing off and twisting into a heap. The next image chilled her blood and squeezed her throat.

"The former Saint Joseph's Church took a hit when its steeple was torn from the roof and a small addition in the back of the building was demolished by a falling tree."

The video clearly showed Blake's car parked

at the entrance. Eden's heart pounded and electrical jolts of fear shot through her nerves. She was faintly aware of Jackie putting her arm around her shoulders. Eden stared at the phone in her hand and tried again to call Blake.

Her knees buckled and she sank into a chair. "He was there. In the middle of it. What if…?"

"Shh. Don't think like that. They haven't mentioned anyone being inside. Let's not jump to conclusions. Blake is a resourceful guy and he's been in dozens of worse situations. I'm sure he took the right precautions."

In her heart she knew Jackie was right, but her heart also was revealing just how much she cared for Blake. She couldn't bear the thought of losing him.

"Owen. What's wrong?"

Yanked from her internal turmoil, Eden faced her father-in-law and saw an expression on his craggy features she'd never seen before. She wasn't sure how to interpret it. Shock. Horror. Grief.

"Owen, are you in pain?" Jackie asked. "Do you want me to call the doctor?"

When he didn't respond, Jackie reached for the nurse call button. He appeared quickly and made a cursory check of Owen, who kept trying to wave off the examination.

The diversion temporarily diverted Eden's emotions, but a glance at the TV brought it all back. She tried again, fighting tears and a hole in her heart that was growing by the second. She tried to ignore all the horrible scenarios that kept forming in her mind, of Blake lying unconscious on the floor or trapped under the fallen tree.

Unable to remain still, she picked up her purse and slung the strap over her shoulder. "I'm going to the museum."

"Eden, no. Stay here."

"I can't, Jackie. I have to know if he's all right." The woman started to protest, then sighed and nodded.

"Okay, but be careful. Sounds like lots of streets are blocked with fallen trees and power lines. Let us know when you get there."

"Owen?" Eden asked.

"He's fine. Go."

Blake carried the wet book into the kitchen and opened it on the table. At first glance only the top few pages were wet. Maybe they could dry them out and hope that the underlying pages weren't too severely damaged.

"Blake."

He turned at the sound of his name. What was Eden doing here? He hurried out into the

main room and was wrapped in a fierce hug. Eden clung to him like a vine. "Why did you come? Has something happened?"

She spoke against his chest. "I was afraid I'd lost you."

All the breath in his chest whooshed out. Had he heard her right? Did she care that much?

He gently cradled her head with one palm. "I'm fine, but I confess to having a moment there when the tree fell. Sounded like a bomb going off."

She looked up at him. "How bad is it?"

"See for yourself." He walked her into the sanctuary, where the steeple had left a split in the ceiling. "Thankfully, the hole didn't go all the way through. A stained glass window near the entrance was shattered. The worst is in the back." He stopped at the door to the small room that had once been a nursery. The room was pancaked into the ground, the trunk of the tree and broken branches filling the space.

Eden moaned softly. "Oh no. This is awful. If that tree had fallen in a different direction…" She turned and looked at him, her eyes moist. "I'm glad you're safe."

"Me, too." Blake held her gaze, warmed by the softness in her eyes. He allowed himself

to believe she cared for him more than just a friend or family member. She placed her hand on his cheek and slowly stroked her thumb over his skin. He sucked in a surprised breath.

"Careful, lady. You'll start giving me ideas."

"Maybe that's what I want to do," she whispered.

He smiled tenderly down at her. "I wouldn't protest."

"You wouldn't?"

"No. I care for you, Eden. A great deal. More than I should. Keep looking at me like that and I won't be responsible for my actions."

"You're always responsible, aren't you?"

"No." The temptation was too great. He lowered his head, his gaze locked on her blue eyes. She lifted her face, her hand still on his cheek. Eden whispered his name and he captured her lips. She leaned into him, returning his kiss and sending his heart rate soaring. He raised his head. "Eden, I want to tell you…"

Her eyes widened and she lifted her palm to her throat. "No. Don't."

Her cheeks were flushed as she stepped away. He held on to her arms, searching her eyes for confirmation of what they'd shared. "We need to talk about this. About what's happening between us."

"No we don't. There's nothing between us.

There can't be. Ever." She turned and hurried toward the door.

He caught up with her before she could open it. "Eden, you can't keep ignoring this."

"Yes I can. I have to. For Mark."

Her words burned like a hot poker in his chest. She walked out and Blake watched her drive away in the mist.

The kiss replayed in Blake's mind a thousand times as he drove home to the studio. Eden loved him. He was certain of that. And in those few seconds, he'd seen his heart's desire. A future with Eden and Lucy. A future that could never be because neither one knew how to deal with the memory of his brother.

Blake stood on the porch of the studio the next day watching as Jackie and Eden escorted Owen into the house. Thankfully, he'd recovered quickly and had been released this morning. From where he stood, his father looked spryer than he had since Blake had arrived. Almost as if the health scare had sent him in a new direction.

Blake waited for fifteen minutes after the family had gone inside. He wanted to give Owen a chance to settle in. Then he'd assess his situation and decide whether to confront him about the pressure he put on Mark.

Eden's words came to mind. Maybe he should leave well enough alone. Maybe he should never have come home in the first place. He'd upset the applecart and accomplished nothing in the process. Worst of all, he'd never found a way to reconcile with his father.

All in all, a useless homecoming.

With the exception of meeting Eden and Lucy and losing his heart to both of them, of course. But they were Mark's family, even if Mark was no longer here. Eden would always see him as the bad guy, the man she shouldn't care for because he was the brother.

Blake had his own reservations about that. He carried a bag of guilt for falling for his brother's wife, though technically, there was nothing wrong with them being together. On the other hand, he hated to think what Owen would say about Eden loving the wrong son.

He couldn't deny the kiss they'd shared. While they'd acknowledged their mutual attraction, the word *love* hadn't been spoken yet. He doubted it would now.

Grabbing hold of his cane, Blake went to the main house and found the family gathered in the living room. Owen looked unusually pleasant as he met his gaze. There was no fire in his eyes this time, only a question.

"I was wondering about the museum. How badly was it damaged?"

Blake winced inwardly and tried to hide his irritation. He should have known his father's first thought would be for the museum. "Bad. I've called someone to cover the holes in the roof with tarps. I'll have Eden look over the displays tomorrow and see what can be done, but it won't be open for the bicentennial if that's what you're wondering."

Owen nodded thoughtfully but didn't comment further.

Blake set his jaw. Some things never changed.

Chapter Twelve

Eden met Jackie in the hallway the next morning as she was coming down the stairs. "How's our patient this morning?"

"Surprisingly well. He seems almost contented. Though, he still doesn't like taking his medicine." She slipped her arm through Eden's. "But I have high hopes for the old goat. I think this scare might have opened his eyes to certain things."

"Like what?"

"Let's wait and see, huh? So, how are things between you and Blake?"

Eden averted her gaze. "Fine. Why wouldn't they be?"

"Any further developments on your relationship? Like maybe admissions of affection or maybe a kiss."

Her cheeks flamed. "Jackie, you are talk-

ing nonsense." She moved to the counter and started to wipe it down.

"You can deny it until your last breath, sweet girl, but we both know that you and Blake have been playing emotional dodgeball ever since the day he knocked on that back door. You can't keep your eyes off one another. Blake's heart falls out of his chest whenever he looks at you or Lucy. The man is seeing you as part of his future."

"He's not a family type of guy," Eden protested.

"Oh? Sure seems that way to me. I've seen him with Lucy. The joy on that man's face is a sight to behold. And, from what you've told me, he's been a comfort and support to you now and again."

She couldn't deny that. Despite her fierce resistance, she'd fallen in love with Blake, but it was futile. Eden could feel Jackie's gaze pinned on her back. She knew the woman too well and that she wouldn't let this rest until she got an answer that satisfied her.

Eden gripped the damp rag in her hand. "Even if you're right and there are...*feelings*...between us, it can never happen."

"Why?"

"Because of Mark. Blake is my brother-in-law. I can't fall for him."

"Why?" Jackie repeated.

"Because it's wrong. It's disgraceful. Sinful even."

Jackie grinned. "You know, in biblical times, the brother of the deceased was supposed to assume the care of his brother's family."

Eden frowned at her friend. "This isn't biblical times, and anyway, it's too soon to jump into anything."

"I wouldn't call two years jumping. Let me ask you, were you unfaithful to Mark? Did he cheat on you?"

Eden set her jaw. The woman was going too far. "No. We honored our vows."

"Uh-huh. And what is the last line of the marriage vows?"

Eden frowned. She had no idea what Jackie was leading up to. She thought about it a moment. "Uh, till death do us part."

"Exactly. You're parted. The marriage severed. The covenant fulfilled. You're free to move on to a relationship with his brother." Jackie held her gaze. "No condemnation."

"Mommy, Uncle Blake taught Cuddles a new trick. Watch."

Eden breathed a sigh of relief when Blake entered the kitchen holding Lucy in his arms with the puppy trotting along at his heels.

The look of pure happiness on Blake's face brought a lump to her throat. One thing she was sure of. Blake adored little Lucy. He'd be a wonderful father.

She shut down that thought and smiled. "A new trick. Let me see it."

Blake put Lucy down and she squatted, pointing a finger at the dog. "Okay, Cuddles, show Mommy your new trick. Roll over." Lucy made circular motions with her fingers. "Roll over. You can do it."

Cuddles stared at her a moment, then sat down. Lucy looked up at her uncle. "Uncle Blake, make him do his trick."

He chuckled and leaned down. "Cuddles. Roll over." He made a quick movement with his finger and the little dog executed a perfect doggie roll. The child squealed in delight and hugged the fuzzy pup.

Eden giggled. "Good job, Lucy! That was wonderful." She looked at Blake and his gaze told her clearly that he thought she was wonderful, too. She quickly looked away.

Jackie gave Cuddles a scratch behind his ears. "Blake, I'm glad you're here. Owen wants to have a family meeting. Might as well do it now since we're all together. I'll tell Owen."

Blake frowned and looked at her with a shrug.

"Have you ever had a family meeting before?" Eden asked.

He scratched his chin. "Never. I'm guessing he'll want to remind us to speed up the museum repairs so it will be open for the bicentennial."

"You're probably right. I can't think of anything else that would concern the family, though he has acted differently since he got home. I can't believe the change in him. It's almost like the anxiety attack has scrubbed off all his rough edges. I suppose the rest and regular medications these last few days have helped. I just hope he doesn't go back to work and put himself at risk again."

"He won't," he said.

"How can you be so sure?"

"Because he won't be the Sinclair going to the office each day," Blake told her.

Eden studied his expression. Something was wrong. She could see it in his eyes. "What do you mean?"

Blake sat down beside her. "Norman is leaving so I thought it would be a good idea to take his place and see if I can get the business back on track. I let Owen down once. I don't want to do it a second time. Not after all he's been through."

Eden touched his arm. Was he serious? "But what about your job in Mobile?"

"I turned it down. It didn't really suit me anyway. Too much time at a desk."

"You said there would be more time with trainees and—"

"I know. But I'm a Sinclair. I need to shoulder this. Besides, you were right—my coming home upset everything. That was never my intention."

Eden sighed. "Oh, Blake. I need to apologize for what I said. I was surprised, that's all. I wasn't prepared for you to go away. I was hoping…"

"What?"

"I assumed you'd stay around. Lucy likes having you here." Why was she such a coward? Why couldn't she just tell him how she felt?

"Is that the only reason?"

"I'd miss you, too."

Blake took her hand in his and gently squeezed it. "Good."

"So why are you sacrificing your future, Blake? You're not fooling me. I know how much that job meant to you. I know you never wanted to take over the company."

Eden reclaimed her hand. "I'm sorry for the way I've been acting since you came home. I

always believed that if you'd joined the company, been the other son, that it would have made everything right. But I know now that I was wrong. Things wouldn't have ended differently. I think it was my way of explaining Mark's behavior." She touched his cheek. "Now I feel so sad. It's not right that you have to give up your dream for your father's."

"It's not such a sacrifice." He gazed into her eyes. "I'll be able to see you and Lucy as much as I want. That's compensation enough."

She hugged him. "You are a noble man. And I know what you did. Norman told me about your other sacrifice. I know how much that bike meant to you."

"Unfortunately, it was only a stopgap but I don't regret it. I need to stop walking away and stand and confront my demons."

Eden leaned over and gave him a brief kiss and watched the emotion bloom in his eyes. Fear and shame gathered in hers. She moved away. Soon, she'd have to make a decision about her relationship with Blake. She couldn't keep playing this yo-yo game with their feelings.

But what was the right decision? And how did she remove Mark from her thoughts without feeling disloyal?

* * *

Jackie entered the kitchen as they were ending their conversation and gave them a knowing smile. "I put Lucy down for a nap so we won't be disturbed. Owen is ready for us now." She smiled and motioned them to follow.

Blake placed a possessive hand on her arm. "So, I guess King Owen is ready to hold court."

Eden grinned. "I should have practiced my curtsy."

"Maybe a kowtow would be more appropriate."

She giggled and poked her elbow in his side.

In the living room, Owen was seated in the wingback chair, looking every bit the king. The only odd note was Jackie, who was standing beside him with a very unusual smile on her face.

Blake and Eden positioned themselves on the sofa. Blake's chest was tight from anxiety. What could be going on? He studied his father a moment. There was a peculiar twinkle in his eyes that was unnerving. Did he have some other big scheme in mind he was going to dump on them?

Owen took a deep breath. "I asked you here

to tell you about changes that I've decided to make. My recent health scare has opened my eyes to things I've been ignoring. No, that's not true. Things I chose to deny." He directed his gaze at Blake.

Blake braced for another dressing-down. What had he failed to do now?

"I've come to realize that pride and greed led me down a dead-end trail. I've done you all an injustice and I'm going to try and correct that going forward." He glanced at Jackie before continuing. "To begin with, I've arranged to have the Blessing Historical Society take over the museum. They'll pack up the contents and return them to us, with the exception of the items that generally pertain to the town's history."

Eden gasped and clutched Blake's arm. So typical. Decide but don't discuss. "Dad, Eden has worked hard getting that museum set up."

"I know and she's done a wonderful job considering the burden I placed on her shoulders. That was one of my big mistakes."

Eden exchanged a puzzled look with him. "That's very generous. I'm sure the people in this community will be grateful."

Owen nodded. "They were. I also have to admit to making a series of misjudgments over the last few years. I realize now that

after my wife died, I lost my compass. She was the one who kept me from falling prey to my flaws. As a result, I've been blind and unfair to my sons. I've also taken steps to rectify that."

Eden leaned forward. "Owen, I don't understand."

"I'm in the process of finalizing the sale of Sinclair Properties to a company out of Jackson. They are a large firm, and they have a lot of experience managing small-town interests like ours."

Blake's vision blurred and his chest caved inward from the air leaving his lungs. "You sold the company?"

"It's all but a done deal."

His mind whirled. He never anticipated his father would sell out. It was *unthinkable*. He was barely aware of Eden gripping his arm.

"Owen, what will you do with your time if you're not going to go back to work?"

Jackie lowered her hand and Owen took hold of it with a smile. "I'm going traveling. Jackie and I are going to be married. We've both been alone a long time. She convinced me that it was time to turn a new page in my life and to let go of the old dreams and find new ones." He stood and pulled Jackie against his side. "I hope you'll be happy for us. And

I hope you'll forgive me for being such a single-minded old—" he looked at Jackie "—goat."

Eden went to them and gave them a hug. "I'm so happy for you. I should have seen this coming." She smiled at Jackie. "You told me you were falling for the widower of an old friend. I never guessed it was Owen."

"Good. Because that would have complicated things even more."

Blake took advantage of the distraction to leave the room. He walked through the kitchen and out to the porch only vaguely aware of what he was doing. His father had just destroyed his future. He'd been unceremoniously kicked out in the cold.

Inside the studio, he ran his fingers over his scalp. He'd spent the last few days talking himself into doing the right thing and now he'd lost it all. He wasn't needed at Sinclair Properties because it no longer existed. His job in Mobile was gone, and he had nowhere to go.

Eden. How did she fit into this new reality? He had nothing to offer her now. He had no job, security or promise of a good life ahead for her and Lucy. He'd hoped that they might start a new life together, but he couldn't take that step when he was empty-handed.

A knock sounded on the door. Eden peeked in. "Blake, I'm so sorry. I can't believe Owen is making all these changes."

She came to him and slipped her arm in his.

Blake took comfort from her nearness. "Dad has a way of pulling the rug out from under people. Like your museum."

Eden shook her head. "No. That's a relief. I've always known it was pointless. But I made a promise, and I didn't want to break it. Owen didn't know what you were planning to do. Maybe you could talk to him and he'll change his mind."

Blake shook his head. "No. It's too late. He's already set things in motion. Besides, he has a new life ahead of him. A happy life. He hasn't had that in a long time. I'm glad for him and Jackie. She'll give him the contentment he used to have with Mom. He needs a strong woman to keep him in check."

"Do you think he'll be happy traveling and not having a business to consume his time?" she asked.

Blake huffed out a skeptical breath. "I don't know. This is an Owen I've never seen before."

"Me, either. Do you have any idea what you'll do now?"

"No. I need time to think things through."

She moved in front of him, her eyes soft and brimming with affection. "You could stay here with me and Lucy."

He smiled and touched her chin. "I'm not sure that would go over well with Owen. I'd always be a reminder of the past. Not just because of being the son that failed him, but now, I'd be a reminder of my mother. He doesn't need that to complicate his new marriage. I think it's best if I just move on. Let everyone get on with their lives. I came here with nothing and I'm leaving with nothing."

"That's not true! You have me and Lucy."

"I wish that were true, but we both know that Mark's memory will always be a wall between us." His heart tightened when she didn't deny it.

"Where will you go?" she asked quietly.

"I have a friend in Nashville. I'll see what opens up from there."

Her eyes welled with tears. "Please don't go. Stay here."

"Do I have a reason?"

"Yes. Lucy loves you."

"And her mother?" he asked gruffly.

"Yes. I do. I've just been feeling so guilty. Like I was betraying Mark. But then I realized that I have a right to love again. Being

a widow doesn't mean I can never feel for someone else, even my brother-in-law. Till death do us part. We're parted. I was a good wife to him. He was the best husband he could be until he got sick." She took his hand and held it to her chest. "I believed that loyalty was the most important quality. Loyal to the end. No matter what. But sometimes loyalty can make you blind. I loved Mark and I know he loved me, but he made a mistake and instead of looking for help, he tried to fix it on his own with his own power and he only made it worse. I hated him for that," she said softly.

"You did?"

"Yes," she admitted. "Until I realized I was no better. I was proud of being Mark's wife and thought I could go through life with his memory alone to sustain me." She shook her head. "But the more I saw you with Lucy, the more I came to see what kind of man you really were. I knew what I really wanted was a family again. With you. Loving you shouldn't be any different than if I met someone else who was a stranger. And you were a stranger to me. I didn't know you, only what I'd heard."

Blake pulled her into his arms. "I fell for you the moment you opened the door. I was

so ashamed. It seemed so wrong and disrespectful to have feelings for my brother's wife."

"What are we going to do?"

He brushed a hair from her forehead. "What do you *want* to do?"

She stood on tiptoe and kissed him. A kiss filled with all the emotions she'd been denying. "I want a future with us together."

Blake crushed her to him, holding her close and thanking the Lord for leading him home again.

Eden stared out the window at the studio the next day. It was rainy and cold today. The kind of day you wanted to curl up with a cup of hot chocolate and a good book, or maybe a good friend. Someone you cared for.

Except Blake wasn't in the studio today. He'd left early this morning before she had to take Lucy to school. Her heart had been twisted with worry ever since. What if he didn't come back? He'd talked last night about leaving. He was right. Mark's image would always stand between them unless they could overcome their guilt.

She wished there was something she could do. He'd been blindsided. They all had, but Blake most of all. He'd been prepared to sac-

rifice for the company and instead he'd lost not only his position at Sinclair Properties, but his dream job in Mobile. It wasn't fair. It was wonderful that Owen had realized the error of his ways and tried to make amends, but he should have discussed things with them first, gotten their input. But that wasn't his way. Or Mark's. They'd both made decisions that affected others on their own, assuming everyone would go along.

On the other hand, Blake would never have been happy running the business given its dire condition. Someone had to do something.

Reaching her decision, Eden went in search of her father-in-law. She found him and Jackie in his study looking at the computer. He glanced up and smiled. The sight threw her for a curve. In all the years she'd known him he'd rarely smiled.

"We're researching vacation spots."

A swell of anxiety rose in Eden. Maybe this wasn't such a good idea. "I wanted to talk to you, alone, if I could."

Jackie smiled. "Of course." She kissed Owen and gently touched Eden's arm as she went by.

Her father-in-law looked at her, his bushy brows drawn together. "What is it?"

Suddenly, her courage failed. She'd never,

ever questioned Owen's decisions before. Not about things in the house, or Mark or anything. She had to be prepared for him to lash out and rant again. "I need to talk to you about Blake."

"Oh. What about him?" he asked.

"There are things he's done that you aren't aware of."

The smile faded. "Do I need to call a lawyer?"

Eden filled with indignation. "Why do you always assume that he's done something wrong?"

"Well, I—"

"You've done it ever since I joined the family. Everything Blake did was wrong. You said he was reckless, heartless and dishonored his family. But you were wrong. So was Mark. I don't know what Blake did to make you so angry that you'd ban him from his home, but he's none of the things you said." She narrowed her eyes at her father-in-law. "He's a decorated police detective who has several commendations for bravery and had to resign from the force. He'll always walk with a limp."

"I—I had no idea."

"No, because you could only see your dream and Mark's role in it," she reminded him.

"I'm beginning to see that."

"I'm no better. I believed everything Mark told me. I didn't have a family role model to follow. I thought devotion to work was how my husband showed his love. I know he loved me and Lucy, but it was love from a distance." She took a deep breath and plunged ahead. "Do you know Lucy's favorite thing to do every day? Play soccer with Blake. A man who has to use a cane to stand, but he kicks that ball to her and plays with her and loves her in ways Mark never thought of."

Owen nodded and met her gaze. "You're right. I've made every mistake a father can make. I put my dreams above everyone else's, and it caused me to lose my oldest son. Jackie has made me see things differently." He paused a moment, as if collecting his thoughts. "When we were in the hospital, and I saw that news footage of the museum and realized that Blake might be injured... that I might have lost him, too. It was like a dark cloud being lifted from my eyes. I saw clearly what I'd done, and I hated myself."

"Owen, I know you didn't mean to hurt anyone."

"No, but I was determined to achieve my goal at any cost. My wife tried to warn me but I was too prideful to listen."

Eden nodded. She knew only too well.

"Owen, there's a few more things you need to know. Things Blake and Norman have been doing to try and save your company."

"What do you mean?"

"You know that motorcycle Blake inherited?" Eden shared the story behind Blake's action. "Also, did you know Norman was leaving?"

"Yes, he informed me a few days ago."

"Well, one thing you don't know is that Blake was planning on taking over, and that he turned down his dream job to try and save your business."

Owen's eyes widened. "Why would he do that?"

"Because he's a good man with a huge noble streak and a loving heart. I just thought you should know that selling the company has pulled the rug out from under him."

Eden departed Owen's office later, unsure of whether she'd made things better or worse. Her father-in-law was genuinely surprised about the things she shared with him. They talked about Mark, and she filled him in on the things Blake had uncovered. Through it all Owen had listened and nodded and stared at his hands.

He'd thanked her for telling him these things and she'd left.

She prayed she hadn't complicated things for Blake. She wasn't sure what she'd tried to accomplish, but she couldn't let his dream die without letting Owen know about his part in it.

Eden was anxious to talk to Blake and forewarn him about her talk with his father. But he'd been gone for most of the day, and it was suppertime before he returned and he didn't show up at the house to eat with the family.

She hoped Owen would go and speak with him. An honest father-and-son discussion would do wonders for their relationship. She should have known better. Owen had retreated to his study with Jackie and the pair had been secluded the rest of the day.

Eden made a point to seek out Blake early the next morning before he could get busy. The weather was still cold and drizzly, so she slipped on her heavy sweater and made her way along the covered porch to his door. He didn't answer when she knocked. Noting that his car was still parked nearby, she opened the door and called his name.

"In here."

She found him in the bedroom, stuffing his belongings into his worn duffel bag. The one he'd carried when he'd arrived. "Blake. What are you doing?"

"I'm leaving for Nashville. My friend has a job for me there."

"What? Wait, you mean you're walking out without letting me know."

He didn't respond. "Did you need something?"

"Yes. An explanation. I came to tell you I talked to Owen, and I told him what you've done to try and save the company." She held her breath, anticipating his response.

Blake glowered. "Why would you do that?"

Eden raised her chin and met his gaze. "Because he needed to know that his opinion of you was all wrong. He needed to see the full scope of his narrow point of view."

He set his hands on his hips and frowned. "What did you hope to accomplish?"

She took a few steps toward him. "I thought he might talk to you and apologize. You said you wanted to make amends. Well, you have. Several times. I wanted to see you and Owen reunited."

"That's not going to happen." Blake shoved a few more items into his duffel.

Eden's patience reached the breaking point. "Stop that." She tugged the duffel away from him. "You can't leave. We need to talk about this."

"Nothing to talk about."

She gritted her teeth. "So, you were going to just drive off with no explanation, no good-bye."

Blake exhaled loudly. "We both know it'll never work between us. Not with Mark's shadow looming every moment. He'll always be the third person in the room."

Eden's anger caught fire. "That's a stupid excuse and you know it. This has nothing to do with Mark and everything to do with you being a Sinclair. They make a decision without consulting anyone else, without considering anyone else's feelings or opinions and just go on their way."

He avoided looking at her. "I didn't want to upset you any more than you were already."

She wanted to wring his bullheaded neck. "No. You're not getting off that easily. This wasn't about my feelings. This was all about yours and your inability to face things when they get difficult."

"Eden."

She jabbed a finger in his chest. "Mark didn't tell me about his troubles or his illness because he didn't want me to worry or cause me concern. You turned your back on your family because you didn't want to work for your dad."

"That was different."

He turned away but she forced him back around to face her. "I'm not done.

"Owen started a museum and dumped me in the middle of it. He decided that Sinclair Properties should be a big grandiose company, but he didn't bother to talk to Mark first." She took a deep breath, every nerve in her body shaking. "Then, you come along and pull me out of my shell and make me fall in love with you. But then you decide I'd be less heartbroken if you just rode off into the sunset like some cowboy in an old movie, rather than talking it over with me."

Eden crossed her arms over her chest and shook her head. "I guess I shouldn't be surprised. I've lived my adult life with the Sinclairs and I should have realized none of you are capable of putting others first. I told Mark I wanted an old home. It had been a dream of mine since I was a child. But he decided we needed something new and modern so he picked out the lot and the plan and chose all the details and then just moved me in."

"Eden, let me explain." He reached out to her.

"No. I'm finished." She raised her hands in resignation. "Go. Find your happy life in Nashville."

She spun on her heels and walked out of

the studio, fighting tears as she hurried back to the main house. How could she have been so blind, so naive to think she had a future with Blake?

Jackie looked up as she entered the kitchen. "Eden, honey, what's happened? Are you all right?"

The tears she'd been fighting burst loose. "He's leaving."

Jackie gave her a hug and gently rubbed her back. "Sit down and tell me what's going on."

"I love him and he's leaving."

Blake watched Eden storm out, his heart a twisted mass of pain and regret. Dragging his hand across his face, he berated himself inwardly for his actions. Eden was right. He was acting exactly like a Sinclair. He'd made up his mind on the best course of action and proceeded to move forward without even a thought of talking to Eden first. He'd decided, on his own, that she'd be better off without him. That they could have no future together.

He sank onto the edge of the bed, his face in his hands. He wanted to talk to her and ask for forgiveness. But he'd sealed his fate. She would never listen to him now. He'd lost her trust.

How did he break the cycle? How could

he prove to Eden he could change, that he *wanted* to change?

A knock on the door brought him to his feet. His heart filled with hope that Eden had returned, and he'd have a chance to explain. He opened the door to his father. The last person he wanted to see.

Blake stood his ground. "I'm kind of busy, Dad."

"I want to talk to you. It's something, well, it's long overdue."

Every instinct in him urged him to shut the door, but it was the first time his dad had ever reached out to him. He stepped back and ushered him in. "Have a seat."

Owen perched on the edge of the sofa, facing Blake as he slowly lowered himself into the recliner. Blake waited for his father to speak. When time dragged on, his irritation swelled. "Dad, I got things to do."

Owen nodded, then stared at him a long moment. "You're a lot like your mother."

"I suppose so."

"I was sorry to hear about your…leg."

Where was this going? "Well, things happen."

"Yes. Yes, they do. We aren't always prepared to deal with them."

Blake blew out an inpatient breath. "Dad, is there something you wanted to say?"

"Just that, you might not know… I mean, I didn't want to work for the company when I was younger. I wanted to be a professional golfer. I was good."

It was not what he'd expected to hear from his dad. "I thought you loved the company."

"I did. I was good at it. But no, I had other plans. Like you did. You always were brave. I wish I'd been more like you."

"You hated my rebellious ways," Blake bit out.

"No. I just didn't understand them. Not the way your mother did." Owen rubbed his hands together. "I know what you've done to help the business. The bike, giving up that job…"

"Eden shouldn't have told you."

"She was proud of you and wanted me to know what kind of man you were. And I, uh, appreciate how you've helped her at the museum."

"Happy to do it." Blake studied his father a moment. He was being surprisingly open and forthright. Maybe now was a good time to share what he knew about Mark's behavior. "Dad, there are things I discovered."

Owen held up a hand to forestall him. "I

know what Mark did. I knew he bought that company and I know I pushed him to do it. I'd convinced myself he was brilliant enough to make the whole thing work. He was always so smart with the business." His shoulders sagged. "But it didn't take long to see it was a big mistake, but I chose to ignore it. I had every confidence in my son. Eventually I realized the problem was too big to fix, but I couldn't accept that Mark wasn't perfect. Or that he might be to blame for the whole mess. The realization was too much. Jackie thinks it might have been the cause of my heart attack."

"So all this time you knew and didn't say anything. Didn't warn Norman."

Owen looked at him, his eyes glimmering with pain and regret. "I couldn't face the fact that my perfect son was destroying my family's business."

"What brought this change about, Dad?"

"When Jackie quit, I started to see what I'd been doing. Then when I saw the damage at the museum and knew you were there, I realized I could lose you, too. I didn't want that. I'd been focusing on a false legacy and ignored the real one right in front of me. You and Eden and Lucy." He stared at his hands a moment. "Pride is a terrible sin. It got in the

way of all my relationships. I'm going to try and guard against that going forward. I have a second chance with Jackie, and I'd like a second chance with you, too, son."

"I never meant to hurt you, Dad, I just—"

Owen stood. "Had to live your own life. I see that now. I've been blind and selfish. I hope we can start over. I... I've missed you, son."

Blake's throat tightened. "I'd like that. I've missed you, too."

Owen stepped forward, opened his arms and hugged him. Tears welled up in Blake's eyes. Never in his wildest dreams had he ever imagined this kind of reconciliation with his father. The Lord truly did move in mysterious ways.

"Well, I'd better get back to the house. Jackie will be wondering where I am."

Blake shut the door and walked back into the bedroom. His half-filled duffel mocked him. Eden was right. He'd been walking away because it was easier than trying to talk things through with her.

If he wanted another chance with Eden, then he'd have to set aside his normal way of addressing a situation and allow her to participate in their decision about their future.

Blake wrestled with his predicament

through the night and into the morning. However, after a lot of tossing and turning, he'd finally realized that the only way to talk to Eden was to let her lead the way. He waited until she returned from dropping Lucy off at school before he went to the main house.

She turned away when he entered the kitchen. "I thought you'd be gone by now."

"No. I have a few important things to take care of first."

She shrugged. "Well, I wouldn't know because you never tell anyone what you're going to do."

"Not this time. I need your help."

"You're a Sinclair." She huffed out a breath. "They don't ask for help, remember?"

"I'm a Sinclair but I'm asking for your help. Please, Eden."

She faced him, a puzzled look in her eyes. "Why?"

"Because I'm stuck, and I don't know how to move forward. You're the only one who can help me."

"I doubt that." She crossed her arms over her chest. "So, what do you want?"

"Will you take a walk with me?"

She glanced outside. "It's nice out. I suppose…"

They started at the end of the drive near

the garage and took the path toward the rear of the property. "Where are we going?"

"To my favorite spot."

"I didn't know you had one."

"I'd forgotten about it until last night." They walked across the lawn, stopping near a copse of trees beside the stream that ran along the edge of the property. "When I was a kid, we owned another five acres back there. My view wasn't marred by homes then."

He turned and moved to a large tree whose main trunk had split into four and provided a cozy hollow in the center. "I used to come here and sit when I needed to think things through."

Eden smiled. "I don't think you'll fit anymore."

"No. But there's a fallen log near the stream." He took her hand and steered her through the trees. He helped her up on the log and then sat beside her. "My dad came to see me yesterday. We've made our peace. I thought you'd like to know."

She clutched his arm. "That's wonderful, Blake. I'm happy for you."

"Which means I have a decision to make. One I can't, no, *won't* make without getting your input."

"Since when?"

"Since it involves you. And me. And Lucy." He took her hand. "I want us to be a family. A real family. I love you and I love that little girl."

Eden looked away. "Blake, what about…?"

"Don't. It's time to remove the obstacles. I know we've both been held back by guilt, troubled by the fact that I'm Mark's brother. I learned a long time ago that friends come and go in our lives for a reason. When that reason is fulfilled, we drift apart and move on to a new friendship. Why not the same for spouses? Your marriage to my brother was exactly what you both needed, and you made a life and a child together. But he's gone now and you're free to move on and love again. I admit I've been feeling like I'm stealing something from Mark. That I somehow was dishonoring his life if I loved you."

"And now?"

"I'm asking you to marry me and let me give you and Lucy the life you deserve."

"Where would we start this new life?"

"I don't know yet. At the moment I have no job and no prospects." He leaned toward her and framed her face with his hands. "All I know is that I don't want to spend another day without the two of you in my life. We'll trust the Lord to work out the details. He's pretty good at that sort of thing."

"Yes, I know. I asked Him to remove you from my life at one point. Thankfully, He just laughed at my request."

"Is that a yes?"

She answered him with a kiss, one with no reservations or restraints, a kiss just for him.

A short while later they started back toward the house. Blake held her hand, unwilling to let go. Ever.

Eden slowed her steps as they neared the backyard. "I need to tell Lucy. She'll be so happy."

Blake stopped. "What about Mark? He'll always be her father."

She touched his chest. "Yes, and we can both keep his memory alive for her by sharing our memories of him."

"We'll have to tell Jackie and Owen eventually. I don't want to ruin his happy mood with this. He might be violently against us. Mark will always be his favorite son."

Eden squeezed his hand. "No. He was simply the oldest son."

"There you are."

Blake and Eden looked up to see Owen walking toward them. Blake braced himself. "Uh-oh."

He stopped and studied them a moment, then nodded and looked at Blake. "I have

something for you. I'm glad I found you together." He reached into his pocket and pulled out a piece of paper.

Blake frowned at the number written on there. "What is it?"

"It's the phone number for the human resources office at the academy in Mobile. Call them first thing tomorrow and they'll tell you when to report to work."

Stunned, Blake struggled to grasp what his dad had done. "How did you know?"

Owen winked at Eden. "Someone who cares for you told me about the sacrifices you've made and were willing to make recently."

"I don't understand. I turned the job down."

His father shrugged. "I know some people, made a few calls. They hadn't filled the position yet, so I reminded them of your special qualifications. It didn't take much persuading, so I assume you're a more accomplished man than I ever imagined."

"You know this means we'll be moving to Mobile."

Owen nodded. "I know how to get there. Jackie loves Orange Beach."

Blake tugged Eden closer to his side. "Dad, there's something else…"

Owen held up his hand. "I know. I've

known for a while now. You can't keep a thing like that hidden for long."

Blake glanced at Eden. "And you're okay with us?"

"I got a second chance at love. You two deserve the same."

Eden broke frcc of his hand and wrapped Owen in a hug. "Thank you. You've made us very happy."

Jackie and Lucy came toward them across the lawn. Lucy darted forward and ran to hug Blake. Jackie stopped at Owen's side, a huge smile on her face. "Aha. I see you two finally have come to terms with things. About time. I never saw two people so much in love."

Owen scowled. "Hey."

"Besides us that is. Come on, Owen. Let these lovebirds have some privacy to celebrate."

Eden stooped down to speak to her daughter. "Lucy, how would you like to have Uncle Blake live with us all the time? He'd be your new daddy."

She smiled and nodded, lifting an adoring glance at Blake. She thought a moment, her forehead creased. "Will I have two daddies now? The one in heaven and him?"

Eden smiled. "Yes."

"I have to tell Cuddles." She ran off, and

Eden stood, slipping her arm around Blake's waist.

"It looks like the family is in agreement."

"Are you okay with moving to Mobile?"

She nodded. "They have old houses there I can help save."

"And maybe live in. We'll find a big old house that needs love, and you can fill it with all the antique furniture and chandeliers you want." He grinned. "And maybe a few kids."

"Oh? How many?"

Blake shrugged. "Six or seven."

"Whoa, cowboy. How about we start small, like a brother and sister for Lucy."

"Deal." He pulled her into his arms. "Wherever we end up, I'll be happy and content as long as we're all together."

Eden touched his cheek and placed a kiss on his lips. "I'm so glad you came home, my prodigal lawman."

Blake held her close to his heart and sent up a prayer of gratitude. Yesterday his life was a pile of rubble at his feet. Today he had a future and a family.

God truly did work in mysterious ways.

* * * * *

Dear Reader,

Pride, forgiveness and guilt are all things humans struggle with. Blake Sinclair faces all three when he returns home after a long absence. An unforgiving father and the lovely widow of his older brother complicate things even more. It takes patience and much understanding to work through all the obstacles Blake and Eden face. One by one they are able to break down the barriers.

We all grow impatient and frustrated when things don't go as we plan. Sometimes the best solution is to just take a step back, inhale a deep breath and wait to see what the next day brings. We have to resist our need to take matters into our own hands and allow the Lord to unfold events as He has them laid out.

For Blake and Eden it provides a happy ending and a path around the guilt. For others in the story it provides peace and a new beginning from pride that can destroy a family. Waiting on the Lord is the only way to overcome the difficult parts of life because love is always the answer.

I love to hear from my readers. You can follow me on FB at Lorraine Beatty Author or on Twitter @lorraine_beatty.

Lorraine

Get 3 FREE REWARDS!

We'll send you 2 FREE Books <u>plus</u> a FREE Mystery Gift.

FREE
Value Over
$20

Both the **Harlequin® Special Edition** and **Harlequin® Heartwarming™** series feature compelling novels filled with stories of love and strength where the bonds of friendship, family and community unite.

HARLEQUIN
PLUS

Try the best multimedia
subscription service for romance
readers like you!

Read, Watch and Play.

Experience the easiest way to get
the romance content you crave.

Start your **FREE TRIAL** at
<u>www.harlequinplus.com/freetrial</u>.

HEART *of a* LION

HILLARY FIELDS
Author of *The Maiden's Revenge*

She had once been a beautiful noblewoman called Lady Isabeau, betrothed at birth to the handsome squire Jared de Navarre. But all that changed when the Crusades began, and Isabeau was abducted, transported to the torrid climes of the Mideast, and sold...Jared had journeyed east, vowing to stay until he found his lady...but there his hopes died and his heart hardened. Now called the Black Lion, he was a fierce mercenary, about to begin a dangerous mission in the employ of a mysterious black-veiled renegade warrior...Jared never guessed that Isabeau had survived, fleeing the erotic realms of a harem to become this legendary desert rebel. And as death and betrayal swirl around them, their chance for love may be destroyed...unless they learn that fighting for each other is the most important battle of all...

"Hillary Fields is a fresh new voice that brings a heap of fire and sensuality to sizzle your senses."

—*The Belles and Beaux of Romance*

Available wherever books are sold
from St. Martin's Paperbacks

SHERRILYN KENYON

Dear Reader,

Being cursed into a book as a love-slave for eternity can ruin even a Spartan warrior's day. As a love-slave, I knew everything about women. How to touch them, how to savor them, and most of all how to pleasure them. But when I was summoned to fulfill Grace Alexander's sexual fantasies, I found the first woman in history who saw me as a man with a tormented past. She, alone, bothered to take me out of the bedroom and into the world. She taught me to love again.

But I was not born to know love. I was cursed to walk eternity alone. Yet now I have found Grace—the one thing my wounded heart cannot survive without. Sure, love can heal all wounds, but can it break a two-thousand-year-old curse?

Julian of Macedon

"Fun, fresh, and fabulous! Sherrilyn Kenyon's imagination is as bright as her future."
— Teresa Medeiros, author of A KISS TO REMEMBER

"By turns funny and touching, *Fantasy Lover* is a compelling story that will make you laugh out loud. The gods haven't been this much fun since Xena!"
— Susan Krinard, author of SECRET OF THE WOLF

Available wherever books are sold
from St. Martin's Paperbacks

FANT 2/02

TEMPT ME TWICE

BARBARA DAWSON SMITH

New York Times Bestselling Author of
ROMANCING THE ROGUE

A rogue shrouded in mystery, Lord Gabriel Kenyon returns from abroad to find himself guardian of Kate Talisford, the girl he had betrayed four years earlier. Now sworn to protect her, he fights his attraction to the spirited young woman. Although Kate wants nothing to do with the scoundrel who had once scorned her, Gabriel is the only man who can help her recover a priceless artifact stolen from her late father. On a quest to outwit a murderous villain, she soon discovers her true adventure lies with Gabriel himself, a seducer whose tempting embrace offers an irresistible challenge—to uncover his secrets and claim his heart forever...

"Barbara Dawson Smith is wonderful!"
— *Affaire de Coeur*

"Barbara Dawson Smith makes magic."
— *Romantic Times*

Only by pride cometh contention:
but with the well advised is wisdom.
—*Proverbs* 13:10

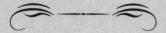

LOVE INSPIRED®
INSPIRATIONAL ROMANCE

Recycling programs
for this product may
not exist in your area.

ISBN-13: 978-1-335-58661-2

The Widow's Choice

For questions and comments about the quality of this book, please contact us
at CustomerService@Harlequin.com.

Love Inspired
22 Adelaide St. West, 41st Floor
Toronto, Ontario M5H 4E3, Canada
www.LoveInspired.com

Printed in U.S.A.

The Widow's Choice

Lorraine Beatty

LOVE INSPIRED
INSPIRATIONAL ROMANCE

Lorraine Beatty was raised in Columbus, Ohio, but now calls Mississippi home. She and her husband, Joe, have two sons and five grandchildren. Lorraine started writing in junior high and is a member of RWA and ACFW and is a charter member and past president of Magnolia State Romance Writers. In her spare time she likes to work in her garden, travel and spend time with her family.

Books by Lorraine Beatty

Love Inspired

The Orphans' Blessing
Her Secret Hope
The Family He Needs
The Loner's Secret Past
The Widow's Choice

Mississippi Hearts

Her Fresh Start Family
Their Family Legacy
Their Family Blessing

Visit the Author Profile page at LoveInspired.com for more titles.

A firm knock sounded on the back door.

Eden opened it to a tall, dark-haired man with deep-set brown eyes. A kernel of concern formed in her chest. "Can I help you?"

The man cleared his throat and shifted his weight. "Is this the Sinclair home?"

Eden debated whether to affirm his question. "Yes."

The man's brown eyes narrowed. "Is Owen Sinclair here?"

Eden's defenses heightened. No one came to visit anymore. Owen had few friends. "May I ask what your business is?"

The man's eyebrows rose as if offended. "Who are you?"

Eden stiffened at the authoritative tone of his voice. "Please state your business or I'll have to ask you to leave."

The man's jaw worked side to side. "I'm Blake. Blake Sinclair. Owen is my father."

Eden blanched. A chill shot up her spine, followed quickly by a jolt of anger. This couldn't be happening. The last thing they needed now was for her coldhearted brother-in-law to suddenly reappear. "What are you doing here?"

He shrugged. "I've come home."

The Tinderbox

A SOLDIER came marching along the highway: One, two! One, two! He had his knapsack on his back and a sword at his side, for he had been to war and now he was on his way home. Then he met an old witch on the highway. She was hideous, and her lower lip hung right down to her chest.

She said, "Good evening, soldier! My, what a pretty sword and a big knapsack you have! You're a real soldier! Now you shall have as much money as you'd like to have!"

"Thanks, old witch!" said the soldier.

"Do you see that big tree?" said the witch, and pointed to a tree beside them. "It's quite hollow inside. You're to climb up to the top. Then you'll see a hole you can slide through, and you'll come down way inside the tree! I'll tie a rope around your waist so I can pull you up again when you call me."

"What'll I do down in the tree, then?" asked the soldier.

"Fetch money!" said the witch. "Now I'll tell you: when you're down at the bottom of the tree, you'll find yourself in a great hall. It's quite light, for over a hundred lamps are burning there. Then you'll see three doors. You can open them: the keys are in them. If you go into the first chamber, you'll see a big chest in the middle of the floor. On top of it sits a dog with a pair of eyes as big as teacups.

But you needn't pay any attention to that. I'll give you my blue-checked apron, which you can spread out on the floor. Then go over quickly and get the dog, put him on my apron, open the chest, and take as many shillings as you like! They're all of copper. But if you'd rather have silver, then go into the next room. There sits a dog with a pair of eyes as big as mill wheels! But you needn't pay any attention to that. Put him on my apron and take the money. On the other hand, if you'd rather have gold, you can also have that, and as much as you can carry, if you just go into the third chamber. But the dog sitting on the money chest here has a pair of eyes each one as big as the Round Tower! That's a real dog, I'll have you know! But you needn't pay any attention to that. Just put him on my apron, so he won't do you any harm, and take as much gold as you like from the chest."

"There's nothing wrong with that!" said the soldier. "But what'll I get for you, old witch? For I daresay you want something too!"

"No," said the witch, "not a single shilling will I have! You can just bring me an old tinderbox, which my grandmother forgot the last time she was down there."

"Well, put the rope around my waist," said the soldier.

"Here it is," said the witch, "and here's my blue-checked apron."

Then the soldier climbed up into the tree, let himself drop down through the hole, and stood now, as the old witch had said, down in the great hall where the many hundreds of lamps were burning.

Now he unlocked the first door. Ugh! There sat the dog with eyes as big as teacups, and it glowered at him.

"You're a pretty fellow!" said the soldier; he put the dog on the witch's apron and then took as many copper shillings as he could get in his pocket. Then he closed the chest, put the dog on it again, and went into the second chamber. Yeow! There sat the dog with eyes as big as mill wheels.

"You shouldn't look at me so hard," said the soldier; "it might strain your eyes!" Then he put the dog on the witch's apron, but when he saw all the silver coins in the chest, he got rid of all the copper money he had and filled his pocket and his knapsack with silver only. Now he went into the third chamber! My, how hideous it was! The dog in there really did have two eyes each as big as the Round Tower, and they rolled around in his head like wheels!

"Good evening," said the soldier, and touched his cap, for he had never seen a dog like that before. But after he had looked at it for a while, he thought, "Now that's enough," and lifted it down to the floor and opened the chest. Well, heaven be praised! What a lot of gold there was! He could buy all of Copenhagen with it, and the sugar pigs of the cake wives, and all the tin soldiers and whips and rocking horses in the world! Yes, that was really a lot of money! Now the soldier threw away all the silver shillings in his pocket and knapsack and took gold instead. Yes, he filled all his pockets and his knapsack, and his cap and boots were so full that he could hardly walk! Now he had money! He put the dog on the chest, shut the door, and then shouted up through the tree: "Pull me up now, old witch."

"Do you have the tinderbox with you?" asked the witch.

"That's right," said the soldier. "I'd clean forgotten it." And then he went and got it. The witch pulled him up, and now he was standing on the highway again with his pockets, boots, knapsack, and cap full of money.

"What do you want that tinderbox for?" asked the soldier.

"That's none of your business!" said the witch. "Why, you've got the money now. Just give me the tinderbox!"

"Fiddlesticks!" said the soldier. "Tell me at once what you want it for, or I'll draw my sword and chop off your head!"

"No!" said the witch.

Then the soldier chopped off her head. There she lay! But he tied all his money in her apron, carried it like a pack on his back, put the tinderbox in his pocket, and went straight to the town.

It was a lovely town, and he put up at the finest inn and demanded the very best rooms and all the food he liked, for he was rich, now that he had so much money.

The servant who was to polish his boots thought, of course, that they were queer old boots for such a rich gentleman to have, for he hadn't bought any new ones yet. The next day he got boots to walk in and pretty clothes. Now the soldier had become a fine gentleman, and they told him about all the things to do in their town, and about their king, and what a lovely princess his daughter was.

"Where can she be seen?" asked the soldier.

"She can't be seen at all," they said. "She lives in a big copper castle with many walls and towers around it. No one but the king is allowed to go in and out, for it has been prophesied that she will be married to a common soldier, and the king can't stand that one bit!"

"I'd like to see her, all right," thought the soldier, but this he wasn't allowed to do at all.

Now he lived merrily and well, went to the theater, drove in the royal park, and gave lots of money away to the poor; and that was well done! He remembered very well from the old days how bad it was to be penniless! Now he was rich and had fine clothes and many friends, who all said what a nice fellow he was, a real cavalier; and the soldier certainly didn't mind hearing that. But as he spent money every day and didn't get any back at all, it happened that at last he had no more than two shillings left and had to move from the nice rooms where he had lived to a tiny little room way up under the roof, and he had to brush his boots himself and mend them with a needle; and none of his friends came to see him, for there were so many stairs to climb.

One evening it was quite dark and he couldn't buy even a candle, but then he remembered there was a little stub in the tinderbox he had taken out of the hollow tree where the witch had helped him. He took out the tinderbox and the candle stub, but just as he struck a light and the sparks flew from the flint, the door flew open and the dog with eyes as big as teacups, which he had seen down under the tree, stood before him and said, "What does my master command?"

"What's that?" said the soldier. "Why, this is a funny tinderbox if I can get whatever I like! Get me some money," he said to the dog. And whoops! It was gone! Whoops! It was back again, holding a bag full of coins in its mouth.

Now the soldier understood what a marvelous tinderbox it was. If he struck it once, the dog that sat on the chest full of copper money came; if he struck it twice, the one with the silver money came; and if he struck it three times, the one with the gold came. Now the soldier moved back down to the lovely rooms again, put on the fine clothing, and then all his friends knew him again right away, and they were so fond of him.

Then one day he thought: "Now, it's really quite odd that no one is allowed to see the princess. Everyone says she's supposed to be so lovely. But what's the good of it when she always has to sit inside that big copper castle with all the towers? Can't I even get to see her at all? Now, where's my tinderbox?" And then he struck a light, and whoops! There stood the dog with eyes as big as teacups.

"I know it's the middle of the night," said the soldier, "but I'd so like to see the princess, just for a tiny moment."

The dog was out of the door at once, and before the soldier had given it a thought, it was back again with the

princess. She sat on the dog's back and was asleep, and
she was so lovely that anyone could see that she was a real
princess. The soldier couldn't resist; he had to kiss her, for
he was a real soldier.

Then the dog ran back again with the princess. But in
the morning, when the king and queen were having their
tea, the princess said that she had dreamed such a remarkable dream last night about a dog and a soldier. She had
ridden on the dog, and the soldier had kissed her.

"That was a pretty story, indeed!" said the queen.

Now, one of the old ladies-in-waiting was to keep watch
by the princess' bed the next night to see if it really were a
dream or what it could be.

The soldier wanted very much to see the lovely princess
again, and so the dog came during the night, took her, and

ran as fast as it could, but the old lady-in-waiting pulled on a pair of rubber boots and ran after it just as fast. When she saw that they disappeared inside a big house, she drew a big cross on the door with a piece of chalk. Then she went home and went to bed, and the dog came back with the princess. But when it saw that a cross had been made on the door, it also took a piece of chalk and made crosses on all the doors in the city, and that was wise, for now, of course, the lady-in-waiting couldn't find the right door when there was a cross on every single one.

Early the next morning the king and the queen, the old lady-in-waiting, and all the officers came to see where the Princess had been.

"There it is!" said the king when he saw the first door with a cross on it.

"No, *there* it is, my dear husband," said the queen, who saw the second door with a cross on it.

"But there's one and there's one!" they all said. No matter where they looked, there was a cross on the door. So then they could see that there was no use searching one bit.

But the queen was a very wise woman, who knew about more than just riding in the royal coach. She took her big golden scissors, cut up a large piece of silk, and sewed a lovely little bag. This she filled with small, fine grains of buckwheat, tied it to the princess' back, and when that was done, clipped a tiny hole in the bag so the grain could dribble out all along the way, wherever the princess went.

That night, the dog came again, took the princess on his back, and carried her straight to the soldier, who had fallen in love with her and gladly would have been a prince so he could make her his wife.

The dog didn't notice at all how the grains dribbled out all the way from the castle to the soldier's window, where it ran up the wall with the princess. In the morning the king and queen saw where their daughter had been, all right, and so they took the soldier and put him in jail. There he sat! Ugh! How dark and dreary it was! And then they said to him, "Tomorrow you're to be hanged!" That wasn't a nice thing to hear, and he had forgotten his tinderbox back at the inn. In the morning, through the bars in the tiny window, he could see the people hurrying out of the city to see him hanged. He heard drums and saw the soldiers marching. Everybody was rushing out, including a shoemaker's apprentice in his leather apron and slippers, who was in such a hurry that one of his slippers flew off and landed nearby the wall where the soldier sat peering out through the iron bars.

"Hey there, shoemaker's boy, you needn't be in such a hurry," said the soldier. "Nothing will happen until I get there. But if you'll run to my lodgings and fetch my tinderbox, you'll get four shillings. But then you must really run." The shoemaker's boy was only too glad to have four shillings, and he scurried away after the tinderbox and gave it to the soldier, and—yes, now we shall hear:

Outside the city a big gallows had been built; around it stood the soldiers and many hundreds of thousands of people. The king and the queen sat on a lovely throne right above the judge and the whole court. The soldier was already on the ladder, but as they were going to put the noose around his neck he said—oh, yes, a sinner is always granted one little innocent wish before he receives his punishment—he would so like to smoke a pipeful of tobacco. After all, it would be the last pipe he'd have in this world.

The king couldn't really say no to that, and so the soldier took out his tinderbox and struck a light: One! Two! Three! And there stood all the dogs: the first with eyes as big as teacups, the second with eyes as big as mill wheels, and the third with eyes each as big as the Round Tower.

"Help me now, so I won't be hanged!" said the soldier. And then the dogs flew right at the judge and the whole court, took one by the legs and one by the nose, and tossed them many miles up in the air so they fell down and broke into pieces.

"I won't!" said the king, but the biggest dog took both him and the queen and threw them after all the others. Then the soldiers were frightened, and all the people shouted: "Little soldier, you shall be our king and have the lovely princess!"

Then they put the soldier in the king's coach, and all three dogs danced in front and shouted, "Hurrah!" And all the boys whistled through their fingers, and the soldiers presented arms. The princess came out of the copper castle, and was made queen, and that she liked very well. The wedding party lasted eight days, and the dogs sat at the table and made eyes at everybody.

Little Claus
and Big Claus

❖ ❖ ❖

IN one town there were two men who had the very same name: they were both called Claus, but one of them owned four horses and the other only a single horse: and so, in order to tell them apart, the one who had four horses was called Big Claus, and the one who had only one horse, Little Claus. Now we shall hear how the two got along, for this is a true story!

All week long Little Claus had to plow for Big Claus and lend him his one horse. Then Big Claus helped him in return with all four of his horses, but only once a week, and that was on Sunday. Huzzah! How Little Claus cracked his whip over all five horses; after all, they were as good as his on that one day. The sun was shining so delightfully, and all the bells in the church tower were ringing for church. People were all dressed up and walked by with their hymn books under their arms, on their way to hear the parson preach. And they looked at Little Claus, who was plowing with five horses, and he was so contented that he cracked his whip again and shouted: "Gee up, all my horses!"

"You mustn't say that," said Big Claus. "After all, only one of the horses is yours!"

But when somebody went by again on the way to church, Little Claus forgot that he mustn't say it, and so he shouted: "Gee up, all my horses!"

16

"Well, now, I'm telling you to stop that!" said Big Claus. "If you say it just one more time, I'll strike your horse on the forehead so he'll be lying dead on the spot, and that'll be the end of him!"

"I certainly won't say it anymore," said Little Claus. But when people went by, nodding and saying, "Good day," he became so contented, thinking it looked so grand for him to have five horses to plow his field with, that he cracked his whip and shouted: "Gee up, all my horses!"

"I'll gee up your horse!" said Big Claus, and he took the tethering mallet and gave Little Claus's horse such a blow on the forehead that it fell down quite dead.

"Oh, woe! Now I haven't got any horse at all!" said Little Claus, and started to cry. Later he flayed the horse, took the hide, and let it dry well in the wind; and then, putting it in a bag that he carried on his back, he went to town to sell his horsehide.

He had such a long way to go, through a deep, dark forest, and now a terrible storm blew up; he completely lost his way, and before he had got back on the right path again it was evening and much too far both from town and from home to arrive at either before nightfall.

Close to the road stood a big farmhouse. The outside shutters were closed, but the light still shone out at the top. "I hope I'll be allowed to spend the night here," thought Little Claus, and went over to knock at the door.

The farmer's wife opened it, but when she heard what he wanted, she told him to be on his way. Her husband wasn't home, and she didn't take in strangers.

"Well, I'll have to sleep outside, then," said Little Claus, and the farmer's wife shut the door on him.

Nearby stood a big haystack, and between that and the house a little shed had been put up, with a flat thatched roof.

"I can lie up there," said Little Claus when he saw the roof. "After all, it's a lovely bed. I daresay the stork won't fly down and bite me in the legs!" For a real live stork was standing on the roof, where it had its nest.

Now Little Claus crawled onto the shed, where he lay twisting and turning in order to make himself comfortable. The wooden shutters in front of the windows didn't go all the way up to the top, and so he could see right into the parlor.

A big table had been laid with wine and a roast and such a delicious fish. The farmer's wife and the parish clerk were sitting at the table, and no one else at all was there. And she poured him a drink, and he prodded the fish, for that was something he liked.

"If only I could have some too!" said Little Claus, and stretched his head all the way over to the window. Heavens! What a lovely cake he could see standing there. That was quite a feast.

Now he heard someone riding along the road toward the house—it was the woman's husband who was coming.

He was such a good man, but he had the singular affliction of not being able to bear the sight of a parish clerk! If he laid eyes on a parish clerk, he would fly into a terrible rage. This was also the reason why the parish clerk had dropped in to pay his respects to the wife when he knew that the husband wasn't at home, and the good wife set before him the most delicious food she had. Now, when they heard the husband coming, they were so terrified that the wife bade the parish clerk crawl down inside a big empty chest that was standing over in the corner. This he did, for he knew, of course, that the poor husband couldn't bear the sight of a parish clerk! The wife quickly hid all the delicious food and wine in her oven, because if the husband had seen it, he certainly would have asked what it was all about.

"Oh, woe!" sighed Little Claus on the shed when he saw all the food disappear.

"Is there someone up there?" asked the farmer, and

peered up at Little Claus. "Why are you lying there? Come in the house with me instead!"

Then Little Claus told how he had lost his way, and he asked if he could spend the night there.

"Why, of course!" said the farmer. "But first we're going to have a bite to eat!"

The wife welcomed them both very warmly, laid a long table, and gave them a big bowl of porridge. The farmer was hungry and ate with a good appetite, but Little Claus couldn't stop thinking about the lovely roast and fish and cake that he knew were standing in the oven.

Under the table at his feet he had put his bag with the horsehide in it—for we know that he had brought it from home to sell in town. He wouldn't enjoy the porridge at all, and so he trod on his bag, and the dry hide inside gave out quite a loud creak.

"Hush!" said Little Claus to his bag, but trod on it again, making it creak louder than before.

"Why, what do you have in your bag?" asked the farmer.

"Oh, it's a sorcerer!" said Little Claus. "He says we shouldn't eat porridge; he's conjured the whole oven full of a roast and fish and cake."

"What's that?" said the farmer, and he quickly opened the oven and saw all the delicious food the wife had hidden, but which he now believed had been conjured up for them by the sorcerer in the bag. The wife dared not say a thing but put the food on the table at once, and then they both ate the fish and the roast and the cake. Without delay Little Claus trod on his bag again so the hide creaked.

"What does he say now?" asked the farmer.

"He says," said Little Claus, "that he has also conjured up three bottles of wine for us, and they're standing in the oven too!" Now the wife had to take out the wine she had hidden, and the farmer drank and became quite merry; he'd be only too willing to own a sorcerer like the one Little Claus had in his bag.

"Can he conjure up the devil too?" asked the farmer. "I'd really like to see him, for now I feel so merry!"

"Yes," said Little Claus. "My sorcerer can do anything I ask him to. Can't you?" he asked, and trod on the bag so it creaked. "Can you hear? He says, 'Of course!' But the devil looks so terrible that it's better not to look at him!"

"Oh, I'm not afraid at all. How do you think he'll look?"

"Well, he'll appear in the shape of a parish clerk!"

"Whew!" said the farmer. "That's awful! You've got to know that I can't bear the sight of parish clerks! But no matter! After all, I know it's the devil, so I guess I'll just have to put up with it. I've got courage now! But he mustn't come too close!"

"Now I'm going to ask my sorcerer," said Little Claus, treading on the bag and holding his ear to it.

"What does he say?"

"He says that you can go over and open the chest standing in the corner, and then you'll see the devil moping inside. But you've got to hold onto the lid so he doesn't get out!"

"Will you help me to hold it?" said the farmer, and went over to the chest where the wife had hidden the real parish clerk, who sat there scared to death.

The farmer lifted the lid a crack and peered in under it. "Yeow!" he shrieked, jumping back. "Yes, now I saw him; he looked just like our parish clerk! My, that was dreadful!"

They had to have a drink after this, and then they kept on drinking far into the night.

"You've got to sell that sorcerer to me!" said the farmer. "Ask whatever you like! Yes, I'll give you a whole bushel of money right away."

"No, I can't do that," said Little Claus. "Think of how much use that sorcerer is to me."

"Oh, I'd so like to have it," said the farmer, and kept on begging.

"Well," said Little Claus at last, "since you've been so kind as to put me up for the night, it's all right. You shall have the sorcerer for a bushel of money, but it has to be heaping full!"

"You shall have it!" said the farmer. "But you'll have to take that chest over there with you. I won't have it in the house another hour—you never can tell if he's still sitting in there."

Little Claus gave the farmer his bag with the dry hide inside, and was given a whole bushel of money—and heaping full, at that. And the farmer even gave him a big wheelbarrow on which to carry the money and the chest.

"Farewell!" said Little Claus, and then off he went with his money and the big chest with the parish clerk still sitting inside.

On the other side of the forest there was a big, deep river; it flowed so fast that one could hardly swim against the current. A large new bridge had been built across it. Little Claus stopped right in the middle of it and said quite loudly, so the parish clerk inside the chest could hear it: "Well, whatever am I going to do with that silly chest? It's as heavy as if it were full of stones. I'm getting quite tired of driving it any farther, so I'm going to throw it out in the river! If it sails home to me, then it's all very well; and if it doesn't, then it doesn't matter."

And taking hold of the chest with one hand, he lifted it up as if he were going to throw it in the water.

"No, stop! Don't do that!" shouted the parish clerk inside the chest. "Just let me come out!"

"Yeow!" said Little Claus, pretending to be afraid. "He's still sitting in there! I've got to throw it in the river right away so he can drown!"

"Oh, no! Oh, no!" shouted the parish clerk. "I'll give you a whole bushel of money if you don't!"

"Well, that's another story!" said Little Claus, and opened the chest. The parish clerk crawled out at once, shoved the empty chest into the water, and then went to his home, where Little Claus received a whole bushel of money—he had already gotten one from the farmer—and now his wheelbarrow was full of money.

"See, I got quite a good price for that horse," he said to himself when he came home to his cottage; then he emptied his bag in the middle of the floor and put all the money into a big pile. "That will annoy Big Claus when he finds out how rich I've become with my one horse. But I'm not going to tell him outright!"

Now he sent a boy over to Big Claus to borrow a bushel measure.

"I wonder what he wants that for!" thought Big Claus, and he smeared the bottom with tar so that a little of what was measured would stick fast. And so it did, too, for when he got the measure back, three new silver florins were stuck to it.

"What's this?" said Big Claus, and ran to Little Claus at once. "Where did you get all that money from?"

"Oh, that's for my horsehide. I sold it yesterday evening."

"I'll say you were well paid!" said Big Claus. He ran home, took an ax, struck all four of his horses on the forehead, flayed them, and drove to town with their hides.

"Hides! Hides! Who'll buy my hides?" he shouted through the streets.

All the shoemakers and tanners came running and asked how much he wanted for them.

"A bushel of money for each one!" said Big Claus.

"Are you mad!" they all said. "Do you think we have tons of money?"

"Hides! Hides! Who'll buy my hides?" he shouted again, but to everyone who asked what the hides cost he replied, "A bushel of money!"

"He's trying to make fun of us!" they all said, and then the shoemakers took their straps and the tanners their leather aprons and started to give Big Claus a thrashing.

"Hides! Hides!" they mimicked him. "Yes, we'll give you a hiding until you look like a flayed pig! Out of town with him!" they shouted, and Big Claus had to get moving as fast as he could. He'd never had such a thrashing before.

"Aha!" he said when he came back home. "I'll get even with Little Claus for this! I'm going to kill him!"

But meanwhile Little Claus's old grandmother had died at his home. To be sure, she had been quite shrewish and nasty to him, but he was still very sad, and taking the old woman, he laid her in his warm bed to see if he could bring her back to life again. She was to lie there all night while he was going to sit over in the corner and sleep on a chair, as he had done before.

Now as he was sitting there during the night the door opened, and Big Claus came in with his ax. He knew very well where Little Claus had his bed, and walking straight over to it, he struck the old grandmother on the forehead, thinking it was Little Claus.

"There now!" he said. "You're not going to fool me again!" And then he went back home again.

"Why, that nasty, wicked man!" said Little Claus. "He wanted to kill me! Still, it was a good thing old Granny was already dead, or else he'd have done away with her!"

Now he dressed old Granny in her Sunday best, borrowed a horse from his neighbor, hitched it to the wagon, and sat the old woman up in the back seat so she couldn't fall out when he was driving, and then they rolled away through the forest. When the sun came up they were outside a big inn. Here Little Claus stopped and went in to get a bite to eat.

The innkeeper had so very very much money; he was also a very good man but as hot-tempered as if he were full of pepper and snuff inside.

"Good morning," he said to Little Claus. "You're up early today in your Sunday best."

"Yes," said Little Claus. "I'm on my way to town with my old grandmother. She's sitting out there in the wagon. I can't get her to come inside. Won't you take a glass of mead out to her? But you'll have to speak quite loudly, as she can't hear very well."

"Indeed I shall," said the innkeeper, and poured out a big glass of mead, which he took out to the dead grandmother, who had been set up in the wagon.

"Here's a glass of mead from your grandson!" said the innkeeper, but the dead woman sat quite still and didn't say a word.

"Don't you hear!" shouted the innkeeper as loud as he could. "HERE'S A GLASS OF MEAD FROM YOUR GRANDSON!"

He shouted the same thing again, and once more after that, but when she didn't budge an inch he flew into a rage and threw the glass right in her face, so the mead ran down over her nose, and she fell over backward in the wagon, for she had only been propped up and not tied fast.

"GOOD LORD!" shouted Little Claus, running out of the door and grabbing the innkeeper by the collar. "You've killed my grandmother! Just look, there's a big hole in her forehead!"

"Oh, it was an accident!" cried the innkeeper, wringing his hands. "It's all because of my hot temper! Dear Little Claus, I'll give you a whole bushel of money if only you'll keep quiet about it, for otherwise they'll chop off my head, and that's so disgusting!"

So Little Claus got a whole bushel of money, and the innkeeper buried the grandmother as if she had been his own.

When Little Claus came back home with all the money, he sent his boy right over to Big Claus to ask if he could borrow a bushel measure.

"What's that?" said Big Claus. "Didn't I kill him? I'll have to go see for myself." And then he took the bushel measure to Little Claus.

"Why, where did you get all this money from?" he asked, his eyes opening wide at the sight of all this additional money that had come in.

"It was my grandmother and not me that you killed!" said Little Claus. "And now I've sold her for a bushel of money."

"You were really well paid!" said Big Claus, and hurrying home, he took an ax and killed his old grandmother straightaway; and putting her in the wagon, he drove off to town, where the apothecary lived, and asked if he wanted to buy a dead body.

"Whose is it, and where did you get it from?" asked the apothecary.

"It's my grandmother," said Big Claus. "I killed her for a bushel of money!"

"Good Lord!" said the apothecary. "You're talking nonsense! But you mustn't say a thing like that, or you can lose your head!" And then he told him what a really wicked deed he had done, and what a terrible man he was, and that he ought to be punished. Big Claus became so terrified at this that he ran right out of the apothecary's shop, right out to the wagon, whipped the horses, and rushed home. But the apothecary and everybody else thought he was mad, and so they let him drive wherever he liked.

"I'll get even with you for that!" said Big Claus when he was out on the highway. "Yes, I'll get even with you for that, Little Claus!" And as soon as he came home he took the biggest sack he could find, went to Little Claus, and said, "Now you've fooled me again! First I killed my horses and then my old grandmother! It's all your fault, but you're never going to fool me again!" And then he grabbed Little Claus by the waist, put him in his sack, threw him on his back, and shouted, "Now I'm going to drown you!"

He had a long way to go before he came to the river, and Little Claus wasn't such a light burden. The road ran by the church; the organ was playing and people were singing so beautifully inside. Then Big Claus placed his sack, with Little Claus in it, close to the church door, and thought it would be a good idea to go in and listen to a hymn first before he went on. After all, Little Claus couldn't get out and everybody else was inside the church, so he went in.

"Oh, woe! Oh, woe!" sighed Little Claus inside the sack. He turned this way and that, but he couldn't open the sack. At that very moment an old cattle drover, with chalk-white hair and a big staff in his hand, came along. He was driving a whole herd of cows and bulls ahead of him; they ran against the sack in which Little Claus was sitting, and it turned over.

"Oh, woe!" said Little Claus. "I'm so young, and I'm going to heaven already!"

"And I, poor soul," said the drover, "am so old and can't get there yet!"

"Open the sack!" shouted Little Claus. "Crawl in, in my place, and you'll get to heaven right away!"

"Yes, I'd be glad to!" said the drover, and untied the sack for Little Claus, who jumped out at once.

"Will you mind the cattle?" said the old man, and crawled down in the sack, which Little Claus tied up and then went on his way with all the cows and bulls.

A little later Big Claus came out of the church and put the sack on his back. Of course he thought it had grown lighter, for the old drover didn't weigh half as much as Little Claus did. "How light he's grown! Yes, I daresay it's because I've listened to a hymn!" Then he went over to the river, which was deep and wide, threw the sack with the old cattle drover in it, into the water, and shouted after him—for of course he thought it was Little Claus: "That's that! You're not going to trick me anymore!"

Then he started for home, but when he came to the crossroads he met Little Claus driving along all his cattle.

"What's that?" said Big Claus. "Didn't I drown you?"

"Yes indeed!" said Little Claus. "You threw me in the river not quite half an hour ago!"

"But where did you get all these fine cattle from?" asked Big Claus.

"They're sea cattle!" said Little Claus. "I'll tell you the whole story, and thanks for drowning me too! Now I'm on top! I'm really rich, I'll have you know! I was so frightened when I was lying in the sack, and the wind whistled about my ears when you threw me down from the bridge into that cold water. I sank straight to the bottom, but I didn't hurt myself, for down there grows the finest soft grass. There I fell, and at once the bag was opened, and the loveliest maiden, in chalk-white clothes and with a green garland on her wet hair, took me by the hand and said, 'Is that you, Little Claus? First of all, here's some cattle! A mile up the road is another herd, which I'm going to give you.' Then I saw that the river was a great highway for the sea people. On the bottom they walked and drove right up from the sea and all the way to land, where the river ends. The flowers there were so lovely and the grass so fresh, and the fish swimming in the water darted past my ears just the way the birds do up here in the air. What handsome people they were, and what a lot of cattle were walking by the fences and in the ditches!"

"But why did you come back up here so fast?" asked Big Claus. "I wouldn't have done that if it was so fine down there!"

"Oh, yes!" said Little Claus. "That was the shrewdest thing I could have done! You'll understand, of course, when I tell you: The mermaid said that about a mile up the road—and by the road she meant the river, of course, because she can't go anywhere else—another herd of cattle is waiting for me. But I know how the river twists and turns, first this way and then that. It's a long detour. Well, you can make it shorter by coming up here on land and driving straight across to the river again. Then I save almost half a mile and come to my sea cattle all the faster."

"Oh, you're a lucky man!" said Big Claus. "Do you think I would get some sea cattle if I went down to the bottom of the sea?"

"Oh, yes, I should think you would!" said Little Claus. "But I can't carry you to the river in the sack. You're too heavy for me. But if you'll walk over there yourself and then crawl into the sack, I'll throw you in with the greatest of pleasure!"

"Thank's a lot!" said Big Claus. "But if I don't get any sea cattle when I get down there, I'll give you a beating, I want you to know!"

"Oh, no! Don't be so mean!" And then they went to the

river. The cattle were thirsty, and when they saw the water they ran as fast as they could so as to have a drink.

"See how they hurry!" said Little Claus. "They're longing to go down to the bottom again!"

"Well, just help me first!" said Big Claus. "Or else you'll get a beating!" And then he crawled into the big sack, which had been lying across the back of one of the bulls. "Put a stone in it, or else I'm afraid I won't sink!" said Big Claus.

"You'll sink, all right!" said Little Claus, but nonetheless he put a big stone in the sack, tied it up tight, and then gave it a push. Plop! There was Big Claus in the water, and he sank to the bottom without delay.

"I'm afraid he won't find the cattle!" said Little Claus, and then he drove home what he had.

The Princess on the Pea

❖ ❖ ❖

THERE was once a prince. He wanted a princess, but it had to be a true princess! So he journeyed all around the world to find one, but no matter where he went, something was wrong. There were plenty of princesses, but whether or not they were true princesses he couldn't find out. There was always something that wasn't quite right. So he came home again and was very sad, for he wanted a true princess so very much.

One evening there was a terrible storm. The lightning flashed, the thunder boomed, and the rain poured down! It was really frightful! Then somebody knocked at the city gate, and the old king went out to open it.

A princess was standing outside, but heavens, how she looked from the rain and the bad weather! Water poured off her hair and clothes and ran in at the toe of her shoe and out at the heel, but she said she was a true princess!

"Well, we'll soon find that out!" thought the old queen, but she didn't say anything. She went into the bedroom, took off all the bedding, and put a pea on the bottom of the bed. Then she took twenty mattresses and laid them on top of the pea and then put twenty eiderdown quilts on top of the mattresses. There the princess was to sleep that night.

In the morning they asked her how she had slept.

"Oh, just miserably!" said the princess. "I've hardly closed my eyes all night! Heaven knows what was in my bed! I've been lying on something so hard that I'm black and blue all over! It's simply dreadful!"

Then they could tell that this was a true princess, be-cause through the twenty mattresses and the twenty eiderdown quilts she had felt the pea. Only a true princess could have such delicate skin.

So the prince took her for his wife, for now he knew that he had a true princess, and the pea was put into the museum, where it can still be seen, if no one has taken it! See, this was a true story!

The Fable Alludes to You

❖   ❖   ❖

THE Sages of Antiquity kindly invented a way of telling people the truth without being rude to their faces: they held before them a singular mirror in which all kinds of animals and strange things came into view, and produced a spectacle as entertaining as it was edifying. They called it "A Fable," and whatever foolish or intelligent thing the animals performed there, the human beings had but to apply it to themselves and thereby think: the fable alludes to you. Let us take an example.

There were two high mountains, and on the very top of each mountain stood a castle. Down in the valley a dog was running. It sniffed along the ground as if, to stay its hunger, it were searching for mice or partridges. Suddenly, from one of the castles the trumpet sounded announcing that dinner was ready. At once the dog started running up the mountain to get a little, too. But just as it had come halfway, the trumpeter stopped blowing, and a trumpet from the other castle began. Then the dog thought, "They will have finished eating here before I come, but over there they will have just begun." And so down it went and ran up the other mountain. But now the trumpet at the first castle started blowing again, whereas the other had stopped. Once more the dog ran down one mountain and up the other, and he kept on in this way

until both trumpets were at last silent and the meal would
be at an end no matter to which place the dog came.

Guess now what the Sages of Antiquity wish to imply by
this fable and which of us it alludes to, who wears himself
out in this fashion without winning either here or there.

The Talisman

A PRINCE and a princess were still on their honeymoon. They felt so extremely happy. Only one thought disturbed them; it was this: will we always be as happy as we are now? And so they wanted to own a talisman that would protect them against every disappointment in marriage.

Now, they had often heard of a man who lived in the forest, and who was held in high esteem by everyone for his wisdom. He knew how to give the best advice for every hardship and misery. The prince and the princess went to him and told him what was troubling them.

When the wise man had heard it, he replied, "Journey through all the lands in the world, and when you meet a truly contented married couple, ask them for a little piece of the linen they wear next to their skin. When you get it, always carry it with you. That is an effective remedy."

The prince and the princess rode off, and soon they heard of a knight who, with his wife, was said to live the happiest of lives. They came up to the castle and asked them, themselves, whether in their marriage they were as extremely happy as rumor would have it.

"Of course!" was the reply. "Except for one thing: we have no children!"

Here, then, the talisman was not to be found, and the

prince and the princess had to continue on their journey to seek out the most perfectly contented married couple.

Next they came to a city in which, they heard, an honest burgher lived with his wife in the greatest harmony and contentment. They went to him, too, and asked whether he really were as happy in his marriage as people said.

"Yes, indeed I am!" replied the man. "My wife and I live the best of lives together. If only we didn't have so many children. They cause us so much sorrow and anxiety!"

The talisman was not to be found with him, either, and the prince and the princess journeyed on through the land and inquired everywhere after contented married couples.

But not one came forward.

One day, as they were riding along fields and meadows, they noticed a shepherd who was playing quite merrily on a shawm. At the same time they saw a woman come over to him with a child on her arm and leading a little boy by the hand. As soon as the shepherd saw her, he went to

meet her. He greeted her and took the child, which he
kissed and caressed. The shepherd's dog came over to the
boy, licked his little hand, and barked and jumped up and
down with joy. In the meantime the wife made ready the
pot that she had brought with her and said, "Papa, come
now and eat."

The man sat down and helped himself to the dishes. But
the first bite went to the little child and he divided the
second between the boy and the dog. All this the prince
and the princess saw and heard. Now they went closer,
talked with them, and said, "Are you truly what might be
called a happy and contented married couple?"

"Yes, indeed we are!" replied the man. "Praise be to
God! No prince or princess could be happier than we are."

"Then listen," said the prince. "Do us a favor that you
will not come to regret. Give us a tiny piece of the linen
that you wear next to your skin."

At this request the shepherd and his wife looked strangely
at each other. At last he said, "Heaven knows we would
gladly give it to you, and not just a tiny piece but the
whole shirt and petticoat if only we had them. But we
don't own a thread!"

So the prince and the princess continued on their journey without any success. At last they grew tired of this
long, fruitless wandering, and so they headed for home.
When they now came to the wise man's hut, they scolded
him for having given them such poor advice. He listened
to the whole story of their journey.

Then the wise man smiled and said, "Has your journey
really been so fruitless? Didn't you come home rich in
experience?"

"Yes," said the prince. "I have learned that contentment is a rare blessing on this earth."

"And I have learned," said the princess, "that in order
to be content, you need nothing more than just that—to
be content."

Then the prince gave the princess his hand. They gazed at each other with an expression of the deepest love. And the wise man gave them his blessing and said, "In your hearts you have found the true talisman. Guard it carefully, and never will the evil spirit of discontent gain power over you!"

The Little Mermaid

❖ ❖ ❖

FAR out to sea the water is as blue as the petals on the loveliest cornflower and as clear as the purest glass. But it is very deep, deeper than any anchor rope can reach. Many church steeples would have to be placed one on top of the other to reach from the bottom up to the surface of the water. Down there live the mermen.

Now, it certainly shouldn't be thought that the bottom is only bare and sandy. No, down there grow the strangest trees and plants, which have such flexible stalks and leaves that the slightest movement of the water sets them in motion as if they were alive. All the fish, big and small, slip in and out among the branches just the way the birds do up here in the air. At the very deepest spot lies the castle of the king of the sea. The walls are of coral, and the long tapering windows are of the clearest amber. But the roof is of mussel shells, which open and close with the flow of the water. The effect is lovely, for in each one there is a beautiful pearl, any of which would be highly prized in a queen's crown.

For many years the king of the sea had been a widower, and his old mother kept house for him. She was a wise woman and proud of her royal birth, and so she wore twelve oysters on her tail; the others of noble birth had to content themselves with only six. Otherwise she deserved much praise, especially because she was so fond of the little princesses, her grandchildren. They were six lovely children, but the youngest was the fairest of them all. Her skin was as clear and opalescent as a rose petal. Her eyes were as blue as the deepest sea. But like all the others, she had no feet. Her body ended in a fishtail.

All day long they could play down in the castle in the great halls where living flowers grew out of the walls. The big amber windows were opened, and then the fish swam into them just as on land the swallows fly in when we open our windows. But the fish swam right over to the little princesses, ate out of their hands, and allowed themselves to be petted.

Outside the castle was a large garden with trees as red as fire and as blue as night. The fruit shone like gold, and the flowers looked like burning flames, for their stalks and leaves were always in motion. The ground itself was the finest sand, but blue like the flame of brimstone. A strange blue sheen lay over everything down there. It was more like standing high up in the air and seeing only sky above and below than like being at the bottom of the sea. In a dead calm the sun could be glimpsed. It looked like a purple flower from whose chalice the light streamed out.

Each of the little princesses had her own tiny plot in the garden, where she could dig and plant just as she wished. One made her flower bed in the shape of a whale. Another preferred hers to resemble a little mermaid. But the youngest made hers quite round like the sun and had only flowers that shone red the way it did. She was a strange child, quiet and pensive, and while the other sisters decorated their gardens with the strangest things they had found from wrecked ships, the only thing she wanted, besides the rosy-red flowers that resembled the sun high above, was a beautiful marble statue. It was a handsome boy carved out of clear white stone, and in the shipwreck it had come down to the bottom of the sea. By the pedestal she had planted a rose-colored weeping willow. It grew magnificently, and its fresh branches hung out over the statue and down toward the blue, sandy bottom, where its shadow appeared violet and moved just like the branches. It looked as if the top and roots played at kissing each other.

Nothing pleased her more than to hear about the world of mortals up above. The old grandmother had to tell everything she knew about ships and cities, mortals and animals. To her it seemed especially wonderful and lovely that on the earth the flowers gave off a fragrance, since they didn't at the bottom of the sea, and that the forests were green and those fish that were seen among the branches there could sing so loud and sweet that it was a pleasure. What the grandmother called fish were the little birds, for otherwise the princesses wouldn't have understood her, as they had never seen a bird.

"When you reach the age of fifteen," said the grandmother, "you shall be permitted to go to the surface of the water, sit in the moonlight on the rocks, and look at the great ships sailing by. You will see forests and cities too."

The next year the first sister would be fifteen, but the others—yes, each one was a year younger than the other; so the youngest still had five years left before she might come up from the bottom of the sea and find out how it looked in our world. But each one promised to tell the others what she had seen on that first day and what she had found to be the most wonderful thing, for their grandmother hadn't told them enough—there was so much they had to find out.

No one was as full of longing as the youngest, the one who had to wait the longest and who was so quiet and pensive. Many a night she stood by the open window and looked up through the dark blue water where the fish flipped their fins and tails. She could see the moon and stars. To be sure, they shone quite pale, but through the water they looked much bigger than they do to our eyes. If it seemed as though a black shadow glided slowly under them, then she knew it was either a whale that swam over her or else it was a ship with many mortals on board. It certainly never occurred to them that a lovely little mermaid was standing down below stretching her white hands up toward the keel.

Now the eldest princess was fifteen and was permitted to go up to the surface of the water.

When she came back, she had hundreds of things to tell about. But the most wonderful thing of all, she said, was to lie in the moonlight on a sandbank in the calm sea and to look at the big city close to the shore, where the lights twinkled like hundreds of stars, and to listen to the music and the noise and commotion of carriages and mortals, to see the many church steeples and spires, and to hear the chimes ring. And just because the youngest sister couldn't go up there, she longed for all this the most.

Oh, how the little mermaid listened. And later in the evening, when she was standing by the open window and looking up through the dark blue water, she thought of the great city with all the noise and commotion, and then it seemed to her that she could hear the church bells ringing down to her.

The next year the second sister was allowed to rise up through the water and swim wherever she liked. She came up just as the sun was setting, and she found this sight the loveliest. The whole sky looked like gold, she said—and the clouds. Well, she couldn't describe their beauty enough. Crimson and violet, they had sailed over her. But even faster than the clouds, like a long white veil, a flock of wild swans had flown over the water into the sun. She swam toward it, but it sank, and the rosy glow went out on the sea and on the clouds.

The next year the third sister came up. She was the boldest of them all, and so she swam up a broad river that emptied into the sea. She saw lovely green hills covered with grapevines. Castles and farms peeped out among great forests. She heard how all the birds sang, and the sun shone so hot that she had to dive under the water to cool her burning face. In a little bay she came upon a whole flock of little children. Quite naked, they ran and splashed in the water. She wanted to play with them, but they ran away terrified. And then a little black animal came; it was a dog, but she had never seen a dog before. It barked at her so furiously that she grew frightened and made for the open sea. But never could she forget the great forests, the green hills, and the lovely children who could swim in the water despite the fact that they had no fishtails.

The fourth sister was not so bold. She stayed out in the middle of the rolling sea and said that this was the loveliest of all. She could see for many miles all around her, and the sky was just like a big glass bell. She had seen ships, but far away. They looked like sea gulls. The funny dolphins had turned somersaults, and the big whales had spouted water through their nostrils so it had looked like hundreds of fountains all around.

Now it was the turn of the fifth sister. Her birthday was in winter, so she saw what the others hadn't seen. The sea looked quite green, and huge icebergs were swimming all around. Each one looked like a pearl, she said, although they were certainly much bigger than the church steeples built by mortals. They appeared in the strangest shapes and sparkled like diamonds. She had sat on one of the biggest, and all the ships sailed, terrified, around where she sat with her long hair flying in the breeze. But in the evening the sky was covered with clouds. The lightning flashed and the thunder boomed while the black sea lifted the huge icebergs up high, where they glittered in the bright flashes of light. On all the ships they took in the sails, and they were anxious and afraid. But she sat calmly on her floating iceberg and watched the blue streaks of lightning zigzag into the sea.

Each time one of the sisters came to the surface of the water for the first time she was always enchanted by the new and wonderful things she had seen. But now that, as grown girls, they were permitted to go up there whenever they liked, it no longer mattered to them. They longed again for home. And after a month they said it was most beautiful down there where they lived and that home was the best of all.

Many an evening the five sisters rose up arm in arm to the surface of the water. They had beautiful voices, sweeter than those of any mortals, and whenever a storm was nigh and they thought a ship might be wrecked, they swam ahead of the ship and sang so sweetly about how beautiful it was at the bottom of the sea and bade the sailors not to be afraid of coming down there. But the sailors couldn't understand the words. They thought it was the storm. Nor were they able to see the wonders down there either, for when the ship sank, the mortals drowned and came only as corpses to the castle of the king of the sea.

Now, in the evening, when the sisters rose up arm in arm through the sea, the little sister was left behind quite alone, looking after them and as if she were going to cry. But a mermaid has no tears, and so she suffers even more.

"Oh, if only I were fifteen," she said. "I know that I will truly come to love that world and the mortals who build and dwell up there."

At last she too was fifteen.

"See, now it is your turn!" said her grandmother, the old dowager queen. "Come now, let me adorn you just like your other sisters." And she put a wreath of white lilies on her hair. But each flower petal was half a pearl. And the old queen had eight oysters squeeze themselves tightly to the princess' tail to who her high rank.

"It hurts so much!" said the little mermaid.

"Yes, you must suffer a bit to look pretty!" said the old queen.

Oh, how happy she would have been to shake off all this magnificence, to take off the heavy wreath. Her red flowers in her garden were more becoming to her, but she dared not do otherwise now. "Farewell," she said and rose as easily and as lightly as a bubble up through the water.

The sun had just gone down as she raised her head out of the water, but all the clouds still shone like roses and gold, and in the middle of the pink sky the evening star shone clear and lovely. The air was mild and fresh, and the sea was as smooth as glass. There lay a big ship with three masts. Only a single sail was up, for not a breeze was blowing, and around in the ropes and masts sailors were sitting. There was music and song, and as the evening grew darker hundreds of many-colored lanterns were lit. It looked as if the flags of all nations were waving in the air. The little mermaid swam right over to the cabin window, and every time the water lifted her high in the air she could see in through the glass panes to where many finely dressed mortals were standing. But the handsomest by far was the young prince with the big dark eyes, who was certainly not more than sixteen. It was his birthday, and this was why all the festivities were taking place. The sailors danced on deck, and when the young prince came out, more than a hundred rockets rose into the air. They shone as bright as day, so the little mermaid became quite frightened and ducked down under the water. But she soon stuck her head out again, and then it was as if all the stars in the sky were falling down to her. Never before had she seen such fireworks. Huge suns whirled around, magnificent flaming fish swung in the blue air, and everything was reflected in the clear, calm sea. The ship itself was so lit up that every little rope was visible, not to mention mortals. Oh, how handsome the young prince was, and he shook everybody by the hand and laughed and smiled while the wonderful night was filled with music.

It grew late, but the little mermaid couldn't tear her eyes away from the ship or the handsome prince. The many-colored lanterns were put out. The rockets no longer climbed into the air, nor were any more salutes fired from the cannons, either. But deep down in the sea it rumbled and grumbled. All the while she sat bobbing up and down on the water so she could see into the cabin. But now the ship went faster, and one sail after the other spread out. Now the waves were rougher, great clouds rolled up, and in the distance there was lightning. Oh, there was going to be a terrible storm, so the sailors took in the sails. The ship rocked at top speed over the raging sea. The water rose like huge black mountains that wanted to pour over the mast, but the ship dived down like a swan among the high billows and let itself be lifted high again on the towering water. The little mermaid thought this speed was pleasant, but the sailors didn't think so. The ship creaked and cracked and the thick planks buckled under the heavy blows. Waves poured in over the ship, the mast snapped in the middle just like a reed, and the ship rolled over on its side while the water poured into the hold. Now the little mermaid saw they were in danger. She herself had to beware of planks and bits of wreckage floating on the water. For a moment it was so pitch black that she could not see a thing, but when the lightning flashed, it was again so bright that she could make out everyone on the ship. They were all floundering and struggling for their lives. She looked especially for the young prince, and as the ship broke apart she saw him sink down into the depths. At first she was quite pleased, for now he would come down to her. But then she remembered that mortals could not live in the water and that only as a corpse could he come down to her father's castle. No, die he mustn't! And so she swam among beams and planks that floated on the sea, quite forgetting that they could have crushed her. She dived deep down in the water and rose up high among the waves, and thus she came at last to the young prince, who could hardly swim any longer in the stormy sea. His arms and legs were growing weak; his beautiful eyes were closed. He would have died had the little mermaid not arrived. She held his head up above the water and thus let the waves carry them wherever they liked.

In the morning the storm was over. Of the ship there wasn't a chip to be seen. The sun climbed, red and shining, out of the water; it was as if it brought life into the prince's cheeks, but his eyes remained closed. The mermaid kissed his high, handsome forehead and stroked back his wet hair. She thought he resembled the marble statue down in her little garden. She kissed him again and wished for him to live.

Now she saw the mainland ahead of her, high blue mountains on whose peaks the white snow shone as if swans were lying there. Down by the coast were lovely green forests, and ahead lay a church or a convent. Which, she didn't rightly know, but it was a building. Lemon and orange trees were growing there in the garden, and in front of the gate stood high palm trees. The sea had made a little bay here, which was calm but very deep all the way over to the rock where the fine white sand had been washed ashore. Here she swam with the handsome prince and put him on the sand, but especially she saw to it that his head was raised in the sunshine.

Now the bells rang in the big white building, and many young girls came out through the gate to the garden. Then the little mermaid swam farther out behind some big rocks that jutted up out of the water, covered her hair and breast with sea foam so no one could see her little face, and then kept watch to see who came out to the unfortunate prince.

It wasn't long before a young girl came over to where he lay. She seemed to be quite frightened, but only for a moment. Then she fetched several mortals, and the mermaid saw that the prince revived and that he smiled at everyone around him. But he didn't smile out to her, for he didn't know at all that she had saved him. She was so unhappy. And when he was carried into the big building, she dived down sorrowfully in the water and found her way home to her father's castle.

She had always been silent and pensive, but now she was more so than ever. Her sisters asked about what she had seen the first time she was up there, but she told them nothing.

Many an evening and morning she swam up to where she had left the prince. She saw that the fruits in the garden ripened and were picked. She saw that the snow melted on the high mountains, but she didn't see the prince, and so she returned home even sadder than before. Her only comfort was to sit in the little garden and throw her arms around the pretty marble statue that resembled the prince. But she didn't take care of her flowers. As in a jungle, they grew out over the paths, with their long stalks and leaves intertwined with the branches of the trees, until it was quite dark.

At last she couldn't hold out any longer, but told one of her sisters. And then all the others found out at once, but no more than they, and a few other mermaids, who didn't tell anyone except their closest friends. One of them knew who the prince was. She had also seen the festivities on the ship and knew where he was from and where his kingdom lay.

"Come, little sister," said the other princesses, and with their arms around one another's shoulders they came up to the surface of the water in a long row in front of the spot where they knew the prince's castle stood.

It was made of a pale yellow, shiny kind of stone, with great stairways—one went right down to the water. Magnificent gilded domes soared above the roof, and among the pillars that went around the whole building stood marble statues that looked as if they were alive. Through the clear glass in the high windows one could see into the most magnificent halls, where costly silken curtains and tapestries were hanging, and all of the walls were adorned with large paintings that were a joy to behold. In the middle of the biggest hall splashed a great fountain. Streams of water shot up high toward the glass dome in the roof, through which the sun shone on the water and all the lovely plants growing in the big pool.

Now she knew where he lived, and many an evening and night she came there over the water. She swam much closer to land than any of the others had dared. Yes, she went all the way up the little canal, under the magnificent marble balcony that cast a long shadow on the water. Here she sat and looked at the young prince, who thought he was quite alone in the clear moonlight.

Many an evening she saw him sail to the sound of music in the splendid boat on which the flags were waving. She peeped out from among the green rushes and caught the wind in her long silvery white veil, and if anyone saw it, he thought it was a swan spreading its wings.

Many a night, when the fishermen were fishing by torchlight in the sea, she heard them tell so many good things about the young prince that she was glad she had saved his life when he was drifting about half dead on the waves. And she thought of how fervently she had kissed him then. He knew nothing about it at all, couldn't even dream of her once.

She grew fonder and fonder of mortals, wished more and more that she could rise up among them. She thought their world was far bigger than hers. Why, they could fly over the sea in ships and climb the high mountains way above the clouds, and their lands with forests and fields stretched farther than she could see. There was so much she wanted to find out, but her sisters didn't know the answers to everything, and so she asked her old grandmother, and *she* knew the upper world well, which she quite rightly called The Lands Above the Sea.

"If mortals don't drown," the little mermaid asked, "do they live forever? Don't they die the way we do down here in the sea?"

"Why, yes," said the old queen, "they must also die, and their lifetime is much shorter than ours. We can live to be three hundred years old, but when we stop existing here, we only turn into foam upon the water. We don't even have a grave down here among our loved ones. We have no immortal soul; we never have life again. We are like the green rushes: once they are cut they can never be green again. Mortals, on the other hand, have a soul, which lives forever after the body has turned to dust. It mounts up through the clear air to all the shining stars. Just as we come to the surface of the water and see the land of the mortals, so do they come up to lovely unknown places that we will never see."

"Why didn't we get an immortal soul?" asked the little mermaid sadly. "I'd gladly give all my hundreds of years just to be a mortal for one day and afterward to be able to share in the heavenly world."

"You mustn't go and think about that," said the old queen. "We are much better off than the mortals up there."

"I too shall die and float as foam upon the sea, not hear the music of the waves or see the lovely flowers and the red sun. Isn't there anything at all I can do to win an immortal soul?"

"No," said the old queen. "Only if a mortal fell so much in love with you that you were dearer to him than a father and mother; only if you remained in all his thoughts and he was so deeply attached to you that he let the priest place his right hand in yours with a vow of faithfulness now and forever; only then would his soul float over into your body, and you would also share in the happiness of mortals. He would give you a soul and still keep his own. But that never can happen. The very thing that is so lovely here in the sea, your fishtail, they find so disgusting up there on the earth. They don't know any better. Up there one has to have two clumsy stumps, which they call legs, to be beautiful!"

Then the little mermaid sighed and looked sadly at her fishtail.

"Let us be satisfied," said the old queen. "We will frisk and frolic in the three hundred years we have to live in. That's plenty of time indeed. Afterward one can rest in one's grave all the more happily. This evening we are going to have a court ball!"

Now, this was a splendor not to be seen on earth. Walls and ceiling in the great ballroom were of thick but clear glass. Several hundred gigantic mussel shells, rosy-red and green as grass, stood in rows on each side with a blue flame, which lit up the whole ballroom and shone out through the walls so the sea too was brightly illuminated. One could see the countless fish that swam over to the glass wall. On some the scales shone purple; on others they seemed to be silver and gold. Through the middle of the ballroom flowed a broad stream, and in this the mermen and mermaids danced to the music of their own lovely songs. No mortals on earth have such beautiful voices. The little mermaid had the loveliest voice of all, and they clapped their hands for her. And for a moment her heart was filled with joy, for she knew that she had the most beautiful voice of all on this earth and in the sea. But soon she started thinking again of the world above her. She couldn't forget the handsome prince and her sorrow at not possessing, like him, an immortal soul. And so she slipped out of her father's castle unnoticed, and while everything inside was merriment and song she sat sadly in her little garden. Then she heard a horn ring down through the water, and she thought: "Now he is sailing up there, the one I love more than a father or a mother, the one who remains in all my thoughts and in whose hand I would place all my life's happiness. I would risk everything to win him and an immortal soul. I will go to the sea witch. I have always been so afraid of her, but maybe she can advise and help me."

Now the little mermaid went out of her garden toward the roaring maelstroms behind which the sea witch lived. She had never gone that way before. Here grew no flowers, no sea grass. Only the bare, gray, sandy bottom stretched on toward the maelstroms, which, like roaring mill wheels, whirled around and dragged everything that came their way down with them into the depths. In between these crushing whirlpools she had to go to enter the realm of the sea witch, and for a long way there was no other road than over hot bubbling mire that the sea witch called her peat bog. In back of it lay her house, right in the midst of an eerie forest. All the trees and bushes were polyps—half animal, half plant. They looked like hundred-headed serpents growing out of the earth. All the branches were long slimy arms with fingers like sinuous worms, and joint by joint they moved from the roots to the outermost tips. Whatever they could grab in the sea they wound their arms around it and never let it go. Terrified, the little mermaid remained standing outside the forest. Her heart was pounding with fright. She almost turned back, but then she thought of the prince and of an immortal soul, and it gave her courage. She bound her long, flowing hair around her head so the polyps could not grab her by it. She crossed both hands upon her breast and then off she flew, the way the fish can fly through the water, in among the loathsome polyps that reached out their arms and fingers after her. She saw where each of them had something it had seized; hundreds of small arms held onto it like strong iron bands. Rows of white bones of mortals who had drowned at sea and sunk all the way down there peered forth from the polyps' arms. Ships' wheels and chests they held tightly, skeletons of land animals, and— most terrifying of all—a little mermaid that they had captured and strangled.

Now she came to a large slimy opening in the forest where big fat water snakes gamboled, revealing their ugly yellowish-white bellies. In the middle of the opening had been erected a house made of the bones of shipwrecked mortals. There sat the sea witch letting a toad eat from her mouth, just the way mortals permit a little canary bird to eat sugar. She called the fat, hideous water snakes her little chickens and let them tumble on her big spongy breasts.

"I know what you want, all right," said the sea witch. "It's stupid of you to do it. Nonetheless, you shall have your way, for it will bring you misfortune, my lovely princess! You want to get rid of your fishtail and have two stumps to walk on instead, just like mortals, so the young prince can fall in love with you, and you can win him and an immortal soul." Just then the sea witch let out such a loud and hideous laugh that the toad and the water snakes fell down to the ground and writhed there. "You've come just in the nick of time," said the witch. "Tomorrow, after the sun rises, I couldn't help you until another year was over. I shall make you a potion, and before the sun rises you shall take it and swim to land, seat yourself on the shore there, and drink it. Then your tail will split and shrink into what mortals call lovely legs. But it hurts. It is like being pierced through by a sharp sword. Everyone who sees you will say you are the loveliest mortal child he has ever seen. You will keep your grace of movement. No dancer will ever float the way you do, but each step you take will be like treading on a sharp knife so your blood will flow! If you want to suffer all this, then I will help you."

"Yes," said the little mermaid in a trembling voice, thinking of the prince and of winning an immortal soul.

"But remember," said the witch, "once you have been given a mortal shape, you can never become a mermaid again. You can never sink down through the water to your sisters and to your father's castle. And if you do not win the love of the prince so that for your sake he forgets his father and mother and never puts you out of his thoughts and lets the priest place your hand in his so you become man and wife, you will not win an immortal soul. The first morning after he is married to another, your heart will break and you will turn into foam upon the water."

"This I want!" said the little mermaid and turned deathly pale.

"But you must also pay me," said the witch, "and what I demand is no small thing. You have the loveliest voice of all down here at the bottom of the sea, and you probably think you're going to enchant him with it. But that voice you shall give to me. I want the best thing you have for

my precious drink. Why, I must put my very own blood in
it so it will be as sharp as a two-edged sword."

"But if you take my voice," said the little mermaid,
"what will I have left?"

"Your lovely figure," said the witch, "your grace of
movement, and your sparkling eyes. With them you can
enchant a mortal heart, all right! Stick out your little
tongue so I can cut it off in payment, and you shall have
the potent drink!"

"So be it!" said the little mermaid, and the witch put
her kettle on to brew the magic potion. "Cleanliness is a
good thing," she said, and scoured her kettle with her
water snakes, which she knotted together. Now she cut
her breast and let the black blood drip into the kettle. The
steam made strange shapes that were terrifying and dreadful to see. Every moment the witch put something new
into the kettle, and when it had cooked properly, it was
like crocodile tears. At last the drink was ready, and it was
as clear as water.

"There it is," said the witch, and cut out the little
mermaid's tongue. Now she was mute and could neither
speak nor sing.

"If any of the polyps should grab you when you go back
through my forest," said the witch, "just throw one drop
of this drink on them and their arms and fingers will burst
into a thousand pieces." But the little mermaid didn't
have to do that. The polyps drew back in terror when they
saw the shining drink that glowed in her hand like a
glittering star. And she soon came through the forest, the
bog, and the roaring maelstroms.

She could see her father's castle. The torches had been
extinguished in the great ballroom. They were probably
all asleep inside there, but she dared not look for them
now that she was mute and was going to leave them
forever. It was as though her heart would break with grief.
She stole into the garden, took a flower from each of her

sisters' flower beds, threw hundreds of kisses toward the castle, and rose up through the dark blue sea.

The sun had not yet risen when she saw the prince's castle and went up the magnificent marble stairway. The moon shone bright and clear. The little mermaid drank the strong, burning drink, and it was as if a two-edged sword were going through her delicate body. At that she fainted and lay as if dead. When the sun was shining high on the sea, she awoke and felt a piercing pain, but right in front of her stood the handsome prince. He fixed his coal-black eyes upon her so that she had to cast down her own, and then she saw that her fishtail was gone, and she had the prettiest little white legs that any young girl could have, but she was quite naked. And so she enveloped herself in her thick long hair. The prince asked who she was and how she had come there, and she looked at him softly yet sadly with her dark blue eyes, for of course she could not speak. Each step she took was, as the witch had said, like stepping on pointed awls and sharp knives. But she endured this willingly. At the prince's side she rose as easily as a bubble, and he and everyone else marveled at her graceful, flowing movements.

She was given costly gowns of silk and muslin to wear. In the castle she was the fairest of all. But she was mute; she could neither sing nor speak. Lovely slave girls, dressed in silk and gold, came forth and sang for the prince and his royal parents. One of them sang more sweetly than all the others, and the prince clapped his hands and smiled at her. Then the little mermaid was sad. She knew that she herself had sung far more beautifully, and she thought, "Oh, if only he knew that to be with him I have given away my voice for all eternity."

Now the slave girls danced in graceful, floating movements to the accompaniment of the loveliest music. Then the little mermaid raised her beautiful white arms, stood up on her toes, and glided across the floor. She danced as no one had ever danced before. With each movement, her beauty became even more apparent, and her eyes spoke more deeply to the heart than the slave girl's song.

Everyone was enchanted by her, especially the prince, who called her his little foundling, and she danced on and on despite the fact that each time her feet touched the ground it was like treading on sharp knives. The prince said she was to stay with him forever, and she was allowed to sleep outside his door on a velvet cushion.

He had boys' clothes made for her so she could accompany him on horseback. They rode through the fragrant forests, where the green branches brushed her shoulders and the little birds sang within the fresh leaves. With the prince she climbed up the high mountains, and despite the fact that her delicate feet bled so the others could see it, she laughed at this and followed him until they could see the clouds sailing far below them like a flock of birds on their way to distant lands.

Back at the prince's castle, at night while the others slept, she went down the marble stairway and cooled her burning feet by standing in the cold sea water. And then she thought of those down there in the depths.

One night her sisters came arm in arm. They sang so mournfully as they swam over the water, and she waved to them. They recognized her and told her how unhappy she had made them all. After this they visited her every night, and one night far out she saw her old grandmother, who had not been to the surface of the water for many years, and the king of the sea with his crown upon his head. They stretched out their arms to her but dared not come as close to land as her sisters.

Day by day the prince grew fonder of her. He loved her the way one loves a dear, good child, but to make her his queen did not occur to him at all. And she would have to become his wife if she were to live, or else she would have

no immortal soul and would turn into foam upon the sea
on the morning after his wedding.

"Don't you love me most of all?" the eyes of the little
mermaid seemed to say when he took her in his arms and
kissed her beautiful forehead.

"Of course I love you best," said the prince, "for you
have the kindest heart of all. You are devoted to me, and
you resemble a young girl I once saw but will certainly
never find again. I was on a ship that was wrecked. The
waves carried me ashore near a holy temple to which
several young maidens had been consecrated. The youngest of them found me on the shore and saved my life. I
only saw her twice. She was the only one I could love in
this world. But you look like her and you have almost
replaced her image in my soul. She belongs to the holy
temple, and so good fortune has sent you to me. We shall
never be parted!"

"Alas! He doesn't know that I saved his life!" thought
the little mermaid. "I carried him over the sea to the
forest where the temple stands. I hid under the foam and
waited to see if any mortals would come. I saw that
beautiful girl, whom he loves more than me." And the
mermaid sighed deeply, for she couldn't cry. "The girl is
consecrated to the holy temple, he said. She will never
come out into the world. They will never meet again, but
I am with him and see him every day. I will take care of
him, love him, lay down my life for him!"

But now people were saying that the prince was going to
be married to the lovely daughter of the neighboring king.
That was why he was equipping so magnificent a ship. It
was given out that the prince is to travel to see the
country of the neighboring king, but actually it is to see
his daughter. He is to have a great retinue with him.

But the little mermaid shook her head and laughed. She
knew the prince's thoughts far better than all the rest. "I
have to go," he had told her. "I have to look at the lovely

princess. My parents insist upon it. But they won't be able to force me to bring her home as my bride. I cannot love her. She doesn't look like the beautiful girl in the temple, whom you resemble. If I should ever choose a bride, you would be the more likely one, my mute little foundling with the speaking eyes!" And he kissed her rosy mouth, played with her long hair, and rested his head upon her heart, which dreamed of mortal happiness and an immortal soul.

"You're not afraid of the sea, are you, my mute little child!" he said as they stood on the deck of the magnificent ship that was taking him to the country of the neighboring king. And he told her of storms and calms and of strange fish in the depths and of what the divers had seen down there. And she smiled at his story, for of course she knew about the bottom of the sea far better than anyone else.

In the moonlit night, when everyone was asleep—even the sailor at the wheel—she sat by the railing of the ship and stared down through the clear water, and it seemed to her that she could see her father's castle. At the very top stood her old grandmother with her silver crown on her head, staring up through the strong currents at the keel of the ship. Then her sisters came up to the surface of the water. They gazed at her sadly and wrung their white hands. She waved to them and smiled and was going to tell them that all was well with her and that she was happy, but the ship's boy approached and her sisters dived down, so he thought the white he had seen was foam upon the sea.

The next morning the ship sailed into the harbor of the neighboring king's capital. All the church bells were ringing, and from the high towers trumpets were blowing, while the soldiers stood with waving banners and glittering bayonets. Every day there was a feast. Balls and parties followed one after the other, but the princess had not yet come. She was being educated far away in a holy temple, they said; there she was learning all the royal virtues. At last she arrived.

The little mermaid was waiting eagerly to see how beautiful she was, and she had to confess that she had never seen a lovelier creature. Her skin was delicate and soft, and from under her long dark eyelashes smiled a pair of dark blue faithful eyes.

"It is you!" said the prince. "You, who saved me when I lay as if dead on the shore!" And he took his blushing bride into his arms. "Oh, I am far too happy," he said to the little mermaid. "The best I could ever dare hope for has at last come true! You will be overjoyed at my good fortune, for you love me best of all." And the little mermaid kissed his hand, but already she seemed to feel her heart breaking. His wedding morning would indeed bring her death and change her into foam upon the sea.

All the church bells were ringing. The heralds rode through the streets and proclaimed the betrothal. On all the altars fragrant oils burned in costly silver lamps. The priests swung censers, and the bride and bridegroom gave each other their hands and received the blessing of the bishop. The little mermaid, dressed in silk and gold, stood holding the bride's train, but her ears did not hear the festive music nor did her eyes see the sacred ceremony. She thought of the morning of her death, of everything she had lost in this world.

The very same evening the bride and bridegroom went on board the ship. Cannons fired salutes, all the flags were waving, and in the middle of the deck a majestic purple and gold pavilion with the softest cushions had been erected. Here the bridal pair was to sleep in the still, cool night. The breeze filled the sails, and the ship glided easily and gently over the clear sea.

When it started to get dark, many-colored lanterns were lighted and the sailors danced merrily on deck. It made the little mermaid think of the first time she had come to the surface of the water and seen the same splendor and festivity. And she whirled along in the dance, floating as the swallow soars when it is being pursued, and everyone applauded her and cried out in admiration. Never had she danced so magnificently. It was as though sharp knives were cutting her delicate feet, but she didn't feel it. The pain in her heart was even greater. She knew this was the last evening she would see the one for whom she had left her family and her home, sacrificed her beautiful voice, and daily suffered endless agony without his ever realizing it. It was the last night she would breathe the same air as he, see the deep sea and the starry sky. An endless night without thoughts or dreams awaited her—she who neither had a soul nor could ever win one. And there was gaiety and merriment on the ship until long past midnight. She laughed and danced, with the thought of death in her heart. The prince kissed his lovely bride and she played with his dark hair, and arm in arm they went to bed in the magnificent pavilion.

It grew silent and still on the ship. Only the helmsman stood at the wheel. The little mermaid leaned her white arms on the railing and looked toward the east for the dawn, for the first rays of the sun, which she knew would kill her. Then she saw her sisters come to the surface of the water. They were as pale as she was. Their long beautiful hair no longer floated in the breeze. It had been cut off.

"We have given it to the witch so she could help you, so you needn't die tonight. She has given us a knife; here it is. See how sharp it is? Before the sun rises, you must plunge it into the prince's heart! And when his warm blood spatters your feet, they will grow together into a fishtail, and you will become a mermaid again and can sink down into the water to us, and live your three hundred years before you turn into the lifeless, salty sea foam.

Hurry! Either you or he must die before the sun rises. Our old grandmother has grieved so much that her hair has fallen out, as ours has fallen under the witch's scissors. Kill the prince and return to us! Hurry! Do you see that red streak on the horizon? In a few moments the sun will rise, and then you must die!" And they uttered a strange, deep sigh and sank beneath the waves.

The little mermaid drew the purple curtain back from the pavilion and looked at the lovely bride asleep with her head on the prince's chest. She bent down and kissed his handsome forehead; looked at the sky, which grew rosier and rosier; looked at the sharp knife; and again fastened her eyes on the prince, who murmured the name of his bride in his dreams. She alone was in his thoughts, and the knife glittered in the mermaid's hand. But then she threw it far out into the waves. They shone red where it fell, as if drops of blood were bubbling up through the water. Once more she gazed at the prince with dimming eyes, then plunged from the ship down into the sea. And she felt her body dissolving into foam.

Now the sun rose out of the sea. The mild, warm rays fell on the deathly cold sea foam, and the little mermaid did not feel death. She saw the clear sun, and up above her floated hundreds of lovely transparent creatures. Through them she could see the white sails of the ship and the rosy clouds in the sky. Their voices were melodious but so ethereal that no mortal ear could hear them, just as no mortal eye could perceive them. Without wings, they floated through the air by their own lightness. The little mermaid saw that she had a body like theirs. It rose higher and higher out of the foam.

"To whom do I come?" she said, and her voice, like that of the others, rang so ethereally that no earthly music can reproduce it.

"To the daughters of the air," replied the others. "A mermaid has no immortal soul and can never have one

unless she wins the love of a mortal. Her immortality depends on an unknown power. The daughters of the air have no immortal souls, either, but by good deeds they can create one for themselves. We fly to the hot countries, where the humid, pestilential air kills mortals. There we waft cooling breezes. We spread the fragrance of flowers through the air and send refreshment and healing. After striving for three hundred years to do what good we can, we then receive an immortal soul and share in the eternal happiness of mortals. Poor little mermaid, with all your heart you have striven for the same goal. You have suffered and endured and have risen to the world of the spirits of the air. Now by good deeds you can create an immortal soul for yourself after three hundred years."

And the little mermaid raised her transparent arms up toward God's sun, and for the first time she felt tears. On the ship there was again life and movement. She saw the prince with his lovely bride searching for her. Sorrowfully they stared at the bubbling foam, as if they knew she had thrown herself into the sea. Invisible, she kissed the bride's forehead, smiled at the prince, and with the other children of the air rose up onto the pink cloud that sailed through the air.

"In three hundred years we will float like this into the kingdom of God!"

"We can come there earlier," whispered one. "Unseen we float into the houses of mortals where there are children, and for every day that we find a good child who makes his parents happy and deserves their love, God shortens our period of trial. The child does not know when we fly through the room, and when we smile over it with joy a year is taken from the three hundred. But if we see a naughty and wicked child, we must weep tears of sorrow, and each tear adds a day to our period of trial!"

The Emperor's New Clothes

❖   ❖   ❖

MANY years ago there lived an emperor who was so exceedingly fond of beautiful new clothes that he spent all his money just on dressing up. He paid no attention to his soldiers, nor did he care about plays or taking drives in the woods except for the sole purpose of showing off his new clothes. He had a robe for every hour of the day, and just as it is said of a king that he is "in council," so they always said here: "The emperor is in the clothes closet!"

In the great city where he lived everybody had a very good time. Many visitors came there every day. One day two charlatans came. They passed themselves off as weavers and said that they knew how to weave the most exquisite cloth imaginable. Not only were the colors and the pattern uncommonly beautiful but also the clothes that were made from the cloth had the singular quality of being invisible to every person who was unfit for his post or else was inadmissably stupid.

"Well, these are some splendid clothes," thought the emperor. "With them on I could find out which men in my kingdom were not suited for the posts they have; I can tell the wise ones from the stupid! Yes, that cloth must be woven for me at once!" And he gave the two charlatans lots of money in advance so they could begin their work.

They put up two looms, all right, and pretended to be working, but they had nothing whatsoever on the looms. Without ceremony they demanded the finest silk and the most magnificent gold thread. This they put in their own pockets and worked at the empty looms until far into the night.

"Now I'd like to see how far they've come with the cloth!" thought the emperor. But it made him feel a little uneasy to think that anyone who was stupid or unfit for his post couldn't see it. Of course he didn't believe that he himself needed to be afraid. Nonetheless he wanted to send someone else first to see how things stood. The whole city knew of the remarkable powers possessed by the cloth, and everyone was eager to see how bad or stupid his neighbor was.

"I'll send my honest old minister to the weavers," thought the emperor. "He's the best one to see how the cloth looks, for he has brains and no one is better fitted for his post than he is!"

Now the harmless old minister went into the hall where the two charlatans sat working at the empty looms.

"Heaven help us!" thought the old minister, his eyes opening wide. "Why, I can't see a thing!" But he didn't say so.

Both the charlatans asked him to please step closer and asked if it didn't have a beautiful pattern and lovely colors. Then they pointed to the empty loom, and the poor old minister kept opening his eyes wider. But he couldn't see a thing, for there was nothing there.

"Good Lord!" he thought. "Am I supposed to be stupid? I never thought so, and not a soul must find it out! Am I unfit for my post? No, it'll never do for me to say that I can't see the cloth!"

"Well, you're not saying anything about it!" said the one who was weaving.

"Oh, it's nice! Quite charming!" said the old minister,

and peered through his spectacles. "This pattern and these colors! Yes, I shall tell the emperor that it pleases me highly!"

"Well, we're delighted to hear it!" said both the weavers, and now they named the colors by name and described the singular pattern. The old minister paid close attention so he could repeat it all when he came back to the emperor. And this he did.

Now the charlatans demanded more money for more silk and gold thread, which they were going to use for the weaving. They stuffed everything into their own pockets. Not a thread went onto the looms, but they kept on weaving on the empty looms as before.

Soon afterward the emperor sent another harmless official there to see how the weaving was coming along and if the cloth should soon be ready. The same thing happened to him as to the minister. He looked and he looked, but as there was nothing there but the empty looms, he couldn't see a thing.

"Well, isn't it a beautiful piece of cloth?" both the charlatans said, and showed and explained the lovely pattern that wasn't there at all.

"Well, I'm not stupid!" thought the man. "Then it's my good position that I'm unfit for? That is strange enough, but I must be careful not to show it!" And so he praised the cloth he didn't see and assured them how delighted he was with the beautiful colors and the lovely pattern. "Yes, it's quite charming!" he said to the emperor.

All the people in the city were talking about the magnificent cloth.

Now the emperor himself wanted to see it while it was still on the loom. With a whole crowd of hand-picked men, among them the two harmless old officials who had been there before, he went to where the two sly charlatans were now weaving with all their might, but without a stitch or a thread.

"Yes, isn't it *magnifique?*" said the two honest officials. "Will your majesty look—what a pattern, what colors!" And then they pointed to the empty looms, for they thought that the others were certainly able to see the cloth.

"What's this?" thought the emperor. "I don't see anything! Why, this is dreadful! Am I stupid? Am I not fit to be emperor? This is the most horrible thing that could happen to me!"

"Oh, it's quite beautiful!" said the emperor. "It has my highest approval!" And he nodded contentedly and regarded the empty looms. He didn't want to say that he couldn't see a thing. The entire company he had brought with him looked and looked, but they weren't able to make any more out of it than the others. Yet, like the emperor, they said, "Oh, it's quite beautiful!" And they advised him to have clothes made of the magnificent new cloth in time for the great procession that was forthcoming.

"It is *magnifique!* Exquisite! Excellent!" passed from mouth to mouth. And every one of them was so fervently delighted with it. Upon each of the charlatans the emperor bestowed a badge of knighthood to hang in his buttonhole, and the title of "Weaver-Junker."

All night long, before the morning of the procession, the charlatans sat up with more than sixteen candles burning. People could see that they were busy finishing the emperor's new clothes. They acted as if they were taking the cloth from the looms, they clipped in the air with big scissors, they sewed with needles without thread, and at last they said, "See, now the clothes are ready!"

With his highest gentlemen-in-waiting the emperor came there himself and both the charlatans lifted an arm in the air as if they were holding something and said, "See, here are the knee breeches! Here's the tailcoat! Here's the cloak!" And so on.

"It's as light as a spider's web! You'd think you had
nothing on, but that's the beauty of it!"

"Yes," said all the gentlemen-in-waiting, but they couldn't
see a thing, for there was nothing there.

"Now, if your majesty would most graciously consent to
take off your clothes," said the charlatans, "we will help
you on with the new ones here in front of the big mirror!"

The emperor took off all his clothes, and the charlatans

acted as if they were handing him each of the new garments that had supposedly been sewed. And they put their arms around his waist as if they were tying something on—that was the train—and the emperor turned and twisted in front of the mirror.

"Heavens, how well it becomes you! How splendidly it fits!" they all said. "What a pattern! What colors! That's a magnificent outfit!"

"They're waiting outside with the canopy that is to be carried over your majesty in the procession," said the chief master of ceremonies.

"Well, I'm ready!" said the emperor. "Isn't it a nice fit?"

And then he turned around in front of the mirror just one more time, so it should really look as if he were regarding his finery.

The gentlemen-in-waiting, who were to carry the train, fumbled down on the floor with their hands just as if they were picking up the train. They walked and held their arms high in the air. They dared not let it appear as if they couldn't see a thing.

And then the emperor walked in the procession under the beautiful canopy. And all the people in the street and at the windows said, "Heavens, how wonderful the emperor's new clothes are! What a lovely train he has on the robe! What a marvelous fit!" No one wanted it to appear that he couldn't see anything, for then of course he would have been unfit for his position or very stupid. None of the emperor's clothes had ever been such a success.

"But he doesn't have anything on!" said a little child.

"Heavens, listen to the innocent's voice!" said the father, and then the child's words were whispered from one to another.

"He doesn't have anything on! That's what a little child is saying—he doesn't have anything on!"

"He doesn't have anything on!" the whole populace shouted at last. And the emperor shuddered, for it seemed to him that they were right. But then he thought, "Now I must go through with the procession." And he carried himself more proudly than ever, and the gentlemen-in-waiting carried the train that wasn't there at all.

The Steadfast Tin Soldier

❖ ❖ ❖

THERE were once five-and-twenty tin soldiers; they were all brothers, for they had been born of an old tin spoon. They shouldered their arms, they faced straight ahead, and their uniforms—red and blue—were ever so lovely. The very first thing they heard in this world, when the lid was taken off the box in which they were lying, were the words: "Tin soldiers!" It was shouted by a little boy, and he clapped his hands. They had been given to him for his birthday, and now he was lining them up on the table. Each soldier looked exactly like the other. Only one was slightly different: he had but one leg, for he was the last one to be cast and there hadn't been enough tin. And yet he stood just as firmly on his one leg as the others did on their two, and he is the very one who turns out to be unique.

On the table where they had been lined up there were many other playthings, but the one that stood out most was a lovely paper castle. Through the tiny windows you could look right into the halls. Outside were tiny trees standing around a little mirror that was supposed to look like a lake. Wax swans were swimming on it and being reflected there. It was all lovely, and yet the loveliest of all was a little maiden who was standing in the open door of the castle. She too had been cut out of paper, but she was wearing a skirt of the sheerest lawn and a narrow ribbon over her shoulder just like a drapery; in the very center of it was a shining spangle as big as her whole face. The little maiden was stretching out both her arms, for she was a dancer, and then she had raised one leg so high in the air that the tin soldier couldn't find it at all, and he thought she had but one leg, just like himself.

"That's the wife for me!" he thought. "But she's very highborn. She lives in a castle and I have only a box, and then it must do for five-and-twenty of us—that's no place for her. Still, I must see about making her acquaintance!" And then he stretched out at full length behind a snuffbox that stood on the table. From here he could look right at the little highborn lady, who continued to stand on one leg without losing her balance.

Later in the evening all the other tin soldiers went back in their box, and the people of the house went to bed. Now the toys began to play—at "Visitors," waging war, and holding balls. The tin soldiers rattled in their box because they wanted to join in, but they couldn't get the lid off. The nutcracker turned somersaults, and the slate pencil did monkeyshines on the slate; there was such a racket that the canary bird woke up and joined in the talk—and in verse, at that! The only two who didn't budge an inch were the tin soldier and the little dancer. She held herself erect on the tip of her toe and with both arms outstretched; he was just as steadfast on his one leg and his eyes never left her for a moment.

Now the clock struck twelve, and crash! The lid of the snuffbox flew off, but there wasn't any snuff in there—no, but a little black troll, and that was quite a trick.

"Tin soldier!" said the troll. "Will you keep your eyes to yourself!"

But the tin soldier pretended not to hear.

"Well, wait until tomorrow!" said the troll.

Now, when it was morning and the children got up, the

tin soldier was placed over in the window; and whether it was caused by the troll or the draft, the window suddenly flew open and the tin soldier went headlong out from the third floor with a terrible speed. He turned his leg up in the air and landed on his cap, with his bayonet stuck between the paving stones.

The maid and the little boy went right down to look for him, but despite the fact that they nearly stepped on him, they couldn't see him. If the tin soldier had shouted "Here I am!" they would have found him, all right. But he didn't think it proper to shout when he was in uniform.

Now it started to rain; the drops fell thick and fast. It turned into a regular downpour. When it was over, two street urchins came along.

"Look!" said the first. "There's a tin soldier. He's going out sailing!"

And so they made a boat out of a newspaper and put the tin soldier in the middle of it, and now he sailed down the gutter. Both the boys ran alongside and clapped their hands. Heaven help us! What waves there were in that gutter and what a current! But, then, the rain had poured down. The paper boat bobbed up and down, and now and then it turned around, sending a shudder through the tin soldier. But he was just as steadfast, didn't bat an eyelash, looked straight ahead, and shouldered his gun.

All at once the boat drifted in under a long gutter plank; it was just as dark as if he were in his box.

"I wonder where I'm going now," he thought. "Well, well, it's the fault of the troll. Alas, if only the little maiden were sitting here in the boat, then it could be twice as dark for all I'd care!"

At the same moment a big water rat came along, who lived under the gutter plank.

"Do you have a passport?" asked the rat. "Hand over your passport!"

But the tin soldier remained silent and held the gun

even tighter. The boat flew away with the rat right behind it. Whew! How it gnashed its teeth and shouted to sticks and straws: "Stop him! Stop him! He hasn't paid the toll! He hasn't shown his passport!"

But the current grew stronger and stronger; the tin soldier could already see daylight ahead where the gutter plank ended, but he could also hear a roaring sound that was enough to frighten a brave man. Just think, where the gutter plank ended, the gutter poured right out into a big canal! It was just as dangerous for him as it would be for us to sail down a great waterfall.

Now he was already so close to it that he couldn't stop. The boat shot out; the poor tin soldier held himself as stiffly as he could. No one was going to say that he had blinked his eyes. The boat whirled around three or four times and filled with water right up to the edge. It had to sink. The tin soldier stood in water up to his neck. The boat sank deeper and deeper; the paper grew soggier and soggier. Now the water went over the tin soldier's head. Then he thought of the lovely little dancer, whom he would never see again, and in the ears of the tin soldier rang the song:

> Fare forth! Fare forth, warrior!
> Thou shalt suffer death!

Now the paper was torn to pieces and the tin soldier plunged through—but at the same moment he was gobbled up by a big fish.

My, how dark it was in there! It was even worse than under the gutter plank, and then too it was so cramped! But the tin soldier was steadfast and lay at full length, shouldering his gun.

The fish darted about; it made the most terrible movements. At last it was quite still. It was as if a flash of

lightning had streaked through it. The light was shining quite brightly and someone shouted: "A tin soldier!"

The fish had been caught, taken to market, and sold, and had ended up in the kitchen, where the maid had cut it open with a big knife. With two fingers she picked the tin soldier up by the middle and carried him into the parlor, where they all wanted to see this remarkable man who had journeyed about in the stomach of a fish. But the tin soldier wasn't proud at all. They stood him up on the table, and there—my, what strange things can happen in this world! The tin soldier was in the very same room he had been in before! He saw the very same children and the playthings standing on the table, and the lovely castle with the beautiful little dancer. She was still standing on one leg and holding the other high in the air—she was stead-fast too. The tin soldier was so moved that he could have cried tears of tin, but it wasn't proper! He looked at her and she looked at him, but they didn't say anything.

At the same moment one of the little boys took the tin soldier and threw him right into the tiled stove without giving any reason for doing so. It was decidedly the troll in the box who was to blame.

The tin soldier stood all aglow and felt the terrible heat—but whether it was from the real fire or from love, he didn't know. His colors were all gone, but whether that had happened on the journey or from sorrow, no one could tell. He looked at the little maiden, she looked at him, and he felt he was melting. But still he stood steadfast and shouldered his gun. Then a door opened, the wind took the dancer, and like a sylphid she flew right into the tiled stove to the tin soldier, blazed up, and was gone. Then the tin soldier melted to a clump, and when the maid took out the ashes the next day, she found him in the shape of a little tin heart. Of the dancer, on the other hand, only the spangle was left, and that was burned as black as coal.

The Garden of Paradise

❖   ❖   ❖

THERE was once a king's son. No one had so many or such beautiful books as he had. He was able to read about everything that had taken place in this world and see it depicted in magnificent pictures. He was able to learn about every nation and every land. But about where the Garden of Paradise was to be found there wasn't a word, and that was the very thing he thought of most.

When he was still quite young, but was going to start his schooling, his grandmother had told him that every flower in the Garden of Paradise was the sweetest cake, and the filaments were the choicest wine. On one flower was written "History," on another "Geography" or "Tables." You had only to eat cake and you knew your lesson. Indeed, the more you ate, the more history or geography or tables you knew.

He believed it then, but as he grew bigger and learned more and became much wiser he understood very well that there had to be far different delights in the Garden of Paradise.

"Oh, why did Eve pick from the Tree of Knowledge? Why did Adam partake of the forbidden fruit? It should have been me, then it would never have happened! Never would sin have entered the world!"

He said it then, and he was still saying it when he was seventeen. The Garden of Paradise filled his thoughts.

One day he went into the forest; he went alone, for that gave him the greatest pleasure.

It grew dark, the sky clouded over, and then it began to rain as if the whole sky were one big sluice from which the water was pouring. It was as dark as it usually is at night in the deepest well. Now he was slipping on the wet grass, now he was falling over the bare stones that jutted out of the rocky ground. Everything was wringing wet. There wasn't a dry stitch left on the unfortunate prince. He had to crawl up over huge blocks of stone, where the water seeped out of the deep moss. He was just about to drop when he heard a strange rushing sound, and ahead of him he saw a huge brightly lit cave. In the middle burned a fire big enough to roast a stag by, and this was being done too. The most magnificent stag, with its high antlers, had been stuck on a spit and was being slowly turned around between two felled fir trees. An elderly woman, tall and husky like a man in disguise, was sitting by the fire throwing on one piece of wood after another.

"Just come closer!" she said. "Sit by the fire so you can dry your clothes!"

"There's a terrible draft here!" said the prince, and sat down on the floor.

"It'll be even worse when my sons come home!" answered the woman. "You're in the Cave of the Winds; my sons are the Four Winds of the world. Can you grasp that?"

"Where are your sons?" asked the prince.

"Well, it's not so easy to give an answer when you ask a stupid question!" said the woman. "My sons are on their own. They're playing ball with the clouds up there in the parlor!" And then she pointed up in the air.

"Oh, is that so!" said the prince. "By the way, you speak

quite harshly and not so gently as the womenfolk I usually see about me."

"Well, as likely as not, they don't have anything else to do! I've got to be harsh if I'm to keep my boys under control! But I can do it, even if they are pigheaded! Do you see those four sacks hanging on the wall? They're just as afraid of them as you were of the rod behind the mirror. I can double the boys up, I'll have you know, and then into the sack they go. No fuss about it! There they sit, and they don't come out to go gallivanting until I see fit! But here comes one of them!"

It was the North Wind, who strode in with an icy chill. Huge hailstones bounced across the floor and snowflakes whirled about. He was clad in bearskin pants and jacket, a sealskin hood went down over his ears, long icicles hung from his beard, and one hailstone after another slid down from the collar of his jacket.

"Don't go over to the fire right away," said the prince. "You can easily get chilblains on your face and hands."

"Chilblains!" said the North Wind, and gave quite a loud laugh. "Chilblains! Why, that's just what I enjoy most! But what sort of a milksop are you? How did you get into the Cave of the Winds?"

"He's my guest!" said the old woman. "And if you don't like that explanation, you can just go in the sack! You're familiar with my judgment!"

See, it helped, and now the North Wind told where he had come from and where he had been for almost a whole month.

"I come from the Arctic Ocean," he said. "I've been on Bering Island with the Russian walrus hunters. I sat and slept at the helm when they sailed out from the North Cape. Now and then, when I woke up for a little while, the stormy petrel was flying about my legs. That's a funny bird: it gives a quick flap of the wings and then holds them outstretched, motionless, and now it has enough speed."

"Just don't make it so long-drawn-out!" said the Mother of the Winds. "And then you came to Bering Island!"

"It's lovely there! There's a floor to dance on as flat as a plate, half-thawed snow and moss, and sharp stones with skeletons of walruses and polar bears, lay there. They looked like the arms and legs of giants, moldy and green. You'd think the sun had never shone on them. I blew on the fog a little to get a glimpse of the hut. It was a house built of wreckage and covered with walrus hide, the fleshy side turned out—it was all red and green. A live polar bear was sitting on the roof growling. I went to the shore, looked at the birds' nests, looked at the bald nestlings shrieking and gaping. I blew into the thousands of throats, and they learned how to shut their mouths. Down below, the walruses were tumbling about like living entrails or giant maggots with heads of pigs and teeth a yard long!"

"You tell the story well, my boy," said the mother. "It makes my mouth water to listen to you."

"Then the hunt began! The harpoon was plunged into the breast of the walrus so the steaming jet of blood spurted onto the ice like a fountain. Then I also thought of my game. I started to blow and let my sailing ships—the icebergs as high as a cliff—crush the boats. Whew! How the men sniveled and how they shrieked, but I shrieked louder! They had to unload the whale carcasses, the chests, and the ropes onto the ice. I shook the snowflakes over them and let them drift south in the wedged-in vessels to have a taste of salt water. They'll never come back to Bering Island!"

"Then you've been up to mischief!" said the Mother of the Winds.

"The others can tell you of the good I've done," he said. "But there's my brother from the West. I like him best of all—he smacks of the sea and brings a heavenly chill along with him."

"Is that little Zephyrus?" asked the prince.

"Yes, that's Zephyrus, all right!" said the old woman. "But he's not so little after all. In the old days he was a handsome boy, but that's over now!"

He looked like a wild man, but he had on a baby's cap so as not to hurt himself. In his hand he carried a mahogany club, chopped down in the mahogany forests of America. It could be no less!

"Where do you come from?" asked his mother.

"From the forest wilderness," he said, "where the thorny lianas make a fence between each tree, where the water snake lies in the grass and mankind seems to be unnecessary."

"What were you doing there?"

"I was looking at the deep river and saw how it plunged down from the cliff, turned to spray, and flew up to the clouds to carry the rainbow. I was watching the wild buffalo swimming in the river, but the current dragged him along with it, and he drifted with a flock of wild ducks that flew in the air where the water went over the edge. The buffalo had to go over. I liked that, so I blew up a storm so the ancient trees went sailing and were dashed to shavings."

"And you haven't done anything else?" asked the old woman.

"I've been turning somersaults in the savannas, and I've been patting the wild horse and shaking down coconuts. Oh, yes, I've got stories to tell, but one shouldn't tell everything one knows. You're well aware of that, old lady!" And then he gave his mother such a kiss that she almost fell over backward. He was really a wild boy.

Now the South Wind came in, wearing a turban and a flowing burnoose.

"It's mighty cold in here!" he said, throwing a log on the fire. "It's easy to tell that North Wind has come first."

"It's hot enough to roast a polar bear in here!" said the North Wind.

"You're a polar bear yourself!" said the South Wind.

"Do you want to be put in the sack?" asked the old woman. "Sit down on that stone and tell us where you've been."

"In Africa, Mother!" he replied. "I was hunting lions with the Hottentots in the land of the Kaffirs. My, what grass is growing on the plain there, as green as an olive! There the gnu was dancing and the ostrich ran races with me, but I'm still more nimble-footed. I came to the desert, to the golden sand that looks like the bottom of the sea. I met a caravan. They were butchering their last camel to get water to drink, but they got only a little. The sun blazed up above, and the sand roasted down below. The vast desert has no boundaries. Then I frolicked about in the fine loose sand and whirled it up into tall pillars! What a dance that was! You should have seen how dispiritedly the dromedary stood and how the merchant drew his caftan over his head. He prostrated himself before me, as before Allah, his god. Now they're buried. A pyramid of sand stands over them all. Someday, when I blow it away, the sun will bleach their bones. Then the travelers will be able to see that people have been here before; otherwise you wouldn't think so in the desert!"

"Then you've just been doing harm too!" said the mother. "March into the sack!" And before he knew it, she had the South Wind by the middle and into the sack! It rolled about on the floor, but she sat on it and then it had to lie still.

"You've got some lively boys here, I must say!" said the prince.

"Yes, so I have," she replied, "but I know how to handle them! There's the fourth!"

It was the East Wind. He was clad like a Chinese.

"So, you've come from that direction!" she said. "I thought you'd been to the Garden of Paradise."

"I'm not flying there until morning. It'll be a hundred

years tomorrow since I was there! Now I've just come
from China, where I've been dancing on the porcelain
tower so all the bells tinkled. Down in the street the
officials were being flogged. Bamboo poles were being
worn out on their shoulders, and they were people from
the first to the ninth rank. They shrieked, "Many thanks,
my fatherly benefactor!" But they didn't mean a thing by
it; and I tinkled the bells and sang 'Tsing tsang tsu!' "

"You're a wild one!" said the old woman. "It's a good
thing you're going to the Garden of Paradise tomorrow.
That always improves your manners. Drink deeply of the
Spring of Wisdom, and bring home a little flaskful for
me."

"That I'll do!" said the East Wind. "But why did you
put my brother from the South down in the sack? Out
with him! He's going to tell me about the Phoenix. The
princess in the Garden of Paradise always wants to hear
about that bird when I pay a visit every hundred years.
Open the sack, that's my sweet mother, and I'll make you
a present of two pocketsful of tea, as green and fresh as it
was on the spot where I picked it."

"Well, for the sake of the tea and because you're mother's darling, I'll open the sack!" And so she did! And the
South Wind crawled out, but he looked quite crestfallen
because the strange prince had seen it.

"Here's a palm leaf for you to give to the princess!" said
the South Wind. "That leaf has been given to me by the
old Phoenix, the only one in the world. With his beak he
has scratched on it the whole account of his life, the
hundred years he has lived; now she can read it for herself. I saw how the Phoenix himself set fire to his nest, sat
on it, and burned up like the Hindu's widow. My, how
the dry branches crackled, what smoke and fragrance there
was! At last it all went up in flames. The old Phoenix
turned to ashes, but his egg lay red in the fire. It cracked
with a loud bang and the youngster flew out. Now he's the

ruler of all the birds and the only Phoenix in the world. He has bitten a hole in the palm leaf I gave you. That's his greeting to the princess."

"What about a bit to eat!" said the Mother of the Winds, and then they all sat down to dine on the roasted stag. The prince sat beside the East Wind, and thus they soon became good friends.

"Listen, tell me now," said the prince, "just who is this princess there has been so much talk about, and where is the Garden of Paradise?"

"Ho! Ho!" said the East Wind. "If you'd like to go there, just fly with me tomorrow. But otherwise I'd better tell you that no mortal has been there since the time of Adam and Eve. I daresay you know about them from your Scriptures!"

"Yes, of course!" said the prince.

"At the time they were driven out, the Garden of Paradise sank into the earth. But it kept its warm sunshine, its gentle breeze, and all its splendor. The queen of the fairies dwells there. There lies the Isle of Bliss, where Death never comes; it's a delightful place to be. Sit on my back tomorrow and I'll take you with me. I daresay it can be done! But now you mustn't talk anymore, for I want to go to sleep!"

And then they all went to sleep.

Early in the morning the prince woke up, and he was not a little dumbfounded to find himself already high above the clouds. He was sitting on the back of the East Wind, who was holding onto him quite squarely. They were so high in the sky that forests and fields, rivers and lakes, looked like an enormous illustrated map.

"Good morning," said the East Wind. "You could just as well have slept a little longer; there's not much to look at on the flatland beneath us unless you like to count churches! They stand out like pricks of chalk on the green board

down there." The fields and meadows were what he called
"the green board."

"It was very impolite of me not to say good-bye to your
mother and your brothers," said the prince.

"Allowances are made for one who's sleeping," said the
East Wind, and then they flew faster than ever. You could
tell by the treetops in the forest that they were rushing
over them: all the leaves and branches rustled; you could
tell by the seas and lakes, for wherever they flew, the
waves rolled higher and the great ships curtsied deep
down in the water like floating swans.

Toward evening, as it was growing dark, the big cities
were a delight to behold: the lights were burning, now
here, now there—just as when someone burns a piece of
paper and sees the myriads of tiny sparks, like children on
their way from school! And the prince clapped his hands,
but the East Wind told him to stop that and hang on tight
instead, or else he could easily fall down and find himself
hanging on a church spire.

The eagle from the dark forest flew quite easily, but the
East Wind flew easier still. The cossack on his horse
dashed along over the steppes, but the prince was dashing
along in another fashion.

"Now you can see the Himalayas!" said the East Wind.
"They're the highest mountains in Asia. We should be
coming to the Garden of Paradise soon!" Then they veered
in a more southerly direction, and soon there was the
scent of spices and flowers. Figs and pomegranates were
growing wild, and the wild grapevines had blue and red
grapes. Here they both came down and stretched out in
the soft grass, where the flowers nodded to the wind as if
they wanted to say, "Welcome back!"

"Are we in the Garden of Paradise now?" asked the
prince.

"No, not at all!" replied the East Wind. "But we should
be there soon. Do you see that wall of rock there, and the

big grotto with the grapevines hanging around it like a huge green curtain? We're going in through there! Wrap yourself up in your cloak. The sun is scorching hot here, but one step away and it's as cold as ice. The bird that sweeps past that grotto has one wing out here in the heat of summer and the other in there in the cold of winter!"

"So that's the way to the Garden of Paradise?" asked the prince.

Now they went into the grotto. Whew! How icy cold it was! But it didn't last long. The East Wind spread out his wings, and they shone like the brightest fire. My, what a grotto that was! Huge blocks of stone, from which water dripped, hung over them in the most fantastic shapes. Now the grotto was so narrow that they had to crawl on their hands and knees; now it was as high and spacious as if they were out in the open. It looked like a sepulchral chapel with mute organ pipes and petrified banners.

"I daresay we're taking the Road of Death to the Garden of Paradise," said the prince, but the East Wind didn't answer a word; he pointed ahead, and the loveliest blue light was shining at them. The blocks of stone overhead were fading more and more into a haze that at last was as bright as a white cloud in the moonlight. Now they were in the loveliest gentle breeze, as refreshing as in the mountains, as fragrant as in a valley of roses.

A river was flowing there, as clear as the air itself, and the fish were like silver and gold. Violet eels, which shot off blue sparks at every turn, were frolicking down in the water, and the broad leaves of the water lily were the colors of the rainbow. The flower itself was a reddish-yellow burning flame, which was fed by the water, just as oil constantly keeps the lamp burning. A massive bridge of marble—but as remarkably and delicately carved as if it were of lace and glass beads—spanned the water to the Isle of Bliss, where the Garden of Paradise was blooming.

The East Wind took the prince in his arms and carried him across. There the flowers and leaves were singing the most beautiful songs from his childhood, but in swelling tones more delightful than any human voice can sing.

Were they palm trees or huge water plants that were growing here? The prince had never seen such lush and enormous trees before. There, in long garlands, hung the most remarkable twining vines, such as are to be found only in gold and color in the margins of the ancient books about the saints or threading in and out of the initial letters. It was the strangest combination of birds, flowers, and flourishes. Nearby, in the grass, stood a flock of peacocks with outspread, iridescent tails. Of course, that's just what they were! But no, when the prince touched them, he realized that they weren't animals but plants; they were huge dock plants that were as radiant here as the peacock's lovely tail. The lion and tiger were gamboling about like supple cats among the green hedges, which had a fragrance of olive blossoms, and the lion and the tiger were tame. The wild wood pigeon, as lustrous as the most beautiful pearl, flapped the lion's mane with its wings and the antelope, which is usually so timid, stood nodding its head as if it too wanted to join in the play.

Now the Fairy of Paradise came; her raiment shone like the sun and her face was as mild as that of a happy mother whose child has brought her joy. She was so young and fair, and attending her were the loveliest maidens, each with a shining star in her hair.

The East Wind gave her the inscribed leaf from the Phoenix, and her eyes sparkled with joy. She took the prince by the hand and led him into her castle, where the walls were the color of the most magnificent tulip petal when held up to the sun; the ceiling itself was one big lustrous flower, and indeed, the more you stared into it, the deeper its calyx seemed to be. The prince stepped over to the window and looked through one of the panes.

Then he saw the Tree of Knowledge with the serpent, and Adam and Eve were standing nearby. "Weren't they driven out?" he asked. And the Fairy smiled and explained to him that Time had thus burned its picture onto every pane, but not the way one usually saw it. No, there was life in it, the leaves on the trees moved. The people came and went, as in a reflected image. And he looked through another pane, and there was Jacob's dream, with the ladder going straight up to heaven, and the angels with big wings were hovering up and down. Yes, everything that had happened in this world was living and moving in the panes of glass. Time alone could burn such remarkable pictures.

The Fairy smiled and led him into a huge, lofty hall. Its walls seemed to be transparent paintings, with each face lovelier than the next. There were millions of happy faces that smiled and sang until it blended into a single melody. The ones at the very top were so tiny that they appeared to be tinier than the tiniest rosebud when it is drawn as a dot on the paper. And in the middle of the hall stood a huge tree, with luxuriant, hanging branches; golden apples, big and small, hung like oranges among the green leaves. This was the Tree of Knowledge, of whose fruit Adam and Eve had partaken. From each leaf dripped a glistening red drop of dew! It was as if the tree were crying tears of blood.

"Now let us get the boat," said the Fairy. "There we will enjoy refreshments out on the billowing water. The boat rocks, and yet it doesn't budge from the spot. But all the lands of the world will glide past our eyes." And it was strange to see how the whole coast moved. Here came the high snow-capped Alps, with clouds and black fir trees. The horn rang out, deep and melancholic, and the shepherd yodeled prettily in the valley. Now the banana trees bent their long drooping branches over the boat, coal-black swans were swimming on the water, and the most curious animals and flowers came into sight on the shore. This was New Holland, the fifth continent, that was gliding past and offering a view of the blue mountains; you could hear the chants of the priests and see the wild men dance to the sound of drums and bone pipes. The pyramids of Egypt, soaring to the clouds, and overturned columns and sphinxes half buried in the sand sailed past. The Aurora Borealis blazed over the glaciers of the North; it was a display of fireworks that none could match. The prince was so blissful. And indeed, he saw a hundred times more than we have described here.

"And can I stay here always?" he asked.

"That depends on yourself!" answered the Fairy. "If you don't, like Adam, allow yourself to be tempted to do what is forbidden, then you can always stay here."

"I won't touch the apples on the Tree of Knowedge!" said the prince. "Why, there're thousands of fruits here as lovely as they are."

"Test yourself, and if you're not strong enough, then go back with the East Wind, who brought you; he is flying back now and won't be coming here again for a hundred years. The time here in this place will pass for you as though it were only a hundred hours, but that's a long time for temptation and sin. Every evening, when I leave you, I must call out to you: 'Follow me!' I must beckon to you with my hand—but remain where you are. Don't come with me, for with every step your yearning will increase. You will enter the hall where the Tree of Knowledge grows. I sleep beneath its fragrant, drooping boughs. You will bend over me and I must smile. But if you press one kiss upon my lips, Paradise will then sink deep into the earth and be lost to you. The biting wind of the desert will whistle around you, the cold rain will drip from your hair. Trial and tribulation will be your lot."

"I'm staying here!" said the prince. And the East Wind kissed his forehead and said, "Be strong, and we'll meet here again in a hundred years. Farewell! Farewell!" And the East Wind spread out his mighty wings; they shone like heat lightning in the summer, or the Northern Lights in the cold winter. "Farewell! Farewell!" came the echo from flowers and trees. Storks and pelicans flew in rows like fluttering streamers and accompanied him to the boundary of the garden.

"Now our dance begins," said the Fairy. "At the end, when I dance with you, you will see me beckoning to you as the sun goes down; you will hear me calling you: 'Follow me!' But don't do it! For a hundred years I must repeat it every evening. Every time that hour is past you will gain more strength; at last you will never think of it again. This evening is the first time. Now I have warned you."

And the Fairy led him into a great hall of white transparent lilies. The yellow filament of each was a tiny harp of gold, which rang out with the sound of strings and flutes. The most beautiful maidens, graceful and willowy, clad in billowing gauze that revealed their lovely limbs, hovered in the dance and sang of how delightful it is to live, of how they would never die, and of how the Garden of Paradise would bloom in all eternity.

As the sun went down the entire sky turned a golden hue that tinged the lilies like the loveliest roses. And the prince drank of the sparkling wine handed to him by the maidens, and he felt a bliss he had never known before. He saw how the back of the hall opened, and the Tree of Knowledge stood in a radiance that blinded his eyes! The song coming from it was soft and lovely, like his mother's voice, and it was as if she were singing, "My child, my beloved child!"

Then the Fairy beckoned and called so affectionately, "Follow me! Follow me!" And he plunged toward her, forgetting his vow, forgetting it already on the very first evening. And she beckoned and smiled. The fragrance, the spicy fragrance all around, grew headier; the harps rang out far more beautifully; and the millions of smiling heads in the hall where the tree was growing seemed to be nodding and singing: "One should know everything! Man is the lord of the earth!" And they were no longer tears of blood that fell from the leaves of the Tree of Knowledge; they were red, twinkling stars, it seemed to him. "Follow me! Follow me!" echoed the tremulous strains, and at every step the prince's cheeks burned hotter and his blood flowed faster. "I must!" he said. "Why, that's no sin. It can't be! Why not follow beauty and happiness! I will look at her asleep. After all, nothing is lost as long as I don't kiss her, and I won't do that, I am strong! I have a strong will!"

And the Fairy let drop her dazzling raiment, bent back the branches, and a moment later was hidden inside.

"I haven't sinned yet!" said the prince. "And I'm not

going to, either." And then he drew the branches aside. She was already asleep, as lovely as only the Fairy in the Garden of Paradise can be. She smiled in her dreams. He bent over her and saw the tears welling up between her eyelashes.

"Are you crying over me?" he whispered. "Don't cry, you lovely woman! Only now do I comprehend the happiness of Paradise! It pours through my blood and through my thoughts. I can feel the might of cherubs and of eternal life in my mortal limbs! Let there be everlasting night for me; one moment such as this is riches enough!" And he kissed the tears away from her eyes, and his lips touched hers. . . .

Then there was a thunderclap louder and more dreadful than had ever been heard before, and everything fell down: the lovely Fairy and the blossoming Paradise sank. It sank so deep, so deep. The prince saw it sink in the black night; like a tiny gleaming star, it sparkled far away. A deathly chill went through his limbs; he closed his eyes and lay as if dead for a long time.

The cold rain was falling on his face and the biting wind was blowing about his head when he regained his thoughts. "What have I done?" he sighed. "I have sinned like Adam! Sinned so that Paradise has sunk deep down there!" And he opened his eyes. He could still see the star in the distance, the star that twinkled like the sunken Paradise—it was the Morning Star in the sky.

He got up and found that he was in the great forest close to the Cave of the Winds, and the Mother of the Winds was sitting by his side. She looked angry, and she lifted her arm in the air. "Already on the very first evening!" she said. "I thought as much! Yes, if you were my boy, you'd go down in the sack now!"

"That's where he's going," said Death; he was a strong old man with a scythe in one hand and with huge black wings. "He'll be laid in a coffin, but not now. I'll just mark him and then let him wander about the world for a while, atone for his sin, grow better and improve! I'll come one day. When he least expects it, I'll put him in the black coffin, place it on my head, and fly up toward the star. The Garden of Paradise is blooming there too. And if he is good and pious, he shall enter there; but if his thoughts are evil and his heart is still full of sin, he will sink in the coffin deeper than Paradise sank and only once every thousand years will I fetch him up again, so that he may sink deeper or remain on the star, the twinkling star on high!"

The Flying Trunk

❖ ❖ ❖

THERE was once a merchant; he was so rich that he could pave the whole street, and most of a little alleyway too, with silver money. But he didn't do it; he knew of other ways to use his money. If he spent a shilling, he got back a daler. That's the sort of merchant he was—and then he died.

Now the son got all this money, and he lived merrily—going to masquerade balls every night, making paper kites out of rixdaler bills, and playing ducks and drakes on the lake with golden coins instead of stones. So I daresay the money could go, and go it did. At last he had no more than four shillings left, and he had no other clothes than a pair of slippers and an old bathrobe. His friends no longer bothered about him now, as, indeed, they couldn't walk down the street together. But one of them, who was kind, sent him an old trunk and said, "Pack it!" Now, that was all very well, but he had nothing to pack, and so he seated himself in the trunk.

It was a funny trunk. As soon as you pressed the lock, the trunk could fly—and fly it did! Whoops! It flew up through the chimney with him, high above the clouds, farther and farther away. The bottom creaked, and he was afraid it would go to pieces, for then he would have made quite a big *jolt!* Heaven help us! And then he came to the

land of the Turks. He hid the trunk in the woods under
the dried leaves and then went into the town. He could do
this easily, for among the Turks everyone, of course, walked
around like he did, in a bathrobe and slippers. Then he
met a nurse with a baby.

"Listen, you Turkish nurse," he said, "what big castle is
this close to the city? The windows are so high!"

"The king's daughter lives there!" she said. "It has been
prophesied that a sweetheart is going to make her very
unhappy, so no one can come in to see her unless the king
and the queen are there!"

"Thanks!" said the merchant's son. And then he went
out in the woods, seated himself in his trunk, flew up on
the roof, and crawled in through the window to the princess.

She was lying on the sofa asleep. She was so lovely that
the merchant's son had to kiss her. She woke up and was
quite terrified, but he said that he was the God of the
Turks, who had come down to her through the air, and
she liked that very much.

Then they sat next to each other, and he told her tales
about her eyes: they were the loveliest dark pools, and her
thoughts swam about there like mermaids. And he told
her about her forehead: it was a snow-capped mountain
with the most magnificent halls and pictures. And he told
her about the stork that brings the sweet little babies.

Yes, those were some lovely tales! Then he proposed to
the princess, and she said yes right away.

"But you must come here on Saturday," she said. "Then
the king and the queen will be here with me for tea! They
will be very proud that I am getting the God of the Turks.
But see to it that you know a really lovely story, for my
parents are especially fond of them. My mother likes it to
be moral and decorous, while my father likes it jolly, so
you can laugh!"

"Well, I'm bringing no other wedding present than a
story!" he said, and then they parted. But the princess

gave him a saber that was encrusted with golden coins—and he could particularly use those.

Now he flew away, bought himself a new bathrobe, and then sat out in the woods and started making up a story. It had to be ready by Saturday, and that's not at all easy.

Then he was ready, and then it was Saturday.

The king and the queen and the whole court were waiting with tea at the princess'. He was given such a nice reception!

"Now, will you tell a story!" said the queen. "One that is profound and imparts a moral."

"But one that can still make you laugh!" said the king.

"Yes, of course!" he said, and started his tale. And now you must listen very carefully.

"There was once a bunch of matches that were so exceedingly proud of their high descent. Their family tree—that is to say, the big fir tree of which each one was a tiny stick—had been a huge old tree in the forest. The matches were now lying on the shelf between a tinderbox and an old iron pot, and they were telling them about their youth.

" 'Yes, when we lived high on the green branch,' they said, 'we were really living high! Every morning and evening, diamond tea—that was the dew. All day we had sunshine—when the sun was shining—and all the little birds had to tell us stories. We were very well aware that we were rich too, for the leafy trees were clad only in the summer, but our family could afford green clothes both summer and winter. But then came the woodcutters—that was the Great Revolution—and our family was split up. The head of the family was given a post as the mainmast on a splendid ship that could sail around the world—if it wanted to. The other branches ended up in other places, and it is now our task to provide light for the rank and file. That's why people of rank like ourselves happen to be in the kitchen.'

" 'Well, it's been different with me!' said the iron pot, which was lying beside the matches. 'Ever since I came out into the world, I've been scoured and boiled many times! I attend to the substantial things, and as a matter of fact, I really come first in this house. My only joy—next to the table—is to lie nice and clean on the shelf and carry on a sensible chat with my companions. But—with the exception of the water pail, which occasionally goes down in the yard—we always live indoors. Our only news bringer is the market basket, but it talks so alarmingly about the government and the people. Yes, the other day an elderly pot was so upset by it all that it fell down and broke to bits! That's liberalism, I tell you!'

" 'Now you're talking too much!' said the tinderbox, and the steel struck the flint so the sparks flew. 'Weren't we going to have a cheerful evening?'

" 'Yes, let's talk about which of us is the most aristocratic!' said the matches.

" 'No, I don't enjoy talking about myself!' said the earthenware pot. 'Let's have an evening's *divertissement*. I'll begin. I'm going to tell about the sort of thing each one of us has experienced; you can enter into it so nicely, and that's such a delight. On the Baltic Sea, by the Danish beeches! . . .'

" 'That's a delightful beginning!' said all the plates. 'This is decidedly going to be the kind of story I like!'

" 'Well, there I spent my youth with a quiet family. The furniture was polished, the floors washed; clean curtains were put up every fourteen days!'

" 'My, what an interesting storyteller you are!' said the mop. 'You can tell right away that it's being told by a lady. Such cleanliness pervades!'

" 'Yes, you can feel it!' said the water pail, and then it gave a little hop for joy, so it went splash on the floor.

"And the pot went on with the story, and the end was just as good as the beginning.

"All the plates rattled with delight, and the mop took green parsley out of the sand bin and crowned the pot with it, for it knew this would irritate the others. 'And if I crown her today,' it said, 'then she'll crown me tomorrow!'

" 'Well, I want to dance,' said the fire tongs, and dance she did. Yes, heaven help us, how she could lift one leg up in the air! The old chair cover over in the corner split just from looking at it. 'May I be crowned too?' said the fire tongs, and then she was.

" 'All the same, they're only rabble!' thought the matches.

"Now the samovar was to sing, but it had a cold, it said—it couldn't unless it was boiling. But that was plain snobbishness; it wouldn't sing except when it was standing on the table in the room with the family.

"Over in the window sat an old quill pen, which the maid usually wrote with. There was nothing exceptional about it except that it had been dipped too far down in the inkwell. But because of this it now put on airs. 'If the samovar won't sing,' it said, 'then it needn't. Hanging outside in a cage is a nightingale. It can sing. To be sure, it hasn't been taught anything, but we won't malign it this evening!'

" 'I find it highly improper,' said the tea kettle, who was a kitchen singer and half sister to the samovar, 'that such an alien bird is to be heard! Is that patriotic? I'll let the market basket be the judge!'

" 'I'm simply vexed!' said the market basket. 'I'm as deeply vexed as anyone can imagine! Is this a fitting way to spend an evening? Wouldn't it be better to put the house to rights? Then everyone would find his place, and I'd run the whole caboodle! Then there'd be another song and dance!'

" 'Yes, let's raise a rumpus!' they all said. At the same moment the door opened. It was the maid, and so they stood still. There wasn't a peep out of anyone. But there wasn't a pot there that didn't know what it was capable of doing or how distinguished it was.

" 'Yes, if only I'd wanted to,' each thought, 'it really would have been a lively evening!'

"The maid took the matches and made a fire with them! Heavens, how they sputtered and burst into flames!

" 'Now,' they thought, 'everyone can see that we're the first! What a radiance we have! What a light!' And then they were burned out."

"That was a delightful story!" said the queen. "I felt just as if I were in the kitchen with the matches! Yes, now thou shalt have our daughter!"

"Certainly!" said the king. "Thou shalt have our daughter on Monday!" They said "thou" to him now that he was going to be one of the family.

And thus the wedding was decided; on the evening before, the entire city was illuminated. Buns and cakes were thrown out to be scrambled for. The street urchins stood on tiptoe, shouted "Hurrah!" and whistled through their fingers.

It was truly magnificent.

"Well, I guess I'd better see about doing something too," thought the merchant's son, and then he bought rockets, torpedoes, and all the fireworks you can imagine, put them in his trunk, and flew up in the air with them.

SWOOOOOOOOSH! How they went off! And how they popped!

It made all the Turks hop in the air so their slippers flew about their ears. They'd never seen a vision like this before. Now they could tell that it was the God of the Turks himself who was going to marry the princess.

As soon as the merchant's son had come back down in the forest again with his trunk, he thought, "I'll just go into the city to find out how it looked!" And of course it was only reasonable that he wanted to do that.

My, how people were talking! Every last person he asked had seen it, in his own fashion, but they all thought it had been delightful!

"I saw the God of the Turks himself!" said one. "He had eyes like shining stars and a beard like frothy water!"

"He flew in a fiery robe!" said another. "The loveliest cherubs were peeking out from among the folds!"

Indeed, those were delightful things he heard, and on the following day he was to be married.

Now he went back to the forest to seat himself in the trunk—but where was it?

The trunk had burned up! A spark from the fireworks had remained and set it on fire, and the trunk was in

ashes. No longer could he fly, no longer could he come to his bride.

She stood all day on the roof and waited. She's waiting still while he's wandering about the world telling stories. But they're no longer as gay as the one he told about the matches.

The Rose Elf

❖   ❖   ❖

IN the middle of a garden there grew a rosebush. It was
quite full of roses, and in one of these, the most beautiful of them all, there dwelled an elf. He was so teeny-
weeny that no human eye could see him; behind each
petal of the rose he had a bedchamber. He was as well
shaped and delightful as any child could be, and he had
wings from his shoulders all the way down to his feet. Oh,
what a fragrance there was in his chamber, and how bright
and lovely were the walls! After all, they were the pale
red, delicate rose petals.

All day long he amused himself in the warm sunshine
flying from flower to flower, dancing on the wings of the
fluttering butterfly, and counting the number of steps he
had to take to run across all the highways and paths to be
found on a single linden leaf. He regarded what we call
the veins of the leaf as highways and paths, and indeed
they were endless roads to him. Before he had finished,
the sun had gone down, but then he had started so late.

It grew so cold; the dew was falling and the wind was
blowing. The best thing to do now was to go home! He
hurried as fast as he could, but the rose had closed and he
wasn't able to come in—not a single rose was open; the
poor little elf became so frightened, for he had never been
out at night before and had always slept so soundly behind
the sheltered rose petals. Oh, this would certainly be the
death of him!

At the other end of the garden, he knew, there was a bower of lovely honeysuckle. The flowers looked like big painted horns; he would climb into one of these and sleep until morning.

He flew there. Shhhh! Two people were inside: a hand-

some young man and the loveliest of maidens. They were sitting side by side, wishing that they would never be parted. They were so much in love with each other, much more than the best of children can love his father and mother.

"And yet we must part!" said the young man. "Your brother has it in for us, so he's sending me on an errand far away over the mountains and seas! Farewell, my sweet bride, for that is what you are to me!"

And then they kissed each other, and the young maiden

wept and gave him a rose. But before she handed it to him she pressed so firm and fervent a kiss upon it that the flower opened. Then the little elf flew inside and leaned his head against the delicate, fragrant walls. But he could hear very well that they were saying: "Farewell! Farewell!" And he could feel the rose being placed at the young man's breast. Oh, how his heart was pounding inside! The little elf couldn't fall asleep, it was pounding so!

The rose didn't remain at the young man's breast long. He took it off, and as he walked alone through the dark forest he kissed the flower so often and so fervently that the little elf came close to being crushed to death. He could feel through the petals how the young man's lips were burning, and the rose had opened as in the heat of the strongest noonday sun.

Now came another man, dark and angry. He was the lovely maiden's evil brother. He drew a big sharp knife, and as the other was kissing the rose the evil man stabbed him to death, cut off his head, and buried it with the body in the soft earth under a linden tree.

"Now he's gone and forgotten!" thought the evil brother. "He'll never come back again. He was going to take a long journey over mountains and seas. Then it's easy to lose one's life, and so he has! He won't be back, and my sister will never dare to ask me about him!"

Then with his foot he scattered withered leaves over the upturned earth and went back home in the dark night. But he didn't go alone as he thought—the little elf went with him. He was sitting in a withered, curled-up linden leaf that had fallen on the hair of the evil man as he was digging the grave. The hat had been placed over him now. It was so dark in there, and the elf was trembling with fright and rage at that odious deed.

The evil man came home at daybreak; he took off his hat and went into his sister's bedroom. There lay the lovely maiden, in the bloom of youth, dreaming about the one she loved so much, and who she now thought was going over mountains and through forests. And the evil brother leaned over her, laughing nastily as only a devil can laugh. Then the withered leaf fell out of his hair and onto the cover, but he didn't notice it and went out, to get a little sleep in the early-morning hours. But the elf popped out of the withered leaf, went into the sleeping girl's ear, told her—as if in a dream—about the horrible murder, described the spot to her where the brother had killed him and left his body, told about the blossoming linden tree close by, and said, "So that you do not think what I have told you is a dream, you will find a withered leaf on your bed." And this is what she found when she awoke.

Oh, how she cried salt tears now! And she dared not confide her grief in anyone. The window stood open all day; the little elf could easily have gone out into the garden to the roses and all the other flowers, but he didn't have the heart to leave the grief-stricken girl. In the window was standing a bush of monthly roses. He seated himself in one of the flowers and looked at the poor girl. Her brother came into the room many times, and he was merry and evil, but she dared not say a word about her broken heart.

As soon as it was night she slipped out of the house, went into the forest to the spot where the linden tree stood, swept the leaves away from the dirt, dug down in it, and found at once the one who had been killed. Oh, how she wept and prayed to the Lord to let her die soon.

She wanted to take the body home with her, but she wasn't able to do it. But then she picked up the pale head with the closed eyes, kissed the cold lips, and shook the dirt out of his beautiful hair.

"I want this!" she said, and after covering the dead body with dirt and leaves, she took home with her the head and a little twig of the jasmine that blossomed in the forest where he had been killed.

As soon as she was in her room, she fetched the biggest flowerpot she could find, and putting the dead man's head in it, she covered it with earth and then planted the twig of jasmine in the pot.

"Farewell! Farewell!" whispered the little elf. He could no longer bear to see so much grief, and so he flew out into the garden to his rose. But it had withered, and only a few pale petals were hanging to the green hip.

"Alas, how soon everything that is beautiful and good comes to an end!" sighed the elf. At last he found another rose. This became his dwelling, behind its delicate, fragrant petals he could stay.

Every morning he flew over to the window of the unfortunate girl, and she was always standing there crying by the flowerpot. The salt tears fell on the jasmine branch, and for every day that she grew paler and paler, the branch became fresher and greener; one shoot after the other grew out; little white buds turned into blossoms and she kissed them. But the evil brother scolded her and asked if she weren't being silly; he didn't like it, nor could he know whose eyes had been closed and whose red lips had turned to dust. And she rested her head against the flowerpot, and the little elf from the rose found her dozing there. Then he climbed into her ear and told her about the evening in the bower, about the fragrance of the roses, and the love of the elves. She had such a sweet dream, and as she was dreaming her life faded away. She had died a peaceful death; she was in heaven with the one she loved.

And the jasmine blossoms opened their big white bells and shed a strange fragrance; this was their only way of weeping for the dead.

But the evil brother looked at the beautiful flowering tree and took it for himself as an inheritance. He put it in

his room next to his bed, for it was so lovely to look at and
the fragrance was so sweet and delicious. The little rose elf
went along too, flying from blossom to blossom. In each
one dwelled a tiny soul, and he told them all about the
murdered young man, whose head had now turned to
dust, and about the evil brother and the unfortunate sister.

"We know it," said all the souls in the blossoms. "We
know it! Haven't we sprung forth from the dead man's
eyes and lips? We know it! We know it!" And they nodded
their heads in such a curious fashion.

The rose elf couldn't understand how they could remain
so calm, and he flew out to the bees, who were gathering
honey, and told them the story about the evil brother.
And the bees told their queen, who ordered them all to
kill the murderer the next morning.

But that night—it was the first night after the sister's
death—as the brother was sleeping in his bed next to the
fragrant jasmine tree, each flower opened its cup; and
invisible, but with a poisonous spear, each flower soul
climbed out. First they sat by his ear and told him bad
dreams, and then they flew over his lips and stuck his
tongue with the poisonous spears. "Now we have avenged
the dead!" they said, and returned to the jasmine's white
bells.

In the morning, when the window to the bedroom was
suddenly thrown open, the rose elf and the queen bee
with the whole swarm of bees flew in to kill him.

But he was already dead. People were standing around
the bed, and they said, "The jasmine odor has killed him!"

Then the rose elf understood the revenge of the flowers.
And he told the queen bee, and she and the whole swarm
flew buzzing around the flowerpot. The bees were not to
be ousted. Then a man took the flowerpot away, but one
of the bees stung him on the hand, making him drop the
pot, and it broke.

Then they saw the white skull and knew that the dead man in the bed was a murderer.

And the queen bee buzzed in the air and sang about the revenge of the flowers and about the rose elf, and that behind each tiny petal there dwells one who knows how to reveal and to avenge evil.

The Evil Prince
(A Legend)

❖　❖　❖

THERE was once an evil and overbearing prince whose
only thought was to conquer all the lands of the world
and strike terror with his name; he fared forth with fire
and sword; his soldiers trampled down the grain in the
field; they set fire to the farmer's house and saw the red
flame lick the leaves from the trees and the fruit hang
scorched on the black, charred branches. Many a poor
mother hid with her naked, nursing babe behind the
smoking wall, and the soldiers hunted for her; and if they
found her and the child, their fiendish pleasures began.
Evil spirits could not have behaved worse; but the prince
thought that this was just as it should be. Day by day his
power grew; his name was feared by everyone and success
followed him in all his deeds. From the conquered cities
he took gold and great treasures. In his royal residence
were amassed riches, the like of which was nowhere to be
found. Now he had erected magnificent castles, churches,
and arches, and everyone who saw these splendors said,
"What a great prince!" They did not think of the misery he
had brought upon other lands; they did not hear the sighs
and the wails that went up from the scorched cities.

The prince looked at his gold, looked at his magnificent
buildings, and thought, as the mob, "What a great prince!
But I must have more! Much more! No power must be

mentioned as equal to mine, much less greater!" And he went to war against all his neighbors and conquered them all. He had the vanquished kings fettered to his carriage with golden chains as he drove through the streets, and when he sat down at the table, they had to lie at his feet and at the feet of his courtiers and take the pieces of bread that were thrown to them.

Now the prince had his statue erected in the squares and in the royal palace. Yes, he even wanted it to stand in the churches before the altar of the Lord. But the priests said, "Prince, you are mighty, but God is mightier. We dare not do it."

"Well," said the evil prince, "then I am going to conquer God too!" And with overweening pride and folly in his heart, he had a remarkable ship built that he could fly through the air with. It was as brightly colored as the tail of a peacock and appeared to be encrusted with a thousand eyes. But each eye was the barrel of a gun. The prince sat in the middle of the ship; he had only to push a spring and a thousand bullets flew out, and the guns were again loaded as before. A hundred strong eagles were attached to the front of the ship, and in this fashion he flew up toward the sun. The earth lay far below; at first, with its mountains and forests, it resembled a plowed-up field where the green peeps forth from the overturned turf. Then it looked like a flat map, and soon it was quite hidden in fog and clouds. Higher and higher flew the eagles. Then God dispatched a single one of his myriads of angels, and the evil prince let fly a thousand bullets at him. But the bullets fell off the angel's shining wings like hail. A drop of blood—only a single one—dripped from the wing feather, and this drop fell on the ship in which the prince was sitting. It burned itself fast; it was as heavy as a thousand hundredweights of lead and swept the ship down toward the earth at breakneck speed. The strong wings of the eagles were broken, the wind rushed around

the prince's head, and the clouds that were all around—
after all, they were from the burned cities—took on threatening shapes, like mile-long crayfish that stretched out
their strong claws after him, like rolling boulders or fire-
spouting dragons. Half dead, he lay in the ship, which was
caught at last among the thick branches of the forest.

"I will vanquish God!" he said. "I have sworn it; my will
shall be done!" And for seven years he had remarkable
ships constructed that would fly through the air. He had
thunderbolts forged from the hardest steel, because he
wanted to blow up the fortress of heaven. From all his
lands he gathered a great army, which covered a radius of
several miles when the men stood lined up. They climbed
into the remarkable ships. The prince himself was approaching his when God sent out a swarm of mosquitoes, a

little swarm of mosquitoes. They buzzed around the prince
and bit him on the face and hands. In a rage he drew his
sword, but struck out at the empty air. He couldn't touch
the mosquitoes. Then he ordered costly carpets to be
brought. They were to be wrapped around him—no mosquito could penetrate them with its sting—and this was
done as he ordered. But a single mosquito was sitting on
the innermost carpet. It crawled into the prince's ear and
bit him there. It seared like fire; the poison surged up to
his brain. He tore himself loose, yanked off the carpets,
ripped his clothes to shreds, and danced naked in front of
the brutal, barbarous soldiers that were now mocking the
mad prince, who wanted to pester God and was vanquished by a single little mosquito.

The Swineherd

THERE was once a poor prince. He had a kingdom that was quite small, but then it was big enough to get married on, and marry he would.

Now it was, of course, a bit presumptuous of him to dare to say to the emperor's daughter: "Will you have me?" But that he dared, all right, for his name was known far and wide, and there were hundreds of princesses who would have been glad to have him. But see if she was!

Now we shall hear.

On the grave of the prince's father there grew a rosebush. Oh, such a lovely rosebush! It bore flowers every fifth year, and then only a single rose. But it was a rose that smelled so sweet that by smelling it one forgot all one's cares and woes. And then he had a nightingale that could sing as though all the lovely melodies in the world were in its little throat. That rose and that nightingale the princess was to have, and so they were put into two big silver cases and sent to her.

The emperor had them brought in before him to the great hall, where the princess was playing "Visitors" with her ladies-in-waiting—they had nothing else to do—and when she saw the big cases with the presents inside, she clapped her hands for joy.

"If only it were a little pussycat!" she said—but then out came the lovely rose.

"My, how nicely it has been made!" said all the ladies-in-waiting.

"It is more than nice," said the emperor, "it is beautiful!"

But the princess touched it, and then she was on the verge of tears.

"Fie, Papa!" she said. "It's not artificial! It's real."

"Fie!" said all the ladies-in-waiting. "It's real!"

"Now, let us first see what is in the other case before we lose our tempers," thought the emperor, and then the nightingale came out. It sang so sweetly that to begin with no one could find fault with it.

"*Superbe! Charmante!*" said the ladies-in-waiting, for they all spoke French, each one worse than the other.

"How that bird reminds me of the late-lamented empress' music box," said one old courtier. "Ahhh yes, it is quite the same tune, the same rendering."

"Yes," said the emperor, and then he cried like a little baby.

"I should hardly like to think that it's real," said the princess.

"Why, yes, it is a real bird," said the people who had brought it.

"Well, then, let that bird go!" said the princess, and she would in no way permit the prince to come.

But he didn't lose heart. He stained his face brown and black, and pulling his cap down over his eyes, he knocked at the door.

"Good morning, Emperor!" he said. "Can't you take me into your service here at the palace?"

"Well, there are so many who apply here," said the emperor. "But—let me see—I need someone to keep the pigs, for we have a lot of them."

And so the prince was hired as the imperial swineherd. He was given a wretched little room down by the pigsty, and there he had to stay. But the whole day he sat working, and by the time it was evening he had made a pretty little pot. Around it were bells, and as soon as the pot boiled they started ringing delightfully and played an old tune:

> *Ach, du lieber Augustin,*
> *Alles ist weg! Weg! Weg!*[1]

But the most curious thing of all, however, was that anyone holding his finger in the steam from the pot could smell at once what food was cooking on every stove in the town, so that was certainly a far cry from a rose.

Now the princess came walking along with all her ladies-in-waiting, and when she heard the tune, she stood still and looked very pleased, for she could also play "Ach, du lieber Augustin." It was the only tune she knew, and she played it with one finger.

"Why, that's the tune I can play!" she said. "This must be a cultivated swineherd! Listen! Go in and ask him what that instrument costs."

And then one of the ladies-in-waiting had to run in, but she put on wooden shoes.

"What will you have for that pot?" said the lady-in-waiting.

"I want ten kisses from the princess," said the swineherd.

"Heaven help us!" said the lady-in-waiting.

"Well, it can't be less," said the swineherd.

"Now! What does he say?" asked the princess.

"That I really can't tell you!" said the lady-in-waiting. "It is too horrible!"

"Then you can whisper!" And so she whispered.

"Why, how rude he is!" said the princess, and left at once. But when she had gone a little way, the bells tinkled so prettily:

[1] Ah, dear Augustine,
All is over and done! Done! Done!

Ach, du lieber Augustin,
Alles ist weg! Weg! Weg!

"Listen," said the princess. "Ask him if he will take ten kisses from my ladies-in-waiting."

"No, thanks!" said the swineherd. "Ten kisses from the princess, or else I keep the pot."

"How really vexatious!" said the princess. "But then you must stand around me so that no one sees it."

And the ladies-in-waiting lined up in front of her and spread out their skirts, and then the swineherd got the ten kisses and she got the pot.

Oh, what fun they had! All that evening and the next day the pot had to boil. They knew what was cooking on every stove in the whole town, whether at the chamberlain's or at the shoemaker's. The ladies-in-waiting danced and clapped their hands.

"We know who's going to have fruit soup and pancakes! We know who's going to have porridge and meatballs! Oh, how interesting!"

"Extremely interesting," said the mistress of the robes.

"Yes, but keep it a secret, for I am the emperor's daughter!"

"Heaven help us!" they all said.

The swineherd—that is to say, the prince, but they didn't know, of course, that he was anything but a real swineherd—didn't let the next day pass before he had made something else, and this time he made a rattle. Whenever anyone swung it around, it played all the waltzes and quadrilles and polkas that were known since the creation of the world.

"But that is *superbe!*" said the princess as she went by. "I have never heard a lovelier composition! Listen, go in and ask what that instrument costs. But no kissing!"

"He wants a hundred kisses from the princess!" said the lady-in-waiting who had been inside to ask.

"I do believe he's mad!" said the princess. And then she left. But after she had gone a little way, she stopped. "One should encourage the arts!" she said. "I *am* the emperor's daughter. Tell him he shall get ten kisses just like yesterday. The rest he can take from my ladies-in-waiting."

"Yes, but not unless we have to!" said the ladies-in-waiting.

"That's just talk!" said the princess. "If I can kiss him, then you can too! Remember, I give you board and wages!" And then the lady-in-waiting had to go in to him again.

"One hundred kisses from the princess," he said, "or else each keeps what he has!"

"Stand in front!" she said. So all the ladies-in-waiting lined up in front of her, and then he started kissing.

"What can all that commotion be down by the pigsty?" said the emperor, who had stepped out onto the balcony. He rubbed his eyes and put on his glasses. "Why, it's the ladies-in-waiting! They're up to something. I certainly must go down to them!" And then he pulled his slippers up in back, for they were shoes that he had worn down at the heel.

My, how he hurried!

As soon as he came down into the courtyard he walked quite softly, and the ladies-in-waiting were so busy counting the kisses to make sure there was fair play—so he shouldn't get too many, but not too few, either—that they didn't notice the emperor at all. He stood up on tiptoe.

"What on earth!" he said when he saw them kissing, and then he hit them on the head with his slipper just as the swineherd got the eighty-sixth kiss. "*Heraus!*"[2] said the emperor, for he was furious, and both the swineherd and the princess were put out of his empire.

There she stood now and cried, the swineherd swore, and the rain poured down.

[2] "Get out!"

"Ohhhh, what a miserable soul I am," said the princess. "If only I'd taken that lovely prince! Ohhhh, how unhappy I am!"

And the swineherd went behind a tree, wiped away the brown and black from his face, threw away the ugly clothes, and stepped forth in his prince's clothing, looking so handsome that the princess had to curtsy to him.

"I have come to despise you," he said. "You wouldn't have an honest prince! You didn't understand about the rose and the nightingale, but you could kiss the swineherd for a mechanical music box! Now it serves you right!"

And then he went into his kingdom and closed and bolted the door, so she really could stand outside and sing:

"*Ach, du lieber Augustin,*
Alles ist weg! Weg! Weg!"

The Nightingale

❖ ❖ ❖

IN China, you know of course, the emperor is Chinese, and everyone he has around him is Chinese too. Now this happened many years ago, but that is just why the story is worth hearing, before it is forgotten. The emperor's palace was the most magnificent in the world. It was made entirely of fine porcelain, so precious and so fragile and delicate that one really had to watch one's step. In the garden the most unusual flowers were to be seen, and the most beautiful had fastened to them silver bells that tinkled so that no one would go past without noticing them. Yes, everything had been very well thought out in the emperor's garden, and it stretched so far that even the gardener didn't know where it stopped. If one kept on walking, one came to the loveliest forest with great trees and deep lakes. The forest stretched all the way down to the sea, which was blue and so deep that great ships could sail right in under the branches. And in these branches lived a nightingale that sang so sweetly that even the poor fisherman, who had so many other things to keep him busy, lay still and listened when he was out at night pulling in his net.

"Good heavens! How beautiful!" he said. But then he had to look after his net and forgot the bird, although the next night, when it sang again and the fisherman came out there, he said the same thing: "Good heavens! How beautiful!"

From every land in the world travelers came to the emperor's city. They admired the city, the palace, and the garden. But when they heard the nightingale, they all said: "But this is really the best thing of all!" And the travelers told about it when they got home, and scholars wrote many books about the city, the palace, and the garden. But they didn't forget the nightingale—it was given the highest place of all. And those who were poets wrote the loveliest poems, each one about the nightingale in the forest by the sea.

These books went around the world, and once some of them came to the emperor. He sat in his golden chair, reading and reading and nodding his head, for he was pleased by the lovely descriptions of the city, the palace, and the garden. "But the nightingale is really the best thing of all"—there it stood in print.

"What's that?" said the emperor. "The nightingale? Why, I don't know anything about it! Is there such a bird in my empire, in my very own garden? I have never heard of it before! Fancy having to find this out from a book!"

And then he summoned his chamberlain, who was so grand that if anyone of lower rank dared speak to him or ask about something, he would only say: "P!" And that doesn't mean anything at all.

"There is supposed to be a highly remarkable bird here called a nightingale!" said the emperor. "They say it's the very best thing of all in my great kingdom! Why hasn't anyone ever told me about it?"

"I have never heard it mentioned before!" said the chamberlain. "It has never been presented at court!"

"I want it to come here this evening and sing for me," said the emperor. "The whole world knows what I have, and I don't!"

"I have never heard it mentioned before!" said the chamberlain. "I shall look for it! I shall find it!"

But where was it to be found? The chamberlain ran up and down all the stairs, through great halls and corridors. But no one he met had ever heard of the nightingale, and the chamberlain ran back again to the emperor and said it was probably a fable made up by the people who write books. "Your Imperial Majesty shouldn't believe what is written in them. They are inventions and belong to something called black magic!"

"But the book in which I read it was sent to me by the mighty emperor of Japan, so it cannot be false. I will hear the nightingale! It shall be here this evening! I bestow my highest patronage upon it! And if it doesn't come, I'll have the whole court thumped on their stomachs after they have eaten supper!"

"Tsing-pe!" said the chamberlain, and again ran up and down all the stairs and through all the great halls and corridors. And half the court ran with him, for they weren't at all willing to be thumped on their stomachs. They asked and asked about the remarkable nightingale that was known to the whole world but not to the court.

Finally they met a little peasant girl in the kitchen. She said, "The nightingale? Heavens! I know it well. Yes, how it can sing! Every evening I'm permitted to take a few scraps from the table home to my poor sick mother—she lives down by the shore. And on my way back, when I'm tired and stop to rest in the forest, I can hear the nightingale sing. It brings tears to my eyes. It's just as though my mother were kissing me."

"Little kitchen maid!" said the chamberlain. "You shall have a permanent position in the kitchen and permission to stand and watch the emperor eating if you can lead us to the nightingale. It has been summoned to appear at court this evening."

And so they all set out for the part of the forest where

the nightingale usually sang. Half the court went with them. As they were walking along at a fast pace a cow started mooing.

"Oh!" said a courtier. "There it is! Indeed, what remarkable force for so tiny an animal. I am certain I have heard it before."

"No, that's the cow mooing," said the little kitchen maid. "We're still quite a long way from the spot."

Now the frogs started croaking in the marsh.

"Lovely," said the Chinese imperial chaplain. "Now I can hear her. It's just like tiny church bells."

"No, that's the frogs!" said the little kitchen maid. "But now I think we'll soon hear it."

Then the nightingale started to sing.

"That's it!" said the little girl. "Listen! Listen! There it sits!" And then she pointed to a little gray bird up in the branches.

"Is it possible?" said the chamberlain. "I had never imagined it like this. How ordinary it looks! No doubt seeing so many fine people has made it lose its *couleur!*"

"Little nightingale," shouted the little kitchen maid quite loud, "our gracious emperor would so like you to sing for him!"

"With the greatest pleasure," said the nightingale, and sang in a way to warm one's heart.

"It is just like glass bells!" said the chamberlain. "And look at that tiny throat. How it vibrates! It's remarkable that we have never heard it before. It will be a great success at court."

"Shall I sing for the emperor again?" said the nightingale, who thought the emperor was there.

"My enchanting little nightingale," said the chamberlain, "it gives me the greatest pleasure to command you to appear at a court celebration this evening, where you will delight his High Imperial Eminence with your *charmante* song!"

"It sounds best out of doors," said the nightingale, but it followed them gladly when it heard it was the emperor's wish.

The palace had been properly polished up. Walls and floors, which were of porcelain, glowed from the lights of thousands of golden lamps. The loveliest flowers, which really could tinkle, had been lined up in the halls. There was such a running back and forth that it caused a draft that made all the bells tinkle so one couldn't hear oneself think.

In the middle of the great hall, where the emperor sat, a golden perch had been placed for the nightingale to sit on. The whole court was there, and the little kitchen maid had been given permission to stand behind the door, for now she really did have the title of kitchen maid. Everyone was wearing his most splendid attire. They all looked at the little gray bird, to which the emperor was nodding.

And the nightingale sang so sweetly that tears came to the emperor's eyes and rolled down his cheeks. And then the nightingale sang even more sweetly. It went straight to one's heart. And the emperor was so pleased that he said the nightingale was to have his golden slipper to wear around its neck. But the nightingale said no, thank you—it had been rewarded enough.

"I have seen tears in the emperor's eyes. To me, that is the richest treasure. An emperor's tears have a wondrous power. Heaven knows I have been rewarded enough!" And then it sang again with its sweet and blessed voice.

"That is the most adorable *coquetterie* I know of," said the ladies standing around. And then they put water in their mouths so they could gurgle whenever anyone spoke to them, for now they thought that they were nightingales too. Yes, even the lackeys and chambermaids let it be known that they were also satisfied, and that was saying a lot, for they are the hardest to please. Yes indeed, the nightingale had really been a success.

Now it was to remain at court and have its own cage as well as freedom to take a walk outside twice during the day and once at night. It was given twelve servants, too, each one holding tightly to a silken ribbon fastened to its leg. That kind of walk was no pleasure at all.

The whole city talked about the remarkable bird, and whenever two people met, the first merely said "Night!" and the other said "Gale!" And then they sighed and understood each other! Yes, eleven shopkeepers' children were named after it, but not one of them could ever sing a note in his life!

One day a big package came for the emperor. On the outside was written "Nightingale."

"Here's a new book about our famous bird," said the emperor. But it was no book, it was a little work of art in a case: an artificial nightingale made to resemble the real one, except that it was encrusted with diamonds and rubies and sapphires! As soon as the artificial bird was wound up it could sing one of the melodies the real one sang, and then its tail bobbed up and down, glittering with gold and silver. Around its neck hung a ribbon, and on it was written: "The emperor of Japan's nightingale is poor compared to the emperor of China's."

"How lovely!" said everyone. And the person who had brought the artificial nightingale immediately had the title of chief-imperial-nightingale-bringer bestowed upon him.

"Now they must sing together! What a duet that will be!"

And then they had to sing together, but it didn't really come off because the real nightingale sang in its own way and the artificial bird worked mechanically.

"It is not to blame," said the music master. "It keeps time perfectly and according to the rules of my own system!" Then the artificial bird had to sing alone. It was as much of a success as the real one, and besides, it was so much more beautiful to look at: it glittered like bracelets and brooches.

Thirty-three times it sang one and the same melody, and still it wasn't tired. People were only too willing to hear it from the beginning again, but the emperor thought that now the living nightingale should also sing a little. But where was it? No one had noticed it fly out of the open window, away to its green forest.

"But what kind of behavior is that?" said the emperor. And all the courtiers berated it and said the nightingale was a most ungrateful bird.

"We still have the best bird," they said, and again the artificial bird had to sing. And it was the thirty-fourth time they had heard the same tune, but they didn't know it all the way through yet, for it was so hard. And the music master praised the bird very highly—yes, even assured them that it was better than the real nightingale, not only as far as its clothes and the many diamonds were concerned, but internally as well.

"You see, my lords and ladies, and your Imperial Majesty above all! You can never figure out what the real nightingale will sing, but with the artificial bird everything has already been decided. This is the way it will be, and not otherwise. It can be accounted for; it can be opened up to reveal the human logic that has gone into the arrangement of the works, how they operate and how they turn one after the other!"

"Those are my thoughts precisely!" they all said. And on the following Sunday the music master was allowed to show the bird to the people. They were also going to hear it sing, said the emperor. And they heard it and were as happy as if they had all drunk themselves merry on tea, for that is so very Chinese. And then they all said "Oh" and held their index fingers high in the air and nodded. But the poor fisherman, who had heard the real nightingale, said: "It sounds pretty enough, and it is similar too. But something is missing. I don't know what it is."

The real nightingale was banished from the land.

The artificial bird had its place on a silken pillow close to the emperor's bed. All the gifts it had received, gold and precious stones, lay around it, and its title had risen to high-imperial-bedside-table-singer. It ranked Number One on the left, for the emperor considered the side where the heart lies to be the most important. And the heart of an emperor is on the left side too. The music master wrote a treatise in twenty-five volumes about the artificial bird. It was very learned and very long and contained the biggest Chinese words, and all the people said they had read and understood it, for otherwise they would have been considered stupid and would have been thumped on their stomachs.

It went on like this for a whole year. The emperor, the

court, and all the other Chinese knew every little "cluck" in the song of the artificial bird by heart. But this is why they prized it so highly now: they could sing along with it themselves, and this they did! The street boys sang "Zizizi! Cluck-cluck-cluck!" And the emperor sang it too. Yes, it was certainly lovely.

But one evening, as the artificial bird was singing away and the emperor was lying in bed listening to it, something went "Pop!" inside the bird. "Whirrrrrrrrrrr!" All the wheels went around, and then the music stopped.

The emperor sprang out of bed and had his personal physician summoned. But what good was he? Then they summoned the watchmaker, and after much talk and many examinations of the bird he put it more or less in order again. But he said it must be used as sparingly as possible. The cogs were so worn down that it wasn't possible to put in new ones in a way that would be sure to make music. What a great affliction this was! Only once a year did they dare let the artificial bird sing, and even that was hard on it. But then the music master made a little speech, with big words, and said it was just as good as new, and then it *was* just as good as new.

Five years passed, and then a great sorrow fell upon the land. They were all fond of their emperor, but now he was sick and it was said he could not live. A new emperor had already been picked out, and people stood out in the street and asked the chamberlain how their emperor was.

"P!" he said, and shook his head.

Cold and pale, the emperor lay in his great magnificent bed. The whole court thought he was dead, and they all ran off to greet the new emperor. The lackeys ran out to talk about it, and the chambermaids had a big tea party. Cloths had been put down in all the halls and corridors to deaden the sound of footsteps. And now it was so quiet, so quiet. But the emperor was not yet dead. Stiff and pale, he lay in the magnificent bed with the long velvet curtains and the heavy gold tassels. High above him a window stood open, and the moon shone in on the emperor and the artificial bird.

The poor emperor could hardly breathe. It was as though something heavy were sitting on his chest. He opened his eyes and then he saw that Death was sitting on his chest. He had put on his golden crown and was holding the emperor's golden sword in one hand and his magnificent banner in the other. All around from the folds of the velvet curtains strange faces were peering out. Some were quite hideous, others so kindly and mild. These were all the emperor's good and wicked deeds that were looking at him now that Death was sitting on his heart.

"Do you remember that?" whispered one after the other. "Do you remember that?" And then they told him so much that the sweat stood out on his forehead.

"I never knew that!" said the emperor. "Music! Music! The big Chinese drum!" he shouted. "So I don't have to hear all the things they're saying!"

But they kept it up, and Death nodded, just the way the Chinese do, at everything that was being said.

"Music! Music!" shrieked the emperor. "Blessed little golden bird, sing now! Sing! I've given you gold and costly presents. I myself hung my golden slipper around your neck. Sing now! Sing!"

But the bird kept silent. There was no one to wind it up, so it didn't sing. But Death kept on looking at the emperor out of his big empty sockets, and it was so quiet, so terribly quiet.

Suddenly the loveliest song could be heard close to the window. It was the little real nightingale sitting on the branch outside. It had heard of the emperor's need and had come to sing him comfort and hope. And as it sang the face became paler and paler, and the blood started flowing faster and faster in the emperor's weak body, and Death himself listened and said, "Keep on, little nightingale, keep on!"

"If you will give me the magnificent golden sword! If you will give me the rich banner! If you will give me the emperor's crown!"

And Death gave each treasure for a song, and the nightingale kept on singing. And it sang about the quiet churchyard where the white roses grow and the scent of the elder tree perfumes the air and where the fresh grass is watered by the tears of the bereaved. Then Death was filled with longing for his garden and drifted like a cold, white mist out of the window.

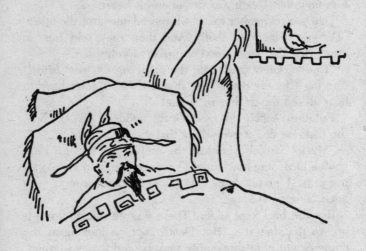

"Thank you, thank you!" said the emperor. "Heavenly little bird, I know you, all right. I have driven you out of my land and empire, and still you have sung the bad visions away from my bed and removed Death from my heart! How can I reward you?"

"You have already rewarded me!" said the nightingale. "You gave me the tears from your eyes the first time I sang. I will never forget that. Those are the jewels that do a singer's heart good. But sleep now, and get well and strong. I shall sing for you."

And it sang, and the emperor fell into a sweet sleep, which was calm and beneficial.

The sun was shining in on him through the windows when he awoke, refreshed and healthy. None of his servants had returned yet, for they thought he was dead, but the nightingale still sat there and sang.

"You must always stay with me," said the emperor. "You shall sing only when you yourself want to, and I shall break the artificial bird into a thousand bits!"

"Don't do that!" said the nightingale. "Why, it has done what good it could. Keep it as before. I cannot build my nest and live at the palace, but let me come whenever I want to. Then in the evening I will sit on the branch here by the window and sing for you. I shall sing about those who are happy and those who suffer. I shall sing of good and evil, which is kept hidden from you. The little songbird flies far, to the poor fisherman, to the farmer's roof, to everyone who is far from you and your court. I love your heart more than your crown, and yet your crown has an odor of sanctity about it. I will come. I will sing for you. But you must promise me one thing!"

"Everything!" said the emperor, standing there in his imperial robe, which he himself had put on, and holding the heavy golden sword up to his heart.

"One thing I beg of you. Tell no one that you have a little bird that tells you everything! Then things will go even better!"

And then the nightingale flew away.

The servants came in to have a look at their dead emperor. Yes, there they stood, and the emperor said, "Good morning!"

The Sweethearts
(The Top and the Ball)

❖ ❖ ❖

THE top and the ball were lying in a drawer together among other playthings, and so the top said to the ball, "Shouldn't we be sweethearts, as long as we're lying in a drawer together?"

But the ball, who had been sewn of morocco leather and who put on just as many airs as a fashionable young lady, would not reply to such a thing.

The next day the little boy who owned the playthings came. He painted over the top red and gold, and ham-

132

mered a brass nail right in the middle. It was a magnificent sight when the top spun around.

"Look at me!" he said to the ball. "What do you say now? Shouldn't we be sweethearts? We go so well together. You spring and I dance! Happier than we no two could ever be!"

"So that's what you think!" said the ball. "I daresay you're unaware that my father and mother have been morocco leather slippers and that I have a cork inside!"

"Yes, but I am made of mahogany wood!" said the top. "And the bailiff himself has turned me out! He has his own lathe, and it afforded him great pleasure!"

"Indeed! Can I rely on that?" said the ball.

"May I never be whipped again if I'm lying!" said the top.

"You speak up quite well for yourself," said the ball, "but I can't, all the same. I'm as good as half engaged to a swallow. Every time I go up in the air he sticks his head out of the nest and says, 'Will you? Will you?' And now I've said yes to myself, and that's as good as being half engaged. But I promise I shall never forget you!"

"Well, that'll be a great help!" said the top, and then they stopped speaking to each other.

The next day the ball was taken out. The top saw how she flew high up in the air, just like a bird. At last she couldn't be seen at all. She came back again every time, but she always made a high jump when she touched the ground. And this came either from longing or because she had a cork inside. The ninth time the ball disappeared and didn't come back again. The boy searched and searched, but gone she was.

"I know where she is, all right," sighed the top. "She's in the swallow's nest and is married to the swallow!"

Indeed, the more the top thought about it, the more infatuated he became with the ball. Just because he couldn't have her, love began. And the queer thing about it was the fact that she had taken another! And the top danced and spun around, but he was always thinking of the ball, who, in his imagination, grew lovelier and lovelier. Thus many years passed—and then it was an old love affair.

And the top was no longer young! But one day he was gilded over. Never had he looked so lovely! Now he was a golden top, and he whirled until he hummed. Indeed, that was something! But all at once he whirled too high, and gone he was!

They searched and searched, even down in the cellar, but still he was nowhere to be found.

Where was he?

He had hopped up into the trash can, where all kinds of things were lying: cabbage stalks, sweepings, and rubble that had fallen down from the drainpipe.

"A fine place for me to be lying in, I must say! The gilding will soon come off. And what sort of rabble have I come among?" And then it stole a look at a long cabbage stalk that had come much too close and at a strange round thing that looked like an old apple. But it wasn't an apple. It was an old ball that had been lying in the drainpipe for many years, and through which the water had been oozing.

"Heaven be praised! Here comes one of my own kind that I can talk to!" said the ball, and regarded the gilded top. "I'm really of morocco leather, sewn by the hands of a maiden, and I have a cork inside! But no one can tell that by looking at me! I was just going to marry a swallow when I fell in the drainpipe, and there I've been lying for five years oozing water. For a maiden that's a long time, believe me!"

But the top didn't say a thing! He was thinking of his old sweetheart. And indeed, the more he listened, the more certain he became that this was she.

Then the serving girl came to empty the trash can. "Hey, now! There's the gold top!" she said.

And the top came back in the house, to high esteem and

honor. But no one heard anything about the ball, and the top never spoke about his old sweetheart again. That goes over when the sweetheart has been lying in a drainpipe oozing water for five years. Indeed, you never recognize her again if you meet her in the trash can!

The Ugly Duckling

❖ ❖ ❖

I T was so lovely out in the country—it was summer. The wheat stood golden, the oats green. The hay had been piled in stacks down in the green meadows, and there the stork went about on his long red legs and spoke Egyptian, for that is the language he had learned from his mother. Around the fields and meadows were great forests, and in the midst of the forests were deep lakes. Yes, it really was lovely out there in the country.

Squarely in the sunshine stood an old manor house with a deep moat all around it, and from the walls down to the water grew huge dock leaves that were so high that little children could stand upright under the biggest. It was as dense in there as in the deepest forest, and here sat a duck on her nest. She was about to hatch out her little ducklings, but now she had just about had enough of it because it was taking so long and she seldom had a visitor. The other ducks were fonder of swimming about in the moat than of running up and sitting under a dock leaf to chatter with her.

Finally one egg after the other started cracking.

"Cheep! Cheep!" they said. All the egg yolks had come to life and stuck out their heads.

"Quack! Quack!" she said, and then they quacked as hard as they could and peered about on all sides under the green leaves. And their mother let them look about as much as they liked, for green is good for the eyes.

"My, how big the world is!" said all the youngsters, for now, of course, they had far more room than when they were inside the eggs.

"Do you think this is the whole world?" said the mother. "It stretches all the way to the other side of the garden, right into the parson's meadow. But I've never been there! Well, you're all here now, aren't you?" And then she got up. "No, I don't have them all! The biggest egg is still there. How long will it take? Now I'll soon get tired of it!" And then she settled down again.

"Well, how's it going?" said an old duck who had come to pay her a visit.

"One egg is taking so long!" said the duck who was hatching. "It won't crack! But now you shall see the others. They're the prettiest ducklings I've seen. They all look just like their father, the wretch! He doesn't even come to visit me."

"Let me see that egg that won't crack!" said the old duck. "You can be certain it's a turkey egg! I was fooled like that myself once. And I had my sorrows and troubles with those youngsters, for they're afraid of the water, I can tell you! I couldn't get them out in it! I quacked and I snapped, but it didn't help! Let me have a look at that egg! Yes, it's a turkey egg, all right. You just let it lie there and teach the other children how to swim."

"Oh, I still want to sit on it a little longer," said the duck. "I've been sitting on it for so long that I can just as well wait a little longer!"

"Suit yourself!" said the old duck, and then she left.

Finally the big egg cracked. "Cheep! Cheep!" said the youngster, and tumbled out. He was very big and ugly. The duck looked at him.

"Now, that's a terribly big duckling!" she said. "None of the others looks like that! Could he be a turkey chick after all? Well, we'll soon find out. Into the water he'll go if I have to kick him out into it myself!"

The next day the weather was perfect. The sun shone on all the green dock leaves. The mother duck came down to the moat with her whole family. Splash! She jumped into the water. "Quack! Quack!" she said, and one duckling after the other plumped in. The water washed over their heads, but they came up again at once and floated splendidly. Their feet moved of themselves, and they were all out in the water. Even the ugly gray youngster was swimming too.

"That's no turkey," she said. "See how splendidly he uses his legs, how straight he holds himself. That's my own child! As a matter of fact, he is quite handsome when one looks at him in the right way. Quack! Quack! Now come with me, and I'll take you out in the world and present you to the duck yard. But always keep close to me so that no one steps on you. And keep an eye out for the cat!"

And then they came to the duck yard. There was a terrible commotion, for two families were fighting over an eel's head, and then the cat got it, of course.

"See, that's the way it goes in this world," said the mother duck, and smacked her bill, for she would have liked to have had the eel's head herself. "Now use your legs," she said. "See if you can't step lively and bow your necks to that old duck over there. She's the most aristocratic of anyone here: she has Spanish blood in her veins. That's why she's so fat. And see? She has a red rag around her leg. That is something very special and is the highest honor any duck can receive. It means that no one wants to get rid of her and that she is to be recognized by animals and men! Be quick! Out with your toes! A well-brought-up duck places his feet wide apart, just like his father and mother. Now, then! Bow your necks and say 'Quack!' "

This they did, but the other ducks all around looked at

them and said quite loudly, "Look there! Now we're to
have one more batch, as if there weren't enough of us
already! And fie, how that duckling looks! We won't put
up with him!" And at once a duck flew over and bit him in
the neck.

"Leave him alone!" said the mother. "He's not bothering anyone."

"Yes, but he's too big and queer!" said the duck who
had bitten him. "So he has to be pushed around."

"Those are pretty children the mother has," said the old
duck with the rag around her leg. "They're all pretty
except that one; he didn't turn out right. I do wish she
could make him over again."

"That can't be, your grace," said the mother duck.
"He's not pretty, but he has an exceedingly good disposition, and he swims as well as any of the others; yes, I
might venture to say a bit better. I do believe he'll grow
prettier or in time a little smaller. He's lain in the egg too
long, so he hasn't got the right shape!" And then she
ruffled his feathers and smoothed them down. "Besides,
he's a drake, so it doesn't matter very much. I think he'll
grow much stronger. He'll get along all right."

"The other ducklings are lovely," said the old duck.
"Just make yourselves at home, and if you can find an eel's
head, you may bring it to me!"

And so they made themselves quite at home.

But the poor duckling, who had been the last one out of
the egg and looked so ugly, was bitten and shoved and
ridiculed by both the ducks and the hens. "He's too big!"
they all said. And the turkey cock, who had been born
with spurs on and so believed himself to be an emperor,
puffed himself up like a ship in full sail, went right up to
him, and gobbled until he got quite red in the face. The
poor duckling didn't know whether to stay or go. He was
miserable because he was so ugly and was the laughingstock of the whole duck yard.

So the first day passed, but afterward it grew worse and worse. The poor duckling was chased by everyone. Even his brothers and sisters were nasty to him and were always saying: "If only the cat would get you, you ugly wretch!" And his mother said, "If only you were far away!" And the ducks bit him, and the hens pecked him, and the girl who fed the poultry kicked at him.

Then he ran and flew over the hedge. The little birds in the bushes flew up in fright. "It's because I'm so ugly!" thought the duckling, and shut his eyes, but he still kept on running. Then he came out into the big marsh where the wild ducks lived. He was so exhausted and unhappy that he lay there all night.

In the morning the wild ducks flew up and looked at their new comrade. "What kind of a duck are you?" they asked, and the duckling turned from one side to the other and greeted them as best he could.

"How ugly you are!" said the wild ducks. "But it makes no difference to us as long as you don't marry into our family!"

Poor thing! He certainly wasn't thinking about marriage. All he wanted was to be allowed to lie in the rushes and to drink a little water from the marsh.

There he lay for two whole days, and then there came two wild geese, or rather two wild ganders, for they were both males, not long out of the egg, and therefore they were quite saucy.

"Listen, comrade!" they said. "You're so ugly that you appeal to us. Want to come along and be a bird of passage? In another marsh close by are some sweet lovely wild geese, every single one unmarried, who can say 'Quack!' You're in a position to make your fortune, ugly as you are!"

Bang! Bang! Shots suddenly rang out above them, and both the wild geese fell down dead in the rushes, and the water was red with blood. Bang! Bang! It sounded again, and whole flocks of wild geese flew up out of the rushes, and the guns cracked again. A great hunt was on. The hunters lay around the marsh. Yes, some were even sitting up in the branches of the trees that hung over the water. The blue smoke drifted in among the dark trees and hovered over the water. Into the mud came the hunting dogs. Splash! Splash! Reeds and rushes swayed on all sides. The poor duckling was terrified. He turned his head to put it under his wing and at the same moment found himself standing face to face with a terribly big dog! Its tongue was hanging way out of its mouth, and its eyes gleamed horribly. It opened its jaws over the duckling, showed its sharp teeth, and—splash!—went on without touching him.

"Oh, heaven be praised!" sighed the duckling. "I'm so ugly that even the dog doesn't care to bite me!"

And then he lay quite still while the buckshot whistled through the rushes and shot after shot resounded.

Not until late in the day did it become quiet, but even then the poor duckling didn't dare get up. He waited several hours before he looked around, and then he hurried out of the marsh as fast as he could. He ran over field and meadows, and there was such a wind that the going was hard.

Toward evening he came to a wretched little house. It was so ramshackle that it didn't know which way to fall, and so it remained standing. The wind blew so hard around the duckling that he had to sit on his tail to keep from blowing away. Then he noticed that the door was off one of its hinges and hung so crookedly that he could slip into the house through the crack, and this he did.

Here lived an old woman with her cat and her hen. And the cat, whom she called Sonny, could arch his back and purr, and he even gave off sparks, but only if one stroked him the wrong way. The hen had quite short tiny legs, so she was called Chicky Low Legs. She laid good eggs, and the old woman was as fond of her as if she were her own child.

In the morning the strange duckling was noticed at once, and the cat started to purr and the hen to cluck.

"What's that?" said the old woman, and looked around, but she couldn't see very well, so she thought the duckling was a fat duck that had lost its way. "Why, that was a fine catch!" she said. "Now I can get duck eggs, if only it's not a drake. That we'll have to try!"

So the duckling was accepted on trial for three weeks, but no eggs came. And the cat was master of the house, and the hen madam. And they always said, "We and the world," for they believed that they were half of the world, and the very best half, at that. The duckling thought there might be another opinion, but the hen wouldn't stand for that.

"Can you lay eggs?" she asked.

"No!"

"Then keep your mouth shut!"

And the cat said, "Can you arch your back, purr, and give off sparks?"

"No!"

"Well, then keep your opinion to yourself when sensible folks are speaking."

And the duckling sat in the corner in low spirits. Then he started thinking of the fresh air and the sunshine. He had such a strange desire to float on the water. At last he couldn't help himself; he had to tell it to the hen.

"What's wrong with you?" she asked. "You have nothing to do. That's why you're putting on these airs! Lay eggs or purr, then it'll go over."

"But it's so lovely to float on the water!" said the duckling. "So lovely to get it over your head and duck down to the bottom."

"Yes, a great pleasure, I daresay!" said the hen. "You've gone quite mad. Ask the cat, he's the wisest one I know, if *he* likes to float on the water or duck under it. Not to mention myself. Ask our mistress, the old woman; there is no one wiser than she in the whole world. Do you think she wants to float and get water over her head?"

"You don't understand me," said the duckling.

"Well, if we don't understand you, who would? Indeed, you'll never be wiser than the cat and the old woman, not to mention myself. Don't put on airs, my child! And thank your Creator for all the good that has been done for you. Haven't you come into a warm house, into a circle from which you can learn something? But you're a fool, and it's no fun associating with you! Believe you me! When I tell you harsh truths it's for your own good, and this way one can know one's true friends. See to it now that you start laying eggs or learn to purr and give off sparks."

"I think I'll go out into the wide world!" said the duckling.

"Yes, just do that!" said the hen.

So the duckling went out. He floated on the water and dived down to the bottom, but he was shunned by all the animals because of his ugliness.

Now it was autumn. The leaves in the forest turned golden and brown. The wind took hold of them and they danced about. The sky looked cold, and the clouds hung heavy with hail and snow. A raven stood on the fence and shrieked "Off! Off!" just from the cold. Merely thinking of it could make one freeze. The poor duckling was really in a bad way.

One evening as the sun was setting in all its splendor, a great flock of beautiful large birds came out of the bushes. The duckling had never seen anything so lovely. They were shining white, with long supple necks. They were swans, and uttering a strange cry, they spread their splendid broad wings and flew away from the cold meadows to warmer lands and open seas. They rose so high, so high, and the ugly little duckling had such a strange feeling. He moved around and around in the water like a wheel, stretching his neck high in the air after them and uttering a cry so shrill and strange that he frightened even himself. Oh, he couldn't forget those lovely birds, those happy birds; and when he could no longer see them, he dived right down to the bottom, and when he came up again he was quite beside himself. He didn't know what those birds were called or where they were flying, but he was fonder of them than he had ever been of anyone before. He didn't envy them in the least. How could it occur to him to wish for such loveliness for himself? He would have been glad if only the ducks had tolerated him in their midst—the poor ugly bird.

And the winter was so cold, so cold. The duckling had to swim about in the water to keep from freezing. But each night the hole in which he swam became smaller and smaller; it froze so the crust of the ice creaked. The duckling had to keep his legs moving so the hole wouldn't close, but at last he grew tired, lay quite still, and froze fast in the ice.

Early in the morning a farmer came along. He saw the duckling, went out and made a hole in the ice with his wooden shoe, and then carried him home to his wife. There he was brought back to life.

The children wanted to play with him, but the duckling thought they wanted to hurt him, and in his fright he flew into the milk dish so the milk splashed out in the room. The woman shrieked and waved her arms. Then he flew into the butter trough and down into the flour barrel and out again. My, how he looked now! The woman screamed and hit at him with the tongs, and the children knocked each other over trying to capture him, and they laughed and shrieked. It was a good thing the door was standing open. Out flew the duckling among the bushes, into the newly fallen snow, and he lay there as if stunned.

But it would be far too sad to tell of all the suffering and misery he had to go through during that hard winter. He was lying in the marsh among the rushes when the sun began to shine warmly again. The larks sang—it was a beautiful spring.

Then all at once he raised his wings. They beat more strongly than before and powerfully carried him away. And before he knew it, he was in a large garden where the apple trees were in bloom and the fragrance of lilacs filled the air, where they hung on the long green branches right

down to the winding canal. Oh, it was so lovely here with the freshness of spring. And straight ahead, out of the thicket came three beautiful swans. They ruffled their feathers and floated so lightly on the water. The duckling recognized the magnificent birds and was filled with a strange melancholy.

"I will fly straight to them, those royal birds, and they

will peck me to death because I am so ugly and yet dare approach them. But it doesn't matter. Better to be killed by them than to be bitten by the ducks, pecked by the hens, kicked by the girl who takes care of the poultry yard, or suffer such hardships during the winter!" And he flew out into the water and swam over toward the magnificent swans. They saw him and hurried toward him with ruffled feathers.

"Just kill me," said the poor creature, and bowed down his head toward the surface of the water and awaited his death. But what did he see in the clear water? Under him he saw his own reflection, but he was no longer a clumsy, grayish-black bird, ugly and disgusting. He was a swan himself!

Being born in a duck yard doesn't matter if one has lain in a swan's egg!

He felt quite happy about all the hardships and suffering he had undergone. Now he could really appreciate his happiness and all the beauty that greeted him. And the big swans swam around him and stroked him with their bills.

Some little children came down to the garden and threw bread and seeds out into the water, and the smallest one cried, "There's a new one!" And the other children joined in, shouting jubilantly, "Yes, a new one has come!" And they all clapped their hands and danced for joy and ran to get their father and mother. And bread and cake were thrown into the water, and they all said, "The new one is the prettiest! So young and lovely!" And the old swans bowed to him.

Then he felt very shy and put his head under his wing—he didn't know why. He was much too happy, but not proud at all, for a good heart is never proud. He thought of how he had been persecuted and ridiculed, and now he heard everyone saying that he was the loveliest of all the lovely birds. And the lilacs bowed their branches right down to the water to him, and the sun shone so warm and bright. Then he ruffled his feathers, lifted his slender neck, and from the depths of his heart said joyously:

"I never dreamed of so much happiness when I was the ugly duckling."

The Snow Queen
(An Adventure in Seven Tales)

FIRST TALE:
WHICH IS ABOUT THE MIRROR
AND THE FRAGMENTS

SEE, there! Now we're going to begin. When we come to the end of the tale, we'll know more than we do now, because of an evil troll! He was one of the worst of all, he was the "Devil." One day he was in a really good humor because he had made a mirror that had the quality of making everything good and fair that was reflected in it dwindle to almost nothing, but whatever was worthless and ugly stood out and grew even worse. The loveliest landscapes looked like boiled spinach in it, and the best people became nasty or stood on their heads without stomachs; the faces became so distorted that they were unrecognizable, and if you had a freckle, you could be certain that it spread over nose and mouth. "That was highly entertaining," said the Devil. Now, if a person had a good, pious thought, a grin would appear in the mirror, and the troll Devil had to laugh at his curious invention. Everyone who went to the troll school—for he ran a school for trolls—spread the word that a miracle had occurred: now, for the first time, they believed, you could see how the world and mortals really looked. They ran about with the mirror, and at last there wasn't a land or a person that hadn't been distorted in it. Now they also wanted to fly up to Heaven itself, to make fun of the angels and Our Lord. Indeed, the higher they flew with the mirror, the harder it grinned! They could hardly hold onto it. Higher and higher they flew, nearer to God and the angels. Then the mirror quivered so dreadfully in its grin that it shot out of their hands and plunged down to the earth, where it broke into a hundred million billion— and even more—fragments. And now it did much greater harm than before, for some of the fragments were scarcely bigger than a grain of sand; and these flew about in the wide world, and wherever they got into someone's eyes, they remained there; and then these people saw everything wrong or had eyes only for what was bad with a thing—for each tiny particle of the mirror had retained the same power as the whole mirror. Some people even got a little fragment of the mirror in their hearts, and this was quite horrible—the heart became just like a lump of ice. Some of the fragments of the mirror were so big that they were used as windowpanes, but it wasn't advisable to look at one's friends through those panes. Other fragments came into spectacles, and when people put these spectacles on, it was hard to see properly or act fairly. The Evil One laughed until he split his sides, and that tickled him pink.

But outside tiny fragments of glass were still flying about in the air. Now we shall hear!

SECOND TALE:
A LITTLE BOY AND A LITTLE GIRL

In a big city—where there are so many houses and people that there isn't enough room for everyone to have a little garden, and where most of them have to content themselves with flowers in pots—there were two poor children, however, who did have a garden somewhat bigger than a flowerpot. They weren't brother and sister, but they were just as fond of each other as if they had been. Their parents lived next to each other; they lived in two garrets; there, where the roof of one house adjoined the other, and the gutter ran along the eaves, from each house a tiny window faced the other. One had only to step over the gutter to go from one window to the other.

Outside, the parents each had a big wooden box, and in it grew potherbs, which they used, and a little rosebush; there was one in each box, and they grew so gloriously. Now, the parents hit upon the idea of placing the boxes across the gutter in such a way that they almost reached from one window to the other, and looked just like two banks of flowers. The pea vines hung down over the boxes, and the rosebushes put forth long branches, twined about the windows, and bent over toward each other. It was almost like a triumphal arch of greenery and flowers. As the boxes were quite high, and the children knew that they mustn't climb up there, they were often allowed to go out to each other and sit on their little stools under the roses, and here they played quite splendidly.

During the winter, of course, this pleasure was at an end. The windows were often frozen over completely; but then they warmed up copper coins on the tiled stove, placed the hot coin on the frozen pane, and thus there would be a wonderful peephole as round as could be. Behind it peeped a lovely, gentle eye, one from each window. It was the little boy and the little girl. He was called Kay and she was called Gerda. In summer they could come to each other at one jump; in winter they first had to go down the many flights of stairs and then up the many flights of stairs; outside the snow was drifting.

"The white bees are swarming," said the old grandmother.

"Do they have a queen bee too?" asked the little boy, for he knew that there was one among the real bees.

"So they have!" said the grandmother. "She flies there where the swarm is thickest! She's the biggest of them all, and she never remains still on the earth. She flies up again into the black cloud. Many a winter night she flies through the city streets and looks in at the windows, and then they freeze over so curiously, as if with flowers."

"Yes, I've seen that!" said both the children, and then they knew it was true.

"Can the Snow Queen come in here?" asked the little girl.

"Just let her come," said the boy. "I'll put her on the hot stove and then she'll melt."

But the grandmother smoothed his hair and told other tales.

In the evening, when little Kay was back home and half undressed, he climbed up on the chair by the window and peeped out through the tiny hole. A few snowflakes were falling out there, and one of these, the biggest one of all, remained lying on the edge of one of the flower boxes. The snowflake grew and grew, and at last it turned into a complete woman, clad in the finest white gauze, which seemed to be made up of millions of starlike flakes. She was so beautiful and grand, but of ice—dazzling, gleaming ice—and yet she was alive. Her eyes stared like two clear stars, but there was no peace or rest in them. She nodded to the window and motioned with her hand. The little boy became frightened and jumped down from the chair. Then it seemed as if a huge bird flew past the window.

The next day there was a clear frost—and then a thaw set in—and then came the spring. The sun shone, green sprouts appeared, the swallows built nests, windows were opened, and again the little children sat in their tiny garden way up high in the gutter above all the floors.

The roses bloomed so wonderfully that summer; the

little girl had learned a hymn and there was something
about roses in it, and these roses made her think of her
own; and she sang it to the little boy, and he sang it along
with her:

> "Roses growing in the dale
> Where the Holy Child we hail."

And the children took each other by the hand, kissed the
roses, and gazed into God's bright sunshine and spoke to
it as if the Infant Jesus were there. What glorious summer
days these were, how wonderful it was to be out by the
fresh rosebushes, which never seemed to want to stop
blooming.

Kay and Gerda sat looking at a picture book of animals
and birds. It was then—the clock in the big church tower
had just struck five—that Kay said, "Ow! Something stuck
me in the heart! And now I've got something in my eye!"

The little girl put her arms around his neck; he blinked
his eyes. No, there wasn't a thing to be seen.

"I guess it's gone," he said. But it wasn't gone. It was
one of those fragments of glass that had sprung from the
mirror, the troll mirror. I daresay we remember that
loathsome glass that caused everything big and good that
was reflected in it to grow small and hideous, whereas the
evil and wicked duly stood out, and every flaw in a thing
was noticeable at once. Poor Kay! He had got a particle
right in his heart. Soon it would be just like a lump of ice.
It didn't hurt anymore now, but it was there.

"Why are you crying?" he asked. "You look so ugly!
There's nothing wrong with me after all! Fie!" he suddenly
cried. "That rose there is worm-eaten! And look, that one
there is quite crooked! As a matter of fact, that's a nasty
batch of roses! They look just like the boxes they're standing in!" And then he gave the box quite a hard kick with
his foot and pulled out the two roses.

"Kay! What are you doing!" cried the little girl. And when he saw how horrified she was, he yanked off yet another rose and then ran in through his window away from dear little Gerda.

When she came later with the picture book, he said it was for babies! And if grandmother told stories, he would always come with a "But—" Yes, if he got a chance to, he would walk behind her, put on glasses, and talk just the way she did. It was exactly like her, and he made people laugh. Soon he could copy the voice and gait of everyone on the whole street. Everything queer or not nice about them Kay knew how to imitate, and then people said, "He's certainly got an excellent head on him, that boy!" But it was the glass he had got in his eye, the glass that sat in his heart; and that is why he even teased little Gerda, who loved him with all her heart.

His games were now quite different from what they had been, they were so sensible; one winter's day, as the snowflakes piled up in drifts, he took a big burning glass, and holding out a corner of his blue coat, he let the snowflakes fall on it.

"Now look in the glass, Gerda!" he said. Each snowflake became much bigger and looked like a magnificent flower or a ten-sided star. It was a delight to behold.

"Do you see how funny it is?" said Kay. "That's much more interesting than real flowers! And there isn't a single flaw in them; they're quite accurate as long as they don't melt."

A little later Kay appeared in big gloves and with his sled on his back. He shouted right in Gerda's ear: "I've been allowed to go sledding in the big square where the others are playing." And off he went.

Over in the square the most daring boys often tied their sleds to the farmer's wagon, and then they rode a good distance with it. It was lots of fun. As they were playing there a big sleigh came up. It was painted white, and there was someone sitting in it, swathed in a fleecy white fur and wearing a white fur cap. The sleigh drove twice around the square, and Kay quickly managed to tie his little sled to it, and now he was driving along with it. It went faster and faster, straight into the next street. The driver turned his head and gave Kay a kindly nod; it was just as if they knew each other. Every time Kay wanted to untie his little sled, the person would nod again and Kay remained seated. They drove straight out through the city gate. Then the snow began tumbling down so thickly that the little boy couldn't see a hand in front of him as he rushed along. Then he quickly let go of the rope in order to get loose from the big sleigh, but it was no use. His little vehicle hung fast, and it went like the wind. Then he gave quite a loud cry, but no one heard him; and the snow piled up in drifts and the sleigh rushed on. Now and then it gave quite a jump, as if he were flying over ditches and fences. He was scared stiff; he wanted to say the Lord's Prayer, but the only thing he could remember was the Big Multiplication Table.

The snowflakes grew bigger and bigger; at last they looked like huge white hens; suddenly they sprang aside. The big sleigh stopped, and the one who was driving it stood up—the furs and cap were all of snow. It was a lady, so tall and straight, so shining white. It was the Snow Queen.

"We've made good progress," she said. "But is it freezing? Crawl into my bearskin." And then she seated him in the sleigh with her and wrapped the fur around him; it was as if he were sinking into a snowdrift.

"Are you still freezing?" she asked, and then she kissed him on the forehead. Ugh! That was colder than ice; it went straight to his heart, which of course was half a lump of ice already. He felt as if he were going to die—but only for a moment, then it only did him good; he no longer felt the cold around him.

"My sled! Don't forget my sled!" Only then did he remember it, and it was tied to one of the white hens. And it flew along behind with the sled on its back. The Snow Queen kissed Kay once again, and by then he had forgotten little Gerda and grandmother and all of them at home.

"Now you're not getting any more kisses," she said, "or else I'd kiss you to death!"

Kay looked at her; she was so very beautiful. A wiser, lovelier face he couldn't imagine; and now she didn't seem to be of ice, as she had seemed that time she had sat outside his window and motioned to him. In his eyes she was perfect, nor did he feel afraid at all. He told her that he knew how to do mental arithmetic, and with fractions, at that; and he knew the square mileage of the countries and "how many inhabitants." And she always smiled. Then it occurred to him that what he knew still wasn't enough. And he looked up into the vast expanse of sky. And she flew with him, flew high up on the black cloud; and the storm whistled and roared—it was like singing the old lays. They flew over forests and lakes, over sea and land; down below the icy blast whistled, the wolves howled, the snow sparkled. Over it flew the black screeching crows, but up above the moon shone so big and bright; and Kay looked at it all through the long winter night. By day he slept at the Snow Queen's feet.

THIRD TALE:
THE FLOWER GARDEN OF THE WOMAN WHO WAS VERSED IN SORCERY

But how did little Gerda get on when Kay didn't come back again? Where was he after all? Nobody knew. Nobody could send word. The boys related only that they had seen him tie his little sled to a beautiful big sleigh,

which drove into the street and out of the city gate. Nobody knew where he was; many tears flowed and little Gerda cried hard and long. Then they said that he was dead, that he had fallen in the river that flowed close by the city. Oh, what truly long dark winter days they were.

Now the spring came and warmer sunshine.

"Kay is dead and gone!" said little Gerda.

"I don't think so!" said the sunshine.

"He's dead and gone!" she said to the swallows.

"I don't think so," they replied, and at last little Gerda didn't think so, either.

"I'm going to put on my new red shoes," she said early one morning, "the ones that Kay has never seen, and then I'll go down to the river and ask it too!"

It was quite early. She kissed the old grandmother, who was sleeping, put on the red shoes, and walked quite alone out of the gate to the river.

"Is it true that you've taken my little playmate? I'll make you a present of my red shoes if you'll give him back to me again!"

And it seemed to her that the billows nodded so strangely. Then she took her red shoes, the dearest things she owned, and threw them both out into the river. But they fell close to the shore, and the little billows carried them back on land to her right away. It was just as if the river didn't want to take the dearest things she owned. Then it didn't have little Kay after all. But now she thought she hadn't thrown the shoes out far enough, and so she climbed into a boat that was lying among the rushes. She went all the way out to the farthest end and threw the shoes, but the boat wasn't tied fast, and her movement made it glide from land. She noticed it and hastened to get out, but before she reached the back of the boat, it was more than an alen out from shore and now it glided faster away.

Then little Gerda became quite frightened and started to cry, but nobody heard her except the sparrows, and they couldn't carry her to land. But they flew along the shore and sang, as if to comfort her: "Here we are! Here we are!" The boat drifted with the stream. Little Gerda sat quite still in just her stockings; her little red shoes floated along behind, but they couldn't catch up with the boat, which gathered greater speed.

It was lovely on both shores, with beautiful flowers, old trees, and slopes with sheep and cows, but not a person was to be seen.

"Maybe the river is carrying me to little Kay," thought Gerda, and this put her in better spirits. She stood up and gazed at the beautiful green shores for many hours. Then she came to a big cherry orchard, where there was a little house with curious red and blue windows and—come to think of it—a thatched roof and two wooden soldiers outside who shouldered arms to those who sailed by.

Gerda shouted to them—she thought they were alive—but naturally they didn't answer; she came close to them, for the boat drifted right in to shore.

Gerda shouted even louder, and then out of the house came an old old woman leaning on a crooked staff. She was wearing a big sun hat, which had the loveliest flowers painted on it.

"You poor little child!" said the old woman. "However did you come out on that great strong stream and drift so far out into the wide world?" And then the old woman went all the way out in the water, hooked the boat with her staff, pulled it to land, and lifted little Gerda out.

And Gerda was glad to be on dry land, but, all the same, a little afraid of the strange old woman.

"Come, now, and tell me who you are and how you came here," she said.

And Gerda told her everything, and the old woman shook her head and said, "Hm! Hm!" And when Gerda had told her everything and asked if she hadn't seen little Kay, the old woman said that he hadn't come by, but he'd

be along, all right; she just shouldn't be grieve
should taste her cherries and look at her flowers
were prettier than any picture book and each one could
tell a complete story. Then she took Gerda by the hand;
they went into the little house and the old woman locked
the door.

The windows were so high up, and the panes were red,
blue, and yellow. The daylight shone in so strangely there
with all the colors, but on the table stood the loveliest
cherries, and Gerda ate as many as she liked, for this she
dared to do. And while she ate, the old woman combed
her hair with a golden comb, and the yellow hair curled
and shone so delightfully around the lovely little face,
which was so round and looked like a rose.

"I've been really longing for such a sweet little girl!"
said the old woman. "Now you shall see how well we two
are going to get along!" And as she combed little Gerda's
hair Gerda forgot her playmate, little Kay. For the old
woman was versed in sorcery, but she wasn't a wicked
sorceress, she only did a little conjuring for her own
pleasure, and now she so wanted to keep little Gerda. And
so she went out in the garden and held out her crooked
staff at all the rosebushes, and no matter how beautifully
they were blooming, they sank down into the black earth,
and no one could see where they had stood. The old
woman was afraid that when Gerda saw the roses, she
would think of her own and then remember little Kay and
run away.

Now she led Gerda out in the flower garden. My, how
fragrant and lovely it was here! Every conceivable flower,
for every season of the year, stood here blooming magnificently. No picture book could be gayer or lovelier. Gerda
sprang about for joy and played until the sun went down
behind the tall cherry trees. Then she was given a lovely
bed with red silken coverlets; they were stuffed with blue

violets, and she slept there and dreamed as delightfully as any queen on her wedding day.

The next day she could again play with the flowers in the warm sunshine—and so many days passed. Gerda knew every flower, but no matter how many there were, it still seemed to her that one was missing. But which one it was she didn't know. Then one day she was sitting, looking at the old woman's sun hat with the painted flowers on it, and the prettiest one of all was a rose. The old woman had forgotten to take it off the hat when the other flowers had sunk down in the ground. But that's the way it goes when one is absentminded.

"What?" said Gerda. "Aren't there any roses here?" And she ran in among the flower beds, searching and searching; but her hot tears fell on the very spot where a rosebush had sunk, and as the warm tears moistened the ground the tree suddenly shot up as full of blossoms as when it had sunk. And Gerda threw her arms around it, kissed the roses, and thought of the lovely roses at home and of little Kay.

"Oh, how I've been delayed!" said the little girl. "Why, I was going to find Kay! Don't you know where he is?" she asked the roses. "Do you think he's dead and gone?"

"He's not dead," said the roses. "To be sure, we've been in the ground, where all the dead are, but Kay wasn't there."

"Thank you!" said little Gerda, and she went over to the other flowers and looked into their chalices and asked: "Don't you know where little Kay is?"

But each flower was standing in the sunshine and dreaming of its own fairy tale or history; little Gerda was told so very many of these, but no one knew anything about Kay.

And then what did the tiger lily say?

"Do you hear the drum? Boom! Boom! There are only two notes—always 'Boom! Boom!' Listen to the dirge of the women! Listen to the cry of the priests! In her long red kirtle, the Hindu wife stands on the pyre, as the flames leap up about her and her dead husband. But the Hindu wife is thinking of the one still alive here in the ring, the one whose eyes burn hotter than the flames, the one whose burning eyes come closer to her heart than the flames that will soon burn her body to ashes. Can the flames of the heart die in the flames of the pyre?"

"I don't understand that at all!" said little Gerda.

"That's my story!" said the tiger lily.

What does the convolvulus say?

"Overhanging the narrow mountain trail is an old baronial castle; the thick periwinkles grow up around the ancient red walls, leaf for leaf about the balcony, and there stands a lovely girl. She leans out over the balustrade and peers at the road. No rose hangs fresher on its branch than she. No apple blossom borne by the wind from the tree is more graceful than she; how the magnificent kirtle rustles! 'Isn't he coming after all!' "

"Is it Kay you mean?" asked Little Gerda.

"I'm speaking only about my tale, my dream," replied the convolvulus.

What does the little snowdrop say?

"Between the trees the long board is hanging by ropes; it is a swing. Two lovely little girls—their dresses are as white as snow, long green silken ribbons are fluttering from their hats—sit swinging. Their brother, who is bigger than they are, is standing up in the swing. He has his arm around the rope to hold on with, for in one hand he has a little bowl and in the other a clay pipe; he is blowing soap bubbles; the swing is moving and the bubbles are soaring with lovely changing colors. The last one is still hanging to the pipe stem and bobbing in the wind; the swing is moving. The little black dog, as lightly as the bubbles, stands up on its hind legs and wants to get on the swing; it soars, the dog tumbles down with an angry bark, it is teased, the bubbles burst—a swinging board, a picture of flying lather, is my song."

"It may be that what you tell is beautiful, but you tell it so sorrowfully and make no mention of Kay at all. What do the hyacinths say?"

"There were three lovely sisters, so ethereal and fine: one's kirtle was red, the second's was blue, the third's was all white. Hand in hand they danced by the calm lake in the bright moonlight. They were not elfin maidens, but mortal children. There was such a sweet fragrance, and the maidens vanished in the forest. The fragrance grew stronger: three coffins—in them lay the three lovely girls—glided from the forest thicket across the lake. Fireflies flew twinkling about, like tiny hovering candles. Are the dancing maidens asleep or are they dead? The fragrance of the flowers says they are corpses. The evening bell is tolling for the dead!"

"You make me miserable," said little Gerda. "You have such a strong fragrance. It makes me think of the dead maidens. Alas, is little Kay really dead, then? The roses have been down in the ground, and they say no!"

"Dingdong," rang the hyacinth bells. "We're not ringing for little Kay; we don't know him. We're just singing our song, the only one we know!"

And Gerda went over to the buttercup, which shone out among the glistening green leaves. "You're a bright little sun!" said Gerda. "Tell me, if you know, where I shall find my playmate."

And the buttercup shone so prettily and looked back at Gerda. Which song, by chance, could the buttercup sing? That wasn't about Kay, either.

"In a little yard Our Lord's sun was shining so warmly on the first day of spring. The beams glided down along the neighbor's white wall; close by grew the first yellow flowers, shining gold in the warm sunbeams. Old granny was out in her chair; the granddaughter—the poor, beautiful serving maid—was home on a short visit. She kissed her grandmother. There was gold, a heart of gold in that blessed kiss. Gold on the lips, gold on the ground, gold in the morning all around. See, that's my story!" said the buttercup.

"My poor old grandmother!" sighed Gerda. "Yes, she's probably grieving for me, just as she did for little Kay. But I'm coming home again, and then I'll bring little Kay with me. There's no use my asking the flowers. They know only their songs; they're not telling me anything." And then she tucked up her little dress, so as to be able to run faster, but the narcissus tapped her on the leg as she jumped over it. Then she stopped, looked at the tall flower, and asked, "Do you, by any chance, know something?" And she stooped all the way down to it. And what did it say?

"I can see myself! I can see myself!" said the narcissus. "Oh! Oh! How I smell! Up in the tiny garret, half dressed, stands a little dancer. Now she's standing on one leg, now on two! She kicks out at the whole world. She's only an optical illusion. She pours water from the teapot onto a piece of cloth she's holding. It's her corset. Cleanliness is a good thing. The white dress hanging on the peg has also been washed in the teapot and dried on the roof; she puts it on and the saffron-yellow kerchief around her neck. Then the dress shines even whiter. Leg in the air! See how she rears up on a stalk! I can see myself! I can see myself!"

"I don't care at all about that!" said Gerda. "That's not anything to tell me!" And then she ran to the edge of the garden.

The gate was locked, but she wiggled the rusty iron hook, then it came loose and the gate flew open. And then little Gerda ran barefooted out into the wide world. She looked back three times, but no one came after her. At last she couldn't run anymore, and sat down on a big stone. And when she looked around her, summer was at an end. It was late autumn. You couldn't tell this at all inside the lovely garden, where the sun was always shining and flowers of every season were blooming.

"Heavens! How I've held myself up!" said little Gerda. "Why, it's autumn! I dare not rest!" And she got up to go.

Oh, how sore and tired her little feet were, and on all sides it looked cold and raw. The long willow leaves were quite yellow and dripping wet in the fog: one leaf fell after the other. Only the blackthorn bore fruit, but so sour that it puckered the mouth. Oh, how gray and bleak it was in the wide world!

FOURTH TALE:
PRINCE AND PRINCESS

Gerda had to rest again. Then a huge crow hopped on the snow right in front of where she sat. For a long time it had been sitting looking at her and wagging its head. Now it said, "Caw! Caw! Go da! Go da!" It wasn't able to say it any better. But it meant well by the little girl and asked where she was going all alone out in the wide world. Gerda understood the word "alone" very well and felt rightly all that it implied. And so she told the crow the whole story of her life and asked if it hadn't seen Kay.

And the crow nodded quite thoughtfully and said, "Could be! Could be!"

"What? Do you think so?" cried the little girl, and nearly squeezed the crow to death, she kissed it so.

"Sensibly! Sensibly!" said the crow. "I think it could be little Kay. But now he's probably forgotten you for the princess!"

"Is he living with a princess?" asked Gerda.

"Yes, listen!" said the crow. "But it's hard for me to

speak your language. If you understand crow talk, then I can tell it better."

"No, I haven't learned that," said Gerda. "But grandmother could, and she knew Double Dutch too. If only I'd learned it."

"No matter!" said the crow. "I'll tell you as well as I can, but it'll be bad all the same." And then it told what it knew.

"In the kingdom where we are sitting now, there dwells a princess who is exceedingly wise. But then she has read all the newspapers there are in the world and forgotten them—so wise is she. The other day she was sitting on the throne—and that's not so much fun after all, they say. Then she started humming a song, the very one that goes: 'Why shouldn't I wed . . .'

" 'Listen, there's something to that!' she said, and then she wanted to get married. But she wanted a husband who was ready with an answer when he was spoken to. One who didn't just stand there looking aristocratic, because that's so boring. Now she got all her ladies-in-waiting together, and when they heard what she wanted, they were so pleased.

" 'I like that!' they said. 'That's just what I was thinking the other day!' You can believe every word I say is true," said the crow. "I have a tame sweetheart who walks freely about the castle, and she has told me everything!"

Naturally this was a crow too, for birds of a feather flock together, and one crow always picks another.

"The newspapers came out right away with a border of hearts and the princess' monogram. You could read for yourself that any young man who was good-looking was free to come up to the castle and talk to the princess. And the one who talked in such a way that you could hear he was at home there, and talked the best, he was the one the princess would take for a husband! Well, well!" said the crow. "You can believe me, it's as true as I'm sitting here, people came in swarms. There was a jostling and a scurrying, but it didn't prove successful, neither on the first day nor on the second. They could all talk well when they were out in the street, but when they came in the castle gate and saw the guards in silver and the lackeys in gold up along the stairs, and the great illuminated halls, then they were flabbergasted. And if they stood before the throne where the princess was sitting, they didn't know of a thing to say except for the last word she had said, and she didn't think much of hearing that again. It was just as if people in there had swallowed snuff and fallen into a trance until they were back out in the street. Yes, then they were able to speak. There was a line all the way from the city gate to the castle. I was inside to look at it myself!" said the crow. "They became both hungry and thirsty, but from the castle they didn't get so much as a glass of lukewarm water. To be sure, some of the smartest had taken sandwiches with them, but they didn't share with their neighbor. They thought, 'Only let him look hungry, then the princess won't take him!' "

"But Kay! Little Kay!" said Gerda. "When did he come? Was he among the multitude?"

"Give me time! Give me time! Now we're just coming to him. It was the third day. Then a little person, without horse or carriage, came marching dauntlessly straight up to the castle. His eyes shone like yours; he had lovely long hair, but shabby clothes."

"That was Kay!" Gerda shouted jubilantly. "Oh, then I've found him!" And she clapped her hands.

"He had a little knapsack on his back!" said the crow.

"No, that was probably his sled," said Gerda, "for he went away with the sled!"

"That's very likely!" said the crow. "I didn't look at it so closely! But I do know from my tame sweetheart that when he came in through the castle gate and saw the bodyguard in silver and the lackeys in gold up along the stairs, he didn't lose heart a bit. He nodded and said to them, 'It must be boring to stand on the steps, I'd rather go inside!' There the halls were ablaze with light. Privy councillors and excellencies were walking about barefoot, carrying golden dishes. It was enough to make one solemn. His boots were creaking so terribly loudly, but still he didn't become frightened.'"

"That certainly is Kay!" said Gerda. "I know he had new boots. I've heard them creaking in Grandmother's parlor."

"Well, creak they did!" said the crow. "But nothing daunted, he went straight in to the princess, who was sitting on a pearl as big as a spinning wheel. And all the ladies-in-waiting, with their maids and maids' maids, and all the gentlemen-in-waiting, with their menservants and menservants' menservants who kept a page boy, stood lined up on all sides. And indeed the closer they stood to the door, the haughtier they looked. And the menservants' menservants' boy, who always goes about in slippers, is hardly to be looked upon at all, so haughtily does he stand in the door.'"

"That must be horrible!" said little Gerda. "And yet Kay has won the princess?"

"If I hadn't been a crow, I'd have taken her—despite the fact that I'm engaged. He's supposed to have spoken just as well as I speak when I speak crow talk. I have that from my tame sweetheart. He was dauntless and charming; he hadn't come to woo at all, only to hear the princess' wisdom; and he found that to be good, and she found him to be good in return."

"Of course! That was Kay!" said Gerda. "He was wise. He could do Mental Arithmetic with fractions! Oh, won't you take me into the castle?"

"Well, that's easily said," said the crow, "but how are we going to do it? I shall speak to my tame sweetheart about it. I daresay she can advise us, although I must tell you that a little girl like you will never be allowed to come in the proper way."

"Oh, yes, so I will!" said Gerda. "As soon as Kay hears I'm here he'll come right out and fetch me."

"Wait for me by the stile there!" said the crow, wagging its head, and it flew away.

Not until it was late in the evening did the crow come back again. "Rah! Rah!" it said. "She asked me to give you her love! And here's a little loaf for you. She took it from the kitchen, and there's bread enough there, and you're probably hungry. It's impossible for you to come into the castle. Why, you're barefoot. The guard in silver and the lackeys in gold wouldn't allow it, but don't cry. You'll come up there after all. My sweetheart knows of a little back stairway that leads to the royal bedchamber, and she knows where to get hold of the key!"

And they went into the garden, into the great avenue where the leaves fell one after the other; and when the lights were put out in the castle, one after the other, the crow led little Gerda over to a back door that stood ajar.

Oh, how little Gerda's heart was pounding with fear and longing! It was just as if she were going to do something wrong, and yet she only wanted to know whether it was little Kay. Indeed, it had to be him; she could picture vividly to herself his wise eyes, his long hair. She could clearly see the way he smiled, as he did when they sat at home under the roses. Of course he would be glad to see her, and he would want to hear what a long way she had walked for his sake and learn how miserable everyone at home had been when he hadn't come back. Oh, how frightened and glad she was.

Now they were on the stairs; there was a little lamp burning on a cupboard. In the middle of the floor stood the tame crow, turning its head on all sides and regarding Gerda, who curtsied the way her grandmother had taught her.

"My fiancé has spoken so nicely about you, my little miss," said the tame crow. "Your vita, as it is called, is also very touching! If you will take the lamp, then I will lead the way. We go here as the crow flies, so we don't meet anyone!"

"It seems to me that someone is coming right behind me!" said Gerda, and something swished past her; it was just like shadows along the wall, horses with flowing manes and thin legs, grooms, and ladies and gentlemen on horseback.

"It's only the dreams!" said the tame crow. "They come to fetch the royal thoughts out hunting. It's a good thing, for then you can have a better look at them in bed. But if you do come into favor, see to it then that you reveal a grateful heart!"

"Why, that's nothing to talk about!" said the crow from the woods.

Now they entered the first hall. The walls were covered with rose-red satin and artificial flowers. Here the dreams were already sweeping past them, but they went so fast that Gerda didn't catch a glimpse of the royal riders. Each hall was more magnificent than the last—indeed it was enough to made one astonished—and now they were in the bedchamber. The ceiling in here was like an enormous palm tree with leaves of glass, costly glass. And in the middle of the floor, hanging from a stalk of gold, were two beds that looked like lilies. One of them was white and in it lay the princess. The other was red, and it was in this one that Gerda was to look for little Kay. She bent one of the petals aside, and then she saw the nape of a brown neck. Oh, it was Kay! She shouted his name quite loudly and held the lamp up to him. The dreams on horseback rushed into the room again—he awoke, turned his head, and . . . it wasn't little Kay.

Only the prince's nape of the neck resembled little Kay's, but he was young and handsome. And from the white lily bed the princess peeped out and asked what was wrong. Then little Gerda cried and told her whole story and all that the crows had done for her.

"You poor little thing!" said the prince and princess. And they praised the crows and said that they weren't angry at them at all. But still they weren't to do it often. In the meantime they were to be rewarded.

"Do you want to fly away free?" asked the princess. "Or would you rather have permanent posts as Court Crows— with everything that falls off in the kitchen?"

And both the crows curtsied and asked for permanent positions, for they were thinking of their old age, and said, "It's good to have something for a rainy day," as they called it.

And the prince got out of his bed and let Gerda sleep in it, and he could do no more. She folded her little hands and thought, "Indeed, how good people and animals are." And then she closed her eyes and slept so delightfully. All the dreams came flying back in, looking like God's angels, and they pulled a little sled and on it Kay sat and nodded. But they were only reveries, and for that reason they were gone again as soon as she woke up.

The next day she was clad from top to toe in silk and velvet. She was invited to stay at the castle and be in clover, but all she asked for was a little cart with a horse in front, and a pair of tiny boots. And then she wanted to drive out into the wide world and find Kay.

And she was given both boots and a muff. She was dressed so beautifully. And when she was ready to go, a new coach of pure gold was standing at the door. The coat of arms of the prince and princess shone from it like a star, and the coachman, footmen, and outriders—for there were outriders too—sat wearing golden crowns. The prince and princess themselves helped her into the coach and wished her all good fortune. The crow from the woods, who was now married, accompanied her the first twelve miles. It sat beside her, for it couldn't stand to ride backward. The other crow stood in the gate and flapped its wings. It didn't go with them as it suffered from headaches, since it had been given a permanent post and too much to eat. The inside of the coach was lined with sugared pretzels, and in the seat were fruits and gingersnaps.

"Farewell! Farewell!" shouted the prince and princess. And little Gerda cried and the crow cried—thus the first miles passed. Then the crow also said farewell, and that was the hardest leave-taking of all.

It flew up into a tree and flapped its black wings as long as it could see the coach, which shone like the bright sunshine.

FIFTH TALE:
THE LITTLE ROBBER GIRL

They drove through the dark forest, but the coach shone like a flame; it hurt the eyes of the robbers and they couldn't stand that.

"It's gold! It's gold!" they cried, and rushing out, they grabbed hold of the horses, killed the little outriders, the coachman, and the footmen, and then they dragged little Gerda out of the coach.

"She's fat! She's sweet! She's been fattened on nut kernels!" said the old robber crone, who had a long bristly beard and eyebrows that hung down over her eyes. "That's as good as a little fat lamb. Oh, how good she'll taste!" And then she pulled out her burnished knife—and it glittered so horribly.

"Ow!" said the crone at the same moment; she had been bitten in the ear by her own little daughter, who hung on her back and was so wild and naughty that it was a joy to behold. "You nasty brat!" said the mother, and didn't have time to slaughter Gerda.

"She shall play with me!" said the little robber girl. "She shall give me her muff, her pretty dress, and sleep with me in my bed!" And then she bit her again, so the robber crone hopped in the air and whirled around, and all the robbers laughed and said, "See how she's dancing with her young!"

"I want to get in the coach!" said the little robber girl, and she would and must have her own way, for she was so spoiled and so willful. She and Gerda seated themselves inside, and then they drove, over stubble and thickets, deeper into the forest. The little robber girl was the same size as Gerda, but stronger, with broader shoulders and darker skin. Her eyes were quite black, and they looked almost mournful. She put her arm around little Gerda's waist and said, "They're not going to slaughter you as long as I don't get angry with you. I expect you're a princess?"

"No," said little Gerda, and told her everything she had gone through and how fond she was of little Kay.

The robber girl looked at her quite gravely, nodded her head a little, and said, "They're not going to slaughter you even if I do get angry with you—then I'll do it myself." And then she dried little Gerda's eyes and put both her hands in the beautiful muff that was so soft and so warm.

Now the coach came to a standstill. They were in the middle of the courtyard of a robber's castle. It had cracked from top to bottom. Ravens and crows flew out of the open holes, and huge ferocious dogs—each one looking as if it could swallow a man—jumped high in the air. But they didn't bark, for that was forbidden.

In the big old sooty hall a huge fire was burning in the middle of the stone floor. The smoke trailed along under the ceiling and had to see about finding its way out itself. Soup was cooking in an enormous brewing vat, and both hares and rabbits were turning on spits.

"You shall sleep here tonight with me and all my little pets!" said the robber girl. They got something to eat and drink and then went over to a corner, where straw and rugs lay. Overhead nearly a hundred pigeons were sitting on sticks and perches; they all seemed to be sleeping, but still they turned a bit when the little girls came.

"They're all mine," said the little robber girl, and quickly grabbed hold of one of the nearest, held it by the legs, and shook it so it flapped its wings. "Kiss it!" she cried, and beat Gerda in the face with it. "There sit the forest rogues!" she went on, pointing behind a number of bars that had been put up in front of a hole in the wall high above. "They're forest rogues, those two! They fly away at once if you don't lock them up properly. And here stands my old sweetheart, baa!" And she pulled a reindeer by the horns. It had a bright copper ring around its neck and was tied up. "We always have to keep hold of him, or else he'll run away from us! Every single evening I tickle his neck with my sharp knife—he's so afraid of it!" And the little girl drew a long knife out of a crack in the wall and ran it along the reindeer's neck. The poor animal lashed out with its legs, and the robber girl laughed and then pulled Gerda down into the bed with her

"Do you want to take the knife along when you're going to sleep?" asked Gerda, and looked at it a bit uneasily.

"I always sleep with a knife!" said the little robber girl. "One never knows what may happen. But tell me again now, what you told before about little Kay, and why you've gone out into the wide world." And Gerda told from the beginning, and the wood pigeons cooed up there in the cage; the other pigeons were asleep. The little robber girl put her arm around Gerda's neck, held the knife in her other hand, and slept so you could hear it. But Gerda couldn't shut her eyes at all: she didn't know whether she was going to live or die. The robbers sat around the fire, singing and drinking, and the robber crone turned somersaults. Oh, it was quite a horrible sight for the little girl to look upon.

Then the wood pigeons said, "Coo! Coo! We have seen little Kay. A white hen was carrying his sled. He was sitting in the Snow Queen's carriage, which rushed low over the forest when we were in the nest. She blew on us squabs, and all died save the two of us. Coo! Coo!"

"What are you saying up there?" cried Gerda. "Where did the Snow Queen go? Do you know anything about that?"

"As likely as not she journeyed to Lappland. There's always snow and ice there. Just ask the reindeer, who stands tied with the rope."

"That's where the ice and snow are; that's a glorious and a grand place to be," said the reindeer. "That's where you can spring freely about in the great shining valleys. That's where the Snow Queen has her summer tent, but her permanent castle is up near the North Pole on the island they call Spitzbergen!"

"Oh, Kay, little Kay!" sighed Gerda.

"Now you're to lie still!" said the robber girl. "Or else you'll get the knife in your belly!"

In the morning Gerda told her everything that the wood pigeons had said, and the robber girl looked quite grave, but nodded her head and said, "No matter! No matter! Do you know where Lappland is?" she asked the reindeer.

"Who should know that better than I do?" said the animal, and its eyes danced in its head. "That's where I was born and bred; that's where I frolicked on the snowy wastes."

"Listen!" said the robber girl to Gerda. "You see that all our menfolk are away, but Mama's still here, and she's staying. But a little later in the morning she'll have a drink from the big bottle, and afterwards she'll take a little nap upstairs. Then I'm going to do something for you." Now she jumped out of the bed, flung herself on her mother's neck, yanked her moustache, and said, "My own sweet nanny goat, good morning!" And her mother tweaked her nose so it turned both red and blue, but it was all out of pure affection.

Now, when the mother had taken a drink from her bottle and was having a little nap, the robber girl went over to the reindeer and said, "I'd so like to keep on tickling you a lot more with that sharp knife, for then you're so funny. But no matter. I'm going to untie your knot and help you outside so you can run to Lappland. But you're to take to your heels and carry this little girl for me to the Snow Queen's castle, where her little playmate is. I daresay you've heard what she said, for she talked loud enough and you eavesdrop."

The reindeer jumped high for joy. The robber girl lifted little Gerda up and was prudent enough to tie her fast— yes, even give her a little pillow to sit on. "No matter," she said. "There are your fleecy boots, for it's going to be cold. But I'm keeping the muff, it's much too lovely! Still, you won't freeze. Here are my mother's big mittens; they reach up to your elbows. Put them on! Now your hands look just like my nasty mother's!"

And Gerda wept for joy.

"I can't stand your sniveling!" said the little robber girl. "Now you should looked pleased! And here are two loaves and a ham for you so you can't starve." Both were tied to the reindeer's back. The little robber girl opened the door, called in all the big hounds, and then cut through the rope with her knife and said to the reindeer, "Now run! But take good care of the little girl!"

And Gerda stretched out her hands in the big mittens to the robber girl and said farewell, and then the reindeer flew away, over bushes and stubble, through the great forest, over marsh and steppes, as fast as it could. The wolves howled and the ravens screeched. "Sputter! Sputter!" came from the sky. It was just as if it sneezed red.

"They're my old Northern Lights!" said the reindeer. "See how they shine!" And then it ran on even faster, night and day. The loaves were eaten, the ham too, and then they were in Lappland.

SIXTH TALE:
THE LAPP WIFE AND THE FINN WIFE

They came to a standstill by a little house; it was so wretched. The roof went down to the ground, and the door was so low that the family had to crawl on their stomachs when they wanted to go out or in. There was nobody home except an old Lapp wife, who stood frying fish over a train-oil lamp. And the reindeer told her Gerda's whole story, but first its own, for it thought that was more important, and Gerda was so chilled that she couldn't speak.

"Alas, you poor wretches!" said the Lapp wife. "You've still got a long way to run! You have to go hundreds of miles into Finnmark, for that's where the Snow Queen stays in the country and burns blue lights every single evening. I'll write a few words on a piece of dried cod—I don't have paper. I'll give it to you to take to the Finn wife up there; she can give you better directions than I can!"

And now, when Gerda had warmed up and had something to eat and drink, the Lapp wife wrote a few words on a piece of dried cod, told Gerda to take good care of it, and tied her onto the reindeer again, and away it sprang. "Sputter! Sputter!" it said up in the sky. All night the loveliest blue Northern Lights were burning—and then they came to Finnmark and knocked on the Finn wife's chimney, for she didn't even have a door.

It was so hot in there that the Finn wife herself went about almost completely naked. She was small and quite swarthy. She loosened little Gerda's clothing at once, took off the mittens and the boots (or else she would have been too hot), put a piece of ice on the reindeer's head, and then read what was written on the dried cod. She read it three times, and then she knew it by heart and put the fish in the food caldron, for it could be eaten and she never wasted anything.

Now the reindeer told first its own story and then little Gerda's. And the Finn wife blinked her wise eyes, but didn't say a thing.

"You're so wise," said the reindeer. "I know that you can bind all the Winds of the World with a sewing thread. When the skipper unties one knot, he gets a good wind; when he unties the second, a keen wind blows; and when he unties the third and fourth, there's such a storm that the forest falls down. Won't you give the little girl a draft so she can gain the strength of twelve men and overpower the Snow Queen?"

"The strength of twelve men!" said the Finn wife. "Indeed, that'll go a long way!" And then she went over to a shelf and took a big, rolled-up hide, and this she unrolled. Curious letters were written on it, and the Finn wife read it until the water poured down her forehead.

But again the reindeer begged so much for little Gerda, and Gerda looked with such beseeching tearful eyes at the Finn wife, that the latter started to blink her eyes again and drew the reindeer over in a corner, where she whispered to it while she put fresh ice on its head.

"Little Kay is with the Snow Queen, to be sure, and finds everything there quite to his liking and believes it's the best place in the world. But that's because he's got a fragment of glass in his heart and a tiny grain of glass in his eye. They have to come out first, or else he'll never become a man and the Snow Queen will keep him in her power."

"But can't you give little Gerda something to take so she can gain power over it all?"

"I can't give her greater power than she already has. Don't you see how great it is? Don't you see how mortals and animals have to serve her, how, in her bare feet, she has come so far in the world? She mustn't be made aware of her power by us. It's in her heart, it's in the fact that she is a sweet, innocent child. If she herself can't come in to the Snow Queen and get the glass out of little Kay, then we can't help! About ten miles from here the garden of the Snow Queen begins. You can carry the little girl there and put her down by the big bush with red berries that's standing in the snow. Don't linger to gossip, but hurry back here!" And then the Finn wife lifted little Gerda up onto the reindeer, which ran with all its might.

"Oh, I didn't get my boots! I didn't get my mittens!" cried little Gerda. She could feel that in the stinging cold, but the reindeer dared not stop. It ran until it came to the big bush with the red berries. There it put little Gerda down and kissed her on the mouth, and big shining tears ran down the animal's cheeks, and then it ran back again with all its might. There stood poor Gerda, without shoes, without gloves, in the middle of the dreadful, ice-cold Finnmark.

She ran forward as fast as she could; then along came a whole regiment of snowflakes. But they didn't fall down from the sky, for it was quite clear and shone with the Northern Lights. The snowflakes ran along the ground, and indeed, the nearer they came, the bigger they grew. Gerda probably remembered how big and queer they had looked that time she had seen the snowflakes through the burning glass. But here, of course, they were much much bigger and more horrible—they were alive. They were the Snow Queen's advance guard. They had the strangest shapes. Some looked like huge loathsome porcupines, others like whole knots of snakes that stuck forth their heads, and others like little fat bears with bristly hair—all shining white, all living snowflakes.

Then little Gerda said the Lord's Prayer, and the cold was so intense that she could see her own breath; it poured out of her mouth like smoke. Her breath grew denser and denser until it took the shape of little bright angels that grew bigger and bigger when they touched the ground. And they all had helmets on their heads and spears and shields in their hands. More and more of them appeared, and when Gerda had finished her prayers there was a whole legion of them. And they hacked at the horrible snowflakes with their spears until they flew into hundreds of pieces, and little Gerda walked on quite safely and fearlessly. The angels patted her feet and hands, and then she didn't feel the cold so much, and walked quickly on toward the Snow Queen's castle.

But now we should first see how Kay is getting along. To be sure, he wasn't thinking of little Gerda, and least of all that she was standing outside the castle.

SEVENTH TALE:
WHAT HAPPENED IN THE SNOW QUEEN'S CASTLE AND WHAT HAPPENED AFTERWARD

The castle walls were of the driven snow, and the windows and doors of the biting winds. There were more than a hundred halls, according to the way the snow drifted; the biggest stretched for many miles, all lit up by the intense Northern Lights; and they were so big, so bare, so icy cold, and so sparkling. Never was there any merriment here, not even so much as a little ball for the bears, where the storm could blow up and the polar bears could walk on their hind legs and put on fancy airs. Never a little game party, with muzzle tag and touch paw; never the least little bit of gossiping over coffee by the white lady-foxes; empty, big, and cold it was in the halls of the Snow Queen. The Northern Lights flared up so punctually that you could figure out by counting when they were at their highest and when they were at their lowest. In the middle of that bare, unending snow hall there was a frozen sea. It had cracked into a thousand fragments, but each fragment was so exactly like the next that it was quite a work of art. And in the middle of it sat the Snow Queen—when she was at home—and then she said that she was sitting on the Mirror of Reason and that it was the best and the only one in this world.

Little Kay was quite blue with cold, yes, almost black; but still he didn't notice it, for after all she had kissed the shivers out of him, and his heart was practically a lump of ice. He went about dragging some sharp, flat fragments of ice, which he arranged in every possible way, for he wanted to get something out of it—just as the rest of us have small pieces of wood and arrange these in patterns, and this is called the "Chinese Puzzle." Kay also made patterns, a most curious one; this was the "Ice Puzzle of Reason." To his eyes the pattern was quite excellent and of the utmost importance. This was due to the grain of glass that was sitting in his eye! He arranged whole figures that made up a written word, but he could never figure out how to arrange the very word he wanted: the word "eternity." And the Snow Queen had said, "If you can arrange that pattern for me, then you shall be your own master, and I shall make you a present of the whole world and a pair of new skates." But he wasn't able to.

"Now I'm rushing off to the warm countries!" said the Snow Queen. "I want to have a look down in the black caldrons!" Those were the volcanoes Etna and Vesuvius, as they are called. "I'm going to whiten them a bit; that's customary; it does good above lemons and wine grapes!" And then the Snow Queen flew off, and Kay sat quite alone in the big bare hall of ice many miles long, and looked at the pieces of ice, and thought and thought until he creaked. He sat quite stiff and still—you'd have thought he was frozen to death.

It was then that little Gerda came into the castle through the huge doors of the biting winds; but she said an evening prayer, and then the winds abated as if they were going to sleep, and she stepped into the big bare cold hall. Then she saw Kay. She recognized him, flung her arms around his neck, held him so tight, and cried, "Kay! Sweet little Kay! So I've found you, then!"

But he sat quite still, stiff, and cold. Then little Gerda cried hot tears. They fell on his chest, they soaked into his heart, they thawed out the lump of ice, and ate away the little fragment of mirror that was in there. He looked at her and she sang the hymn:

> "Roses growing in the dale
> Where the Holy Child we hail."

Then Kay burst into tears. He cried until the grain of the mirror rolled out of his eye. He knew her and shouted jubilantly, "Gerda! Sweet little Gerda! Where have you been all this time? And where have I been?" And he looked about him. "How cold it is here! How empty and big!" And he clung to Gerda, and she laughed and cried for joy. It was so wonderful that even the fragments of ice danced for joy on all sides. And when they were tired and lay down, they arranged themselves in the very letters the Snow Queen had said he was to find, and then he would be his own master and she would give him the whole world and a pair of new skates.

And Gerda kissed his cheeks and they blossomed; she kissed his eyes and they shone like hers; she kissed his hands and feet and he was well and strong. The Snow Queen was welcome to come home if she liked. His release stood written there in shining pieces of ice.

And they took each other by the hand and wandered out of the big castle; they talked about Grandmother and about the roses up on the roof. And wherever they walked, the winds abated and the sun broke through. And when they came to the bush with the red berries, the reindeer was standing there waiting. It had with it another reindeer, whose udder was full, and it gave the little ones its warm milk and kissed them on the mouth. Then they carried Kay and Gerda, first to the Finn wife, where they warmed themselves in the hot room, and were told about the journey home, and then to the Lapp wife, who had sewed new clothes for them and put her sleigh in order.

And the reindeer and the young reindeer sprang alongside and accompanied them all the way to the border of the country, where the first green sprouts were peeping forth. There they took leave of the reindeer and the Lapp wife.

"Farewell!" they all said.

And the first little birds began to twitter; the forest had

green buds; and out of it, riding on a magnificent horse, which Gerda recognized (it had been hitched to the golden coach), came a young girl with a blazing red cap on her head and pistols in front. It was the little robber girl, who had become bored with staying at home and now wanted to go North first and later in another direction if she weren't content.

She recognized Gerda at once, and Gerda recognized her! They were delighted.

"You're a funny one to go traipsing about!" she said to little Kay. "I'd really like to know whether you deserve someone running to the ends of the earth for your sake!"

But Gerda patted her on the cheek and asked about the prince and princess.

"They've gone away to foreign lands," said the robber girl.

"But the crow?" asked little Gerda.

"Well, the crow is dead!" she replied. "The tame sweetheart has become a widow and goes about with a bit of woolen yarn around her leg. She complains pitifully, and it's all rubbish! But tell me now how you've fared and how you got hold of him!"

And Gerda and Kay both told her.

"And snip, snap, snee, go on a spree!" said the robber girl, and taking them both by the hand, she promised that if she ever came through their city, she would come and pay them a visit.

And then she rode out into the wide world. But Kay and Gerda walked hand in hand. It was a lovely spring, with flowers and greenery. The church bells rang, and they recognized the high towers, the big city. It was the one in which they lived, and they went into it and over to Grandmother's door, up the stairs into the room where everything stood in the same spot as before, and the clock said, "Ticktock!" and the hands went around. But as they went through the door they noticed that they had become grown people. The blooming roses from the gutter were coming in through the open window, and there stood the little baby chairs. And Kay and Gerda sat on their own chairs and held each other by the hand. They had forgotten the cold, empty splendor of the Snow Queen's castle like a bad dream. Grandma was sitting in God's clear sunshine and reading aloud from the Bible: "Except ye become as little children, ye shall not enter into the Kingdom of Heaven."

And Kay and Gerda gazed into each other's eyes, and they understood at once the old hymn:

> Roses growing in the dale
> Where the Holy Child we hail.

And they both sat, grown up and yet children—children at heart. And it was summer—the warm, glorious summer.

The Darning Needle

❖　❖　❖

THERE was once a darning needle who put on such a lot of airs that she fancied she was a sewing needle.

"Now, just mind what you're holding!" said the darning needle to the fingers that took her out. "Don't drop me! If I fall on the floor I'm capable of never being found again, I'm so fine!"

"Well, I wouldn't go so far!" said the fingers, and then they squeezed her around the middle.

"Do you see, here I come with a suite!" said the darning needle, and then she drew a long thread after her—though it didn't have a knot.

The fingers guided the needle straight at the kitchen maid's slipper, where the vamp had been torn and was now going to be sewn together.

"That is degrading work!" said the darning needle. "I'll never go through. I'm breaking! I'm breaking!" And then she broke. "What did I tell you!" said the darning needle. "I'm too fine!"

"Now she's no good for anything," thought the fingers, but still they had to hold her tight. The kitchen maid dripped sealing wax on her, and then stuck her in the front of her kerchief.

"See, now I'm a brooch!" said the darning needle. "I knew very well that I would come into favor. When one is something, one always becomes something." And then she laughed deep down inside, for you can never tell from the outside that a darning needle is laughing. There she sat now, as proud as if she were driving in a carriage, and looked around on all sides.

"May I have the honor of inquiring whether you are of gold?" she asked the pin who was her neighbor. "You're lovely to look at, and you have your very own head. But it is small! You must see to it that it grows out, because not everyone can have sealing wax dripped on his end!" And then the darning needle drew herself up so proudly that she fell out of the kerchief and into the sink just as the kitchen maid was rinsing it out.

"Now we're going on a journey!" said the darning needle. "As long as I don't get lost!" But so she did.

"I'm too fine for this world!" she said as she sat in the gutter. "I'm fully aware of it, and that's always a slight pleasure!" And then the darning needle held herself erect and didn't lose her good spirits.

All sorts of things were sailing over her: sticks, straws, pieces of newspaper. "See how they sail!" said the darning needle. "Little do they know what's behind it all. I'm behind it all! I'm sitting here. See, there goes a stick now. It thinks of nothing but 'sticks,' and it is one itself. There floats a straw—see how it whirls, see how it twirls! Don't think about yourself so much, you'll bump against the paving stones! There floats a newspaper; everything in it is forgotten and still it spreads! I sit patiently and quietly! I know what I am, and this I shall remain."

One day something nearby shone prettily, and so the darning needle thought it was a diamond, but it was a fragment of a broken bottle. And as it was shining, the darning needle spoke to it and presented herself as a brooch. "I daresay you're a diamond, aren't you?" "Well, something like that." And then each one thought the other was quite costly, and so they talked about the arrogance of the world.

"Yes, I lived in a box belonging to a maiden," said the darning needle. "And that maiden was a kitchen maid. On each hand she had five fingers, but I've never known anything as conceited as those five fingers, and yet they existed for the sole purpose of holding me, taking me out of the box, and putting me in the box."

"Did they shine?" asked the bottle fragment.

"Shine? No," said the darning needle. "No. That was arrogance for you! They were five brothers, born 'fingers' all of them. They carried themselves erect, side by side, although they were of different lengths. The outermost one, Thumbkin, was short and fat. He went outside the row, and then he had but one joint in his back and could bow only once. But he said that if he were chopped off of somebody, then the whole of the person was ruined for military duty. Lick Pan made its way into sweet and sour alike, pointed at the sun and moon, and he's the one who squeezed when they wrote. Longman looked over the heads of the others. Ringman wore a golden ring around his belly, and Little Per didn't do a thing and was proud of it. Boast they did and boast they always will, so I went in the sink!"

"And now we're sitting here, glittering!" said the fragment of glass. At the same moment more water came into the gutter; it overflowed, dragging the bottle fragment along with it.

"See, now it has been promoted!" said the darning needle. "I'll stay where I am; I'm too fine, but I'm proud of it, and that is worthy of respect!" And then she held herself erect and thought of many things.

"I'm inclined to believe I was born of a sunbeam, I'm so fine! And then too, the sun always seems to seek me out under the water. Alas, I'm so fine that my own mother can't find me! If only I had my one eye that broke off, I think I could cry—even though I wouldn't do it, crying just isn't done!"

One day some street urchins were poking about in the gutter, where they found old nails, shillings, and the like. It was a messy pastime, but they enjoyed it.

"Ow!" said one, sticking himself on the darning needle. "There's a fellow for you!"

"I'm not a fellow, I'm a miss!" said the darning needle, but nobody heard it. The sealing wax had come off and she had turned black. But black is slimming, and so she thought she was finer than ever.

"Here comes an eggshell sailing along!" said the boys, and then they stuck the darning needle firmly in the shell.

"White walls, and black myself!" said the darning needle. "That's becoming! At least I can be seen! If only I don't become seasick, for then I'll throw up!" But she didn't become seasick, and she didn't throw up.

"It's good for seasickness to have a stomach of steel and to remember that one is a little more than a human being. Now mine has passed over. Indeed, the finer one is, the more one can endure!"

"Crack!" said the eggshell as a loaded cart went over it. "My, how it squeezes!" said the darning needle. "Now I'm going to be seasick all the same! I'm breaking! I'm breaking!" But she didn't break, even though a whole cart load had gone over her. She was lying at full length—and there she can stay!

The Red Shoes

THERE was once a little girl, so delicate and fair; but in summer she always had to go barefoot, because she was poor, and in winter she wore big wooden shoes, so her little insteps turned quite red—and horribly red at that.

In the middle of the village lived old Mother Shoemaker; she sat and sewed, as well as she could, out of strips of old red cloth, a pair of little shoes. They were quite clumsy, but they were well meant, and the little girl was to have them. The little girl was named Karen.

On the very day her mother was buried she was given the red shoes, and had them on for the first time. To be sure, they weren't the sort of thing to mourn in, but she had no others, and so she walked barelegged in them behind the poor straw coffin.

At that very moment a big old carriage came up, and in it sat a big old lady. She looked at the little girl and felt sorry for her, and so she said to the parson, "Listen here, give that little girl to me and I will be good to her!"

And Karen thought it was all because of the red shoes. But the old lady said they were horrid, and they were burnt. But Karen was given clean, neat clothes to wear; she had to learn to read and sew, and people said she was pretty, but the mirror said, "You're much more than pretty, you're lovely!"

Once the queen journeyed through the land, and she took with her, her little daughter, who was a princess. People streamed to the castle, and Karen was there too. And the little princess stood at a window, dressed in white, and showed herself; she wore neither a train nor a golden crown, but she had on lovely red morocco-leather shoes. To be sure, they were prettier by far than the ones old Mother Shoemaker had made for little Karen. After all, there was nothing in the world like red shoes!

Now Karen was old enough to be confirmed. She was given new clothes, and she was to have new shoes too. The rich shoemaker in the city measured her little foot at home in his own parlor, and there stood big glass cases full of lovely shoes and shiny boots. It was a pretty sight, but the old lady couldn't see very well, and so it gave her no pleasure. In the middle of all the shoes stood a pair of red ones, just like the shoes the princess had worn. How beautiful they were! The shoemaker said that they had been made for the daughter of an earl, but they didn't fit.

"I daresay they're of patent leather!" said the old lady. "They shine!"

"Yes, they shine!" said Karen. And they fit and they were bought, but the old lady had no idea that they were red, for she would never have permitted Karen to go to confirmation in red shoes. But that is exactly what she did.

Everybody looked at her feet, and as she walked up the aisle to the chancel it seemed to her that even the old pictures on the tombs—the portraits of parsons and parsons' wives, in stiff ruff collars and long black robes—fixed their eyes on her red shoes. And she thought only of these when the parson laid his hand upon her head and spoke of the holy baptism, of the covenant with God, and said that now she was to be a grown-up Christian. And the organ played so solemnly, and the beautiful voices of children sang, and the old choirmaster sang. But Karen thought only of the red shoes.

By afternoon the old lady had been informed by everyone that the shoes had been red, and she said it was shameful! It wasn't done! And after this, when Karen went to church, she was always to wear black shoes, even if they were old.

Next Sunday was communion, and Karen looked at the black shoes and she looked at the red ones—and then she looked at the red ones again and put the red ones on. It was beautiful sunny weather. Karen and the old lady took the path through the cornfield, and it was a bit dusty there.

By the door of the church stood an old soldier with a crutch and a curious long beard. It was more red than white, for it was red. And he bent all the way down to the ground and asked the old lady if he might wipe off her shoes. And Karen stretched out her little foot too. "See what lovely dancing shoes!" said the soldier. "Stay put when you dance!" And then he struck the soles with his hand.

The old lady gave the soldier a shilling, and then she went into the church with Karen.

And all the people inside looked at Karen's red shoes, and all the portraits looked at them, and when Karen knelt before the altar and lifted the golden chalice to her lips, she thought of nothing but the red shoes; and it seemed to her that they were swimming about in the chalice, and she forgot to sing her hymn, forgot to say the Lord's Prayer.

Now everybody went out of the church, and the old lady climbed into her carriage. Karen lifted her foot to climb in behind her, when the old soldier, who was standing nearby, said: "See what lovely dancing shoes!" And Karen couldn't help it, she had to take a few dancing steps! And once she had started, her feet kept on dancing. 't was just as if the shoes had gained control over them.

She danced around the corner of the church; she couldn't stop! The coachman had to run after her and grab hold of her, and he lifted her up into the carriage. But the feet kept on dancing, giving the old lady some terrible kicks. At last they got the shoes off, and the feet came to rest.

At home the shoes were put up in a cupboard, but Karen couldn't stop looking at them.

Now the old lady was ill in bed. They said she couldn't live. She had to be nursed and taken care of, and Karen was the proper person to do it. But over in the city there was a great ball. Karen had been invited. She looked at the old lady, who wasn't going to live after all, she looked at the red shoes, and she didn't think there was anything sinful in that. She put the red shoes on, too; surely she could do that—but then she went to the ball, and then she started to dance.

But when she wanted to go to the right, the shoes danced to the left, and when she wanted to go up the floor, the shoes danced down the floor, down the stairs, through the street, and out of the city gate. Dance she did and dance she must—straight out into the gloomy forest.

Then something was shining up among the trees, and she thought it was the moon, for it was a face. But it was the old soldier with the red beard. He sat and nodded, and said, "See what lovely dancing shoes!"

Now she became terrified and wanted to throw away the red shoes, but they stayed put; and she ripped off her stockings, but the shoes had grown fast to her feet. And dance she did and dance she must, over field and meadow, in rain and sunshine, by night and by day. But the night-time was the most horrible.

She danced into the graveyard, but the dead there didn't dance; they had something better to do than dance. She wanted to sit down on the pauper's grave where the bitter tansy grew, but there was no peace or rest for her. And when she danced over toward the open door of the church, she saw an angel there in a long white robe, with wings that reached from his shoulders down to the ground. His face was hard and grave, and in his hand he held a sword, so broad and shining.

"Dance you shall!" he said. "Dance in your red shoes until you turn pale and cold! Until your skin shrivels up like a skeleton! Dance you shall from door to door, and where there are proud and vain children, you shall knock so they will hear you and fear you! Dance you shall, dance!"

"Mercy!" cried Karen. But she didn't hear the angel's reply, for the shoes carried her through the gate, out in

the field, over roads, over paths, and she had to keep on dancing.

One morning she danced past a door she knew well. The sound of a hymn came from inside, and they carried out a coffin decorated with flowers. Then she knew that the old lady was dead, and she felt that she had been abandoned by everyone and cursed by God's angel.

Dance she did and dance she must. Dance in the dark night. The shoes carried her off through thorns and stubble, and she scratched herself until the blood flowed; she danced on, over the heath, to a lonely little house. She knew that the executioner lived here, and she knocked on the pane with her finger and said, "Come out! Come out! I can't come in because I'm dancing!"

And the executioner said, "You probably don't know who I am, do you? I chop the heads off wicked people, and I can feel my ax quivering!"

"Don't chop off my head," said Karen, "for then I can't repent my sin! But chop off my feet with the red shoes!"

And then she confessed all her sins, and the executioner chopped off her feet with the red shoes. But the shoes danced away with the tiny feet, over the field and into the deep forest.

And he carved wooden feet and crutches for her and taught her a hymn that sinners always sing; and she kissed the hand that had swung the ax, and went across the heath.

"Now I've suffered enough for the red shoes!" she said. "Now I'm going to church so they can see me!" And she walked fairly quickly toward the church door. But when she got there, the red shoes were dancing in front of her, and she grew terrified and turned back.

All week long she was in agony and cried many heavy tears. But when Sunday came she said: "That's that! Now I've suffered and struggled enough. I daresay I'm just as good as many of those who sit there in church putting on airs!" And then she went bravely enough, but she got no farther than the gate. Then she saw the red shoes dancing ahead of her, and she grew terrified and turned back, and deeply repented her sin.

And she went over to the parsonage and begged to be taken into service there; she would work hard and do anything she could. She didn't care about the wages, only that she might have a roof over her head and stay with good people. And the parson's wife felt sorry for her and took her into her service. And she was diligent and pensive. She sat quietly and listened when the parson read aloud from the Bible in the evening. All the little ones were quite fond of her, but when they talked of finery and dressing up, and of being as lovely as a queen, she would shake her head.

The next Sunday they all went to church, and they asked her if she wanted to come with them. But she looked miserably at her crutches with tears in her eyes, and so they went to hear the word of God while she went in her little chamber alone. It was just big enough for a bed and a chair, and here she sat with her hymn book; and as she was piously reading in it the wind carried the strains of the organ over to her from the church. And with tears in her eyes, she lifted up her face and said, "O God, help me!"

Then the sun shone brightly, and right in front of her stood the angel of God in the white robe, the one she had seen that night in the door of the church. He was no longer holding the sharp sword, but a lovely green branch full of roses. And with it he touched the ceiling, and it rose high; and where he had touched it there shone a golden star. And he touched the walls, and they expanded, and she saw the organ that was playing; she saw the old pictures of the parsons and the parsons' wives. The congregation was sitting in the ornamented pews and singing from the hymn books; for the church itself had come home to the poor girl in the tiny, narrow chamber, or else she had come to it. She was sitting in the pew with the rest of the parson's family, and when they had finished singing the hymn and looked up, they nodded and said, "It was right of you to come, Karen."

"It was by the grace of God!" she said.

And the organ swelled, and the voices of the children in the choir sounded so soft and lovely. The bright sunshine streamed in through the window to the pew where Karen sat. Her heart was so full of sunshine and contentment and happiness that it broke. Her soul flew on the sunshine to God, and there was no one there who asked about the red shoes.

The Jumpers

❖ ❖ ❖

THE flea, the grasshopper, and the skipjack once wanted to see which of them could jump the highest, and so they invited the whole world—and anybody else who wanted to come—to see the fun. And they were three proper jumpers who came together in the room.

"Well, I'm giving my daughter to the one who jumps the highest!" said the king. "For it's poor consolation that those persons should jump for nothing!"

The flea stepped forward first. He had genteel manners and bowed on every side, for he had spinster blood in his veins and was used to associating with people. And that, after all, means a lot.

The grasshopper came next. He, of course, was considerably bigger, but still he had quite good manners. He was wearing a green uniform, which he had been born with. What's more, this personage said that he came of a very old family in the land of Egypt, and that back home he was prized very highly. He had been taken right out of the field and put in a house of cards, three stories high— all face cards, with the colored side turned in. It had both doors and windows that had been cut out of the waist of the Queen of Hearts.

"I sing so well," he said, "that sixteen local crickets, who have been chirping ever since they were small and

have not yet been given a house of cards, were so vexed
that they became even thinner after listening to me sing."

Both of them—the flea and the grasshopper—thus gave
a good accounting of who they were and why they thought
they could indeed wed a princess.

The skipjack said nothing, but it was said that he thought
all the more; and the court hound sniffed at him alone
because he recognized that the skipjack came of a good
family. The old alderman, who had been given three
orders for keeping silent, maintained that the skipjack had
the gift of prophecy: one could tell from his back whether
the winter would be mild or severe, and one can't even
tell that from the back of the man who writes the Almanac.

"Well, I'm not saying a thing," said the old king, "but
then I always did go about this way and keep my thoughts
to myself!"

Now the jumping was to begin. The flea jumped so high

that no one could see him, and so they contended that he
hadn't jumped at all. And this was unfair.

The grasshopper only jumped half as high, but he landed right in the king's face, so the king said that was revolting!

The skipjack stood still and meditated for a long time. At last they thought he couldn't jump at all.

"If only he hasn't become indisposed!" said the court hound, and then he sniffed at him again: SWOOOOOOOSH! The skipjack jumped a tiny, wobbly jump right into the lap of the princess, who was sitting on a low golden stool.

Then the king said, "The highest jump is to jump up to my daughter, for that's the very point! But a head is needed to hit upon such a thing, and the skipjack has shown that he has a head. He has legs in his forehead!"

And so he got the princess.

"Nonetheless I jumped the highest!" said the flea. "But it doesn't matter. Just let her have that contraption of pegs and wax. I jumped the highest! But in this world one needs a body if one is to be seen."

And then the flea went abroad to the wars, where it is said he was killed.

The grasshopper sat down in a ditch and thought over the way of the world as it really is. And then he also said, "What's needed is a body! What's needed is a body!"

And then he sang his own melancholy song, and this is where we have taken the story from. But it could very well be a lie, even if it has appeared in print.

The Shepherdess and the Chimney Sweep

❖ ❖ ❖

HAVE you ever seen a really old wooden cupboard, quite black with age and carved with scrolls and foliage? Just such a cupboard was standing in a parlor. It had been inherited from a great-grandmother and was carved with roses and tulips from top to bottom. There were the most curious scrolls, and here and there among them tiny stags were sticking out their antler-covered heads. But in the middle of the cupboard had been carved a whole man; just looking at him was enough to make you grin. And grin he did—you couldn't call it laughing. He had the legs of a billy goat, tiny horns in his forehead, and a long beard. The children of the house called him "Billygoatlegs Chiefandsubordinategeneralwarcommandersergeant," for it was a hard name to say, and there aren't many who receive that title. But to have him carved out was also something! Yet there he stood! He was always staring over at the table under the mirror, for there stood a lovely little shepherdess of porcelain. Her shoes were gilded, her dress was daintily tucked up with a red rose, and she had a golden hat and a shepherd's crook. She was delightful! Close by her side stood a little chimney sweep, as black as coal, but of porcelain too, for that matter. He was just as clean and handsome as anybody else—a chimney sweep was only something he was supposed to be. The porcelain-

201

maker could just as well have made him a prince, it made
no difference.

There he stood so nicely with his ladder, and with a face
as rosy and as fair as a girl's. And this was really a mistake,
for at least he could have been made a little black. He
stood quite close to the shepherdess. They had both been
placed where they were standing, and as they had been
placed like this, they had become engaged. After all, they
were well suited to each other: they were young, they

were both made of the same porcelain, and they were
equally as fragile.

Close by them stood yet another doll, which was three
times as big. This was an old Chinaman who could nod.
He was also made of porcelain and said he was the little
shepherdess' grandfather. But he certainly couldn't prove
it! He insisted that he had authority over her, and this is
why he nodded to Billygoatlegs Chiefandsubordinategeneralwarcommandersergeant, who had been courting the
little shepherdess.

"You'll be getting a man there!" said the old Chinaman.
"A man I'm almost certain is made of mahogany. He can
make you 'Mrs. Billygoatlegs Chiefandsubordinategeneralwarcommandersergeant,' and he has the whole cupboard
full of silver—in addition to what he has in secret drawers."

"I won't go inside that dark cupboard!" said the little
shepherdess. "I've heard it said that he has eleven porcelain wives in there!"

"Then you can be the twelfth!" said the Chinaman.
"Tonight, as soon as the old cupboard starts to creak, the
wedding will be held—as sure as I'm Chinese." And then
he nodded his head and fell asleep.

But the little shepherdess cried and looked at her dearly
beloved, the porcelain chimney sweep.

"I do believe I will ask you," she said, "to go out into
the wide world with me, for we can't stay here!"

"I'll do anything you wish!" said the little chimney
sweep. "Let us go right away; I daresay I can support you
by my profession!"

"If only we were safely down off the table!" she said. "I
won't be happy until we're out in the wide world!"

And he comforted her and showed her where to place
her little foot on the carved edges and the gilded foliage
down around the table leg. He also used his ladder, and
then they were down on the floor. But when they looked
over at the old cupboard, there was quite a commotion!

All the carved deer were thrusting out their heads even farther and raising their antlers and craning their necks. Billygoatlegs Chiefandsubordinategeneralwarcommandersergeant hopped high in the air and shouted to the old Chinaman, "There they run! There they run!"

This frightened them a little, and they quickly jumped up into the drawer of the dais. Here lay three or four packs of cards that weren't complete and a little toy theater that had been set up as well as possible. A play was being performed, and all the queens—diamonds and hearts, clubs and spades—were sitting in the first row, fanning themselves with their tulips. And behind them stood all the jacks and showed that they had heads both right side up and upside down, the way playing cards do. The play was about two sweethearts who couldn't have each other, and it made the shepherdess cry, for it was just like her own story.

"I cannot bear it!" she said. "I must get out of the drawer!" But when they were down on the floor and looked up at the table, the old Chinaman was awake and his whole body was rocking—for his lower half was a single lump.

"Now the old Chinaman is coming!" screamed the little shepherdess, and she was so miserable that she fell right down on her procelain knees.

"I've got an idea!" said the chimney sweep. "Let's crawl down in the big potpourri crock that stands in the corner. There we could lie on roses and lavender and throw salt in his eyes when he comes."

"That would never do," she said. "And besides, I know that the old Chinaman and the potpourri crock were once engaged, and there's always a little feeling left when you've been on such terms. No, there's nothing left to do but to go out into the wide world!"

"Do you really have enough courage to go out into the wide world with me?" asked the chimney sweep. "Have you ever thought of how big it is and that we could never come back here again?"

"I have!" she said.

Then the chimney sweep gave her a steady look and said, "My way goes through the chimney. Do you really have enough courage to crawl with me through the tiled stove, through both the drum and the flue? Then we come out in the chimney, and from there I know what to do. We'll climb so high that they can't reach us. And at the very top there is a hole out to the wide world."

And he led her to the door of the tiled stove.

"It looks black!" she said, but still she went with him, through the drum and through the flue, where it was as black as pitch.

"Now we're in the chimney!" he said. "And look! Look! The loveliest star is shining up above!"

And there in the sky was a real star that shone all the way down to them, as if it wanted to show them the way. And they crawled and they crept—it was a terrible way—so high, so high! But he lifted her and he helped her; he held her and pointed out the easiest places for her to put her tiny porcelain feet. Then they came all the way up to the edge of the chimney. And there they sat down, for they were really tired—and so they should be too.

The sky with all its stars was overhead, and the city with all its rooftops lay down below. They could see far around them, so far out into the world. The poor shepherdess had never imagined it was like this. She lay her little head against her chimney sweep, and then she cried so hard that the gold popped off her sash.

"It's much too much!" she said. "I cannot bear it! The world is much too big! If only I were back there again. I have followed you out into the wide, wide world, so now you can just follow me home again if you have any feelings for me!"

And the chimney sweep tried to talk sense into her. He

talked about the old Chinaman, and about Billygoatlegs Chiefandsubordinategeneralwarconmandersergeant. But she sobbed so bitterly, and kissed her little chimney sweep so, that the only thing he could do was to do as she said, even though it was wrong.

And so with considerable difficulty they crawled back down through the chimney, and they crept through the flue and the drum—it wasn't at all pleasant. And then they were standing in the dark stove, eavesdropping behind the door to find out how things stood in the room. It was quite still. They peeked out. Alas! There in the middle of the floor lay the old Chinaman. He had fallen down off the table while trying to go after them, and lay broken in three pieces. His back had come off in one piece, and his head had rolled over in a corner. Billygoatlegs Chiefandsubordinategeneralwarcommandersergeant stood where he always stood, thinking everything over.

"It's gruesome!" said the little shepherdess. "Old grandfather is smashed to bits, and we're to blame! I can never live it down!" And then she wrung her teeny-weeny hands.

"He can still be riveted," said the chimney sweep. "He can be riveted very well. Don't carry on so! After they glue his back and put a good rivet in his neck, he'll be just as good as new and be able to tell us many unpleasantries!"

"Do you think so?" she said. And then they crawled back up on the table where they had stood before.

"See how far we've come!" said the chimney sweep. "We could have spared ourselves all that bother!"

"If only old grandfather were riveted," said the shepherdess. "Can it be too expensive?"

And he was riveted. The family had his back glued, and a good rivet was put in his neck. He was just as good as new, but he couldn't nod.

"You've certainly become high and mighty since you were broken!" said Billygoatlegs Chiefandsubordinategeneralwarcommandersergeant. "Although I don't think that's anything to be so proud of! Am I to have her or am I not?"

And the chimney sweep and the little shepherdess gave the old Chinaman such a piteous look. They were afraid he was going to nod. But he couldn't. And it was unpleasant for him to have to tell a stranger that he would always have a rivet in his neck. So the porcelain people remained together, and they gave grandfather's rivet their blessing and loved each other until they broke into bits.

The Little Match Girl

❖ ❖ ❖

IT was so bitterly cold. It was snowing, and the evening was growing dark. It was also the last evening of the year: New Year's Eve. In this cold and in this darkness a poor little girl was walking along the street. Her head was uncovered and her feet were bare. To be sure, she had been wearing slippers when she left home, but what was the good of that? The slippers were quite big; her mother had used them last, they were so big. And the little girl had lost them when she hurried across the street, just as two carriages went rushing past at a frightful speed. One slipper was nowhere to be found, and a boy had run off with the other. He said he could use it for a cradle when he had children of his own.

There walked the little girl now on her tiny bare feet, which were red and blue with the cold. In an old apron she had a lot of matches, and she carried a bunch in her hand. No one had bought any from her the whole day. No one had given her a single shilling. Hungry and frozen, she looked so cowed as she walked along, the poor little thing. The snowflakes fell on her long golden hair, which curled so prettily about her neck. But of course she didn't think about anything as fine as that. The lights were shining out from all the windows, and there in the street was such a delicious odor of roast goose. After all, it was New Year's Eve. Yes, she did think about that.

Over in a corner between two houses—one of them jutted a little farther out in the street than the other—she sat down and huddled. She tucked her tiny legs under her, but she froze even more, and she dared not go home. She hadn't sold any matches, hadn't received a single shilling. Her father would beat her, and then too it was cold at home. They had only the roof above them, and the wind whistled in even though the biggest cracks had been stuffed with straw and rags. Her tiny hands were almost numb with cold. Alas! One little match would do so much good! Did she dare to pull just one out of the bunch, strike it against the wall and warm her fingers? She pulled one out. Scratch! How it spluttered, how it burned! It was a warm clear flame, just like a tiny candle when she held her hand around it. It was a strange light. It seemed to the little girl that she was sitting before a huge iron stove, with shining brass knobs and a brass drum. The fire burned so wonderfully, was so warming. No, what was that? The little girl was already stretching out her feet to warm them too when the flame went out. The stove disappeared. She sat with a little stump of the burnt-out match in her hand.

A new one was struck. It burned, it shone, and where the light fell on the wall it became transparent like gauze. She looked right into the room where the table was set with a gleaming white cloth, fine china, and a splendid, steaming roast goose stuffed with prunes and apples. And what was even more splendid, the goose hopped down from the platter and waddled across the floor with a fork and a knife in its back. Right over to the poor girl it came. Then the match went out, and only the thick cold wall could be seen.

She lit a new match. Now she was sitting under the loveliest Christmas tree. It was even bigger and had more

decorations on it than the one she had seen through the glass door of the rich merchant's house last Christmas. A thousand candles were burning on the green branches, and gaily colored pictures—like the ones that decorate shop windows—looked down at her. The little girl stretched out both hands in the air. Then the match went out; the many Christmas candles went higher and higher; she saw that they were now bright stars. One of them fell and made a long fiery streak in the sky.

"Now someone is dying!" said the little girl, for her old grandmother—the only one who had ever been good to her, but now was dead—had said that when a star falls, a soul goes up to God.

Again she struck a match against the wall. It shone around her, and in the glow stood the old grandmother, so bright and shining, so blessed and mild.

"Grandma!" cried the little one. "Oh, take me with you! I know you'll be gone when the match goes out, gone just like the warm stove, the wonderful roast goose, and the big, heavenly Christmas tree!" And she hastily struck all the rest of the matches in the bunch. She wanted to keep her grandmother with her. And the matches shone with such a radiance that it was brighter than the light of day. Never before had grandmother been so beautiful, so big. She lifted up the little girl in her arms, and in radiance and rejoicing they flew so high, so high. And there was no cold, no hunger, no fear—they were with God.

But in a corner by the house, in the early-morning cold, sat the little girl with rosy cheeks and a smile on her face—dead, frozen to death on the last evening of the old year. The morning of the New Year dawned over the little body sitting with the matches, of which a bunch was almost burned up. She had wanted to warm herself, it was said. No one knew what lovely sight she had seen or in what radiance she had gone with her old grandmother into the happiness of the New Year.

The Drop of Water

❖ ❖ ❖

YOU are familiar, of course, with a magnifying glass, a round spectacle lens that makes everything a hundred times larger than it is. When you hold it up to your eye and look at a drop of water from the pond, you can see more than thousand strange creatures that are otherwise never seen in the water; but they are there and it is real. It looks almost like a saucer full of shrimps frisking about one another, and they are so gluttonous that they tear arms and legs and bottoms and edges off one another— and yet they are happy and contented in their own fashion.

Now, there was once an old man whom everyone called Wiggle-Waggle, for that was his name. He always wanted the best of everything, and when he couldn't get it, he used magic.

One day he was sitting there, holding his magnifying glass to his eye and looking at a drop of water that had been taken from a puddle in the ditch. My, what a wiggling and a waggling there was! All the thousands of tiny creatures were jumping about, stepping on one another and taking bites out of one another.

"Why, how abominable that is!" said old Wiggle-Waggle. "Can't they be made to live in peace and quiet, and each one mind his own business?" And he thought and he thought, but it wouldn't work. And then he had to start

212

conjuring. "I must give them color so they can be seen plainly," he said, and then he poured something resembling a tiny drop of red wine into the drop of water. But it was witch's blood, the very best sort at two shillings. Then all the strange creatures turned a rosy-red all over their bodies. It looked like a whole city of naked wild men.

"What have you there?" asked an old troll who had no name, and that was what was so fine about him.

"Well, if you can guess what it is," said Wiggle-Waggle, "I shall make you a present of it. But it's not so easy to find out as long as you don't know."

And the troll who had no name looked through the

magnifying glass. It really did look like a whole city, where all the people ran about with no clothes on! It was frightful, but it was even more frightful to see how each one shoved and jostled the other, how they nipped and nibbled at one another and dragged one another forth. The ones at the bottom had to be at the top, and the ones at the top had to be at the bottom. "See! See! His leg is longer than mine! Biff! Away with it! There's one who has a tiny pimple behind his ear, a wee little innocent pimple, but it plagues him, and so it shall not plague him anymore!" And they hacked at it and they tugged at him and they ate him for the sake of that tiny pimple. One was sitting there so still, like a little maiden, and desired only peace and quiet, but the maiden had to come forth, and they tugged at her and they pulled at her and they ate her up!

"It's extremely amusing!" said the troll.

"Yes, but what do you think it is?" asked Wiggle-Waggle. "Can you figure it out?"

"Why, that's easy to see," said the other. "It's Copenhagen, of course, or another big city. They all resemble one another, to be sure. A big city it is!"

"It's water from a ditch!" said Wiggle-Waggle.

The Happy Family

❖　❖　❖

THE biggest green leaf here in the land is, to be sure, a dock leaf. If you hold it in front of your little tummy, it's just like a whole apron; and if you put it on your head, then in rainy weather it's almost as good as an umbrella, for it's so terribly big. A dock plant never grows alone. No, where one grows, there grow more. It's a great delight, and all that delightfulness is food for snails—those big white snails that fashionable people, in the old days, had made into a fricassee, ate, and said, "Yum! How good it tastes!" because they thought it tasted so delicious. The snails lived on dock leaves, and for that reason the dock plants were sown.

Now there was an old manor house where snails were no longer eaten; they were quite extinct. But the dock plants were not extinct. They grew and grew over all the paths and all the beds. It was no longer possible to cope with them. There was a whole forest of dock plants. Here and there stood an apple tree or a plum tree, otherwise you would never have thought it was a garden. Everything was dock plants, and in there lived the last two exceedingly old snails.

They themselves didn't know how old they were; but they could well remember that there had been many more, that they belonged to a family from foreign parts, and that the entire forest had been planted for them and theirs. They had never been beyond it, but they knew that there was one thing more in the world, called The Manor House. And up there you were cooked and then you turned black and then you were placed on a silver platter. But what happened next no one knew. For that matter they couldn't imagine how it felt to be cooked and lie on a silver platter, but it was supposed to be delightful and particularly distinguished. Neither the cockchafer, the toad, nor the earthworm, whom they asked about it, could give them any information. None of them had ever been cooked or placed on a silver platter.

The old white snails were the most aristocratic in the world, they knew; the forest existed for their sakes, and the manor house existed so that they could be cooked and laid on a silver platter.

They now lived quite happily and secluded, and as they had no children themselves, they had adopted an ordinary little snail, which they reared as their own. But the little one wouldn't grow, for he was ordinary. Yet the old folks, especially Mama—Mama Snail—still thought they could see that he was progressing. And she asked Papa, in case he couldn't see it, to feel the little shell. And so he felt it and found out that Mama was right.

One day there was a heavy downpour.

"Listen to how it rub-a-dub-dubs on the dock leaves!" said Papa Snail.

"Drops are coming in too!" said Mama Snail. "Why, it's running right down the stalks! You'll see how wet it's going to be here! I'm so glad we have our good houses, and the little one has his too! More has certainly been done for us than for any other creatures. It's plain to see that we're the Lords and Masters of the world! We have a house from birth, and the dock forest has been sown for our sakes. I'd so like to know how far it stretches and what is beyond it."

"There's nothing beyond it!" said Papa Snail. "There can be no better place than here where we are, and I have nothing else to wish for!"

"Oh, yes," said Mama. "I'd so like to come up to the manor house and be cooked and laid on a silver platter. All our ancestors have, and you can imagine there's something special about that."

"It's possible the manor house may have fallen down," said Papa Snail. "Or else the dock forest has grown up over it so the people can't come out. There's no need to be in such a hurry, either. But you're always in such a terrible rush, and now the little one is starting too. For three days he's been crawling up that stalk. It gives me a headache when I look up at him!"

"Now, you mustn't fuss!" said Mama Snail. "He's crawling so steadily; he'll be a great joy to us, all right, and we old folks have nothing else to live for! But have you thought of where we're going to find a wife for him? Don't you think that far, far inside the dock forest there might be some of our own kind?"

"I daresay there are plenty of black slugs!" said the old snail. "Black slugs without a house. But that would be such a comedown—and they put on airs! But we could commission the ants to look into it. They scurry back and forth as if they had something to do. They certainly must know of a wife for our little snail!"

"Of course, we know of the loveliest one!" said the ants. "But we're afraid it won't do, for she's a queen!"

"That doesn't matter!" said the old snails. "Does she have a house?"

"She has a castle!" said the ants. "The loveliest ant castle, with seven hundred halls!"

"No, thank you!" said Mama Snail. "Our son is not going into an ant hill! If you haven't got better sense, we'll give the commission to the white gnats. They fly far and wide, in sunshine and in rain. They know the dock forest inside and out."

"We have a wife for him!" said the gnats. "A hundred human paces from here, sitting on a gooseberry bush, is a little snail with a house. She is quite alone and old enough to get married. It's only a hundred human paces."

"Well, let her come to him," said the old snails. "He has a forest of dock plants; she has only a bush!"

And so they fetched the little snail maiden. It took eight days for her to get there, but that was just what was so nice about it—one could tell she belonged to the same species.

And then the wedding was held. Six glow worms shone as well as they could, but otherwise it all proceeded quietly, for the old snails couldn't stand carousing and merry-making. But a lovely speech was made by Mama Snail—Papa couldn't, he was so moved. And then they passed on the entire forest of dock plants to them and said what they had always said: that it was the best forest in the world, and as long as they led honest and unpretentious lives and multiplied, then they and their children would one day come to the manor house, be cooked black, and laid on a silver dish.

And after that speech had been made, the old folks crawled into their houses and never came out again; they had gone to sleep. The young snail couple reigned in the forest and had a huge progeny. But they were never cooked, and they never came onto a silver dish. And from this they concluded that the manor house had fallen down, and that all the people in the world were extinct. And as no one contradicted them, it was true, of course. And the rain beat upon the dock leaves to make music for their sakes, and the sun shone on the dock forest to give color for their sakes. And they were very happy, and the whole family was happy. Indeed it was!

The Collar

❖ ❖ ❖

THERE was once a fashionable cavalier whose entire inventory consisted of a bootjack and a comb. But he had the finest collar in the world, and it is about the collar that we are going to hear a tale.

Now, the collar was so old that he was thinking of getting married, and then it happened that he was put in the wash along with a garter.

"My!" said the collar. "I've never seen anyone so slender and so elegant, so soft and so cuddly! May I ask your name?"

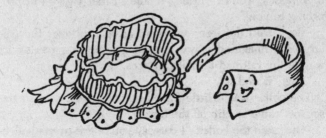

"I'm not saying!" said the garter.

"Where do you belong?" asked the collar.

But the garter was shy and thought this was an odd question to reply to.

"I daresay you're a waistband!" said the collar. "One of those waistbands that are worn underneath! I can see very well that you're both useful and decorative, little maid!"

"You mustn't talk to me!" said the garter. "I don't think I've given you any occasion to!"

"Oh, yes! When anyone's as lovely as you are," said the collar, "then it's occasion enough!"

"Stop coming so close to me!" said the garter. "You look so masculine!"

"I'm a fashionable cavalier too!" said the collar. "I have a bootjack and a comb!" Now that, of course, wasn't true. It was his master who had them, but he was bragging.

"Don't come near me!" said the garter. "I'm not used to it!"

"Prude!" said the collar, and then he was taken out of the wash. He was starched, hung on a chair in the sunshine, and then placed on an ironing board. Along came the hot iron.

"Madame!" said the collar. "Little widow lady! I'm turning quite warm! I'm becoming quite another! I'm losing my creases! You're burning a hole in me! Ugh—I'm proposing to you!"

"Rag!" said the iron, and went arrogantly over the collar; for it imagined it was a steam engine that was on its way to the railroad to pull carriages.

"Rag!" it said.

The collar was a little frayed at the edges, and so the scissors came to clip off the fuzz.

"Oh!" said the collar. "I daresay you're the prima ballerina! My, how you can stretch your legs! That's the most adorable sight I've ever seen! No human being can ever equal you!"

"I know that!" said the scissors.

"You deserve to be a countess!" said the collar. "All I

have is a fashionable cavalier, a bootjack, and a comb! If only I had an estate!"

"He's proposing!" said the scissors, growing angry. And then it gave him a proper clip, and so he was discarded.

"I daresay I must propose to the comb!" said the collar. "It's incredible the way you keep all your teeth, little miss! Haven't you ever thought of becoming engaged?"

"I'll say I have!" said the comb. "I'm engaged to the bootjack!"

"Engaged!" said the collar. Now there were no more to propose to, and so he scorned proposing.

A long time passed. Then the collar ended up in a box at the paper mill. The rags were having a party, the finer ones for themselves, the rougher ones for themselves— just as it should be. They all had a lot to tell, but the collar had the most—he was a real braggart!

"I've had such a lot of sweethearts!" said the collar. "I was never left in peace! But then I was a fashionable cavalier—with starch! I had both a bootjack and a comb, which I never used! You should have seen me then, seen me when I lay on my side! I'll never forget my first sweetheart! She was a waistband, so fine, so soft, so cuddly! She threw herself into a tub of water on my account! Then there was a widow lady who became red hot, but I let her stand there and turn black! Then there was that prima ballerina, she gave me the scar that I still carry. She was so wild! But my heart bleeds most for the garter—I mean the waistband—who ended up in the tub of water. I have so much on my conscience. It's time I turned into white paper."

And so he was—all the rags turned into white paper. But the collar was made into the very piece of white paper we are looking at here. And that was because he bragged so dreadfully about all the things he had never been. And we should keep this in mind, so that we don't carry on in the same way. For we never can tell if we too won't end up in the rag box and be made into white paper—and have our whole story printed on it, even the most secret, and have to go about and relate it ourselves, just like the collar.

It's Quite True

❖ ❖ ❖

"IT'S a frightful affair!" said a hen, and this was over on the side of town where the business hadn't taken place. "It's a frightful affair in a hen house! I dare not sleep alone tonight! It's a good thing there are a lot of us on the roost together!" And then she went on to tell, and the feathers of the other hens stood on end and the cock dropped his comb! It's quite true!

But we will begin at the beginning, and that was in a hen house on the other side of town. The sun went down and the hens flew up. One of them—she had white feathers and bandy legs—laid her prescribed number of eggs and, as a hen, was respectable in every way. When she came to the roost she preened herself with her beak, and then a tiny feather fell out.

"There it went," she said. "Indeed, the more I preen myself, the more beautiful I become!" Now, it was said in jest, for of all those hens she had the merriest disposition, but otherwise, as has been said, she was quite respectable. And then she went to sleep.

It was dark all around. Hen sat beside hen, and the one who sat next to her did not sleep. She heard and she didn't hear, as indeed you should in this world if you are to have peace of mind. But still she had to tell it to her other neighbor. "Did you hear what was said here? I'm

223

not naming any names, but there's a hen who wants to pluck out all her feathers just to look good. If I were a cock, I'd despise her!"

And right above the hens sat the owl, with owl-husband and owl-children. They had sharp ears in that family. They heard every word the neighbor hen said. And they rolled their eyes, and Mama Owl fanned herself with her wings.

"Just don't pay any attention! But I daresay you heard what was said? I heard it with my own ears, and it'll take a lot before *they* fall off. One of the hens has forgotten what is proper for a hen, to such an extent that she's sitting there plucking out all her feathers and letting the cock look on!"

"*Prenez garde aux enfants!*" said Papa Owl. "That's not for the children!"

"I just want to tell the owl across the way. It's such a worthy owl to associate with." And away Mama flew.

"Whoooo! Hooooo! Whoooo! Hooooo!" they both hooted right down to the doves in the neighboring dovecote.

"Have you heard? Have you heard? Whoooo! Hoooo! There's a hen who's plucked out all her feathers for the cock's sake. She's freezing to death, if she hasn't already! Whoooo! Hoooo!"

"Where? Where?" cooed the doves.

"In the hen yard across the way! I've as good as seen it myself! It's almost an improper story to tell, but it's quite true!"

"Believe! Believe every last word!" said the doves. Then they cooed down to their own hen yard: "There's a hen— yes, some say there are two who have plucked out all their feathers so as not to look like the others, and thus attract the attention of the cock. It's a risky game. You can catch a cold and die of a fever, and they're both dead!"

"Wake up! Wake up!" crowed the cock, and flew up on the fence. Sleep was still in his eyes, but he crowed all the same: "Three hens have died of unrequited love for a cock! They have plucked out all their feathers. It's a dreadful affair! I don't want to keep it! Let it go on!"

"Let it go on!" squeaked the bats. And the hens clucked and the cocks crowed: "Let it go on! Let it go on!" And so the story flew from hen house to hen house, and at last it came back to the spot from which it had originally gone out.

"There are five hens," so it went, "who have all plucked out their feathers to show which of them had grown the shinniest because of an unhappy love affair with the cock! And then they hacked at one another until the blood flowed, and fell down dead, to the shame and disgrace of their families, and a great loss to the owner!"

And the hen who had lost the tiny loose feather naturally did not recognize her own story again. And as she was a respectable hen, she said, "I despise those hens! But there are more of that sort! Such a thing should not be hushed up, and I will do my best to see to it that the story appears in the newspaper. Then it will be known throughout the land. Those hens have deserved it, and their families too!"

And the story did appear in the newspaper; it was printed. And it's quite true: one tiny feather can indeed turn into five hens!

In a Thousand Years

❖ ❖ ❖

Y ES, in a thousand years they'll come on wings of
steam, through the air and across the ocean! America's young inhabitants will visit old Europe. They will
come to the ancient monuments here and to places falling
to ruin, just as we in our day journey to the smoldering
splendors of southern Asia.

In a thousand years they'll come!

The Thames, the Danube, the Rhine, are rolling still:
Mont Blanc is standing with a snowy cap; the Aurora
Borealis is shining over the lands of the North. But generation after generation has turned to dust, rows of the
mighty of the moment are forgotten, like those who already slumber in the mound, where the prosperous flour
merchant, on whose land it is, makes himself a bench on
which to sit and look out across the flat, rippling fields of
grain.

"To Europe!" is the cry of America's young generation.
"To the land of our fathers, the lovely land of memory and
imagination, Europe!"

The airship comes. It is overcrowded with travelers, for
the speed is faster than by sea. The electromagnetic thread
under the ocean has already telegraphed how large the air
caravan is. Europe is already in sight—it is the coast of
Ireland—but the passengers are still asleep. They are not

to be awakened until they are over England; there they will set foot on European soil in the Land of Shakespeare, as it is called by the sons of the intellect; the Land of Politics or the Land of Machinery is what others call it.

The sojourn here lasts a whole day; so much time the busy generation has for the great England and Scotland.

On they speed through the Channel Tunnel to France, the land of Charlemagne and Napoleon. Molière is mentioned, the learned speak of a Classical and a Romantic school in the far-distant past, and there is jubilation over heroes, bards, and men of science unknown to our time, but who will be born on the crater of Europe: Paris.

The airship flies on, over the land where Columbus sailed forth, where Cortez was born, and where Calderón sang dramas in flowering verse. Lovely dark-eyed women still dwell in the flowering vale, and ancient songs tell of El Cid and the Alhambra.

Through the air, across the sea to Italy, where ancient Eternal Rome once lay; it has been wiped out, the Campagna is a wilderness. Of St. Peter's Church, only the remains of a solitary wall are shown, but its authenticity is doubted.

To Greece, in order to sleep for one night at the luxurious hotel high on the top of Mount Olympus—just to say they've been there. The journey continues to the Bosporus, to get a few hours' rest and see the spot where Byzantium lay. Poor fishermen spread their nets where legend tells of the harem garden in the time of the Turks.

Remains of mighty cities by the foaming Danube, cities our age never knew, are crossed in flight; but here and there—places rich in memory, those still to come, those yet unborn—the air caravan alights only to take off again.

Down there lies Germany, once encircled by the tightest network of railways and canals—the land where Luther spoke and Goethe sang, and where Mozart in his day wielded the scepter of music. Great names shine out in science and art, names unknown to us. A one-day stop for Germany, and one day for Scandinavia, the native lands of Ørsted and Linnaeus, and Norway, the land of the ancient heroes and the young Norwegians. Iceland is taken on the homeward journey; geysers no longer boil, Hekla is extinguished, but, as an eternal monument to the Sagas, the rocky island stands firm in the roaring sea.

"There's a lot to see in Europe!" says the young American. "And we have seen it in eight days. And it can be done, as the great traveler"—the name of a contemporary is mentioned—"has shown in his famous work: *Europe Seen in Eight Days*."

The Nisse at
the Sausagemonger's

❖   ❖   ❖

THERE was a real student; he lived in a garret and owned nothing. There was a real sausagemonger; he lived on the ground floor and owned the whole house. And the nisse stuck to him, for here every Christmas Eve he received a dish of porridge with a big lump of butter in it—the sausagemonger could afford it. And the nisse remained in the shop, and that was quite instructive.

One evening the student came in the back door to buy himself candles and cheese. He had no one to send, so he came himself. He got what he ordered and paid for it, and the sausagemonger and the missus nodded "good evening." And that was a woman who could do more than nod: she had the gift of gab! And the student nodded back and then stood there, engrossed in reading the leaf of paper that had been wrapped about the cheese. It was a page torn out of an old book that should not have been torn to pieces, an old book full of poetry.

"There's more of it lying about," said the sausagemonger. "I gave an old woman some coffee beans for it. If you'll give me eight shillings, you can have the rest."

"Thanks," said the student. "Let me have that instead of the cheese! I can eat the bread and butter plain. It would be a sin for the whole book to be torn to shreds and tatters. You're a splendid man, a practical man, but

you don't understand any more about poetry than that tub!"

And that was a rude thing to say, especially about the tub. But the sausagemonger laughed, and the student laughed. It was said, of course, as a kind of joke. But it annoyed the nisse that anyone dared to say such a thing to a sausagemonger who was a landlord and who sold the best butter.

When it was night, and the shop was closed and everyone was in bed except the student, the nisse went in and took the missus' gift of gab. She didn't use it when she was asleep. And no matter which object in the room he put it on, it acquired speech and language; it could express its thoughts and feelings just as well as the missus. But only one could have it at a time, and that was a blessing, for otherwise they would have been speaking all at once.

And the nisse put the gift of gab on the tub in which the old newspapers lay. "Is it really true," he asked, "that you don't know what poetry is?"

"Of course I know," said the tub. "That's the sort of thing that stands at the bottom of the page in the newspaper and is clipped out. I should think I have more of that in me than the student, and I'm only a lowly tub compared to the sausagemonger."

And the nisse put the gift of gab on the coffee grinder. My, how it chattered! And he put it on the butter measure and on the till. They were all of the same opinion as the tub, and what the majority agrees upon must be respected.

"Now the student's going to catch it!" And then the nisse went softly up the backstairs to the garret where the student lived. There was a light inside, and the nisse peeped through the keyhole and saw that the student was reading the tattered book from below. But how bright it was in there! From the book shone a clear ray of light that turned into the trunk of a mighty tree that soared so high and spread its branches far out over the student. Every leaf was so fresh, and each blossom was the head of a lovely maiden—some with eyes so dark and radiant, others with eyes so blue and wondrously clear. Each fruit was a twinkling star, and a wonderfully lovely song rang out.

No, the little nisse had never imagined such splendor, much less seen or experienced it. And so he remained standing on tiptoe, peeping and peeping until the light inside went out. The student probably blew out his lamp and went to bed. But the nisse stood there all the same, for the song could still be heard so softly and sweetly—a lovely lullaby for the student who had lain down to rest.

"How wonderful!" said the little nisse. "I never expected that! I believe I'll stay with the student." And he thought—and thought quite sensibly—and then he sighed: "The student has no porridge!" And so he went—yes, he went back down to the sausagemonger. And it was a good thing he came, for the tub had used up almost all the missus' gift of gab by declaring on one side all the things it contained. And now it was just on the point of turning, in order to repeat the same thing on the other side, when the nisse came and brought the gift of gab back to the missus. But from then on, all the inhabitants of the whole shop, from the till to the kindling wood, were of the same opinion as the tub, and so high was their esteem and so great was their confidence in it that from then on, whenever the sausagemonger read the "Art and Theater Reviews" in his *Times*, the evening one, they believed it came from the tub.

But the little nisse no longer sat quietly and listened to all the wisdom and intelligence down there. No, as soon as the light shone from the chamber in the garret, the rays were like a strong anchor rope that dragged him up there, and he had to go and peep through the keyhole. And a feeling of grandeur engulfed him, such as we feel on the rolling sea when God strides across it in the storm. And he burst into tears. He didn't know himself why he was

crying, but there was something so refreshing in those
tears. How wonderfully delightful it must be to sit with
the student under that tree! But that could never happen.
He was happy at the keyhole. He was still standing there
on the cold landing when the autumn wind blew down
from the trap door in the loft, and it was so cold, so cold.
But the little fellow didn't feel it until the light was put
out in the garret room and the tones died before the wind.
Brrrrr! Then he froze, and he crept back down to his
sheltered corner where it was so cozy and warm. And
when the Christmas porridge came with the big lump of
butter in it, well, then the sausagemonger was master.

But in the middle of the night the nisse was awakened by
a terrible commotion at the shutters. People were pounding outside! The night watch was blowing his whistle!
There was a big fire; the whole street was ablaze! Was it
here in the house or at the neighbor's? Where? It was
terrifying! The sausagemonger's missus was so upset that
she removed her golden earrings and put them in her
pocket, just to have something to save! The sausagemonger
ran to get his bonds, and the serving maid ran to get her
silk mantilla. And the little nisse ran too. In a couple of
bounds he was up the stairs and in the room of the
student, who was standing quite calmly at the open window, watching the fire in the house across the way. The
little nisse grabbed the wonderful book on the table, put it
in his red cap, and held onto it with both hands. The
greatest treasure of the house was saved! And then he
rushed all the way out on the roof, all the way up to the
chimney. And there he sat, lit up by the burning house
right in front of him. And with both hands he held onto
his red cap with the treasure in it. Now he knew where
his heart lay, to whom he really belonged. But then, when
the fire had been put out and he had regained his
composure—well, "I'll divide myself between them!" he

said. "I can't give up the sausagemonger completely for the sake of the porridge!"

And that was quite human! The rest of us also go to the sausagemonger—for the porridge!

Two Virgins

❖　❖　❖

HAVE you ever seen a virgin? That is to say, what the street pavers call a virgin: something to pound down the cobblestones with. She is solid wood, broad at the bottom with iron rings all around, and small at the top with a stick for her arms.

Two such virgins stood in the tool yard. They stood among shovels, cordwood measures, and wheelbarrows, and it had been rumored there that the virgin was no longer going to be called a virgin, but a "stamper" instead. And this is the latest and only correct term in the street-paver language for what, in days gone by, we all called a virgin.

Now, among us mortals there exist "emancipated females," among which are included headmistresses of institutions, midwives, dancers (who, by virtue of their office, can stand on one leg), modistes, and night nurses; and behind these ranks of "The Emancipated," the two virgins in the tool yard also ranged themselves. They were Virgins of the Highway Authority, and under no circumstances were they going to give up their good old name and allow themselves to be called stampers!

"Virgin is a human name," they said, "but a stamper is a thing, and we will not allow ourselves to be called a thing. That is the same as being called names."

236

"My fiancé is capable of breaking up with me," said the youngest, who was engaged to a pile driver, one of those big machines that drives down piles and consequently does on a large scale what the virgin does on a small one. "He will have me as a virgin, but he might not as a stamper, and so I cannot permit them to rechristen me."

"Yes, I'd sooner have my two arms broken off!" said the eldest.

The wheelbarrow, on the other hand, was of another opinion, and the wheelbarrow regarded itself as one-fourth a cart because it went on one wheel.

"I must indeed tell you that to be called a virgin is fairly commonplace, and not nearly as fine as being called a stamper; for in being called by that name one joins the rank of the signets, and think of the Signet of the Law. This is what affixes the judicial seal. In your place I would give up the virgin!"

"Never! I am too old for that!" said the eldest.

"You are certainly not aware of something called 'The European Necessity,'" said the honest old cordwood measure. "One must be kept within bounds, subordinate oneself; one must yield to time and necessity. And if there is a law that the virgin is to be called a stamper, then she must be called a stamper. Everything has a standard by which it is measured."

"Then if worst comes to worst," said the youngest, "I would sooner allow myself to be called 'Miss' instead. Miss smacks a little of virgin."

"But I would rather let myself be chopped into kindling wood!" said the old virgin.

Now they went to work. The virgins were driven; they were put on the wheelbarrow, and that was always fine treatment. But they were called stampers.

"Vir——!" they said as they stamped against the cobblestones. "Vir——!" And they were just about to say the whole word "Virgin"! But they bit the word off short.

They caught themselves in time, for they found that they needn't once bother to answer. But among themselves they always addressed one another by the name virgin and praised The Good Old Days, when everything was called by its right name and one was called a virgin when one *was* a virgin. And virgins they remained—both of them—for the pile driver, the great machine, really *did* break off with the youngest. He would not have anything to do with a stamper!

The Piggy Bank

❖ ❖ ❖

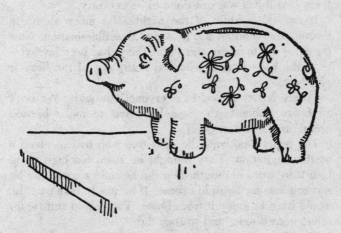

THERE were such a lot of playthings in the nursery; on the top of the cupboard stood the bank. It was made of clay in the shape of a pig. It had a natural crack in its back, and the crack had been made bigger with a knife so that silver dalers could also go in. And two had gone in, in addition to lots of shillings. The piggy bank was stuffed so full that he could no longer rattle, and that is the utmost a piggy bank can do. There he stood now, on top of the shelf, and looked down on all the things in the room.

He knew very well that with what he had in his stomach he could buy it all, and that is what is known as being well aware of oneself.

The others thought about it too, even if they didn't say so. Indeed, there were other things to talk about. The bureau drawer stood halfway open, and a big doll could be seen. She was quite old, and her neck had been riveted. She looked out and said, "Shall we play at being people? At least that's something!"

Now there was a commotion! Even the pictures turned around on the wall to show that there was another side to them too. But it was not done to be contrary.

It was the middle of the night. The moon shone in through the window and provided free illumination. Now the game was to begin, and all the things had been invited— even the baby buggy, who was really one of the heavier playthings.

"There is some good in everyone!" he said. "We can't all be of noble birth. Somebody has to make himself useful, as the saying goes."

The piggy bank was the only one who had received a written invitation. They thought he stood too high up to hear it by word of mouth. Nor did he send a reply that he was coming, for he didn't come. If he was to take part, he would have to enjoy it from home. They could suit themselves accordingly, and so they did.

The little toy theater was immediately set up so he could look right into it. They were going to begin with a play, and then there would be tea and intellectual exercise. But they started with this first. The rocking horse talked about training and thoroughbreds, the baby buggy about railroads and steam power. Indeed, it all had something to do with their professions, which they could talk about. The clock talked about politic-tic-tics! It knew the hour had struck! But it was said that it did not keep the correct time! The rattan cane stood, and was proud of his ferrule and his silver knob, for, indeed, he was capped above and below. On the sofa lay two embroidered pillows—they were beautiful and dumb. And now the play could begin.

They all sat and watched, and they were asked to crack and smack and rumble, all according to how pleased they were. But the riding whip said he never cracked for the aged, only for those who were not engaged.

"I crack for everything!" said the firecracker.

"After all, one has to be somewhere," thought the cuspidor.

Indeed, this was everyone's idea in attending a play. The play was no good, but it was well acted. All the players turned their painted sides out; they could be looked at only from one side—not the wrong side—and they all performed excellently, all the way out in front of the theater. Their strings were too long, but this made them all the more noticeable. The riveted doll was so moved that her rivet came loose; and the piggy bank was so impressed by it, in his fashion, that he decided to do something for one of them: include him in his testament as the one who was to lie buried with him when the time came.

It was such a treat that the tea was abandoned, and they went on with the intellectual exercise. It was called "Playing People." There was no malice intended, for they were only playing; and each one thought of himself and of what the piggy bank was thinking. And the piggy bank thought the most. He, of course, was thinking about the testament and the funeral, and when it was to be held—always before one expects it. CRASH! He fell down from the cupboard and lay on the floor in bits and pieces, and the coins danced and sprang. The smallest spun, the biggest rolled—especially one of the silver dalers. He really wanted to go out into the world, and so he did! And so did every last one of them! And the fragments of the piggy bank ended up in the basket. But the next day, on the cupboard stood a new piggy bank made of clay. There wasn't a shilling in it yet, and so it couldn't rattle, either! In this he resembled the other. It was always a beginning, and with that we shall end.

Cloddy Hans

❖   ❖   ❖

OUT in the country there was an old manor, and in it lived an old squire who had two sons. They were so witty that they were too witty by half. They wanted to propose to the king's daughter, and this they dared to do because she had proclaimed that she would take for a husband the one she found who could best speak up for himself.

Now the two made their preparations for eight days. This was all the time they had for it, but it was enough. They had previous learning, and that is useful. One of them knew the whole Latin dictionary by heart and the city newspaper for three years—both forward and backward. The other had acquainted himself with all the Guild Articles and what every alderman should know. So he was able to discuss Affairs of State, he thought. And what's more, he also knew how to embroider suspenders, for he had delicate hands and was clever with his fingers.

"I'm going to win the king's daughter!" they both said, and so their father gave them each a splendid horse; the one who knew the dictionary and the newspapers by heart was given a coal-black horse, and the one who knew about aldermen and did embroidery got a milk-white steed. And then they smeared the corners of their mouths with cod-liver oil to make them more flexible. All the servants were down in the yard to see them mount their steeds. At the same moment the third brother came up—for there were three of them, but no one counted him as a brother because he didn't have the same kind of learning as the other two, and they only called him "Cloddy Hans"!

"Where are you off to, since you're wearing your Sunday best?" he asked.

"To court to talk the princess into marrying us! Haven't you heard what's being proclaimed throughout the land?" And then they told him.

"My word! Then I've got to come along too!" said Cloddy Hans, but the brothers laughed at him and rode off.

"Father, let me have a horse!" shouted Cloddy Hans. "I'd so like to get married. If she'll take me, she'll take me; and if she won't, I'll take her all the same!"

"That's just twaddle!" said the father. "I'm not giving any horse to you! Why, you don't know how to talk! No, your brothers are real gentlemen."

"Well, if I can't have a horse," said Cloddy Hans, "I'll just take the billy goat! It's mine, and it can carry me very well!" And then he straddled the billy goat, dug his heels into its sides, and rushed off down the highway. Whew! How he flew!

"Here I come!" said Cloddy Hans, and then he sang so the forest rang.

But the brothers rode ahead quite silently. They didn't utter a word. They had to think over all the clever retorts they were going to make, for it had to be so well thought out.

"Hey hallo!" shouted Cloddy Hans. "Here I come! Look what I found on the highway!" And then he showed them a dead crow he had found.

"Clod!" they said. "What do you want with that?"

"I'm going to present it to the king's daughter!"

"Yes, just do it!" they said, and laughed and rode on.

"Hey hallo! Here I come! Look what I found now! You don't find this on the highway every day!"

And the brothers turned around to see what it was. "Clod!" they said. "Why, it's an old wooden shoe that has lost its top. Is the king's daughter going to have that too?"

"Yes, indeed!" said Cloddy Hans. And the brothers laughed and rode until they were way ahead of him.

"Hey hallo! Here I am!" shouted Cloddy Hans. "My! Now it's getting worse and worse! Hey hallo! It can't be beat!"

"What have you found now?" said the brothers.

"Oh," said Cloddy Hans, "it's nothing to speak of! How happy the king's daughter will be!"

"Ugh!" said the brothers. "Why, it's just mud that's been thrown up out of the ditch!"

"Yes, so it is!" said Cloddy Hans. "And it's the finest sort! You can't hold it!" And then he filled his pocket.

But the brothers rode as hard as they could, and they came to the city gates a whole hour ahead of him. There the suitors were given numbers as they arrived and were placed in rows six abreast—so close together that they couldn't move their arms. And it was just as well, for otherwise they would have stabbed one another in the back, just because one was standing in front of the other.

The rest of the populace was standing around the castle, right up to the windows, to see the king's daughter receive the suitors. But just as each one came into the room, his eloquence failed him.

"Won't do!" said the king's daughter. "Scram!"

Now came the brother who knew the dictionary by heart. But while standing in line he had clean forgotten it. And the floor creaked, and the ceiling was of mirrors so he saw himself upside down on his head. And at each window stood three scribes and an alderman, who wrote down everything that was said, so it could go right into the newspaper and be sold for two shillings on the corner. It was terrible! And then they had made up such a roaring fire that the stove was red hot.

"It's pretty warm in here!" said the suitor.

"That's because my father's roasting cockerels today!" said the king's daughter.

Bah! There he stood. He hadn't expected that speech. He didn't know a word to say, for he had wanted to say something amusing! Bah!

"Won't do!" said the king's daughter. "Scram!" And then he had to go. Now the second brother came.

"It's terribly hot here!" he said.

"Yes, we're roasting cockerels today!" said the king's daughter.

"I beg your . . . I beg! . . ." he said, and all the scribes wrote: "I beg your. . . . I beg! . . ."

"Won't do!" said the king's daughter. "Scram!"

Now Cloddy Hans came. He rode the billy goat straight into the hall.

"Well, this is a scorcher!" he said.

"That's because I'm roasting cockerels!" said the king's daughter.

"Well, now, that is strange!" said Cloddy Hans. "Then maybe I can roast a crow!"

"Indeed you can, quite well!" said the king's daughter. "But do you have anything to roast it in? For I have neither a pot nor a pan!"

"Oh, I have!" said Cloddy Hans. "Here's a cooker with a tin cramp!" And then he pulled out the old wooden shoe and put the crow in the middle of it.

"That's enough for a whole meal," said the king's daughter, "but where will we get the drippings from?"

"I've got that in my pocket!" said Cloddy Hans. "I've got so much that I can dribble some on." And then he poured a little mud out of his pocket.

"Now you're talking!" said the king's daughter. "Why, you know how to answer! And you know how to talk!

You're the one I'll have for my husband! But do you know that every word we're saying and have said is being written down and will appear in the newspaper tomorrow? At each window you can see three scribes and an old alderman. And the alderman is the worst of all because he doesn't understand a thing." Now, she said this just to frighten him. And all the scribes snickered and threw blots of ink on the floor.

"Those are the high and mighty, all right!" said Cloddy Hans. "Then I must give the best to the alderman." And then he turned out his pockets and gave him the mud right in his face!

"That was well done!" said the king's daughter. "I couldn't have done it, but I'm certainly going to learn how!"

And so Cloddy Hans became king and got a wife and a crown and a throne of his own. And we got it straight from the alderman's newspaper—but that's not to be trusted.

Soup from a Sausage Peg

❖ ❖ ❖

"THAT was an excellent dinner yesterday!" said an old she-mouse to one who hadn't been to the banquet. "I sat number twenty-one from the old Mouse King; that's not so bad, after all! Now, shall I tell you the courses? They were put together very well: moldy bread, bacon rind, tallow candles, and sausage, and then the same thing all over again. It was as good as getting two meals. There was a convivial atmosphere and a delightful twaddling, as in a family circle. Not a bit was left except the sausage pegs, and so we talked about them, and then the making of soup from a sausage peg came up. Everybody, of course, had heard about it, but no one had tasted the soup, much less knew how to make it. A charming toast was proposed for the inventor: he deserved to be Purveyor to the Needy! Wasn't that witty? And the old Mouse King stood up and promised that the young mouse who could make the soup in question the tastiest would become his queen. They were to have a year and a day to think it over in."

"That wasn't so bad, considering!" said the other mouse. "But how do you make the soup?"

"Yes, how do you make it?" They asked about that too, all the she-mice young and old. They all wanted to be queen, but they didn't want to take the trouble of going out into the wide world to learn how, and that'll probably be necessary! But, then, it isn't everyone who can leave his family and the old nooks and crannies too. One doesn't go out every day on a cheese rind and the smell of bacon. No, one can end up starving—yes, perhaps be eaten alive by a cat.

I daresay these thoughts also frightened most of them out of sallying forth after knowledge; only four mice—young and pretty, but poor—presented themselves for departure. Each of them wanted to go to one of the four corners of the earth, so it was a question of which one of them Dame Fortune would follow. They each took a sausage peg with them, as a reminder of what they were traveling for; it was to be their pilgrim's staff.

Early in May they set out, and early in May the following year they came back—but only three of them. The fourth one didn't turn up and didn't send any word, and now the day of decision was at hand.

"There always has to be something sad bound up with one's greatest pleasures!" said the Mouse King, but gave orders to invite all the mice for miles around; they were to gather in the kitchen. The three traveling mice stood in a row, by themselves. For the fourth, who was missing, a sausage peg with black crepe around it had been put up. No one dared speak his mind before the three of them had spoken—and the Mouse King had said what more there was to be said.

Now we shall hear!

WHAT THE FIRST LITTLE MOUSE HAD SEEN AND LEARNED ON THE JOURNEY

"When I went out into the wide world," said the little mouse, "I thought, like so many of my age, that I knew everything. But one doesn't; it takes a year and a day before that happens. I went to sea at once; I went with a

ship that was going to the North. I had heard that at sea
the cook has to look after himself, but it's easy to look after
oneself when one has plenty of sides of bacon, barrels of
salt provisions, and flour full of mites. The food is delicious, but one doesn't learn anything that can produce
soup from a sausage peg. We sailed for many days and
nights; we were subjected to a rolling and a drenching.
Then, when we came to where we should, I left the
vessel. That was far up in the North.

"It's strange to come away from home, from your own
nook and cranny, to go by ship—which is also a kind of
nook and cranny—and then suddenly be more than a
hundred miles away and stand in a foreign land! There
were trackless forests of fir and birch! They gave off such a
strong odor! I'm not fond of it! The wild herbs had such a
spicy fragrance that I sneezed; it made me think of sausage! There were big forest lakes; close at hand the water
looked clear, but seen from a distance as black as ink.
White swans were floating there—I took them for foam,
they were lying so still. But I saw them fly and I saw them
walk, and then I recognized them. They belong to the
goose family; you can certainly tell by the gait. No one can
repudiate one's kinship! I kept to my own kind; I attached
myself to the field and meadow mice, who, for that matter, know exceedingly little—especially as far as treating is
concerned. And that, of course, is what I journeyed abroad
for. That soup could be made from a sausage peg was such
an extraordinary thought to them that it spread through
the entire forest at once. But that the problem could be
solved they relegated to the impossible. Least of all did I
think then that here and on that very same night I was to
be initiated in the making of it. It was midsummer, and
that was why the forest gave off such a strong odor, they
said; that was why the herbs were so spicy, the lakes so
clear and yet so dark with the white swans on them. At
the edge of the forest, between three or four houses, a

pole as high as a mainmast had been set up, and from the
top of it hung garlands and ribbons: it was the Maypole.
Lads and lasses were dancing around it and singing to it,
vying with the fiddler's violin. Things got lively at sun-
down and in the moonlight, but I didn't join in. What
business has a little mouse at a forest ball? I sat in the soft
moss and held onto my sausage peg. The moon shone on
one spot in particular where there was a tree, and moss as
fine—yes, I daresay as fine as a Mouse King's hide! But it
was of a green color that was a balm to the eyes. All at
once the loveliest little people, who reached no higher
than my knee, came marching up; they looked like human
beings, but were better proportioned. They called themselves 'elves' and had delicate garments of flower petals,
with fly- and gnat-wing trimmings—not bad at all. Right
away they seemed to be looking for something, I didn't
know what, but then a couple of them came over to me.
The noblest of them pointed to my sausage peg and said,
'That's just the kind we use! It has been carved out, it's
excellent!' And he became more and more delighted as he
looked at my pilgrim's staff.

" 'Borrow, of course, but not keep!' " I said.

" 'Not keep!' they all said. And taking hold of the sausage
peg, which I released, they danced over to the fine mossy
spot and set up the sausage peg right there in the open.
They wanted to have a Maypole too, and it was as if the
one they had now had been carved out for them. Now it
was decorated, yes, then it was a sight to behold.

"Tiny spiders spun threads of gold around it, and hung
up fluttering veils and banners so finely woven and bleached
so snowy white in the moonlight that it dazzled my eyes.
They took colors from the wings of butterflies and sprin-
kled them on the white linen, and flowers and diamonds
were sparkling there. I didn't recognize my sausage peg
anymore. I daresay a Maypole like the one it had turned
into was nowhere to be found in the world. And not until

then did the really great company of elves arrive. They
were quite without clothes; it could be no finer. And I was
invited to look at the doings—but from a distance, as I was
too big for them.

"Now the playing began! It was as if a thousand glass
bells were ringing out so loud and strong; I thought it was
the swans that were singing. Indeed, it seemed to me that
I could also hear the cuckoo and thrush. At last it was as if
the entire forest were resounding along with it; there were
children's voices, the sound of bells and the song of birds—
the sweetest melodies. And all that loveliness rang out
from the Maypole of the elves. It was a whole carillon, and
it was my sausage peg. Never had I believed that so much
could come out of it, but I daresay it depends on whose
hands it falls into. I was really quite moved. I cried, as
only a little mouse can cry, for pure joy.

"The night was all too short! But, indeed, it isn't any
longer up there at that time of the year. At daybreak a
breeze sprang up, rippling the mirrored surface of the
forest lake; all the delicate, fluttering veils and banners
blew away in the air; the swaying gossamer pavilions,
suspension bridges, and balustrades—or whatever they're
called—that had been erected from leaf to leaf blew away
at once. Six elves came and brought me my sausage peg,
asking as they did so whether I had any wish they could
grant. Then I asked them to tell me how soup from a
sausage peg is made.

" 'The way we go about it!' said the noblest of them, and
laughed. 'Yes, you saw that just now! I daresay you hardly
recognized your sausage peg again!'

" 'You mean in that fashion?' I said, and told outright
why I was on a journey and what was expected of it at
home. 'Of what advantage is it to the Mouse King, and the
whole of our mighty kingdom, that I have seen this magnificence? I can't shake it out of the sausage peg and say:

"See, here's the peg, now comes the soup! Still, it was a course of sorts when one was full!" '

"Then the elf dipped his little finger down in a blue violet and said to me, 'Take care, I'm stroking your pilgrim's staff, and when you come home to the Mouse King's castle, touch your staff at the king's warm breast. Then violets will spring out all over the staff, even in the coldest wintertime. See, there's something for you to take home with you and a little more besides.' "

But before the little mouse said what this little more could be, she touched her staff at the king's breast, and the loveliest bouquet of flowers really did spring out. It had such a strong odor that the Mouse King ordered the mice standing closest to the chimney to stick their tails into the fire right away, in order that there might be a slight smell of something burning, for that odor of violets was unbearable. That wasn't the sort of thing one set store by.

"But what was that 'little more besides' you mentioned?" asked the Mouse King.

"Well," said the little mouse, "I daresay that's what is called 'the effect'!" And then she gave the sausage peg a turn, and then there were no more flowers. She was holding only the bare peg, and she raised it just like a baton.

"Violets are for Sight, Smell, and Touch, the elf told me, but Hearing and Taste still remain!" And then she beat time: there was music, not the way it resounded in the forest during the festivities of the elves, no, but as it can be heard in the kitchen. My, what a to-do! It came suddenly, just as if the wind were whistling through all the flues. Kettles and pots boiled over; the fire shovel pounded on the brass kettle. And then, all at once, it was quiet. You could hear the subdued song of the teapot. So strange, you couldn't tell at all whether it was stopping or starting; and the little pot bubbled and the big pot bubbled; one took no heed of the other. It was as if there wasn't a thought in the pot. And the little mouse swung her baton, wilder and wilder—the pots foamed, bubbled, boiled over; the wind whistled; the chimney squeaked. Hey! Hey! It was so dreadful that the little mouse even dropped the baton.

"That was quite a soup!" said the old Mouse King. "Doesn't the main course come now?"

"That was all!" said the little mouse, and curtsied.

"All! Well, then, let us hear what the next one has to say!" said the Mouse King.

WHAT THE SECOND LITTLE MOUSE RELATED

"I was born in the castle library," said the second mouse. "I, and others of my family there, have never had the good fortune of coming into the dining room, not to mention the larder; only when I journeyed out, and now here today, did I see a kitchen. We often suffered real hunger and privation in the library, but we acquired much knowledge. Up there the rumor reached us about the royal prize that had been offered for making soup from a sausage peg, and it was then that my old grandmother pulled out a manuscript. She couldn't read it, but she had heard it read. On it was written: 'If one is a poet, then one knows how to cook soup from a sausage peg!' She asked me if I were a poet. My conscience was clear, but then she said that I had to go and see about becoming one. But what was needed for that, I asked. For it was just as difficult for me to find that out as it was to make the soup. But Grandma had listened to reading; she said that three main components were needed: 'Intelligence, fantasy, and feeling! If you can go and get those inside you, you're a poet, and then I daresay you'll find that out about the sausage peg!'"

"And so I headed West, out into the wide world to become a poet.

"I knew that in all things intelligence is the most important; the two other components are not held in the same esteem. And accordingly I set out after intelligence. Well, where does it dwell? 'Go to the ant and be wise,' a great king in the Holy Land is supposed to have said. This I knew from the library, and I didn't stop until I came to the first big anthill. There I lay in wait, in order to be wise.

"The ants are quite a respectable race; they are all brain. Everything about them is like a correctly worked problem in arithmetic that comes out right. Working and laying eggs, they say, is the same as living in the present and providing for the future, and that is just what they do. They divide themselves into the clean ants and the dirty ants. Rank consists of a number; the ant queen is number one, and her opinion is the only correct one. She knows everything, and that was essential for me to find out. She said so much that was so wise that I thought it was stupid. She said that their anthill was the tallest thing in the world. But close to the anthill stood a tree. It was taller, much taller; that couldn't be denied and so it wasn't mentioned at all. One evening an ant had strayed over there and crawled up the trunk, not even to the top, and yet higher than any ant had ever been before. And when it had turned around and made its way home, it told in the mound about something taller outside. But all the ants found this to be an insult to the entire society, and so the little ant was sentenced to wear a muzzle, and to everlasting solitude. But shortly afterward another ant came to the tree and made the same journey and discovery, and talked about it, as it is said, with deliberation and articulation. And, as it was an esteemed ant into the bargain—one of the clean ants—they believed it. And when it died, they put up an eggshell to it as a monument to the venerated sciences.

"I saw," said the little mouse, "that the ants perpetually ran about with their eggs on their backs. One of them dropped hers. She did her utmost to get it up again, but without success. Then two others came and helped with all their might, so they very nearly dropped their own eggs. But then they stopped at once, for one has to look after oneself. And concerning this, the ant queen said that both heart and intelligence had been displayed here. The two establish us ants as the highest of the rational beings. Intelligence must and should predominate, and I have the most!' And then she stood up on her hind legs; she was so recognizable that I couldn't make a mistake! And I swallowed her. Go to the ant and be wise! Now I had the queen!

"Now I went closer to the big tree in question. It was an oak, it had a tall trunk and a mighty crown, and was very old. I knew that a living creature dwelled here, a woman. She is called a 'dryad' and is born with the tree and dies with it. I had heard about that in the library. Now I was looking at such a tree, looking at such an oak maiden. She let out a terrible shriek when she saw me so close. Like all females, she had a great fear of mice, but then she had more of a reason than the others: for I could gnaw through the tree, and therein, of course, hung her life. I talked to her, kindly and sincerely, and gave her courage, and she picked me up in her delicate hand; and when she found out why I had gone out into the wide world, she promised that, perhaps the same evening, I should obtain one of the two treasures for which I was still looking. She told me that Phantasus was her very good friend, that he was as beautiful as the God of Love, and that many a time he had rested here under the leafy branches of the tree, which rustled even louder above them both. He called her his dryad, she said, the tree his tree. The gnarled, mighty, beautiful oak was just to his liking. The roots spread deeply and firmly down in the ground; the trunk and the crown soared high in the fresh air, and felt the drifting snow and the biting wind the way they should be felt. Yes, this is the way she spoke: 'The birds sing up there and tell about the foreign lands! And on the only dead limb the stork has built a nest; that's a good trimming, and one can hear a little from the land of the pyramids. Phantasus likes it all very well. But even that is not enough for him; I must tell him about life in the forest from the time I was small and the tree was tiny enough to be hidden by a nettle, and up to now, when it has grown so big and mighty. Now, if you just sit over there under the woodruff and pay close attention, when Phantasus comes I daresay I'll have a chance to tweak him in his wing and yank out a little feather. Take it; no poet ever received a better one. Then you'll have enough!'

"And Phantasus came, the feather was yanked out, and I grabbed it," said the little mouse. "I kept it in water until it became soft! It was still quite hard to digest, but I managed to gnaw it up! It's not at all easy to gnaw oneself into a poet, there's so much that has to be taken in. . . . Now I had the two: intelligence and fantasy, and through them I knew now that the third was to be found in the library. For a great man has said and written that there are novels that are produced for the sole purpose of releasing mankind from superfluous tears; that is to say, they are a kind of sponge in which to absorb emotions. I remembered a couple of these books; they had always looked quite appetizing to me—they were so well read, so greasy; they must have absorbed an unending flood.

"I went home to the library, immediately ate practically a whole novel—that is to say, the soft part, the novel proper; the crust, on the other hand, the binding, I left alone. Now, when I had digested that and one more, I was already aware of the way it was stirring inside me. I ate a little of the third, and then I was a poet. I said so to myself, and the others said so along with me. I had a headache, a bellyache—I don't know all the aches I had. Now I thought of the stories that might be connected with sausage pegs, and then so many pegs came to my mind— the ant queen had had exceptional intelligence. I remembered the man who'd been taken down a peg; I thought of old beer with a peg in it; standing on one's pegs; a peg for hanging a claim on; and then the pegs to one's coffin. All my thoughts were wrapped up in pegs! And it should be possible to make up something about them as long as one is a poet. And that's what I am, that's what I've struggled to be. Thus, every day in the week, I'll be able to serve you a peg—a story. Well, that's my soup!"

"Let us hear the third," said the Mouse King.

"Squeak! Squeak!" it said in the kitchen door, and a little mouse—it was the fourth, the one they thought was dead—scurried in. It bowled over the big sausage peg with the band of mourning on it. It had been running night and day; it had gone by rail, on a freight train when the opportunity presented itself, and still had come almost too late. It pushed its way forward, looking disheveled; it had lost its sausage peg but not its voice. It started talking right away, just as if everyone had been waiting for it alone and only wanted to listen to it. Everything else was of no concern to the world. It spoke at once and said what it had to say. It came so unexpectedly that no one had time to take exception to it or to its speech while it was talking. Now we shall hear!

WHAT THE FOURTH MOUSE—
WHO SPOKE BEFORE THE THIRD—HAD TO RELATE

"I went right away to the biggest city," it said. "I don't remember the name. I'm not good at remembering names. I came from the train to the City Hall along with confiscated goods, and there I ran to the jailer. He told about his prisoners, especially about one who had let fall rash words. These words, in turn, had been commented on, and now he'd been given a dressing down. 'The whole business is soup from a sausage peg!' he said. 'But that soup can cost him his neck!' This made me interested in that prisoner," said the little mouse, "and I seized the opportunity and slipped in to him. There's always a mousehole behind locked doors. He looked pale, had a great beard and big flashing eyes. The lamp smoked, and the walls were used to it—they grew no blacker. The prisoner scratched both pictures and verse, white on black. I didn't read them. I think he was bored. I was a welcome guest. He coaxed me with bread crumbs, with whistling, and with kind words. He was so happy because of me; I trusted him, and so we became friends. He shared bread and water with me, gave me cheese and sausage; I was living in great style, but, I must say, it was really the good company in particular that kept me there. He let me run on his hand and arm, all the way up in his sleeve. He let me crawl in his beard, called me his little friend. I grew really fond of him; I daresay that sort of thing is mutual. I forgot my errand out in the wide world, forgot my sausage peg in a crack in the floor; it's lying there still. I wanted to stay where he was; if I went away, the poor prisoner would have no one at all, and that's not enough in this world. I stayed, he didn't. He talked to me so sorrowfully that last time, gave me twice as much bread and cheese rinds, then blew kisses to me; he left and never came back. I don't know his story. 'Soup from a sausage peg!'

the jailer said, and I went to him. But I shouldn't have
believed him. To be sure, he picked me up in his hand,
but he put me in a cage, on a treadmill. That's dreadful!
You run and run, you come no farther, and you only make
a fool of yourself.

"The jailer's grandchild was a lovely little thing, with
golden curls, the happiest eyes, and a laughing mouth.
'Poor little mouse!' she said, and peered into my nasty
cage, and pulled away the iron peg—and I leaped down
onto the windowsill and out into the gutter. Free! Free! I
thought of that alone, and not of the journey's goal.

"It was dark, night was falling. I took shelter in an old
tower. There lived a nightwatch and an owl. I didn't trust
either of them, least of all the owl. It looks like a cat, and
has the great shortcoming that it eats mice. But one can
be mistaken, and I was. This was a respectable, exceedingly well-bred old owl; she knew more than the nightwatch
and just as much as I did. The owlets found fault with
everything. 'Don't make soup from a sausage peg!' she
said. That was the harshest thing she could say here, she
was so devoted to her own family. I gained such confidence in her that I said 'Squeak!' from the crack where I
was sitting. She found that confidence to her liking and
assured me that I would be under her protection. No
creature would be allowed to do me harm. She herself
would do that in winter, when food became scarce.

"She was wise about each and every thing. She convinced me that the nightwatch couldn't hoot except through
a horn that hung loosely at his side. 'He puts on such
terrible airs because of that; he thinks he's an owl in the
tower! That's supposed to be grand, but it's only a little.
Soup from a sausage peg!'

"I asked her for the recipe, and then she explained it to
me: 'Soup from a sausage peg is only a human way of
talking, and can be interpreted in various ways. And each

one thinks that his way is the most correct, but the whole thing is really much ado about nothing!'

" 'Nothing!' I said. It struck me! The truth isn't always pleasant, but the truth is the highest. The old owl said so too. I thought it over and realized that when I brought the highest, then I was bringing much more than soup from a sausage peg. And so I hurried off in order to come back home in time and bring the highest and the best: the truth. The mice are an enlightened race, and the Mouse King is above them all. He is capable of making me queen for the sake of the truth."

"Your truth is a lie!" said the mouse who hadn't yet been allowed to speak. "I can make the soup, and so I shall!"

HOW IT WAS MADE

"I didn't go on a journey," said the fourth mouse. "I remained in the land; that's the proper thing to do. One doesn't need to travel; one can get everything here just as well. I remained. I haven't learned what I did from supernatural beings, or eaten my way to it, or talked with owls. I've thought it out all by myself. Now, if you'll just have the kettle put on and fill it all the way up with water! Make a fire under it! Let it burn; let the water come to a boil—it has to boil furiously! Now throw in the peg! Now if the Mouse King will be so kind as to stick his tail down in the bubbling water and stir. Indeed, the longer he stirs, the stronger the soup will be. It doesn't cost a thing. No additions are needed—just stir!"

"Can't someone else do it?" asked the Mouse King.

"No," said the mouse, "the stock is in the tail of the Mouse King alone!"

And the water bubbled furiously, and the Mouse King took his stand close to it—it was nearly dangerous—and he stuck out his tail the way the mice do in the dairy when they skim the cream from a dish and afterward lick their tails. But he only got it into the hot steam, then he jumped down at once.

"Naturally you are my queen!" he said. "We'll wait with the soup until our Golden Wedding Anniversary. Then the needy in my kingdom will have something to look forward to—and a protracted pleasure!"

And so the wedding was held. But when they came home, several of the mice said, "You couldn't very well

call that 'soup from a sausage peg'; it was more like 'soup from a mouse's tail'!"

They found that one thing or another, of what had been said, had been presented quite well, but the whole thing could have been different. "Now, *I* would have told it like this and like that! . . ."

That was the criticism, and that's always so wise—afterward!

And the story went around the world. Opinions about it were divided, but the story itself remained intact. And that is what is best—in matters great and small—in soup from a sausage peg. It's just that one shouldn't expect thanks for it!

The Girl Who Trod on the Loaf

❖   ❖   ❖

YOU'VE probably heard of the girl who trod on the loaf so as not to soil her shoes, and of how badly she fared. It has been written down and printed as well.

She was a poor child, vain and overbearing; she had an ornery disposition, as they say. As quite a little child she delighted in catching flies and picking off their wings to make crawling things out of them. She took the cockchafer and the dung beetle, stuck them each on a pin, and then held a green leaf or a tiny scrap of paper up to their feet. The wretched creatures would thereby cling to it, twisting and turning it, to get off the pin.

"Now the cockchafer's reading!" said little Inger. "See how it's turning the page!"

As she grew she became worse, if anything, instead of better. But she was pretty, and that was her undoing, or else in all likelihood she would have been given a good many more cuffs than she was.

"It'll take a desperate remedy to cure your ailment!" her own mother would say. "As a child you've often trod on my apron. I'm afraid when you're older you'll often come to tread on my heart."

And that is precisely what she did.

Now she went out in the country to enter the service of a gentle family. They treated her as if she had been their very own child and dressed her in the same fashion. She looked good, and her arrogance increased.

She had been out there for a year when her mistress said, "Really, you should pay your parents a visit one day, little Inger!"

She went too, but only to show off. They were to see how grand she had become. But when she came to the village gate and saw the maidens and young lads gossiping by the pond—and her mother was sitting right there, resting with a bundle of twigs that she had gathered in the forest—Inger turned around. She was ashamed that she, who was so finely dressed, should have such a ragamuffin for a mother, who went about gathering sticks. She didn't regret turning back at all, she was merely irritated.

Now another half year passed.

"Really, you should go home for a day and see your old parents, little Inger!" said her mistress. "Here's a big loaf of white bread for you; you can take it to them. They'll be delighted to see you."

And Inger put on her best finery and her new shoes, and she lifted her skirts and walked so carefully in order to keep her feet nice and clean—and she couldn't be blamed for that. But when she came to where the path went over boggy ground, and a long stretch of it was wet and muddy, she tossed the loaf into the mud so as to tread on it and get across dry-shod. But as she was standing with one foot on the bread and lifting the other, the bread sank with her, deeper and deeper, until she had disappeared completely, and only a black, bubbling pool was to be seen.

That's the story.

But where did she come to? She came down to the Marsh Wife, who was brewing. The Marsh Wife is paternal aunt to the elfin maidens—they're well enough known: ballads have been written about them and pictures have been painted of them. But the only thing people know about the Marsh Wife is that when the meadows are

steaming in the summertime, the Marsh Wife is brewing. It was down into her brewery that Inger sank, and you can't stand being there for long. The cesspool is a bright, elegant salon compared with the Marsh Wife's brewery! The stink from each vat is enough to make people swoon, and then too the vats are jammed so close together. And if there is a little opening somewhere through which you could squeeze, you can't because of all the wet toads and fat snakes that become matted together here. Down here sank little Inger; all that loathsome, writhing matting was so freezing cold that she shivered in every limb; indeed, she became more and more rigid. She stuck to the loaf, and it dragged her just as an amber button drags a bit of straw.

The Marsh Wife was at home. That day the brewery was being inspected by the Devil and his great-grandma, and *she's* a most virulent old female, who's never idle. She never goes out unless she has her needlework with her, and she had it along here too. She sewed unrest to put in people's shoes so they couldn't settle down; she embroidered lies and crocheted thoughtless remarks that had fallen to the ground—anything to cause harm and corruption. Oh, yes, great-grandma really knew how to sew, embroider, and crochet!

She saw Inger, held her eyeglass up to her eye, and had another look at her. "That's a girl with aptitude!" she said. "Give her to me as a token of my visit here! She'll be a suitable pedestal in my great-grandchild's anteroom!"

And she got her. And this is how little Inger came to Hell. People don't always rush straight down there, but they can get there by a roundabout way—when they have aptitude!

It was an anteroom that went on forever. It made you dizzy to look ahead and dizzy to look back; and here stood a miserable host waiting for the Door of Mercy to be opened, and they would have a long wait! Big fat waddling spiders spun thousand-year webs over their feet, and these webs clamped like footscrews and held like copper chains. And added to this was an eternal unrest in every soul, a tormenting unrest; there was the miser who had forgotten the key to his moneybox, and he knew it was sitting in the lock. Indeed, it would be too long-winded to rattle off all the various torments and tortures that were endured here. It was a dreadful feeling for Inger to stand as a pedestal; it was as if she had been toggled to the loaf from below.

"That's what you get for wanting to keep your feet clean!" she said to herself. "See how they glower at me!" Indeed, they were all looking at her. Their evil desires flashed from their eyes and spoke without a sound from the corners of their mouths. They were dreadful to behold.

"It must be a pleasure to look at me!" thought little Inger. "I have a pretty face and good clothes." And now she turned her eyes—her neck was too stiff to move. My, how dirty she had gotten in the Marsh Wife's brewery. She hadn't thought of that! It was as if one big blob of slime had been poured over her clothes. A snake had got caught in her hair and was flapping down the back of her neck. And from every fold of her dress a toad was peering out, croaking like a wheezy pug dog. It was quite unpleasant. "But the others down here look just as horrible," she consoled herself.

Worst of all, however, was the dreadful hunger she felt. Couldn't she even bend down and break off a piece of the bread she was standing on? No, her back had stiffened, her arms and hands had stiffened; her entire body was like a pillar of stone. She could turn only her eyes in her head, turn them completely around so they could see backward— and that was a terrible sight, that was. And then the flies came. They crawled over her eyes, back and forth. She blinked her eyes, but the flies didn't fly away—they couldn't. Their wings had been picked off; they had turned into crawling things. That was a torment. And then there was the hunger—at last it seemed to her as if her entrails were devouring themselves, and she became so empty inside, so horribly empty.

"If this keeps up for long, I won't be able to stand it," she said. But she had to stand it, and it did keep up.

Then a burning tear fell on her head; it trickled down her face and breast, straight down to the loaf. Yet another tear fell, and many more. Who was crying over little Inger? Didn't she have a mother up on earth? The tears of grief that a mother sheds over her child always reach it, but they don't redeem it, they burn. They only add to the torment. And now this excruciating hunger, and not being able to reach the loaf she was treading with her foot! At last she had a feeling that everything inside her must have devoured itself. She was like a thin hollow tube that sucked every sound into it. She heard clearly everything up on earth that concerned her, and what she heard was ill-natured and harsh. To be sure, her mother wept deeply and sorrowfully, but she added, "Pride goes before a fall! That was your undoing, Inger! How you have grieved your mother!"

Her mother and everyone else up there knew about her sin: that she had trod on the loaf and sunk down and disappeared. The cowherd had told about it; he had seen it himself from the hillside.

"How you have grieved your mother, Inger!" said the mother. "But then I always thought you would!"

"If only I'd never been born!" thought Inger. "Then I'd have been much better off. My mother's sniveling can't be of any help now."

She heard how her master and mistress, those gentle souls who had been like parents to her, spoke: "She was a sinful child," they said. "She paid no heed to the gifts of the Lord, but trod them under her feet. The Door of Mercy will be hard for her to open."

"They should have minded me better," thought Inger, "cured me of my whims—if I had any!"

She heard that a whole ballad had been written about her: "The arrogant lass who trod on the loaf in order to have pretty shoes!" And it was sung throughout the land.

"Imagine hearing so much about it and suffering so much for it!" thought Inger. "I daresay the others ought to be punished for what they've done too! Yes, then there'd be a lot to punish! Ugh, how tormented I am!"

And her soul grew even harder than her shell.

"One won't grow any better in this company! And I don't want to grow any better! See how they glower!"

And her heart was filled with wrath and spite for everybody.

"Well, now they have something to tell up there! Ugh, how tormented I am!"

And she heard that they told her story to the children,

and the little ones called her "Ungodly Inger." "She was so nasty," they said, "so wicked! She really ought to be tormented!"

There were always hard words against her on the children's lips.

Yet one day, as resentment and anger were gnawing at her hollow shell, and she was hearing her name being mentioned and her story being told to an innocent child, a little girl, she became aware that the little one burst into tears at the story of the arrogant Inger who loved finery.

"But is she never coming up again?" asked the little girl.

And the reply came: "She is never coming up again!"

"But if she were to ask forgiveness and never do it again?"

"But she will never ask forgiveness," they said.

"I'd so like for her to do it!" said the little girl, and was quite inconsolable. "I'll give my doll's wardrobe if only she can come up! It's so gruesome for poor Inger."

And those words reached all the way down to Inger's heart; they seemed to do her good. It was the first time that anyone had said "Poor Inger!" without adding the least little thing about her shortcomings. A tiny innocent child was crying and praying for her. It made her feel so strange; she would have gladly cried, but she couldn't cry. And that was also a torment.

As the years went by there was no change down below; she seldom heard sounds from above, and less was said about her. Then one day she was aware of a sigh: "Inger, Inger, how you have grieved me! But I always said you would!" It was her mother, who had died.

Now and then she heard her name mentioned by her old master and mistress, and the mildest words the housewife said were: "Will I ever see you again, Inger? One never knows where one is going."

But Inger realized very well that her gentle mistress would never be able to come to where she was.

Thus another long and bitter time elapsed.

Then Inger again heard her name being mentioned and saw something shining above her like two bright stars. They were two mild eyes that were closing on earth. So many years had gone by since the time the little girl had cried inconsolably over "poor Inger" that the child had become an old woman whom the Lord now wanted to call up to himself. And at that very moment, when the thoughts from her whole life rose before her, she also remembered how bitterly she had cried as a little girl on hearing the story of Inger. The time and the impression appeared so lifelike to the old woman in the hour of her death that she exclaimed aloud, "Lord, my God, haven't I too, like Inger, often trod on your blessed gifts without a thought? Haven't I too gone with pride in my heart? But you, in your mercy, didn't let me sink. You held me up. Don't desert me in my final hour!"

And the eyes of the old woman closed, and the eyes of her soul opened to what is hidden; and as Inger had been so vivid in her last thoughts, she saw her, saw how far down she had been dragged. And at the sight the pious soul burst into tears. In the Kingdom of Heaven she was standing like a child and crying for poor Inger. Those tears and those prayers rang out like an echo in the hollow, empty shell that encased the imprisoned, tortured soul. It was overwhelmed by all this unthought-of love from above; one of God's angels was crying over her! Why was this being granted to her? It was as if the tortured soul collected in its thoughts every deed it had performed in its earthly life, and it shook with tears such as Inger had never been able to cry. She was filled with anguish for herself; she felt that the Door of Mercy could never be opened for her. But as she acknowledged this with a broken heart, at the same moment a beam of light shone

down into the abyss. The beam was stronger than the
sunbeam that thaws the snowman put up in the yard by
the boys. And then, much faster than the snowflake falling
on the warm mouth of the child melts away to a drop,
Inger's petrified figure faded away. A tiny bird, zigzagging
like lightning, soared up to the world of mortals. But it
was afraid and wary of everything around it; it was ashamed
of itself and ashamed to face all living creatures, and
hurriedly sought shelter in a dark hole it found in the
decayed wall. Here it sat huddled, trembling all over. It
couldn't utter a sound—it had no voice. It sat for a long
while before it was calm enough to look at and be conscious of all the magnificence out there. Yes, it was magnificent: the air was so fresh and mild, the moon shone so
brightly, trees and bushes gave off such a fragrance; and
then too it was so pleasant there where it sat. Its feathered
kirtle was so clean and fine. My, how all creation had been
borne along in love and glory! All the thoughts that were
stirring in the breast of the bird wanted to vent themselves in song, but the bird was unable to do it. It would
gladly have sung like the cuckoo and nightingale in spring.
The Lord, who also hears the worm's silent hymn of
praise, was here aware of the hymn of praise that soared in
chords of thought, the way the Psalm resounded in Da-
vid's breast before it was given words and music.

For weeks these silent songs grew and swelled in its
thoughts; they had to burst forth at the first flap of the
wings in a good deed; such a deed had to be performed.

Now the holy celebration of Christmas was at hand.
Close to the wall the farmer set up a pole and tied an
unthreshed sheaf of oats to it so the birds of the air could
also have a joyous Christmas and a gratifying meal at this
time of the Savior's.

The sun came up on Christmas morning and shone on
the sheaf of oats, and all the twittering birds flew about
the feeding pole. Then a "cheep-cheep" rang out from the

wall as well! The swelling thoughts had turned into sound;
the feeble cheeping was a complete hymn of rejoicing. An
idea for a good deed had awakened, and the bird flew out
from its shelter. In the Kingdom of Heaven they knew
very well what kind of bird this was.

Winter set in with a vengeance, the waters were frozen
deep. The birds and animals of the forest had a hard time
finding food. The little bird flew along the highway, searching in the tracks of the sleighs, and here and there it found
a grain of corn; at the resting places it found a few bread
crumbs. Of these it ate only a single one, but called to all
the other starving sparrows that they could find food here.
It flew to the cities and scouted about, and wherever a
loving hand had strewn bread by a window for the birds, it
ate but a single crumb itself and gave everything to the
others.

In the course of the winter the bird had gathered and
given away so many bread crumbs that, altogether, they
weighed as much as the whole loaf of bread that little
Inger had trod on so as not to soil her shoes. And when
the very last bread crumb had been found and given away,
the bird's gray wings turned white and spread out wide.

"A tern is flying over the sea!" said the children who
saw the white bird. Now it ducked down into the sea, now
it soared in the bright sunshine; it shone, it wasn't possible to see what had become of it. They said that it flew
straight into the sun.

Pen and Inkwell

THE words were uttered in a poet's chamber as someone was looking at his inkwell, which was standing on
the table: "It's remarkable, all the things that can come
out of that inkwell I wonder what will be next. Yes, it's
remarkable!"

"So it is!" said the inkwell. "It's incomprehensible! That's
what I always say!" it said to the quill pen and to anything
else on the table that could hear it. "It's remarkable, all

the things that can come out of me! Yes, it's almost incredible! And I don't really know myself what will be next, when the human being starts drawing from me. One drop of me is enough for half a page of paper, and what can't appear there? I'm something quite remarkable! All the poet's works emanate from me! These living beings that people think they know, these profound emotions, this good humor, these lovely descriptions of nature. I can't comprehend it myself, because I'm not familiar with nature. But after all it's in me. From me has originated—and does originate—this host of hovering, lovely maidens, gallant knights on snorting chargers! Indeed, I'm not aware of it myself! I assure you, I don't give it a thought!"

"You're right about that!" said the quill pen. "You don't think at all. Because if you did, you'd understand that you merely provide fluid. You provide moisture so that I can express and render visible on the paper what I have in me, what I write down. It's the pen that writes! Not a soul has any doubts about that, and most mortals have as much of an understanding about poetry as an old inkwell!"

"You have only a little experience!" said the inkwell. "You've scarcely been on duty a week, and already you're half worn out. Are you pretending that you're the poet? You're only hired help, and I've had many of that sort before you came—both of the goose family and of English fabrication! I know both the quill pen and the steel pen. I've had many in my employ, and I'll have many more when he, the human being who makes the motions for me, comes and writes down what he gets out of my insides. I wonder what will be the next thing he draws out of me!"

"Inkpot!" said the pen.

Late in the evening the poet came home. He had been to a concert, heard an excellent violinist, and was quite engrossed and entranced by his incomparable playing. He had produced an amazing flood of tones from his instrument; now they sounded like tinkling drops of water, pearl upon pearl, now like twittering birds in chorus as the storm raged through a forest of spruces. He seemed to hear his own heart crying, but in a melody, the way it can be heard in the lovely voice of a woman. It was as if not only the strings of the violin rang out but also the bridge, yes, even the pegs and the sounding board as well—it was extraordinary; and it had been difficult, but it looked like play, as if the bow could leap back and forth over the strings. You would have thought that anyone could imitate it. The violin rang out by itself, the bow played by itself; it was these two who did it all. The maestro who guided them, gave life and soul to them, was forgotten; the maestro was forgotten! But the poet thought of him; he named him by name and thereby wrote down his thoughts: "How absurd if the bow and the violin were to put on airs about their performance! And yet, that is what we mortals do so often: the poet, the artist, the scientific inventor, the general. We put on airs ourselves, and yet we are all merely the instruments upon which the Lord plays. To him the honor alone! We have nothing to put on airs about!"

Yes, this is what the poet wrote; he wrote it as a parable and called it "The Maestro and the Instruments."

"You had it coming to you, madame!" said the pen to the inkwell when the two were alone again. "I daresay you heard him read aloud what I wrote down!"

"Yes, what I gave you to write," said the inkwell. "After all, it was a dig at you because of your arrogance. You can't even understand when someone is making fun of you! I've made a dig at you straight from my insides. I daresay I should know my own malice!"

"Ink holder!" said the pen.

"Writing stick!" said the inkwell.

And they both had the feeling that they had answered well. And it's a good feeling to know that you've answered well. You can go to sleep on it, and they did sleep on it. But the poet didn't sleep. The thoughts poured forth like the tones from the violin, rolled like pearls, raged like the storm through the forest. He felt his own heart in there; he was aware of the glimmer from the eternal Master.

To him the honor alone!

The Barnyard Cock and the Weathercock

There were two cocks, one on the dunghill and one on the roof; both of them arrogant; but which one accomplished the most? Tell us your opinion, we'll keep ours all the same.

A plank fence separated the chicken yard from another yard, in which there was a dunghill, and on it grew a huge cucumber that was fully convinced that it was a hothouse plant.

"One is born to that," it said deep down inside. "Not everyone can be born a cucumber. There must be other living species too! The hens, the ducks, and the entire stock of the neighboring farm are also creations. For my part, I look up to the barnyard cock on the fence. To be sure, he is of quite another significance than the weathercock, which has been placed so high. It can't even creak, much less crow! It has neither hens nor chicks. It thinks only of itself and sweats verdigris! The barnyard cock, now, is quite a cock! Look at him strut—that's dancing! Listen to him crow—that's music! No matter where he goes you can hear what a trumpeter is! If he were to come in here, if he were to eat me up—leaves, stalk, and all—if I were to enter his body, what a rapturous death that would be!" said the cucumber.

Later on in the night there was a terrible storm. Hens,

chicks, and even the cock sought shelter. The fence between the yards blew down with a great crash. Tiles fell down from the roof, but the weathercock was firmly fastened and not once did it turn around—it couldn't! And yet it was young, newly cast, but staid and sober-minded; it had been born old, and did not resemble the flighty birds of the air, the sparrows and swallows. It despised them, ". . . those dickybirds, small of size and *ordinaire*." The doves were big, glossy, and shiny, like mother-of-pearl; they resembled a kind of weathercock, but were fat and stupid. Their only thought was to get something in their craws, said the weathercock. They were bores to associate with. The birds of passage had also paid a visit and told of foreign lands and of caravans in the air, and dreadful cock-and-bull stories about birds of prey. It was new and interesting the first time, but later the weathercock knew that they repeated themselves, and it was always the same. And this is tedious. They were bores, and everything was a bore. No one was worth associating with, every last one of them was insipid and vapid!

"The world's no good!" he said. "Drivel, the whole thing!"

The weathercock was what is known as blasé, and this would have made him decidedly interesting to the cucumber had she known. But she looked up only to the barnyard cock, and now he was in the yard with her.

The fence had blown down, but the lightning and thunder were over.

"What do you have to say about that cockcrow?" said the barnyard cock to the hens and chicks. "It was a bit unpolished. The elegance was lacking."

"Garden plant!" he said to the cucumber, and in that one expression all his extensive breeding was revealed to her, and she forgot that he was pecking at her and eating her.

"Rapturous death!"

And the hens came and the chicks came. And when one comes running, the others run too! And they clucked and they "cheeped." And they looked at the cock and were proud of him. He was one of their kind.

"Cock-a-doodle-do!" he crowed. "The chicks turn at once into big hens when I say that in the hen yard of the world."

And hens and chicks clucked and "cheeped" behind him.

And the cock proclaimed great news: "A cock can lay an egg! And do you know what lies in that egg? A basilisk! No one can bear the sight of it. The human beings know that, and now you know it too—know what's inside me, know what a terribly fine barnyard-cock-of-the-walk I am!"

And then the barnyard cock flapped his wings, lifted his comb, and crowed again. All the hens and little chicks shuddered, but they were terribly proud that one of their kind was such a terribly fine barnyard-cock-of-the-walk. They clucked and they "cheeped" until the weathercock

had to hear it, and hear it he did. But he wasn't impressed by it!

"It's all nonsense!" he said to himself. "The barnyard cock will never lay an egg, and I can't be bothered to! If I wanted to, I could certainly lay a wind egg, but the world's not worth a wind egg! It's all nonsense! I can't even be bothered to sit here."

And then the weathercock broke off, but he didn't kill the barnyard cock.

"Even though that's what he counted on doing!" said the hens.

And what does the moral say? "Indeed, it's better to crow than to be blasé and break off!"

The Dung Beetle

❖   ❖   ❖

THE emperor's horse was getting golden shoes, a golden shoe on every single foot.

Why was he getting golden shoes?

He was the loveliest animal, had fine legs, the most intelligent eyes, and a mane that hung about his neck like a silken veil. He had borne his master through clouds of gunpowder and a rain of bullets, heard the bullets sing and whistle; he had bitten, kicked, and fought when the enemy pressed closer; with his emperor he had sprung over the fallen horse of the fiend, saved his emperor's crown of red gold, saved his emperor's life, which was worth more than red gold, and for this reason the emperor's horse was getting golden shoes, a golden shoe on every single foot.

Then the dung beetle crawled out.

"First the big, then the small," it said. "After all, it's not the size that counts." And then it held out its thin legs.

"What do you want?" asked the smith.

"Golden shoes!" replied the dung beetle.

"You're certainly not very bright!" said the smith. "Do you want to have golden shoes too?"

"Golden shoes!" said the dung beetle. "Aren't I just as good as that great beast who is to be waited on, groomed,

283

looked after, and given food and drink? Aren't I a part of the emperor's stables too?"

"But why is the horse getting golden shoes?" asked the smith. "Can't you understand that?"

"Understand? I understand that it's an affront to me!" said the dung beetle. "It's an insult! So now I'm going out into the wide world!"

"Scram!" said the smith.

"Vulgar oaf!" said the dung beetle. And then it went outside and flew a little way, and then it was in a beautiful little flower garden where there was a scent of roses and lavender.

"Isn't it lovely here?" said one of the little ladybugs that flew about with black dots on its red shieldlike wings. "How sweet it smells, and how beautiful it is here!"

"I'm used to better things!" said the dung beetle. "Do you call this beautiful? Why, there isn't even a dunghill here!"

And then on it went, into the shade of a big cabbage. A caterpillar was crawling on it.

"How glorious the world is!" said the caterpillar. "The sun is so warm! Everything is such a delight! And one day, when I go to sleep and die, as they call it, I will wake up a butterfly!"

"Don't give yourself ideas!" said the dung beetle. "Now we're flying about like butterflies! I come from the emperor's stables, but no one there—not even the emperor's favorite horse, who, after all, wears my cast-off golden shoes—has such delusions! Get wings! Fly! Yes, now we'll fly!" And then the dung beetle flew. "I will not be vexed, but it vexes me all the same!"

Then it plumped down on a big plot of grass. Here it lay for a little while, then it fell asleep.

Heavens, how the rain poured down! The dung beetle was awakened by the splashing and wanted to burrow down in the ground at once, but couldn't. It overturned; it swam on its stomach and on its back. Flying was impossible! It would never come away from here alive! It lay where it lay, and there it stayed.

When it had cleared a bit, and the dung beetle had blinked the rain out of its eyes, it caught a glimpse of something white. It was linen spread out to bleach. It went over to it and crawled into a fold of the wet cloth. It certainly wasn't like lying in the warm heap in the stable, but there was nothing better; so here it stayed for a whole day and a whole night, and the rainy weather stayed too. Early in the morning the dung beetle crawled out. It was so vexed by the weather.

Two frogs were sitting on the linen; their bright eyes beamed with pure joy. "What delightful weather!" said the first. "How refreshing it is! And the linen holds the water so wonderfully! My hind legs tickle just as if I were swimming!"

"I wonder," said the other, "if the swallow—who flys so far and wide on its many journeys abroad—has found a better climate than ours: such a drizzle, such humidity! It's just like lying in a wet ditch. If that doesn't make one glad, then one doesn't really love one's country!"

"Then you've never been in the emperor's stables?" asked the dung beetle. "The moisture there is both warm and spicy! That's what I'm accustomed to! That's my kind of climate, but you can't take it with you on your journey. Isn't there any hotbed in the garden where persons of rank, such as myself, can put up and feel at home?"

But the frogs didn't understand him—or else they didn't want to understand him.

"I never ask a second time," said the dung beetle after it had asked three times without receiving an answer.

Then it walked a bit; there lay a fragment of a flowerpot. It shouldn't have lain there, but lying where it did, it provided shelter. Several earwig families were living there; they don't insist upon a lot of room, only company. The

females are especially endowed with maternal love, and for this reason the youngsters of each were the prettiest and the most intelligent.

"Our son has become engaged," said one mother, "the sweet innocent! His highest ambition is to crawl, once, into a clergyman's ear! He's so adorably childish, and the engagement keeps him from running wild! That's so gratifying to a mother."

"Our son," said another mother, "was up to mischief the moment he came out of the egg. He's bubbling over! He's sowing his wild oats! That's a tremendous consolation to a mother! Isn't it, Mr. Dung Beetle!" They recognized the stranger by its figure.

"You're both right," said the dung beetle, and then it was invited inside—as far as it could come under the fragment of pottery.

"Now you're also going to see my little earwig," said a third and a fourth mother. "They're the most lovable children, and so entertaining! They're never naughty—except when they have a pain in their stomachs, but one gets that so easily at their age!"

And then each mother talked about her youngsters, and the youngsters talked along with them and used the little fork they have on their tails to tug at the dung beetle's whiskers.

... always up to something, the little ... king of motherly love. B... so it asked if it wer... ...world, on the other side of ... none of my children ..." said the ... ...ung beetles. ...we live!" they said. "It's quite cozy. May we invite you down in the rich dirt? No doubt the journey has worn you out."

"So it has," said the dung beetle. "I've been lying on linen in the rain, and cleanliness in particular takes a lot out of me! I've also got rheumatism in the joint of my wing from standing in a draft under a fragment of pottery. It's really quite refreshing to find oneself among one's own kind."

"Are you by any chance from the hotbed?" asked the oldest.

"Higher up," said the dung beetle. "I come from the emperor's stables, where I was born with golden shoes on. I'm on a secret errand that you mustn't pump me about, as I'm not talking!"

And then the dung beetle crawled down in the rich mud. There sat three young female dung beetles. They snickerered, because they didn't know what to say.

"They're not engaged," said the mother, and then they snickered, because they didn't know what to say.

"I've never seen them prettier in the emperor's stables," said the traveling dung beetle.

"Don't lead my girls astray! And don't speak to them unless your intentions are honorable. But so they are, and I give you my blessing!"

"Hurrah!" said all ... Hans Ch... ...prise!" it said.

was engaged. First ... ...prise in return!"

After all, there w...

The next day ...

but on the th it was. Gone the whole day, gone the

perhaps t...

"I've

"So ...ight. And the wife was left a widow. The other
dung beetles said they had taken a regular tramp into the
family; the wife was now a burden to them.

"Then she can become a maiden again," said the mother,
"remain my child. Fie on that dastardly wretch who abandoned her!"

In the meantime it was on its way, having sailed across
the ditch on a cabbage leaf. Early in the morning two
people came. They saw the dung beetle, picked it up, and
twisted and turned it. They were both very learned,
especially the boy. "Allah sees the black dung beetle in
the black stone in the black mountain! Isn't that the way
it's written in the Koran?" he asked. And he translated the
dung beetle's name into Latin and gave an account of its
genus and nature. The older scholar voted against taking it
home with them. The examples they had there were just
as good, he said. The dung beetle didn't think this was a
polite thing to say, and so it flew out of his hand and flew a
good distance—its wings had become dry—and then it
reached the hothouse. One of the windows had been
pushed up, so it could pop in with the greatest of ease and
burrow down in the fresh manure.

"How luscious it is!" it said.

Soon it fell asleep and dreamed that the emperor's
horse had fallen and that Mr. Dung Beetle had been given
its golden shoes and the promise of two more. That was a
pleasure, and when the dung beetle awoke it crawled out

and looked up. How magnificent it was in the
Enormous fan palms spread out overhead, t
them transparent. Beneath them was a luxuria
ery, and flowers glowed as red as fire, as golden as amber,
and as white as the driven snow.

"What wonderfully magnificent plants! How marvelous
it all will taste when it starts to rot!" said the dung beetle.
"This is a fine dining room. No doubt some of the family
dwells here. I will track them down and see if I can find
anyone worth associating with. I have my pride and I'm
proud of it!" Then off it went, thinking of its dream about
the dead horse and the golden shoes it had won.

All at once a hand grabbed the dung beetle. It was
squeezed and turned over and over.

The gardener's little boy was in the hot house with a
friend; they had seen the dung beetle and were going to
have some fun with it. It was wrapped in a grape leaf and
put down in a warm pants pocket. It wriggled and crawled
until it received a squeeze from the hand of the boy, who
went quickly over to the big lake at the end of the garden.
Here the dung beetle was placed in a broken old wooden
shoe with the instep missing. A stick was made fast for a
mast, and the dung beetle was tied to it with a woolen
thread. Now it was a skipper and was going out sailing.

The lake was very large. The dung beetle thought it was
the ocean, and it was so astonished that it fell over on its
back with its feet kicking in the air.

The wooden shoe sailed, for there was a current in the
water; but if the ship went too far out, one of the boys
rolled up his pants right away and went out and fetched it.
But the next time it drifted, the boys were called—called
in earnest—and they hurried away, leaving the wooden
shoe a wooden shoe. It floated farther and farther from
land. It was terrifying for the dung beetle; it couldn't fly
because it was tied fast to the mast.

A fly paid it a visit.

What glorious weather we're having," said the fly. Here I can rest and sun myself. You are quite comfortable."

"You're talking as if you were not in possession of your senses! Don't you see I'm tied up?"

"I'm not tied up!" said the fly, and then it flew away.

"Now I know what the world is like," said the dung beetle. "It's an ignoble world! I'm the only respectable soul in it. First I'm refused golden shoes, then I have to lie on wet linen and stand in a draft, and in the end they foist a wife upon me. Then, when I take a quick trip out in the world to see how it is, and how it should be for me, along comes a human whelp and ties me up and puts me in the raging sea! And in the meantime the emperor's horse goes about with golden shoes on! It's enough to make one croak! But one can't expect sympathy in this world. The story of my life is quite interesting, but what's the good of that when no one knows about it? Nor does the world deserve to know about it, otherwise it would have given *me* golden shoes in the emperor's stables when the steed held out its feet and was shod. Had I been given golden shoes, I would have been a credit to the stables. Now it has lost me and the world has lost me. Everything is finished."

But everything wasn't finished yet. A boat came along with some young girls in it.

"A wooden shoe is sailing there," said one.

"A little bug is tied fast to it," said the other.

They were right alongside the wooden shoe. They picked it up, and one of the girls took out a pair of scissors and cut the woolen thread without harming the dung beetle, and when they came ashore she put it in the grass.

"Crawl, crawl! Fly, fly if you can!" she said. "Freedom is a wonderful thing."

And the dung beetle flew right in through the window of a large building and sank exhausted in the fine, soft, long mane of the emperor's charger, who was standing in the stable where he and the dung beetle belonged. It clung fast to the mane and sat for a while to collect its thoughts. "Here I sit on the emperor's charger, sit like a rider. What am I saying? Yes, now it's clear to me! It's a good idea and a correct one at that. Why did the emperor's horse get golden shoes? The smith asked me about that too. Now I see it! The emperor's horse was given golden shoes for my sake!"

And now the dung beetle was in good spirits.

"Travel clears one's head!" it said.

The sun shone on it, shone very beautifully. "The world hasn't gone so mad yet," said the dung beetle. "You just have to know how to take it." The world was lovely: the emperor's charger had been given golden shoes because the dung beetle was to be its rider.

"Now I'm going to climb down and tell the other beetles how much has been done for me. I'll tell of all the pleasures I've indulged in on my journey abroad, and I'll say that now I'm going to remain at home until the horse has worn out its golden shoes!"

What Papa Does
Is Always Right

❖ ❖ ❖

NOW I'm going to tell you a story I heard when I was a boy, and every time I've thought of it since, it struck me as being much nicer, for it's the same with stories as with many people: they grow nicer and nicer with age, and that's so delightful!

Of course you've been out in the country! You've seen a really old farmhouse with a thatched roof. Mosses and herbs are growing on it of their own accord. There's a stork's nest on the ridge—you can't do without the stork. The walls are crooked, the windows low—indeed, there's only one that can be opened. The oven juts out just like a little pot belly, and the elder bush hangs over the fence, where there's a little puddle of water with a duck or ducklings on it, right under the gnarled willow tree. Yes, and then there's a dog on a chain that barks at each and every one.

Just such a farmhouse was out in the country, and in it there lived a couple: a farmer and the farmer's wife. No matter what little they had, there was still one thing they could do without: a horse that grazed in the ditch by the side of the road. Papa rode to town on it, the neighbors borrowed it, and one good turn was repaid by another. But I daresay it was more profitable for them to sell the horse or swap it for something or other that could be of even more use to them. But what was that to be?

"You'll be the best judge of that, Papa!" said the wife. "Now, there's a fair on in town. Ride there and get money for the horse, or else make a good bargain. Whatever you do is always right! Ride to the fair!"

And then she tied his neckerchief, for after all she knew how to do that better than he did; she tied it in a double bow—it looked so perky—and then she brushed his hat with the flat of her hand, and she kissed him on his warm lips. And then he rode off on the horse that was to be sold or swapped. Yes, Papa was the best judge of that.

The sun blazed down; there wasn't a cloud above. The dust whirled up from the road, for there were so many people on their way to the fair—in carts, on horseback, and on their own two feet. It was sizzling hot, and there wasn't a bit of shade along the way.

A man was walking along driving a cow; it was as pretty as a cow can be. "I daresay that cow gives delicious milk!" thought the farmer. "It could be quite a bargain to get that!" He said, "Look here, you with the cow! Shouldn't the two of us have a little chat together? Here's a horse, which I do believe costs more than a cow, but it doesn't matter! A cow is of more use to me. Shall we swap?"

"I'll say!" said the man with the cow, and so they swapped.

Well, that was settled, and now the farmer could have turned back. After all, he'd done what he'd set out to do. But as long as he'd made up his mind to go to the fair, then to the fair he wanted to go, just to have a look at it. So he went on with his cow. He walked along at a good clip, and the cow walked along at a good clip, and soon they were walking alongside a man who was leading a ewe. It was a fine ewe, with plenty of meat and plenty of wool.

"I'd like to own that!" thought the farmer. "It'd never

be without something to graze on by the side of our ditch, and in the winter we could bring it into the house with us. As a matter of fact, it would be better for us to keep a ewe than a cow. Shall we swap?"

Well, the man with the ewe was only too willing, and so this swap was made, and the farmer went on down the road with his ewe. There by the stile he saw a man with a big goose under his arm.

"That's a big fellow you've got there!" said the farmer. "It has both feathers and fat. It'd look good tethered by our pond. This is something for Mama to gather peelings for! She's often said, 'If only we had a goose!' Now she can have one—and she shall have one! Do you want to swap? I'll give you the ewe for the goose, and thanks into the bargain!"

Well, the other man was only too willing, and so they swapped. The farmer got the goose. He was close to town; the crowds on the road increased. It was teeming with men and beasts. They walked on the road, and in the ditch, all the way up to the tollman's potato patch, where his hen stood tied, so that she wouldn't run away in her fright and get lost. It was a bobtail hen that blinked with one eye and looked good. "Cluck! Cluck!" it said. What it meant by that I cannot say. But when the farmer saw her, he thought: "She's the prettiest hen I've ever seen. She's prettier than the parson's sitting hen. I'd so like to own her! A hen can always find a grain of corn. She can almost look after herself! I think that would be a good bargain if I got her for the goose." "Shall we swap?" he asked. "Swap?" said the other. "Why, yes, that wasn't such a bad idea!" And so they swapped: the tollman got the goose, the farmer got the hen.

He'd done quite a lot on that journey to town, and it was hot and he was tired. A dram and a bite to eat were what he needed. Now he was by the inn. He wanted to go in, but the innkeeper's hired hand wanted to go out. He met him right in the doorway with a sack heaping full of something.

"What have you got there?" asked the farmer.

"Rotten apples!" answered the fellow. "A whole sackful for the pigs."

"Why, that's an awful lot! I wish Mama could see a sight like that. Last year we had only a single apple on the old tree by the peat shed. That apple had to be kept, and it stood on the chest of drawers until it burst. 'There's always plenty!' said Mama. Here she could really see plenty!"

"Well, what'll you give?" asked the fellow.

"Give? I'll give you my hen in exchange!" And then he gave him the hen for the apples and went into the inn and right over to the bar. He leaned his sack of apples up against the tiled stove. There was a fire in it, but he didn't give that a thought. There were lots of strangers here in the room: horse traders, cattle dealers, and two Englishmen—they're so rich that their pockets are bursting with golden coins, and they love to make wagers!

Now you shall hear.

"Ssssssss! Ssssssss!" What was that noise over by the stove? The apples were beginning to roast.

"What's that?" Well, they soon found out about the whole story—about the horse that had been swapped for the cow, all the way down to the rotten apples.

"Well," said the Englishmen, "you'll be getting a cuff from Mama when you come home! There'll be the devil to pay!"

"I'll get a kiss and not a cuff!" said the farmer. "Our Mama's going to say, 'What Papa does is always right!'"

"Shall we wager?" they said. "A barrelful of gold coins! A hundred pounds to a ship's pound!"

"A bushel is enough," said the farmer. "I can put up only the bushel of apples—and myself and Mama into the bargain! But that's more than a level measure; that's a heaping measure!"

"Heaping! Heaping!" they said, and then the wager was made.

The innkeeper's wagon was brought out, the Englishmen got in, the farmer got in, the rotten apples got in, and then they came to the farmer's house.

"Good evening, Mama!"

"Same to you, Papa!"

"Well, I've made a swap!"

"Yes, you're the best judge of that," said the wife, putting her arm around his waist and forgetting both the sack and the strangers.

"I've swapped the horse for a cow!"

"Heaven be praised for the milk!" said the wife. "Now we can have milk dishes and butter and cheese on the table. That was a lovely swap!"

"Yes, but I swapped the cow for a ewe!"

"That's decidedly better too!" said the wife. "You're always considerate. We've plenty of fodder for a ewe. Now we can have ewe's milk and cheese and woolen stockings— yes, even a woolen nightshirt. The cow doesn't give that. She loses her hair. You're the most considerate man!"

"But I swapped the ewe for a goose!"

"Are we really going to have a goose this year for Martinmas, little Papa? You're always thinking up ways to please me! That was sweet of you. The goose can stand tethered and grow fatter by Martinmas."

"But I swapped the goose for a hen!" said the husband.

"A hen! That was a good swap," said the wife. "The hen lays eggs; it hatches them out—we'll have chickens, we'll have a hen yard! That's just what I've always wanted!"

"Yes, but I swapped the hen for a sack of rotten apples!"

"Now I've got to give you a kiss!" said the wife. "Thank you, my own husband! Now I'm going to tell you something. While you were gone I thought I'd make a really good meal for you—an omelet with chives. I had the eggs, but no chives. So I went over to the schoolmaster's. They have chives there, I know. But the wife is so stingy, that sweet she-ass! I asked if I could borrow! 'Borrow!' she said. 'Nothing grows in our garden, not even a rotten apple! I can't even lend you that!' Now I can lend her ten—yes, a whole sackful. What a joke that is, Papa!" And she kissed him squarely on the mouth.

"Now you're talking!" said the Englishmen. "Always down and out, and always without a care! That's certainly worth the money!" And so they paid a ship's pound of golden coins to the farmer, who received a kiss instead of a cuff.

Yes, indeed, it always pays for the wife to realize and

explain that Papa is the wisest, and whatever he does is right.

See, that's a story! I heard it when I was a boy, and now you've heard it too and know that What Papa Does Is Always Right.

The Snowman

"I'M fairly creaking inside, it's so delightfully cold!" said
the snowman. "The wind can really bite life into one!
And how that glowerer there can glower!" This was the
sun that he meant; it was just about to go down. "She's not
going to make me blink! I daresay I can hang onto the
fragments!"

He had two big triangular fragments of tile for eyes; the
mouth was a piece of an old rake, and so he had teeth.

He had been born to the cheers of the boys and greeted
by the jangle of bells and the crack of whips from the
sleighs.

The sun went down; the full moon came up, round and
big, bright and lovely in the blue air.

"There she is from another angle," said the snowman.
He thought the sun was showing itself again. "I've made
her stop glowering! Now she can just hang there and shine
so I can have a look at myself. If only I knew what one
does to move! I'd so like to move! If I could, I'd go down
now and slide on the ice, the way I saw the boys doing it!
But I don't understand how to run!"

"Gone! Gone!" barked the old watchdog. He was somewhat hoarse. He'd been that way ever since the time he
was a house dog and had lain under the tiled stove. "The
sun'll soon teach you how to run! I saw it with your

predecessor last year, and with *his* predecessor. Gone! Gone! And they are all gone!"

"I don't understand you, friend!" said the snowman. "Is that one up there going to teach me how to run?" He meant the moon. "Well, of course she can run. She ran before, when I glared at her. Now she's sneaking around from another side."

"You don't know anything!" said the watchdog. "But then you've only just been made! The one you're looking at now is called the moon; the one that left was the sun. She'll be back tomorrow. I daresay she'll teach you how to run down in the moat. We'll soon be getting a change in the weather. I can tell by my hind leg—it's aching. The weather's going to change."

"I don't understand him," said the snowman, "but I've

got a feeling that he's saying something unpleasant. That one who glowered and went down—the one he calls the sun—she's not my friend, either. I can feel it."

"Gone! Gone!" barked the watchdog, turning on his tail three times and lying down in his house to go to sleep.

There really was a change in the weather. Early in the morning a thick, clammy fog settled over the entire countryside. At daybreak the wind started to blow. It was biting cold; the frost really nipped. But what a sight to behold when the sun rose! All the trees and bushes were covered with rime. It was like an entire forest of white coral, as if every branch had been heaped with sparkling white blossoms. The myriads of delicate twigs, which cannot be seen in summer for the many leaves, now came into their own—each and every one. It was like lace, and as shining white as if a radiant white light were streaming from every branch. The weeping birch stirred in the wind; it seemed to be as alive as the trees in summer. It was incomparably lovely; and when the sun shone—my, how it all sparkled! It was as if it had been powdered over with diamond dust, while the big diamonds glittered on the earth's blanket of snow. One might even believe that myriads of tiny candles were burning, whiter than the white snow.

"How incredibly lovely!" said a young girl who came out in the garden with a young man, and stopped close to the snowman to look at the glittering trees. "There's no lovelier sight in summer," she said, and her eyes beamed.

"And there aren't any fellows like this one at all," said the young man, pointing to the snowman. "He's splendid!"

The young girl laughed, nodded to the snowman, and danced on with her friend across the snow, which creaked beneath them as if it were starch.

"Who were those two?" the snowman asked the watchdog. "You've been here in the yard longer than I have. Do you know them?"

"That I do!" said the watchdog. "After all, she has petted me and he has given me a bone. I don't bite them."

"But what are they supposed to be?" asked the snowman.

"Sweeeeeeethearrrrrrrrts!" said the watchdog. "They're going to move into a doghouse and gnaw bones together. Gone! Gone!"

"Are those two just as important as you and I?" asked the snowman.

"Why, they belong to the family," said the watchdog. "I must say, there's very little one knows when one was born yesterday. I can tell by the way you act! I have age and knowledge; I know everybody here. And I've known a day when I didn't stand outside chained up in the cold! Gone! Gone!"

"The cold is delightful!" said the snowman. "Tell! Tell! But you mustn't rattle your chain, for it makes me crack inside."

"Gone! Gone!" barked the watchdog. "I was once a puppy—tiny and sweet, they said. Then I lay on a velvet stool inside the house, lay on the lap of the head of the family. I was kissed on the chaps and had my paws wiped with an embroidered handkerchief. I was called "the most delightful" and "cuddly-wuddly." But then I grew too big for them, so they gave me to the housekeeper. I came down to the basement! You can see in there from where you're standing. You can look down into the room where I was lord and master, for that's what I was at the housekeeper's. It was probably a humbler place than above, but it was more comfortable here. And I wasn't mauled and hauled about the way I was by the children upstairs. The food I got was just as good, and there was more of it! I had my own pillow, and then there was a tiled stove—the most wonderful thing in the world at this time of year. I crawled all the way in underneath it until I was out of sight. Oh, I still dream about that tiled stove! Gone! Gone!"

"Does a tiled stove look so lovely?" asked the snowman. "Does it look like me?"

"It's the very opposite of you! It's as black as coal and has a long neck with a brass drum. It eats wood until the flames pour out of its mouth. You have to stay beside it, close up to it, underneath it; it's an infinite pleasure! You must be able to see it through the window from where you're standing!"

And the snowman looked, and he really did see a black highly polished object that had a brass drum. The fire shone out at the bottom. The snowman felt very queer. He had a feeling that he was unable to account for; something had come over him that he had never known before, but which everyone has known who isn't a snowman.

"And why did you leave her?" said the snowman—he felt that it had to be of the female persuasion. "How could you leave such a place?"

"I had to," said the watchdog. "They threw me outside and put me here on a chain. I'd bitten the youngest Junker in the leg for kicking away the bone I was gnawing on. And bone for bone, I thought. But they took exception to this, and I've been chained up out here ever since. And I've lost my clear voice. Listen to how hoarse I am. Gone! Gone! That was the end of that!"

The snowman was no longer listening. He gazed steadily into the housekeeper's basement, down into her parlor, where the stove stood on its four legs and seemed to be as big as the snowman himself.

"I'm creaking so strangely inside," he said. "Will I never come in there? It's a harmless wish, and our harmless wishes ought to be granted. It's my greatest wish, my only wish, and it would almost be unjust if it weren't granted. I must come in there, I must lean up against her, even if I have to break the window."

"You'll never get inside there," said the watchdog. "And if you did get to the tiled stove, you'd be gone! Gone!"

"I'm as good as gone!" said the snowman. "I think I'm breaking in two!"

All day long the snowman stood gazing in through the window. In the twilight the room was even more inviting. From the tiled stove came a gentle glow, as could never come from the moon or the sun; no, it glowed as only a tiled stove can glow when it has something inside it. If the door was opened, the flames shot out as they were in the habit of doing. The snowman's white face turned a scarlet hue, he was red all the way down to his chest.

"I can't stand it," he said. "How it becomes her to stick out her tongue!"

The night was very long, but not for the snowman. He stood deep in his own lovely thoughts, and they froze so they creaked.

In the early-morning hours the basement windows were frozen over; they were covered with the loveliest flowers of ice that any snowman could wish for, but they hid the tiled stove. The panes wouldn't thaw; he couldn't see her. It creaked and it crunched; it was just the sort of frosty weather to satisfy any snowman, but he wasn't satisfied. He could and he should have felt so happy, but he wasn't happy: he had what is known as the "tiled-stove-yearning."

"That's a bad sickness for a snowman to have," said the watchdog. "I've had a little of the same sickness myself, but I've got over it. Gone! Gone! Now we're going to have a change in the weather."

And there was a change in the weather: a thaw set in.

The thaw increased, the snowman decreased. He never said a word, he never complained, and that's a sure sign.

One morning he fell over. Something like the handle of a mop was sticking in the air where he had been standing. This is what the boys had built him around.

"Now I can understand his longing," said the watchdog. "The snowman had a poker inside him. That's what has affected him; now it's over! Gone! Gone!"

And soon the winter was over too.

"Gone! Gone!" barked the watchdog.
But in the yard the little girls sang:

> "Hurry forth woodruff, fresh and fair,
> Willow, hang your woolen tassels there,
> Come cuckoo, lark! Sing, be merry,
> Spring has come in February.
> Cuckoo! Tweet-tweet! I sing too!
> Come, dear sun, the way you often do!"

So no one is thinking about the snowman!

In the Duck Yard

❖　❖　❖

A duck came from Portugal, some said from Spain. It makes no difference—she was called "The Portuguese." She laid eggs, was butchered and served for dinner; that's the course of her life. All those who crawled out of her eggs were called "The Portuguese," and that meant something. Now, of the entire stock only one was left in the duck yard—a yard to which the chickens also had access, and where the cock behaved with infinite arrogance.

"That violent crowing of his outrages me!" said The Portuguese. "But he is handsome. That cannot be denied, despite the fact that he is no drake. He should control himself, but controlling oneself is an art. It reveals breeding. That's what the little songbirds up in the linden tree in the neighboring garden possess. How sweetly they sing! There's something so moving in their song. I'd call it *Portugal!* If I had a little songbird like that, I'd be a mother to him, affectionate and good. It's in my blood, in my Portuguese!"

And at the same moment as she was speaking, a little songbird did come. It came headlong down from the roof. The cat was after it, but the bird escaped with a broken wing and fell down in the duck yard.

"That's just like the cat, the scoundrel!" said The Portuguese. "I know him from the time I had ducklings myself! That such a creature is permitted to live and walk about on the rooftops! I don't believe it would happen in Portugal!"

And she took pity on the little songbird, and the other ducks, who weren't Portuguese, took pity on him too. "The poor little mite," they said, and came one after the other. "It's true that we're not singers ourselves," they said, "but we do have internal sounding boards, or something like that; we feel it even if we don't talk about it."

"Then I want to talk about it," said The Portuguese. "And I want to do something for it, for that is one's duty!" And then she went up to the drinking trough and flapped in the water, so that she almost drowned the little songbird in the deluge he received. But it was well meant. "That's a good deed!" she said. "The others can look at it and follow its example."

"Peep!" said the little bird; one of his wings was broken. It was hard for him to shake himself, but he quite understood that well-meant deluge. "You're so tenderhearted, madame!" he said, but he insisted on nothing more.

"I've never given the tenderness of my heart a thought!" said The Portuguese. "But I do know that I love all my fellow creatures with the exception of the cat. But then no one can ask that of me! I myself am from foreign parts, as you probably can tell by my carriage and my feathered gown. My drake is a native, doesn't have my blood, but I don't put on airs! If you're understood by anybody in here, then I daresay it's by me."

"She was a *portulaca*[1] to the craw," said one ordinary little duckling who was witty, and the other ordinary ducklings thought that *portulaca* was quite splendid—it sounded like Portugal; and they nudged one another and

[1] Purslane.

said, "Quack!" He was so incomparably witty. And then they took up with the little songbird.

"True, The Portuguese has the language at her command," they said. "Our bills are not given to big words, but we participate just as much. If we don't do anything for you, we keep quiet about it, and we find that to be most agreeable."

"You have a sweet voice," said one of the oldest. "It must be delightful to be aware that one gives so much pleasure to so many, the way you do. Of course I don't know anything about that! And so I keep my mouth shut, and that's always better than saying something stupid, the way so many others say to you."

"Don't pester him!" said The Portuguese. "He needs rest and care. Little songbird, shall I splash you again?"

"Oh, no, let me stay dry!" he begged.

"The water cure is the only thing that helps me," said The Portuguese. "Diversion is also quite good! Now the neighboring hens will be coming soon to pay a visit. There are two Chinese hens. They wear pantaloons and have considerable breeding, and they've been imported—which elevates them in my esteem."

And the hens came, and the cock came! He was so polite today that he wasn't rude.

"You're a real songbird," he said, "and with your little voice you do as much as can be done with such a little voice! But something more locomotive is needed for it to be heard that one is of the male sex!"

The two Chinese hens stood enraptured over the sight of the songbird. He looked so disheveled from the deluge he had received that they thought he resembled a Chinese chicken. "He's lovely!" And then they took up with him. They spoke in whispers, and the *p*-sound in proper Chinese.

"Now, we belong to your species. The ducks—even The Portuguese—belong to the web-footed birds, as you no doubt have observed. You don't know us yet, but how many do know us or take the trouble to! No one, not even among the hens, even though we're born to sit on a higher perch than most of the others. Of course it doesn't matter—we go our silent way among the others whose principles are not our own. But we look only at the good qualities and talk only about the good, despite the fact that it's hard to find where none exists. But with the exception of the two of us and the cock, there's no one in the hen house who is gifted. But they are respectable. You can't say this about the occupants of the duck yard. We warn you, little songbird, don't believe the one there with the short tail—she's perfidious! That speckled one there, with the uneven wing bows, she loves to argue and never permits anyone to have the last word. And then she's always wrong! That fat duck talks badly about everybody, and that's contrary to our nature. If you can't say something nice, then you should keep your mouth shut. The Portuguese is the only one who has a little breeding, and with whom one can associate. But she's passionate, and talks too much about Portugal!"

"What a lot the two Chinese have to whisper about!" said a couple of the ducks. "They bore me; I've never talked with them!"

Now the drake came. He thought the songbird was a house sparrow. "Well, I can't tell them apart," he said. "And besides, it makes no difference! He's one of the mechanical musical instruments, and if you've got them, then you've got them."

"Pay no attention to what he says!" whispered The Portuguese. "He's worthy of respect in business, and business is everything! But now I'm going to lie down to rest. One owes it to oneself to be nice and fat until one is ready to be embalmed with apples and prunes."

And then she lay down in the sunshine, blinking one eye. She lay so well, she behaved so well, and then she slept so well. The little songbird pecked at his broken

wing and lay down next to his protectress; the sun shone
warm and delightful; it was a good place to be.

The neighbor hens continued to scrape. As a matter of
fact, they had come there solely for the sake of the food.
The Chinese left first and then the others. The witty
duckling said, about The Portuguese, that the old one
would soon be going into her "Duckage." And then the
other ducks cackled, "Duckage! He's so incomparably witty!"
And then they repeated the first witticism: "*Portulaca!*"
That was very funny. And then they lay down.

They lay there for a while, then all at once some slops
were thrown down in the duck yard. It made such a splash
that the entire sleeping company flew up and flapped their
wings. The Portuguese woke up too and fell over, crushing the little songbird quite dreadfully.

"Peep!" he said. "You tread so hard, madame!"

"Why are you lying in the way?" she said. "You mustn't
be so thin-skinned! I have nerves too, but I've never said
'Peep'!"

"Don't be angry," said the little bird. "That 'Peep' slipped
out of my beak."

The Portuguese paid no attention to this, but flew to the
slops and had her good meal. When it was over and she
had lain down, the little songbird came and wanted to be
pleasant:

> "Twittery-twing!
> About your heart
> I'll always sing,
> Far, far, far on the wing!"

"Now I'm going to rest after the food," she said. "You've
got to learn the house rules in here! Now I'm going to
sleep."

The little songbird was quite taken aback, for he had
meant so well by it. When madame later awoke, he was

standing in front of her with a little grain of corn he had found. He put it in front of her, but she hadn't slept well and of course she was cross.

"You can give that to a chicken!" she said. "Don't stand there and hang over me!"

"But you're angry with me," he said. "What have I done?"

"Done!" said The Portuguese. "That expression is not of the finest sort, I'll have you know!"

"Yesterday there was sunshine here," said the little

bird, "but today it's dark and gray! I'm so deeply grieved."

"You certainly don't know enough about measuring time," said The Portuguese. "The day isn't over yet, so don't stand there and pretend to be so stupid."

"You're looking at me so angrily, the way those two evil eyes looked when I fell down here in the yard."

"Impudence!" said The Portuguese. "Are you comparing me with the cat, that beast of prey? There's not one drop of evil blood in me. I've taken care of you, and I'm going to teach you how to behave!"

And then she bit off the songbird's head. He lay dead.

"Now what's that?" she said. "Couldn't he take it! Well, he certainly wasn't much for this world, then! I've been like a mother to him, that I know, for I do have a heart."

And the neighboring cock stuck his head into the yard and crowed with the power of a locomotive.

"You'll be the death of somebody with that crowing!" she said. "It's all your fault! He lost his head, and I'm about to lose mine!"

"He doesn't take up much room where he lies," said the cock.

"Talk about him with respect!" said The Portuguese. "He had manners and song and good breeding! He was affectionate and softhearted, and that's just as becoming to the animals as to those so-called human beings."

And all the ducks gathered around the little dead songbird. The ducks have strong passions, no matter whether it's envy or compassion. And as there was nothing here for them to be envious of, they were compassionate. And so were the two Chinese hens.

"We'll never have a songbird like that again! He was almost Chinese!" And they cried so they clucked, and all the hens clucked. But the ducks went about with the reddest eyes.

"We have heart," they said. "There's no denying that!"

"Heart!" said The Portuguese. "Yes, that we have—almost just as much as in Portugal."

"Now let's see about getting something in the carcass!" said the drake. "That's more important! If one of the mechanical musical instruments breaks down, we'll still have enough."

The Butterfly

❖ ❖ ❖

THE butterfly wanted to have a sweetheart. Naturally he wanted one of the pretty little flowers. He looked at them; each one was sitting so prim and proper on its stalk, the way a maiden should sit when she is not engaged. But there were so many to choose from that it proved irksome. The butterfly couldn't be bothered, and so he flew to the daisy. The French call her Marguerite. They know that she can foretell the future, and she does it when sweethearts pick petal by petal off her, and with each one they ask a question about the beloved: "Loves me? Loves me not? Loves me a lot? A teeny-weeny bit? Not at all?" Or something like that. Each one asks in his own language. The butterfly also came to ask. He didn't nip off the petals, but kissed each one—it being his opinion that one comes the farthest without resorting to force.

"Sweet Marguerite!" he said. "Of all the flowers, you are the wisest woman! You understand how to foretell the future. Tell me, am I to marry this one or that? When I find it out, I can fly straight over and propose!"

But Marguerite did not reply at all. She could not bear his calling her a woman, for of course she was a maiden, and then one is not a woman. He asked a second time and he asked a third. And when he didn't get a single word out of her, he couldn't be bothered with asking her anymore and flew off to woo without further ado.

It was early spring. There were snowdrops and crocuses in abundance.

"You are quite nice!" said the butterfly. "Lovely, small candidates for confirmation! But a bit green!" Like all other young men, he was looking for older girls. Then he flew to the anemones. They were a little too tart for him, the violets a little too soulful, the tulips too gaudy, the white narcissus too bourgeois, the lime blossoms too small—and they had so many kinfolk. To be sure, the apple blossoms looked like roses, but they stood today and fell off tomorrow—all according to the way the wind blew.

That was too short a marriage, he thought. The sweet pea was the most pleasing: she was white and red, pure and delicate—one of those homey maidens who look good and yet are cut out for the kitchen. He was just going to propose to her when, at the same moment, he saw hanging close by a pea pod with withered flowers on the top.

"Who's that?" he asked.

"That's my sister," said the sweet pea.

"Well, that's the way you're going to look later!" This frightened the butterfly, and so he flew away.

The honeysuckles were hanging over the fence. There were plenty of those maidens—with long faces and sallow complexions. They weren't his type at all.

Well, what was his type? Ask him!

Spring passed. Summer passed, and then it was autumn. He had made just as much headway. And the flowers appeared in the loveliest garments. But what good was that? The fresh, fragrant lightness of heart was lacking. Fragrance is just what the heart needs, and there is not very much fragrance to dahlias and hollyhocks. So the butterfly turned to the mint.

"Now it has no flower at all. But it is all flower, gives off a fragrance from root to top, and has a flower scent in every leaf. She is the one I will take!"

And so he proposed at last.

But the mint stood still and stiff, and at last she said, "Friendship, but no more. I am old and you are old. We could quite well live for each other. But marry? No! Let us not make fools of ourselves at our great age!"

And so the butterfly got no one at all. He had searched too long, and one should not do that. The butterfly became a bachelor, as it is called.

It was late autumn, with rain and drizzle. The wind sent cold shivers down the spines of the old willow trees, making them creak. It was not good flying outside in summer clothes—you'd be in for an unpleasant surprise, as they say. But the butterfly did not fly outside, either. By chance he had come indoors, where there was a fire in the stove. Indeed, it was as warm as summer. He could live.

"But living isn't enough!" he said. "One must have sunshine, freedom, and a little flower!"

He flew against the pane, and was seen, admired, and stuck on a pin in the curio chest. More could not be done for him.

"Now I too am sitting on a stalk, just as the flowers do!" said the butterfly. "But it is not very pleasant. Indeed, it is like being married—one is stuck!" And then he consoled himself with that.

"That is poor consolation," said the potted plants in the parlor.

"But one cannot quite believe the potted plants," thought the butterfly. "They associate too much with people."

The Snail and
the Rosebush

AROUND the garden was a hedge of hazlenut bushes, and beyond it were fields and meadows with cows and sheep. But in the middle of the garden stood a flowering rosebush, and under it sat a snail. It contained a lot: it contained itself.

"Wait until my time comes!" it said. "I shall accomplish something more than sending forth roses, bearing nuts, or giving milk, as cows and sheep do."

"I'm expecting a great deal from you," said the rosebush. "May I ask when it's coming?"

"I'm biding my time," said the snail. "You, now, are in such a hurry! It doesn't raise one's expectations."

The next year the snail was lying in just about the same spot in the sunshine, under the rosebush, which was budding and sending forth roses—always fresh, always new. And the snail crawled halfway out, stretched out its horns, and drew them back again.

"Everything looks the way it did last year! There has been no progress. The rosebush keeps on sending forth roses; it makes no further headway."

The summer passed and autumn came. The rosebush kept on sending forth flowers and buds until the snow fell. The weather turned raw and wet. The rosebush bent down to the ground; the snail crawled into the earth.

Now a new year began, and the roses came forth and the snail came forth.

"Now you're an old rose stock!" it said. "You must soon see about dying. You've given the world everything you had in you. Whether it was of any consequence is a question I haven't had time to think over. But still it's clear that you haven't done the slightest thing about your inner development, or else you would have produced something else. Can you justify that? Soon you'll end up as kindling. Can you understand what I'm saying?"

"You frighten me," said the rosebush. "I've never given it a thought."

"No, I daresay you never were much prone to thinking. Have you ever figured out for yourself why you put forth flowers and how the flowering came about? Why this way and not another way?"

"No," said the rosebush. "I flowered for the joy of it. I couldn't help myself. The sun was so warm, the air so invigorating. I drank the clear dew and the strong rain. I breathed, I lived! A force came up in me from the earth and from above; I sensed a joy always new, always great, and for that reason I had to blossom. That was my life—I couldn't help myself."

"You have led a very easy life," said the snail.

"Assuredly! Everything has been handed to me!" said the rosebush. "But even more has been given to you! You are one of those thoughtful, profound natures, one of the highly gifted who wants to astound the world."

"That has never crossed my mind at all," said the snail. "The world is of no concern to me! What have I to do with the world? I have enough with myself and enough in myself."

"But shouldn't each one of us here on earth give the best we have to others, bring what we can? To be sure, I have only given roses—but you, you who have received so much, what have you given to the world? What are you giving to it?"

"What have I given? What am I giving? I spit at it! It's no good! It is of no concern to me! You send forth roses. You can go no further! Let the hazelnut bush bear nuts. Let cows and sheep give milk. They each have their public; I have mine in myself! I withdraw into myself, and there I stay. The world is of no concern to me!"

And then the snail went inside its house and sealed it up.

"It's so sad," said the rosebush. "As much as I'd like to, I cannot crawl inside. I must always come out, come out in roses. The petals fall off; they fly about in the wind. And yet I saw one of the roses being put in the housewife's hymnbook; one of my roses was placed on the breast of a lovely young girl; and one was kissed by the lips of a child in blissful joy. It did me so much good! It was truly a blessing. This is my reminiscence, my life!"

And the rosebush bloomed in innocence, and the snail languished in its house. The world was of no concern to him.

And the years went by.

And the snail was dust in the earth. The rosebush was dust in the earth; even the keepsake rose in the hymnbook had withered away. But in the garden new rosebushes bloomed; in the garden new snails grew; they crawled into their houses and spit—the world was of no concern to them.

Shall we read the story again from the beginning? It will be no different.

The Teapot

❖ ❖ ❖

THERE was a proud teapot—proud of its porcelain, proud of its long spout, proud of its broad handle. It had something in front and something behind, the spout in front and the handle behind, and it talked about that. But it didn't talk about its lid; that was cracked and had been riveted. It had a flaw, and one is not fond of talking about one's flaws—the others are sure to do that. Cups, cream pitcher, and sugar bowl, the whole tea service, would be sure to remember more the frailty of the lid, and to talk about it, than about the good handle and the excellent spout. And the teapot was aware of this.

"I know them!" it said to itself. "I am also well aware of my flaw, and I acknowledge it. Therein lies my humility, my modesty. We all have flaws, but one also has talents. The cups were given a handle, the sugar bowl a lid. I, of course, was given both, and one thing in front that they will never receive: I was given a spout. That makes me the queen of the tea table. The sugar bowl and the cream pitcher have been granted the privilege of being hand-maidens of palatability. But I am the dispenser, the mistress. I diffuse the blessing among thirsting humanity. In my interior the Chinese leaf is prepared in the boiling, tasteless water."

All this the teapot said in its intrepid youth. It stood on

the ready-laid table. It was lifted by the most delicate hand. But the most delicate hand was clumsy: the teapot fell, the spout broke off, and the handle broke off. The lid is not worth mentioning—enough has been said about that. The teapot lay in a swoon on the floor, the boiling water running out of it. It had received a hard blow. And the hardest blow of all was that they laughed at it, and not at the clumsy hand.

"That memory I will never lose," said the teapot when it later related the course of its life to itself. "I was called an invalid and put over in a corner, and on the following day I was given away to a woman who came begging for drippings. I sank down into destitution, stood speechless, both inside and out. But as I stood there my better life began. You are one thing and turn into quite another. Dirt was put inside me. To a teapot this is the same as being buried, but a flower bulb was put in the dirt. Who put it there, who gave it I do not know. It was given a compensation for the Chinese leaves and the boiling water a com-

pensation for the broken-off handle and spout. And the
bulb lay in the dirt, the bulb lay inside me. It became my
heart, my living heart. I had never had one like that
before. There was life in me, there was vigor and vitality;
the pulse beat, the bulb sprouted. It was bursting with
thoughts and emotions. It bloomed. I saw it, I bore it, I
forgot myself in its loveliness. How blessed it is to forget
oneself in others! It did not thank me. It did not think of
me: it was admired and praised. I was so happy because of
that: how happy it must have been then. One day I heard
someone say that it deserved a better pot. I was broken in
two. It hurt terribly, but the flower was put in a better
pot—and I was thrown out in the yard, to lie there like an
old fragment. But I have a memory that I cannot lose."

The Candles

❖   ❖   ❖

THERE was once a big wax candle that was well aware
of itself.

"I am born of wax and cast in a mold!" it said. "I shine
better and burn longer than any other candle! My place is
in a chandelier or a silver candlestick!"

"That must be a delightful existence," said the tallow
candle. "I am merely of tallow, only a taper. But I take
comfort in the thought that it's always a little more than
being a tallow dip! It is dipped only twice, whereas I am
dipped eight times to arrive at my proper thickness. I am
content! To be sure, it is finer and more fortunate to be
born of wax and not of tallow, but after all one doesn't put
oneself into this world. They go into the parlor in a crystal
chandelier; I remain in the kitchen. But that is a good
place too. From there the whole house is fed!"

"But there's something far more important than food!"
said the wax candle. "Festivity! To see the radiance and to
be radiant oneself! There's going to be a ball here this
evening. Soon my whole family and I are going to be
fetched!"

The words were scarcely uttered before all the wax
candles were fetched. But the tallow candle came along
too. The mistress herself picked it up in her delicate hand
and carried it out into the kitchen. A little boy was stand-

ing there with a basket. It was filled with potatoes, and a few apples had been added. All this the good woman gave to the poor boy.

"Here's a candle for you too, my little friend!" she said. "Your mother sits working far into the night; she can use it!"

The little daughter of the house was standing nearby, and when she heard the words "far into the night," she said with heartfelt joy, "I too am going to stay up until far into the night. We're going to have a ball, and I'm going to wear my big red bows!"

How her face shone! This was happiness! No wax candle can shine like the two eyes of a child!

"What a blessed sight!" thought the tallow candle. "I will never forget it, and I daresay I will never see it again."

And then it was put in the basket under the lid, and the boy left with it.

"Where am I going now?" thought the candle. "I'm going to poor people. Perhaps I won't even be given a brass candlestick, whereas the wax candle is sitting in silver and looking at the most fashionable people. How wonderful it must be to shine for the most fashionable people. After all, it was my fate to be of tallow and not of wax!"

And the candle did come to poor people, a widow with three children in a lowly little cottage right across from the house of the rich family.

"God bless the good mistress for her gift," said the mother. "Why, there's a lovely candle! It can burn until far into the night!"

And the candle was lighted.

"Sputter, phooey!" it said. "What a nasty, smelly match she lit me with! Such a match would hardly have been offered to a wax candle over in the rich family's house!"

There too the candles were being lighted; they shone

out into the street. The rumbling carriages brought the elegantly clad ball guests. The music rang out.

"Now they're beginning over there!" observed the tallow candle, and thought of the little rich girl's radiant face, more radiant than all the wax candles. "I'll never see a sight like that again!"

Then the youngest child of the poor family came, a little girl. She flung her arms around the necks of her brother and sister—she had something very important to tell them and it had to be whispered: "This evening . . . Imagine! . . . This evening we're going to have hot potatoes!"

And her face shone with bliss. The candle shining there saw a joy, a happiness, as great as that it had seen over in the house of the rich family, where the little girl had said, "We're going to have a ball, and I'm going to wear my big red bows!"

"Is having hot potatoes equally as important?" thought the candle. "The children here are just as happy." And then she sneezed; that is to say, she sputtered, a tallow candle can do no more.

The table was set; the potatoes were eaten. Oh, how delicious they tasted! It was quite a feast! And afterward each child received an apple, and the youngest child recited the little verse:

> "Again, dear Lord, my thanks to thee,
> For giving so much food to me! Amen!"

"Wasn't it nice of me to say that, Mother?" the little one now cried.

"You must neither ask nor say such a thing," said the mother. "You should think only of the good Lord, who has given you enough to eat."

The little ones went to bed, received a kiss, and fell asleep right away, and the mother sat sewing until far into the night to earn a livelihood for them and for herself. And

from the house of the rich family, the candles shone and the music rang out. The stars twinkled above all the houses, above those of the rich and those of the poor, just as bright, just as lovely.

"Come to think of it, this was a strange evening," thought the tallow candle. "I wonder if the wax candles were any better off in silver candlesticks. I wish I could find that out before I burn down."

And it thought of the two children—equally as happy—one illuminated by wax candles, the other by a tallow candle!

Yes, that's the whole story!

The Most Incredible Thing

❖   ❖   ❖

WHOEVER could accomplish the most incredible thing was to have the king's daughter and half the kingdom. The young people—indeed, the old ones too—strained all their thoughts, tendons, and muscles. Two ate themselves to death and one drank himself to death to accomplish the most incredible thing—each according to his own taste—but that wasn't the way in which it was to be done. Little street urchins practiced spitting on their own backs—they considered this to be the most incredible thing.

On a given day each one had to show what he considered to be the most incredible thing. Children from the age of three to people in their nineties had been appointed as judges. There was a whole exhibition of incredible things, but everyone soon agreed that the most incredible thing of all was a huge clock in a case, remarkably contrived inside and out. At each stroke of the clock appeared living pictures that depicted the hour. There were twelve performances in all, with movable figures and with song and speech.

"This was the most incredible thing!" people said.

The clock struck one, and Moses stood on the mount and wrote down the First Commandment on the Tables of the Law: "Thou shalt have no other gods before me."

The clock struck two: now appeared the Garden of
Paradise, where Adam and Eve met, both happy without
owning so much as a clothes closet, nor did they need
one, either.

On the stroke of three, the three Wise Men appeared,
one as black as coal—he couldn't help that, the sun had
blackened him. They came bearing incense and precious
objects.

On the stroke of four came the Seasons: Spring with a
cuckoo on a beech branch in full leaf; Summer with a
grasshopper on a ripe sheaf of grain; Autumn with an
empty stork's nest—the bird had flown away; Winter with
an old crow, which could tell stories and old memories in
the corner by the tiled stove.

When the clock struck five, the Five Senses appeared:
Sight came as an optician, Hearing as a coppersmith,
Smell sold violets and woodruff, Taste was a chef, and
Touch was an undertaker with mourning crepe down to
his heels.

The clock struck six: there sat a gambler casting a die.
The highest side turned up and on it stood six.

Then came the Seven Days of the Week or the Seven
Deadly Sins—people couldn't agree. After all, they belonged together and weren't easy to tell apart.

Then came a choir singing matins.

On the stroke of nine followed the Nine Muses: one was
employed in Astronomy, one at the Historical Archives,
and the rest were in the theater.

On the stroke of ten, Moses again appeared with the
Tables of the Law. There stood all of God's Command-
ments, and there were ten of them.

The clock struck again: now little boys and girls were
hopping and jumping. They were playing a game, and
with it they sang: "Digging, delving, the clock's struck
eleven!" And this is the hour it had struck.

Then it struck twelve. Now the nightwatch appeared in

a fur cap and with a spiked mace. He sang the old night-watch cry:

> " 'Twas at the midnight hour
> Our Savior, Lord was born."

And as he sang roses sprang up, and they turned into the heads of cherubs borne by rainbow-hued wings.

It was a delight to hear, it was a joy to behold. The entire clock was such an incomparable work of art—the most incredible thing, all the people said.

The artist was a young man, tenderhearted, fond of children, a loyal friend, and helpful to his poor parents. He deserved the princess and half the kingdom.

The day of decision was at hand, the entire city was decked out, and the princess was sitting on the throne of the land—it had been given a new horsehair stuffing, but this didn't make it any more comfortable or any easier to sit on for that. The judges on all sides stole sly glances at the one who was going to win, and he stood confident and happy—his success was assured: he had accomplished the most incredible thing!

"No! That's what I'm going to do now!" cried a tall, rawboned, strapping fellow at the same moment. "I'm the man to accomplish the most incredible thing!" And then he swung a huge ax at the work of art.

CRASH! SMASH! SHATTER! There it all lay. Wheels and springs flew about. The whole thing was destroyed!

"I was capable of doing that!" said the man. "My deed has surpassed his and overwhelmed you all. I have accomplished the most incredible thing!"

"To destroy such a work of art!" said the judges. "Yes, that was the most incredible thing!"

The entire populace agreed, and so *he* was to have the princess and half the kingdom! For a law is a law, even if it is the most incredible thing.

From the ramparts and from all the city towers it was proclaimed: "The wedding is to be solemnized!" The princess wasn't at all pleased with it, but she looked lovely and she was richly dressed. The church was ablaze with light—it looks its best late in the evening. The noble maidens of the city sang and ushered in the bride. The knights sang and accompanied the bridegroom. He was swaggering as if he could never be brought to his knees.

Now the singing stopped. It grew so quiet that you could have heard a pin drop on the ground. But in the midst of all that silence the church doors flew open with a rumble and a bang, and BOOM! BOOM! The entire time-piece came marching down the middle of the aisle and lined up between the bride and bridegroom. Dead people cannot come back again—we know this very well—but a work of art can come back again. The body had been smashed to bits, but not the spirit. The Art Spirit had returned as a ghost, and this was no joke.

The work of art stood there as lifelike as when it had been whole and untouched. The strokes of the clock rang out, one after the other, all the way to twelve, and the figures swarmed in. First came Moses. Flames seemed to flash from his forehead. He threw the heavy Tables of the Law onto the bridegroom's feet, pinning them to the floor of the church.

"I cannot lift them again!" said Moses. "You have broken off my arms! Remain now as you are!"

Next came Adam and Eve, the Wise Men from the East, and the Four Seasons, and they all told him unpleasant truths: "Be ashamed of yourself!"

But he wasn't ashamed of himself.

All the figures that had been revealed with each stroke of the clock stepped out of the timepiece, and they grew to a terrible size; it was as if there weren't room for the real people. And when the nightwatch stepped out on the stroke of twelve, with fur cap and mace, there was a strange commotion. The nightwatch went straight over to the bridegroom and struck him on the forehead with the mace.

"Lie there!" he said. "One good turn deserves another! We are avenged and the master too! We are disappearing!"

And then the entire work of art vanished. But all the candles around the church turned into huge flowers of light, and from the gilded stars under the roof were shining long bright shafts of light. The organ pealed by itself. All the people said that this was the most incredible thing they had ever experienced.

"Then, will you summon the right one?" said the princess. "The one who constructed the work of art—he is to be my husband and my lord!"

And he was standing in the church. The entire populace was his retinue. Everyone rejoiced, everyone gave him his blessing. There wasn't a soul who was envious.

Indeed, *that* was the most incredible thing!

The Gardener and the Lord and Lady

❖ ❖ ❖

ABOUT four or five miles from the capital stood an old manor house with thick walls and towers and a corbie gable.

Here there lived—but only during the summer—a rich lord and lady who belonged to the high nobility. This manor was the best and finest of all the manors they owned. It looked like new on the outside and was cozy and comfortable on the inside. The family coat of arms had been carved in stone above the gate; beautiful roses twined about the shield and the bay; a whole carpet of grass stretched out in front of the manor; there were red hawthornes and mayflowers; there were rare flowers even outside the greenhouse.

The lord and lady also had a clever gardener. It was a delight to behold the flower garden, the orchard, and the kitchen garden. Adjoining this was what was left of the original old garden of the estate, with several box hedges trimmed to form crowns and pyramids. Behind these stood two enormous old trees. They were almost always bare of leaves, and it was easy to believe that a gale or a waterspout had strewn them with big clumps of dung. But each clump was a bird's nest.

From time immemorial, swarms of shrieking rooks and crows had built their nests here: it was a complete bird

city, and the birds were the aristocrats, the landed propri-
etors, the oldest stock of the family seat, the real lords and
ladies of the estate. None of the human beings down
below was any concern of theirs, but they put up with
these low-flying creatures even though they banged away
with guns now and then, sending chills up the spines of
the birds, so that each one flew up in fright, shrieking:
"Caw! Caw!"

The gardener often spoke to his lord and lady about
having the old trees chopped down; they didn't look good,

and once they were gone, in all likelihood, they would be
rid of those shrieking birds, which would go somewhere
else. But the lord and lady had no desire to be rid of the
trees or the swarm of birds. This was something the estate
couldn't be without; it was something from bygone days,
and that shouldn't be wiped out at all.

"Those trees, after all, are the inheritance of the birds. Let them keep it, my good Larsen!"

The gardener's name was Larsen, but that is of no further consequence here.

"Isn't your sphere of operation big enough, little Larsen? The entire flower garden, the greenhouses, the orchard, and the kitchen garden?"

Those he had; those he tended, looked after, and cultivated with zeal and skill. And the lord and lady admitted this. But they never hesitated to let him know that, while visiting, they had often eaten fruit or seen flowers that surpassed those they had in their own garden; and this distressed the gardener, for he wanted to do the best and he did the best he could. He had a good heart and did a good job.

One day the lord and lady sent for him and told him blandly and superciliously that on the previous day, while visiting distinguished friends, they had been served a species of apples and pears so succulent and tasty that they and all the guests had expressed their admiration. To be sure, the fruits were not domestic, but they ought to be imported, made to thrive here if our climate permitted it. It was known that they had been purchased from the first fruit dealer in the city. The gardener was to ride in and find out where these apples and pears had come from and then write for cuttings. The gardener knew the fruit dealer well. It was to this very dealer that, on behalf of the lord and lady, he sold the surplus of fruit that grew in the garden of the estate.

And the gardener went to the city and asked the fruit dealer where he had gotten these highly praised apples and pears from.

"They're from your own garden!" said the fruit dealer, and showed him both apples and pears, which he recognized.

My, how happy this made the gardener; he hurried

back to the lord and lady and told them that both the apples and the pears had come from their own garden.

The lord and lady couldn't believe this at all. "It's not possible, Larsen! Can you obtain a declaration in writing from the fruit dealer?"

And this he could; he brought back a written attestation.

"How very extraordinary!" said the lord and lady.

Every day now bowls of these magnificent apples and pears from their own garden appeared on the table of the lord and lady. Bushels and barrels of these fruits were sent to friends in the city and beyond, yes, even abroad. It afforded them great pleasure! And yet they had to add that, after all, there had been two remarkably good summers for tree fruit. These had turned out well everywhere in the land.

Some time passed. The nobility dined at the court. On the following day the gardener was summoned to his lord and lady. At the royal table they had been served such luscious, tasty melons from their majesties' greenhouse.

"You must go to the court gardener, my good Larsen, and obtain for us some of the seeds from these priceless melons!"

"But the court gardener has got the seeds from us!" said the gardener, quite pleased.

"Then that man has discovered a way of bringing the fruit to a higher stage of development," replied the lord and lady. "Each melon was excellent."

"Well, then, I can be proud!" said the gardener. "You see, my lady and my lord, this year the court gardener hasn't had any luck with his melons, and when he saw how splendidly ours were standing, and tasted them, he ordered three to be sent up to the castle."

"Larsen! Don't get the idea into your head that they were the melons from our garden!"

"I think so!" said the gardener, and went to the court

gardener and obtained from him written proof that the
melons on the royal table had come from the manor.

This was really a surprise to the lord and lady, and they
did nothing to keep the story quiet. They showed the
attestation; indeed, melon seeds were sent far and wide,
just as the cuttings had been sent previously.

They received word that the seeds took and bore quite
excellent fruit, and it was named after the lord and lady's
family seat, so that this name was now to be read in
English, German, and French. This had never occurred to
them before.

"As long as the gardener doesn't get too many big
notions about himself!" said the lord and lady.

It affected him in another way: now he made every
effort to make a name for himself as one of the best
gardeners in the land, to try each year to produce something outstanding from every garden variety; and this is
what he did. And yet he was often being reminded that
the very first fruit he had raised, the apples and the pears,
had really been the best; all later varieties were quite
inferior. To be sure, the melons had been very good, but
after all they were of an entirely different sort. The straw-
berries could be called excellent, but still they weren't any
better than the ones grown on the other estates. And
when the radishes failed one year, then only those unsuccessful radishes were mentioned, and not the other good
things that had been raised.

It was almost as if the lord and lady found relief in
being able to say, "It didn't turn out well this year, my
little Larsen!" They were quite happy in being able to say,
"It didn't turn out well this year."

Once or twice a week the gardener brought fresh flowers up to the drawing room, always tastefully arranged; it
was as if the colors grew stronger by being placed side by
side.

"You have taste, Larsen," said the lord and lady. "That is a gift that has come from Our Lord, not from yourself."

One day the gardener brought a big crystal bowl. In it was lying a water lily leaf. On top of this, with its long thick stalk down in the water, had been placed a dazzling blue flower as big as a sunflower.

"Hindustani lotus!" exclaimed the lord and lady.

They had never seen such a flower before, and during the day it was put in the sunshine and in the evening in reflected light. Everyone who looked at it found it to be remarkably lovely and rare; indeed, the highest young lady of the land said so, and she was a princess; she was wise and tenderhearted.

The lord and lady took pride in making her a present of the flower, and it went with the princess up to the castle.

Now the lord and lady went down in the garden themselves to pick a flower just like it if there were any more left. But it was nowhere to be found, so they called the gardener and asked where he had got that blue lotus from.

"We have searched in vain!" they said. "We have been in the greenhouses and all around the flower garden!"

"No, it's not there, all right!" said the gardener. "It's only a lowly flower from the kitchen garden! But how beautiful it is, isn't it! It looks like a blue cactus, and yet it's only the blossom of the artichoke!"

"You should have told us so right away!" said the lord and lady. "We were convinced that it was a rare foreign flower. You have made fools of us in the eyes of the young princess! She saw the flower here and found it to be quite lovely. She didn't recognize it, and she is well versed in botany. But that science has nothing to do with vegetables. What on earth were you thinking of, good Larsen, to put such a flower in the drawing room? It makes us look ridiculous!"

And the magnificent blue flower, which had been taken from the kitchen garden, was thrown out of the lord and lady's drawing room, where it didn't belong. Yes, the lord and lady apologized to the princess and told her the flower was only a vegetable and that the gardener had taken it into his head to display it. But for that reason he had been severely reprimanded.

"That was a shame and an injustice!" said the princess. "Why, he has opened our eyes to a magnificent flower that we would never have noticed at all. He has shown us loveliness where it didn't occur to us to look for it! Every day, as long as the artichokes are in bloom, the castle gardener shall bring one up to me in my drawing room."

And this was done.

The lord and lady informed the gardener that he again could bring a fresh artichoke blossom to them.

"As a matter of fact, it is pretty," they said. "Highly unusual!" And the gardener was praised.

"Larsen likes that!" said the lord and lady. "He's a pampered child!"

In the autumn there was a dreadful storm. It started during the night and was so violent that many big trees on the outskirts of the forest were torn up by the roots. And to the great sorrow of the lord and lady—sorrow as they called it, but to the gardener's delight—the two big trees with all the birds' nests blew down. The shrieking of the rooks and the crows could be heard above the storm. They beat on the panes with their wings, said the servants at the manor.

"Well, you're happy now, aren't you, Larsen!" said the lord and lady. "The storm has blown down the trees, and the birds have taken to the forest. Not a vestige remains of bygone days; every sign and every trace are gone! We are grieved!"

The gardener didn't say anything, but he was thinking of what had been on his mind for a long time: the best way of utilizing the splendid sunny spot, which had not been at his disposal before. It was going to be the pride of the garden and the joy of the lord and lady.

The huge, blown-down trees had crushed and broken the old box hedges, with all their fancy shapes. Here he raised a thicket of plants, domestic plants from field and forest.

What no other gardener had thought of planting in the garden of an estate he planted here in profusion, in the kind of soil each one was to have, and in shade and in sunshine, as each species required. He tended them with affection, and they grew in splendor.

The juniper bush, from the heath of Jutland, rose, in shape and color like the Italian cypress; the shiny, prickly Christ's-thorn, always green in the cold of winter and in the summer sun, was a beautiful sight. Many different species of ferns were growing in front, some looking like the offspring of palm trees and others as if they were the parents of that delicate, lovely plant that we call Venushair. Here stood the despised burdock, which, in its freshness, is so pretty that it would enhance a bouquet. The burdock grew in dry soil, but farther down in moister earth grew the dock plant—a plant also held in low esteem, and yet, with its height and its enormous leaf, so picturesquely beautiful. Waist-high, with flower upon flower like a mighty many-armed candelabra, soared the great mullein, replanted from the meadow. Here stood woodruffs, primroses, and hellebore, the wild calla lily and the delicate three-leaved wood sorrel. It was a delight to behold.

In front, supported by strings of steel wire, growing in rows, were quite small pear trees from French soil. They received sunshine and good care, and soon bore big, juicy fruits, as in the country from which they had come.

In place of the two leafless trees, a tall flagpole had been erected, from which Dannebrog[1] waved, and nearby

[1] The Danish flag.

yet another pole, around which, in summer and autumn, twined the hop with its fragrant, conelike catkins, but on which in winter—according to ancient custom—was hung a sheaf of oats so that the birds of the air might have their feast in the joyous Yuletide season.

"Our good Larsen is growing sentimental in his old age!" said the lord and lady. "But he is faithful and devoted to us!"

Around the beginning of the New Year, in one of the illustrated periodicals of the capital, a picture of the old manor appeared. One could see the flagpole and the sheaf of oats for the birds in the joyous Yuletide season. And it was referred to, and emphasized, as a lovely thought that such an ancient custom had here been restored to such prominence and veneration, so characteristic of precisely this old family seat.

"Everything Larsen does," said the lord and lady, "they beat a drum for! What a happy man! Why, we should almost be proud to have him!"

But they weren't proud at all. They felt that they were the master and mistress. They could give Larsen notice, but they didn't do it. They were good people. And there are so many good people of their sort, and that is gratifying to every Larsen.

Well, that's the story of "The Gardener and the Lord and Lady."

Now you can think it over!

The Flea and
the Professor

❖   ❖   ❖

THERE was a balloonist who came to grief. The balloon burst; the man dropped down and was dashed to smithereens. Two minutes earlier he had sent his boy down by parachute. This was the boy's good fortune. He was unharmed and went about with considerable knowledge for becoming a balloonist. But he had no balloon, nor had he any means of acquiring one.

He had to live, and so he went in for legerdemain and talking with his stomach—this is called "being a ventriloquist." He was young and easy on the eyes, and when he had acquired a goatee and put on fashionable clothing, he could be mistaken for the offspring of a count. The ladies found him handsome. Indeed, one maiden was so taken by his good looks and his legerdemain that she accompanied him to foreign lands and cities. There he called himself "professor"; nothing less would do.

His constant thought was to get hold of a balloon and go aloft with his little wife. But they did not yet have the money.

"It will come!" he said.

"If only it would!" she said.

"After all, we're young, and now I am a professor. Crumbs are also bread!"

She helped him faithfully, sat by the door, and sold

tickets to the performance—and this was a chilly pleasure in the wintertime. She also helped him in one of his tricks. He put his wife in the drawer of a table, a huge drawer. There she crawled into the back drawer, and then she could not be seen in the front drawer. It was a kind of optical illusion.

But one evening, when he pulled out the drawer, she had disappeared from him too. She was not in the front drawer, not in the back drawer, not anywhere in the house, nowhere to be seen or heard. This was her leger-demain. She never came back again. She was tired of it all, and he grew tired of it all; he lost his good humor and could not laugh or perform tricks any more, and then no one came. The earnings became poor, the clothes became shabby, and at last the only thing he owned was a big flea—an inheritance from his wife, and for this reason he was quite fond of it. So he trained it, taught it tricks; he taught it to present arms and shoot off a cannon—but a tiny one.

The professor was proud of his flea, and the flea was proud of itself. It had learned something and had human blood in its veins. It had been in the greatest cities, had been seen by princes and princesses and won their highest acclaim—this stood in print in newspapers and on plac-ards. It knew it was a celebrity and could support a professor, indeed, even a whole family.

It was proud and it was famous, and yet, when the flea and the professor traveled by railway, they went fourth class. It arrives just as quickly as first. There was an unspoken promise between them that they would never be parted, never marry. The flea would remain a bachelor and the professor a widower. It all adds up to the same thing.

"One should never revisit the scenes of one's greatest success!" said the professor. He was a judge of human nature, and that too is an art.

At last he had traveled to every land except the land of the Wild Men, and so he wanted to go to the land of the Wild Men. The professor knew, of course, that they ate Christian people there. But he wasn't really a Christian, and the flea wasn't really a person, so he thought they could risk journeying there, for they could make a good profit.

They traveled by steamship and by sailing ship. The flea performed its tricks, and so they had a free passage on the way and came to the land of the Wild Men.

A little princess reigned there. She was only eight years old, but she reigned. She had taken the power away from her father and mother, for she had a will of her own and was so adorably sweet and naughty.

At once, when the flea presented arms and shot off the cannon, she fell so in love with it that she said, "Him or no one!" She became quite wild with love, and indeed, she was already quite wild to begin with.

"Sweet little sensible child," said her father, "if only one could first make a person out of it!"

"You just leave that to me, old boy!" she said, and that wasn't a nice thing for a little princess to say to her father. But she was wild.

She put the flea on her little hand.

"Now you're a human being. You'll rule with me. But you will do as I wish, or else I'll kill you and eat the professor."

The professor was given a big hall to live in. The walls were of sugarcane. He could go and lick them, but he didn't have a sweet tooth. He was given a hammock to sleep in; it was as if he were lying in a balloon—the one he had always wanted and which was his constant thought.

The flea remained with the princess and sat on her little hand and on her delicate throat. She had taken a hair from her own head. The professor had to tie it around the flea's leg, and then she kept the flea tied to the piece of coral she wore in the lobe of her ear.

What a wonderful time for the princess, and for the flea too, she thought. But the professor didn't like it there. He was a traveling man, was fond of going from city to city and reading in the newspapers about his wisdom and patience in teaching human tasks to a flea. Day in and day out he loafed in the hammock and received his good food: fresh birds' eggs, elephant eyes, and roast thigh of giraffe. The cannibals do not live on human flesh alone—that's a delicacy.

"Children's shoulders with piquant sauce," said the princess' mother, "are the tastiest!"

The professor was bored and only too willing to leave the land of the Wild Men, but he had to have the flea with him. It was his prodigy and his livelihood. How was he going to capture it and get hold of it? That was not so easy.

He strained all his powers of concentration, and then he said, "Now I have it! Princess' Papa, permit me to do something! May I train the inhabitants of the land in the art of presentation? This is what, in the biggest countries of the world, is called breeding."

"And what can you teach me?" said the princess' father.

"My greatest skill," said the professor, "is to fire off a cannon so the whole world trembles, and all the most delicious birds of the skies fall down roasted! That's quite a bang!"

"Out with the cannon!" said the princess' father.

But in the whole land there was no cannon except for the one the flea had brought, and it was too small.

"I'll cast a bigger one!" said the professor. "Just give me the means. I must have fine silken cloth, a needle and thread, rope and string, and stomach drops for balloons: they inflate, alleviate, and elevate! They give the bang to the cannon stomach!"

He was given everything he asked for.

The entire population gathered to see the great cannon. The professor didn't send for them before the balloon was all ready to be filled and sent aloft.

The flea sat on the princess' hand and watched. The balloon was filled; it swelled out. It was so uncontrollable that it could hardly be held down.

"I must have it aloft so it can cool off," said the professor, and seated himself in the basket that hung below it.

"I can't possibly manage to steer it alone. I must have an expert companion along to help me. There's no one here who can do it except the flea."

"I'd rather not allow it!" said the princess, but still she handed the flea to the professor, who put it on his hand.

"Let go of the string and the ropes!" he said. "Here goes the balloon!"

They thought he said "the cannon!"

And then the balloon went higher and higher, up above the clouds, away from the land of the Wild Men.

The little princess, her father and mother, the entire
population, stood and waited. They are waiting still. And
if you don't believe it, just go to the land of the Wild Men.
There every child speaks of the flea and the professor and

believes they are coming back when the cannon has cooled off. But they are not coming. They are back home with us. They are in their native land, riding on the railroad—first class, not fourth; they earn good money; they have a large balloon. No one asks how they got the balloon or where it came from. They are prosperous folk, esteemed folk—the flea and the professor.

The Gate Key

❖ ❖ ❖

EVERY key has its story, and there are many keys: the chamberlain's key, the watch key, St. Peter's key; we could tell about all the keys, but now we're just going to tell about the Civil Servant's gate key.

It had been made by a locksmith, but it could very well believe it had been a blacksmith, the way the man took hold of it, hammering and filing. It was too big for a pants pocket, so it had to go in a coat pocket. Here it often lay in the dark—but, come to think of it, it did have its fixed place on the wall beside the silhouette of the Civil Servant from his childhood. There he looked like a dumpling in shirt frills.

They say that every human being acquires in his makeup and conduct something of the sign of the Zodiac under which he is born: Taurus, Virgo, Scorpio, as they are called in the Almanac. Madame Civil Servant mentioned none of these. She said that her husband had been born under the "sign of the Wheelbarrow": he always had to be pushed ahead.

His father had pushed him into an office, his mother had pushed him into matrimony, and his wife had pushed him up to the rank of Civil Servant; but she never mentioned the latter. She was a level-headed, good wife, who hauled in the right places, talked and pushed in the right places.

Now he was well on in years, "well proportioned," as he said himself, a well-read, good-natured man, who was as "bright as a key" to boot—something we will be able to understand later on. He was always in good spirits; he liked everybody and was only too fond of talking to them. If he were walking in the town, it was hard to get him home again if Mama wasn't along to give him a push. He had to talk to everyone he knew, and the dinner suffered.

From the window Madame Civil Servant kept watch. "Now he's coming!" she would say to the maid. "Put on the pot! Now he's standing still, talking to somebody, so take off the pot, or else the food will be cooked too much! Now he's coming, so put on the pot again!"

But still he didn't come.

He could stand right under the window of the house and nod up; but then if somebody he knew happened to come by, he couldn't help it, he had to have a few words with him. And if another acquaintance came along while he was talking with this one, then he would hang onto the first by the buttonhole and take the second by the hand while he shouted to a third, who wanted to go by.

It was enough to try the patience of Madame Civil Servant. "Civil Servant! Civil Servant!" she would shout. "Yes, that man is born under the sign of the Wheelbarrow: he can't budge unless he's given a push ahead!"

He was very fond of going to bookshops and browsing in books. He paid his bookseller a tiny fee for permitting him to read the new books at his home, that is to say, for being allowed to cut open the pages of the books lengthwise, but not across the top, for then they couldn't be sold as new. He was a walking newspaper, though an inoffensive one, and knew all about engagements, weddings, and funerals, literary gossip and gossip of the town; indeed, he would let drop mysterious hints that he knew of things that no one else knew. He had got it from the gate key.

Even as newlyweds the Civil Servant and his wife were

living in their own home, and from that time they had had the same gate key. But they were not aware then of its remarkable powers; they found out about those later.

It was during the reign of King Frederick the Seventh. At that time Copenhagen had no gas, it had train-oil lanterns: it had no Tivoli or Casino, no trolley cars and no railroads. There were few diversions as compared with what there are now. On Sunday one went for a walk out of the city gate to the churchyard, read the inscriptions on the graves, sat down on the grass, ate from one's lunch hamper, and drank one's schnapps with it; or else one went to Frederiksberg, where there was a regimental band in front of the castle and crowds of people to look at the royal family rowing about in the tiny narrow canals, where the old king steered the boat; he and the queen nodded to everyone without making any distinction in rank. Well-to-do families went out there from town to drink their afternoon tea. They could obtain hot water from a little farmhouse beyond the gardens, but they had to bring their own samovars with them.

The Civil Servant and his wife took a trip out there one sunny Sunday afternoon; the maid went ahead with the samovar and a hamper of provisions and "a drop to wash it down with."

"Take the gate key," said Madame Civil Servant, "so we can get in our own gate when we come back. You know it's locked here at dusk, and the bellpull has been broken since this morning! We'll be late getting home! After we've been to Frederiksberg, we're going to Casorti's Theater at Vesterbro to see the pantomime: 'Harlequin, Foreman of the Threshers,' where they come down in a cloud; it costs two marks per person!"

And they went to Frederiksberg, listened to the music, watched the royal family go bathing with banners waving, saw the old king and the white swans. After drinking a cup of good tea, they hurried away, but still they didn't get to the theater on time.

The tightrope walking was over, the stilt walking was over, and the pantomime had begun. As always, they had arrived too late, and for this the Civil Servant was to blame; every moment along the way he had stopped to talk to someone he knew; inside the theater he also met good friends, and when the performance was over, he and his wife had to accompany them to a family on the bridge to have a glass of punch; it was only going to be a ten-minute stop, but this, of course, stretched out to a whole hour. They talked and talked. Especially entertaining was a Swedish baron—or was he German? The Civil Servant didn't remember exactly, but on the other hand, the trick with the key—which the baron taught him—he retained for all time. It was extraordinarily interesting; he could make the key reply to everything it was asked about, even the most secret.

The Civil Servant's gate key was especially suited for this purpose. The bit was heavy, and it had to hang down. The baron let the bow of the key rest on the index finger of his right hand. It hung there loosely and lightly; each beat of the pulse in the tip of the finger could set it in motion, so that it turned—and if it didn't, then the baron knew very well how to make it turn as he wished. Each turning was a letter of the alphabet, from A and as far down in the alphabet as one cared to go. When the first letter had been found, the key turned to the opposite side; in this way one sought the next letter, and thus one arrived at complete words, complete sentences—an answer to the question. It was all a fraud, but always an amusement. And that was precisely what the Civil Servant thought at first, but he didn't stick to it: he became completely wrapped up in the key.

"Husband! Husband!" cried Madame Civil Servant. "The

West Gate closes at twelve o'clock! We won't get in; we have only a quarter of an hour left in which to hurry!"

They had to get a move on; several people, who wanted

to go in the town soon passed them by. At last they reached the outermost guardhouse. Then the clock struck twelve and the gate slammed shut, a large number of people stood locked out, and among them stood the Civil Servant and his wife, with maid, samovar, and empty lunch hamper. Some standing there were thoroughly frightened, others were irritated; each one took it in his own fashion. What was to be done?

Fortunately it had been decided of late that one of the city gates, the North Gate, was not to be locked; here the pedestrians could slip through the guardhouse into the town.

The way was not at all short, but the weather was fine, the sky was clear with stars and shooting stars, the frogs were croaking in ditch and marsh. The party began to sing, one ballad after the other; but the Civil Servant didn't sing, nor did he pay any attention to the stars—no, not even to his own two feet; he fell at full length right by the side of the ditch. One would have thought he'd had too

much to drink, but it wasn't the punch, it was the key that
had gone to his head and was turning there.

At last they reached the guardhouse of the North Bridge;
they went across the bridge and entered the town.

"Now I'm happy again!" said Madame Civil Servant.
"Here's our gate!"

"But where's the gate key?" said the Civil Servant. It
was in neither the back pocket nor the side pocket.

"Good gracious!" cried Madame Civil Servant. "Haven't
you got the key? You've lost it doing those key tricks with
the baron! How are we going to get in now? You know the
bellpull has been broken ever since this morning. The
nightwatch hasn't got a key to the house! Why, this is a
desperate situation!"

The maid began to wail; the Civil Servant was the only
one who maintained his composure.

"We must break one of the windowpanes at the sausagemonger's," he said. "Get him out of bed and come in that
way."

He broke a windowpane; he broke two. "Petersen!" he
shouted, and stuck the handle of his umbrella in through
the opening. Then the daughter of the family in the basement gave a loud shriek. The sausagemonger threw open
the door to the shop, crying, "Nightwatch!" And before
he'd rightly seen the family, recognized them and let
them in, the nightwatch was blowing his whistle, and in
the next street another nightwatch answered and started
blowing. People came to their windows. "Where's the
fire? Where's the riot?" they asked, and were asking still
when the Civil Servant, who was already in his parlor, was
taking off his coat—and in it lay the gate key, not in the
pocket but in the lining. It had fallen down through a hole
that shouldn't have been in the pocket.

From that evening the gate key acquired a singularly
great importance, not only when they went out in the
evening but also when they stayed home and the Civil

Servant showed off his sagacity by letting the gate key provide answers to questions.

He made up the most plausible answer, and then let the gate key supply it. At last he believed in it himself; but not the apothecary, a young man closely related to the Civil Servant's wife.

This apothecary had a good head on his shoulders, a critical head; already as a schoolboy he had written reviews of books and plays, but without his name being mentioned—and that means such a lot. He was what is called a *belesprit*, but he didn't believe in spirits at all—least of all key spirits.

"Of course I believe, I believe," he said. "Blessed Mr. Civil Servant, I believe in the gate key and all the key spirits just as firmly as I believe in the new science that is beginning to make itself known: table-turning, and the spirits in old and new furniture. Have you heard about that? I have! I've had my doubts. You know I'm a skeptic, but I've been converted after reading a frightful story in a quite reputable foreign publication. Mr. Civil Servant! Can you imagine! Yes, I'll tell you the story the way I read it; two bright children have seen their parents arouse the spirit in a big dining table. The little ones were alone, and now they wanted to try to rub life into an old chest of drawers in the same fashion. It came to life; the spirit awoke, but it couldn't tolerate the commands of children. It got up—the chest of drawers creaked—it shot out its drawers—and with its chest-of-drawer legs it put each of the children into a drawer. And then the chest of drawers ran out through the open door with them, down the stairs and out in the street, over to the canal, where it threw itself in and drowned both the children. The tiny bodies were placed in consecrated ground, but the chest of drawers was brought to the town hall, convicted of infanticide, and burned alive in the square! I've read it!" said the apothecary. "Read it in a foreign publication. It's not something I've made up myself; I swear by the key that it's true! Now I swear by all that's holy!"

The Civil Servant found such a tale to be too coarse a jest; the two of them could never talk about the key—the apothecary was "key-stupid."

The Civil Servant made progress in key wisdom; the key was his entertainment and his enlightenment.

One evening, as the Civil Servant was about to go to bed, he was standing half undressed when someone knocked on the door to the entryway. It was the sausagemonger in the basement who had come so late; he too was half undressed; but, he said, a thought had suddenly occurred to him, which he was afraid he couldn't keep overnight.

"It's my daughter, Lotte-Lene, who I must talk about. She's a pretty girl; she has been confirmed and now I want to see her make a good marriage!"

"I'm not yet a widower," said the Civil Servant with a chuckle, "and I have no son that I can offer her!"

"You understand what I mean, Civil Servant!" said the sausagemonger. "She can play the piano and she can sing— you must be able to hear it up here in the house. You have no idea of all the things the girl can do. She can mimic the speech and walk of everyone. She's made for playacting, and that's a good career for pretty girls of good family—they could marry into a family with an estate, although such a thing has never entered my mind or Lotte-Lene's! She can sing and knows how to play the piano! The other day I went up to the Song Academy with her. She sang, but she doesn't have what I call a 'beery-bass voice' in ladies or a canary-bird screech up in the highest registers, which so many songstresses are required to have now. And so they advised her not to choose this career at all. Well, I thought, if she can't be a singer, then she can always be an actress, for a voice is the only thing needed for that. Today I talked about it to the director, as he's called. 'Is she well read?' he asked. 'No,' I said, 'not in the least!' 'Reading is necessary for an artist!' he said. 'She can still acquire that,' I thought, and then I went home. 'She can go to a rental library and read what is there,' I thought. But this evening, while I'm sitting and getting undressed, it occurs to me: why rent books when you can borrow them? The Civil Servant has lots of books; let her read those. There's enough to read there, and she can have it free!"

"Lotte-Lene is a strange girl," said the Civil Servant, "a pretty girl! She shall have books to read! But does she have what is called 'get-up-and-go,' ingenuity, genius? And if she does, what is equally as important, is she lucky?"

"She has won twice in the Merchandise Lottery," said the sausagemonger. "Once she won a wardrobe and once six pairs of sheets! That's what I call luck, and that's what she has!"

"I'll ask the key!" said the Civil Servant.

And then he placed the key on the index finger of his right hand and then on the index finger of the sausagemonger's right hand, and let the key turn and supply letter after letter.

The key said, "Triumph and happiness!" And so Lotte-Lene's future was decided.

The Civil Servant gave her two books to read right away: *Dyveke*[1] and Knigge's *Associating with People*.

From that evening a closer acquaintanceship of sorts grew up between Lotte-Lene and the Civil Servant and his wife. She came often to the family, and the Civil Servant discovered that she was a sensible girl—she believed in him and in the key. Madame Civil Servant found, in the openness with which every moment she revealed her extreme ignorance, something childish and

[1] A tragedy by Ole Johan Samsøe.

innocent. The married couple, each in his own fashion, was fond of her, and she was fond of them.

"It smells so delightfully up there!" said Lotte-Lene.

There was an odor, a scent, a fragrance of apples in the hall, where Madame Civil Servant had stored a whole barrel of Gravenstein apples. There was also a smell of rose and lavender incense in all the rooms.

"It produces an atmosphere of quality!" said Lotte-Lene. And then she feasted her eyes upon all the beautiful flowers that Madame Civil Servant always had. Yes, even in midwinter, lilacs and cherry blossoms were blooming here. The cut, leafless branches were placed in water, and in the warm room they soon bore leaves and blossoms.

"You'd think there was no life in those bare branches, but see how they rise up from the dead."

"It has never occurred to me before," said Lotte-Lene. "Why, Nature is lovely!"

And the Civil Servant let her look at his "Key Book," in which had been written down remarkable things said by the key, even about half an apple cake that had disappeared from the pantry on the very evening the maid's sweetheart came calling.

And the Civil Servant asked his key: "Who has eaten the apple cake, the cat or the sweetheart?" And the gate key replied, "The sweetheart." The Civil Servant believed it even before he asked, and the maid confessed—why, that damned key knew everything!

"Yes, isn't it remarkable!" said the Civil Servant. "That key! That key! And it has said 'triumph and happiness' about Lotte-Lene. Now we'll soon see! I'll vouch for that!"

The Civil Servant's wife wasn't so confident, but she didn't express her doubts when her husband was listening. But later she confided to Lotte-Lene that, as a young man, the Civil Servant had been completely addicted to the theater. If someone had given him a push then, he would decidedly have appeared as an actor. But the family dis-

missed the idea. He wanted to go on the stage, and in
order to get there he wrote a play.

"This is a great secret that I'm confiding to you, little
Lotte-Lene. The play wasn't bad. It was accepted by the
Royal Theater and booed off the stage, so it has never
been heard of since, and I'm glad of it. I'm his wife and I
know him. Now you want to follow the same career. I
wish you well, but I don't think it'll work. I don't believe
in the gate key!"

Lotte-Lene believed in it, and in that belief she and the
Civil Servant found each other.

Their hearts understood each other in all propriety.

Moreover, the girl had other skills that Madame Civil
Servant set store by. Lotte-Lene knew how to make starch
from potatoes, sew silk gloves out of old silk stockings,
recover her silk dancing slippers—even though she could
afford to buy all her clothes new. She had what the
sausagemonger called "shillings in the table drawer and
bonds in the safe." This was really a wife for the apothecary, thought Madame Civil Servant. But she didn't say
so, nor did she let the key say so, either. The apothecary
was soon going to settle down and have his own pharmacy
in one of the larger provincial towns of the land.

Lotte-Lene was constantly reading *Dyveke* and Knigge's
Associating with People. She kept these two books for two
years, and by then she had learned one of them—*Dyveke*
—by heart, all the roles. But she wanted to perform only
one of them, that of Dyveke, and not in the capital, where
there is so much envy—and where they didn't want her.
She wanted to start her artistic career, as the Civil Servant
called it, in one of the larger provincial towns. Now it
happened, by a strange coincidence, that this was in the
very same town in which the young apothecary had settled
down as the town's youngest, if not only, apothecary.

The great evening of expectation was at hand: Lotte-
Lene was to perform and win triumph and happiness, as

the key had said. The Civil Servant wasn't there; he was in bed and Madame Civil Servant was taking care of him. He was to have hot napkins and chamomile tea—the napkins on his tummy, the tea inside his tummy.

The couple didn't attend the *Dyveke* performance, but the apothecary was there, and he wrote a letter about it to his relation, Madame Civil Servant.

"Dyveke's collar was the best!" he wrote. "If the Civil Servant's gate key had been in my pocket, I would have taken it out and hissed through it! That's just what she deserved and just what the key deserved for having lied so shamefully to her about 'triumph and happiness'!"

The Civil Servant read the letter. It was all spite, he said, a "key hatred" with that innocent girl as the victim.

As soon as he was out of bed and human again, he sent a short but venomous letter to the apothecary, who wrote a reply as if he had interpreted the whole epistle as nothing more than a high-spirited joke.

He expressed his thanks for this, as well as for every well-meant contribution in the future to making public the key's incomparable value and importance. Then he confided to the Civil Servant that, in addition to his profession as apothecary, he was working on a long "key novel," in which all the characters were keys and keys alone. The gate key, of course, was the leading character and had been patterned after the Civil Servant's gate key—it had the gift of prophecy; all the other keys had to revolve around it: the chamberlain's old key, which had known the pomp and festivity of the court; the watch key, tiny, elegant, and important, at four shillings from the ironmonger's; the key to the box pew, which counts itself as one of the clergy, and which, after sitting all night in a keyhole in the church, has seen spirits; the keys to the pantry and to the fuel and wine cellars all make their appearance, curtsying and circulating around the gate key. The sunbeams make it shine like silver; the wind—the spirit of the world—flies into it and makes it float. It is the Key of all Keys, it was the Civil Servant's gate key, and now it is the key to the Pearly Gates, it is a papal key, it is "infallible"!

"Gall!" said the Civil Servant. "Unmitigated gall!"

He and the apothecary never saw each other again. Oh, yes, except at Madame Civil Servant's funeral.

She died first.

She was mourned and missed in the house. Even the cut cherry branches, which sent out fresh shoots and blossoms, grieved and withered away; they stood forgotten, for she no longer took care of them.

The Civil Servant and the apothecary walked behind her coffin, side by side as the two oldest relations.

There was neither the time nor the mood here for bickering.

Lotte-Lene tied a band of mourning around the Civil Servant's hat. She had long since returned to the house, without winning triumph and happiness in an artistic career. But it could come; Lotte-Lene had a future. The key had said so, and the Civil Servant had said so.

She came to see him. They talked about the deceased and they wept—Lotte-Lene was soft; they talked about the arts, and Lotte-Lene was strong.

"The life of the stage is lovely," she said, "but there's so much unpleasantness and envy! I shall go my own way instead. First myself and then the arts!"

Knigge had told the truth in his chapter about actors; she realized this. The key had not told the truth, but she didn't speak of this to the Civil Servant. She loved him.

As a matter of fact, during his entire period of mourning, the gate key had been his consolation and encouragement. He asked it questions and it gave him answers. And when the year was up, and he and Lotte-Lene were sitting together one sentimental evening, he asked the key: "Shall I get married and whom shall I marry?"

There was no one to give him a push, so he gave the key a push and it said: "Lotte-Lene!"

Now it had been said, and Lotte-Lene became Madame Civil Servant.

"Triumph and happiness!"

These words had been said in advance—by the gate key.

Afterword

❖   ❖   ❖

WE start on a journey. The journey teaches us
and we teach the journey, and slowly, unalter-
ably, the journey changes and then the destination
changes. Andersen began his professional life as a
novelist and he continued writing novels and plays
until his death—thirty plays and six novels. Even
with all that energy expended, his name would never
have left Denmark but for the short folk tales he used
to bridge the childhood and grown-up worlds, in neither of which he felt he belonged. He yearned to
explain what of himself he could. There were traditional tales recast, written between his serious professional works, and other stories of his own. The plays,
on which he spent so much energy and for which he
had so much hope, weren't popular and few were
produced. The novels earned him praise when they
were published and are now almost all out of print.
The "fairy" tales . . .

It's difficult to think of childhood without them.
The stories have been told and retold, translated into
dozens if not hundred of languages. They have been
bowdlerized, modified, made into ballets, modern

dances, poems, cartoons and animated films, children's plays, and holiday costumes. Andersen himself has been represented as part of a folk tale, a happy-go-lucky wanderer and lover of children, and luckiest of all, well loved and famous in his own lifetime. That part is true.

Andersen was following a trend, a watershed in Victorian literature: the mining of the vast treasures of the oral tale. The brothers Grimm had published *Kinder- und Hausmärchen* in 1812–15, and the English soon followed, recognizing the depth and psychological penetration of many of these previously neglected tales. In Denmark, the trend had been begun by N.F.A. Grundtvig (1783–1872). It's worthwhile to take a moment to look at the work of this extraordinary man.

Grundtvig, a Lutheran minister, composed most of the hymnody used to this day in Danish churches. He was an enthusiastic reader of Kierkegaard and worked for a revival of Christianity that would ease the dry rationalism of its former expression. This trend was widespread in Europe and in America was expressed in the spiritualism that produced the Christian Science, Seventh Day Adventist, and Jehovah's Witness movements. Grundtvig also wrote poetry and in 1820 translated *Beowulf* into Danish. In 1832, he published *Nordens Mytologi,* which introduced many Danes to their own superb heritage of myth. Andersen had certainly been exposed to this trend and to Grundtvig's work. Kierkegaard said, "Reasoned philosophy fails to account for the depths and tragedies of human existence." The Norse classics harked back to an older age, one of violence and bloodshed but one also of feeling and an open-eyed assessment of human possibilities of courage, heroism, pain, and loss.

The Teutonic folklore gathered by the brothers Grimm shared many stories and much tradition with the Norse tales. Their work was translated and read with great interest. Andersen, one of the most traveled men of his time, was exposed to these trends all over Europe as well as in Denmark. "The Tinderbox," "Little Claus and Big Claus," "Cloddy Hans," "The Girl Who Trod on a Loaf," and "What Papa Does Is Always Right," among others, are folk tales familiar at all European hearths. Andersen didn't copy these tales; he retold them.

There are two conflicting philosophies in storytelling, especially in the oral form. One is that the ancient tale or myth must be told exactly as heard, being borne as an almost sacred responsibility from generation to generation. Modification or elaboration of any kind is a violation of the story's provenance. The story is preeminent; its power is enhanced by its purity, even though it may, over centuries, cease to be understood by its ordinary hearers, and be available only to the specialist or dedicated student.

The other is that each teller understands the story differently, comes to it from a different background and point of view, and therefore makes modifications to explicate and clarify it to himself before presenting it to his hearers. The teller interacts with his audience and, if he is good at what he does, brings forth elements of the story that may have been hidden. The story does change, but its basic elements remain in place.

The danger in the first case is that the living story may become "classic," removed from the ordinary audiences for whom it was first created. The danger in the second is that, in attempting to make it relevant, its point may be changed beyond recognition over time, or it might become so chatty and forced that its magic is lost and its informality of speech dates it almost before it's out of the teller's mouth.

Andersen, in translation, has been subjected to excesses on both sides. I've been reading these tales since I was a child, and I've come on both the stuffed nightingale and the pop version. The new translation is, I think, a middle way. Andersen adopted an informal, oral style, which was later gussied up by many of his translators in a desire to make the work classic and to clean it up for Victorian children's ears. The work here gets much of the spirit back. "In China, you know, of course, the Emperor is Chinese," and "A duck came from Portugal, some said from Spain. It makes no difference. She was called The Portuguese." There's a Dickensian love of little details, flourishes or grace notes that add a hominess to what builds the story. "Here they lived—but only during the summer."

Andersen used details and an easy style, but he walked a narrow line and never went over it into the kind of pandering to kid vocabularies and pop slang that Disney movies do. Compare the language used in *The Little Mermaid* animated film with the language Andersen used in the story itself. "Wow, cool," the fish tells the mermaid, who says, "My father's gonna kill me." "She's got it bad," another mermaid observes, trivializing a yearning that in the Andersen story is tragic.

When Andersen's stories are serious, the language used to dress them is serious, and when the story is lighter, the language lightens and the characters pay homage to the form that surrounds them. In one, a proud princess renounces her unfit suitors. Princesses and unfit suitors abound in all European traditions of storytelling. Andersen's princess looks at one of them: "Won't do," she says, "scram."

Hans Christian was anything but the simple teller of childhood tales his readers imagine, or perhaps want him to be. He never married; he had no children. He was a shy man, easily depressed, but convinced by a hard childhood that it was a desperate necessity to proclaim and exalt himself, to work against the odds, and he expected very long odds indeed.

He was born in Odense, in 1805. Odense was then the second largest city in Denmark, but it was on an island, Furen. In 1807, Denmark joined the Napoleonic War, siding with Russia. After being defeated by Sweden, it was forced to give up its rights to Norway. The loss caused great poverty in the cities of this primarily agricultural country. Hans Christian's father was a cobbler, a man embittered by his low status, poor education—although he could read—and scant prospects. He married Hans Christian's mother two months before her son was born. This casual approach to the calendar wasn't uncommon in the class to which the family belonged.

Hans Christian's mother was illiterate, but a loving presence. His father was also devoted to him and tried to give him the education he had been denied. The couple was ill-matched—he, a rationalist-atheist, she, a superstitious theist. These trends were never resolved

in the family or in Hans Christian. I think the para-
doxes and ambiguities of the home situation provided
the motive force for the flowering of his gifts and prepared the arena in which the gifts would find their
expression.

Hans Christian's grandfather was mentally ill, and
Hans Christian was both ashamed and terrified of
the inheritance. His grandmother tended the garden
of the mental hospital and Hans Christian was in
touch with the inmates there and other old people
in the area who provided him with every kind of
verbal expression. He was used to conundrums,
metaphor, personification, and a slipping away of
reality against which the rationalist part of his nature supplied the necessary corrective.

The island was also a bit of a cultural backwater,
removed from the more sophisticated world of Copenhagen. Many of the old styles of speech and folk-
ways had been preserved there, as well as the best-
maintained Renaissance castle in Europe, where it
can still be seen, with its moat, battlements, and perfect fairy tale setting.

In the class in which Hans Christian was raised,
children were worked long and hard. Even though
he was allowed to go to school, he must have seen
children at brutal and backbreaking labor in long
hours of unskilled work. In none of his stories is
childhood romanticized as it is by other writers. Seldom is it made wonderful. "The Little Match Girl"
is only one of the visions we have of childhood as
cold, lonely, and treated with offhand cruelty and
rare sympathy.

To the extent that he was a schoolboy, Hans
Christian was privileged. The schooling itself was

marginal, a charity affair, but he did have time to
play and dream, rare for poor children in those
days. He seldom made his games with other children. His father gave him a puppet theater and he
spent hours constructing lives for his characters.

When he was seven, his father gave up the cobbler shop and went into Napoleon's army, hoping
to better himself and return a war hero. The elder
Andersen never saw action, but the two years he
was away must have been very hard on his wife
and son. He came home broken in health and died
in 1816. His widow supported herself and Hans
Christian by cleaning houses and taking in washing.

It was a custom among the titled nobility of the
time to sponsor or promote one or two of the gifted
sons of the poor. Someone would notice or recommend a musical or literary prodigy, and he would
be invited up to the castle to perform. My grandfather had been such a boy and to the end of his
life he would describe the wonder of being sent for
by the baron on the hill on various occasions to sing,
recite, or supply wit for the parties at the castle,
away from the mud and ugliness of the village. Not
only was the performance paid for with food or
money enough to feed the family for a week, but
the culture shock provided a valuable experience.
The gleaming floors of the reception hall, the rooms
on rooms, the heavy velvet drapes, and the profusion of lamps, food, and warmth were a world away
from his familiar dirt floor, the single room odorous
with the sweat, cooking, closeness of the whole family, the freezing privy.

Hans Christian drew the interest of such people
in Odense's upper class and was often asked to per-

form, singing and declaiming. He had a high, clear soprano voice, a joke to his schoolfellows, a boon to his starving mother.

She married again to another cobbler and apprenticed Hans Christian to a tailor, but that ended in failure. Her second husband died several years later, leaving the widow in the starkest circumstances.

When Hans Christian was thirteen, a repertory company came to the theater in Odense and he got a job as an extra. His short stint convinced him that the theater was his calling. That meant Copenhagen. Over his mother's objections, he left home.

That road was (and is) rocky, full of failure and rejection. The letter of introduction he had led nowhere. The Royal Theater manager told him that with no more than his rudimentary schooling, he had no place there. After a dozen fits and starts he began to submit plays.

These plays were refused, but a member of the theater's board became interested in Hans Christian. Such an interest seems as miraculous as the transformations in one of his stories. By all accounts, Hans Christian was at that time all bumptious boy-man, a callow show-off, using big words incorrectly, demanding attention, all persistence and no experience. He was every mentor's nightmare: the writer with true talent and deep gifts he wasn't showing and who comes on like a steam calliope at a funeral.

Luckily for the world, James Collin, the board member, saw past this desperate overreaching of an essentially reclusive person who was trying too hard and ruining his own chances. Collin arranged for schooling and a stipend.

Hans Christian graduated in 1829, at the age of

twenty-four, and must have felt like a battle-scarred veteran whose best years had been spent getting to the place to which everyone else in his world had already been given easy access years before.

He had written a poem about a dying child, one of the earliest of the flood of that genre, echoed in Dickens, Harriet Beecher Stowe, Louisa May Alcott, and dozens of photographers who made endless studies of dead children. Although written for himself, the poem became an instant worldwide success, printed and reprinted. There were no laws or copyright controlling the artistic product at the time. Hans Christian would have fame, but not money.

The poem was a beginning, but seemed an ending. The second beginning was *A Walking Tour from the Holman Canal*, a comic, satirical fantasy, a bit like *The Pickwick Papers* in its approach, but without Dickens' sure hand. The elements were there: fantasy, concern with the life-death divide, a sense of the absurd. The work did very well and gave Hans Christian enough money to send some to his mother. He was, by then, light-years separated from the class in which he had been raised. That summer he passed two university degree exams and bid good-bye to the schoolroom.

Here began the travels that would take him all over Europe and last on and off for the rest of his life. He had fallen in love, faithful to the ideal of the German Romanticism he was adopting as his own—hopelessly. All of his loves would be hopeless. She married. He suffered and wrote and saw himself very much in the Goethe-Heine tradition. Of course, his first big trip outside Denmark would be to Germany. He visited all the major cities there.

Then he went to Italy in 1833, north to Prague, Bohemia, Austria, and back to Denmark, where he began the first of his stories, a book of four: "The Tinder Box," "Little Ida's Flowers," "Little Claus and Big Claus," and "The Princess and the Pea." Three were folk stories, "Little Ida's Flowers," his own. The book was an immediate success. The tales were newly approached:

> A soldier was marching along, left, right! Left, right. He had his knapsack on his back and a sword at his side, for he had been to the wars and was going home. And on the way he met an old witch. Oh, she was horrid: her bottom lip came right down to her chest.

In those days, tales for children were for the purpose of moral instruction and no extras. These stories in which flowers talked and toys and figurines came to life were brand-new and a window flung wide-open on the way children actually think and feel.

By 1836, Hans Christian was an established writer with a novel and two volumes of tales. He was working on a second novel. The next years would be prolific, adding to his fame, which was, even then, international, but Andersen wasn't a man destined for happiness. Ambition, self-doubt, and an almost childish self-centeredness crippled his relationships and chilled the delight he might have felt with his gifts and his fame.

He traveled constantly in those years: Greece, the Balkans, and Constantinople, at a time when travel was difficult and often dangerous.

All of Hans Christian's loves were hopeless, all importunate, passionate, self-defeating, and doomed. Now it was Jenny Lind.

She was very like him: poor, orphaned, gifted, and able to catch the interest of exalted patrons at an early age. She was needy, neurotic, and terrified of losing the gift on which she and her family depended, a gift like mercury in the palm.

She became an icon, a rage. Barnum brought her to America; she was the toast of Europe. Her relationship with Hans Christian was hopeless. Labile, highstrung individuals with intangible gifts usually need the presence of stable, reasonable, and balanced friends and lovers who moderate their excesses and smooth their feathers. Whom do they pick? She realized the impossibility of a more than friendly relationship. He didn't. As with his other loves, he suffered loudly and publicly. Such effusions went with the romantic bravura of the time, and so they didn't do him much harm.

Andersen's libido was more erotic than sexual, anyway. He courted both genders and established triangles with both, but the objects of his desire were always unattainable. His relationship with Jenny, if doomed, resulted in his emergence from being a refashioner of folk stories to a creator of his own best tales, using the children's story form without its content, so as to make a new genre. "The Ugly Duckling," "The Nightingale," "The Snow Queen," and "The Fir Tree" were all written under the Jenny spell, and the content was that of transformed autobiography, his own life made metaphor. "The Nightingale" is a direct tribute to Jenny, who was, after all, the Swedish Nightingale.

"The Snow Queen" is Andersen's longest and most involved tale: love and loss. The characters are children: Kay and Gerda, who are best friends. Kay receives the splinter of a broken Devil's mirror in his eye. This renders the world and all its creatures ugly and evil. Later, he is kidnapped by the ice-hearted Snow Queen and driven into the lands of ice. Gerda sets out to rescue him. After great dangers, she almost loses hope, but never quite. The story is pervaded with a homesick anguish that is almost palpable. That emotion is at its most intense in childhood and is seldom captured by an adult writer. The closest description of it is in *Heidi*, by Johanna Spyri. A gift Andersen shared with Dickens was his ability to remember childhood in all its intensity and all its pain. Anyone who remembers childhood as a golden time has memory loss. We seal those years off not because of their irrelevance but because of their anguish. "The Snow Queen" ends with Gerda finding Kay and her tears flushing away the hateful shard in his eye, but Andersen is no fool. There is a huge price to pay. The two have lost their childhoods. He tells us that they remain children at heart, but all that means is that the homesickness has gone soul-deep in both of them. You don't make up lost years, he says. Andersen's fantasy is grounded with both feet in the hard facts of reality, which is what makes it so compelling. The Little Mermaid is told:

The very thing that is so lovely here in the sea, your fishtail, they find so disgusting up there on earth. They don't know any better. Up there they have to have two clumsy stumps, which they call legs, to be beautiful!

Andersen's later life was one of travel and stay-overs at the homes of the rich and famous, of universal fame and adulation, but his joy was marred by his self-centered blindness and straitjacketed by the persona he had made for himself. He wrote autobiographies that concealed more than they showed. Dickens prepared his way and fame in England, where he traveled in triumph and he, in turn, paved the way for Lewis Carroll, Charles Kingsley, and George McDonald. His work succeeded in English in spite of awful translations and Victorian bowdlerizations. The dying Elizabeth Barrett Browning made him the hero of her last poem.

The European revolutions of 1848–51 changed the cultural climate there, but these washed over Andersen, who saw his reputation outlive the chaos. He traveled widely for the rest of his life and his talent matured in later tales. "The Marsh King's Daughter" and "Anne Lizbeth" are products of this later, wider style.

As egocentric and eccentric as Hans Christian was, he continued to be welcome in the homes of wealthy and generous families. Happy families gave him the security at the end of his life that he lacked at the beginning. He continued to have crushes on members of both sexes, but the Victorian talent for overlooking the specific while damning the general came to his rescue. Even when his behavior was indiscreet, it was never a public trouble to him. In his last years, he was able to discuss his bisexuality, and to write of it, more freely than he had before. His final stories produce overtly effeminate men and mannish women.

He also continued to travel, although with age's

complaints, including fear of the poverty that was long years past. Dickens died, other friends and contacts died, but his support system to the very end was chrome steel. He died in the presence of loving and caring friends, at five past eleven in the morning, the fourth of August 1875.

> And it was summer—the warm, glorious summer.   —"The Snow Queen"

> —JOANNE GREENBERG